MYTHBORN

Fate of the Sovereign

Book I

by

V. Lakshman

Dedication

This book is dedicated to Wendy, Aidan, & Noble.

They were my first champions,
and I am grateful for their love, faith, guidance,
and unending support.

I love them with all my heart.

MYTHBORN
Fate of the Sovereign, Book 1

Cover art by Raymond Lei Jin and Na Sun
Map by Ralf Schemmann

Certificate of Copyright Registration: TXu 1-796-339

ISBN-13: 978-0-9850620-2-6

For more information please go to:
www.mythbornbook.com

TABLE OF CONTENTS

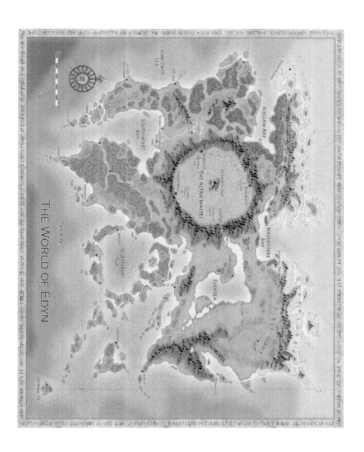

THE WORLD OF EDYN

*"Any sufficiently advanced technology
is indistinguishable from magic."*

—*Arthur C. Clarke*

HISTORIES: SOVEREIGN'S FALL

"War is not about who is right,

it is about who is left."

—*General Valarius Galadine, High Marshal*

The final battle lasted for days, leaving the ash slopes littered with dead. Bodies lay strewn about with the casual haphazardness of violence passed. King Mikal Galadine stepped his horse forward carefully, mindful not to trod upon those who had fallen in his name. His gray eyes drank in the scene, the dark earth of the volcano's slope now stained with the blood of men. In that gaze, the toll the past years had taken was there for all to see. New lines creased his face, and his shoulders slumped with the weariness of a man who had labored far too long at the task of war.

Too many sacrificed, he thought, and now one final duty. He motioned to his armsmark.

"My lord?" the armsmark grunted.

Mikal sighed, then ordered, "Bring your men forward."

"At once, sire." The mounted armsmark turned and cantered back to the lines, barking commands at the assembled soldiers.

The ground shuddered. Mikal's horse whinnied, then stepped to the left, the animal's senses attuned to the minor rifts occasionally snapping into and out of existence around them. He'd been told to expect small quakes, by-products of the magic that allowed a space between their world and the demon plane to open. The tremors would pass, now that the Gate was closed.

Mikal gave his horse a few pats on the neck then turned his attention back to the slope and the ragtag band of men and women descending it. They stumbled along slowly, supporting each other, with barely the energy to breathe, much less walk. Hundreds had gone up to do battle with the demonlord Lilyth, but barely twenty staggered down from that final struggle, their black uniforms gray with soot.

But they had succeeded, and the demon was dead, buried in the volcano's smoking pit. Lilyth had destroyed vast stretches of the land in her quest to subjugate and rule, and much work remained to bring back what her all-consuming hate had perverted. An army of lore-masters had bought new hope, but the price of their service had cut deep.

So many signs had been missed, and so many mistakes made.

A younger Mikal Galadine might have dwelt on such regrets and allowed them to change his heart, but the elder king's sense of justice took over, silencing any doubt. Mistakes had indeed been made, but some debts are paid for in blood.

The survivors came down the last rise. At their lead was Mikal's friend Duncan, who raised his hand in greeting. The king could see the effort it cost him.

"Rai'stahn has pulled the dragon-knights back. The gods be praised, we were successful. Lilyth is no more." Duncan lowered his pale eyes. "I am sorry... for the loss of your brother."

The king brushed off the concern that was plain in his friend's voice, and said, "Whatever was left of him died years ago. We do what we must."

Duncan turned his attention to the people behind him, missing the look of determination on his friend's face. "Your leave to move to shelter? Sonya is especially drained." Pride shone in his eyes and a slight smile escaped, despite his immense weariness. His leaden arms moved automatically to support his wife, who stood a bit unsteadily beside him, though her eyes were clear and alert. "She truly is the Lore Mother to us all." At his touch, she leaned into the comfort of his embrace.

"A moment," King Galadine said, holding up a mailed hand. His armsmark cantered forward and handed him a scroll. After he'd backed away, the king undid the black ribbon and unrolled the parchment.

Confusion ran for a moment across Duncan's face. "My lord, can this not wait?"

For the first time, the king met his eyes. "No, it cannot." He looked down at the parchment and began to read:

"On this day, the twentieth of Peraat, I, King Mikal Petracles Galadine, proclaim the Way of Making false. It shall no longer be practiced in the lands of Edyn. Those who continue to adhere to and follow its teachings shall be put to death. Those who exhibit the Talent shall be sacrificed for the greater good of the land."

The king met his friend's confused gaze, "Never again shall we find ourselves under the yoke of the Way." A breath passed, then two, and in that instant the two knew each other's hearts. Then Mikal bellowed, "Archers, forward!"

The armsmark repeated the command and one hundred archers moved forward in lines on either side of the king.

Duncan looked about in alarm, then shook his head in disbelief. "What are you doing?"

"I killed my brother for the safety of this land, archmage. Why would I spare you?"

Duncan dropped all pretense of mannered speech and exclaimed, "We fought side by side! Now we are to be executed?"

"No. Just as my brother, you are a casualty of war." The king turned and nodded.

Bows bent and released, their strings thrumming as deadly shafts sped to their targets. Having defeated Lilyth, few mages had any strength left to defend themselves. Arrows pursued the few who tried to flee, ripping through flesh and finding vital organs. Most died where they stood.

Sonya screamed, diving at her husband, who had not moved. She caught hold of his chest, placing herself in the way of coming death. In a moment the sound of bowstrings stopped. She cautiously opened her eyes and found the rest of her friends and compatriots scattered about. All were dead or dying. Only she and Duncan remained.

Duncan looked around in shock. "You ... they defend you with their lives." He looked up numbly. "They were heroes. They had children, families..."

"No," the king said.

His answer caught the archmage off guard. The king's dead gaze never shifted, as he watched a sickening realization set in across Duncan's features.

"You killed their families, too?"

Mikal remained silent, his eyes searching the blasted landscape for an answer. Then he looked back at his friend and said, "I cannot allow this to happen again."

Duncan shook his head, "Women and children?" He paused for a moment, then added, "Why have we been spared?"

The king motioned with his hand and a runner came forward with Valor, the fabled bow of House Galadine. "You have not, for I share the burden of my law." He grasped the weapon, rune-carved and ancient. Its black wood seemed to soak up the little light left. "Hold each other. I will make it quick."

Sonya stepped forward, her hands protectively over her belly and said, "You'll be killing three of us."

It was simply said, but delivered with such an intensity it swept aside any royal formalities, speaking directly to the man she had called friend these many years, instead of a king who now sat in judgment.

Mikal's gaze fell to her stomach, her meaning instantly clear. Slowly, his chin dropped to his chest and he slumped forward, every part of him physically echoing the grief he felt. He sat there for a moment in silence, then answered her from under his helm, his voice sounding hollow even to himself. "It is the worst thing I have done," he said, even as he slowly nocked an arrow. "But not the worst I will ever do."

"How can you live with yourself?" she accused.

The king took a deep breath, then raised himself and met her incredulous stare without flinching. "Make no mistake, my lady, for I am damned as well. I have killed the innocent, those pledged to my service, even children. Unborn shall be put to death for no crime they can control. Is this justice, fairness, or misery I now spread in the name of safety?"

Neither answered, but the battlefield replied with the moans of the dying, and the cawing of crows. Duncan turned to his wife and held her close. Their eyes met, the years behind their gaze speaking more than any words could. Their hands touched tenderly and a small blue spark jumped from her to him. Duncan looked at her, first with astonishment, then with anguish.

She grabbed him tighter, then whispered something in his ear, to which he slowly nodded. Their embrace lasted only a moment before Duncan met Mikal's eyes and said, "Nothing dies." It was an age-old adage, warning of the ghosts injustice raised.

The king's grip tightened, but he said nothing. He sighted down the shaft, his hands steady, and slowly drew back. Valor groaned, as if the runebow knew what was about to happen and ached for release. Then, its *twang* and *thrum* echoed across the battlefield, the sound scattering a few black-winged thieves, their bellies full of the flesh of his men. Two bodies fell, pierced by one arrow.

The king looked down, drew a shuddering breath, then turned back to his handiwork. His eyes, however, did not waver with remorse or regret, for there was none. They remained hard, like the granite rocks surrounding him, and just as dead.

Many years passed while King Galadine descended further into grief. Some heard a cawing of crows whenever the king was near. Others, something like screams echoing from a far off battlefield. The word, 'scythe', was cautiously whispered, but no one knew why. Perhaps none wanted to say, 'curse' – that the king now reaped what he had sown.

Madness soon overcame grief, ghosts of a friend's last words haunting Mikal's every waking moment. No one knew exactly when he decided to take his own life, only that the deed was done after an heir had been born.

Darker times, though, were still to come . . .

Part I

THE LORE FATHER

In combat, make every intention

to kill your opponent.

Every cut, every strike, every breath

must feed victory.

—*Kensei Tsao, The Book of Blades*

Y ou ask me to put my apprentice in harm's way,"
Silbane Petracles addressed the council, his voice
firm. Second only to the lore father, none doubted
his wisdom or power. That power now ran through his
voice, echoing with an undercurrent of anger.

His hair stood cropped close to his head, and a goatee
framed a lean face. His body followed suit, with dark
clothing, functional and well-used. Silbane's flesh, where it
showed, had the weather-beaten look of a man who spent
much time in the sun, with corded muscles bunched tightly
around a thin, tall frame. His eyes sparkled with
intelligence. Normally they would be laughing, as if an
unspoken joke lay forever at the tip of his tongue. But the
mood of the council now reflected in Silbane's eyes: hard,
cold slate.

"We have not interfered in the land's business since Sovereign's Fall," Silbane continued, turning to address the lore father directly, "and now you want us to help the Galadine royal family? You and Thera suffered the most under their rule. Are not two hundred years of persecution and loss enough? What madness is this?" His arms opened, demanding an answer.

The other adepts stared at the lore father. Though they mostly agreed with Silbane, a hesitation hung in the air, an unspoken acknowledgment that if Lore Father Themun Dreys himself petitioned the council for action, the need must be dire indeed. Themun picked his weathered frame up and took hold of his runestaff of office. He made his way around the table until he stood side by side with Silbane who, with a respectful bow, released the floor and retreated.

Themun did not look as ancient as his years would indicate. Power still coursed through his veins. The same power that earned him his place as lore father also gave him the appearance of a man in his late fifties, though he was centuries old. Still, compared to the other adepts, Themun Dreys looked ancient and tired.

He let his gaze sweep the arc of the chamber, fixing each of the council members with an icy stare. As the others waited, he started to speak, his surprisingly deep voice cutting through the room. "Silbane speaks truly. I am two-hundred years or more on blessed land, yet I have never taken action without reason." He encompassed the watching adepts with a gesture, his eyes softening. "We are all that's left."

Themun paused, then in a fluid motion brought his runestaff up and slammed the black metal heel onto the floor. Sparks flew and in a blinding flash of light, a knight appeared. Tall and outfitted in plated armor, distinctive for both its archaic form and the single, circle-shaped sigil emblazoned on his chest, he stood motionless yet commanded the attention of everyone in the room. Even without the trappings of knighthood, though, they all knew instantly who he was. Beneath a visored helm stared pale blue eyes glowing with malice and hatred.

A few adepts instinctively raised their flameskins at the first hint of violence, colored fire igniting around their bodies in protective halos. The lighter the fire, the more powerful the Adept. It was a gesture not lost on the lore father, who nodded and said, "You'll protect yourselves, at least. Maybe *that* will be worth something." He turned to an adept, this one built like a bear. "Name him."

The adept, Giridian Alacar, stood in response, long brown hair falling below his muscular shoulders. His face was square cut, with bright eyes beneath dark, bushy brows. His ursine form moved with grace, and as he strode out to the center floor one could see he was a man accustomed to his own size.

Giridian knew the question was rhetorical, the lore father's way of setting them in their place. He quenched his green flameskin without a thought. "I don't need the history lesson," he growled in answer, the lore father's theatrics obviously both frustrating and angering him.

A strikingly beautiful woman chose then to speak. Long black hair spilled down to her waist while blue eyes called to mind ocean waves. Thera Dawnlight radiated an air of steadfastness in a storm. "I think it safe to say none of us do. Lore Father, this ill becomes you."

Themun smiled, ignoring Thera, his eyes never wavering from Giridian's own. "Then I shall name him." He walked around the image of the knight, his runestaff glowing faintly. "He is General Valarius Galadine, brother to the king who decreed we be killed on sight." Themun's staff hit the granite floor at the end of his statement, punctuating the point.

"How have the last two hundred years passed for you?" the lore father went on. "In safety, raising families to love and cherish?" He spat these words, knowing the sacrifice each of the gathered adepts had made to keep their knowledge alive. "Or have those two centuries been spent in hiding? Here, if lucky, alone and hunted if not? What of the children in the land born with Talent?"

Giridian shook his head then addressed the lore father, "The persecutions are over! The latest Galadine has put an end to them."

Themun scoffed. "You think we are now welcome in the land?"

Giridian answered, "Master Silbane is right. You ask him to take his apprentice into harm's grasp? I, too, cannot agree."

Rubbing his beard, Silbane said, "And you have not yet told me why he's so important." Silbane referred to his own apprentice, but the statement could just as easily have applied to the conjured image of the general in armor.

Themun nodded, then said to the assembled adepts, "I have a simple question. You know of the destruction caused by Valarius and the demonlord Lilyth. Would any of you allow such a tragedy to replay itself if you could prevent it?"

Giridian shook his head, angry, ignoring the question and pointing instead at the image. "There has not been a fully trained adept of that power in centuries! Even you, Lore Father, have mastered only a fraction of the Old Lore." Giridian bowed in apology and quickly added, "I do not discount the very strength it took for you to survive, but it would be folly to call ourselves their peers. For all our training, we are still a shadow of what we once were."

There was steel in his voice as Giridian continued, "Perhaps it is the Lore Father who requires a history lesson." He looked at the assembled adepts. "We can lay devastation to dozens of men, but who can still call lightning from the sky?" His eyes wandered until they met Thera's. "Who has the oceans at their command?" He shook his head, and in a sad voice said, "Two centuries under the yoke of Galadine persecution have forged us into deadly warriors, but not one of us wields the might of the Old Lords."

Themun replied in a low and dangerous voice, "We may not have the Old Lords' knowledge, but we still serve the land. It has need of us now." He searched the familiar faces, hoping to find allies. He finally came to Silbane, who held his gaze for a moment before breaking contact and looking away.

It was then, Themun realized, that without some answers that even his old friend had reached his limit. He paused, then took a breath, reminding himself a patient hand was needed. What they were about to learn would require each adept's commitment to its fullest.

"I stand here now only by chance," he started to say but then stopped, looking at the image he had conjured for the first time. He stood there in silence, then came to a decision. Better they know what they faced, now. In a forthright voice that did not waver he said simply, "The demon, Lilyth, was not destroyed."

Stunned silence followed. Dragor Dahl, a powerfully built adept whose dark skin bespoke of an ancestry from the southern continent of Koorva, motioned for permission to speak. With a nod from Themun, he said smoothly, "And you bring this up now? Your timing seems . . . convenient."

Themun's eyes hardened at the implied challenge and in a low voice he replied, "Would you tell a people weary of war, who blamed you for the summoning of such a creature, that you were unable to eradicate it?" He waited for a response but there was none. Dragor stood firm, his skepticism plainly written on his face and stance for all to see, waiting for the lore father to continue.

A moment passed, then Themun said, "I thought not. For what it is worth, we will never know what the First Council planned to do. King Galadine saw to that.

"My father taught me much before he passed, but I also learned from the world itself. I grew in power, and over the years became one with the Way. When that happened, the knowledge of the lore fathers who came before me sparkled, like points of light before my eyes. Through this, I learned the fate of Lilyth. I know the demon still lives."

Themun wished this burden had fallen upon another council, one better prepared to shoulder the responsibility. He sighed but continued, his voice firm, "I share this knowledge with you now, hoping you can see the need for action."

Silbane looked at the lore father and simply asked, "Bara'cor?"

The lore father nodded. "A Gate rests at Bara'cor, once under King Bara's watchful eye."

Giridian asked, "Why worry? None were left after Sovereign's Fall, so who could know of its existence?"

Themun sighed then answered, "None but Bara. We assume he guarded it, but when he and the dwarves of Bara'cor disappeared, the guarding of this rift ended with them."

"What is it you would have us do, challenge the king's forces?" challenged Master Kisan Talaris. "I have dealt with their ilk more than you, Lore Father. They do not parley."

Kisan Talaris looked no more than thirty, though she was in fact close to her fiftieth year. Her appearance was a study in composed lethality. Her features were lithe, her eyes bright and alert, and though she was opposite to Thera in most ways, Themun still considered her quite beautiful. But she was as stubborn as the day they first met, an irksome trait undiminished by age or experience.

Yet Kisan was the only other besides Silbane to have earned the rank of Master, having progressed quickly. Next to Silbane or the lore father, she was perhaps the most powerful adept in the room.

Still, Themun ignored her challenge and directed his answer instead to the listening adepts. "King Bara was as old as the rock around him and as wise. This rift was nothing new or special. Its existence had been known since the fortress's forging by the first *builders,* but its purpose remained a mystery. I believe Bara waited for the Old Lords to return from battle, to determine what to do next. Bara'cor is dwarven-made, naturally resistant to magic, so I doubt it overly concerned him. That is, until no one returned."

Themun looked down for a moment, gathering his thoughts to outline their tenuous position. He began haltingly, almost speaking to himself, "A moment ago I wished this problem had fallen to others, a childish thought." He raised his head and looked at the assembled adepts, his gaze hardening, his voice finally finding the strength to become firm once again, "This task falls to us, and we carry the burden."

When none responded, he shook his head and said simply, "Indulge me."

He gestured with his runestaff and the middle of the chamber's floor glowed in response, a pulsing blue spreading outward from the center. Slowly, a featureless expanse of sand and desolation became visible, as if seen from high above.

"You know the Altan Wastes . . . roughly circular, and at each cardinal point—" Themun pointed at a miniature castle, no bigger than his thumb, which rose on his map— "lies one of the great strongholds. The middle area is barren, deadly to those not desert bred."

Kisan said, "The nomads are the only people known to be able to survive there. They have little regard for outsiders."

"It is not just Bara'cor that lies besieged," Themun went on, "but some force has attacked and destroyed the other fortresses of the desert." He turned on the shocked faces surrounding him. "Shornhelm, Dawnlight, now EvenSea, *gone*. Something has overcome inconceivable odds, a fact I find both frightening, and hard to comprehend. By chance or design, Bara'cor stands alone."

The council chamber fell silent, each adept weighing this new information. They knew Themun had the ability to see things happening elsewhere in the world. It was this power that had saved so many, bringing them to Meridian Isle. Now he used the same Sight to warn them of a danger they could not have seen themselves. To have Bara'cor under siege was believable. To hear something had destroyed the other ancient guardians of the desert was unimaginable.

Giridian leaned back, a question in his eyes. "You believe whatever force this is, it seeks the Gate hidden within Bara'cor? But what does Silbane's apprentice have to do with this?"

"If this were an isolated incident, with one fortress under attack, I would likely ignore it. The Galadine line seems to enjoy waging war whenever the outcome favors the royal black and gold. The siege of Dawnlight not even twenty years is testament to that."

Giridian countered Themun with, "Bara'cor is a natural target, as it defends the one pass to the lower, fertile plains, and the capital city." He waited, but the lore father did not have an answer.

In the silence, Kisan asked, "How do we aid Bara'cor without revealing ourselves? And assuming we are successful, how do we close this Gate?" She took a moment to make sure she had everyone's attention, then said, "Instead of risking an apprentice, why not infiltrate the nomad encampment and kill their leaders? Two of us could do this and escape, unseen and unscathed." Her indifferent proclamation of death hung in the air, a task that could be accomplished as easily as saying the words.

Themun was silent, leaving the rest of the council to wonder if the lore father weighed Kisan's suggestion seriously or not.

Dragor was the first to break the silence. "You would murder people who had done nothing—"

"According to the lore father, they are responsible for the destruction of three other fortresses," retorted Kisan. "They've killed thousands already. In my mind, that is enough. We hunt them down and do what we must."

"We do not know it was the nomads," said Thera. "And, Kisan, is this not crossing the line? We have never meted out punishment in such a manner. Even the First Council never took it upon themselves to be both judge *and* executioner."

"They might have lived longer if they had," Kisan replied.

"Is that your answer to everything? Kill?" Thera shot back.

Looking at Kisan was to look death in the eye, and still feel a strange elation when that gaze was returned. To Themun it was like comparing the beauty one found in a flower with a finely crafted blade. Both were beautiful, but the blade represented a deadly simplicity, an instrument forged for only one purpose. Kisan dealt death, and in doing so insured change.

But Thera nurtured life, and in doing so cherished harmony between all living things. They each represented complementary ideals that while necessary, were philosophically antithetical. Because of this, no deep friendship had formed between the two, for neither could truly understand the other. Yet life and death had their places, and when channeling the Way in its purest form, each were stunning to behold.

"What of Themun's father, who was certainly responsible for saving *you?*" Kisan replied, realizing that Themun wouldn't yet intervene. She fell back into her chair and planted the barb, arms crossed. "Quite a killer, Themun's father, from what I understand."

"You're right," Themun finally said, icily, "my father *was* a killer. But before you attack Thera or his memory, you'd be wise to remember his sons are, too."

He locked eyes with the younger master, who tried to meet his gaze but could not, breaking contact to inspect the tips of her fingers. "No offense was meant," she said coolly.

Silbane held up a hand, then said in a measured voice, "There are other things to consider. Getting into and out of the nomad camp will not be so easy. If the other fortresses have been defeated, someone or something is clearly helping them."

Themun waited a moment longer, until he was satisfied that Kisan knew her place, then nodded, "I agree."

"Now *he's* all knowing?" Kisan scoffed, clearly meaning Silbane.

"These nomads are horsemen and traders," Silbane retorted, "not experts in siege warfare. Perhaps the lore father is correct and they are being helped, by someone with knowledge, experience, and power."

Dragor stepped forward and asked, "Are we not the last?"

Silbane turned to the questioning adept and said, "Think. We have created hundreds of disciples, both wayward students and those with true Talent, who failed to achieve the Black. Our last combat instructor, Keren, makes her home near Moonhold. She seems at peace with her life, but others bear watching." He paused, thinking, then said, "We are here, so we must conclude there are others."

The lore father shrugged and said, "Perhaps, but we don't know this as fact, and none of our errant students have the power to destroy a stronghold. It comes to this: Three of the four fortresses have fallen, I know the Gate is hidden somewhere within Bara'cor, and the nomads now besiege that same fortress."

Themun looked at each council member. "Perhaps Kisan is correct," he offered, attempting to soothe his earlier treatment of the younger master. "Mayhap we need a falcon for this mission." He gave her a small smile, which she gratefully returned.

Silbane shook his head. "I can't believe the answer lies in, 'kill first and ask questions later.' If we follow that line of thinking, we should engineer the destruction of Bara'cor herself, just to be sure."

"Perhaps we should," said the lore father after a moment's thought.

"Themun, this is insane!" Silbane exclaimed.

As if sensing the council would need a solution rather than another problem, Giridian said, "While destroying Bara'cor may be out of the reach of our knowledge, there are artifacts in the vaults below that could accomplish it."

"You speak so easily of power and strength, but what of right and wrong?" Thera asked, sadness plain in her voice. "Should we not ask ourselves what is the right thing to do?"

Silbane paced a slow circle. "Bara'cor is the path for trade between the lower plains and the upper desert region. It would disrupt the trade routes and throw the entire land into turmoil. All this, on the *suspicion* of a Gate opening? We need to be more careful in our response."

"Perhaps we should consider Kisan's suggestion then, as distasteful as it may seem," Giridian said. "Kill the leaders of the nomads before they enter Bara'cor. It will buy us the time necessary to determine what we should do next." The adept then looked at Themun and continued, "As she says, they are responsible for the deaths of many. This would be fit punishment and limit any collateral damage."

Themun sighed with true sadness, then responded in a soft voice, "I never meant for things to come to this. I would like to aid Bara'cor." He knew the seed had been planted, and with it the steps necessary to ensure the land's safety. Now all he needed was time for his council to accept his line of reasoning. After that, he could address the need for Silbane's apprentice, another subject sure to cause controversy.

Kisan stood, emboldened by the seeming support of her idea, and asked, "Can we not *control* Lilyth? I realize we speak of a demon, but with our knowledge—"

"Lilyth would possess you," Themun replied. "You would be but a vessel for it to dominate and occupy. Once taken, it gains access to all your knowledge and powers, but most importantly, permanence on this plane of existence."

Themun looked pointedly at Kisan, his gaze brooking no argument, then he went on, "We will not risk ourselves to Lilyth's influence. If the demonkind re-enter this world, they will seek possession on a scale vaster than any in the past." He then looked at Silbane and said, "And as it has been so eloquently pointed out, we are not what we once were."

He stood and raised his staff, bringing it at arm's length before him. "We shall recess for the afternoon and reconvene at dusk. When we meet again, I will explain about Silbane's apprentice and his pivotal role in our decision. Your insight is needed if we are to plan a course of action."

Bowing once, he excused the other council members, sinking wearily into his chair. He watched as they filed out, Kisan being the first out the door. Themun cleared his throat and caught the attention of his friend, "Silbane, a moment of your time."

Silbane remained, a questioning look on his face.

"You must be wondering what Arek has to do with all this. As his master, you have the most insight into his abilities." He avoided Silbane's gaze, fingering the runes on his staff.

"You flatter me," Silbane replied, "but despite Arek's talent in combat, we both know he has significant shortcomings when it comes to the Way."

Themun shook a dismissive hand and took a different tact. "It is opening. I sense it," he said, referring now to the Gate.

Silbane furrowed his brow, a disbelieving look on his face. "As Dragor said, you have a knack for timing. It must feel nice to play us, but I don't have the power you do. Even I can sense nothing at this distance. And claiming my apprentice is somehow pivotal and yet expendable does not help your position. At least," he added, "not with me."

"And what of Kisan's suggestion?"

Silbane pursed his lips, clearly annoyed at the way Themun kept changing the subject. "You seemed overly eager to put her in her place."

"She insults the man who made it possible for all of us to live. Stubborn and mule-headed, nothing with her has changed."

"You are still the same, so easily angered when it comes to your father." Silbane offered a sad smile then said, "One or two of us could get in and out of the camp with little to fear. And while trained, I do not relish the role of assassin yet again."

"It may come to that, if no other solution is found."

Silbane looked into his friend's eyes. "I know, but you keep feeding us bits of information, so get comfortable with the idea of waiting." The last bit was delivered with a good measure of sarcasm, a clear indication that Silbane was in no mood to bandy words back and forth.

Themun closed his eyes, wishing the dull headache that had recently become a part of his life would recede for just a moment. As he heard Silbane get up, he put out a restraining hand and said, "Whoever is helping the nomads could be formidable. Furthermore, the Gate *is* opening, and we need a way to seal it before it does." Themun hesitated, then added, "We would need something to mask your approach, *and* disrupt the Gate itself."

Silbane stared at the lore father for what seemed an eternity, then a cold weariness stole over him. This had been a charade, a game played for his benefit. It was a puerile gift from a friend who owed him more than this, more than his life. "He's just a boy." Silbane looked away, his eyes shut as if this physical act could keep the inevitable at bay. "He would never survive."

Themun's gaze fell and in a soft voice he said, "Don't be melodramatic. He's certainly not helpless."

Silbane had no answer. Almost as an afterthought, likely to confirm what he already suspected, Silbane asked, "Has this decision already been made?"

Themun sensed his friend's frustration and held up a forestalling hand. "Circumstances would have to be truly dire for us to allow the Gate to remain unchecked and unheeded. I did not come to this lightly." He blew out a gust of air and leaned back in his chair, rubbing his forehead as he thought about his choices. "Yes. I will do what is best for the land. If that means sending your apprentice on a dangerous but vital mission, so be it."

"And if I refuse?"

Dead silence.

Then Themun barked, "Refuse? We act for the good of this land. *All of us!* That includes you *and* your apprentice!" The same anger that told Kisan she had dared too much, now fell upon Silbane. Themun made sure the master knew there was no doubt he would make good on his next promise as he said coldly, "I will assign Kisan to the task, if you decide to ignore your Oath."

Silbane was speechless, the Lore Father's sudden anger shocking him. He stepped back, making his way to the double doors that led out of the chamber,. There, he stopped, as though not trusting himself to speak, the sickening realization setting in that Arek's only hope lay on what he did next.

Then, something caught his eye. The master detected a wavering of the air, as when the sun bakes the earth, except this stood in the shadows behind Themun. His gaze narrowed, but then the mirage was gone, dissipating like the release of a breath long held.

"What was that?" Silbane motioned to the space behind the lore father.

Themun paused then said smoothly, "I thought it best our conversation remained private."

"You *warded* us? For this?"

Themun nodded, leaning on his armrest, but saying nothing else.

Silbane shook his head then turned and left, his stride betraying the anger he felt at being manipulated.

Themun watched him go, sure that the master had seen through his lie. Regardless, events were unfolding, and if Rai'stahn was to be believed, the fate of their world hung in the balance. His mind spun through every permutation to come up with a solution that did not involve sacrificing one of their own, but came back to the same place.

"You have to be more careful," Themun said aloud to the empty chamber. Silence was the only answer, though he had expected something more. Nonetheless, it was not his place yet to question the will of the Conclave.

What, he wondered, would you have counseled, Father, and am I now living by your lessons? Privately, he doubted his father would have been proud of anything he had done today.

Journal Entry 1

Banished. It is with a heavy heart that I share my thoughts, but history has a way of remembering us as she wants, and she is a fickle mistress. Having been branded tyrant, usurper, and worse, this may be my only voice.

Dragons are traitors, and first amongst these is Rai'stahn. I name him so you can greet him with death, for he deserves no better absolution than cold steel. He never understood his place, and now survives on the victory I seized.

It is a wish, and I admit a selfish one that you know of the sacrifices I made for all of us. Though they think me dead, I gain an immortality of sorts, for my legend will never die.

It is a small solace, perhaps noble to you, hollow sounding to me. I am not content with the way the dice have rolled. I do not accept my fate. It does not sit well with me. Let those who pray for my death continue to do so. Nothing they do will change who I am.

And just whose tribute do you read? Will knowing impugn your sense of fairness? Will you wish for the axe on my neck, or place the garland at my feet? We will walk the road a bit longer, so you may be more charitable to my memory, in light of my many sacrifices.

It will not be the first time a hero stood maligned, nor a common man such as yourself learns the truth.

Come, there will be much to tell you in the pages ahead . . .

THE NOMADS

Remember, those who show no fear

tend to inspire it.

—*Altan proverb*

The desert dunes glowed red in the setting sun, shimmering from the day's heat. Occasionally a small *windspin* would swirl the sand into a cloud of grit and dust, working under any amount of protection a weary traveler might have. The Altan Wastes were inhospitable at best, deadly at worst.

A lone figure stood atop a dune, his robes streaming behind him in the hot wind. Raising a massive arm, he unhooked a pack from his heavily muscled back and dropped it to the sandy floor, grunting as he released its weight.

Hemendra, leader of the clans, tribes, families, and kinsmen who called themselves the Altan, unwound the light cotton *shahwal* from his face. His eyes squinted at the wavering image of the fortress, rising just out of catapult range. He wore the loose fitting robes favored by the desert nomads to protect himself from the harsh wind and sun. As it beat down on the sands, he reached to his belt, detaching his water skin. Taking a small sip, he then corked and replaced it with the efficiency of a man who had survived fifty years under the desert's baleful yellow eye.

He was soon joined by two other men dressed much as he was. Though both would be considered large, they were almost tiny compared to the sheer size of the clanchief. He acknowledged the leader Paksen's bow with a grunt before turning to look back at the fortress.

"Mighty U'Zar," said the lead man, addressing Hemendra, "I come to ask if you wish to pull our troops back. The Redrobe has begun the summoning of the storm and wishes our men to be ready."

Hemendra inwardly grimaced at the mention of the strange man amongst them, but was careful in his response, especially in front of clanfists as ambitious as these were. The twenty or so clans they alone controlled, the largest number under one man besides himself, had come to worship the man in red robes with an almost religious zeal, thinking him chosen by the Great Sun itself. Hemendra worried this Redrobe commanded too much consideration, but had to be careful how he dealt with it. As long as Bara'cor's walls remained intact, this man was necessary. As long as *that* remained true, his lifewater would remain unspilled.

Turning from the sight of the fortress, he addressed the lead clanfist, "We shall camp, Indry. Have the brothers dig themselves in for the storm and shield the fires." Hemendra paused for a moment, looking out over the Altan Wastes. So beautiful, he reflected, yet as deadly as a *sarinak*'s sting. Turning back to the two waiting chieftains he finished, "Tell the sun sages to begin the bloodletting for their spells. Tomorrow, under cover of the storm, we advance on Bara'cor again."

"And the Redrobe's orders?" Indry asked, looking at Bara'cor with hunger in his eyes.

Hemendra eyed this nomad chieftain, his hand casually straying to rest on the bone hilt of his fighting knife, a knife that never left his side. He saw Paksen's eyes widen as the second clanfist realized his companion's error and prayed the chieftain would react so he could kill him, too. Wisely, Paksen did not move.

"Tell me of the *asabiyya.*"

The other chieftain spun to face the u'zar, the simple question laced with deadly undertones, and realized his error. He fell to his knees and touched his forehead to the sand. "Mighty U'Zar—"

"Tell me, Indry."

The man stammered, then said, "Me against my brothers; my brothers and me against our cousins; my brothers, cousins, and me against the world."

"And what family is the Redrobe to you?"

Indry shook his head slowly, almost as if he knew his fate. "He is nothing, Mighty U'Zar."

Slowly, Paksen also fell to his knees and touched his forehead to the sand. "Of course, Mighty U'Zar, your orders are not to be questioned."

Hemendra waited for a moment, looking towards the camp. He could hear the priests chanting their spells, ones that banished fatigue or called up springlets of fresh water from the dry, wind-blown wastes. Looking down, he growled, "Look at me, Indry." At first he thought the man would refuse, as what could only be a stifled sob ran quickly through him. Then, as Indry's head slowly came up, Hemendra kicked him under the chin.

Blood spurted as the ill-fated clanfist bit through his tongue and went tumbling backward down the dune, landing in a heap at the bottom. Hemendra strode down and grabbed him by his neck, picking him up like a rag doll. Dark blood ran freely in rivulets out of the nomad's mouth, dripping off his chin and staining the front of his robes. He was on the verge of screaming when Hemendra's grip tightened like a vise, choking off any sound. "Your lifewater is accepted."

The man fought, his desire for life overcoming any fear he had for the clanchief. He tried punching, kicking, and pushing the gargantuan man, trying to find any kind of purchase or weakness, but Hemendra's grasp was like iron, unyielding. Indry's punches soon became lethargic, then feeble. Finally, they stopped all together.

Hemendra waited, watching until life drained from the man's eyes, then he released his hold. He flung the dead nomad to the desert floor, feeling his fingers stick together where blood had congealed. Stalking back up the dune he stooped to grab a handful of sand and began to rub off the drying blood. Paksen, who he noticed had not moved, slowly came to his feet and paid the proper homage, palms to forehead. I will have to watch this one, he thought, angry at himself for letting the Redrobe's presence affect him so.

He could have let Indry's lapse go unpunished—killing nomads for slight transgressions was not sustainable, not for a true leader of the Altan—and Indry had brothers and cousins who would now feel obligated to retaliate. They would die too, in a ripple of violence, but to what purpose? He had been foolhardy, he knew.

Yet another part of him forgave his harsh action. Indry *had* given him what he needed most, a show of strength in front of a clanfist as powerful as Paksen. Fear was a strong motivator, and killing one to maintain order and discipline was valuable in its own way. It also stripped Paksen of an ally, should he think to challenge the u'zar. And it was clear to Hemendra that Paksen's ambition would soon exceed his caution. He nodded permission as Paksen bowed and went to see to his orders.

His eyes followed the retreating form of the clanfist, flat and empty of emotion. That day, he knew with cold certainty, would be the day Paksen died. For now, though, he would carry the word of the killing back to the men, and sprinkle the waters of doubt into their cups of ambition.

Behind him, over eight thousand nomads made ready to assault the walls of Bara'cor again. As the Great Sun dipped below the western horizon, he could see the fortress's minarets, the flags atop unfurled and rippling in the wind: a golden lion on a black field. Hemendra rewrapped the *shahwal,* careful to cover his mouth and nose. Tomorrow the storm would be here in full force and his nomads would hide in its swirling sands.

"Once again we follow you, Redrobe," he whispered into the warm desert breeze, but the words came out like a curse.

Casting one last look around, Hemendra made his way down the dune and back to his tent to perform his evening ablutions. Storms, spells, or not, he vowed, Bara'cor would soon see its last sunset.

THE MASTER

In preparation for close combat,

take heed of your opponent's stance;

in making a strike, his arms;

in giving and taking blows, his chest;

in all else, watch your opponent's eyes.

—*Tir Combat Academy, Basic Forms & Stances*

Silbane moved through the wide hallway toward the stairwell that would take him to his quarters. This is insanity, he thought. Using Arek could not be the only answer. There were always other options. Still, the danger to Edyn was great. Were they not pledged to serve that need? And as the lore father had pointed out, his apprentice intended to take the same oath of service as an adept, a Binding Oath. It was not a decision taken lightly.

In fact, the Binding Oath did much more once uttered, for it combined the true intent of the two who pledged it, heard and enforced by the Way. Breaking the oath had varying degrees of punishment, from something as simple as blindness or deafness, to complete annihilation. A dark cloud would appear, and the person would be forever changed. None had ever escaped its punishment, so the uttering of such an oath was taken with the utmost sincerity.

Was Arek not already committed by his allegiance to the council, and his intention to test for the rank of adept? Was he not governed by his intention to take this very same oath, whether uttered or not? Silbane did not trust himself to answer that question now.

Another thing troubling the master was that the other fortresses of the land had been destroyed. This only strengthened the argument that something was happening, and it was not some random testing of strength. There were many other targets, ones more convenient and easier to defeat than an armed and guarded fortress of granite. Regardless of his opinion of nomad strength, Silbane knew that desert warriors armed with horn bows would not survive an assault on a fortress stronghold. At least, not without help. Themun had surely gone through the same line of reasoning, and staged that charade for his benefit. Silbane inwardly cursed, then asked himself, what had been the point?

He strode up the circular stairway, exiting on a level high above the main training halls. He ignored the bows of respect protocol demanded students and servants offer as he passed, his mind deep in thought. If Bara'cor is the last fortress standing, then the nomads have combined their strength with someone else, and Themun is correct … it did not bode well for the security of the Gate.

Silbane strode through the double doors to his quarters, which swung silently shut behind him. Placing his things in a corner, he made his way into his personal library. There he searched the stacks for a particular manuscript on the history of Bara'cor, snapping his fingers when his eyes fell on its faded brown leather cover. Retrieving it, he settled into a plush chair near a window and began to read.

Bara'cor, it stated, stood at the southwest corner of the Altan Wastes, straddling Land's Edge, aptly named for the two thousand foot cliff face separating the upper desert region from the lush, abundant grasslands surrounding the capital city of Haven below. The fortress stood with its back to Land's Edge protecting the one safe way down, a wide road cut out of the sheer face of the cliff.

As a result, Bara'cor had found an ever-increasing amount of people traveling through its walls, the pass between the upper and lower regions creating the perfect atmosphere for trade to flourish and grow. The fortress served as the protective nexus for traders from the Wastes and those from the lower, fertile valleys to meet in a neutral place that welcomed all.

It was dwarven-made, with towers and minarets reaching gracefully into the desert sky. The stone itself was shaped in a manner unlike any known in the land, as if poured and then hardened in place. It was beautiful, and bespoke of a mastery of stonemasonry long since lost.

Still, the citizens of Bara'cor could not entirely dismiss the obvious intent of the original builders to protect their work of art. Bara'cor held a strong military presence and surrounding its fragile inner city were hundred-foot walls of solid granite, rising out of the desert floor. It stood alone along the cliff's edge like a great stone fist so only the walls facing the desert were open to possible attack.

Atop those walls were catapults, standing like silent sentinels. The area in front of the stronghold was mostly sand with a few boulders strewn haphazardly, as if some giant had upended a sack of rocks, none of which were big enough to afford any protection against the deadly barrage of missile fire Bara'cor could bring to bear.

One of the most astounding facts about the fortress, Silbane read, was the natural lake within its walls. Fed through underground springs, Bara'cor had an unlimited supply of fresh water, a commodity worth more than gold to inhabitants of the Wastes. Silbane sat back for a moment, the last thought repeating in his head.

Closing the book, he moved out into the main room and settled down near another large window. The afternoon sun shone with its usual springtime intensity. In the distance, he could hear the rumble of the waves crashing onto the surf. He noticed a few of the older apprentices gathering for informal practice on the hill behind the tower, their brown uniforms contrasting with the bright green of the grass.

The nomads could be after that source of water. Though it did not seem logical, no explanation could be ruled out. But there were easier ways to get water, including trading between the people of the desert and those of the fortresses—a practice well respected and known.

Also, it failed to answer how the nomads had already destroyed three other fortresses, and now looked to the fourth. Nothing about this fit with the ways of nomadic life, nor with their favored style of warfare, fast-moving and mounted. It gave him a very uneasy feeling.

Opening the window, Silbane breathed in the cool sea air and watched the initiates gathered on the hill, not without a bit of envy. Simpler times, with simpler pleasures, he remembered fondly. Silbane had been brought here almost eighty years ago, a wide-eyed lad of perhaps nine. He had expected to see all sorts of magical beasts and eldritch incantations of power. Instead, much to his disappointment, his first years exposed him to stacks of books, none of which were magical. Themun and the other teachers had pounded the basics of reading, writing, history, and mathematics into his young mind until finally he passed his entrance examinations, proving he was intelligent enough to continue. Mathematics in particular had been emphasized. For some reason, it had been shown that those with the highest aptitude in numbers had the greatest connection to the Way.

From that day forth, Silbane had been subjected to intense physical and mental conditioning, something he had not at all expected. Each day had been dedicated to hardening his body in unarmed and bladed combat, and sharpening his mind on logic and numerical puzzles. The mantra of this phase of his training was repetition, an ideology Themun in particular seemed to inflict upon him with a special zeal.

When the time came, he had taken the Test of Potential, proving once again he had a connection to the Way. His formal apprenticeship had begun that very same day, with him turning in his old white uniform for dark green. During this time he had been regaled with the histories of the land, and the Demon Wars.

The First Council had been ill-prepared for the war. They had not concentrated nearly as much on the physical aspects of combat, instead investing much of their time on more arcane manifestations of power. This decision, in Silbane's opinion, rendered them incapable of protecting themselves when they needed it the most. Their bodies, lacking in physical endurance and stamina, had succumbed to the immense needs of facing Lilyth and the armies of demonkind that followed.

Themun and his Second Council had vowed never to let their adepts face such a situation unprepared. "A fool expects the same song to end on a different note," was another favorite saying of his instructors.

As a result, a significant portion of an adept's training now lay in the physical arts of combat. This ensured their ability to survive in situations a pure scholar could not, regardless of magical potential. The path to the Way was often thought of as hanging onto a rope, with an adept's stamina eventually wearing out. To combat this, one needed to train both the mind *and* the body, before they could truly master the Way and the arcane energies flowing unseen throughout the world.

Silbane wondered how the lords of the First Council had ever made the journey to Sovereign's Fall, leaving their cloistered lives behind. Their bodies could not have been ready for the hardships they would face.

In truth, the Second Council's adoption of physical and mental excellence had made them better prepared in some ways for this crisis than their forebears. Their bodies were at the peak of conditioning, and enhanced by magical energy, could accomplish feats most would consider impossible. What they lacked in raw, overt, power they partially made up for with enhanced speed and strength. If the sham of the upcoming council "vote" went the way the lore father had engineered, the final task would come down to infiltration and assassination, something Silbane was especially well trained to do.

He cursed himself for daydreaming and moved away from the open window. His apprentice's life lay in the balance, for Themun would not hesitate to send Arek with Kisan. If the Gate had opened, then Themun's solution would be to push Arek through. To Silbane, it was clear the lore father believed Arek's peculiar ability to dampen or disrupt magical energies was the reason behind this.

It *might* close the Gate, he conceded, but if successful would leave Arek stranded in Lilyth's world. Silbane could not live that. His only choice would be to find a way to protect his apprentice, and that meant he would have to accompany him. He could no longer trust the lore father or anyone else to keep the boy safe, and this was exactly what the lore father had counted on. Silbane could see he was being manipulated and hated it.

Putting down the leather-bound tome, he rose and went back into his library. Searching the stacks, he retrieved another book, *The Altan Nomads*. He moved back to his chair and sat down, preparing for some intensive research. Being angry at the lore father was a waste of time, he semi-chastised himself. If there is an answer to the nomad's actions, and a chance to safeguard Arek, it will be in here. Opening the old book, Silbane leaned back in the afternoon sun and began to read.

HISTORIES: MAGEHUNTERS

A bladesman does not kill by using a sword; he

allows his opponents to live

when wielding his blade.

He kills or grants life, by his own will.

—*The Bladesman Codex*

How often have you done this?" His voice came out nervously, looking to his lieutenant. He wore the dark mail and cloak of the king's Magehunters, blue edged with silver. In his right hand he carried a torch, its dancing flame sputtering and hissing in the light rain. It painted his young face a lurid splash of orange and black, as light and shadow danced in the dismal night. He didn't want to do this, but talking to his lieutenant kept him in good spirits.

"Half a dozen, Stiven, maybe more. Stop worrying." He was not much older than the boy he spoke to. He rubbed his face clear of rain and looked up, silently cursing the weather and the clutch of new recruits like Stiven he had to look after. Dumber than a bag of onions, and not even as useful, but he could not afford to have the boy panic at the wrong time. He put a conciliatory hand on Stiven's shoulder and said, "The king's mark is with us. She'll deal with any trouble. Just worry about your shieldmates."

Stiven gulped, looking at the storm clouds, then turned a wide-eyed stare back to his commander and said, "Garis said they have powers . . . that we can be turned into things . . . *unnatural* things."

Lieutenant Kearn shook his head and smiled. "What makes you think you're so normal now?"

Another soldier bumped the kid with an elbow and said, "Don't worry Stiv, you'll likely be turned into a man. That'll be a real trick." Good-natured laughter followed as the platoon of men moved through the forest toward the village. Then the rain began to fall in earnest, ruining the moods of many. They had spent close to a fortnight on the hunt and wanted nothing more than a roof that didn't leak and a dry, warm bed.

Their mood was further darkened by the woman who rode next to them on her black destrier. Her name was Alion Deft, the king's mark, and her job was to hunt down and kill those who would threaten Edyn again. She wheeled her horse, then signaled Kearn to stop. She cantered over and met the young lieutenant's unvoiced question with a flat statement. "I'll address the men here."

Lieutenant Kearn nodded, then motioned to his sergeant to have them form up but keep silent. At this distance, sound could still carry to the village, though the rain had muffled much of their progress through the undergrowth.

The men shambled into a loose square facing their sergeant. The fact the order had been obeyed instantly was the only indication these were seasoned fighting men. Some pulled their hoods farther forward as the rain fell harder. Lieutenant Kearn looked at the ragtag grouping and scowled at the lax formation, but then said, "Shield rest." The men relaxed, but only a bit, waiting for their commander to speak.

Deft moved her warhorse forward to face the men and dismounted. Her cloak was the same dark blue as the others, but her armor was silver and steel, with a circular symbol stamped upon her breastplate. Her fingers rubbed it absentmindedly, a ritual before every cleansing. She looked at the assembled soldiers and asked, "Why are we here?"

There was no answer, and she seemed to expect none. She pulled her sword from its scabbard, the steel ringing its own note of death, and continued, "There is a pestilence. I mean to remove it." Her gaze swept the men while the clearing remained silent. The only sound, rain falling through the trees. "I act on the king's order, and by his grace and our Fathers, so do you." Her eyes hardened. "No mercy."

The men shuffled a bit, but nothing they heard was new. At a nod from the king's mark, they all knelt. Deft raised a circled hand in supplication and said, "Let us pray."

The men lowered their heads as the king's mark intoned, "Fathers, bless our acts tonight. Aid us to smite the demons who wish harm upon your good lands. Let us be the hand that delivers justice, in peace."

"In Peace." The men responded. They slowly rose, some making the sign of the Circle and kissing their fists. Soon, they knew, it would be over.

Kearn watched Stiven look at the king's mark as she stood there in the rain. "She's beautiful," he heard him whisper, to no one in particular.

"Aye," said the sergeant who had lost an eye during one of the many border fights following Lilyth's defeat, "and deadly. Stay away from her when it starts."

"Why?" Stiven asked, in a voice that sounded like a boy more than a man.

The one-eyed man turned back and said, "Just stay out of her way." He cinched Stiven's pauldron closer, tapping it with a mailed fist to be sure it sat securely on his shoulder, then walked away, disappearing into the wet gloom.

Stiven stared at the sergeant's back until Kearn thumped him out of his reverie. "Come on, Stiv. You're assigned to the catchers. Grab some torcs." He motioned to a basket holding dozens of metal collars, dull and gray. Still, every so often the light would catch one just so, and the coppery orange metal would flash into life.

Stiven moved over and grabbed one of the collars, holding it as he had been taught. It didn't weigh much, but Kearn knew Stiven had seen what it could do. He clutched it tighter, making the thrusting motion once, twice, as if to remind his own arm how it was used. Then he took two more and hooked them onto his belt, within easy reach, and was obviously relieved to see the others do the same. Everyone knew Stiven hated standing out.

The sergeant whispered a command to douse the torches, and Stiven's went into the wet ground with a hiss. The clearing where they stood fell into inky darkness, until his eyes adjusted and Kearn could make out the rest of the men. They looked like shadows, disappearing between the rain, leaves, and trees, and death followed their every step.

* * * * *

Alion Deft stood where she had delivered her prayer, scanning until her eyes came to rest on an older man, grizzled and gray. He had the look of one who scowled regardless of the weather. His mouth worked a repetitive chewing motion that spoke to the wad of *hazish* within. He stood near a small cart they had wheeled along with them. It was made of wood, and along one side held a small door, bolted closed. The king's mark nodded her chin at the cart and said, "Malioch, bring her out."

"Royal whelp." He said the words like they were a private curse, talking *at* Alion, but not about her.

The king's mark moved in front of him, her eyes fixed on the man until he acknowledged her with a spit to one side. She waited a moment longer then said, "Bring her out."

It was the flatness of her voice, the dead calm that gave the man pause. He spat again, a brown liquid, foul smelling and pungent, then produced a large iron key. The bolt unlocked with a snap and he pulled wide the door. He waited a moment, then thrust his hand inside. "Come on!"

A squeal sounded from inside the box and Malioch cursed, then grabbed a handful of hair and yanked. Out came a girl, dumped unceremoniously into the wet mud. He kicked her so she tumbled forward again, falling face down. "Curse you, witch."

Alion watched this without care, waiting for the girl to rise. Slowly, as the desire to stand and stretch overcame her inherent fear, the girl came to her feet. What was once a white robe was now matted with filth and stains, hanging from her bony shoulders. Dark hair that had not felt a loving hand in weeks fell in clumpy strings. When she finally looked up, what had been a face filled with laughter held only the frightened gaze of someone trying desperately to avoid another beating. The girl cringed with her entire body and spirit, looking far younger than her twelve summers would indicate.

The king's mark stepped forward and stooped so her eyes were level with the girl's own. She noted the prisoner still wore the torc around her neck. As she neared, the girl stepped back but Alion held up a hand, "Steady now, Galadine. You know your job, yes?"

The girl looked as if she were about to cry, but nodded vigorously.

"Do as I say and you may have your father's love again." Alion lied without a second thought. This vermin, along with the rest, would be food for worms long before the king forgave her sins. Alion did not care. Using these magelings had become a necessary evil. How else would they be able to find others like her?

The Talent ran strong in the Galadine line, their curse to bear for being faithful stewards of the land, and the king's willingness to sacrifice his own blood spoke to his character and nobility. Still, the need to consort with this *thing* filled her with disgust. She could only imagine the royal family's shame that they should be so afflicted.

Despite these thoughts, her revulsion, along with the deepest desire to thrust her blade into the heart of the creature, never reached her eyes. She said the words with utter sincerity, allowing the briefest hint of a smile to play across her features, reassurance that everything would be all right.

She stood and motioned to Kearn. "Take the torc off."

As the lieutenant obeyed, she looked back at the girl and said, "Kalissa, you know what happens if you run?"

* * * * *

Kalissa Galadine nodded again, not saying a word. The instant the lieutenant touched the torc, it unlatched with a small *click* and the metal collar opened.

Power flooded through Kalissa's senses, reawakening her connection to the Way. It sang into her heart, healing minor injuries, succoring her weariness, and cleansing her soul. The pain fell as if washed away like her mud stains. She felt reborn, but knew this was only temporary. If she did not obey, her father would keep her here. Nothing she did, no connection to the Way, would ease the pain of what she had to do next.

She opened her eyes and Saw, then pointed and stammered, "Th-through the trees. There are two you want."

Alion looked at the girl for a moment then asked, "Just two? Are you sure?"

She nodded.

Alion looked up, her eyes calculating. "You stay near me for this." She handed the reins of her warhorse to a nearby soldier who secured it to the cart, which would remain behind.

Kalissa came forward, standing woodenly next to the king's mark. She never took her eyes off the glowing folk she could see, amongst the less bright signs of the people in the village around them. They stood not more than two hundred paces away, beacons of Talent marking them for death.

Next to them, she saw a third, brighter than they were, someone with the potential for true power. Her eyes flicked once to the knight standing next to her, then back to the village. This third one was young, a girl not more than five or six summers old. Kalissa did not know who she was, only that if the girl were discovered, it would likely mean her own death.

Why would the king's mark need her Talent if another, younger child were found to do her bidding? The shame of the decision to let this girl be put to the sword along with the rest of her village would have caused her anguish in the past, but now it barely registered. If her own father could give her away to someone like Malioch, why should she be any more merciful?

Adults with Talent were killed, but children were harvested and put to work, just as she had been. She would not take the chance these men would choose this new child of power over herself, and she did not care anymore about the consequence to her own soul. She would live and that was all that mattered. It was not the first time she had chosen her own safety over others and she knew it would not be her last. It was simply a matter of survival.

* * * * *

The village was small, counting no more than ten huts arranged around a central fire pit that still held glowing embers, protected by a rain shield made of some sort of metal. The rain hit it with a *pang* that sounded at once both hollow and strangely muffled. Alion could almost hear the drops slide down the shield, before they joined their brothers on the soaked earth. At best, the king's mark estimated, there were less than fifty people here. She looked to Kalissa, who pointed to the second hut on her right. Alion put two fingers up and pointed.

The men broke into smaller squads of four, each taking station silently at the entrance to each hut. The remainder of her men melded into the shadows in case any tried to sneak out, a strategy they had practiced and perfected over dozens of raids.

When they were in position, Lieutenant Kearn signaled to the king's mark, who strode into the center of the village and its fire pit. Grabbing a metal poker, she stoked the embers, then grabbed some wood from the pile. She threw this onto the fire, watching as it lit, growing slowly into a warm, orange dance of flames. Then, she casually ran the poker across the rain shield, the metal on metal creating a cacophony of sound.

A few villagers to poke their heads out to see what was happening. At that moment those under Deft's command exploded into action, streaming into each house and grabbing the people inside. Screams ensued as the village realized it was suddenly under attack, yet there was little defense offered, as the attackers were both well-trained and alert in comparison with these simple, sleep-addled folk.

Three entered each house and battered people into submission. A fourth would move in quickly and collar them, the torc snapping into place before they knew what was happening. Instantly, any path to their powers would vanish, or at least that was the promise. These torcs could only be removed by one without Talent. It made for an infallible test of who exactly was a mage and who wasn't. If they had no power, they could remove their torc easily. If not, the king's mark would deal with them.

* * * * *

Stiven raced in behind his team, torcs ready. He saw a man go down with a strike to his forehead, the flat of the blade hitting him with a dull thud. Stiven was upon him, dropping his torch and snapping a torc in place with a simple thrust of his hand. He fumbled to make another ready and looked up, only to see a woman slashing downward with something. He raised his blade instinctively, hearing the strike of steel on steel and feeling the shock of impact. The sword tumbled from his cold, wet fingers as he fell onto his back.

The woman carried a cleaver and raised her hand to strike again, but two swords plunged into her back as his squadmates came to his aid. They struck repeatedly as the woman let out a low groan, falling to her knees. They stabbed her even after she fell forward, face down and lifeless, pinning her body to the ground with their blades.

One leaned on his sword, thrust through the back of the dead woman's body, then looked up at Stiven and laughed, "She had some swing in that arm!"

He didn't answer, his mind still reeling from the speed of the attack and everything happening around him. Sitting on the ground, he watched numbly as the little girl who ran up to her dead mother's body was torced, then pulled out of the hut along with her unconscious father.

Alion smiled at the brutal efficiency of her men. The villagers put up little resistance and were soon rounded up and left kneeling in the mud of the central square. Those who were unconscious were dumped to the side under the watchful eyes of the guards. Those who had been killed were dragged from where they fell and laid out for the count, a grisly sight for the survivors. Within a few moments, the raid was over and the people of the village were fully accounted for, one way or another.

* * * * *

"Wake them," Alion said, motioning to the unconscious.

Guards went to the well and roped up buckets of cold water. With these they doused the fallen, following with kicks and slaps until all were at least semi-conscious and able to kneel next to their friends.

When the king's mark was satisfied she had everyone's attention, she said, "You know why we are here. You harbor those decreed by the King's Law as a threat to this land. Point them out, and we will release you."

None said a word, which did not surprise Alion Deft at all. Simple folk often saw those with Talent as some kind of benefit and harbored them, a mistake she would not allow to go unpunished. She moved slowly until she stood silhouetted by the fire, which blazed like a mantle of yellow power behind her. "Separate them."

At her command, the children were grabbed and moved to one side, while the adults were held at sword point. Screams ensued and one mother ran forward to grab her son. Alion moved with the swiftness of a cat. Her blade licked out, slicing the woman's head from her shoulders before returning to her scabbard in one smooth motion. The body and head fell separately, and the villagers instantly sank into a stifled hush of broken sobs and muttered curses.

"You are in violation of the King's Law, a decree designed to safeguard your lives! I bring justice and order. Where are they?" Alion knew she could have asked Kalissa, but this was the interesting part. She always wondered why people had such faith in their friends, when it took so little to turn them against each other.

"Justice?" a kneeling man asked. "The king's brother summons a demon and the land is plunged into war. For that, we pay with *our* lives?"

Alion nodded, and a guard picked the man up and brought him before her. Her eyes narrowed. "Lilyth destroyed our world. King Galadine saved it. You owe him your respect."

The man shook his head, clearly distraught, "My wife . . ."

The king's mark looked at the headless body and shrugged. "She chose her path, as will you." Alion grabbed him by the chin, forcing him to meet her eyes. "Where are the mages? Answer, or your son dies."

Two guards snatched up the boy in question and brought him to where the man could see him. It was clear this was the boy the dead woman had tried to save. They shoved him down to a kneeling position, and one placed his sword point at the nape of his neck.

"No!" The man looked back at the king's mark, pleading, "No, please." He then looked about the group and pointed to a man near one end. "He is the one you seek. He and his wife!"

Alion looked to where the man pointed and saw one of the men who had been unconscious. He knelt now, holding one hand to his bleeding forehead. She looked back at the man, then shoved him away. "Well done." She then looked at the guards near the accused man and said, "Bring him here."

The guards obeyed, and the man was dragged before the king's mark and dumped at her feet. Alion looked at the man and said, "Kalissa?"

The girl walked forward, a small tremble in her lips. She came slowly, fear dragging at her feet.

"Is this man one of your kind?" Alion asked.

The girl looked at the man, who now focused his eyes on her with hatred. Because he was collared, she would not be able to see his aura, a sure sign he had Talent. Normal people always shone, regardless of the collar or not, just not as brightly as those with Talent. "Yes, King's Mark. He is one of us."

"And the other?" Deft had pulled a dagger, wicked and sharp, absentmindedly picking at her nails.

Kalissa looked at the pile of bodies and pointed. "Dead. His wife w-was the other," she stammered.

Alion watched the girl, then the man. When Kalissa mentioned his wife, she caught the look of anguish that flitted behind his eyes. So, she thought, the girl speaks truly, or at least it is true his wife is dead. We shall see.

The king's mark addressed the kneeling man. "Take off the torc, and you will be released."

The man turned his attention from the girl who had pointed him out and now looked at the tall woman before him. She was square-jawed and horse-faced, her voice without emotion. There was no love or compassion in her eyes, only apathy and death. "The Lady curses you," he said weakly, knowing his fate.

"My Kalissa is seldom wrong. If your wife had lived, maybe I could have persuaded you to work for me, but with her dead, there is little to compel your obedience." Alion paused, "Unless, you have a child?"

The man shook his head. "No," he spat, and the king's mark could see he wished her death, or worse.

"Then take off the torc and you will be absolved in the eyes of your Fathers."

The man slumped into the ground, head in his hands. Then he grabbed the torc in both and pulled, his neck and face straining until red. When he could pull no more, he gave up, exhausted. "What does it prove?" he muttered.

Alion turned and faced the man kneeling before her and said, "It proves you have been judged, found guilty, and served the King's Justice."

She brought the blade up in a short, brutal arc, stabbing under the man's neck and through the back of his skull. The man coughed a gout of blood, clutching at the Mark's hands. His grip was at first strong, but as his life gushed out, became weak, feeble pulls on her wrist. His last breath gurgled out of him as he died.

Alion pulled the dagger from his neck and wiped it clean, shoving the dead man onto his back with her booted foot. Then she grabbed the torc, which came undone easily at her touch, and tossed it into a basket sitting some feet away. Sheathing her dagger, she looked to Lieutenant Kearn. "Get them up."

At his command, the villagers were lined up facing the king's mark. She watched them without emotion. These were worse than the ones who sullied themselves with magic. They turned their backs on the Almighty Fathers, embracing instead the work of demons.

Her men grabbed the large basket she had tossed the torc into and placed it on the ground near the standing villagers. Alion motioned to the basket and said, "Take off your torcs and put them in the basket. Then go wait in that hut." She pointed to the back of the village. "Once I have satisfied the king's decree, we will release you and depart."

The survivors moved slowly, stiffly, reaching up and pulling off their torcs with numb fingers, tossing them into the basket. Unlike the man before them, they had no Talent, and the torcs came off easily at their touch. As each collar came off, that person was ushered into the hut to stand with his neighbors.

From the back of the line came a child's squeal. Alion looked and saw a small girl, no more than five, pulling at her torc. A nearby adult reached down, but the king's mark stopped her with a word: "Hold!"

Four men formed a circle around the girl, who looked more frightened now than ever. She sat down in the mud and buried her face in her hands. Alion moved in closer and said, "Little one, what is the matter?"

She looked up, with eyes so blue they almost glowed. Soft black hair spilled down her shoulders, and Alion found herself stunned by the child's simple beauty. The girl stifled her tears, then sobbed, "You hurt him!"

The king's mark looked back at the dead man and thought, Not as truthful as I was led to believe.

She turned slowly and faced Kalissa, a little satisfied when the girl shook uncontrollably, her eyes showing white. "Did we miss one?"

With a scream, Kalissa turned to run, but was grabbed by Malioch. He punched her once in the face, then slapped the torc back on her before she tried any more mischief.

Alion grabbed Kalissa by the scruff of her neck and dragged her back to the little girl, then threw her to the ground. "Did you think to save one of your own?"

When the girl did not answer, the king's mark looked to the other villagers. "Remove your torcs, now!"

The townsfolk scrambled to obey, and within a few heartbeats there were no more wearing the king's metal collar. They were pushed and shoved back to the hut, until all were crammed inside. Guards stationed themselves at the entrance, as others circled the hut to ensure none escaped.

Alion turned her attention back to the little girl Kalissa had not mentioned. "The collar, it won't come off?" she said sweetly.

The girl looked up, then shook her head, pulling at it. "I want my da," she said in a small voice.

The king's mark drew her blade. "You'll join him in a moment."

"Hold your arm, Deft." The strident command came from behind her, the voice strong and composed. She saw her men turn and look. Any undrawn weapons sang out of their scabbards now with the ring of steel. She blinked once, then turned to the voice.

At the village's entrance path stood three men. No, not men, she corrected herself, one man and two boys. They were dressed in dark, close fitting clothes without armor. They carried swords strapped across their backs, the hilts jutting up defiantly over their shoulders. Even as she watched, the man in the center stepped forward into the light of the village fire.

Recognition sparked and she paused, thinking through her options. This man was an outlaw, a malcontent, but dangerous. Her eyes narrowed and she drawled, "Captain Davyd Dreys, what a pleasant surprise." Suddenly a simple evening's culling had turned into a fight for her very survival, and Alion was too pragmatic to lie to herself. Still, she had to buy time and asked while readying her weapons, "How does it feel, knowing you are both a traitor and cursed?"

The man she had called Davyd looked about and said simply, "I'm no longer captain and don't serve your king. That doesn't make me a traitor."

"Really? What would your men say, the ones lying dead at Sovereign's Fall?" A smirk pulled at the corner of her mouth, for Captain Drey's desertion was a well-known fact.

Davyd ignored her jibe and looked about, taking in the whole scene. "Still consorting with children? Have you found no better work since your days in court?"

"This is better suited to my particular tastes, but what of you? Do you not care for the mark you still wear?" She raised her arms and displayed the two interlocked circles worn by all king's marks, tattooed on her forearms.

Davyd was hit with a fit of coughing, a phlegm-covered sound emanating from deep within his chest, and held a hand to his mouth. Beneath his sleeve, she could still see the same tattoos on his forearm, twin to hers. After a moment, his coughing subsided and he rasped, "Circumstances have dictated I intervene. I was too late to help my brothers, but will not allow you to kill their children. You will face justice today."

Alion's eyes took on a calculating stare, and she nodded slowly. "The wasting sickness is upon you, judgment from the Fathers' hands." She moved to one side and motioned to her men, who moved forward in a loose semicircle. "Why chance your sons' lives? They do not have the benefit of the training you've received."

Davyd signaled to his sons to remain steady. They, in turn, drew weapons and came to stand by their father. "I've taught them what I know. Shall we demonstrate?"

Alion Deft, the king's mark and magehunter, bowed to the outlaw and said, "By all means, have at us." She looked to the brace of men still guarding the hut with the villagers inside and screamed, "Release them to their Fathers!"

At her order, her men hefted long spears and began stabbing through the thin hut walls, killing any within reach of the leafed blades. Normally they would have set the hut afire, but the accursed rain had put an end to that plan. The men at the entrance waited, stabbing any who ventured near the opening. The screams of the dead and dying soon filled the night air.

Davyd and his sons exploded into action, summoning the Way. Their forms flashed in a burst of blue fire, a flame-like skin protecting them as armor would. Without speaking they ran in three directions, with Davyd taking the shortest route to Alion and the other two winging toward the hut where the soldiers continued massacring the townsfolk. To the assembled men, the three looked like angels, shining like blue stars in the dismal night.

It was not a moment too soon, for guards began flinging their torcs at them, lethal rings aimed at the mages. The torcs did not need to fasten themselves to be effective, only loop around a limb, and Alion's men knew it. They had practiced this sort of maneuver too, and the air soon filled with the weapons of the Magehunters, seeking any kind of contact to deaden a connection to the Way.

Davyd blocked one, deflecting it with his sword, then ducked and rolled under another as a soldier swiped at him with his weapon. The mage raised his blade and blocked the soldier's, then opened his palm.

Blue flame engulfed the man, incinerating him in less than a heartbeat. Davyd did not slow as he dived through the dying man's ashes and stabbed another through the eye. He yanked his blade free and spun, slicing with his arm. A thin blue light arced out, like a line with a weight at the end, severing anything it touched. Soldiers fell screaming, their legs cut out from under them.

Alion felt the blue line come her way and dodged, rolling through it. Her armor shone, bending Davyd's spell and protecting her from its lethal cut. She thanked the king's priests and their ability to bring the power of her Fathers to protect her.

Over the blue devastating line streaked the elder of Davyd's sons, Armun. He landed lightly, swinging his blade in a tight arc and swatting aside two rings. He knelt and punched his fist downward. The ground erupted in a circle from the impact point, cracking under the soldiers' feet, but leaving the villagers unharmed.

The men caught in the spell fell into crevasses appearing suddenly beneath them. Armun stood and clenched his fist, and the earth closed again on the trapped men, crushing them in its black embrace. He looked to his father and smiled, then made his way toward the hut, cutting men in half with his blade as if they were made of paper.

Davyd leaped at Alion again, weaving a net of silver steel around the king's mark. The strikes were lethal, but each time they came near, his sword bent and twisted in his hand as if it had a life of its own. Her armor acted as if it were a reversed lodestone, repelling his blade at every thrust. He cursed, then pointed his finger and a bolt of pure lightning, blue and white, flashed at his opponent.

Alion stabbed her sword into the ground, then knelt behind it. The arc of lightning hit the air in front of her and curved around, bending the stroke into a sphere of power surrounding the king's mark, but not touching her. The lightning danced until it gathered at the hilt of her sword, then followed the blade down, channeling itself into the ground and leaving Alion entirely unharmed.

The ground around her exploded outward from the force of the lightning strike, scorching the earth in a radial pattern of force. From its smoking center rose the king's mark, smiling, blade in hand.

While Davyd combated Alion, his youngest son, Themun, leapt away from the clearing and began cutting down sentries and those who had managed to escape their swath of destruction through the camp. As he rounded a tree, a blade came whipping out, only to be caught on the hilt of Themun's steel.

Lieutenant Kearn pulled a shorter blade and faced his opponent, who looked no older than his new recruits. This would be simple work. "I've never heard of a mage who can fight." To his side came Stiven, holding a cudgel he had found to replace his lost sword. He held one in one shaking fist, a torc in the other.

Kearn motioned to him to attack. "Easy kill," he cajoled, "they can't stand against our—"

Themun's form blurred, moving faster than the man could blink. His blade sliced effortlessly through the torso of the hapless lieutenant, the body falling in two pieces even as he kicked the other man in the face.

Stiven tumbled and landed on his back. He threw the torc blindly at his attacker, then rolled and began feverishly crawling into the undergrowth, trying to hide.

Themun deflected the torc away, then placed a booted foot on the boy's back. He heard him scream, then watched as he rolled over and begged, "Mercy! Please, this is my first time! I knew it was wrong! From the very beginning!"

The look on the boy's face made it clear he had not expected to be facing someone his own age, but Themun didn't care. He could hear the lies fall from the man's tongue even as he spoke it. Magehunters were despicable and the song of retribution sang in Themun's heart. Only blood would quench it.

"Please, don't kill me," begged the boy again. He began to grab for a dagger.

"I'm not my father," the Themun said, then sliced twice with his blade, opening Stiven's bowels. "I'm not as good at making this painless."

Stiven screamed in agony and fell back, the dagger falling from nerveless fingers.

Themun stabbed him once in the neck, then held the boy's hand to the spurting wound. "Hold here, it'll be slow; let go, and you'll die quick. More mercy than you Magehunters have shown these people." With that, he stood up and literally vanished into the undergrowth, never looking back to see what the boy chose. He simply did not care.

Alion and Davyd battled back and forth, their swords an intricate dance of death. When Davyd pressed, Alion pulled back, forcing the other to commit. Davyd however was too well trained to allow her to draw him in. Worse, she knew his sons would be done soon, then it would be three against one.

*****

Armun did not hesitate, speeding to the hut holding the villagers. He knew his father battled Alion and that he could not get there in time, so he did the next best thing. At least saving some of the villagers was still within his power. He grabbed the soldiers at the door and flung them away, his touch sending a surge of lightning through their bodies. They fell in smoking husks, dead before they hit the ground.

He pushed forward with both hands and the hut exploded outward. The grass and thatching detonating with such force that many of the larger pieces sliced into exposed skin and blinded those soldiers unlucky enough to have been looking in that direction. Armun had a special affinity with earth and trees.

He snapped his fingers and every piece of grass or wood lodged within a soldier or on their person burst. The force was not huge, but enough to break bone, tear flesh, and incapacitate them. Literally dozens of men fell dead or dying from Armun's touch. He let out a sigh and surveyed the area. In a few heartbeats he and his brother had laid waste to almost fifty men.

*****

Alion watched this, knowing her time was running out. When Davyd's sons returned, her life would be over. She cursed her luck again at having the errant king's mark appear now, during *her* raid. Alion was no fool, and though Davyd Dreys had not participated in the final battle against Lilyth, he was not one to be trifled with. He had been trained by the best, before going outside the law.

Had she been assigned a full complement of troops, they might have prevailed, but against one who had the combined training of a bladesman *and* the lore of the Way, this was no longer about winning, it was about survival. It didn't help that his sons were turning out to be as lethal as he was. What she needed now was leverage if she was going to get out of this with her skin intact.

At that moment, Davyd was wracked by a fit of coughing, so Alion took the advantage. She pushed forward and kicked him in the chest, then bolted to one side. In an instant, she dived and rolled, snatching up the little girl they had found. Alion put her back to a tree, a blade to the girl's throat. She did not have to wait very long.

Davyd Dreys was joined by his two sons, neither of whom seemed particularly winded, a testament to their own training. He clapped them on their shoulders, then came to stand in front of Alion. He sheathed his blade and opened his hands. "What do you hope to accomplish?"

"Another mage, dead before she bears more filth!" Alion spat this out, her hand tightening on the hilt as she prepared to slit the girl's throat.

"Wait. You must want something." Davyd gestured to the open forest and asked, "Free passage?"

Themun looked to his father in astonishment. "She can't live!"

Another bout of coughing erupted, bending Davyd over. When the attack subsided, he let loose a breath and wheezed, "Her armor . . . It bends the Way. Do we take that chance?"

Themun's eyes met Alion's own, and she could almost hear his thoughts. She would do this again if left alive. He looked back at his father, "For one girl?"

Father and son regarded each other, and Alion knew Themun saw the death of this hostage as a small price to pay for eradicating someone like her. "Trust me?" He put a hand on his son's shoulder and then turned back to the woman holding the knife. "Free passage, for her life."

"You would trade? After telling me I will see justice today?" Alion laughed. "Do you think me a fool?" Still, a part of her began to believe she might yet gain her freedom.

"I would trade even scum like you if it meant saving her," Davyd said, looking at the little girl. "Release her and I will grant you safe passage."

"Your Oath, then? And my other girl, Kalissa? You *know* who she is." Alion raised a bushy eyebrow. "Protect the innocent I understand, even the child of a Galadine. She must return to her father."

Davyd stepped back, sighing. Alion knew that to let her go was against every fiber of his being, but he would not mete out justice in the same manner as the king's men. It simply was not what he believed in. He needed to know that in some things, he and his sons were different. And she would use that against him. She remained silent, knowing he could only come to one decision, and was not surprised to hear him utter the Oath.

"By the blood of my forefathers, I bind myself," he said. "My oath as Keeper of the Lore, no harm will befall you by my hands." A small flash of yellow encompassed the mage at the uttering of the Binding Oath, then disappeared. "Now, do what your honor demands."

Alion stood and released the girl, shoving her forward with a booted foot. "You'll never survive the King's Law, honor or not, and neither will your sons." She looked around the camp. Of the villagers, perhaps ten survived and she had killed the two that *had* been mages. An incomplete victory, but one she could accept with her honor intact.

Armun stepped forward and said, "Be thankful we value his Oath, or your blood would water the ground here."

"Your father is a fool," Alion replied with a smile. She limped over to Kalissa, who lay unconscious on the ground, paused to sheathe her blade, then picked up the girl and slung her over a shoulder. Looking back at Davyd, she said, "You can't win."

"Perhaps, but that depends on what 'winning' means." Davyd nodded to the trees. "Be gone, dog. I took the Oath, but my sons did not."

Alion clenched her jaw at that, but said nothing. She adjusted the weight of the girl over one armored shoulder, then made her way into the trees and disappeared.

* * * * *

"You're letting her go?" A villager exclaimed. "She is a murderer and she goes free?"

Davyd turned to the voice and said, "The message she carries back, without her men, without accomplishing what she set out to do, will strike fear into the hearts of the Magehunters."

Though he believed this, none of the people around him did. They had lost those they loved most dearly and now sorted through the memories of their lives, strewn about because of one night's casual violence. This was not a time to accept his point, much less care. Only their shock at this attack and their fear stopped them from exacting their own vengeance on the king's mark.

He looked to Armun and said, "Help them, check the wounded, heal who you can." He coughed again and spat out a dark phlegm that looked bloody, but neither of his sons commented. His healing had done what it could to slow the sickness, buying him maybe a few more years. Nevertheless, the outcome was inevitable.

He wiped his mouth and smiled at his youngest, barely fifteen. "Go, see to the young girl. One of the villagers can take that torc off her."

The boy scampered away and landed lightly at the girl's feet. "Come on." He had a shock of brownish-blonde hair standing out from his head and the little girl smiled at him. It looked funny.

"What's your name?" she asked, not understanding that this boy had argued to sacrifice her life just a moment ago.

He turned, then offered a very formal bow and said, "Themun. Themun Dreys, and you?" He gave her a small smile, but Davyd watched his son carefully. He knew the boy's mind was still on his father and his decision to let Alion Deft go.

She smiled back and answered, "My name is Thera." She looked about a little sheepishly then added, "I don't have a last name."

"No matter." Themun looked toward the north and said, "The fortress of Dawnlight lies not too far away. We'll call you that. Thera Dawnlight."

* * * * *

Some distance away, Alion reached her horse and untied the reins. Dumping Kalissa's leaden weight across the saddle, she mounted, then hurried along the path that led back the way they had come. She heard a groan and realized the treacherous girl had come awake. Alion slowed and grabbed her by the back of her head, pulling her upright.

"Sit up, or I'll carry you across it all the way home."

Kalissa looked about in confusion, then said, "Where are we?"

"Alive," said Alion dispassionately. "Don't thank me." She didn't say anything else, but counted herself lucky. Losing the girl might have meant her neck in a Galadine noose, regardless of her affliction of Talent.

They rode slowly for a short distance while she adjusted to sit in the saddle as Alion had commanded.

Then both their attentions were taken by a man standing on the path, the moonlight streaming through the clearing, clouds painting his red robes the color of dried blood. Alion kicked her horse, intending to ride him down, but he raised a hand. For some reason the horse obeyed his command to stop, pulling up short with a whinny.

The man said, "Well met, Alion Deft, king's mark."

Alion vaulted off her saddle, the sword clearing its sheath as her feet touched the ground. If this person knew her, he was likely in league with Davyd. She would deal with his treachery now and be on her way.

She pulled her arm back to strike and felt her muscles go stiff. Normally her armor would have bent enchantments around it, but this time she felt as if she were encased in stone.

The man tilted his head to the side, as if examining something, and said, "Your armor won't protect you, king's mark, and neither will your simple faith in the gods. They don't care, they never did."

She tried to move, but her muscles were frozen tight, still locked in paralysis. Only her mouth seemed to work. She snarled, "So much for honor. Had I known Davyd to be so craven, I would have slit that girl's throat when I had the chance."

The man stepped forward past her blade and pulled his hood back, revealing blond hair and pale blue eyes. His gaze told her this man had nothing to do with Davyd Dreys.

His eyes gripped hers and he said, "I am the Scythe. Like the reaper's tool, I *ascend* those found worthy, or wanting." He then reached up and tapped her forehead lightly. The flesh began to blacken and shrivel away.

"I judge you wanting. You have much to atone for, Alion Deft. This spell will take several hours to kill you, and you will feel every moment of it. Call to your gods. Perhaps they will grant you solace in the next world."

* * * * *

He stepped past her and came to stand by the girl, Kalissa, who had dismounted with a grimace that gave testament to the punishment she had suffered at the hands of Alion Deft and her men. She ran to and hugged the man, saying, "She deserves it. They all do."

Scythe laid a gentle hand on her head, stroking the soft hair. His eyes looked back through the forest to the mountain of Dawnlight, a black silhouette of jagged rock climbing up to stand illumed in the clear moonlight. There were forces at work in the ancient city that could aid him on his quest, ones he meant to investigate.

He looked away from those moonlit peaks and could sense Davyd and the others hard at work in the decimated village. The youngest in particular bore watching, for he had Talent far beyond his father and elder brother. He could sense others too, doing what they could to create a better life far from the king's Justice. He looked down, sadness in his eyes, then knelt in front of Kalissa.

He froze her in place, then tapped her forehead lightly, watching the blackness spread like an inky stain. "I am the Scythe. Like the reaper's tool, I ascend those found worthy, or wanting. I judge you wanting, Kalissa Galadine. You have hunted your own kind, killed others so you might live, and sown sorrow in your wake."

He looked again in the direction of Dawnlight, took a deep, cleansing breath and said, "Like your father, I do not show mercy."

THE KING

Be not so eager to strike first,

but have a solid stance.

Lethality comes from those who understand,

the pillars that support them.

—*Tir Combat Academy, Basic Forms & Stances*

Niall's father, Imperial King Bernal Galadine, paced the walls of Bara'cor, watching the barbarian horde with disgust written upon his torchlit features. One hundred feet below him spread a moonlit ocean of sand, dunes mimicking motionless waves washing toward the shore of his fortress walls. Running his fingers through his short, iron-gray hair, he readjusted his sword belt for what seemed like the hundredth time. Niall was sure that it was the waiting that drove his father mad, the knowledge of the inevitable clash with the nomads encamped at his doorstep.

Niall, too, looked out over the wastes, breathing in the cool night air, his eyes striving to discern individual shapes in the campfires and tents of the barbarian horde, his hand on the hilt of his saber.

"Will they attack again so soon?" he asked, looking to his father, and noting the deep lines of worry etched in his sun-darkened face. The barbarians had been encamped outside the walls for the past fortnight, a black, inky smudge on the white desert floor.

Niall squeezed the hilt of the saber at his side for reassurance yet again, the leather wrapping soft and worn from summers of practice. He was, however, very conscious that the closest he had ever come to crossing live blades with an opponent was at practice with the firstmark. A mix of fear and anticipation had prompted his earlier question. He didn't want his father thinking he was still a child, and he longed for a chance to prove the opposite.

The firstmark would not have recommended me for duty if he had any doubts, he reminded himself.

"They will wait until tomorrow, attacking under cover of the storm," the king explained. Then to Niall's unasked question he added, "It is the tactic I would use if I commanded their troops."

"But if you know that already, why not do something to stop them?"

"And what, my prince, would you have your father do?"

Niall spun at the deep voice, coming face to chest with Firstmark Jebida Naserith. The ursine man stood almost seven feet tall, his eyes flashing in humor. Jebida hailed from the lower reaches of the Shornhelm Expanse, where it was said giant's blood still flowed in the veins of men. Looking at the firstmark, one could believe it was true. Moving forward, he bowed to the king before turning on the wide-eyed prince.

"Shall we dispense with all you have learned in military strategy and leave the cover of Bara'cor's walls? Or should we try the catapults and archers? A few might hit, though the godless heathens are out of range. We might get lucky."

Niall looked down and with a sigh he intoned, "Luck should not be your only partner."

Jebida straightened, peering out at the nomads. His experienced eye measured the strength, distance, and disposition of the nomad army out of habit, then flicked over to the king. He met the gray-eyed stare and nodded.

Turning his attention back to Niall, Jebida placed one thick-callused finger on the boy's chest and said, "Aye, you have the right of it." Then his eyes softened and he continued, "But sometimes, a jester's luck is the only thing between a blade and your heart. Do not worry, my prince. When they attack, we will be ready."

Niall responded with a nod, moving back against the wall and out from between the two veterans. The king gazed down the outer face of the wall pointing to a section hit hard with what could only have been a rock larger than a man's head. Beckoning to Jebida, he asked, "Will it hold?"

The firstmark peered intently for a moment then said, "I'm no builder, but it was made by dwarven hands and they have a way with rock." Placing his meaty hand on the king's shoulder, Jebida steered his friend away from the edge. "We number about eight hundred men. I would estimate the horde fields over ten times that. While we haven't seen it, something in my bones tells me there's sorcery involved or they wouldn't even attempt the walls."

* * * * *

Twenty summers ago, Jebida had left to fight alongside Bernal in the Dawnlight campaigns, a successful effort to solidify the northern borderlands. The king had liberated the fortress of Dawnlight, and in the process, won himself a new bride and queen, Yevaine.

The firstmark, elated at their victory and the king's good fortune, had returned to his village only to find it in smoking ruins, the houses smashed and burned into charcoal caricatures of the beautiful homes they once were. He recalled with perfect clarity the sight of his own home, reduced to a bed of gray ash like freshly fallen snow, barely covering the blackened bodies of his wife and daughter.

The village blacksmith had been the only survivor. She wailed of winged creatures pouring through an opening in the air, what they now knew to be a small rift. Each creature was insubstantial, but fearsome in form. They dived *into* people, who then lost themselves. Their eyes glowed white and they walked mindlessly away, back through the rift and were never heard from again. Those few that fought or resisted were killed.

Part of him had died then, with his family and people. The village had been decimated and as a result, nothing of the Naserith name had survived, except for him.

Swallowing the knot of anger that had begun to form in his throat, the firstmark concentrated on finishing his report. "I have evacuated all the elderly and children down the pass to the lowlands, escorted by Captain Kalindor with Fourth Company. Any who passed their third blade are here, reporting for duty. The younger ones were given the chance to volunteer to stay if they wished."

Both Jebida and the king knew Tyrus Kalindor well, a straightforward man who had served the Galadines for over a quarter of a century. He was a seasoned veteran with a steady hand, a soldier who would bear even the underhanded maneuverings and political intrigues of Haven to watch over the queen and the evacuees.

The king asked, "How many volunteers?"

Jebida smiled crookedly, "All of them. What did you expect?" He paused, a glint of pride shining in his eyes, then finished, "Tyrus and the queen's party should arrive in Haven soon."

The smile was short-lived, though, as the firstmark's eyes drifted back to the nomad line, and his mood darkened at the thoughts of magic being used against them. But Jebida's loss to the demons and hatred of magic was no secret to the king. They both focused on the desert.

The king replied, "The nomads will attack on the morrow with this storm."

"Aye, it is the wisest course," Jebida agreed, "but hard on our archers. I do not underestimate their commander. Barbarian or not, he has attacked us with cold efficiency and camped well out of catapult range. Only the fact that our backs are to a cliff and we have water has allowed us to hold this long. Makes me wonder how they manage to stay camped at our door this long without the same."

* * * * *

With the conversation between his father and the firstmark receding into the back of his awareness, Niall imagined what his first real battle would be like. So far, all the assaults against the wall had been warfare at range, the archers of First and Third Companies dueling with their counterparts from the barbarian lines.

However, if his father was right, they would see hand-to-hand combat tomorrow. Niall ran his hand over the waist-high lip of the outer wall. The rough, gritty surface felt good against the hard calluses on his palm. Niall hoped to serve with Armsmark Rillaran. His heart beat hard at the thought of working the front wall, where undoubtedly the harshest fighting would be. Most on duty there were seasoned veterans, well versed in the art of repelling a siege.

"Niall."

Niall gave a start at hearing his name. Shaking off the visions of battle, he found both his father and Jebida staring at him. He moved over to the pair, watching as Jebida nodded his massive head in answer to some command his father whispered.

"Niall, I shall be down in the council room. Jebida has your orders for tomorrow." The king clasped his son's hand in an iron grip, apparently satisfied he would do as he was told, and confident in the firstmark's ability to keep him safe. With a thin smile he walked across the battlements to the inner stairwell, heading into the deep coolness of the interior.

The firstmark cleared his throat, motioning for Niall to come closer. "Well, boy. You'll be working with Captain Fenrith."

"Fenrith! Wha—?"

"Silence," snapped Jebida, fire in his eyes. "The first lesson a soldier must learn is to follow orders. Tomorrow you will be working under Captain Fenrith, supporting Fifth Company."

The boy dropped his gaze, disappointment etched in his young features.

A conciliatory hand came up, clapping the young warrior on the shoulder as the firstmark continued, "I understand your disappointment, lad, but you are not yet experienced enough to stand at the point of the spear. It is not yours, but the lives of those next to you that are in jeopardy, as each would extend himself to protect the Imperial heir. You understand this?" A small smile escaped his lips, "You have my word I will do what is within my power to allow you a chance on the wall. Just be patient."

Niall nodded once, dejected. He knew Jebida would keep his word, but put little faith in the firstmark's chances against his father's will. He was too disappointed to think others might endanger themselves for him. "If you will excuse me, sir." He saluted, right fist to chest, then spun on his heel, heading for the stairwell where his father had disappeared.

THE APPRENTICE

In studying the Way,

accept that learning it is hard.

Once learned, accept that

wielding it is hard.

Accept that mastery of the Way is hard,

and your journey will be made easier.

—*Lore Father Argus Rillaran, The Way*

Arek Winterthorn sat at an oaken desk situated deep in the back of the large library in the main tower, his blond head bent in concentration over the book in front of him. Looking up, he rubbed his pale blue eyes and squinted as the full strength of the afternoon sun shone through a slotted portal high above, pooling its yellow brilliance on the top of his desk.

He rose and stretched, his brown practice uniform feeling both warm and used, as he moved to another table, and a platter of cold meats. Sandwiching a piece of meat between some hard bread, he sat down and began his repast. The spells he had been given to research by his master, Silbane, swam like clickfish through his head. Finding himself unable to concentrate, he hoped food would bring clarity to his thinking, a state particularly elusive today. How math and numbers had anything to do with spells made no sense to him, but he continued learning every equation and transformation by rote.

He was interrupted by Piter Winterthorn, a fellow apprentice who was under Master Kisan's tutelage. Piter made his way over to Arek's books and looked down, the familiar smirk already forming on his mouth. "Is my brother-in-name still muddling through matrices? With the Test of Ascension so close at hand, I would think you would be with the other apprentices on the hill, practicing."

Piter moved slowly around the desk and lowered his wiry frame onto Arek's notes. "Will your master let you have help with these? They're pretty simple."

Arek looked sidelong at Piter, his taunting nothing new, and removed his gloves. Then he said simply, "Get off my notes."

"Of course," Piter backed away quickly with both hands up. "I didn't mean it the way it came out."

Arek had a unique Talent, one that none of the masters on the Isle yet understood. For some reason, anything he touched that was magical found itself disrupted for hours. This made it necessary for Arek to wear thin gloves whenever he was around anyone who had magical abilities, or items of a magical nature, which included almost everything on the Isle. Arek's interactions with his fellow students had quickly become strained. Piter in particular seemed to enjoy making Arek feel different, somehow damaged.

Forbidden from participating in unsupervised combat practice, Arek could not establish an equanimous balance with his peers. Had he been allowed to fight, he might have asserted himself in the natural pecking order. Competition in all things was naturally intense amongst the students as they vied for recognition or attention from their instructors. His strange Talent had resulted instead in more one-on-one tutelage and attention from the adepts, something he hadn't "earned."

He hated having to back down again, but Master Silbane had been extremely clear. Real fighting amongst students was strictly forbidden, punishable by chores, extra homework, possibly even expulsion from the Isle, something every apprentice knew. Arek straightened out his notes and turned to face the other boy, "Nothing you say ever comes out the way you mean." Arek knew Master Kisan would not look kindly upon this incident if Arek reported it. He nodded, affecting an air of nonchalance, and finished, "And I don't need your help."

Piter backed up a bit, nodding. When Arek didn't continue, he turned to go, but stopped. Looking back he asked, "Have you ever considered you may not be a jinx, like everyone says?" A heartbeat, then two passed. When Arek made it clear he was not going to reply, Piter shrugged and said, "Well... good luck with your studying." He continued to back away, then turned and left.

Once again, it seemed like a nice thing to say. Then came that familiar smirk painting Piter's face, and Arek knew he was being ridiculed. His face grew hot from a flush of anger. Even though competition between apprentices was tolerated, at times even encouraged, it seemed Piter had a special dislike for him. What frustrated Arek more than Piter's arrogance, was that deep down inside he knew Piter was one of the more gifted apprentices on the Isle. When given the chance, Piter would certainly earn the black uniform to mark him as having passed from initiate to adept.

Arek was not so confident of his own chances. Truth be told, he didn't know why he was even on the list to test. In his opinion, he was far from ready. He stared at his notes, anger still clenching his jaw. Then, his ability to concentrate ruined, he gathered his notes and left the library. The confrontation with Master Kisan's apprentice was the perfect interruption to what was becoming a truly pointless day.

Walking down the wide hallways, he made his way to the Hall of Apprentices. Divided into three levels, the lowest was a large area for the newest arrivals. Arek wove in and out of the small cots placed side by side, trying to get through quickly. The last thing he wanted now was to get waylaid by some youngster full of questions.

He rounded one bed, promptly smacked his toe into a footlocker, and fell. Out spilled school supplies and a white robe. He sat there for a moment, clutching his foot, his eyes watering. Massaging the pain out with a hand, he looked about the isolated carnage he'd wrought, then began grabbing things. He put everything back, knowing it didn't look as neat and orderly as before, but better than it did a moment ago. New candidates would spend many years here, learning mathematics, reading, and writing. No sense in ruining someone else's day because of his clumsiness.

Getting back to his feet, he brushed himself off and continued through the Hall. He still remembered where his cot had been and often checked up on its newest occupant, a small girl named Lissah. He did not see her as he passed, and silently thanked the Lady. He didn't have the patience just then to sit down and engage in a conversation with that talkative little girl, barely eight summers old. He limped over to the stairwell, shaking his foot to lessen his toe's throbbing, and made his way gingerly up.

The next level was dedicated to the intermediate apprentices, or "Greens," those who were selected to stay after a rigorous testing of both basic skills and magical potential. They slept three to a room, offering a little more privacy than that of the Whites.

Greens studied the basics of the Way, armed combat, and a multitude of herbs, medicines, and other techniques for healing the sick and injured. They also began learning more complex mathematical concepts, for the instructors seemed to believe the Way was strongest in a logically trained mind. While Arek had learned quite a bit, he still couldn't see the connection.

These Greens did not learn anything but the most rudimentary of fatigue-banishing spells, nor fight with anything but wooden weapons. They would stay Greens for as many years as it took to earn them the right to move on. No apprentice knew how long he or she would train at any level, and no promises were made that they would ever advance. When the right time came and their instructors felt they were ready, they traded in their uniforms of green and donned close-fitting dark brown ones, moving themselves up to the third level of the hall.

Each Brown slept in his own room and carried the responsibility of teaching the rudiments of mathematics, reading, and writing, as well as the basics of combat and magic to those below them. Arek himself conducted two classes in blade combat, a beginner's course in mathematics, and an advanced course in multi-opponent combat strategy. In this way Browns kept their knowledge up to date, as they could be called upon anytime to teach Whites or Greens.

Browns also began rudimentary efforts at combining their combat training with magic. They learned the same spells, though of much less power, that they would use as full adepts. Their primary focus was to learn to create a path to the Way and sustain it. It took intense concentration at first, but as with all things, became easier as students practiced and time passed. Eventually the council recommended the more promising of these initiates to take the Test of Ascension and be recognized once they passed as a full adept of the council.

Unfortunately, the intervening years after the King's Law had been enacted had seen fewer and fewer children with Talent born in the land. Fewer still found their way to safety from the Magehunters and whatever else preyed on those newly born to the Way. Many children disappeared into the rifts: unexplained events that never hinted at their impending appearance, and over the years had grown more frequent.

The result had been a slow dwindling of students to teach and masters to teach them. These six adepts and their students were the only ones left to carry on the knowledge and learning of a once proud and powerful Order. It also didn't help that passing the Test to become an adept was extremely difficult, even if one were strong with the Way.

Arek's knowledge of the Test was hazy at best and subject to the rumors that inevitably filtered throughout the school. If half of those rumors were true, becoming an adept required ludicrous feats of power, like slaying an elder dragon barehanded. Arek doubted that masters Silbane or Kisan had ever done anything quite so legendary.

However, every student who aspired to don the black uniform knew one fact. They knew they were an adept when they heard their true name uttered for the first time. It came to them as they Ascended to the rank of adept, whispered on the wind, and with it came their power.

Arek continued his climb up to the third level. He paused for a moment at the top of the stairs, listening. He did not want to meet up with any of the other Browns, least of all Piter, who had a habit of inexplicably showing up at the most inopportune times, like in the library. Making his way to his door, he eased it open, careful not to make too much noise. Then he closed the door behind him and plopped down on his bed, staring out the window. To be an adept had been Arek's dream since he had first begun his training.

He did not remember much of his life before the Isle. What he did remember came as brief flashes, a feeling, or a smell. He recalled someone with a gruff voice, and the smell of fresh cut leaves. Arek remembered a feeling like stone against his skin, but colored a strange blue and warm to the touch, as if alive.

They said he had been found by Master Silbane, abandoned in the forest near Winters Thorn, on the east side of Neverthere Bay. For this reason the name "Winterthorn" became his last, shared with the other orphan of that same forest, Piter. Now, nearing the date of what he had adopted as his seventeenth birthday, he had spent all his life on Meridian Isle.

In all that time, he thought, I have yet to see any example of my power. Negating magic seemed to be the only evidence he could do anything at all. Every student learned minor spells, like how to clean dirt off their clothes, stay warm, heat water, or clear dust. These were necessary to help with upkeep and chores. Arek, however, could not even cast the simplest enchantment. It didn't help his self-esteem that even Lissah, the little White of eight years old, could do more than he could.

The most perplexing thing about his time at the Isle was that he had been formally apprenticed to Master Silbane before becoming an initiate. This was an honor supposedly reserved for only the most gifted of students, such as Piter, whom Master Kisan had apprenticed when he was just a Green.

Arek was sure the only reason he had been apprenticed so early was because he was a danger to other students. Of course they would want him looked after, to make sure he didn't hurt anyone else. He shook his head and pushed open the glass pane, breathing in the cool sea air that rushed in.

His room, much like any of the others on this level, was sparsely decorated, one wall dedicated to a bookshelf crowded with training manuals and texts he had accumulated with the passage of time. A small washbasin and mirror stood against the wall between his bed and the bookshelf. In the far corner stood a small sword stand holding his *bohkir*, a two-handed wooden practice sword, the handle worn smooth and dark with years of practice and sweat. At least in that, he knew he had some talent.

When he held his sword, calmness came over him, a peace he could not explain. He had heard some other Greens say they dreaded combat. That made no sense to him. Why learn a martial discipline, but not wish to use it? It was like being a great swimmer, but not wanting to swim. The entire illogic of it frustrated him, and he tended to deal with those students who were afraid to fight more harshly than those who were clearly eager to test themselves, blade against blade.

Arek rolled over on his back and stared at the ceiling. His ability to disrupt magic had been a constant annoyance in his life. More than once, he had ruined his study partner's experimental conjuration in class, or caused an instructor's example to go awry.

He knew Piter wasn't the only one who called him a jinx. He was bad luck on anyone trying to cast a spell and as a result, rarely chosen as a partner for any schoolwork. Rarer still was being asked to participate in the festivals marking many of the most joyous times of year. Who wanted someone who could ruin an evening with a touch? Only Master Silbane seemed to care about teaching him. Arek rolled onto his stomach and sighed. Some days, he thought sullenly, it just did not make sense to get out of bed.

Laughter drifted up from the courtyard, pulling his gaze. Sitting up, he braced his elbows on the windowsill and watched as two apprentices squared off for a game of *rhan'dori*. One he recognized immediately as Jesyn, her slight frame hidden beneath her leather combat uniform. In her right hand, she carried her *bohkir*, glowing faintly blue as she concentrated her magical power through the wooden blade.

This slight conjuration helped to teach each apprentice how to channel their power, and served as part of the *rhan'dori* rules. Whatever part of the body the blade touched would become temporarily immobile, paralyzed by the magic channeled in the wood. Unconsciousness was the result of a strike to the head. Arek often wondered what color his *bohkir* would glow if he could channel power the way his friends could.

The paralyzing effect channeled into the *bohkir* served another important purpose. Injuries were kept to a minimum since the victor was clear. It made the blade work easier to follow and learn from, as each blade would leave behind a quickly dissipating colored trail in the air. Instructors could then reconjure the trails and walk the students through the fight, showing where a strike or block was correct, or out of place. When two evenly matched opponents paired, the cuts and parries often painted an intricate image of their struggle that was beautiful to behold.

Arek didn't recognize Jesyn's opponent until he shrugged off his cloak and raised his *bohkir*, glowing purple in the fading light. That would be Piter. Even as he watched, Piter's sword flashed brighter for a moment, an obvious sign he was channeling more power into the wooden blade, either to lighten it or to increase its speed.

Piter was always showing off, in one way or another. Arek grimaced at the thought. Even as the flash faded, the two combatants grabbed their swords in both hands and moved toward each other, measuring stance and pace. Soon the sounds of their blocks and parries echoed from the circle, along with the occasional cheer from one group of students or another, each supporting their favorite.

The game of *rhan'dori* was as ancient as the council itself, and Arek had heard rumor that it was part of the Test of Ascension. At the time a student became a Green, he or she began learning the basics of sword and spell. By the time the student was ready for Ascension, they would have gained enough knowledge to blend these two disciplines together.

Part of every formal test before Black was the *rhan'dori,* where a student faced multiple opponents. Only by successfully defending themselves and defeating their opponents with controlled killing strikes, could a student pass.

Of course, these were against real people. Arek had no idea what one faced when testing for the Black. The mark of a true master was to use nothing at all. They had trained to a point where their very bodies were honed as weapons. Arek assumed the Test of Ascension would be fought unarmed.

And he certainly would not be required to kill anyone. That would be an unsustainable way to advance the teachings, for it called for losing a member at each test. Furthermore, he reminded himself, believing the *rhan'dori* was part of the final test was still purely conjecture, as no one except the one being Ascended and the adepts witnessed anything. Only they had an idea of what was required, and to date no one had talked about their test after it concluded.

Those who failed their first attempt, and this seemed to be almost everyone, were unable or unwilling to voice any recollection of the test itself. They claimed they remembered everything, but just couldn't speak it aloud. It was likely, Arek thought, that they took a Binding Oath that prevented them from speaking.

A few, a very few, were never seen or heard from again. The other students whispered that these unfortunate souls had failed and as a result, died. The thought brought a certain fervor to their training, for no student took the chance their life might be forfeit due to laziness.

One thing was clear. If they failed and survived, it was not considered a mark against the student. They were encouraged to continue teaching classes, their knowledge invaluable to the younger students, until such a time when they were ready to test again. Strangely, very few ever did, and most left the Isle within a year.

Arek also reminded himself, being at the Brown rank did not mean one was not formidable. Indeed, Browns were accomplished and deadly fighters, dangerous to the extreme. Arek had once heard Adept Dragor say he worried more about facing Browns than adepts, because they would try anything, with little regard to their own safety.

This could result in disaster, as evidenced by stories passed down from student to student, whispered tales about the statue on Prayer's Rock actually being a Brown who had tried to enhance his skin by merging with the energies of the surrounding stone itself. The adepts did little to discourage this sort of gossip, content it kept the more adventurous in line.

It was clear though to the other students that something fundamental changed when a Brown failed their final test for the Black. Something altered deep within them, a strange indifference to the world. It was as if they were going through the motions, but their minds were a thousand leagues away.

Arek's only exposure to this had been a few years back, when their combat instructor, Keren, had tested and failed to achieve the Black. She hadn't said anything, but the normally talkative and vibrant trainer had become more silent and withdrawn, given to bouts of prolonged introspection. She had continued teaching for a few months, then one day had simply left the Isle. Once a Brown left, they were seldom heard from again, and the memory of Initiate Keren had faded from detailed stories and feats to a soft patchwork of nondescript feelings.

Silbane had often told him the outcome of the Test of Ascension seldom hinged on the raw magical power of a particular initiate, but more on his or her ability to understand weakness and be observant. Arek knew with a cold certainty that if his admission into the adepts' elite circle rested on his ability to merge the arcane with the mundane, he would never wear the Black, regardless of what his master thought. It was more likely he would leave the Isle, just as Keren had, an errant disciple of the Way, out in the world on his own.

Arek shook his head; this was no way to think. He would not have been accepted into the Isle or been apprenticed by Master Silbane if he didn't have potential. Through hard work and training, he had achieved the rank of Brown, a feat that put him in an already rarified level of expertise. Still, his inability to cast even the simplest charms infuriated him and made him feel incompetent in front of the others.

Then there were the informal *rhan'dori* practices. He understood the touch of his bare skin caused the paralyzing effect, which was followed by unconsciousness or feeling dizzy.

However, Arek argued, wasn't that exactly what the enchanted *bohkir's* touch did? No, it didn't *disrupt* magic, but it did cause the person hit to become incapacitated. He didn't see the difference between that and his touch. When he had ventured to ask why, his master had scoffed, "You will learn nothing from these mock combats other than imitating other people's mistakes. Practice perfection and you will learn perfection."

As a result, while Arek had participated in practice combats during classes, he had never competed in an informal test against his friends. This frustrated and relieved him; frustrated because he couldn't show off his skills and prowess, relieved because he had the perfect excuse not to have to compete against the other Browns and perhaps lose.

The fear of losing was his darkest secret, one he did not mull over, but that grew the moment he found himself across blades. He did not fear combat, as others did. Actually, he longed for it, but he was more afraid of losing than of fighting.

Strangely enough, Arek's lack of participation in the *rhan'dori* and his obvious skill in class had given him a reputation as a dangerous opponent with the sword, something he had not anticipated. He enjoyed the reputation, but because it was unearned, being asked by his friends for advice on technique still made him feel uncomfortable, as though they were actually mocking him.

A yell of triumph caught his attention as Jesyn cut quickly downward, forcing Piter back to block. The force of the blow caused him to go down to one knee, his sword raised horizontally above him. Jesyn took that opportunity to kick upward, catching the back of Piter's blade from underneath. His sword spun out of his hand in an arc of purple, leaving him defenseless.

Jesyn's leg went numb from the strike. Arek could tell she knew this would happen, and had bet her victory on it. Her sword leapt high, then cut straight at Piter's head. However, the numb leg slowed her by a heartbeat, an eternity in a sword fight.

Piter was too well trained to let the slip go unanswered. As Jesyn attacked, he timed himself perfectly, flipping sideways from the blow, landing more than a sword's length away. He stretched out his hand and his wooden *bohkir* flew from across the circle into his palm. Then from a crouch he moved forward, his legs pumping as he quickly covered the short distance between himself and his opponent.

Jesyn tried to retreat, but her leg impeded her motion and she took a painful whack on her left arm. That arm went limp as the magic of the blade deadened it. Jesyn quickly spun on the heel of her good leg with a dancer's grace, her training taking hold. The blade in her right hand whizzed horizontally through the air behind her, completing a blue circle and singing for Piter's head.

He raised his *bohkir* vertically and caught her blade, forcing it out and downward. His sword leapt from hers to tap her right arm, deadening that as well. Jesyn's sword dropped from nerveless fingers, but not before she flung her head backward and caught Piter full in the face. With a cry, he fell onto his back, his nose a spattered ruin.

Jesyn knew where Piter was and kicked backward like a mule. She both felt the impact and heard the satisfied "whuff," as her heel caught him in the stomach.

As he fell backward, she fell with him and landed straddling Piter's prostrate form, her numb shin under his throat, the other pinning his outstretched sword arm to the ground. Without using her arms, she leaned her weight forward onto her shin, closing Piter's windpipe. One word hissed from her mouth, "Yield?"

Piter's face turned purple, as his left hand tried to claw Jesyn's knee off, but it was useless. Jesyn had positioned herself well and had her entire body's weight on Piter's chest. By leaning forward, she had brought that weight to bear on this throat. Only a few heartbeats passed before he realized the futility of trying to break free and croaked out, "Yield."

She leaned back, letting him breathe, and smiled. "I figured you'd not want to be dragged to the infirmary unconscious." Jesyn stood up and limped back, her arms dangling at her sides. The feeling had started to return in her leg, pins and needles prickling it back to life. Her arms, however, were still completely numb. She turned and took a bow.

Arek sighed and whispered to himself, "Finish him, Jes. I've told you a hundred times. You're too nice."

Piter slowly rose, growling, "The winner is the one who walks from the circle."

"You yielded." Jesyn spun, facing him.

"And you left me armed." Before Jesyn could move, he swung his glowing blade, still in his right hand, in a tight arc. It caught her under her chin on the left side of her face. Jesyn went down in a heap and lay still, unconscious.

Arek looked around, but there were no other senior Browns on the hill. Piter bowed once and walked out of the circle toward a small copse of trees, and Arek could imagine the smirk already growing on his face. A few of the watching Greens were at Jesyn's side, helping her back to consciousness. She finally stood on unsteady legs and staggered out of the circle supported by a brace of Greens as they headed toward the nearest doors.

Damn him, Arek thought as a cold anger settled over his heart. It was one thing to be arrogant, but to cheat to win a stupid practice match! A part of Arek knew no adept would think what Piter did was wrong, instead they would chastise Jesyn for dropping her guard and not incapacitating her opponent.

The rules of *rhan'dori* were simple. You continue until your opponent is disabled, then you leave the circle. They were constantly reminding the apprentices there were no rules in the *rhan'dori*, just as there were no rules in war. Jesyn failed to disable her opponent, trusting his word instead.

Still, though nothing Piter did was technically wrong, Arek could not let him get away with it, ready to accept whatever punishment his master gave him. He raced toward his door, only to be brought up short by a chime sounding. He sighed, then turned to face his washbasin mirror. Slowly, on the mirrored surface appeared an image of his master, Silbane. Straightening his robe, Arek bowed once and stood still, only his eyes betraying the anger he felt.

"I have need of you, Apprentice. Please come to my quarters."

Arek licked his lips and replied, "Of course, Master . . ." He tried to think of a way to meet Piter first. When no excuse came to mind he felt his master would accept, he inwardly cursed and bowed again. "Yes, Master." It was not often he was called upon and once done, it was not his place to disobey, regardless of his current situation. Piter would have to wait. Arek watched the image fade and then left for the Hall of Adepts.

Between his quarters and the Hall of Adepts lay a square expanse of green, a courtyard of sorts with a nice open area that contained little to interrupt its serenity. This was the quad, where his friends and he spent many hours lounging when chores, adepts, and other students failed to beckon.

The quad was also where the Spring and Fall Festivals were held each year. The Spring Festival had only been a moon ago, the square decorated with all the new blossoms the students could gather. He could still remember the exhibitions of martial prowess by the adepts, reenacting the great battles of the land. They heard tales of the Crystal Mountains and the dragon Rai'kesh, of the Battle of Ice at Dawnlight, and of Argus the Sunlord and the Rending of Shornhelm.

The adepts performed feats of strength, speed, and agility that would have left most in stunned silence. They reduced a boulder to a pile of rubble, shattered by an adept's withering palm, or leapt through rings of fire while extinguishing candle flames with thrown darts at fifty paces. It seemed nothing lay beyond their honed expertise. They were forged by their training to be weapons of the most lethal sort: ones that could think.

He cursed himself for daydreaming, then ran across the green expanse and made his way up the many levels to his master's chambers without breathing hard. He took this for granted, a luxury of energy that only the young or highly-trained did not appreciate. He found his master's door ajar and after knocking discreetly, he entered. He bowed as his master turned from the open window.

The sun was setting over the Shattered Sea, spilling red-orange light into the room. Arek could feel a strong breeze whip through, ruffling some of the dry parchment held down by a weight on the desk. He had forgotten how high up his master's quarters were. Somewhere the sound of a gull cawing added to the serenity of the scene. Arek drank in the sea air, its coolness slowly easing the anger he had held at Piter.

Silbane moved to a chair, motioning for him to sit across from him. "Tell me, Apprentice, what do you know of Bara'cor?"

Arek, not surprised by the question, raced to dredge up all he could from the name. His master often tested him this way, pulling something from a lesson taught many years ago. His frustrations at the many events of this day were forgotten as the information came flooding into his mind. That seemed another of his peculiar talents. He could remember anything he saw or heard with perfect clarity.

Clearing his throat he began, "It is a fortress on the western edge of the Altan Wastes. Legend has that it was built by the dwarven lords. It defends the pass to the lower plains and the capital city of Haven.

"It is currently held by King Bernal Galadine, with an unbroken lineage that can trace its ancestors back more than two hundred years, to the summoning and defeat of the demonlord, Lilyth. Mikal Galadine enacted the King's Law then, which put people with Talent, people like us, to death."

He paused for a moment, thinking if there was anything else he knew. "It is said the Galadine line runs strong in the Way, and every Galadine has magic to some degree, whether or not they choose to acknowledge it. I doubt this, however." Arek watched his master, waiting for any remark.

"Really? Why?" countered Silbane.

"If you have power, why not use it? I cannot believe the Galadines could be so strong in the Way and still reject its might. More likely they are mundane."

Silbane looked out over the Shattered Sea before replying. "Having power doesn't require its use."

"Easy to say, for those *with* power," countered the younger apprentice. He knew his master encouraged debate as a way of learning, and therefore said what was on his mind.

"Perhaps," Silbane said, looking sidelong at his apprentice, "but forbearance is also a sign of strength." He sighed, then stood up. "Bara'cor stands as you said, guarding the pass to the lowlands and though no longer inhabited by dwarves, still contains many mysteries."

Silbane moved over and picked up the book on his desk, opening it to a previously marked section. He passed it over to Arek who took it gingerly, careful of the delicate pages showing a detailed map of the known world.

"There." Silbane stabbed his thin finger down, creasing a spot on the map with his nail. "There stands Bara'cor, along the two thousand foot drop known as Land's Edge. Take this with you to your quarters. You have until tomorrow to learn all you can of Bara'cor, her history, the surrounding area, and people."

Mystified, Arek closed the book and stood up, his mind whirling. He bowed once and took two steps toward the door before turning back to his master and asking, "Why?"

Silbane pursed his lips, his eyes narrowing. "Why ask a question to an answer you already know, apprentice?"

Arek's pale eyes met his master's faded blue ones. Perhaps there was still some simmer in his blood, some anger at Piter taking advantage of Jesyn. Something was going on that his master was not sharing. He stood for a moment, unsure of whether this was another debate, or a true question.

In either case, he did not like feeling the fool, and replied, "The assumption is I will need this information in the near future, Master."

Sketching a bow, the apprentice retreated from the room, his mind whirling. He knew his master wasn't telling him everything and that scared him more than any upcoming test.

* * * * *

Silbane watched his apprentice leave, troubled by the mix of emotions that flashed across Arek's face. Oh, it was gone in an instant, but the boy was hard to read. Harder still because of his peculiar Talent, which blocked the empathic sense adepts usually employed when teaching their apprentices. With Arek, he could get surface feelings, but the boy's Talent clouded anything deeper. And now, he thought, we will use him . . . I hope for a greater good.

Gathering his notes, Silbane left for the council chamber. Behind him, the sun finished its graceful demise into the west, the sky flaming orange in its fading light.

Journal Entry 2

The vision granted to me by the dragonkind gives me an advantage. I can see particles of thought, like small points of light. They flow and weave at my every gesture, as if they know I am here.

Anything is possible, it seems. The land is beautiful, but empty. I will first find a safe place to make camp, and from there a way to survive. I hear creatures around me, scurrying things I cannot see. Their presence fills me with unease, as if they hunt.

Supplies should not be an issue, so long as nothing steals them. Many a fool has ventured into combat without adequate provisions for his men. If I am to do combat here, I must first fortify a camp, but somewhere safe. These small points of light gather and glow around dangers, making them easy beacons against my inattention and inexperience.

My very thoughts are sustenance, and merely the wish for food or water (within reason!) brings it forth from the ground around me. I sleep, and upon rousing find myself surrounded by a bounty of fruits and vegetables. Yet no plants have sprouted and no obvious source shows itself. Something, it seems, wants me alive. Still, I must stockpile. I do not know yet if the lean wolf of starvation may stalk my nights.

But my mission has not changed. I must free our world of these Aeris.

THE PRINCE

In a drawn out or extended combat,

pay attention to your breathing.

Exhale when you strike,

but conserve your energy.

Victory will be achieved only if you can

continue to fight.

—*Tir Combat Academy, Basic Forms & Stances*

Niall descended the stairs and exited on one of the archers' balconies, his face set in grim lines. "Supplies? It would have been more dangerous with my mother," he complained to himself.

Around him, the signs of siege showed themselves in the soldiers camped on the balcony, just inside and above the main gates. In times of war, they took rest wherever and whenever they could.

Weaving his way between sleeping forms, Niall ran down a small flight of stairs spiraling down the inside wall of the keep, then crossed the inner courtyard with determined strides.

He soon found himself near the Warriors Hall, a place reserved for unit drills and training. The square building stood near the back of the fortress, separate from the main buildings and quarters.

Behind the training hall was the pool of Shimmerene, its glassy surface reflecting the moonlit sky with quiet dignity. Ancient stonebinders had fed this pool, cut from the very earth, through carefully redirected underground streams. The runoff from the waters flowed down Land's Edge and joined with the real Lake Shimmerene, a much larger body of water with the capital city of Haven nestling along its southeastern side. Niall took a deep breath, smelling the water in the air, and made his way for the Lady's Hands.

The Hands were a thin strip of rock extending to the center of the pool, ending in two cupped hands in the act of scooping water out of Shimmerene. The bowl shaped by the Hands was large enough to comfortably hold a small ceremony inside it. Niall often wondered why the dwarves had built the Hands, envisioning secret rituals or sacrifices to the glimmering waters. But the secret of the Lady's Hands, along with the fate of the obdurate dwarves, was lost with their disappearance over two hundred summers ago. The stillness of the mirror-like surface making him feel as if he floated on a sea of stars, Niall came here whenever he needed to think. Now was definitely one of those times.

He was not surprised to find his cousin, Yetteje, already there. They had agreed to meet at moonrise, eager to discuss Niall's station assignment for tomorrow, though that was before he'd talked to Jebida, he recollected. He walked up the wide pier to the Hands, stepped down into the bowl, and seated himself on one of the benches carved into the rough granite palms. "Don't even ask, Tej. I don't want to talk about it."

Yetteje Tir smiled, her amber eyes filled with mirth. She was the daughter of King Ben'thor Tir, lord of Bara'cor's sister stronghold, EvenSea, which lay thirty days' ride to the east. Yetteje looked at Niall, almost matching in height, and brushed some hair away from her face. Arching an eyebrow, she asked, "I'm sure my mother spoke to yours long before this."

Niall pursed his lips, "You can't be serious. Why?"

Yetteje shrugged, "You're her favorite. If it wasn't required, even the Walk of Kings would be chaperoned." She plopped down next to her cousin and added, "At least your father and mine won that argument, else you'd be stuck here when I leave."

"Like anything is getting out of the fortress now." He sighed then leaned back, looking at the stars. The Walk of Kings allowed the heirs of each fortress to meet and learn the different aspects of governing their respective domains-to-be, and served to renew the ancient peace the four fortresses shared. It also tested their resolve and forced them to survive on their wits and strength. Thirty days in the Altan Wastes was no easy journey.

As was often the case, the heirs of Bara'cor and EvenSea formed a fast and strong friendship, given they were of equal station and "suffered" the same things as most would-be rulers. It had been almost three months since Yetteje had heard any news from her father, however, a fact that had brought faint lines of worry to her usually carefree visage.

Before the nomads laid siege to Bara'cor, Niall had planned to return with Yetteje to EvenSea to begin his own three-summer long tour of the land, one summer spent at each of the other three fortresses that ringed the Altan Wastes. It now seemed nothing was getting in or out of the stronghold.

Heaving another dramatic sigh, Niall said, "I'm assigned to Fenrith and supplies, can you believe it?"

"Are you surprised?" Yetteje moved to the opposite end of the bowl, "You didn't really expect to fight, did you?" The expression on Niall's face obviously told her this was *exactly* what he had expected. Yetteje seemed to regret the words, though a part of her still had to smile at the humor of it.

"I've earned my third blade, one of the best in the class."

Yetteje arched one delicate eyebrow at this, "Indeed, almost a bladesman then."

Niall quickly put up the open palm warding gesture and exclaimed, "Bladesmen!" He spat out his next word with distaste, "Traitors."

"I'm sorry," laughed the princess, "I just can't believe you would think your father would risk you to some stray arrow. You're a *prince,* by the Lady, and the only heir to his throne. Plus, imagine every recruit trying to keep you alive. They'll be jumping over each other to be the one who saves you."

Niall shook his head, hating that her words echoed the firstmark's sentiments. "You assume I'll need saving." He climbed to his feet, thinking about the absurdity of men actually putting themselves into harm's way for him. "Why would anyone do that?'

Yetteje shook her head. "You really don't get people, do you?"

Niall looked around a bit before continuing, ignoring her last comment. He began slowly, "You know, Father speaks of Haven, some sort of retirement." He carefully avoided Tej's inquisitive stare.

"Why does that...?" Then her eyes brightened and laughter she couldn't help spilled out. "Wait, you think he's going to leave *you* in charge?"

"What?" Niall replied, exasperated, though now it sounded a bit stupid when he heard it out loud.

"You are going to be in charge of the greatest military and civilian bastion in the world... at sixteen?"

Niall cursed, then vaulted lightly over the lip of the bowl, landing on the stone walkway. His patience with his cousin was close to its limits. "Leave it, please."

"He's going to skip over the Firstmark, the Armsmark, *all* the officers, and put you—"

"Just shut up!" he exclaimed, not looking back.

* * * * *

Yetteje smiled at Niall's retreating form, then followed him down the walkway in silence. She didn't want to poke more fun at what was obviously something important to Niall, but surely he knew better.

His desire to fight now made a little more sense, in that he thought to prove to his father that he, too, was a fighting man. She could empathize, but unlike her cousin, had no qualms about staying as far from the fighting as possible. It was not fear, for Yetteje had spent countless hours training with blade, bow, and staff, as any royal heir would. She was just more pragmatic about her role in life, and her aspirations were higher than being a soldier of the line.

Though her participation in the siege was involuntary, as a ward of Bara'cor, her participation in the defense was not expected. The king had made it quite clear she could not stray onto the wall without permission.

"You know," Niall said, turning to face her, "sometimes soldiers are promoted in battle, right on the spot." His finger stabbed down in emphasis.

Clearly, thought Yetteje, he had continued the argument between them in his head. She decided not to respond directly, Niall wasn't listening anyway. She was curious, however, about why he was so set on fighting *now*. The nomads didn't seem to be going anywhere. After a moment's consideration, she asked him just that.

Niall stopped, then turned and said, "No one will respect a ruler who hasn't fought, no matter what people say and no matter what royal lineage we're from. People follow heroes. Plus, aren't you sick of being thought of as kids? Even my father and the firstmark treat us like children."

Yetteje stopped at that, considering. It had not occurred to her that combat might be a prerequisite of leadership, as Niall had said. Her thoughts narrowed with focused intensity.

* * * * *

Niall, for his part, looked back at Shimmerene, trying to articulate how he felt. He hadn't been entirely truthful. He also sought fame and glory. But combat was the only way he could see to get that, too. His cousin would never understand. Her gaze seemed to be focused on the Warriors Hall, not far from where they stood. He smiled and shoved her shoulder a little harder than playfully, but still in jest. His anger at her was never long-lived. "Never mind. How about a little sparring before we go to sleep?"

"Sure, unless that might endanger your upcoming promotion." She quickly ducked as Niall swung at her, then ran up the slight slope leading to the Warriors Hall.

As they neared, they could again hear the faint clack of the wooden practice *bohkir* striking each other. Motioning Niall to be silent, she moved closer to one of the portals looking onto the training grounds. She felt Niall come up behind her, cursing softly as he jostled for a better view.

"That's Ash! What's he doing?" In answer to Yetteje's annoyed look, Niall added, "I know, stupid question."

Still, it was unusual for the man who was second-in-command of all of Bara'cor's forces to be out on the practice grounds at this hour. Pushing Yetteje and her muffled curses out of the way, Niall pulled up close to the portal to get a better view.

In the center of the torchlit ground stood Armsmark Ash Rillaran, his eyes narrowed in concentration. He held two *bohkir*, low and away from his body. Stripped to the waist, Ash's lean form was sheened with sweat. Dark, close-cropped hair glistened from his exertions. Circling around him ranged his three opponents, their sashes marking them as captains of different companies. They held their weapons in front of their midsections, the blades angled up. Even as the prince and princess watched, two switched their stance and attacked with their *bohkir* held high, the third thrusting in at Ash's neck.

Ash ducked inside the first overhead strike, shoving his muscular shoulder into his opponent's stomach and driving him into his comrade. As they went sprawling in a tangle of arms and legs, he charged the third, heading straight for the *bohkir*'s tip. At the last possible moment, he twisted his left shoulder forward, the sword passing inches away from the right side of his neck, and struck with his left *bohkir* to the captain's wrist.

The wooden sword fell from nerveless fingers, even as the captain dived into a roll to avoid Ash's second strike as it whizzed by his ear.

Niall grabbed Yetteje. "Come on, let's go inside!"

They ran around to the front of the Warriors Hall, pausing only to pull their boots off as custom dictated, before entering. They found, much to their disappointment, that they were not the only spectators.

The dozens of soldiers, watching as their captains took on the young armsmark quickly dashed Niall's hopes for a private lesson. Moving over to one side of the combat circle, he found a seat and pulled Yetteje next to him. "I think the armsmark should test for his Seventh."

Yetteje looked at Niall, pursing her lips, "You don't even know what that takes. By the Lady, you've only passed your Third and you're talking like a master."

"So what? I was just..." Niall began to say more, but a sudden flurry caused Yetteje to make shushing gestures, her attention plainly on the combatants. "...making an observation," he finished quietly.

The armsmark had positioned himself to one side of the circle, and the three captains crouched in a semicircle in front of him, having retrieved their weapons. Then, with a shout, all three attacked together, clearly hoping to overwhelm their opponent.

Ash blocked the first's overhead strike with his left sword and put his body close to the captain's, using him as a shield. Spinning in place, he shoved the captain into the second attacker, who made the fatal mistake of trying to catch his friend. Two quick blows from Ash's *bohkir* dispatched them even as he pivoted to block the third captain's thrust at his stomach. Parrying it past him, he hooked his foot behind the man's forward ankle and pulled, sweeping him to the floor. Ash placed his *bohkir* on the man's throat, smiled, and said, "Durbin, you were always impatient. Yield?"

A slow smile broke out on Captain Durbin's face, bringing new creases to an already sun-lined visage, and in a gruff voice he replied, "Yes, yes, you wet-behind-the-ears pup! I yield."

The armsmark pulled his sword away and helped Durbin up, clapping him on the back. Around them, the crowd laughed as jokes flitted back and forth between the rival companies, and chores changed hands as wagers were lost or won.

Turning to the other two captains, Ash bowed once, thanking them, then walked over to an earthen water bowl set to one side of the Warriors Hall. The three captains made their way out of the circle, meeting the good-natured jeering with smiles and comments of their own.

Ash watched them for a moment, and Niall could see the armsmark appeared content that there were no hidden animosities. Ash grabbed a wet towel and began to scrub his face and neck. As he replaced his weapons on the rack, he noticed Niall and Yetteje approaching. Niall saw his eyes linger on the hilt of the prince's saber poking out from behind his right shoulder.

Shaking his head at the boy's youthful enthusiasm, Ash greeted the pair with a smile. "It seems you are already preparing for tomorrow, my prince." He then nodded to Yetteje and added, "Princess."

Niall grimaced. "Father has assigned me to Captain Fenrith."

The armsmark nodded in understanding, but said, "An important position."

"What position?" Niall spread his arms in exasperation.

Ash narrowed his ice blue eyes, nodding more slowly. He then held out a callused hand and asked, "Does this hurt?"

Niall yelped in surprise as the armsmark's finger poked him in the chest, then he laughed. "No, of course not. It's only your finger."

Slowly Ash closed his fingers into a tight fist and then addressed Niall again. "And if I hit you with *this?*"

"Wha—!" Niall backed up a step, then stopped. "I mean, no . . . That could hurt." Actually, Ash's finger *had* felt like an iron rod, and hurt quite a bit, but Niall didn't want to admit that in front of Yetteje.

The armsmark straightened and asked, "Why?"

"That would hurt a lot more than your finger. Even that didn't feel so good." His hand had unconsciously begun rubbing the spot Ash had poked.

Ash spread the fingers of his hand in front of Niall. "Each of my fingers represents one facet of defending this fortress. No one part can succeed by itself." The armsmark closed his fingers slowly. "Together, we form a fist the nomads cannot break." He looked at the prince thoughtfully. "Do you understand?"

Niall stood for a moment, dumbfounded. "I think so."

"I hope so. Do not forget that we, who repel the attackers from the wall cannot do so without arrows, or survive the heat without water. There is no station beneath your respect, my prince. The men will be heartened to see the Prince of Bara'cor perform such menial duties for them. It is important and noble. It is the stuff of leaders."

The armsmark looked thoughtfully at Niall, then his face broke into a grin, "It is one of the many things you will have to master if someday you wish to command these men. By your leave?"

As Niall nodded, the armsmark scooped up his shirt and made his way out of the Warriors Hall, into the cool night.

Yetteje came up behind Niall, who stood alone now, deep in thought. "Maybe *he'll* promote you," she said.

"Shut up, Tej, seriously."

Council's Choice

If an opponent is frustrating you

by fighting well,

consider adopting her strategy.

—*Altan proverb*

S ilbane entered the council chamber and took his seat. Looking about, he saw the other adepts had already arrived, and an expectant murmur ran around the table as views were debated back and forth. He watched all this in silence, waiting for the lore father to make his appearance. *He has played us well, like a master at the game of Kings.* The thought came with more than a little anger and Silbane wondered if their opinions had ever really mattered.

A few moments later, Themun Dreys entered, took his place at the head of the chamber, and tapped his runestaff three times to call the council to order. Once everyone had been seated, he sat down and took a moment, mentally assessing each adept before speaking.

"The problem is simple. We have a fortress besieged, within which I sense a Gate opening. I believe the attackers are being helped by someone of power, and wish to send Silbane and his apprentice into the area to investigate. I would hear what counsel you have to offer."

Kisan was the first to speak, stating, "It is simple, my opinion has not changed. Forget investigating Bara'cor, or sending Silbane's apprentice. If the problem is the nomads, deal with it there. Let us take direct action." Everyone understood by this she meant, *kill the nomad command.* This simple declaration had a palpable effect on the gathered adepts and the room itself seemed to hold its breath, waiting for the lore father's reaction.

One adept could not contain herself any more, rebutting, "And what of our Oath? *Shield of the Weak,* as I recall, is still one of our duties. Is that so easily dismissed?" This was from Thera, who in the gathered silence chose to stand in answer to Kisan's statement. "We cannot dismiss it just because it is convenient to do so, else we would be no better than those who first drove us from the land. I have felt that pain and do not wish to be the arbiter of justice."

Giridian stood now, a deep rumble echoing from his throat. As the eyes of the council turned to him, he bowed to the lore father and said, "As Thera says, our very existence is based upon the nurturing of the land *and* its people. To turn our backs on them now is not why I became an adept."

He paused for a moment, casting his eyes at Kisan and said, "However, I can see merit in Master Kisan's suggestion. What would our ancestors do if given the choice of killing a few to save our world? I think they would have taken it. Now we have the same choice. Do we do any less?"

Themun paused, then looked to Dragor and said, "I would hear Adept Dragor's thoughts."

The others turned to the dark-skinned adept, waiting. Dragor was already known for being more quiet than most. These events, however, had driven him to near silence. Now he bowed his head and wiped the sweat from his face with a large hand. The firelight of the torches gleamed on his bald pate and hung sparkling from a gold earring he wore, but distress showed in his every move.

Slowly, Dragor stood and addressed the council, his voice troubled. "You know I prefer a peaceful solution. Lore Father, is the Gate protected by wards of the Old Lords' making?"

Themun shook his head, "Basic warding spells completed before they were cut down. As I said before, they had not expected to be butchered."

Dragor nodded once, his expression hinting to the fact that he did not find this surprising. Much of the old lore about gates indicated that making and warding them was difficult work, requiring advanced skill and intense concentration. The fact that the First Council even had the wherewithal to raise any protective measures spoke of their incredible competence.

This fact surely didn't make his next announcement any easier. "Then I have no choice but to agree with the lore father. If the Gate can be found, we must attempt it. We should come to Bara'cor's aid."

"The noble-born Galadines, who enacted laws that killed mothers and fathers and hunted innocent children?" Kisan retorted, looking at Dragor. "Shall we help them, too?"

"We aid Bara'cor by killing the nomads, as *you* just advocated. Can we not first determine what is necessary? You seem bent on killing," said Dragor, icily. "What harm comes in letting Silbane investigate?"

Themun cleared his throat, then raised a hand. "I understand Kisan's point, for she seeks to avoid sending an apprentice. Unfortunately, we do not have an option. The Bara'cor Gate, if found, cannot be allowed to open. We cannot leave it for the nomads to find and we cannot ignore it." He looked at Giridian and continued, "Despite your confidence, we have not the means in our Vaults to destroy it."

Giridian paused, about to retort, but then nodded hesitantly. "Yes, but none of us have that kind of power either. The Old Lords and their knowledge would be necessary."

Thera jumped in before the lore father could answer Giridian and said, "How do you know the Gate is even at Bara'cor?"

This was not really a question and the lore father knew it. Thera was cunning and sought to create doubt, when there was none in his heart. He could not afford to let her influence the others.

Themun said, "With the other three fortresses now laying in ruin, I *know* it is there. I have no way of proving it to *you,* but I know the Gate has awakened somewhere in Bara'cor." He looked at the council and said, "Let us focus on what I said last, these other fortresses. These nomads are being helped by someone of power."

Kisan nodded. "Investigating the fortress or killing the nomad command is still easily accomplished."

Themun shook his head. "Not without revealing yourselves. Until we know who they are, they are a danger to us and potentially anyone living on the Isle."

"King Galadine rescinded the laws against magic some years back," said Giridian. "What danger?"

"They've hunted us for close to two hundred years. The law has little to do with our safety, if you act outside it. Do you truly believe the Magehunters are gone, just because they stand outlawed? We cannot risk knowledge of us coming to light until we know who is behind the strength of the nomads." Themun looked pointedly at Silbane. "We need to hide our presence during this mission."

Giridian shook his head. "You are asking the impossible. We cannot hide our life auras. The Magehunters used that fact to hunt us quite effectively."

Themun looked at Silbane, then said simply, "Tell them about Arek."

From the moment the lore father had spoken with him privately, Silbane knew it would come to this. Still, he had to try to dissuade him, and with a matter-of-factness that belied his anguish he said, "He would never survive."

Themun's eyes did not waver. "You don't know that. He's not helpless, and you must think of the benefit of the people of Edyn over the needs of one boy."

Silbane shook his head. "It cannot have come to this." He knew the lore father meant what he had said. One look into his friend's eyes showed him a man who would stand by this course of action because he believed in it. He *would* send Arek with Kisan and Silbane felt his heart grow heavy, the burden of their planning now exacting its own personal debt.

Then he drew a deep breath, calming himself, centering his thoughts, purging the fear. He took another, then another, each bringing with it the calm needed to explain to the others what the lore father requested of him. His ability to think was crucial to this council acting with alacrity, and for Arek's survival.

Slowly, he turned and addressed the assembled adepts, his voice heavy but measured. "As many of you know, I apprenticed Arek at a very young age, much earlier than normal. As you've seen from his performance in your classes, while he is quite accomplished in many of the physical arts, his ability to command the Way is ... limited."

Kisan scoffed, "'Limited' is being generous."

"Nonetheless," Silbane continued, "all of you know why. His ability to disrupt magic is unique, and none of us has yet understood how he does it. Conveyed by touch, it causes those who are further along in their mastery of the Way more danger. However, Arek has another ability, one the lore father and I think is an offshoot of this magical disruption."

Silbane paused, gathering his thoughts, then said, "The lore father can sense magical potential, even at far distances." He looked at Thera. "I believe Themun when he says he can sense the Gate come to life. He has saved many of us in much the same way."

He turned back to the adepts and went on, "I, too, have this ability, though to a much lesser degree. When Arek first came to the Isle, we noted two things were very peculiar about him. One was the magical disruption his touch causes. We are all familiar with this. The other trait is when anyone of magical potential stood within close proximity to Arek, they *faded* from our awareness."

Dragor leaned forward and asked, "Faded?"

Silbane nodded. "Anything near Arek tends to have its magical aura suppressed. We do not know why. Further, it persists for some time even after Arek leaves the area, like the ground after a rainstorm, slowly drying in the sun. I apprenticed Arek early to try and understand the reasons, for it could have great value in hiding us from persecution." He paused, then added, "In this I have not made much progress."

Kisan looked back at the lore father and asked, "This is the reason you brought up his apprentice?"

"Yes," Themun replied. "The fate of the world rests on our success. To ensure that, no sacrifice is too great. Getting to Bara'cor undetected, past whomever or whatever is helping the nomads, is critical. Staying out of the demon's notice if the Gate is open is paramount. Arek guarantees both these things."

Silbane shook his head. "Themun, I can't do this."

Themun looked at his longtime friend, noting in his eyes what his mind already knew. "Yes, you can, and that frightens you. You know risking Arek to keep our existence safe and close this Gate is choosing life for the land and her people."

The anguish in Silbane's eyes told Themun he had guessed right, but his voice softened when he asked, "He seeks to become an adept, does he not? What oath will he take then? Will it be the same one you and I took, pledging our fealty and service to this land? You think him young, but he may wish to stand by his pledge of service, though he has not yet achieved the Black."

Silbane forced a laugh. "Then test him! Promote him to adept and let him reaffirm the Oath! Will that not be better?"

Themun's eyes hardened, "We do not know what will happen when spells are cast *at* him. What if he is incapacitated, or killed? Gone will be any chance of achieving this mission."

"Wait," said Thera, hesitancy in her voice, like an instinct that something was not being said. "What do you mean? Silbane acts as if his apprentice is doomed, when all you've asked is they investigate the Gate. Can they not achieve that and return easily?" The rest of the adepts nodded, Thera's question a valid one.

Themun looked at Silbane. A moment passed and finally the lore father said, "If you wish me to state Silbane's orders fully so there is no confusion, fine." Themun met Silbane's gaze unflinchingly and said, "If it is open, he will use Arek to close the Gate."

Shock followed that last statement and Thera leapt to her feet. "What will happen to the boy?"

Themun looked at Thera and said simply, "The *initiate* may be in danger, but he is not helpless, and his master accompanies him."

"You know what is likely," Silbane responded. "He will either die, or be trapped on the other side of the Gate, in Lilyth's world." Then he looked meaningfully at the lore father and said, "And you seem quite sure his touch won't open the Gate further. How can you suggest something so potentially disastrous?"

Themun answered, "Arek's power has never increased magic, nor created more from less. That would be like saying soaking cloth in water creates more water than when you started. Clearly that does not happen."

"But you don't know."

He held his hand up to Silbane and said, "Yes, I do. Arek does not increase or magnify magic in any way whatsoever. He has *never* done so. The only thing he does is nullify it. You know this better than any of us."

The council remained silent, but Silbane didn't have an answer to that. What the lore father said was true, for he had never seen his apprentice create anything, only disrupt the Way with his touch.

Kisan raised a hand, her head bowed in thought. When she looked up again, one could see the sincerity in her eyes. "Danger is our job . . . *all of us.* Even our apprentices, for they have the freedom to leave with coin in their pockets if they do not wish to remain here. Some leave of their own accord and still we give them every means to survive, should they choose that path. Others choose to stay."

She looked at Silbane and said, "I would ask we consider what indecision will mean to the people of Edyn. We cannot hesitate to seal a wound because of the pain. Doing so will only cause the patient to die."

"Then should we not give *him* this choice?" Thera implored. "Service is our oath. Danger is a by-product, and we accept this risk. Even if Arek's touch can close this Gate, Themun is asking the boy to go in blind, not knowing the possible consequences. Should he be sacrificed for the greater good?"

"You speak of sacrifice and forget those who have not yet been born. Do they not deserve better than this? Have we not killed in the past?" Kisan retorted, looking around the council chamber. "The mistakes of the Old Lords are well known to us. When they failed in their duty, how many innocent children—and *parents*—died in the war and the persecutions that followed? Who killed them?"

Kisan looked at each adept before speaking. "We did. Our arrogance caused Lilyth's blight on the land and the resulting persecutions against us. Now we hesitate again, much as the First Council must have done. Had they the benefit of hindsight, would they have hesitated with the life of one initiate? I doubt not, seeing the price it would exact." She paused, then intoned, "A fool expects the same song to end on a different note."

Thera shook her head at this, looking down and saying, "I cannot believe I am hearing this. Have we become so fearful we sacrifice our own at the slightest hint of danger? Is that easier than thinking?"

Kisan looked at Thera, exasperation in her eyes. "What option is left to us? If closing the Gate means sacrificing lives, or even *one* life, you are against it?"

"What if it were Piter?" she retorted.

Kisan sat back, disbelief written plainly on her face. She did not say anything, but Silbane could see on her face that her mind worked quickly against the sudden reversal brought on by Thera's words. What would she do if it were Piter? Perhaps a part of her began sympathizing with Silbane's plight. She grew silent, apparently not trusting herself to answer immediately.

Thera continued, her voice a mixture of disbelief and anger, now directed at all the assembled adepts, "I cannot believe what I have just heard from this 'council'." Her words fell like acid. "We pledge ourselves to the service of the land. 'Shields and blades, healers and spirit,' these words are part of our oath, but at the first hint of trouble, we offer our children as acceptable casualties. I—"

"We are the land's last hope!" Themun exclaimed, his voice like thunder. "Do you not understand?" He slammed his staff into the ground in frustration. "You were ever cautious, Thera, from the day my father rescued you till now, always holding back! That is why you sit as adept, and not yet a full master, though you have twice the teachings of anyone here. Do you think this day is one of simple problems and easy solutions?"

Thera looked down, abashed by Themun's words. Her will was strong though and in a voice supported by her convictions, she continued, "I know you think me yielding and soft, but after a storm, it is the whiplash tree that remains standing. As for this, I cannot in good conscience agree."

She looked at the gathered adepts, then back at the lore father. "I excuse myself," she said softly. She made her way to the large double doors and stopped. She kept her back to Themun and dropped her head, but her voice echoed throughout the large chamber. "Your father would be ashamed of you." Themun stepped forward, but before he could say anything, the doors opened and she swept out of them in a swirl of black hair and blue silk.

As the doors shut again, Themun stood in silence. Silbane knew it did not bode well for them that Thera had left and yet he also knew the lore father couldn't bring himself to blame her, no matter how her words had hurt him.

Themun turned to the remaining adepts, anger in his eyes. "Does anyone else share Thera's dilemma? If so, you should excuse yourselves as well. Lay down this burden and share not in the load. Make your lives easier, stand aside, decide you cannot sacrifice your own comfort and moral certitude for *service.*

"This is the hard path, the path of the Way. This is a day where we must all make difficult choices, and for that I need only those who can bear the weight. I need those willing to serve."

When no one stepped forward, his features softened. He looked down, but when his head rose, the remaining adepts could see the weariness, fear, and sadness that framed Themun's face. With a sigh, he said, "These are trying times. I hold no anger at Thera, except for the delays in judgment her doubt will surely cause. We do not have the luxury of time, or being sure of ourselves."

He sighed, then his voice came out with the surety and certainty of the lore father of this council, "We prepare for Silbane and Arek's journey. Equip the initiate to give him the best chance of surviving."

Giridian said, "What of his ability to disrupt magic? While it is the reason for him going, nothing we give him can withstand his touch."

"Not all the objects in the lower Vaults require physical contact," Silbane offered. "Perhaps we can find something that will aid Arek by its very presence."

Kisan asked Silbane, "And what will you tell him? How will you explain you are taking him into a siege?"

"You can suggest that this is part of his training," Giridian suggested. "It seems cruel, but it would keep him near you, and obedient."

Silbane scoffed. "Arek is powerless, not stupid. When we arrive at Bara'cor, he will look at me as though I've lost my mind."

"Perhaps," Kisan answered, "but to be blunt, who cares? By then he will stay near you to stay safe."

Themun waited, but no answer came from Silbane. Then, he carefully said, "I have an idea. Perhaps what I suggest will also help keep Arek alive." The gathered adepts looked at the lore father, who said one word, "Rai'stahn."

Silbane looked in shock at the lore father, "How will that help Arek?"

Themun looked at Silbane and said, "I cannot speak to what a dragon will do or say, only that if there is another way to close a rift, Rai'stahn will know it."

Silbane pursed his lips, deep in thought. It was a slim chance centered on the ancient creature's willingness to participate. He looked at the lore father and asked, "And you think Rai'stahn will help?"

To this Themun smiled. "I am not without some influence, and as I recall the dragon owes me a favor. I will send word you wish to speak to him."

Silbane nodded, but his attention was caught again by a wavering in the air, a displacement. He took a deep breath and reached for the Way, intending to open his Sight.

"Silbane, a moment of your time, please," Themun interrupted. "You must keep, as your foremost concern, the Gate and the danger it represents. You must keep Arek with you to remain masked to anyone's scrutiny."

"You mean keep Arek alive until Silbane knows the Gate exists, then push his apprentice through and hope for the best." This came from Giridian, the comment uttered before he could help himself. "I agree we must verify the Gate's existence, but the boy . . . it does not sit well with me."

Silbane nodded in agreement, looking again for the sign of that *something,* but it was gone. It was so slight and faint, it truly could be his imagination. It was not a warding, of that he was certain. He decided to keep quiet for now and instead said, "Nor I, but the lore father has presented a plan that may work. What do we know of what a true dragon can do? What is beyond its capabilities? Because of this, I am willing to do my part."

Giridian slowly shook his head. He seemed surprised at Silbane's acceptance. Perhaps to him it brought to mind the desperate actions of a drowning man clinging to a flimsy branch, a branch the lore father had offered. Yet, though the thought disturbed him greatly, he too, said nothing. Something did not ring true with this sudden promise of the dragon's aid.

Themun looked to Silbane and said, "You will make plans to leave as soon as possible."

"And what of Arek? How will you tell him he's going into a war zone?" asked Silbane.

"I won't," Themun said simply. *"You* will. Speak with your apprentice, explain what he needs to know of our plan. Do not speak of how you intend to close the Gate. For all other matters, there is no need to lie to him. He, too, is a servant of this land, as the oath he took requires."

Gathering himself, Themun addressed the adepts around him. "I thank each of you for your guidance. We will prepare for Silbane's departure." With a single rap of his black runestaff, he closed the meeting.

* * * * *

The first to exit the room was Kisan, the air swirling in the wake of her hasty departure. In a moment, the chamber was empty, save for the lore father and Giridian. Themun felt, rather than saw, the latter come to stand beside him.

Giridian cleared his throat, voicing a concern that had not left him since Thera's departure. "This is harder on Thera than the rest of us."

"You think so?" Themun looked away. "I have asked Silbane to sacrifice his apprentice to close the Gate. Are Thera's feelings somehow more important than his young apprentice's life?"

Giridian looked at the lore father, not knowing exactly what to say. "Of course not ... though at these times is it not more important for us to be united?"

Themun looked at the burly adept and asked, "Are we not? You worry about Thera, who even now wonders if she acted correctly." He paused for a moment, then continued, "Do you know what she did after seeing her parents killed? As we moved the villagers to shelter and bedded down for the night, she called upon the earth and eradicated her village. Not a hut, stone, tree, bush, or blade of grass remained, and she was just five years old. She chooses to nurture this world and make it a better place for the living. We need people like her, so Edyn can continue to flourish."

"I had no idea she had such power," Giridian replied.

Themun nodded, and said, "She will come to a place where she can either support our decisions, or not. Regardless, she will feel justified, and we can all stand by *that* decision. Thera is the lucky one. Her fortitude will be unwavering exactly because of the challenges placed on her. We should all be so lucky to earn that kind of conviction."

"Then what hurdles must we endure?"

Themun did not smile when he said, "Faith. In us, in all of this," he said while taking in the room with a gesture.

Giridian bowed to the lore father, excusing himself with, "I'll go see how she's doing."

"Thank you," Themun said, his eyes far away in thought. Faith is a tricky thing, he reminded himself sadly.

Giridian bowed, then gathered his things and made his way to the door.

Themun watched him leave the chamber, knowing the upcoming days would be the hardest his council would ever face.

RESPITE

The slightest tremble can show

a man's weakness.

Once seen, act decisively

or the moment is lost.

Remain alert, strike swiftly.

—The Bladesman Codex

The council chamber lay deep in the heart of the fortress, dominated by an octagonal table large enough for two men to lay head to foot across it without touching either end. It rose from the solid granite floor without seam, a natural extension of the rock forming the fortress. Under skilled artisans' hands, the stone became a work of beauty, flowing from scene to scene, as it depicted what could only be a history of the ancient dwarven people.

Etched on the floor at each of the eight corners of the table lay another octagon, smaller, but no less intricate. Their surfaces were a complex mixture of pictures and dwarven writings, showing strange vistas that could only be distant lands. The true meaning of the inlays was lost, however, to antiquity. Anyone who could have deciphered them had perished long ago.

Bernal had been at the table for much of the night, his eyes absently tracing the rune-carved surface of the Galadine great bow, Valor. It had been in his family for centuries, passed from father to son. His father had trained him for many summers, arduous practice sessions, until he had the strength to string and draw it.

When he could put six arrows into a space no bigger than his hand at four hundred paces, his father had declared him worthy of its name. Soon it would go to Niall, who had been training tirelessly to wield this awesome weapon. Rarely did the king disturb Valor from its holder at one side of the table, but on some occasions, its presence filled him with a sense of purpose.

Now, with the horde encamped at his doorstep, he found himself in this room more frequently, his eyes vacant as he pictured the battles depicted on the floor and wall. His thoughts scattered when Jebida entered the council chamber and sat his large frame down across from him. The king nodded in greeting, his eyes reluctantly leaving the runebow. Jebida answered with a grunt, the day's strain showing.

High above the granite walls the sun rose, coloring the sky pink as it slowly peeked above the horizon, but the air told him a different story. Storm clouds would be brewing, and his bones said there was magic in the air, but he did not mention that to Jebida. He could taste the metallic tang and knew today would bring a tempest of wind and sand, not rain.

"The men are sore pressed, my lord," began Jebida quietly. "It is well the enemy does not have siege engines—"

"Aye, we are fortunate in many respects."

Bernal's bitter interruption elicited a raised eyebrow from the firstmark, who knew the king's moods well. "Nevertheless, we *are* quite lucky. Land's Edge prevents them from surrounding us, and provides us with a means of escape . . . should it come to that."

The king nodded, realizing he was venting his frustration on the one person who would take it, "I am sorry. Just wish we knew why they are here. Why Bara'cor?" Bernal pounded his fist into his palm. "It makes no sense."

"Not much does," he answered, then a thought occurred and he asked, "What of the queen's mission? Will Haven reinforce us?"

"Doubtful," replied the king. He knew the political atmosphere in the capital city and ventured, "Haven will see to its own safety, as it always has. In the end, it will come to a vote of the Senate."

Jebida sighed. "Shornhelm and Dawnlight, for all their willingness to bend their knee, have never truly supported you."

The king nodded, knowing his military actions against both had brought peace, but also difficult relations. They would never openly work against the King of Bara'cor, but during a senatorial vote would certainly not be supportive of his queen. "Yevaine has the right of one vote for Bara'cor. The legates from the other fortresses make up three more and the chancellor for Haven is one. She will need to turn two of them in order for the city to release the militia."

"Can the queen not pull two more besides herself?"

"Never mind the fact that I am repelling a siege on Haven's doorstep," the king replied, "it will not stay the deft hands of Shornhelm and Dawnlight. They will use this to sway the chancellor, if that is even necessary. Only Tir will stand with us."

"They why—?" began Jebida, but a slight smile emerged as the king's motivation became clear. "You're occupying her with something impossible, and keeping her away from here in case Bara'cor should fall." The firstmark shook his head, simultaneously admiring the king's bravery and foolhardiness. "I wouldn't want to be in your boots. You'll have the Lady's price to pay when she finds out."

The king gave a rueful grin and said, "It won't be the first time."

Jebida sighed, "Politics," but it came out like a curse. Then he continued, "I can't say I'm flattered by your faith in me."

With a smile the king replied, "You know I believe we'll prevail, or Niall would have gone with her."

The firstmark scoffed at that. "And somehow Kalindor pulls light duty."

"Strange," the king said with a laugh. "I thought you assigned him."

The giant warrior didn't bother to deny it, knowing the king had somehow heard everything, as usual. The silence stretched on, then he said quietly, "He could have been firstmark had he so desired. You know the man is not happy without a spear in hand and enemies at the gate. His fault, not mine." He paused, then added with a smile, "But he deserves the rest."

"For all your bluster, the men should know you have a kind heart," the king offered, tilting his head in half joke, half praise.

"Tell anyone, and the story of you and that golden-haired dancer from that inn in Moonhold will surface. Innocently, of course."

The king shook his head, laughing. "Younger days, before all this." Then his expression grew more somber.

"When Yevaine and Kalindor return," Jebida said, "at least we'll have Fourth Company back to reinforce us."

Bernal paused, knowing the truth, and said, "Haven will not allow the queen or Kalindor's company to leave. If she fails to turn the vote, they will likely be ordered to support the militia in Haven's defense." He paused, then added softly, "In either case, Yevaine is safe."

"I don't envy Captain Kalindor when your wife sees through your ruse. He'll be paying for your trickery."

"His fault for accepting light duty, and better him than me," stated the king flatly, which elicited a small laugh from Jebida in return.

The firstmark waited for a moment, then asked, "No news from EvenSea? Has Ben sent nothing?"

"Nothing," replied the king. He didn't add the obvious, that no news generally meant bad news, and he feared for the lives of King Ben'thor Tir and the rest of Yetteje's family.

Jebida rose, the stress of the night watch showing in his eyes. "Your leave then, my lord? They will attack soon and I need to review our defenses. Already the wind has picked up and the sands begin to swirl. The storm will hit and we will be effectively blind."

"Ash holds the wall?"

"Aye, my lord. He is prepared for the assault."

Bernal could not miss the pride shining in Jebida's eyes when he spoke of the young armsmark. He suspected that over the summers, Ash had taken the place of Jebida's family and had become the son the gruff firstmark never had. "Well then, you may as well turn in and get some rest."

"Sir?" the firstmark asked in confusion.

Bernal stood, facing the firstmark. "Was I not clear enough? Go to your quarters and get some sleep. Ash and I will handle the wall today," and as Jebida hesitated, the king continued, "or do you not trust us?"

"It is not that, my lord! Just, I had hoped to assist—"

"You're beginning to sound like a certain son of mine," the king interrupted again. "And by that I mean stubborn." He said this while moving around the table and laying a hand on Jebida's massive shoulder, steering the firstmark toward the exit. "You and I both know there is little you can do after a long night watch. Get some rest. If anything happens, I'll send for you."

"What about you?" Jebida paused at the door, looking at his old friend. "There is little you can achieve by staying on the wall when you are in more need of rest than I."

"Perhaps. Still, my presence bolsters the men. Now, be gone. I will not have my commanders falling asleep in their boots. You're ordered to get some rest."

"I'm starting to understand how Kalindor felt," offered Jebida.

The king didn't answer, instead pushing the reluctant firstmark through the door and toward his quarters. He watched Jebida's broad back disappear around a bend in the flickering torchlight before casting his gaze upward, imagining he could see the first dark thunderheads as they raced across the sky to block out the bright rays of the rising sun.

IN HARM'S WAY

In the contest of blades,

each parry and riposte

is opportunity dancing with chance,

and the prize for victory is life.

—*Kensei Shun, The Book of Shields*

Arek awoke early the next morning, sluggishly throwing off the covers and making his way to his washbasin. On his desk lay the book Master Silbane had given him, open to the page he had been studying well into the night. Squinting in the bright sun shining through his window, he began his morning ritual, splashing cold water on his face and neck. I have studied that stupid fortress so much I can't think of anything else, he thought with irritation.

He dried his face and sat down at his desk, his eyes automatically finding the place he had stopped before. Though his eyes stared at the page, his mind wandered, picturing the fortress as it must have been at the time of the dwarves. King Bara had held it then, his ancestors being builders. It was said that between the great fortress and the small trade city within, Bara'cor could hold close to two thousand people. Strangely, it was said everything in Bara'cor was big, as if made for a race of men larger than normal.

Arek leaned back, closing his eyes. What he did not understand was why King Bara had turned the fortress over in the first place. After the final battle, it was rumored the dwarven king had said, "The dwarven people seek their *Sovereign.*"

He had then handed Bara'cor over to a young lieutenant by the name of Thorin Hayden and left the great fortress. They marched into history and oblivion, never to be heard from again.

Arek focused his attention back on the pages before him when a discreet knock on his door caused him to turn his head in consternation. Rising, he beckoned to whomever it was to enter. He was surprised to see a small boy in a white uniform cautiously push his door open.

Arek immediately recognized Benjahmen, a Whiterobe some seven years old. In Ben's hands was a scroll tied with a black cord, signifying the message was from the council. Arek allowed a small smile to crease his face as the boy moved forward and bowed, holding the scroll out with both hands. Kneeling, he tousled the boy's brown hair and said, "Well, Benjahmen, it seems you have grown a bit since I saw you last."

Ben's face lit up in a smile as he answered in a high voice, "But I saw you yesterday!"

"Yes, you did, but is it possible you have grown just a *little* bit between then and now?" Ben's answer was an exaggerated shrug that seemed to take the boy's small shoulders above his ears. Arek took the scroll and pointed to the door with mock severity. "Away with you, then." He laughed as Ben scampered out, nearly tripping on his own feet, clearly happy to get back to his friends.

Arek waited a moment, listening as the little boy's footsteps receded down the stairwell, before untying the cord and unrolling the parchment. He began reading the scroll as he made his way back to his desk. With each sentence, however, his steps began to falter and he finally came to a standstill in the center of the room, despair punched into the base of his stomach.

The Test of Ascension, cancelled? While Arek's confidence in himself may falter, the council cancelling the test must have meant that they lacked confidence in him. And *that* could mean . . .

He clutched the scroll and grabbed his robe, barely pausing to pull it over his head before racing out his door.

He arrived at the central tower's front gate, the scroll still crumpled in one hand. Hastily stuffing it in his pocket he made his way into the tower and up the spiral staircase, finally exiting on the proper level.

All was quiet and for a moment, and Arek hesitated. The hour was early yet, and he loathed the idea of rousing his master's displeasure. Nevertheless, the memory of the scroll's contents set his heart fluttering and with resolve born of desperation, he strode down the wide corridor stopping in front of his master's chambers for only a moment before knocking.

For what seemed an eternity there was no answer, the silence of the corridor building upon itself until even the slight act of wiping his sweating palms on his robe seemed deafening to his ears. Then, finally, just as he made to knock again, the doors to Silbane's chambers swung silently open. Arek stepped in, grabbing the crumpled scroll from his pocket, and stopped, the audacity of his actions suddenly hitting him like a blacksmith's hammer.

Silbane faced the door, observing his apprentice. He could see the fear in the boy's eyes, the scroll clutched in his left hand. Turning, he motioned for Arek to come in and sit, while he himself stood in front of his window.

"What brings you by my chambers?" Silbane asked.

Arek licked his lips nervously, all thoughts of the council's message having fled from his mind. To disturb an adept, a *master* at that, he did not let himself finish the thought. Instead, he held out the scroll, hoping Silbane would understand once he'd read it. Silbane's next words drowned any small hope Arek held in his heart that this might have been a mistake or some cruel joke played on him by the other Browns.

"I already know what the scroll says. I assisted in drafting it. Why does it bother you?"

Arek looked at his master incredulously, anger lending him voice, "What do you mean why does it bother me? Why cancel my test?"

Silbane's eyes softened and he gestured to his apprentice to enter. "We have a mission. One that requires our immediate attention."

"We?" asked Arek. "What about?"

Silbane looked out his window, across the Shattered Sea. "You have studied the lore of gates." It was not a question.

Arek nodded and Silbane continued, "The lore father fears a rift may have opened in the land, connecting our world to another. You and I are being sent to investigate."

Arek shook his head, his eyes darting about as he sought to understand what his master was saying. "Why me?"

"Are you not apprenticed to a Master of the Way? What else is your purpose?" When Arek did not answer, Silbane added, "Your Talent to disrupt magic makes you important for this mission. I wish it were different, but you and I are the best choice to go."

"How can I help?" Arek asked, self-doubt pitching his voice in a whisper.

"Why do you ask that? You know the lessons, your combat skills are good, and you seem to have a natural ability to strategize, a rare skill in anyone. Even Master Kisan has a difficult time across blades with you, and she is one of the very best. You should be more confident."

"More confident?" Arek let out a short laugh. "I cannot cast even the simplest of spells! How could you consider me ready for a mission like this, when a second-year Green can do something as simple as lighting a candle and I—" He remembered the last time he'd tried to light a candle. Adept Dragor had spent considerable time in darkness, trying to coax a flame out of anything in the spell room. It had been as if a force had snuffed the light-giving nature of everything in Arek's vicinity.

"The Way has many manifestations." Silbane paused, then came and stood next to his apprentice. Placing his arm around the boy's shoulders, he said, "Arek, you and I are being trusted to do something very important. It is an honor the lore father even requests us, a service for the land. It is what you are trained to do, whether or not you have the Way. Besides, not everything we do requires magic."

Arek, so caught up in his own argument, did not at first hear his answer. Then the words registered, and he slowly turned unbelieving eyes to his master, "Not required . . . how?"

"I cannot aid you in passing, but it suffices to say when you finally do test for the Black, *you* can pass without casting a single spell."

Arek rose and walked to the door, hesitating for a moment.

"Where are we going?" His voice came out low, but Silbane heard it.

"Why do you insist on asking questions you already know the answers to?" he replied.

Arek let out a sigh. "Bara'cor."

The word had lost all meaning, as if it were just something he had seen written on a piece of parchment. Nothing made sense anymore, but he didn't know what else to do. Bowing, he made his way from his master's chambers, the echo of his leather-soled feet somehow magnified in the silent corridors of the Hall of Adepts, underscoring the palpable dread he felt growing in his heart with each step.

* * * * *

Silbane wondered once again if telling Arek was the correct decision. The boy had without a doubt some kind of power in great magnitude, mused the mage. He had not been lying when he told Arek the Way of Making manifested itself differently for each person. He remembered when the boy had taken his Test for Potential.

The test itself was simple enough. After passing their written examinations for Green, the students assembled outside in a specially prepared testing area. Four concentric circles of increasing diameter stood carved into the stone ground. At a gesture from the administering adept, a barrier sprang up at each circle, made of one of the four elements.

It was the student's task to find a way through each barrier: water, earth, air, then fire. Since most were on the Isle because they had already demonstrated some magical ability, the Test for Potential gauged the intelligence of a student.

It was rare a student could defeat all four barriers, their untrained strength not up to the task. They usually found themselves trapped between the second and third circle, mentally and physically exhausted until the watching adept banished the spell and escorted the student out.

Piter, another student testing on the same day had managed to pass the first three barriers only to find himself trapped behind the wall of fire. Finally, Silbane had banished the final barrier while congratulating him, knowing the boy was destined to be a powerful adept. He then instructed Arek to stand in the hexagonal tile marking the testing ground's center. With a gesture from the adept, the four circles had sprung up again, hiding Arek from view.

Silbane had closed his eyes to concentrate on reading the young boy's state of mind. To his surprise, he could feel nothing from Arek, as if he was not even there. What happened next etched itself in Silbane's memory forever.

Arek relaxed and prepared himself. As he did so, Silbane felt as if a great void had opened up and swallowed all conscious thought within the testing area. Casting his Sight, he could still see Arek, his head bowed in intense concentration, and Silbane had a sudden feeling of something immense building, like flood waters behind a cracked dam. Then Arek opened his eyes, pale blue and flashing with power, and the dam burst.

All four circles imploded inward and collapsed, flickering into nothingness. Silbane watched this in awe, unable to comprehend the resources it would take to be able to disrupt that much power. In all his memory, none had accomplished what Arek had done.

At his own test, Silbane had managed to pass by exploiting the intrinsic weakness of each element. To *extinguish* the energies of all four was a feat unheard of.

Arek looked about himself, confusion in his eyes, as if he had just awakened from a trance. Silbane rushed into the testing area, finding the boy dazed, but unharmed. Then Arek collapsed and fell into a deep sleep, one they could not rouse him from.

He slept for almost a half moon before waking one day and asking for eggs, as if nothing strange had happened. Between plates of food, he claimed no memory of the incident, and had at first refused to believe he had been asleep for two weeks. The results, however, were too astonishing to ignore.

The council unanimously agreed they would watch and guide such power as Arek had demonstrated. Silbane had been appointed his guardian and teacher, and for the next four years served as his mentor. When Arek earned his Brown, Silbane had apprenticed him that very same day.

Since then, Silbane mentally grimaced, there had been maybe one or two minor incidents of Arek's power. Dragor's incident with the candle for one, but there had been no reappearance of anything near the level of energy the boy had channeled during his Test for Potential. It was as if the boy simply had no power except to disrupt magic. Perhaps, Silbane hesitantly began to believe, he had witnessed everything Arek had to offer.

Silbane shook his head and turned his attention to the list of items he wished to take with him on the journey. I will worry about Arek later, he told himself, plenty of time for that on our trip.

Journal Entry 3

Curse Thoth, the dragons, and their ilk. They knew what they did, and did it with pleasure. Imagine seeing things for what they truly are. The very firmament lies now before me, and I do not appreciate this "gift." It makes little sense.

It has been some time since I last wrote. I am surrounded by my own anger, creating dangers I cannot ignore. They come in raids, formless creatures having no purpose except to terrorize and take from me whatever meager provisions I have managed to gather. Unlike our world, these manifestations are much more powerful.

I catch hints of them only, but even in these barest of glimpses, they are fearsome to behold and grow more sophisticated. They are cunning, taking that which I need most, coming upon me when I am most vulnerable.

It is as if they read my thoughts . . .

(I write this later this same day . . .)

I am a fool, the answer and reason before me. Of course they take what I need, for I need it and give life to that fear! They are like wolves or jackals, but made from my mind, like a child's mistfrights.

They react and fulfill my fears and are exact in their punishment. Their master is me. They do only what I fear, to the letter. I am the key.

I must remain focused, I must stay calm . . .

POWER AND DEATH

Bladesman, when your opponent faces you,

assume the same posture and wait.

When he begins his strike,

step into his swing, striking first.

Follow with the killing stroke.

This technique must be honed,

for perfect timing is crucial.

—*The Bladesman Codex*

The day went by quickly, with Arek busy conducting his classes and preparing to leave the Isle. Part of him still could not believe the lore father had requested he go with his master, but despite his feelings to the contrary, he decided to believe his master would not lie to him.

Moreover, the fact that he was not testing had not yet sunk in. Because of this he went about his preparations in a wooden way, his mind watching as his body packed clothes and other supplies into a small, serviceable bundle.

As the afternoon waned, Arek found himself sitting on his bed, staring at his bookshelf, though his eyes focused on nothing. Part of him was secretly relieved he was not dealing with the upcoming test. Another part, however, remembered Piter's words in the library, about how his master trained him in private because he had no faith.

Was that it? Was that the reason for this special consideration? Arek hoped not, for it implied his teacher and the council really did not have any confidence in him at all. Still, he argued with himself, his master shared what he did to demonstrate his faith. He would not have asked me to go if I did not bring some value, he mused.

Rising, he moved over to his closet and started to pick clothes for dinner. A sigh escaped his lips when he realized that everything, except the combat uniforms he had left, had holes in them. He looked to his closet and brought out more serviceable, if close-fitting, clothes: pants and shirts that allowed for freedom of movement but could be layered to keep him comfortable through the desert climate's great swings in temperature between day and night. Throwing a few of these on his bed along with a pair of boots, he closed his closet and walked over to his desk.

He opened a drawer and pulled out a small sewing kit and a dagger, double-edged and keen enough to shave with. He would repair some clothes, then shave, a practice he had recently adopted as soft blond hair had begun sprouting from his cheeks and upper lip. He could then pack this away with his other travel supplies.

The sewing went quickly, and it was only near the end of his shave when a grumble from his stomach told him he had delayed his repast too long. He gave one last look at his face in the mirror to be sure he found all the hair, musing wryly that it wasn't *that* hard yet, then he left his room to make his way down to the refectory.

The dining hall wasn't too crowded, and that suited Arek fine, since the last thing he wanted now was to run into his classmates or students.

Grabbing a plate, he made himself a meal out of scattered remains, mostly buttered bread and honey. Arek found himself a seat near the back of the hall and said a brief prayer to the Lady of Flame, thanking her for his meal. He poured the thick honey over the bread, occasionally stopping to lick his sticky fingers. He had hardly finished half his meal when Jesyn entered, followed by Tomas. Both angled toward him.

Arek grabbed a napkin and began wiping his mouth and fingers, more because he needed something to do with his hands than to clean himself off. Jesyn flashed him a smile, which turned into a grimace as she felt a stab of pain in her swollen jaw. She put a hand over it and pulled over a chair, sitting down.

"You have been most difficult to find of late." Her green eyes danced with amusement. "It's almost as if you've been avoiding us."

The outcome of the *rhan'dori* Arek had witnessed didn't seem to have damaged her enthusiasm. Smiling in return, he said, "I've been busy ... but I didn't mean to ignore you."

Jesyn's presence always made him feel awkward, and he worried something stupid would spout from his mouth before he knew it. It seemed unfair that Tomas was clearly unaffected by her. A pang of jealousy ran through Arek, as it was common knowledge amongst the initiates that Jesyn and Tomas were together.

"You mean you didn't want to ignore Piter?" Tomas asked, spreading his muscular arms in feigned innocence. His eyes gleamed with mischief. "I don't know why you care so much about him."

Arek couldn't help but laugh. "I just hate the way he's always around, like he's following me."

Tomas waved a deprecatory hand and Jesyn laughed. "I know, but both of you are already apprentices. We aren't as lucky. After the test, you'll both be ahead of us by quite a bit."

At the mention of the test, Arek felt his humor drain away, leaving him empty and cold. Suddenly, all the words of his master felt like a lie. He couldn't believe he wasn't testing.

That left a sick feeling in his stomach, one that quickly destroyed his appetite. The last thing he wanted to do was come back an apprentice while all his friends took the Black. His sudden change in manner cast a dark mood over the table, and Arek knew he would have to say something.

Clearing his throat he began, "I suppose even Piter must be a bit nervous, considering the circumstances."

Jesyn scoffed at his comment, replying, "He's the weirdest kid I know. He's probably at the tailor selecting his adept's uniform right now!" Jesyn stood up, pointing to an imaginary set of garments, thoughtfully placing one hand on her chin as if in deep contemplation and shaking her head. "No, not that one, it will clash with my perfectly dark hair. No, no, I'll take the one on the right. It is the most gruesome black I have ever seen."

Arek and Tomas burst out laughing at Jesyn's impersonation. Curtseying once to her small audience she retook her seat and smiled at Arek. "You don't have to worry about Piter. You have more Talent in your little finger than he'll ever have, and he knows it."

Arek wiped tears of laughter from his eyes, saying with mock severity, "Thank you, most noble adept-to-be. Your praise is most deserved, and of course, I'm not going to argue with you." Smiling, he leaned back, these friends of his making him truly happy. He had not realized how much he missed them, which made the fact that he was leaving doubly hard.

Leaning forward again, he made up his mind he would tell them what his master had decided. He needed them to know, to understand, and to see that the idea scared him to death. Magic or not, he knew they would be his friends first.

He realized they must have sensed his mood, for both of them had quieted, waiting for his next words. His face solemn, he began, "I must confess something to both of you, but it's hard. I'm not sure—"

"What are you guys talking about?"

Arek turned his head to the voice, knowing already it belonged to Piter. He stood a table's length away, looking a bit eagerly at the group. Arek sighed, then looking at his friends, said, "Let's go. I can tell you later."

Piter looked down, a hurt expression on his face. Then he looked up and snarled, "What was so funny?"

"Get lost, Piter." Tomas locked eyes on the smaller initiate, tightening his grip on his chair, which creaked in protest. Both knew that in a physical confrontation, Piter was no match for Tomas's muscle and size.

Emboldened by the knowledge that severe punishment faced any fighting this close to a test, though, Piter stood his ground, casually breaking contact and looking at Jesyn, who did not meet his gaze.

She felt uncomfortable any time these three squared off. She didn't like Piter's need to show off, but Tomas and Arek didn't give him much opportunity to join them either. It hadn't always been this way, but cruelty seemed to be the basis of their interactions of late. All that changed was who outnumbered whom.

"Some news has been conveyed to me by my master; news I thought interesting. It concerns those of us who *are* testing." Piter's emphasis on the last part caused a knot of trepidation to form in Arek's stomach, but before he could say anything Piter continued, "He won't be testing with us."

Jesyn looked at Tomas, her unspoken question mirrored in his eyes. Looking back at Piter with confusion and annoyance written on her face, she then saw Piter's smug stare focused on Arek. Tomas saw it too and looked at his friend, who still did not meet his gaze.

"Arek, if this isn't true, say something," Tomas urged in a low voice.

"As usual," Piter sneered, "his master is protecting him."

Arek stood. "That's a lie!" He could feel his heart fluttering, as every fear he had of failing, of not being their equal, seemed to be coming to life.

"Prove it then, Apprentice." Piter's eyes narrowed slightly, as if seeing Arek for the first time. "Do ... anything." Piter spread his arms magnanimously.

A moment went by as Arek stood, watching Piter's unwavering stare, his peripheral vision picking up Jesyn's fidgeting as her nervousness became more apparent. He could feel a small bead of sweat trickle down his back, leaving a wet, cold trail that faintly itched. Somewhere, deep inside, he knew there was nothing he could do or show to contradict Piter.

Finally, it was Tomas who broke the tension by saying, "Do what I said earlier and get lost."

"I have a better idea." Piter looked down at the table, concentrating. "He's a jinx, a defect. In fact, I've been spending time researching a counter to it."

Arek knew Piter was trying to bait him and it was working. "I'm not a defect."

"No?" Piter smiled. "What do you call it then when a mage can't cast spells and interferes with others who can? It is at least . . . inept, no?"

Tomas stepped forward and demanded, "Leave."

Piter glanced at Tomas, then turned back to Arek. "How long will you let others fight your fights?"

Arek stepped forward and said, "You want a fight, you got it." He shook off his gloves and assumed a combat stance.

Piter made a gesture with his hands. Instantly his body encased itself in a shimmering gossamer glow, like a second skin, but this "skin" was a dark blue and faintly reflective.

A collective gasp escaped the group as they realized Piter had learned to create something similar to, but not the same as, an adept's flameskin. An impressive feat, speaking of true artistry on his part. Any appreciation, though, was lost on the gathered group as they squared off.

"This skin amplifies whatever disruptive thing you seem to be doing and sends it back at you," Piter warned.

Arek didn't move. His concentration stayed on Piter's eyes, where he knew any intent to attack or strike would appear first.

Jesyn said, "Please, stop. This is insane!"

"Really?" Piter asked. "Like when you guys laugh at me behind my back? You don't think I hear it?" His attention turned back to Arek and slowly he too raised his hands in front of him, settling into a combat stance. "You won't laugh after this."

Tomas reacted first. He placed his hand on Piter's shoulder, intending to push him out of the way.

Piter did not move. As Tomas touched him, the force of the slight impact was amplified tenfold and redirected back at the hapless initiate. Tomas flew backward, hitting a bookshelf with a dull crack and dropping to the floor unconscious. Only a slight smile betrayed that Piter was happy with the first test of his protective spell. "I'm waiting, jinx."

Time slowed as Arek's focus shifted and his battle sense took over. He could feel the indrawn breath as Piter began to say something. He sensed Jesyn running to Tomas's side, her concern for him overriding anything else. He could feel the weight of the table next to him and knew where every plate and eating utensil lay. Even the tiny dust motes in the air seemed to pause, caught in his heightened awareness. Most of all, he saw where Piter stood and knew where the opening would be.

Then *something* happened. Arek watched as the scene unfolded, slowed by his battle-sense. Something had appeared in the air around Piter. It was a creature, a ghost, barely visible, manifesting itself over the other initiate.

Arek tried to understand what he was seeing. The creature seemed armored, standing superimposed over Piter's frame with enormous wings outstretched to either side. The features were blurred and indistinct, but it lay over him like a gossamer sheet, an ethereal winged knight flaring the same color as Piter's flameskin, a deep, reflective blue. A name sounded then in his head and he knew this creature called itself, *Kaliban.*

Then, to Arek's horror, Piter reached back and the Kaliban mimicked his action. A glow of flame began to form between the creature's hands and Arek knew he only had a moment to interrupt it.

In a liquid motion Arek's hand shot forward, his wrist hitting Piter's, even as his elbow came around that wrist toward Piter's jaw. However, the moment their wrists touched, a black flash occurred, a detonation of force blasting the two apart. Arek had the distinct impression of the winged knight falling backward, the ethereal fireball exploding silently and prematurely.

He felt the heady rush of strength and power flow into him from that contact, infusing his body with a glow that rivaled the sun. It surged into him, powerful, ancient, and unyielding. It echoed through him with a boom, and a feeling of utter triumph and ecstasy flooded his every sense. He knew, for an instant, what he *could* be. This winged creature surrounding Piter, it was his to take. He could feel his body hunger for it like food, like some sort of basic sustenance, ethereal, but real. *He knew it.*

He could hear something gibbering, screaming, pleading for mercy, but years of frustration, of feeling inferior, crystallized into a black dagger of hate. Arek exulted in this feeling of power, of strength, of total control.

In that instant, he knew he held a life in his hands and felt an incoherent thrill as he made a fist and felt it snap! The life-force shattered into an infinite sea of particles and light, then flowed into him. He drank it in, consuming what had been Kaliban utterly. He could feel it become part of him, suffusing him with all it had been.

Then, when there was nothing left, not even a shred within the empty husk that had also once been Piter, blackness surrounded him and Arek felt nothing at all . . .

ASSAULT

In general melee, do not focus too narrowly.

Instead, use the mountain stare,

and drink in all that surrounds you.

Danger comes from all sides.

See, or be feast for the crows.

—*Kensei Tsao, The Book of Blades*

A sh fixed a steely gaze on the horde spread out before him. Turning to Captain Durbin he said, "Have Sevel and your men ready for our signal. Stay under cover and fire on my command."

"The men'll be ready, sir, the Lady willing. Just lay the catapult barrages on their heathen heads and we'll take care of the rest." Saluting smartly, fist to chest, the captain wheeled and made his way to the command tower and Captain Sevel of Second Company.

Ash watched him leave and turned his attention to the desert floor. He could see the barbarians milling about, just out of arrow range. Straining his eyes, he could just see their encampment, a motley collection of tents called *ger* set in a haphazard circle just beyond the main force of nomads. The semblance of order came from the openings, which all faced south. Why this was so was a mystery to him. Still, he thought, if only I had a catapult that could reach that far.

The king exited a stairwell and caught his attention, smiling in greeting.

Ash saluted, then clasped the older man's callused hand. There was a look of tiredness around the king's eyes, a look Ash respectfully did not comment on. Instead, he turned to the outer lip of the wall, encompassing the nomads with a sweep of his arm., "They will attack soon. Look on the horizon, already the clouds gather."

Bernal followed the armsmark's pointing finger to the line of purplish clouds, slowly advancing across the sky like a spreading bruise. The wind had picked up, gusting through the battlements and whipping his cloak out behind him. Soon, the sand itself would become their worst enemy, swirling up in the wind and blinding the archers to their targets.

He turned to the armsmark and said, "Soon the wind and sand will make it impossible to speak or be heard. You'll use the flags?"

Nodding, Ash asked, "I assume you are commanding the center wall, my lord?"

"No, these are your men. Both the Firstmark and I have complete trust in your abilities. Besides, one day you may be Firstmark. Might as well start applying for the post now." He clapped the younger man on the shoulder at the jest. "I won't tell Jebida."

The king paced over to the wall's edge and unslung Valor. "I shall stand with the archers. If the Lady blesses us, we will not see nomad blood touch the walls today."

The armsmark watched the king's corded forearms bulge as he strung the powerful runebow with ease, and checked the weapon for signs of wear. Because of the king's royal heritage, it was sometimes easy to forget he was also a seasoned warrior, a "man of the ranks," so to speak. Ash had a healthy respect for his prowess in battle, knowing that what Bernal had lost with age he made up for in experience. In a low voice he said, "Thank you."

Before the king could comment Ash continued, raising his voice and saluting fist to chest, "Captain Durbin and his men will be honored to have another marksman of your caliber amongst them, my lord."

Bernal gave a small deprecatory laugh at that, hefting the bow and drawing an imaginary arrow as he sighted down his arm, careful not to touch the string without an arrow in place. As he raised his head, a familiar figure ran across the inner courtyard, carrying an armful of arrows. Smiling at the sight, the king addressed the armsmark behind him, "How does Niall like his new duties?"

Ash followed the king's gaze to the courtyard. The prince shuttled between the lower courtyard and the upper archers' loops, unloading neat bundles into quivers at each station. "He is taking the news better than most would. There is much to be said for his maturity."

When the king turned and raised an eyebrow in disbelief, Ash quickly added, "At least, he's working hard and not being petulant."

The king shook his head ruefully. "He is still young and stubborn, just like his mother. And be assured, he will try to get on the wall, whether he has my approval or not."

Whatever Ash's reply was, a warning shout from one of the lookouts cut it short. Racing to the front wall both Bernal and Ash heard the fast chanting coming from the nomads' front line. It droned across the desert like a buzzing of insects.

The sky was already a boiling mass of gray and purple clouds. Diffused flashes of lightning from deep within the thunderheads illuminated the fortress for a moment, before plunging them into the strange twilight created by this unnatural storm.

A howling rose and for an instant Bernal thought the nomads had commenced their attack. Then he realized it was merely the voice of the wind as it sped through the parapets and across the stone. Behind him the flag of Bara'cor, a golden lion rampant on a black field framed by lightning bolts, rippled and cracked in the stiff breeze.

"My king, we need to get to our stations, the attack will come soon." Ash laid a hand on Bernal's arm, trying to urge him toward one of the two archer towers. He felt himself easily shrugged off as the king pointed at the nomads' front line.

Ash looked and gasped at what he saw. The front line parted as eight thousand nomads went to their knees, heads bowed to the sand. It was not this sight that elicited Ash's response, but rather the man who walked out to face the fortress.

Even at this distance, Ash could tell he easily dwarfed even the firstmark in size. He estimated the man to be almost eight feet tall, with legs as thick as his own body. The figure raised its robe-covered arms, displaying open palms. Then slowly, he began to pace forward toward the fortress walls. Behind him the nomads stayed bowed, their heads glued to the sand.

"I think we are finally to meet the leader of the nomads, Armsmark. Tell the archers to hold their fire."

As Ash complied, Bernal waited for the leader of the nomads to come within hailing distance. He then climbed upon the wide battlements, so the figure could have a clear view of him. Around him the fortress grew silent, the only noise coming from the whistling of the wind through the ramparts.

"That will be far enough," Bernal warned. He had a sergeant's voice, the kind that carried through the din of battle. Ash knew the chieftain could hear him.

The figure stopped, then began to undo his mask. As the cloth fell away, he placed his fists on his hips and addressed the king of Bara'cor. His voice was deep and guttural, as if he found it difficult to bend his tongue around trade speech, but judging from his words, he was nonetheless educated. "You are the leader of these men?"

"I am."

"Then you condemn your men to death. If you have any love for them, surrender."

Bernal smiled. "Surrender is no way to show love to *my* men."

The massive figure shrugged. "It is only a matter of time. You will fall and condemn your men to death."

The wind picked up for a moment, making it impossible to answer the man. Bernal waited, his cloak flapping behind him while a distant thunderclap sounded. As the wind died down he yelled, "Your name?"

The figure paused as if considering Bernal's question, then answered, "I am Hemendra, U'Zar of the Children of the Sun, and Clanchief of Sovereign's Fall."

"Then, Hemendra, hear this. I am King Bernal Galadine, and by might and right I hold these walls. Get used to the heat, dog. Lap the water your master gives you." The king undid his water skin and opened it, but did not drink. Instead, he upended it so the water fell down the front wall, soaking into the stone and sand below. "We have plenty." Behind him echoed the cheers of his men, emboldened by his resolute courage and divine right as king.

* * * * *

The silence deepened as Bernal's voice echoed from Bara'cor's walls. Hemendra held himself still, one part of him surprised by the lord of Bara'cor's bravery, the other barely able to restrain his anger at the insult. However, years of living had taught Hemendra that anger led only to ruin.

He took a few moments, seemingly bringing himself under control, more because these men on the wall expected that. To show the extent of his discipline would reveal more than he cared to share at this time. Let them think him uneducated, impetuous, and barbaric. It served his purpose.

When he was ready, Hemendra gestured to his line with one of his muscular arms. Three groups of nomads detached themselves from the main body, each group holding upright a long spear. As they neared the fortress, the men's cheers turned to cries of horror, for each spear held an impaled figure.

At another gesture from Hemendra, the nomads drove the spear ends into receptacles designed especially for this purpose, planting the poles with their gruesome burdens so they faced the fortress's walls.

The u'zar knew Bernal recognized Ben'thor Tir and the other kings of the fortresses ringing the Altan Wastes.

Hemendra raised his voice again. "You say I speak empty words. These others thought the same. Food for the *vulkraith*—"

"Jackal!" cried one of Bernal's captains as he leapt onto the battlements, bow in hand. Before anyone could stop him, he had nocked and released an arrow in the smooth motion of a master archer. It sped true to its mark, toward the clanchief's heart.

The nomads around Hemendra scattered, but the u'zar held his ground, not moving an inch. He heard the hiss of feathered death as the arrow neared. Then, with a quickness that belied his bulk, he caught the arrow in mid-flight, a hand span from his chest.

Looking up at the defenders of Bara'cor with contempt, he crushed the arrow in one meaty fist, hurling its broken pieces to the desert floor. "We shall speak again, when you have had time to consider your words." With that he spun, stalking back to the nomad line and through the parting, which closed behind him.

* * * * *

The king's aide-de-camp, Sergeant Alyx Stemmer, had pulled Durbin off the wall before a second arrow followed the first, holding him pinned against the rear lip. Under the dark gray clouds, she watched the king still standing on the battlement, looking at the impaled figures below. The sergeant quickly motioned to some men to escort Durbin back to his post, and then moved to stand next to the armsmark.

The wind had picked up again, angry rumblings echoed across a leaden sky. Ash and Alyx waited for their king to climb down off the outer lip. When he did so, Ash saw tears in his eyes and politely dropped his gaze.

The king looked at the stones of the battlements for a moment, composing himself, then addressed Ash. "Armsmark, I will need to inform Princess Tir of the death of her father and the fate of EvenSea," he said in a voice tight with grief, "but that will wait till this attack is over. Prepare the catapults. I will await your signal with the other archers."

Ash saluted once, then sprinted for the center wall. The trumpeter sounded the battle ready signal. Ash waited a few moments for his men to get to their positions, then gave the signal for the catapults to be loaded.

The chanting had increased, driving the front nomad line into a frenzy. Like penned animals awaiting release, Ash thought. The clanks and groans of the large winches as they bent the arms of the three catapults back, caught his attention. Engineers scrambled forward to secure them, as others filled the great iron cups with large stones, the size of a man's head.

Raising his right arm, the armsmark looked out over the horde, smiling to himself. It was then that the horde surged forward like a wave during a desert storm, sweeping across the windswept sand with hoots and yells. Some paused to kneel and shoot arrows at those ranged along the wall.

Ash paid no attention to the buzzing shafts, keeping a careful eye on distance, his arm still raised. As the nomads crossed a mental line, Ash dropped his arm, taking cover.

With a crack, the great arms released, swishing upward in an arc and hurling their contents at the attackers. Between twenty and thirty good sized rocks fit into each cup, big enough to crush skulls and break bones. The result was a barrage of missile fire that to the nomads, must have felt like the very heavens opened and rained rocks upon their heads. Ash heard the cries of the dying men below, and stood waving a short red flag.

The captains in the command tower responded. With another quick signal, two hundred archers, bows bent to their limits, loosed arrows. Steel-tipped shafts hummed through the air, cutting into the front ranks of nomads still alive after the first wave of missile stones. While the bowmen nocked and released with deadly accuracy, the engineers started cranking the great arms back again.

Ash watched their practiced efficiency with satisfaction, but knew this was only the first phase. The wind had already doubled in force. Soon the archers would be useless.

Regrouped, the nomads raised large flat shields over their heads and rushed toward Bara'cor's forward gates. Groups of them carried siege hammers and picks. Under the cover of the wind and blinding sand, the nomads started smashing at the gate, hoping to break the great crossbar on the other side. If they could see its size, thought Ash wryly, they would not be so foolhardy. And it was only the first of three barriers leading to the fortress interior.

Ash raised two fingers of one hand, then made a quick slashing motion across his other wrist. The signal passed down to the wall crews, who in turn made their way to the large cauldrons based near the edge of the wall. These cauldrons, filled with a mixture of boiling pitch and oil, stood ready for use.

Once in position, they looked to Ash, who squinted down at the nomads through wind-blown sand and grit. With a downward slash of his hand, the contents of the cauldrons poured down the wall, splashing the nomads below. The screams of burned and dying men were almost drowned out by the now howling wind.

The archers of First and Third Company renewed their assault, sending feathered death among the barbarians. Many found, however, their arrows were caught by the wind, flying wide of their mark. The storm had hit in full force.

Ash pursed his lips, hardly able to make out Bernal in the windstorm. Leaning close to Captain Durbin he yelled, "I fear sappers on the far right, where our vision is least." At this, the captain nodded and then sped off to investigate.

The nomads had pulled their wounded back, taking cover behind large, flat shields. Then they rushed forward again, converging at a point on the main wall: the castle gates. Ash could see they had hammers and picks and smiled to himself at the futility of such a gesture. No one carried a satchel, or anything else that looked like an explosive. Bara'cor's granite walls stood impervious to breach by hand tools, but explosives were another matter entirely.

Ash raised two fingers and the cauldrons refilled, but this time with rocks and stones. It took time to bring oil or water to a boil, time they no longer had. With another signal, these heavy rocks were dumped onto the nomads clustered around the main gate. The lucky ones died never knowing what hit them.

Realizing they could not stand at the base of Bara'cor's walls unprotected much longer, the assault leaders ordered their men to pull back. They had accomplished what their clanfists had ordered, taking the fortress's eyes off the main horde.

Ash watched the retreat in confusion. Though the defenders had inflicted casualties, the barbarians had more than enough to continue their assault. He had expected them to erect a shielded battering ram, then have at the gate in earnest. Then the wind died for a bit and through a gap in the sandstorm, Ash caught a glimpse of something that made his stomach clench with fear.

Six large shapes stood well within arrow range as if they had been magically conjured. Trebuchets! He suddenly realized with dread that the force at the gate had only been a diversion.

"Take cover!" he screamed, just as the first of the attackers' weapons fired, flinging a large boulder easily the weight of a man. Arching high, it came screaming down with a sound like the crack of thunder.

Men stumbled and fell as the wall shook under the impact. Five more boulders came crashing in as the nomads' remaining trebuchets released and the air filled with a mixture of sand, pulverized stone, and dust. Ash took cover from stone shrapnel whizzing by, his mind already formulating a defense. Sprinting to the second tower, the armsmark met Captain Durbin.

"Fire at will! I want those crews dead!" Ash screamed into the rising wind.

"We cannot, Armsmark. The storm!" Durbin gestured around him and Ash realized their predicament. Unlike stones, arrows did not have the weight to combat the heavy wind. The nomads had known this would happen, giving them relative safety to fire their engines at Bara'cor's walls.

Ash nodded to the captain, his mind already looking for alternatives. He noticed two of his catapults were already drawn and secured, filled with missile stones. Ash watched as the engineers took time to aim them at the nomad line. Running over to the crews, he directed them to fire instead on the enemy's trebuchets.

The engineers changed their targets. With a crack, the engines fired. The missiles arced high, carrying much of Bara'cor's hopes. Their shots, however, went wide, burying stones in the soft desert sand.

Five more boulders smashed into Bara'cor's already weakened wall. Ash coughed and spat sand and stone dust, praying for the engineers to find their targets. He watched as the great arm of their lead catapult pulled back with agonizing slowness. Secured, the crew filled the cup once again.

Ash closed his eyes and sent a fervent prayer to the Lady of Flame for this shot to be true. With another crack, the arm released and its contents arced across the desert sky. Ash followed its path, his lips still moving in prayer.

He almost cheered when one of the barbarian's trebuchets splintered and broke apart, crushed beyond repair. The other catapult crews along the wall followed suit and soon the air filled with the sounds of winching and releasing. All missed, but then one trebuchet's crew fell, decimated by Bara'cor's deadly missile fire, as stones smashed through their ranks.

The nomads, seeing the fortress had found its range, pulled their trebuchets back, wisely not wanting to risk them this early in the siege. The remaining barbarians retreated, pulling their wounded after them, back to the main horde.

Though they had held, Ash knew it had been at great cost. The crack in the wall was now wide enough in some places for a man to stand in. Parts lay pulverized, creating huge rents in the stone. Large pieces now littered the area in front of the fortress, giving the nomads partial protection from the archers in the towers.

We cannot take much more and repairs are too slow, Ash thought.

He turned from the scene of carnage and moved to help those wounded nearby. His attempt was interrupted by Lieutenant Galin. The lieutenant held the body of Captain Durbin in his arms. Ash stopped, speechless. Hadn't the man been standing next to him only a moment ago?

"It must've been a piece of stone," Galin mumbled numbly. Ash could see the ragged wound in the captain's neck and his armor soaked in more blood than it seemed one body could hold. Moving forward, he relieved the lieutenant of his burden before turning back to the outer edge of the wall, his eyes hard. The nomads were now out of arrow range, stretched into a ragged line. The faint sound of their cheers carried on the desert wind, stabbing into the armsmark's heart like a cold iron spike.

Suddenly the weight of Captain Durbin's body seemed inconsequential to the crushing weight of confidence from the soldiers of Bara'cor. Their chances were futile, of that he was certain. It would only be a matter of time before the nomads broke through their defenses. Then he felt a warm hand on his shoulder and turned to see the king standing beside him.

"His fate does not rest on your shoulders, Commander."

You think not, my king? Thought Ash. I should have foreseen the nomads and their trebuchets.

But Ash said nothing aloud. His gaze wandered across the peaceful features of his friend, now dead from a piece of shrapnel sent by the Lady's hand.

A shudder passed through him and he turned away from his king, not able to face the trust in those eyes. In a hollow voice, he said, "Lieutenant Galin, select one of your men to take your place. You are now Captain of Third Company."

AFTERMATH

When facing the winds of a storm,

the whiplash tree bends to its force,

and sees tomorrow come

with its roots intact.

—Kensei Shun, *The Book of Shields*

I think he's coming around . . ."

Arek heard a voice through the blackness. Slowly he felt it give way to gray, then a blurry white. He started to reach for his face.

"Don't move yet." A gentle hand redirected his. "Here, sip this."

A bitter brew tipped into Arek's mouth. The acrid taste disappeared quickly, and in its wake he felt his head clearing. He squeezed his eyes shut until purple spots appeared, then opened them again, looking around.

He lay in the infirmary, with Silbane seated next to him. Behind his master stood the lore father, a disapproving look on his face. Arek could sense others in the room, but did not turn his head to look. "What happened?"

Silbane looked carefully at his apprentice, then at the lore father. It seemed like something unspoken flitted between the two. Then Silbane turned back to Arek and asked, "What's the last thing you remember?"

Arek thought about it and recalled going to his master's chambers to discuss the test he was not to take. He said that, adding, "Did I fall somewhere on the way back?"

Silbane paused, then answered, "No, Arek. Do you remember going to dinner?"

Arek thought about it, but his last clear memory was leaving his master's quarters. "No, sir, I don't." The concerned look on everyone's faces plus the fact that he was in the infirmary prompted another: "What happened?"

The lore father stepped forward and said, "It seems you had an altercation with Piter. Do you remember that?"

Arek swallowed, the intense look on his master's and the lore father's face causing him to pause. Still, no memory of a fight emerged. "Considering where I am, I hope I gave as well as I got." The jest seemed to fall flat, as neither master smiled.

Giridian stepped forward into Arek's view, looked squarely at the young apprentice, and said, "Arek, Piter is dead."

Arek felt time slow, each heartbeat in his chest pounding a physical blow. Dead? How could that be?

Silbane motioned for Giridian to step back then said to Arek, "We don't know yet what happened. Tomas is injured, but will survive. Jesyn doesn't have a clear memory either. We were hoping you'd know."

Arek stammered, "I . . . I'll try to remember."

Silbane looked at his apprentice once more, then at the lore father. "We should let him rest some more. The *mhi'kra* he drank will bring sleep."

Themun nodded and turned, only to be confronted by Kisan, who had just arrived. The master was clearly distraught and furious. "We will convene to discuss the punishment of Silbane's apprentice, now."

Silbane shook his head. "The boy does not remember what happened. For all we know, Tomas could have done something. They *were* the only two with injuries."

"You're going to blame *Tomas?*" replied Kisan, incredulous. "Maybe Arek is not the only one to blame." She accused Silbane with her stare and didn't seem to care what came out of her mouth. Someone in this room had cost her young apprentice his life.

"You'd be wise to hold your tongue," said Silbane with deadly intensity.

Themun laid a soft hand on Kisan and Silbane's shoulders, pushing them apart. "Masters, please. For now, let the boy rest. We've already had one tragedy on our hands. I'd rather not rush to judgment on a second."

Arek's vision get blurred again, and a soft, warm feeling stole over his body. He had never felt so tired before. He was unable to fight the feeling of sleep that stole over him, but even as his eyes closed, he heard Master Kisan exclaim, "You're not going to do anything! Lilyth, the Gate, the nomads, all deserve more than Piter!"

Arek thought it funny she would mention the demonlord ... did his master tell them about Bara'cor? Another part of his mind, though, knew this was important to remember, something was not right.

But the effects of the *mhi'kra* dulled his senses and pushed him into a deep, healing sleep. Before he could commit anything to memory or answer his feeling of danger, he fell into darkness for the second time that day.

* * * * *

Themun looked at Silbane and Kisan and said, "You two, come to my chambers." He then looked to Giridian and added, "Please continue with your search of the Vaults. Take Dragor if you need help." Finally, to Thera: "You will administer to the boy and summon us if he wakes."

She nodded in agreement, but both she and Themun knew their argument from the previous day was not yet finished.

"If you hurry, you might be able to send Arek with Silbane before he wakes," Thera could not help but add mockingly.

The sarcasm wasn't lost on the lore father, who turned to confront the adept, but it was Silbane who now gently pushed *him* away. It took a moment, but Themun brought himself under control.

His eyes remained locked on Thera as he repeated, "Silbane, Kisan, my chambers, now."

All bowed in acquiescence, with the two masters following Themun out the door. They made it out of the infirmary without further words to each other, though the clench of Kisan's jaw and unflinching stare showed she was still seething inside.

Once there, Themun took a seat behind his oaken desk, ornately carved with scenes and depictions of the land they sought to protect. He put a hand to his head and said, "She is infuriating, always has been. But you two are worse! You dare threaten each other at a time like this? What honor do you bring Piter's memory?"

Silbane pulled up a chair and sat down, ignoring the lore father's comment. The day had clearly taken its toll, as his weary stance and increasingly lined face could attest. None of them could imagine this, one apprentice killing another. It did not bode well, eroding the sense of security the Isle represented, accentuated by recent events and decisions.

Kisan remained standing, her frustration easy for all to see. As soon as the lore father looked up she blurted, "I see how this will end. Arek is sped off the Isle, the *mission* taking precedence. My apprentice lies dead, and for necessity's sake we will look the other way." She challenged the lore father to contradict her.

Themun sighed then leaned back in his chair. He looked at Silbane, who ran his fingers through his short hair. "What do you think we should do?" Though Themun looked at Silbane, the question hung in the air for either to answer.

Kisan grabbed a chair and pulled it over, sitting down with an expletive and a sigh. "Piter was a hard case, and at times a bully, but he did not deserve this." Her gaze met Silbane's own and in a whisper she said, "He was no different than the rest of us, just looking for a family, a place to be safe. Did he know what would await him at the end of his glittering path?"

Silbane leaned forward and laid a hand on Kisan's shoulder. "You know how sorry I am." He then looked at the lore father and asked, "Is it true neither Tomas nor Jesyn remember anything?"

"When asked what happened by a scullery maid, Jesyn uttered a single word before collapsing. That word was 'Arek'," said the lore father.

Kisan's fist tightened, but she said nothing. She had spent years with Piter, training him, teaching him. Because these children came to the Isle orphaned or abandoned, the adepts adopted them. The servants and the other apprentices became their families. Today, they had lost a brother . . . and Kisan had lost what had become a son.

"Even brothers quarrel, but seldom wish death upon each other." Silbane looked at the younger master and said, "I know you want Piter's death to have meaning. Let's find it together."

Kisan looked up and Themun could see tears in her eyes. She turned to the lore father and said in a choking voice, "I will not interfere with your decision. Silbane is right, and regardless, this mission is already a death sentence." She lowered her gaze, as though her misery centered in her chest, but when she raised her eyes again, they flashed with power. "But I promise you this: Should Arek return alive, I will see him brought to justice for my apprentice's death." Kisan stood, looking at both the lore father and Silbane, before turning and walking out the door.

The chamber remained silent until Silbane broke it, saying, "You'll not let her carry through on that threat, will you?"

"And how would I stop her? Frankly, how would I stop *you* if you got it in your head to kill someone? My hope is that with time, her anger cools and reason returns."

"I won't let Kisan hurt Arek. If any harm befalls him, she will answer to me."

Themun knew civil war now threatened his tiny council. One wrong look, one wrong word, and the masters would face each other, crippling their ability to fight the real enemy. He could not allow that.

Still, though he would not have wished it, these circumstances gave him the freedom to push *another* agenda. "Perhaps Kisan offers a better incentive than any I can to take Arek off this Isle," Themun offered.

Silbane shook his head with disgust. "You'll use this too? Is there nothing beneath you?"

"That would imply the luxury of choice. I serve the land. The question is, do you?"

Silbane stood, his fist pounded the table and a crack appeared in the ornate surface under the force of his blow. "You let her near Arek and you'll see what power is."

Themun didn't move. "I will keep this simple, before you destroy any more of my furniture." He rose slowly and said, "It is best you and Arek left as soon as possible."

Silbane didn't seem to know what to say. Themun had not deigned to say it out loud, but the threat of sending Arek with Kisan was now a veritable death sentence, just as leaving him here on the Isle without Silbane's protection would be, and they both knew it. He came to the only decision he could.

"The *mhi'kra* should accelerate Arek's healing. If we gathered things and made ready, I could leave at sunrise, provided there's nothing wrong with him we haven't already seen," Silbane said.

Themun watched the master, knowing the decision he must come to. Then, with a nod and a wave of his hand he said, "Make your plans. I have reached out to Rai'stahn and explained your coming."

"Already?" When the lore father didn't answer, Silbane continued, "And his response?"

"He did not seem surprised that I sought him out."

"Do you think he knows of the Gate?" asked Silbane. "What do I tell him?"

"I would say as little as possible and stay truthful. It is not in Rai'stahn's interest to see the demonkind set loose upon this world, and in that you may have a powerful ally." The lore father was unconcerned by Silbane's apparent need to convince the dragon to help and instead asked, "Have you given any thought to whether the dragon can fly if Arek touches him?"

"As much as you have about putting my apprentice in the middle of all this," Silbane replied sarcastically, but appeared to regret it. Arek's life hung on his ability to act with consideration. "No, but as long as he covers his bare flesh, nothing dangerous should happen."

"You have another advantage: Arek's ability to mask."

"His mask? You think it will hide an aura as big as a dragon's?

Themun nodded and replied, "We both know it can. Have Rai'stahn fly to another point far from you. When Arek's masking wears off, he will become apparent to any who search."

"And they will be looking in the wrong place," Silbane said. "A cunning plan, almost as if you had given it prior thought."

The lore father shrugged and said, "I would not have reached out to him without a plan."

"So all I have to do is convince him to help us."

"And if you don't?"

"Then this will be a very short mission," answered Silbane. "Rai'stahn will either help us, or kill us, and there is little I can do to stop him."

THE PRINCESS

It is only when the sand quickens

beneath you and you begin to sink,

that you know your true friends.

—*Altan proverb*

Yetteje knew better than to dwell, but she couldn't help it. The faces of her family kept coming to her mind. She remembered her mother, her hair shining black with pearls, her smile flashing white. She always had a laugh for her. Now, she was dead—or worse.

Her father had been a man of great wisdom. He had won the fortress of EvenSea through more than his strength of arms, but also his nobility and character. He had taught Yetteje that the measure of a person had to include their experience, education, and the philosophy by which they ruled. A kingdom should be left better by the Tir hand, not worse, and he lived up to that ideal.

Yetteje had rushed to the wall when she had heard the news and seen the horrible fate her father had suffered. The sight of her father, of the man she loved and respected so deeply, impaled on a spear, was more than she could take. Yet she could not get it out of her head.

Sobs took her again, but no tears accompanied them. In their place was the ache of a throat that had cried for hours through the night, the stabbing pain of lungs that had screamed and sobbed. Now all she wanted was to let this feeling of numbness overcome her. Drift away from all this pain, let her mind cocoon itself in the memories of nothing and sleep the sleep that let her forget.

However, something else grew in that space of emptiness . . . and it was not fear. It was a small flame, but a flame nonetheless, fueled by anger: anger that she would never speak with her father again, anger her family lay murdered by the Altan barbarians. She could feel it getting stronger, intensifying.

A tremor interrupted her thoughts, shaking the very walls and ground. She looked around in panic, wondering what new peril Bara'cor faced, but the shaking subsided quickly. Moments passed in silence and with nothing else amiss, she fell again into her dark misery.

Things had always come easily to the Princess of EvenSea, and her family had never wanted for anything. Between her time at court, the many social events and her own interests, nothing had interfered. She hadn't imagined it could all be taken away so easily, like wind clearing the smoke and haze of an unappreciated life. Her last sixteen years of careless fun had been scattered to the winds.

Her eyes narrowed . . . Wind not only cleared smoke, it also fanned flames, and those who murdered her family would pay with their lives. She took a silent vow between herself and those she loved. Vengeance would be hers before her life ended.

"Are you all right?"

Yetteje started, not realizing someone had been standing at the entrance to her room. For a moment, her mind refused to focus on what her eyes were seeing, but then with a snap of clarity she was in the here and now.

"Niall . . . yes, no." Her face screwed up and try as she might, she could not forget her father, impaled. "No, I'm not."

Niall moved hesitantly into the room. It was obvious he didn't want to be there, but he also didn't want to leave his cousin alone. "I am so sorry. Your father was always so kind to me, and my aunt . . ." He trailed off miserably.

Tej nodded, but said nothing. Each moment seemed to go by both slowly and quickly, taking forever to pass, then impossible to forget. Finally she said, "You don't have to worry. I'm not going to do anything stupid."

"Like what?"

Tej looked up at her friend, as if seeing him for the first time. "Huh?"

Niall cocked his head to the side. "Stupid like try to attack the nomads by yourself? Or stupid like stay in this room?"

"What are you talking about?"

Niall looked in his friend's eyes and said, "Tej, whatever it takes, whatever we have to do, I will help you avenge your family. You are not alone in this."

Tears she didn't know she had welled up in her eyes. She crossed her arms and hugged herself, but clamped down on the sadness threatening to overwhelm her. She would not lose control now ... not ever again. When she looked up, the flame within her gave her strength and there was an intensity in her gaze that even Niall could see.

Without a word, Niall went to one knee and took Yetteje's hand, intoning the oath his father had taken with Tej's father. He said, "I hail you, Queen Tir of EvenSea, and pledge my arm and my life to aid you in times of need. You stand not alone, but always with your brothers of Bara'cor."

"It is as it should be, Queen Tir." King Bernal Galadine stood outside Yetteje's room, along with the firstmark and the armsmark. "We come to pay our respects and fealty to you. I can think of no other I would call daughter. Hail, Queen of EvenSea." Bernal went down on one knee and kissed the hand of Yetteje Tir. He looked up then and said, "My sister would wish no less. You stand not alone."

Jebida stepped forward from behind the king, and he too went down on one knee. "My arm and my life I give to defend you in your times of need, Queen of EvenSea. You stand not alone." He too kissed Yetteje's hand, then moved back to make way for the armsmark.

Ash kneeled in front of the young queen, who looked like nothing more than a tear-wracked sixteen-year-old girl. Breathing deeply he. said, "Hail, Queen of EvenSea. Brighter days are ahead. The sun will shine on your seas again. You do not stand alone." He kissed the girl's hand, then waited.

Yetteje rose, looking at the four lords of Bara'cor before her. At that moment, she knew her duty lay in honoring their oaths and pledges as a royal heir should, not crying like a young girl.

She took a breath and felt it steady her and her breathing calmed. She took another and pushed down those feelings of hatred and vengeance within herself. Then she said, "King Galadine, it is not fit for you to kneel before me. There will be many years before I am your equal. I am not the Queen of EvenSea."

To the puzzled king's look, she replied, "Your sister may not be dead. I only know that the King of EvenSea has fallen. Until I know differently, I am still your humble servant and ward. I accept your pledge of kinship and offer you my own. My arm and my life, such as they are, are yours to command."

She turned to Niall and said, "Prince of Bara'cor, you will always have my sword and my counsel at your side. Please rise and stand with me, as my cousin and my friend."

She then addressed the firstmark and armsmark saying, "Rise, please. My arm and sword are yours. I am the queen of nothing and yet . . . EvenSea will rise again."

As the men rose, Tej moved forward, embraced the king, and said, "My father . . ." Her voice cracked and almost broke, but she continued, "My father said to me he has never had a dearer friend than you. I thank you for that and for honoring me now. I know we are not alone."

Journal Entry 4 (early)

That a simple request for aid could lead to this, and now I am here, but not as a hero.

Shall I be more plain? Very well, Rai'stahn betrayed me. I saved his people, who hid from the very nature of life around them in their caves, their holes in the dirt. They offered me a "vision," as if I needed such charity, yet held themselves back from the bloody work, the warriors' work.

Still, I cannot go so far as to say I do not understand. He did what he thought best, as did the rest. I must find a way to forgive them, but it is hard. Why do we hate those close to us more deeply than strangers? Perhaps because they betray our expectations of fairness, of justice? Nevertheless, I must forgive, for here hate is an emotion and terrible emotions give rise to terrible things.

Thoughts go to my brother. I hope he knows I did not falter or fail in the end. His need for assurance should be well-satisfied by our victory, which I do not doubt was achieved, thanks to me.

In the distance is what seems to be an abode. I make my way there, in hopes that there may be someone unaffiliated with the Aeris who can help me.

Those subjugated by the demon's rule must exist and welcome a chance at freedom. All people of the known world split into factions, and I do not underestimate even the smallest creature's ability to help . . .

SHADOW VOICE

When taking the killing stroke,

kill quickly and cleanly,

and do not mourn the dead.

They brought themselves before your blade.

—*The Bladesman Codex*

Arek awoke to the strange sensation that something was wrong. There was a coldness to the room, a *forlornness*, if that was even possible. In the faint moonlight that streamed in from one tall window, he could see the other infirmary beds were empty.

A cool breeze from the ocean wafted through, but did not settle his unease. He quickly stifled an urge to ask who was there, but his sense of *wrongness* grew. Then the sound of footsteps came from the hallway; purposeful, not hesitant, as if the person knew his destination . . . and he was getting closer. A nameless fear gripped Arek, one that sent him back under the blankets in an infantile attempt at safety.

A figure in a hooded robe moved into the room as if materializing out of thin air. It glided toward him, pausing a few feet away. Arek couldn't see under the hood, but he could feel the malevolence, the danger this person represented. For the first time in his life, he felt what someone meant when they talked about *evil*.

Then the figure did something unexpected. It kneeled and whispered, "I exist to serve." The voice was familiar, though he had never heard anything quite like it. The figure reached with one hand and pulled back the hood concealing its identity, then slowly raised its face into the pale moonlight.

Arek sat dumbfounded, as what he saw and what he knew were in direct conflict. "You're dead," he stated dumbly.

"Astute as always, I see." The mocking voice of Piter echoed softly across the chamber, floating around Arek as if he heard it both in his mind and with his ears.

Arek stuttered, "N-no, I mean the masters told me you are dead."

Piter smiled a cold smile. "I *am* dead, Arek. You killed me." Piter looked around. "I'm surprised you are surprised. I mean, don't you remember the begging, the pleading?" He stared at Arek, as if measuring him, then a sudden understanding seemed to dawn in his eyes and he said, "You have no idea what I'm talking about, do you?"

The shade of Piter rose, laughing. "The most shameful moment of my short life and you don't remember it!" He raised his arms to both sides and shook his head. "Is there no end to the insults I must face?"

Arek said softly, "I'm dreaming this, or you're not dead and this is some sort of sick joke."

Piter focused on Arek, his self-absorption gone. "Yes and all the adepts are in on it . . . does that make sense, you imbecile?" Piter stared at him a moment longer, then said, "They *are* plotting something, just not what you think." He slowly walked over and sat down next to Arek on the bed. "I'll enjoy watching the adepts sacrifice you."

Arek didn't respond to that, his attention completely on the shade's appearance and substance. At this close range, Arek thought he looked quite alive and began to reach out to touch him to confirm it.

Piter jumped awkwardly away, yelling, "Idiot! Your touch will banish me!" The shade said this with an acid hate even Arek could read, as if being here was paramount to something. Piter smiled and pointed at the bed. "Look where I sat."

Arek slowly turned his head and looked. "What? There's nothing there."

"Exactly. You saw me sit down. Are the sheets disturbed? Did I pull the blanket away from you with my weight?" Piter watched him for a few moments as Arek struggled to comprehend what was going on, then said with a smirk, "Quick as ever."

"You're really dead?"

He looked at Arek for a moment longer, then offered, "I am dead, now bound to serve you, and I don't like it." He walked a short distance away and looked out the window. "All I had has been taken from me, by you and your kind."

Arek looked at Piter, still unable to believe his eyes. Clearly the shade was not happy to be here. Yet, Piter was answering his questions ... but why? Arek was not so shocked as to forget that once out of childhood, he and Piter had never really gotten along, so why answer *anything*, especially if Arek truly caused his death? Something wasn't right.

He watched as Piter stood, patiently looking out the window, as if he waited for something, or someone. It also occurred to Arek that he had never seen Piter kneel to anyone, and when this thing had entered the room ... a sudden intuition forced him to his feet.

"Piter, why are you here?"

Piter turned to Arek and stated, "Lilyth has bound me to serve you." He didn't seem to want to answer, but acted as if compelled. "You create an opening ... a *thinness* between the planes. It allows me to appear here, instead of where I should."

Arek continued, "Do you have to answer what I ask?"

Piter hesitated, his eyes darted back and forth, then he curtly replied, "Yes."

"Do you have to tell me the truth?"

To this, Piter smiled and replied sarcastically, "As I see it, *Master.*" Piter walked slowly over to the bed, his arms behind his back. "There is one thing I'll offer: I may escape this wretched servitude on occasion."

Arek said, "When?"

Piter had already started to dissipate. "Whenever I want to frustrate you. You're an imbecile, as always." With a small laugh and a flash, Piter was gone.

"Piter!" Arek looked around the room in confusion. This can't be happening, he thought. I didn't kill Piter and this proves it! He was just here! Arek decided quickly to find Master Silbane and tell him Piter had somehow used a spell or something to make himself look dead . . . that *had* to be the explanation.

What about the sheets? Arek was sure he had sat down and yet he never felt the mattress move. What of the moonlight? Had Piter cast a shadow? He couldn't remember now and his stomach lurched a bit. He sat down on his bed, feeling sick. Had he really killed Piter?

Adept Thera entered the room, clearly awakened by Arek's yell. "What is it?" The young apprentice looked pale and confused. "What's the yelling about?"

He looked at the adept as if seeing her for the first time. He then stammered, "Piter . . . Piter is here."

"What? Arek," she said carefully, "what did he want?"

Arek looked around the room, confused. "What? He wants . . . he said he's bound." He blinked a few times as if waking from a dream, then looked directly at the adept. "I must see my master. I don't think Piter is really dead."

Thera looked at Arek with pity in her eyes. With all the kindness she could muster, she said, "Relax and start from the beginning. If we are to wake the others, I daresay we will need a good explanation."

Arek looked at her, his eyes calculating. "You don't believe me."

"I don't know what to believe yet," Thera replied. "Please, tell me what happened."

Arek fell onto his back, crossing his arms over his eyes, and said, "Piter appeared here. He said he served me."

She moved closer to the bed and sat down next to Arek. "Go on."

Arek couldn't help but notice the bed shift and the mattress move when Thera sat down. It was so easy to discern now, which made Piter's claim seem all the more real. "He said he had to answer my questions, but he didn't like it."

"What makes you say such a thing?"

Arek uncrossed his arms, splaying them out to the sides. He did notice her flinch a bit as his uncovered right hand came close to contacting her arm.

"He only seemed interested in tormenting me."

Arek saw Thera's expression change from one of concern to a more thoughtful stare. He also noticed her proximity, and he pulled the thin gloves from his nightstand and slipped them on. The gesture was automatic, but served to break Thera's contemplation.

"Did Piter say anything else?" she asked.

Arek thought about it then added, "He said Lilyth has bound his service to me. That doesn't sound right, does it?"

Thera stood up, her face in shock. "Arek, get up," she said, a new urgency in her voice where before there had been none.

Arek looked at the adept in confusion. "Why?"

"Get up. We are going to see the council, *now.*"

AREK'S STAND

When your opponent thrusts at you,

divert his stroke by striking outward.

Then ride his blade in

and strike forcefully on his fists to disarm.

—*Tir Combat Academy, Basic Forms & Stances*

H e *what?*" Themun asked. He addressed the full council, which had been awakened and hurriedly gathered in the chamber. They had been summoned instantly by mindspeak, but the effort cost the sending adept dearly in energy. Thera stood shakily near the center of the chamber, ashen-faced and clearly drained, having sent her mental summons the instant Lilyth's name had been mentioned.

She waited as the rest of the council hurriedly took their seats, leaving Arek to wait outside till called for. The servant accompanying him looked more nervous than he, if such a thing were possible.

"He named Lilyth, as if the demon still lived," answered Thera.

Themun looked at Silbane, who raised an eyebrow in return, saying, "You told him about the Gate, yes?"

"Of course," Silbane answered, "but Lilyth's role in the last war is common knowledge. Arek himself recited it to me when I asked him what he knew of Bara'cor. The fact Lilyth was not destroyed is the only secret I know of, and *that* knowledge was not revealed to Arek. He knows we seek a rift, nothing more."

The lore father looked back at Thera and asked, "What exactly did he say?"

"He said Piter came to him," she answered. "At first, I thought he was suffering from shock and trying to rationalize the killing by denial. After all, if Piter appeared, Arek could at least tell himself there was a chance the boy was still alive. Then he said Piter had been ordered to serve him, *by Lilyth.*"

Stunned silence followed Thera's last point. She continued in a low voice, "This isn't an hallucination. Something is going on."

Giridian motioned to speak and asked, "But why would Piter say he served Arek? It makes no sense."

"Perhaps it was the connection Arek and Piter had through his death," Silbane said. "Perhaps it serves as a path the demon can use."

Kisan motioned to speak. "I mentioned the demon's name in the infirmary, but Arek was under the influence of the *mhi'kra.* If he heard anything, he has better ears than we thought." She looked around the room, her gaze finally settling on Silbane as she added sarcastically, "Perhaps we've found another thing your apprentice is good at, something more than just killing his friends."

Silbane started to get up when the lore father put out a restraining hand. "Quarrelling now is of no use. Why would Lilyth care about two apprentices? There are many who have died closer to Bara'cor, and there are other beings of power that still walk this world."

Giridian looked at Themun, then said matter-of-factly, "Then investigating this Gate has become our first priority."

"Why else do I petition to send someone to Bara'cor?" Themun asked. "And I haven't ruled out the possibility Arek has woven this tale out of a desperate need to rationalize his hand in killing his classmate."

"How?" Kisan exclaimed. "The boy is a dullard when it comes to magic and now you think he can suddenly read minds?"

Themun looked pointedly at Thera. "One of us could be trying to influence a different course . . ."

Thera at first could not believe her ears. She had left the last council meeting because she was morally against the path they had chosen for Arek, but to suspect her of betrayal? Her fury grew and she retorted, "You distrust me because I don't agree with you? Who is being childish now, Themun?"

"It was clear you disagreed with the council's last decision regarding Arek," said the lore father.

"Yes, but I wouldn't—" started Thera.

The lore father cut her off, saying, "Betray this council to save the life of what you think of as an innocent boy? How are we to believe that?"

Thera crossed her arms and controlled her indignation. When she spoke, her voice echoed through the chamber with an icy chill. "You have gone too far. Believe what you will, but this boy should not go near Bara'cor. It is clear Lilyth knows of him and that cannot be a good sign. He is not making this up."

Silence followed the last exchange, a silence that grew uncomfortable to many of the adepts, as neither Thera nor the lore father seemed to be willing to concede their position. Finally, it was Silbane who said, "Perhaps we should see what Thera saw, then judge for ourselves."

Thera looked at Silbane, a hint of anger on her lips. She understood what Silbane was suggesting and knew it would set any doubt about her to rest. Still, it galled her that the one person whom she had been friends with for her entire life could so callously abandon her now.

"Very well," she said, "judge for yourselves."

She nodded to the lore father, who extended his staff. The black metal began to glow blue, a soft glow radiating outward to encompass Thera, who in response closed her eyes and motioned with one palm. Much like the vision earlier of the Altan Wastes conjured by the lore father, a new image formed.

The assembled adepts watched the scene with Arek unfold from Thera's viewpoint. They saw Arek standing as if in shock and heard the exchange between the adept and the apprentice. As the scene faded and she opened her eyes, she caught the faintest look of chagrin on the lore father's face. Still, it did little to mollify her.

"I trust you are all satisfied?" she asked no one in particular, but her gaze never left the lore father.

The council remained quiet, only the sputtering of the torches that lit the chamber making any noise. Finally, the lore father coughed once and muttered, "My fear was not too farfetched . . ."

"No, you are within your rights," Thera said, "but stubbornly continue to do what is plainly wrong."

"When it comes to defending this land from the likes of Lilyth, nothing is wrong," answered Themun.

Statements like this make us worse than what we fear, Thera thought sadly. She then turned her attention to the chamber doors and asked, "What of Arek? He waits outside."

"I still have many questions about what he saw," Kisan said. "What did Piter tell him? Does my apprentice still live? If he has a chance of being saved, I must know."

Themun nodded and motioned to Thera, "Bring the boy in."

She bowed and retreated to the chamber doors. A few moments later, she returned with the young apprentice, who was clearly intimidated to be facing the assembled adepts.

Themun looked at Arek for a moment, then motioned to Silbane. The master took his cue and stood beside his apprentice. Laying a hand on his shoulder, he gave him an encouraging smile and said, "Arek, you are not in trouble. Thera has brought you here because of what you saw and what you heard. We would like to hear it from you, to make sure there is no danger." He patted the boy on the shoulder to ease his concern, then asked, "Can you tell us, from the beginning, what happened?"

* * * * *

Arek looked around, nervous. His voice came out small at first, but as he related the tale, it grew in strength. He told the council of Piter's appearance, what he had said, the contempt Piter showed, and his decision to leave when he felt it would hurt him the most. In the end, he appeared more drained than relieved.

The council chamber fell silent as each adept contemplated Arek's recounting, matching it against Thera's shared vision. The fact that an apparition claiming to be following Lilyth's orders appeared *here* was disconcerting to say the least. The fact that it appeared to Arek made no sense to any of them.

Silbane was the first to voice his thoughts. "Arek, you are sure Piter was . . . insubstantial?"

"Yes," Arek replied. "In fact he pointed out himself that he did not disturb the sheets."

"And you think he was compelled to speak?"

"Compelled? No . . . but he answered my questions."

"Do you think he lied?" asked Giridian.

"No, Adept. I think he told me as little as he had to," answered Arek, and to Silbane truthfully, he thought.

Themun asked, "What of this *thinness* Piter mentioned?"

"A byproduct?" Silbane added. "Perhaps he makes the passage easier?" The death of Piter by Arek's hand could be a factor linking them, but what was the link to the demonlord? To that, Silbane had no answer.

Themun interrupted his thoughts when he asked Silbane, "You have spoken to your apprentice of your mission to Bara'cor?"

Silbane gave a hesitant nod feeling a sense of doom that nearly overcame him—the desire to remain here on the Isle that threatened to overwhelm his normally logical demeanor. Silbane was not one to fall prey to superstition or omens, as magic and science were the cornerstones of truth to him. Still, he sensed fear at his very core, and even he did not know why.

Silbane realized that they were all waiting for him to say something. He cleared his throat, then looked at his young apprentice. "We can be ready to leave in the morning. The mission will be brief. Investigate this army besieging the fortress and look for any signs of the Gate. We will avoid all contact, and if I find nothing, we will return here as quickly as possible." The lie felt hollow in Silbane's ears, as he avoided any mention of using Arek to close the Gate.

During this exchange, Arek stood wide-eyed. Before the lore father concluded the meeting, Arek said, "Wait." The adepts turned to listen. "What if my master finds something?"

Themun's eyes narrowed. Arek turned to the lore father and strength seemed to flow into him, emboldening his next words. "My master said we will return here if we find nothing. But what if we find something? What happens to me?"

Silbane looked at Themun and said, "Arek needs to know more if we are to be successful."

"You know of your ability to disrupt magic," Silbane said. "We spoke of its importance when you burst into my quarters, remember?" It was a rhetorical question and Arek answered with downcast eyes and a nod. Silbane continued, "It is not your only power. You also *mask* magic, a necessary advantage if we are to get to Bara'cor undetected."

Silbane then said carefully, "The lore father believes the Gate is linked to Lilyth's world, which lies somewhere near Bara'cor. I am to investigate it undetected, hence your involvement."

Arek's brows knitted and he asked the lore father, "What if we find this Gate? What do we do then?"

Themun looked at Silbane, annoyance showing in his face. He then looked back at Arek and stated, "Your master has his orders."

"I would know my *master's* orders, Lore Father," Arek pressed. "It will best serve the mission."

Themun looked incredulously at the young boy and said, "You presume much."

"If my master finds something and I do not know his orders, I will be a hindrance."

Before the lore father said anything too harsh, Silbane stepped forward to say, "Arek, my orders are to ascertain if the Gate has awakened and if so, to contact the lore father and relate the situation." He knew he had just directly lied to his apprentice, something he did not remember ever doing before. The feeling did not sit well with him.

Arek turned to his master and asked, "And if I choose not to go?"

Themun spread his arms and said, "You are one step away from the rank of adept. You are pledged to learn the Way and complete your training in defense of this land. What oath and service awaits you upon the earning of the Black?"

Silbane laid a hand carefully on Arek's shoulder and said, "I will not let any harm come to you, but you are necessary for me to get to Bara'cor undetected. The fate of the world rests on this." He smiled at his apprentice, though his eyes remained hard.

Arek thought about that. He looked back at the lore father and said, "I'm not an adept, yet."

"Something you seem to have forgotten with your impertinence," the lore father replied. "I had thought you would rise to this service honorably and with courage."

Arek held the lore father's gaze, bowed slowly, and said, "My apologies, Lore Father. I did not mean to question your command. Of course I am honored to serve the land."

Themun looked at the young boy, his face unreadable. To Silbane, Arek's words and demeanor seemed to indicate not an initiate but someone far older, more arrogant, someone of *power.* Crippling them all was Arek's peculiar masking, making his inner emotional state nearly impossible to read. Still, he thought he felt a smoldering anger deep within the boy.

Silbane coughed, gently reminding the lore father that they were waiting on his leave.

Themun motioned with his hand saying, "A better response for one of your rank, Initiate. I trust you will behave in a manner reflecting honor upon this Order."

Arek raised his eyes, meeting the lore father's gaze with his own. "Of course, I will reflect exactly what I have been taught." He then backed away a few steps and stood by the doors, waiting for the other adepts to leave as their rank permitted, before he himself left.

As he grabbed the double doors and pulled them shut, Silbane watched the lore father watching Arek. He thought he saw anger in those eyes, but something else too: fear.

* * * * *

Themun waited for the doors to close before letting himself relax. "You heard, my lord?"

From the darkness came a hiss, then a voice growled, "I did."

The air wavered and from the darkness stepped a massive figure, invisible until now. It came into being like a shadow given substance.

It was a knight, but gargantuan in size, with black plated armor encasing its muscular body. Long black hair fell from a regal face framing an aquiline nose. Out of its back sprang two leathery wings, shining with black scales.

It turned golden reptilian eyes on the lore father and with a voice like low thunder said, "I worried of the Gate, but now Fate twists her rope. Thy hatchling's death leaves me little choice. Dire circumstance walks hand in hand with each step."

"Can we not still accomplish both what you wish and what the land needs?" asked Themun. "The Gate remains and Arek is our best choice."

The dragon-knight turned to face Themun. "What hides it from mine eyes?"

"His masking, my lord. It blankets anything of the Way around him, including himself."

The armored creature took in a deep breath then said, "I had thought to meet upon Silbane's petition for passage to Bara'cor, then I felt thy hatchling swallowed, as if a black maw opened in the Way. The Gate may not be the danger we face."

"Can we not ascertain that *and* answer the need of closing the Gate?"

"I know not. I must *feel* this Arek, to know where our path lies." The creature turned and regarded the chamber doors as if it could see through them. "Silbane is strong in the Way." He paused, surprised that the man had the power to have almost Seen him twice, despite his glamour. He reminded himself again of the role this particular adept was meant to play. "The Conclave prays for his cooperation."

The lore father looked at the dark-armored dragon-knight and with an ache in his voice said again, "We must seal the Gate."

A moment passed, as if the knight weighed the lore father's words against some other hidden voice, then it rumbled, "It will not stay the hand of Lilyth. Already she reaches out, as the shade of thy hatchling portends. She hath many heralds and seeks release."

Themun nodded sadly, then sat down with the weariness of all the events of these past days on his heart. He looked at the dragon-knight and asked directly, "What of Silbane?"

The dragon-knight looked back at the lore father, then looked down. "The Conclave wishes no harm to befall him, but he is a vital part of the tapestry and shall be tested."

"Tested?"

"Stand steady. It is beyond thy purview now." He paused, then continued, "I wilt take them both to the Far'anthi Stones near Bara'cor. There, I test Silbane and judge this Arek."

Themun looked at the dragon-knight, his next words coming out carefully. "And if he is judged wanting?"

The creature shifted its golden gaze, meeting the lore father's own. "I wilt do what I must, as I have ever done. It will be safer, far from the Isle. Give them thy *Finder*. It will aid me should the hatchling attempt to flee." With that, the creature took a step forward and faded from sight in midstride, as if he had never been.

Themun Dreys leaned back, wishing against all hope Arek would survive whatever judgment the dragon-knight rendered. He knew he could not tell Silbane and had to trust this creature would act honorably, as it had for the near two centuries he had known it.

He leaned back, knowing the mission to close the Gate at Bara'cor had just changed to something far more serious and deadly.

LEAVING THE ISLE

Slap the tip of your opponent's blade,

and watch his response.

Watch his feet, his body;

what direction does his weight shift?

Use the mountain stare to learn

the entirety of his behavior,

then strike at his point of weakness.

—*Kensei Tsao, The Book of Blades*

Silbane waited patiently in the courtyard, mentally reviewing the contents of his leather pack for any forgotten items, while the sun rose white and dazzling in the early morning air. He had left a message with his apprentice to meet him at sunrise and hoped the boy had enough sense to do so. That hope was quickly diminishing with each passing heartbeat. Heaving an exasperated sigh, he was not surprised to see Themun and Giridian approaching out of the Hall of Adepts.

Under Giridian's left arm was tucked an oblong box. Silbane nodded to himself in approval. A good choice, he thought. He offered his palm upraised in greeting to the others, and jutted his chin at the box. "Couldn't help it, could you?"

"I could not," Giridian answered in return. It was plain to see this mission did not sit well with Giridian, and Silbane understood that, for they had been friends longer than most men lived. "At least I'll feel better we're not sending the boy into harm's way completely unprotected."

"Unprotected?" Themun looked at the two and said, "Considering recent events, Arek is better at protecting himself than we realize." He looked past Silbane, his eyes searching, "Speaking of that, where is he?"

"Probably still asleep."

Giridian stepped forward and said, "Doubtful. His test is cancelled ... a friend is dead. Now he's leaving the Isle for reasons he never could have anticipated. I imagine he never went to bed."

"Perhaps—" But then the figure of Arek coming out of the Hall, a bag clutched in one hand and walking staff in the other, interrupted Silbane. Even as they watched, he broke into a stumbling run, plainly trying to balance the many various items with the need to hurry. As Arek slid to a stop, Silbane bowed once and asked, "I trust we did not keep you waiting?"

Arek blushed, stammering out an apology while trying, it seemed, to hide behind his own thin staff. A strap chose that moment to betray him, coming undone and spilling half the contents of his pack onto the hard dusty ground. The apprentice fell to his knees in a vain attempt to gather the various knickknacks strewn at his feet.

"I am sorry, Master. There were a few things I wanted to take with me." Arek kept his eyes down waiting for a rebuke, but seemed surprised to see all the gathered adepts solemn, as if their minds were a thousand leagues away.

"No matter," Silbane said softly.

He then turned to Themun, his voice dropping almost to a whisper. "You are sure?" He heaved a sigh and continued, "Something doesn't feel right."

Themun smiled, but there was little humor in his reply. "Would you rather stay here and allow a rift between our world and Lilyth's to open?" He watched the emotions play across his friend's face, but the conclusion was inevitable as the setting sun. "I thought not. You and I are not that different. In the end, duty rules us both."

Silbane didn't answer that. He just looked at the lore father for a moment before saying, "If two days pass without word from me, prepare Kisan."

The two locked eyes for a moment as something unseen passed between them.

"Aye, you have the right of it." A tired smile pulled at the corners of Themun's mouth. "Besides, I find I do not have the strength to argue with you anymore." He clasped his friend on the shoulder and said, "I have one more gift for you." Before Silbane could respond, Themun reached into his tunic and withdrew a small metal wafer, etched with silver and black runes. "I give you this."

Silbane's eyes widened at the sight of the lore father's gift. "The great dragon gave you this, years ago."

"True, and now I give it to you," Themun said. "Perhaps it can help you keep Arek safe." He smiled then, forcing himself to remain resolute in the face of the decisions he knew might already have been made.

Silbane took the charm in his hand and prepared to break it.

Themun put his own hand over the charm, interrupting his friend. "Wait. Use this to keep you and Arek together."

"But leaving one half on the Isle guarantees our safe return." Silbane's eyes narrowed, for what other reason could this Finder be useful?

Themun looked down and said, "And open a portal between the dangers you face and this Isle? I think not. You worried about keeping Arek safe. This keeps you by his side."

Silbane's brows drew together, his eyes flicking back and forth as he thought through the reasoning. Themun's stance didn't make sense unless one thought about the worst case scenario. In that situation the Finder would most certainly be used to escape, potentially bringing some lethal pursuer to the Isle.

Perhaps, he convinced himself, the lore father is right. He grudgingly nodded, saying, "I'd not want to endanger the children here." He clapped his friend on the shoulder and motioned to Arek to get ready. He missed the look of sadness Themun quickly blinked away.

Giridian took that moment to step forward and relieve himself of the burden under his arm. Looking up at Silbane he said, "Master Silbane, this is for Arek."

Knowing what was in the box, Silbane nodded his approval and watched as Giridian traced a symbol in the air. The box flashed blue once then, with a barely audible click, opened. Giridian carefully swung the cover back, revealing a mirror-bright sword, straight with double keen edges. Embedded in the hilt was a small emerald radiating a faint green glow. Smiling, the adept lifted the sword and accompanying sheath, sliding the blade home.

Walking over to the wide-eyed apprentice, Giridian said, "Her name is Tempest. Forged in the fires of Sovereign's Fall, she has certain healing properties, though none know the exact extent of her power. We do know, however, that she can heal the wielder from grave injury."

Silbane added, "Know she is powerful. If you touch her with a bare hand, I do not know what will happen, so keep your gloves on. It is doubtful you will be able to use her healing power because of this, but Tempest has other properties as well, such as lightness and anticipation."

Arek looked at his master and asked, "It can think?"

With a smile, Silbane replied, "*She* can anticipate what you might do, and it won't take very long to appreciate this particular benefit. I have seen the way you wield a blade, and she will be deadly in your hands. You are more than ready for her and if needed, I can tap her healing powers. Guard her well and she will guard you well."

Arek took the blade in his gloved hand, obviously surprised at its lightness. Silbane knew it would feel slightly warm to the touch, almost alive. There was something else as well. He didn't know exactly what it was, but giving the blade to Arek felt somehow 'right.'

Looking at the smiling adepts in confusion, Arek blurted, "This is really mine?"

Giridian laughed, a deep sound that seemed to come right from his belly. "Of course, at least until you return." The comment turned sour in the adept's throat and he shot a hasty glance filled with remorse to Silbane, then continued awkwardly, "Remember, Arek, the greatest weapons are always forged through *sacrifice.* In Tempest's case, legend has it a princess pledged her soul to an angel to save the life of her one true love, binding them together within this blade. Since that time, she protects her wielder from all harm ... if one believes old legends. She won't fight for you, but you won't be fighting alone with her in your hand."

Arek took hold of the leather strap and slung the sword diagonally across his back, securing it there for easy drawing. Then he bowed and moved to Silbane's side. As he moved, Silbane noted the sword did not dangle or jostle about, as if it clung to him. It must have been an interesting feeling for the apprentice.

Still, the boy had not deigned to thank the adept for the blade, confirming Silbane's suspicion that something had happened to the boy. Making a mental note to deal with this later, he said to Giridian, "A most fitting gift, Adept. Our thanks."

"Of course, Master Silbane," Giridian replied awkwardly. "Our pleasure."

Silbane nodded then stooped to get his things. He faced the lore father one last time, but there was little more to be said. Themun's knowledge of the dangers he and Arek were about to face created an awkward distance between them, a distrust Silbane could feel, but could not understand. It served to make their good-byes sound hollow, stilted and out of place, especially for men who had been friends for so long.

Before an uncomfortable silence could fully take hold, Silbane raised a hand in a brief farewell, then turned and made his way to the gate leading out of the council's demesne. Behind him came Arek, eyes downcast and sullen.

Neither looked back, and Silbane couldn't know this would be the last time he would see his friend in this life. If he had, he might have enjoyed the rising sun with Themun for a moment longer, before venturing out into whatever dangers the world held for him and his young apprentice.

Instead, he walked for a distance in silence, until the dirt road curved away and they were no longer in sight of the gate, then he stopped. His mind went back to Arek's behavior with Adept Giridian and he asked, "What bothers you, Apprentice?"

Arek looked down, apparently not expecting his master to ask the question so directly. "You expect me to believe we're going on a . . . secret mission."

He stopped, confused. He had worried Arek would question the council's orders or the safety of going, but never considered his apprentice would doubt they were on a mission entirely. "What do you mean?"

Arek turned and faced his master. "Tell me the truth. You are getting me off the Isle because I am not worthy of testing, or because of what you claim I did to Piter. What happens? I'm taken from the Isle and left somewhere?" His lips quavered at that, the fear they were indeed abandoning him into the world bringing unwanted tears to his eyes. "I don't know what to believe, or who to trust."

Silbane shook his head, never imagining his apprentice could think this way. Then he reminded himself of all that had happened: his test cancelled, Piter's death. It may indeed seem to Arek that banishment was a real possibility. While he knew Arek and Piter had never been close, the full weight of having been involved in Piter's death must only now be setting in. Without the ability to read Arek's emotional state, Silbane had no way of knowing just how close he had come to his young apprentice's exact fears.

"It was uncharacteristic of you to challenge the lore father last night," Silbane said.

Arek looked at his master, then said carefully, "I am not sorry for that."

"No, you aren't, and that is acceptable. In life, one must not always count on others to look out for one's own interests."

Arek's eyes narrowed as he thought about what his master had just said. "Then you will tell me why I am being sent? The *real* reason?"

A small, sad smile escaped Silbane's lips. "We really *are* on a mission of vital importance. You are not being banished or punished. You have been selected to go with me."

"Because of this new so-called 'power' I have to mask our presence?" Arek finished, doubt clear in his voice.

"Trust me when I say you are like a son to me," Silbane said. "I will let no harm come to you." He placed a hand on the boy's shoulder. "I promise."

He saw a glimmer of hope in Arek's eyes, like a small fire caught in a gale. Silbane meant to shelter that fire and see it blossom, succor it against the regret he felt at not speaking of the lore father's belief that Arek's touch might disrupt the Gate. *That* possibility and the sacrifice it might entail, was a bridge Silbane intended to cross when necessary, but only after ascertaining what was going on at Bara'cor. No need to worry his apprentice until he knew exactly what they faced. With that in mind, he changed his tact. "Arek," he began, "do you know how we plan to get to Bara'cor?"

The question took Arek by surprise. "No, Master, I hadn't given it much thought. Something quick, or our mission will be meaningless."

Silbane nodded "Accurate and insightful, if obviously stated. We will be riding Rai'stahn."

"What's a 'rye-stan'?" mumbled Arek, fidgeting with his pack, which threatened again to come loose.

"Rai*stahn,*" Silbane emphasized, "is the name of a dragon."

Turning, the adept continued down the road to the beach, whistling a soft tune. Arek stared after him open-mouthed for a moment before he realized he was fast being left behind. Grabbing his pack, he ran after his master, catching up with him quickly.

"Dragon!" Arek exclaimed.

"Did the lore father not make the need for urgency most plain? How else would we journey to land so quickly and still keep this Isle a secret?" Silbane stopped for a moment and said, "Look there."

From their position above the beach, they could see well up and down the coastline. Arek knew this beach line and the rest of their Isle by heart, having played across its face for many years. Silbane pointed to where the beach slowly gave way to cliffs that reached almost to the water's edge. These had been strictly forbidden to the apprentices, as the water and currents could easily kill someone who slipped and fell in, and apprentices spoke of a vague fear that overcame them as they approached the cliffs.

"We go there, to summon Rai'stahn," Silbane explained, adding, "and hope he will do our bidding."

When the boy had nothing further to say, Silbane resumed his pace, slowly making his way down to the sandy beach.

They walked this way for the better part of the morning, with the breeze gradually increasing as they neared the water. Along the way they passed the small homesteads and farms that dotted the Isle, providing sustenance to the inhabitants. As they looked out over the clear blue waters, they could see no other land, and could taste the salt in the thick sea air.

As the sun rose higher, so too did Arek's mood, or so it seemed to Silbane.

"I acted like a child with Adept Giridian," said the apprentice suddenly.

Silbane raised an eyebrow, then nodded. "I was a bit disappointed you didn't thank him." Silbane looked sidelong at Arek and continued, "But he was once an initiate on the eve of his test. Had his been cancelled, I doubt his behavior would have been any better than yours."

Slowly the beach gave way to rocky ground and soon they stood near one of the large cliffs, a dark opening at its base resembling the black maw of some forgotten creature. Silbane paused, his eyes searching the deep gloom, he then sat down and made an impromptu camp.

"Why are we stopping?" Arek asked, looking hesitantly at the cave mouth. "Will Rai'stahn come here?"

"Silence. I must prepare." Silbane closed his eyes and relaxed his breathing, opening his mind to his surroundings. As the sound of the waves crashing onto the rocks receded, he could feel the dragon, a pulsing node of power, deep in the caverns below. Before he began the summoning, he needed to speak with Arek. Opening his eyes, he looked at his apprentice.

"Rai'stahn is a lord among his kind. He is ancient and powerful, as you shall soon see. It is important you understand this, for he sees us as fleeting wisps of life. Even I, with my extended years, am no more than a wink in time to him."

Arek nodded hesitantly, then asked, "Is he dangerous?"

Silbane ignored that and said, "Do not speak unless he addresses you directly." He rose, turning to the cave entrance. Looking back at his apprentice, he smiled and said, "It is not that I fear for you, only that Rai'stahn looks upon men as we look upon insects. I would not see him brush you aside as an annoyance, and I would be sore-pressed to stop him if he did. Do you understand?"

Arek nodded quickly, unable to hide his apprehension. As his master turned back to the cliff, Arek asked, "But what about you?"

Silbane continued looking straight ahead. "Rai'stahn owes a life debt to our lore father, and he is not one to forget a debt."

Silbane picked his way up the rocky slope until he stood at the mouth of the entrance. He then closed his eyes and opened a path to the Way.

His form was quickly outlined in a thin, yellow flame that grew brightest at his head, then disappeared. Much like a flameskin, this would protect him from the aura of dragonfear surrounding Rai'stahn. He thought of including Arek in the spell's effects, but was quite sure a spell cast on Arek would not work. As he thought on it more, it would serve the boy well to fully experience the majesty of a true dragon.

Arek had followed his master up the slope to stand only a few yards behind Silbane, who could feel the boy's growing apprehension.

"He comes," Silbane said.

Arek took an involuntary step backward, his eyes darting to the cave mouth. A form took shape out of the darkness. As it emerged, it appeared to be a knight, except this one stood almost eight feet tall. Long black hair fell well below his shoulders. Plate armor as black as midnight encased his titanic body. Behind him, folded on his back, were a pair of immense black leather wings that rustled as he moved. His eyes shone golden in the afternoon sun.

The knight looked down at the two men and bared a smile revealing a row of fanged teeth. His voice rasped out, deep and ancient, "Who disturbs the Lord of this Isle?"

"Silbane, Master of the Way." Silbane took a step forward, meeting the knight's gaze. "I have come to ask for his lord's aid."

The knight's golden orbs narrowed a bit, as if he were measuring Silbane, weighing his words with what his eyes revealed. In a moment, he spoke again, his deep voice echoing through the cave behind him. "Thou art remembered, friend Silbane."

The powerful knight bowed once, fist to chest, before straightening. Silbane returned the bow, which brought a smile to the black knight's face.

"You were ever well-mannered, mortal." The knight took a step forward, scanning the horizon. His eyes fell for a moment on Arek, staring at him with an intensity suggesting more than idle curiosity.

Under that golden gaze, Silbane knew Arek would feel for the first time the power of this being, and surely realized that this was Rai'stahn. Dropping his eyes, his apprentice bowed quickly as Silbane had, going to his knee.

The moments beat by with agonizing slowness and Silbane could feel the dragonfear begin to build within his gut; and yet, for all its weight, it seemed to pass over and through him. It was like a cool breeze, a feeling that could find no purchase to anchor itself within him as his flameskin came to his protection. The dragon-knight gestured to the sword on Arek's back. "It carries thy blade, Tempest. What need has it of such a companion?"

"This is Arek, my apprentice. He carries the blade for his own protection," answered the adept. Curious, he thought, Arek seemed to be immune to the dragonfear. Silbane made a mental note of that. True, the boy seemed frightened, but no more so than anyone else in seeing a gigantic, armored knight. Strange indeed, thought the adept.

A silence followed as the dragon returned to his scrutiny of the apprentice, his deep voice rasping out finally, "Come, let us speak of thy need." With that, it strode past them and down the slope. Silbane turned and followed, Arek close behind.

The dragon-knight looked out over the deep blue of the sea and addressed Silbane again. "What task dost thou petition?"

"Safe passage to Bara'cor, my lord," he replied simply.

Rai'stahn turned his sunlit gaze on the adept, measuring him. "What is thy purpose?"

"The lore father senses something stirring, something at Bara'cor. I have been sent to investigate," Silbane offered. As he had discussed with the lore father, he kept his answers brief.

The dragon-knight looked thoughtfully out over the deep blue expanse, his long hair whipped back by the wind. His next words drifted back to them, as if the ancient creature were speaking to himself. The words sent chills into Silbane's heart. "There hath been a stirring in the Way, one that has not occurred during thy life's short length." Rai'stahn turned from watching the sea and looked at Silbane's apprentice, "And what of thy hatchling? Why take it?" He stood there with mailed arms crossed, like an armored god awaiting an answer.

A few moments passed as Silbane debated whether to reveal the nature of Arek's peculiar Talent to the dragon, deciding at last it would continue to be prudent to say as little as possible. Nodding once, he answered, "I seek to teach him more of the world." He watched as the dragon-knight flicked a brief look at Arek again.

Rai'stahn moved forward, towering over Silbane, and said, "I will convey thee, but a sojourn must be made, one of great importance. Dost thou agree?"

Silbane licked his lips, then said carefully, "If we must."

Rai'stahn looked at Arek. He then looked back at Silbane, his golden yellow eyes narrowing. "At the sojourn, we will judge thy next steps." His golden gaze met Silbane's again and he said softly, "Dost thou agree?"

Silbane measured the dragon before him, feeling instinctively that something was being decided here that had more importance than this short question seemed to reflect, but he did not gainsay Rai'stahn. "Of course, my lord."

The dragon-knight turned, motioning for them to stay as he walked away.

Silbane could feel a building of power and realized the dragon was about to assume his true shape. He turned and grabbed Arek, backing away from the armored figure. Behind their retreating backs, the dragon-knight's form exploded in a flash of white fire that for an instant burned brighter than the sun.

Silbane blinked, purple afterimages of the knight's form dancing across his blurred vision. Looking down for a moment, he rubbed his eyes to clear them. Arek held Silbane's arm for support. He felt that arm stiffen and heard the sharp intake of breath from the boy. Nothing, he knew, could have prepared his young apprentice for the sight that met his eyes.

Arek's mouth hung open as he saw Rai'stahn in his true form. The dragon was at least a hundred paces in length from nose to tail, ebony scales encasing its entire body. Razor sharp claws larger than a man's body tipped the ends of his feet and fangs the size of swords revealed themselves as Rai'stahn opened his mouth to sound a tremendous roar. Arek covered his ears at the sound, wincing in pain. They watched as the dragon slowly extended a leathery wing, its tip touching the ground in front of their feet.

Climb and secure yourselves, lest thee lose thy grip.

Arek gave a start as the words formed unbidden in his mind, as they did in Silbane's, in Rai'stahn's strange, archaic tongue. Mindspeak! Arek took an involuntary step back and bumped into Silbane, who, with a wry smile, gently pushed the young apprentice forward.

"Do not be afraid, Arek. Rai'stahn will not harm you." The wizard laid a gentle hand on Arek's shoulder. "Come, we must climb aboard quickly."

Watching his master get on the dragon's wing with no apparent harm seemed to make Arek feel a little better, though Silbane knew that nothing could completely wash away the unease he felt this close to such a creature. Cautiously Arek moved forward and onto the resilient membrane of the wing. Scrambling up to the yard-long spikes emerging from the dragon's spine, he seated himself between two of them and waited for Silbane to do the same.

In moments, all was ready for their departure. Silbane looked back in the direction of the Halls in farewell, though he couldn't see it. Then he said to Rai'stahn, "We are ready, my lord."

To Bara'cor then.

With a mighty leap, the dragon launched himself into the air, his powerful wings catching the ocean breeze and lifting him and his riders over the Shattered Sea. Silbane felt a great weight on his chest and was thankful for the spine spike supporting him from behind. Looking back, he and Arek watched the Isle slowly shrink in size as Rai'stahn gained altitude. Soon, it was nothing but a small speck of brown and green in a vast sea of blue.

Silbane checked their direction against the sun, estimating a northwestern heading. Only a slight wind caressed his face, a by-product of the magic that allowed a dragon of Rai'stahn's size to fly. "Be careful about your bare flesh touching Rai'stahn," he said so to Arek. "I do not know if you could affect such a powerful creature, but I'd rather not have him suddenly change form while we're on his back." Silbane smiled at the joke, but Arek looked at him wide-eyed. "We should be in the air till almost dusk. I would suggest getting some rest."

Though Arek nodded his head, Silbane knew sleep would be far from his mind. Meeting a dragon and flying in one day was too new an experience to allow Arek any rest. Silbane, however, had no such problems. Relaxing against the spine ridge, he allowed himself to doze into a light sleep.

* * * * *

They flew swiftly, Rai'stahn taking advantage of tail winds to increase his already considerable speed. Arek watched with fascination the small whitecaps that appeared on the water below. Because of the dragon's bulk, though, his vision was limited to the sea in front of them.

It's so blue, he thought, as he watched the wide expanse of the ocean through the space between the shoulders and where the dragon's wings met his body.

There's so much water around us, Arek thought, feeling a strange vigor course through his body, a boundless sense of well-being.

His vision sharpened, and gazing at the horizon, Arek fancied he could already see the southern coast of the mainland though Silbane had cautioned him that they were still far from their destination. He thought of eating some of the food he had packed, but dismissed the idea when he realized his pack was wedged behind him.

After a considerable amount of time, Arek found he was able to lean back in the sunshine. The problems of the last few days seemed so far away, as if nothing had ever happened. He took a deep breath of fresh air, felt the wash of energy permeate him, and watched the white, puffy clouds drift by.

Journal Entry 5

Finnow should have listened. Her obstinacy forced my hand. She had the single-minded opinion one only finds in the young and the stupid. Not enough life yet to turn her knife into a spoon. Seeing her fall was difficult, but inevitable. She earned what she wrought. I will think about her no more, for I have no guilt. None.

These things I see, they are significant in some way. I had discounted the dragon's vision, but now appreciate more of what they tried to impart. These points of light are the substance of everything. Could they be the unseen hands I felt, the touch of the Aeris? This is worth rewriting: they are what makes everything. Therefore, I know what the dragons meant, we and the Aeris are somehow linked.

Because I know these things respond to me, I believe they are the basis of the Way. However, here their power is multiplied tenfold. They move and respond to my presence, yet they are invisible to normal sight.

If I can unlock this secret, I will be the most powerful mage in recorded history.

THE WALL

It is difficult for the body

to continue fighting without its head.

Perfect separating the two.

—*The Bladesman Codex*

Sergeant Alyx Stemmer picked her way carefully along the upper tier of the outer wall. The afternoon sun slowly set, blazing yellow to the west, painting her features orange and copper in its ruddy glow. Bara'cor soaked in and then radiated that heat, a warmth the night watch would welcome when the desert turned chill under the gaze of the sun's sister, the moon.

The barbarians waited patiently, camped out of arrow range. When the wind shifted, she could make out the sound of drums and laughter. Well, she thought, at least someone is having fun. Behind her came Yetteje and Niall, each armed and accompanying the sergeant on her rounds. "Walking the wall" had become a habit of Yetteje and Alyx, but including Niall was something the king hoped would give his heir a new appreciation for what the soldiers of Bara'cor went through.

Alyx felt sorry for the princess, who recently became a girl with no family or lands. Still, she had come to know Yetteje had strength within her, a strength that through this period of hardship would temper her like a fine blade, if she allowed it.

They came upon a small square landing cut into the area where two walls joined. It was used as a catapult staging area and served as an unofficial combat ring for those who wanted to try their hand at blades. Though not sanctioned as part of official duty, the unspoken rule was any amount of practice was not just tolerated, but encouraged. Each year the fortresses held the King's Tourney, as teams from each competed for recognition.

Last year, Bara'cor's armsmark had won the King's Thorn. The ceremonial blade would call Bara'cor home until the next annual tournament, but it had been made clear that losing the blade to another fortress would earn the team the "best" of duties. The king liked winning and so did the teams fielded by the Galadines, so practice made perfect and practice was the rule. Still, if rumors of the fate of the other fortresses were true, it would be some time till any tourneys were held.

A few off-duty men had gathered, casting dice and waiting for the shift change. Alyx nodded to them, then picked up two wooden *bohkirs,* tossing one to Yetteje. "Come, some lumps will do you good."

Yetteje caught it automatically, but shook her head, her eyes on the barbarian encampment, "No thanks, Al. I'm not in the mood."

The sergeant's eyes narrowed and a steel came to her voice. "Is that what you'll tell the nomads who killed your father?"

Yetteje's head snapped back, anger flashing to the surface quickly. She started to advance into the square, the *bohkir* twitching in her hand as if it were alive. "Fine."

"Bring what you will," the sergeant said with a smile.

Niall stepped back, a little disappointed the sergeant had not asked him, but then again, he likely didn't relish the idea of being beaten by a woman, even if she was the sergeant-of-the-watch. He made himself content with stepping back and waiting his turn. And given the tourney, it never hurt to get a preview of the other teams' moves.

Yetteje moved in quickly, throwing her weight behind a strike aimed at the sergeant's temple. Though the swords were wooden, a strike would still cause damage, or "love lumps" as known by the men-at-arms.

Sergeant Stemmer caught the wooden blade on the base of her own, pushing it out and forcing Yetteje back.

"You're swinging with anger," Alyx said. "It'll make you—"

She never finished. Yetteje attacked with lightning quick strikes alternating from head to chest and then back to head. Her breathing deepened then became shallow, as Alyx watched her struggle to control it. She knew Tej would have to flow with her weapon, but her anger overrode her training.

For her part, the sergeant took the strikes, alternating her blocks, then jumped forward with a heavy overhand strike to Yetteje's head. It was an easy strike to block, not intended to score but to get the girl to think. Alyx wanted the girl to be in the here and now, and only the physical shock of blocking seemed to get her attention.

Tej brought her blade up, catching the sergeant's inches above her forehead, and pushed it off.

Alyx could see in her eyes that hurt had replaced anger, and her feelings of being alone and abandoned only grew. But the sergeant didn't respond, knowing this was only an excuse for Yetteje to stop and wallow in self-pity. Instead, she pressed her attack, throwing a flurry of slashes the Princess of Tir had no choice but to counter, dodging and twisting to avoid the gruff sergeant's swings.

Yetteje braced, stabbing then spinning her blade in a well-known Tir move, "the flower cut." Instantly her vision exploded in black and she knew she had taken a wallop of a strike to the head. When she opened her eyes, she was on her back, Alyx's blade at her throat.

"Why did you lose?" the sergeant asked, her blade not wavering. When Yetteje didn't answer, the point of the blade poked her chest. "Why?"

"Stop it!" Yetteje cried. "What do you want from me?"

"You fought terribly, like a student hoping for her First Blade."

"You don't care at all for my family, do you?" she said, her eyes squinting as tears started to fall.

"I care about you living, more so than you do." The *bohkir* was withdrawn and a hand replaced it, outstretched, demanding her grasp. Yetteje reached up and was pulled to her feet by the sergeant, but not unkindly. Sergeant Stemmer regarded her for a moment. "Why did you lose?"

Yetteje let loose a huff then said, "I was angry."

"That's right. You were. And in that anger, you let me hit you with a strike a child could have blocked." She put a hand on the princess's shoulder and said, "Now, look at me."

She waited until the princess met her gaze, then said with a smile, "What have you learned?"

Yetteje breathed out again through her nose. "Not to fight angry?"

"Mayhap a better lesson is to understand when the moment is upon you. You may face an opponent who is far more skilled, but when given the chance, remove your emotion. Learn to *strike true.*"

Yetteje nodded, a small smile on her lips. "I'm not as angry now."

"It's not gone, I can see it simmering. You have lost those you love, and that space will feel empty for a time." She looked about the wall, her eyes finally resting on Niall. Then she said so only Yetteje could hear, "Your skill surpasses most—in leadership, diplomacy, even blades. Do not let the actions of others cause you to waste it." She squeezed the princess's shoulder reassuringly. "You are special, Yetteje Tir. Don't forget it."

"I won't. It's just . . . difficult."

Before Alyx could answer, Niall came up to join them. "Do you think they'll attack again tonight?" he asked, his eyes on the barbarian encampment.

"Perhaps . . . perhaps not." Sergeant Stemmer made her way over to a basin and scooped up some water to wash off her face, then threw a wet towel to Yetteje, who touched the knot on her eye gingerly.

"They pushed us hard the other day and continue to test our resolve." Alyx went over to the princess and grabbed the cold towel and folded it into a tight ball. Then she braced the back of the princess's head in one hand and pressed the cold towel into the swelling.

"Ouch! That hurts!"

"Now their leader must be wondering how to get us out of here. With Shimmerene at our back we have water, and the Lowland Pass behind allows us to go for food." She ignored the girl who squirmed under her grasp as she applied pressure to the swelling. "How long will the other kingdoms stand by and let trade be disrupted? Even now the queen must be rallying Haven's forces."

She pulled off the towel and inspected the lump, noting the swelling had reduced significantly. "Hold this here, as I did," she instructed. She turned her attention back to the prince. "We need only hold for a while and they will come to our aid. For us it becomes a waiting game."

"That did *not* feel good," Yetteje complained, but despite that, she held the cold compress to her eye pressing hard, if not harder than the sergeant had.

"Just like most things that are good for us," was the sergeant's response.

"Fine." Tej looked out over the battlements, hating to admit the lump felt smaller and better with her continued ministrations. Instead, she answered Niall's last question. "They'll come ... likely try to sneak in. They know we're not going to just open the doors and invite them in, and they can't get past our walls, so they'll try to sabotage us."

Alyx nodded and smiled. "I see someone is finally thinking. I'm happy for that, else I'd have been talking to myself all this time." Though their contact fit mainly around her regular duties to the king, Alyx and Yetteje had formed a tenuous bond and she had come to be somewhat of an "elder sister" for the young princess while she was at Bara'cor.

Yetteje had proven pragmatic and disciplined, and Alyx was known and respected for the same. It had been no accident that the veteran aide-de-camp had been assigned to see to the princess's needs.

Niall looked at the sergeant and asked, "So we have a plan then? We are prepared for this?"

"We will be vigilant, patrolling the walls with double guards at night." Alyx stopped, replacing the *bohkir* and bracing her hands against the warm stone and looking out over the desert. She took in a deep breath of the dry air and caught the whiff of cinnamon from the camp below. "Do you see that *ger?*" she asked, pointing at a large tent decorated with pennants and animal tokens. It sat well behind the front line. "Their leader sits there, plotting how to bring us out."

"At first I thought he might be weak and cowardly," said Niall. "But seeing him stand against Durbin's arrow was ..."

"What? You think him brave now, or noble?" Yetteje turned on Niall, her amber eyes flashing yellow with anger again. "He killed innocent people ... *my* people." She went over to the wall and stared at the camp, her face barely able to conceal the fury she felt.

Niall came up behind her and said softly, "Sorry, Tej. I didn't mean it like that. I just..." He searched for the words. "I just thought that since he was evil, he'd be craven too."

The sergeant spoke then, knowing something needed to distract the young princess from her own misery again, and this time blade work would not do. "You judge him 'evil,' but by what standard? Because he attacks us?"

Alyx shook her head slowly, though there was still a smile in her eyes. "That is often a mistake, judging your enemy as you would a character in a tale. This is no story, but real life. Here, good people die and not everyone looks the way they act. You must learn to know what is in your enemy's heart if you mean to defeat him. The first place to look is in the eyes, for they are the window to a person's soul."

"And what if I find myself fighting a 'good' man, Sergeant?" asked Niall.

"Niall, no man who is trying to kill you can be good," Alyx said with a small laugh, conceding to her own joke. "But seriously, would you rather see a good man go home and tell his family of his brush with death, instead of you? You have heard it said, 'ask no quarter and give none.' It is sooth, for the only honor you will find across blades is in the King's Tourney. On the field of battle, honor walks away with the living."

Niall was quiet, thinking about what the sergeant had said. His next question came out hesitantly. "So ... you have never granted someone mercy?"

Sergeant Stemmer looked at the two youths, her lips pursed in thought. "Would you think me evil if I said I have not? I do not look for conflict, but if a blade is drawn against me, I will grant no quarter." Alyx turned, her mind on days long gone, and despite her statement to the two she no longer knew if this were really true. "No quarter," she whispered, almost convincing herself.

Yetteje looked at the nomad encampment. They all heard the drums, the laughter. They could smell the food. Normally the night was best for fighting in the desert, the day's heat making any kind of attack unlikely. However, it seemed that as the sun set on this day, the barbarians were going to rest. She turned to Alyx and said, "I want vengeance."

The sergeant looked sidelong at the young princess, knowing she was angry and hurt. "Lives can be brought into focus through tragedy. It gives purpose, direction." Then she looked up at the stars, barely discernible, as the sun slipped below the horizon. "But it cannot sustain you forever. What do the gods care if you or I have been wronged? There are greater ills borne by lesser folk. You have lost your family and I mourn with you. However, think on the tale of the gods Eben and Aaron and their fight against the demonlord Eris. This is a tale, I think, showing the difference between what drives us."

Niall nodded, but Yetteje looked confused. "I remember some of it..." Niall said. "Lord Eben lost his kingdom through trickery. Since there was no shedding of divine blood, he and his consort accepted banishment. But that's all I know."

Alyx nodded at Yetteje's summary, then began to tell the tale. "This was in an ancient time, when our world was embroiled in a bitter war with the demonlord Eris. Remember too that Lord Eben was betrothed to Selene, said to be the most beautiful woman in the world. When he and his wife accepted banishment from the land, Lord Aaron went with them.

"He did this even though he was next in line to sit upon the throne; such was his love for his brother. For years, they wandered the wastes of Winters Thorn, never allowed to return home. Through all this, Lord Aaron always stood by his brother's side.

"When word came that the demons of Eris were looking for Selene, Lord Eben bade his brother to protect her while he went looking for a legendary weapon, said to be hidden in the mountains of Dawnlight."

Alyx turned and leaned her back against the warm stone, continuing, "Lord Aaron knew he could not guard Selene without rest. He would need to sleep at some point and dreaded losing her during these moments of weakness. Therefore, he crafted a spell, placing her within the crude shelter they called home and circling it with magical sand.

"Then he said to her, 'Selene, do not cross this barrier I have constructed, for it shields you from the hosts of Eris. They cannot cross this line, for it is my boon that it protects those I love, so long as they stay within its bounds. I must sleep, but will break the seal in the morning.' With that, Lord Aaron went to take his rest.

"However, he did not understand the deception conspired by the demons. They sent dreams to Selene, dreams of her husband hurt in the mountains, fallen in a crevasse, trapped. They whispered on the wind for anyone who loved Lord Eben to hear, lies saying he was lost in the icy peaks, crippled by the cold and dying alone.

"She could not sleep and did not believe in Lord Aaron's spell of sand. 'How could such a small, fragile line stop true demons?' she reasoned, not knowing it was Lord Aaron's own purity, his faith, manifest in the sand that protected her. She crossed the seal, breaking the spell it contained, hoping to go to her husband in need. No sooner had she done so, than she was taken."

The sergeant paused for a moment, looking at Yetteje. "I do not mean to say the burdens carried by others are somehow greater than what you feel for your family. I only tell you this to remind you of what has driven others, so we may perhaps be inspired."

Seeing Yetteje understood, the sergeant continued, "When Lord Eben returned and saw his beloved gone, he railed on Lord Aaron, 'I asked you to do a simple thing! Guard her! And you could not even accomplish that!'

"When Lord Aaron heard these words, his heart fell to pieces, for he had followed his brother these past years for love's sake, relinquishing title and throne. He had protected and served him dutifully, never once coveting what his brother had and never seeking happiness with another. His happiness was his brother's safekeeping and love. Think how his heart must have broken at this moment, to think he had failed his brother so completely."

Yetteje's eyes fell from the sergeant's face to stare out at the sea of sand. "The problem is Lord Eben's, who is ungrateful . . ."

Alyx turned to the princess and said, "Perhaps. However, Lord Aaron did not give up on his brother and held no ill will on him for those words. He stood fast and firm and did not succumb to the misery he felt, both for losing Selene and for failing his brother. Lord Aaron carried that burden for another year, seeing failure and misery every time his brother looked upon him.

"Lord Eben, for his part, seldom entrusted his brother to another task. He rarely spoke to him and never with the brotherly love they once shared. To him, his brother was dead and their relationship became as you are to your shadow, forever beside each other, but silent. He gave up hope of ever finding Selene again and railed at the gods for punishing him so.

"Now I ask you this. Who suffered more? Lord Aaron, who carried the guilt for losing Selene and bearing Lord Eben's anger in silence, or Eben, who lost his mate *and* brother?"

Yetteje looked at the sergeant thoughtfully, then said, "They both lost, but I judge Lord Eben's loss greater. He can mend things with his brother, for they are still alive. You cannot make amends with the dead."

Alyx looked at the young princess and said, "Lord Aaron never gave up hope. He carried his brother through his darkest hours of hate and self-pity, till at last they found and rescued Selene from Eris's kingdom, alive.

"You see, had he allowed himself to be driven by guilt or hate, it would have eventually destroyed him. I judge that by maintaining hope, a better end was achieved, in which all were healed. But, Princess, what gave him hope?"

Yetteje shrugged, then said, "Stupidity?"

The sergeant smiled at that. With a small laugh she came over and clapped Yetteje on the shoulder, "No. It was *love* that drove him. Love for his brother and the desire to do the right thing. These things can also sustain us through difficult times."

Yetteje seemed to think about that, but the loss of her family was too recent. Alyx knew that every time Yetteje tried to release it, guilt flooded through her. If she didn't hate, who would avenge them? She couldn't abandon them so easily. She wanted to see the blood of the barbarian leader flow. The princess turned, shrugging off the sergeant's hand and looked at the nomad camp.

"Perhaps," Yetteje said, "but hate is an emotion too. It can sustain much, as it did Lord Eben through his darkest hours."

She watched the encampment for a moment longer, missing the look of sorrow that crossed Alyx's face.

"Someone should sneak into that camp and put an end to their leader. See if that makes them feel like singing and dancing," Yetteje said. Then she spat over the wall. "I'll wager we wouldn't hear laughter and drums then. I appreciate the tale but—"

The sergeant held up a forestalling hand. "No, Princess. Do not apologize. In fact, you may have just spoken a truth." She looked over the encampment, her eyes calculating. They could manage the guards ... a small group, perhaps no more than four ...*could it be possible?*

DRAGON VISION

Think of the moon on the water.

Its light shines as if close by,

yet it hangs far above.

You must forge your tactics the same way,

and stay close to your opponent,

yet feel far away.

You must be like the moon's reflection

on the water's surface.

—*Tir Combat Academy, The Tactics of Victory*

Rai'stahn winged low over the desert, sighting a small, vertical stone shaft rising from yellow, sun-stroked dunes. The shaft quickly grew into a tower, its minarets broken and its walls crumbled, open to the gritty winds. The great dragon braked and for all his bulk landed softly, scattering only a little sand and debris. He dipped a wing, allowing Silbane and Arek to disembark.

"What is this place?" Arek asked, drinking in the sight of the ancient ruin.

Having landed, they lacked the benefit of the cool breeze of flight. Hot dry air hit him like the blast of a furnace and he found himself instantly sweating. The desert seemed empty in all directions, a vast flowing sea of dunes set against a deep orange sky. Strange Rai'stahn had chosen such a desolate place for his stop. Still, the motivations of dragonkind were not always apparent, Arek reminded himself, despite their affectation of taking on our form.

Silbane looked about, making sure no one had noted their landing, and said, "This is a Far'anthi Tower. The stone looks dead, though."

Arek had suspected as much when his eyes fell upon a pedestal at the tower's base holding a great globe of ash colored rock in a three-pronged grasp. He looked at Silbane, "It's supposed to glow blue?"

Silbane nodded, "Yes, if active." He motioned to the pile of gear on the dragon's back. "Once Rai'stahn changes, see to our things." He started to move up the slight rise to the tower base, but then remembered something and turned back. He fumbled through his tunic, bringing forth the lore father's small charm. "Before I forget, Tempest was not your only gift."

Silbane held the talisman aloft for Arek to see, then took it between his hands and broke it in half, triggering the enchantment. As he did so, a sparkle of blue surrounded the break, then disappeared. Each half now sought the other. "It is a *Finder* . . . do you understand?"

Arek nodded. One half the adept strung around his neck; the other, Arek slipped into his pocket, careful not to touch it with his bare flesh. "Thank you."

"I assume you understand its use?" Silbane asked. "As long as we live, each half will glow."

Arek did not particularly care for how his master worded that. Still, he knew in an emergency, either could crush their half. Doing so would create a temporary portal between their locations, allowing them instantaneous transport to the other.

"You're expecting we'll lose each other," Arek concluded.

Silbane shook his head. "I'm just trying to keep you safe." With that, he turned to look as the great dragon completed his change, once again becoming the dark-armored knight.

Rai'stahn strode purposefully up to the tower walls and looked at the weathered stone. "It has the scent of magic, though long dead." His yellow eyes mirrored the setting sun, shining like liquid gold, inhuman, but expressive nonetheless.

To Arek it was almost as if all the light had pooled there, giving the dragon-knight's face an unearthly countenance. Just then, Rai'stahn's image wavered for a moment, as if there were two of him, superimposed upon each other.

One stood looking at the Far'anthi Stone, the other staggered a step to the left, taloned hand to head. His wings flexed to steady himself, bat-like and black, then the vision was over. The two images collapsed back into one. Whatever had affected the dragon-knight had passed like a desert breeze. Arek watched, but neither his master nor the dragon said anything about it, almost as if neither had seen it.

Rai'stahn looked sidelong at the adept and said, "Indeed. Come, Silbane."

Rai'stahn turned around, fixing Arek with his golden gaze, brushing past what others saw. His gaze was almost physical, a beam of truth pulling apart Arek's carefully constructed sense of worth. It was almost as if the great dragon knew of the double vision Arek had just seen.

What felt like an eternity swept by as the dragon gauged something not readily apparent to either the adept or his apprentice. He then said, "I wouldst speak with thee privately." Rai'stahn did not wait for a response, walking away from the lone tower and into the Wastes.

Silbane, his brow furrowed, had no choice but to follow. He looked at Arek and motioned for him to stay put and finish setting up camp. His apprentice nodded absentmindedly, clearly engrossed by their exchange, their belongings temporarily forgotten.

* * * * *

Under Rai'stahn's gaze, Arek should have been reduced to a cowering supplicant and yet he withstood the great dragon's Sight, ignoring it as one would an uncomfortable wind. This fact worried Silbane greatly and without another word, he turned and walked in the direction Rai'stahn had gone.

The dragon-knight continued until the tower grew smaller behind them. His long strides ate up the distance, carrying him quickly and surely to whatever destination he had in mind.

Silbane hurried to follow, knowing any emotion the dragon felt was a magnification of whatever emotion he felt himself. Dragons were passionate creatures and their actions were often ruled by need as much as expediency and logic. Dragons do not measure time as we do, he also reminded himself. He crested a small rise and approached the armored knight.

Rai'stahn had stopped and looked back at the tower, his golden eyes narrowing. A moment passed, then another, as he seemed to ponder how best to begin. Of course, Silbane reminded himself, dragons did not hesitate to speak their minds. Still, the expression on Rai'stahn's face reminded Silbane of what a person might look like if an unpleasant subject were about to be broached.

He looked down at the mage, then cleared his throat. "Now that we are clear of the Isle, I am left with a difficult choice. Tell me truly, what is thy purpose?"

"My lord? I have spoken plainly." Silbane hesitated to reveal more about their mission until he knew where Rai'stahn stood. The dragon could be a powerful ally or deadly enemy, depending on how he saw the situation. Moreover, it bothered the adept that the dragon-knight cared to mention they were "clear of the Isle." What did he mean by that? A deepening knot of worry grew in the master's stomach, accentuated by the fact that they were far from anything in this remote place, and alone with a creature of immense power.

"The lore father sensed a stirring in the Way," Silbane said. "Something at Bara'cor." He watched the dragon closely for any signs betraying his inner thoughts.

Rai'stahn's eyes became slits. "Thou speakest of the Gate and slip the question," he stated. "Dost thou know why I brought thee here?"

Silbane looked back at the dragon, the initial shock at the mention of the Gate receding. Dragons were attuned to the Way, and there was little a dragon of Rai'stahn's age would not know. Silbane decided to say more, hoping to find an ally. "Do you oppose our quest to find this Gate?"

"The Gate is not what should concern thee."

Silbane cocked his head. Everyone knew the demons had brought the world to the brink of destruction, flooding into their world through these rifts. They possessed a person in their attempt at life. Nonetheless, he continued, "Our council worries Lilyth may not have been destroyed, but rather banished."

Rai'stahn closed his eyes, searching with his mind. "The doom this world faces is brought by thee, Magus."

Silbane knew dragons were far more sensitive to the magical currents and eddies present in the world. It was possible Rai'stahn sensed things beyond Silbane's ability to comprehend. "What do you mean, my lord?"

The dragon-knight nodded once, a short, hesitant nod that surprised Silbane more *because* of its hesitancy. It occurred to him the dragon's demeanor reflected an emotion he had never thought to see in his kind: fear. Silbane decided to press further. "My lord, if there is something I should know . . . ?"

A moment passed before Rai'stahn answered, "Dost thou seek the truth? The consequences will be high."

Silbane looked down, but when his head rose, there was a steely determination in his slate blue eyes. "Why do you test me? I have done nothing but request conveyance to a destination. Is that so difficult for you, my lord?"

The dragon-knight walked a slow circle around the mage, and his voice barked out, "Difficult? Do not question me, mortal! I have walked this earth when thee and thine were nothing!" The dragon-knight seemed genuinely angry and Silbane found himself wondering why.

He continued, his voice low and deadly, "Thou wouldst hazard all races of this world, save thine own." Rai'stahn looked at Silbane and said, "I hath been given special dispensation for thee, Magus."

Silbane stepped back a pace, sensing deadly intent in those words and said, "For what?"

"Pay heed. I offer thee a chance to see events from thy past. Dost thou accept?"

Silbane looked about the desolation surrounding them, empty and beautiful. It was clear now there could only be one reason Rai'stahn had agreed to transport them. Knowing what the dragon knew was imperative if he was to keep himself and Arek alive, and he knew this had suddenly turned into a life and death situation. He nodded, not trusting himself to speak.

"Very well," Rai'stahn nodded, then placed his fingers at a point on the center of Silbane's forehead. Where the talons met, a yellow fire erupted in a thin line, piercing the master with a light shining like a miniature sun, hanging on Silbane's forehead like a star. "Thou art given Sight. Behold, then choose . . ."

Around Silbane the sand stirred, then rose in a swirling column sealing him and the dragon-knight from sight. Inside, Silbane could hear sibilant female voices, whispers coming from all directions.

Rai'stahn stood facing the mage, his eyes glowing with power. Then, the whispers became a vision filling Silbane's head, and he *Saw* . . .

* * * * *

The leader moved through the darkened tunnels, his armor catching and reflecting the firelight flickering from torches along the cave walls. He was accompanied by two guards, each wide-eyed, their faces covered in sweat from both fear and heat.

"Far enough, General." The voice came from a dwarven soldier, who stepped out of the shadows and held up an armored hand. Though he towered over the men, he seemed somehow smaller.

Perhaps it was the aura of power their leader projected, or the fact his gaze did not waver from the guard's own. After a moment, the dwarf moved back an involuntary step, as if his body had been commanded to do so.

"You'll summon your masters," said the leader in armor, dismissing his men without a sound or gesture. He didn't say anything else, his pale eyes locked straight ahead, as if looking through the stone itself.

Two more dwarves appeared and one bowed deferentially. "General, you have been granted audience. Please, follow me." He turned, accustomed to men of rank and clearly shielded from it by his own station. It was this comfort and his natural skill at diplomacy that had seen him chosen to greet this man, a skill he wielded as deftly as this man did his own power.

The general had no choice but to follow, his eyes drinking in the details of this passage even as the chamber widened into an open basin. Arranged around the upper lip some distance above were shapes, reptilian and massive. They hinted at armored scales and promised fire.

He knew he stood before ancient creatures more powerful in the Way than any known in the land. He looked about the chamber, searching for the greatest of these, the dragon-king, Rai'kesh.

He had ruled his kind for over a thousand years and now turned his glowing red eyes on this mortal, his mere presence an affront to dragonkind and the Way.

As their gazes locked, the man smiled, as if knowing the harm that could befall him, and said, "Coward."

A low rumble resulted and the ancient creature pulled back lips to reveal dagger-like teeth. "Have we not stayed our hand?" His voice was deep and sounded like gravel against stone.

The general nodded. "And thousands die."

The dragon-king raised a taloned claw and asked, "Who hath died?"

The armored man stepped back. "If you can ask that, you have turned your back on this land."

"Then thou dost not understand the war thee wages, nor the Aeris and their nature, *halfling*."

The general cocked his head. "Halfling? Even I, a mere mortal, am not beneath your insults?"

A growl promising menace sounded, followed by, "No insult was meant, General. Without the Aeris, thy kind are but half of what thou couldst be, like the reflection of the moon on water, compared to the moon itself."

"Aeris?" he retorted. "I thought so once and chose a peaceful path. Then this happened. I name them demons now."

Rai'kesh raised himself, his dark red scales glowing in the rocklight of the cavern like smoldering iron. His eyes narrowed and brightened into two embers. "What dost thou want, Archmage? We suffer thy presence because of honor, yet with every breath and word, our patience is tested."

The armored man looked about the chamber and pitched his voice to carry to all those assembled. "The war goes badly. Despite your claim, our people grieve for their dead. Our children disappear, taken by these demons, never to be seen again." His eyes hardened and he stated, "We must have aid."

There was no movement, but the shadows conspired to give the impression that the entire assemblage moved in a bit closer. Rai'kesh looked at the man in armor, then hissed, "Thou presume much, coming before us."

"I would dare even you, if it means victory."

The great dragon leaned in, his head level with the armored warrior. "The Aeris cannot be eradicated. Created by thee and thy people, they are the stuff of dreams, halfling. Thy war is pointless."

If the man understood, he did not show it. Instead, he stamped his foot and an explosion of white power flashed out, cracking the basin upon which he stood and pushing the great dragon king back with a promise of violence. "I will not suffer lies from the likes of you!"

Rai'kesh treated the man's outburst like the misbehavior of a child and did not react except to exhale a blast of smoldering air. Then, he growled, "The blind worry at each step. Mayhap it is Sight thou art lacking."

The general's eyes narrowed and a few moments went by in silence. Then he simply asked, "Sight?"

"Thou shalt *See* the true nature of things. Perhaps only then wilt thou understand war is not thy people's destiny. Peace may yet be achieved. With the gift of Sight, thou wilt come to understand the Aeris and depart this path of recklessness."

The man looked slowly around the basin, somehow understanding that the dragons meant to change him in some fundamental way, then he knelt and said, "I accept your boon."

"Not all survive the giving."

"My survival is of little concern without your aid." He looked up and power flashed in his pale eyes. "Do what you must."

There was a pause, as if the very air went still with anticipation, then Silbane saw yellow power erupt from above, spearing the knight in its fire. It burned bright, utterly consuming the man in armor. He thought he heard a scream, then nothing.

The fire slowly subsided. As it withered and died, the armored man knelt where he had been, the ground around him burned and molten, steam escaping in hisses from its charred surface, melted smooth from the heat.

He looked dead, but then his armor glinted, a small sign of movement from the man within. Silbane thought he heard a slight sigh of disappointment from the gathered dragons, as if they had hoped to end his petition here and now. That was not to be. The man was still alive and about to become more powerful than Silbane could imagine.

He rose, his form still smoking, and his eyes flashed opened. Silbane could see them glow yellow now, infused with the power granted by this Conclave of Dragons. The general looked about, as if seeing things for the first time.

"I had never dreamed—" he began.

"The Aeris are *necessary*," Rai'kesh interrupted. "Look upon them with mercy and thou wilt See that there are better answers than war."

He continued to stare about him, as if drinking in every detail, then his head shook. He took a step back, flanked by the dwarven guards, and said, "These creatures, if they are as you say, cannot be killed. We are dead as a race!"

Rai'kesh looked again at the man to whom they had entrusted with their gift and said, "Neither can they eradicate those who create them, for it will be their undoing as well. Thou canst petition for peace, because neither can survive without the other. Valarius, wilt thou desist in thy path?"

The man in armor, who Silbane realized could only be General Valarius Galadine, shook his head. "You would see us enslaved?"

"How canst thou be a slave to thine own shadow?" Rai'kesh responded, tilting his head quizzically. This halfman was making no sense, and the war with the Aeris had to be put aside. "Thou art thinking within the frame of a single lifetime. Much hath happened since Sovereign's Fall, yet the parting of thee and thine from the Aeris was never intended. Seek peace and unification and all will be as it was meant to be." The great dragon paused, then said, "Forbear." The chamber echoed with his final admonishment.

The general's eyes grew hard as he looked at the assembled dragons and said, "Patience is for the weak, and we are all granted but a single life." He turned and walked away from the basin, but looked back as he neared its edge. "If your children had been taken, would you stand by so idly?" His eyes flashed again with power, as if daring any of the Conclave to act.

When nothing happened, he gave a hesitant bow. It was a strange sign of respect, thought Silbane, given the tone of the exchange. He then turned away from the Conclave and back into the tunnels. Moments passed in silence.

Then the dragon-king said, "Rai'stahn."

The air congealed where the archmage had just stood, a black smoke taking on the kneeling form of the armored dragon-knight Silbane knew. "My lord?"

"He presumes much, doth he not?"

Rai'stahn turned a yellow-golden gaze in the direction of the retreating form and replied, "We should kill him. At least then Azrael wouldst stand free."

Rai'kesh seemed to smile at that, though it could have been a trick of the light. The elder dragon looked around at the Conclave and a silent communion was held. When it was finished, he addressed the younger dragon-knight again. "Perhaps the Sight granted will yet lend him perspective. He should understand what he wishes to destroy. Mayhap it will give him pause." Rai'kesh moved closer and put an armored hand on the kneeling dragon's shoulder. "Thou wilt take a force of knights. Attend the battle, but not to help these halfmen. Thou shalt protect the land should Valarius fail to See the path opened for him."

Rai'stahn nodded, then hesitantly asked, "Dost thou still believe he can bring *unity*?" His was clearly not the place to question the elders, so he did not elaborate, instead waiting in silence. When nothing was offered he began to get up, but Rai'kesh's voice stopped him.

"If he lives, perhaps. If he dies, it will be as thee says. Azrael will walk again amongst us. Either outcome favors a beneficent end." Rai'kesh paused, then added, "There will come a moment. Thou wilt know when. Act as we hath been ordered, for the good of this land."

Then the vision faded from his mind like smoke . . .

* * * * *

Silbane clutched his head, pain pounding inside his skull, his eyes shut. When he opened them, he realized he had fallen to his knees, the swirl of sand and dust gone. Above him, the dusk sky shone orange and gold with a serenity out of place with the import of the visions he had just Seen.

He noticed the sand in front of him, spotted with dark, wet blobs. He reached out a cautious finger and realized it was his own blood, dripping from his nose and ears. A sharp pain in his forehead and a quick inspection with his fingertips revealed something that felt like a small scar where the dragon's claws had touched him, burned in by the searing light of the vision. He quickly rose, wiping his face and looking for the dragon-knight.

As the master rose the dragon-knight grunted, as if acknowledging his strength, and said, "Thou shalt feel the gift come upon you, but slowly. Stand steady."

Silbane shook his head to clear it, still throbbing from the intensity of thought and power. Never in all his previous dealings with dragons had he felt such might. He looked at Rai'stahn and though there were other more critical concerns such as Arek and his mission, he asked the one question burning in his mind, "Who is Azrael?"

Rai'stahn watched the mage, his eyes calculating, then he offered, "As Lilyth, Azrael is a Celestial, the most powerful of the Aeris."

Azrael? The name could be coincidence. Silbane licked his lips and then asked, "He opposed her?"

The dragon shrugged. "Nothing so simple as that. He chose a different path and disappeared in the Ascension."

Silbane swallowed, his mouth suddenly dry. Too much was happening and he needed time to digest it. He closed his eyes, willing the turmoil to end, then took a deep breath, thinking.

Clearly the dragons in the vision thought Azrael and Valarius connected somehow, an impossibility he did not want to pursue just yet, the implications to his own soul too deep to consider.

"The armored man was General Valarius Galadine?" asked Silbane.

The dragon nodded.

"What did he See?"

"If thou wert stronger in the Way, the gift of Sight wouldst already be upon thee. Until then, it suffices to say Valarius wasted his gift and instead created an abomination."

Silbane shook his head. "He petitioned the dragons for aid? He fought for us, *against* Lilyth?"

"Be not foolish, Magus. Shall we recite the entire vision again?" The dragon-knight looked at Silbane a moment longer, then pointed a finger and whispered, "Thou deliver ruin to the Way of this world."

At first, he thought the dragon had been passing judgment on him. Now he knew that despite the dragon's demeanor, he was not the one in immediate danger. Silbane looked with growing dread to where Rai'stahn pointed, his talon stabbing directly at his apprentice. He hesitated, afraid to ask the next question, but knowing he must. "What does Arek have to do with this?"

"Thou hast seen the Vision. How wouldst the Aeris be destroyed?"

Silbane shook his head and admitted, "I don't know."

"What hath Valarius been told? The Aeris are Shaped by thee. They are the Way."

"But the gods—" Silbane started.

Rai'stahn held up his hand and closed his eyes. "Think. Use thy training. What is the danger of thy kind believing in a single, all-powerful being in a world where dreams live, a world filled with Aeris lords and Celestials such as Lilyth?"

A part of Silbane fought for more information. "You said Valarius created an abomination?"

"So much more," the dragon said. "He was an Archmage of the Way. Think of the Conclave and our forbearance. Only his power forced our consideration. He created something even he could not understand."

"What?"

"The death of all of us." Rai'stahn's taloned finger had never wavered from the direction of the tower and Arek. "Look, with thine newfound Sight. Though the gift is still weak, mayhap thou wilt see what the Conclave sees with thine own eyes."

Silbane turned his attention in the direction of the dragon's gaze, drinking in the golden dunes lit orange by the setting sun. Above, the sky painted itself an almost perfect blue, the beauty and peace of this land in such contrast to the dire conversation taking place between them. What did Rai'stahn want him to see?

He closed his eyes and took a deep breath, cleansing his mind and opening himself to the Way. At first, nothing happened different than any other time he centered himself. His body relaxed and time slowed, yet something urged him to continue, and he stood there, staring into a sea of blackness swimming before his closed eyes.

Then, from that sea, points of yellow light appeared. They were like infinitesimally small particles of dust, eddying and flowing in some unseen current. The current took on form and substance, and a landscape took shape: the dunes, the hills, even the tower! It all stood glittering, each particle adhering to everything, painting him a monochromatic picture of the world in front of him in a sparkling shimmer. Though his eyes remained closed, Silbane could see!

He began to narrow his focus, for near the tower something caught his attention. It was an area of blackness, of *wrongness*. It sucked in the particles, pulling them into itself. What was that? Was it the tower doing this, or something else?

Before he could determine what he was seeing, the vision of particles faded from view, then disappeared all together. A sudden wave of lethargy overcame him and he stumbled, only to be steadied by Rai'stahn's armored hand.

"Thy Sight is taxing to the new."

He cautiously opened his eyes, blinking as if waking from a dream. "What is it?" he asked, dumbfounded by what he saw.

The expression on the dragon's face was inscrutable, but his tone was clear. "Thy mettle is tested true. It is the Way in its purest form and thou hast been given the gift to see it. Thou must keep thine own counsel, but I offer thee this: Thou witnessed the blackness? It is a blight upon the land. Should it be allowed to grow, the Way will die."

Silbane drew a breath, feeling his energy replenish itself. A part of him realized he was breathing in the Way, its power suffusing him, and he marveled again at the insight this vision provided. He looked at Rai'stahn and said, "I saw it but did not see its source. Perhaps the tower—"

"T'was not the Far'anthi, but the abomination birthed by Valarius. Fate offered the cruelest of hands, dealt by the Conclave, played by me. Now the world hangs in the balance."

Silbane looked at the dragon, his mind skipping past the absurd suggestion that now Arek was somehow tied to Valarius and said, "What did you do?"

Rai'stahn looked at the mage, then looked away to the west. He took a deep breath, then said, "Valarius hath been a brilliant commander and tactician." The great dragon turned his massive head and met Silbane's stare. "Yet he lived for war and ignored his gift of Sight. The land needed peace. I was told to deliver it."

Silbane missed the implication of the dragon's last statement, blurting, "You show me a vision of him beseeching the dragons for aid, then condemn him in the same breath?"

"Victors write histories, Magus. I acted, and thought Edyn saved."

Suddenly, Silbane understood what the dragon was trying to say. Rai'stahn would act to save this world from any who he perceived would bring it harm. This included Arek, just as it had Valarius. Only the alliance between them had stayed the great dragon's hand this long. It was time he spoke to the dragon about their mission. Somehow, he had to make him understand.

Silbane looked at the dragon-knight, then began haltingly, "My lord, the lore father sensed a Gate may have opened. I have been dispatched to determine the threat."

The dragon took a step back. "Dost thou continue to prattle of this Gate?" he asked, weariness in his voice.

Silbane looked back at the tower and his apprentice, then said simply, "I am to use Arek to seal it."

Rai'stahn followed his gaze and in that look Silbane saw resignation. "If he touches the Gate, it will open. His power shall disrupt the wards placed there so long ago. Just as I did back then, thou dost not ken the danger."

"Arek disrupts magic. The lore father believes if he touches the Gate, it will close," Silbane countered. "If he is indeed this blackness as you say, the Way disappears into it. That would imply the Gate, too, would unravel."

"I know of thy mission. Themun did not believe this, else thou wouldst not be here." Rai'stahn faced the mage and said, "I tell thee again, if this abomination lives, all sustained by the Way dies."

The words hit Silbane like a hammer. He could not believe what Rai'stahn had just said. He shook his head and asked, "Why show me Valarius, then?"

Rai'stahn's golden gaze continued to stare at the tower and Arek. "Mistakes made by another have meaning. Wilt thou relive his path, knowing something of Valarius still survives in thy hatchling? He reaches back from death and exacts retribution on this world, on me, even now."

"Arek is just a boy!"

"A boy in this life," the dragon accused, "the hand of vengeance from another." He looked up, his eyes drinking in the dusk sky. "How often is one given the exact truth? Never wilt thou be given every fact, and thou hast been given more than most. *Think.*" He paused, then added, "I will give thee one more. Let it sway thee to the side of reason. Thine apprentice does not disrupt magic, he *consumes* it. Thou witnessed this."

Silbane did not know what to say. He took a step back, the dragon's next words sinking slowly into him, making him question all he knew about Arek.

"He is born of something selfish, something *unclean.* I sought the lore father out, summoned by the passing of the other hatchling on my Isle. His death was unforeseen, but he was swallowed by the same blackness."

Silbane thought, Piter.

"Providence delivered thine apprentice to me, a sure sign I should now bear this burden, justice for what I wrought on the slopes of Sovereign's Fall so many summers ago."

Silbane shook his head. "The lore father knew?" He could not believe it. "He sent Arek here to be killed?"

The dragon-knight held up an armored hand and said, "Whilst we journeyed here, I felt myself weaken. Ask thyself, how much power hath he taken from me already? Too much perhaps, for us to accomplish what we must? The time for discussion is past. He is dangerous. Heed me and thou wilt save this world." His finger stabbed the ground with finality. "Help me end Valarius's final dream of madness, and set right what my hand put in motion."

Silbane could only stare at the dragon's golden eyes. The lore father knew this and sent Arek here with Rai'stahn to be killed? He could not believe that. Thoughts raced through his head.

The vision didn't show what Valarius did, or that he even survived. The vision given him was from over two hundred years ago, yet Arek had been found comparatively recently. Silbane could not agree with the dragon, at least not without thinking it through, and something told him facts were still missing.

Below his uncertainty also ran an undertow of Silbane's own guilt, threatening to drown him into inaction. Had he not agreed with Themun to a mission calling for the sacrifice of his apprentice? They had bargained Arek's life for the fate of the land. Rai'stahn argued for the fate of the world. How were the two different? How was the council or he any better than the Conclave of Dragons and their actions?

Still, one thing kept coming back to his mind. It had been an immutable fact since the lore father had forced him to hold a figurative dagger to his apprentice's throat. He had never intended on sacrificing Arek, agreeing only to avoid giving his apprentice over to Kisan, or worse. *I can keep Arek alive,* he said to himself, *only I can do this.*

Although Silbane felt each of the dragon's words strike deep within him, it had not yet overcome his reasoning. The turmoil in his soul did not yet reflect in his eyes. He had dealt with dragons too long to make that mistake. Silbane stood his ground and stared at the dragon-knight until one word escaped his lips, said with the obdurate strength of the man behind it, "No."

Rai'stahn took a step forward and laid an armored hand on the mage's shoulder. "Dost thee think I suffer this burden so easily? It falls upon thee to weigh the good of thy world against the life of this one child, yet *thou doth hesitate.* What sacrifice then dost thou deem acceptable against this measure?"

"You condemn a boy on a vision showing nothing but the madness of a dead man, a man I already know was the land's enemy." Silbane's head dropped and a small sigh escaped his lips as the burden of his decision began to sink into his heart. "How are we better than what we fight, if the price is the blood of our children?"

Silence reigned while Silbane looked over the majesty of the Wastes. Had he just condemned them both to death? He did not know, but hoped against all hope his words still held some sway. What came next surprised him.

"Stand steady," The dragon-knight said. "Even now, thine apprentice dreams of power, of dealing death. He is not as innocent as thou wouldst believe..." Rai'stahn's voice trailed off. At first he seemed rooted in place like a statue, but then he wheeled and started walking away from the tower, toward the deep desert.

Silbane looked up, confused for a moment. "You're leaving?" He could not believe the dragon would give up so easily.

The dragon-knight stopped, his gaze sweeping the dunes, still lit golden by the setting sun. With a deep breath he turned and said, "I am drained and cannot recover whilst in that *thing's* presence. Worry for this world, for I fear even I cannot kill him without thy help. I give thee till the full moon rises. Upon my return, I will ask thee one last time."

Rai'stahn prepared to leave, but then turned back to the mage and said, "Thou questioned my actions with Valarius."

"What did you do?" The question came out in the barest whisper and something told him he would not like the answer.

The great dragon locked eyes with the master and said, "I waited for Valarius to stand victorious then struck him a blow, pushing him through the rift and into Lilyth's world. Alone, I delivered the land's greatest hero to his mortal enemies, then condemned his memory with fault for the land's undoing."

The dragon paused, his golden gaze catching the last of the setting sun in a flash of yellow and menace. "What dost thou think I will do to thine apprentice if the land's benefit hangs again on such a balance? Or, for that matter, to thee?"

Without waiting for a response, Rai'stahn leapt into the air and changed back into a dragon. His huge wings beat once, twice, as he gathered speed, arrowing off to the east.

Silbane stood stunned, his mind refusing to believe what had just happened. Rai'stahn's revelation put real meaning to the deadline he gave, for when he returned at the full moon's rise, there was no doubt in Silbane's mind it would be to kill them both.

BLADE DREAMS

Mark the sun, direction of the wind,

feel the earth with your bare feet.

Be one with your surroundings.

Familiarity with the killing ground

is as important as

training with your weapon,

or that ground will become your grave.

—*Tir Combat Academy, Basic Forms & Stances*

While Silbane and Rai'stahn walked off in discussion, Arek busied himself with setting up their camp. He walked over to where their equipment lay in a heap on the sand. They had not brought that much, just a few sleeping mats and some food supplies. He knew they had not planned to be here long. If worse came to worst, he thought, they could probably forage for whatever they needed from the nomads, or the beleaguered fortress's supplies.

A part of him felt guilty at the thought of stealing from a group of people besieged, but whatever he and his master might consume would in no way affect the outcome. If Bara'cor were meant to fall, nothing he or Silbane ate would change that.

He proceeded to move their equipment to a small alcove of rock, made by a partially crumbled wall at the base of the tower. This would provide them with shelter from the wind at night, at least from two directions, Arek thought, his mouth crooked into a wry smile as he took in the wall's dilapidated and pitiful state. He then worked his way up to the tower proper, leaning against the dead Far'anthi Stone.

The great expanse of the Wastes, empty and desolate, pulled his gaze. An ocean of sand stretched as far as his eyes could see, like soft swells frozen by time. The setting sun gave the sky a ruddy orange cast, accentuating the yellow glow of the stark terrain. So different, he thought, from the blue water and green hills of the Isle. Perhaps that was what made this place so beautiful to his eyes.

Arek wondered if a desert nomad had ever stood here, watching his own sunset before moving on to Bara'cor. Did he watch as the golden orb cast its warm light across the sands, thinking this may be his last view of the setting sun before the next day's battle? Would he wonder about his fate, the way Arek himself did now? Looking out at the great expanse before him, he knew the kind of person it would take to survive out here. It was someone very different from anyone he had ever known.

Arek quit his daydreaming with a start, looking back at the pile of gear he had left near the wall. His master would expect the camp to be laid out before he returned. He picked up a handful of sand and let it sift through his fingers as he walked back down the hill. It trailed behind him, caught on the slight hot breeze, and fanned out like a horse's tail.

His mind returned to that imagined nomad, and it struck him at how much sheer ingenuity and willpower it would take to survive in this environment. It was hard to believe anyone could do it for long, but he knew better. The Altan nomads were a hardy people, accustomed to the harsh life the desert demanded. This made them extremely pragmatic and deadly adversaries. Arek did not envy those trapped behind Bara'cor's walls. Perhaps the nomad he dreamed of earlier only thought of the next day's victory. That would not be so hard to believe.

He set to work stowing their gear and arranging a place for them to sleep. Once finished, he collected broken parts of the wall and arranged them into a circle, putting a rock the size of his head in the center. When Silbane returned, he could open a path to the *Way* and use it to heat the rock, providing them warmth tonight as the desert cooled.

A part of him felt shame that he had to wait for his master. Either Tomas or Jesyn could have heated the rock without a thought. But he buried that thought in a place where he put all his frustrations, a silent place deep inside.

His task completed, he sat with his back to the short wall, reaching for Tempest in the pack next to him. The sword almost leapt from its sheath and he marveled again at her beauty. This was truly a wondrous gift and it spoke to the respect the council had for him. He should not have let his self-absorption get the better of him in front of the lore father, his master, or acted so ungratefully in front of Adept Giridian. He resolved to apologize to the latter, once he saw him again.

He inspected the sword again. It was a keen, deadly, double-edged blade with polished metal flowing like water down its silvery length. Silbane had told him during their flight that legends said when one worthy held the sword, its full power would be released. No one had ever caused any change to Tempest on the island, leaving many to believe this part of the old legend was just a myth.

Still, Arek seldom discounted things he heard in old myths. According to Adept Giridian, Tempest was forged during the Demon Wars. He had little doubt it represented a level of magic never to be seen again in his lifetime. He had no illusion about his lack of experience, but secretly hoped the old legends might be true and he was in some way . . . special.

Arek leaned his back against the wall, making himself comfortable. The worn leather wrap of Tempest's hilt warmed in his tight grasp. The blade, extremely well balanced, felt light and quick, as Arek could tell after executing a few half-hearted swings from his seat. Though he had never faced an opponent across blades where his life was truly in danger, he knew he could wield this sword with deadly effect.

A part of him, however, was disappointed when nothing happened as he drew the fine blade. He laughed a little to himself then, the thought of some proclamation declaring he was Tempest's special wielder a bit too childlike a fantasy, even for him. Well, perhaps it would only happen in real combat. Realistic or not, he still held onto some small hope.

Then a thought crept in: What if I touch it with my bare hand? Cautiously, and with furtive glances to see if his master had returned, Arek shook off a glove and brought his hand within inches of the sword's grip. He held his breath, debating if this was worth possibly disenchanting the weapon, but doubting his power could permanently harm an artifact like Tempest. Also, the slight possibility this weapon might be part of his destiny inexorably pulled at him.

With a slight exhale, he grasped the hilt. At first, nothing happened. He watched carefully, thinking about the Way, and wondering if it required a key word of some sort. Just as he was ready to give up, he looked over at the horizon and his world exploded in black.

The desert was gone, as if he floated in a sea of nothing, with no shape, no horizon in sight. A lilting laugh echoed, as if from a great distance. *I am not for you, brother ... though I will protect you.* Another laugh and Arek felt himself pushed out of the blackness by an invisible hand, a quick sensation of falling, then he felt sand beneath him and the rock wall at his back.

The sword still shone with its liquid silver intensity and the gem remained an emerald green. His touch had not disrupted it, but how was that possible? His elation turned to disappointment when he recalled the words he had heard in his head: *Not for you.*

Then, watching the blade, he seemed consumed with visions of combat. What kind of warrior could he be, armed with Tempest? What mighty opponents could he defeat, if only for her?

Arek's mind, consumed by the sword's enchantment, dreamed of how it would be to take another's life, but each time with Tempest. His pale blue eyes narrowed as he imagined Tempest through another man's heart, the recognition in his opponent's gaze at his own impending death, then seeing the light go from those eyes.

Arek shook his head, trying to clear the visions, but they persisted. Dying men pleading for mercy, Arek twisting and cutting through opponents effortlessly, leaving a swathe of blood and death behind. Though the thoughts filled him with revulsion, a small part he could not acknowledge felt something else, something that drove him to be the best blade of his class. As Arek imagined pulling Tempest from the chest of a dead man and cleaning the blood off the blade, a small part of him felt a sense of victory and relished in it.

He raised his eyes and watched as the sun finished its fall from the western sky like a flaming coin, slowly melting onto the horizon. Taking a deep breath, he tightened his grip on Tempest, its heft and balance feeling somehow natural and right, like a long lost extension of his arm. He settled back against the warm wall and allowed himself to doze, his mind running through dozens of blade to blade engagements, each more dangerous than the last.

Each victory brought a sudden smile of satisfaction to his lips, as foe after foe fell before him. Soon, his master would return and the real adventure would begin. Until then, Arek dreamed of blood and fire, where he was the one with power. In his mind, echoed the lilting laugh of Tempest, relishing in the attention she received.

Journal Entry 7

Today I achieved the abode seen in the distance. It revealed itself to be a small castle, a defensible place borne from the dreams of someone long dead, or from my own dreams. I hope it is the former, as my mind has many specters still lurking, dark things I would rather not yet face.

It looks deserted, and it is. Perhaps I saw it change from what it might have been into a desolate place haunted only by the echoes of memories. I will use this as my base camp, from which to research the Aeris and forge their undoing.

Finnow came to me last night, a shade of death. I am not surprised she found her way here. It is likely the one place she has always wished to be, standing in judgment at the right hand of her gods.

She has always been strange, but death makes her worse. At first, I was fascinated and listened to her weave her tale, but I know what Finnow is. She is nothing more or less than I expected and I do not need a shade's words to measure my worth. The world knew my greatness long before she learned the same by dying. I banished her, her incessant yapping more tiresome than informative. Let this place do its best. I have survived worse.

One thing to note: I know not if she is real, or something I conjured with my latest regrets. She formed from a cloud of these same, infinitesimal lights, but they dispersed once my will came to bear. Her appearance has, however, taught me more about this place and the power my will has over it. I shall think on this more.

SOVEREIGN'S HAND

An arrow flies with deadly intent,

whether in combat or practice.

Train to be the same way.

—*Tir Combat Academy, Basic Forms & Stances*

Half a dozen shadows raced up the hillside, their forms blurred and indistinct in the dusk. Each was silent, quickly scaling the cliff with professional efficiency. Their fingers dug into rock and stone as if made of soft clay, providing hand and foot holds as necessary. They had to rely on their speed and stealth. As they neared the top, one turned back to the dark waters below and raised a small gem. It pulsed white for a moment and was answered by its twin from the prow of a blackened ship, waiting just offshore.

The leader turned and with a quick hand motion gathered his group close. Six figures formed a loose circle. At first, they looked like men, but one could see wider torsos and thicker arms and legs than one would find on the men of Edyn. These figures were stronger, bigger, with the obduracy of the very granite that surrounded them.

"We move in quickly. Our primary target is their leader. No survivors." He whispered this, then wrapped his mask in place so only his eyes showed. These began to glow a soft, ethereal blue, another visible sign he and his fellow assassins were no ordinary men.

As a group, they pulled their weapons and checked the dart loads, then inspected the firing mechanisms carefully. Once satisfied, each signaled "ready," then like shadows, the team melted into the darkness of the trees. They flitted from trunk to trunk, unerring as an arrow launched at a distant mark.

In the distance, the sounds of a group of children floated on the ocean breeze, along with the voice of a woman who instructed them in a gentle, but determined voice.

* * * * *

Adept Thera guided her little pupils down an embankment and closer to a small stream. The sun was setting on the second day since Silbane's departure. By now, she mused, they must have just reached the Shornhelm Wastes. She wondered if they fared well, but no communication from the two had been received.

The time since Silbane had left had moved along slowly. An uncomfortable silence descended upon any gathering of the council, as if each dared not second-guess the lore father's choices. The lack of information made the waiting even more difficult. It was only in times like this, when she was alone with her class of Whites that Thera felt at peace.

Lissah, a promising young White, reached down and picked up a small yellow flower with pale petals, raising it triumphantly. "I found it!"

Thera moved a bit closer and squatted in front of the little girl. "And what have you found?"

"Sunbeam." The girl's determined face and clear eyes bespoke a confidence that she knew exactly what she had found and would brook no argument to that fact.

Thera laughed and said, "And sunbeam is good for . . . ?"

Lissah looked down, searching for the answer, then back up again at the adept. "Fevers . . . you boil it in water, like tea."

Thera nodded, still smiling and said, "And it tastes good if you dry it and crush it into soup." She turned her gaze to the left side of the embankment, where the land opened to the beach. She could not see the waves in the distance, but could hear the dim sound as they broke on the shore. If she had the time, she would have made the trek with this group in tow, but the sun had already finished setting, and it would mean picking their way through the dark.

Dusting off her hands, she picked herself up and tousled Lissah's hair. It wasn't often she fell into these melancholy moods, but her recent confrontations with the lore father and her moral sense of wrongness in his sending Arek weighed heavily on her heart. At least, she thought, they should have further investigated his encounter with the apparition of Piter. She no longer thought of it as a fevered dream, and its portent worried her greatly.

She felt a small tug on her sleeve and saw Lissah pointing to the brush.

"Someone's in the bushes."

Before Thera could respond, she heard a number of soft *whuths* and felt a sharp prick on her arm and neck. Sprouting out of her arm as if by magic was a sharp, silver needle, its tail end a small clear glass vial filled with a dark liquid and surrounded by strange fletching.

It took her a moment to come to the realization that it was a dart of some kind, and somehow on this secluded isle, they were under attack. It was a moment she did not have.

The shadows kept moving, dangerous and fast. Then the night was illuminated by Thera's flameskin, her form blazing yellow and powerful. "Who dares . . . ?"

Before she even finished that sentence, she saw the little ones around her crumpling to the ground. Then she felt grass next to her face, her shield dissipating into the night like mist. A small choked sob clawed its way out of her as the poison went to work and her muscles tightened then locked.

She watched as one of the black shapes detached itself and moved across her field of view to check the child who lay in front of her. She could not tell if it was Lissah or not ... the child was not moving. The figure leaned in and then made a quick stabbing motion, pulling something long and thin from the crumpled form. Then it moved over to her.

"No survivors," it whispered, and she felt a punch in her chest and an ice-cold shaft of steel slide between her ribs and into her heart. It twisted once, expertly, then pulled out. At first, she felt fine, then a warm gush of wetness soaked the ground below her. Her sight went dim, then slowly black.

* * * * *

The leader moved over and checked the woman personally, as he had been instructed. It had been made clear to him that if even one lived, they would be taken off the combat line and reslumbered. He had slept long enough, as had his men.

She was dead. The poison had neutralized her as promised. He looked about at the dozen or so crumpled forms. A small part of him felt pity for these children, who had not survived their encounter with his team. Pity was not, however, a luxury he could afford. He signaled to his men and they moved quickly and silently toward the structures illuminated a short distance away. As they neared, he held up a hand and signaled their stop.

Motioning to two of them he pointed to the stairs leading up into the first tower, then two more to back them up. He and his second waited at the entrance to be sure no one went in or out. The four disappeared into the multilevel structure, lethal harbingers of death.

* * * * *

Kisan and Tomas were at the observatory taking readings of the night sky. The injuries Tomas had sustained from Piter's counter-spell had almost faded, leaving behind only a general weakness and malaise. Kisan's attention remained on her direhawk, roosting nearby.

The giant bird's raven black feathers changed to a bright crimson on each trailing edge of its wings and tail. A similar marking ran from deep black at the beak to a crest of crimson, giving the direhawk an almost fiery aspect. The hawk watched a bag Kisan held in her hand, intent on what squirmed inside.

Kisan didn't say anything. She expertly flipped the bag over and slammed it into the stones. Whatever was inside ceased moving and she reached in and withdrew a limp rabbit, either unconscious or dead.

The direhawk had not taken its gaze off its the meal and when Kisan tossed the rabbit into the air, the raptor caught it deftly in its razor-sharp beak. Within moments the direhawk made short work of the rabbit, swallowing, then cocking its head, looking to its master for more.

Kisan ignored the hawk, her thoughts still on the loss of her own apprentice. She took some solace in Tomas's recounting of what had happened, thankful the boy had not been more severely injured. Still, there was a hole in her, a black space Piter used to fill. It felt like a betrayal to her first apprentice's memory to be teaching Tomas, and Kisan didn't know if she could deal with it. She reached up and ruffled the direhawk's proud crimson crest, unafraid of the lethal beak and talons that stood unsheathed so close by.

Oh, she knew the lore father had been correct in assigning her a new apprentice. In a clinical sense, this was the best way to cope with her loss, by occupying her time with someone who needed it. But Kisan didn't want her time occupied and didn't want to be "handled" by the lore father. She'd had quite enough of that lately.

She looked at her new charge, Tomas, who clearly found it hard to stand near so dangerous a predator despite her reassurance it was quite safe. She had raised and cared for over a dozen lethal warbirds, like this direhawk, yet the boy still edged away. No doubt the sight of those glittering black eyes unnerved him, and made him feel more or less like some sort of small prey.

"Does your hawk have a name?" Tomas inquired.

"I do not name my weapons," she replied in a monotone, looking back at the dark-winged predator.

Apparently in an effort to lighten the mood he changed subjects and said, "Funny, but there was a time people thought the stars marked one's adherence to the gods."

Kisan was startled out of her reverie and looked at Tomas askance, as if seeing him for the first time. "What?"

Tomas gestured at the sky with his chin, "The stars, Master ... gods who guide our destiny. I find that amusing." His eyes sparkled with mirth and in another time or place it would have been infectious. Here and now, though, it only served to irritate her further.

Tomas continued, oblivious to Kisan's mood, "Take me, for instance. I was born in the summer under the stars of the Benevolent Ruler, Pious ... or at least that's when my birthday is celebrated." Tomas smiled. "So, I guess I'll be in charge of all this one day," he said, waving his arms about.

Kisan snorted, "Yes. People are a stupid, superstitious lot," missing Tomas's joke entirely. She petted her hawk again, then leaned her head against its breast and closed her eyes, feeling the warmth of its feathers envelope her.

"What about you, Master? What god rules your destiny?"

Something about the easy banter Tomas assumed, so unlike Piter, who had been consumed with memorizing everything Kisan said or did, put the young master at ease. Piter's death was still too recent, but she felt herself responding to the gregarious nature of her new apprentice and answered, "Dyana, the Huntress, believe it or not." She smiled, then said in voice tinged with chagrin, "I was short with you earlier, and perhaps not as forthcoming."

Tomas smiled and offered, "I did not mean to presume."

The master held up a hand and said, "I did not lie, in that I do not name my weapons. However—" she paused, looking at her direhawk—"he names himself, Temairex."

Tomas smiled, his eyes wide. "Really? It sounds noble."

Kisan nodded, feeling for the first time as if a burden had been lifted, "It is, and perhaps—" then her eyes widened and she stopped in midsentence.

Even Temairex sensed something, flapping his wings and sending a whirlwind of air across their small open space. The bird would have already taken flight if not for the harness holding his leg to his tree trunk sized roost. Kisan calmed him with a touch, thinking.

Something was dreadfully wrong. In the back of her mind, there existed a tenuous link, a common bond amongst all the adepts on the Isle. It was so constant it was largely ignored. Even now, she could sense Giridian in his chambers, and Dragor training. *Thera* ... that link had been severed and only one thing could break it.

"Pit—Tomas, get inside. Now!"

She had almost called him "Piter," but the boy understood the message. Without checking to see if he obeyed, Kisan went to the edge of the observatory, looking down into the darkness. She couldn't see anything but that didn't mean there was no danger. Something or someone had silenced Thera. She didn't know what, but she was going to find out. Whatever it was, it was about to face a true Master of the Way.

* * * * *

Time crawled along, but the leader's composure never wavered. They trained for this and knew their opponents' strengths and weaknesses. The key to their success would be their speed and surprise. He had, however, made a calculated deviation from their assignment and detoured to finish this hall first.

His reasoning had been simple. Once the adepts knew of the attack, the conflict would create chaos, and in that chaos, some of the magelings might escape. It was a priority none who used the Way survived, especially the young ones, who dreamed more vividly than did the elders.

A moment later four shapes came racing down the stairs, still silent, and crouched next to the team leader. With hand signals, they made a curt report: *All dead.* The quick hand motion was too short to give full weight to the fact that dozens from the Hall of Apprentices would not wake the next day. The leader nodded once, then looked to the next structure. Like ghosts, they slipped into the darkened spaces along the path and leapfrogged their way to the Hall of Adepts.

As they neared, the leader held up his hand again and the team came to a halt. Reaching into his tunic, he pulled out a small metal cross, carved with runes. He gingerly placed it against the doors and waited.

The metal cross began to glow, then the runes lit. With a flash, the tiny talisman was gone, as was the protective spell that held the door shut. The leader raised two fingers and two men shot past him like black darts, through the now open door. The rear two took positions in the dark recesses of the entryway, to ensure they could proceed uninterrupted. He and his second slid through the doors and joined the two already inside.

The Hall of Adepts had a grand curving staircase on the inside spiraling up through each level to where the masters' chambers lay. Taking those stairs would be suicide, he knew. Too many wards and cantrips designed to alert these so-called, adepts. He looked to his team and flexed his gloved hands. They scintillated for a moment, purple and amethyst. He then moved to the underside of the staircase.

Without hesitation, he grabbed and pulled, flattening himself against it. The magic of his uniform and his training took over and he climbed like a spider rapidly up the underside of the staircase. His team silently followed, the four of them looking like black, four-legged insects.

When they reached the first landing, they grabbed the lip of the floor and vaulted over the banister. Their feet barely touched the rail before they leapt upward to the ceiling. There they clung again like spiders and made their way to the first door.

The first man to the door took out another talisman and affixed it. Silently the device negated any wards on the door, dissipating in a flash and sparkle, leaving no trace of itself. They looked at one another, synchronizing their next move.

Then, without a sound, one pulled the door open while two fired poisoned darts into Giridian's back as the adept replaced a book onto his bookshelf. The poison's double dose went to work immediately, locking his muscles and constricting his breathing. Even without a *coup de grâce*, Giridian would be dead within moments.

As the first two held their positions, a third man entered and punched a lethal dagger into Giridian's back. The blade was cross-shaped, designed to create a wound that would not close. A small *huff* was the only sound the ursine adept made as the knife punched into his heart, then pulled out. His attackers were moving out of the room before Giridian's lifeless body hit the floor.

These adepts were proving to be easier targets than had been indicated. He had thought their element of surprise would have been over with the death of the first … but that did not seem true. No matter, now they needed to find Themun Dreys and put an end to him. At four against one old man, he was confident in the outcome and continued forward toward the main chambers.

* * * * *

Kisan did not have time for the circuitous route down the main stairs of the hall. Instead, she moved with the litheness of a cat, springing from the parapet and falling down the side of the building. At careful measured moments, she reached out and touched the citadel rushing by, slowing her fall using the Way and her own training. Just before she reached the ground her legs snapped out, the balls of her feet kicking the rough stone wall.

In an instant, her downward velocity transformed into a rotation and Kisan used that momentum to flip herself, arcing gracefully over and out from the wall. She landed lightly, crouched in the darkness. Summoning the Way, she sank low to the ground and expanded her senses: sight, hearing, smell, and touch. As she did so, she quickly reviewed what she knew.

Whoever silenced Thera must have known much about the Isle and the people living here. It made sense they had intimate knowledge of adepts, the training ground's layout, and the defenses they could expect. She would be foolish to assume they were any less trained than she. Kisan quickly readied another spell, then cast it.

The air next to her began to darken, then separate into two distinct clouds. They sucked in the surrounding air then sparkled and coalesced. Where Kisan crouched, two duplicates of her now mirrored her stance.

"I speak, you obey," she said to them.

They nodded and said, "Yes, Master." Their voices, exactly like her own, sounded eerie in the night air, but Kisan knew they would serve their purpose. Though they were not alive and could only follow simple verbal commands, they were better than normal mirror images. She could create dozens of those, but they lacked substance and could only follow a single order. These were more complex and served two critical needs.

The most obvious was as decoys ... but because of the increased power spent in making them, Kisan could use their senses as her own, even control them to some degree. As scouts, they would serve to provide her with information, and that would be her key advantage. Should they be discovered and attacked, they would even die, feeling solid and real. It was her only chance.

"We will make our way behind the Hall of the adepts."

"Yes, Master," the doppelgangers whispered.

Kisan looked around. She had purposely fallen into a shadowed area that was almost pitch black. Her line of sight to the front of the hall was obscured by the building itself. Nevertheless, she had no doubt whoever was attacking was just around the corner, waiting.

She looked to the duplicate on her right and said, "Walk to the front of this building. Do not stop for anyone."

The doppelganger nodded, then stood and started walking around the circular hall. Kisan motioned to the other to follow and they started circling the other direction. Her mind opened a path to the Way, and whatever the first doppelganger saw became clear. She then moved to the first defensible position she could find, one that had a clear view of the courtyard in front of the Hall, but where someone hiding in that area could not see her.

Through her simulacrum's eyes, she saw its approach to the front of the building. At first, nothing seemed amiss, and there were no obvious signs of attack. Perhaps she had been wrong. It was then she saw that the front door stood ajar. That would never happen . . .

Before she could do anything, she heard through the doppelganger's ears the sound of something firing with whispers of air. This double had few battle skills, so it was pointless to try to evade. Rather Kisan concentrated on the doppelganger's response.

She felt two small pinpricks on her own skin, letting her know her doppelganger had been hit with two dart-like objects. The grouping was tight, no more than a hand span at fifty paces, and centered on her throat. Within a heartbeat, she felt a numbing paralysis in the doppelganger's body. If those darts had hit her, she would have been helpless.

Quickly, she mentally forced her double to fall facing the door with its eyes open. She could feel what the double felt, hear what it heard, and knew these attackers expected those darts to work. Until she knew what and whom they were facing, she was going to play along. The double collapsed in a heap and turned its head exactly the way she wanted. Now Kisan could watch what happened next.

At first, nothing stirred the night. Neither movement nor sound broke the silence and no one appeared. Kisan realized they were waiting . . . then it dawned on her they were waiting for the poison to take effect. Even as she came to this conclusion, two shadows detached themselves from the dark recesses of the doors. They moved quickly, their wide forms blurring with some sort of magic.

Kisan was shocked at their speed and their seeming ability to use the Way. However, her training took over and she watched dispassionately as these men made quick work of her first scout. One punched a dagger into the base of the skull. The other searched the body. They worked with the practiced efficiency of highly trained thieves. As both finished their gruesome tasks, no word was exchanged. Then they quickly dragged the body out of sight and resumed their stations, melting back into the darkness.

Kisan's resolve hardened as she watched their quick and controlled movements over her double's corpse. She knew two things from observing them. First, she would not underestimate them, for they were highly disciplined. This would have been her fate had she rounded that corner without a plan. Second, no parley had been offered, no terms, nor discussion. She was facing someone with the clear objective to kill them all.

She was not worried that the ease with which they dispatched her doppelganger would arouse their suspicion. The fact was that given the right circumstances, anyone could be killed by surprise, even a disciple of the Way as well trained as she.

Inwardly, Kisan smiled. She was no longer surprised, and that meant these men would be facing a full master in battle. She motioned to her remaining double and together they moved forward into the night. Nothing these assassins did now would save them.

* * * * *

Dragor finished the end of his *kata* with a fast spin kick, his mind and body one. His breathing came easy, exhaling on time with each point of impact while he continued his practice movements. The point of *kata* was to allow him to train his body and mind for that perfect strike, against a perfect opponent.

He knew that in reality, there was no such thing . . . but fighting against his own mind helped him learn what strikes should look like when unencumbered by the clash and din of battle. His body remaining loose until the point of impact occurred, then tightening with the strength of steel to focus all the power into one small area. It was this point, this focus, that caused all the damage.

He spun, ducking under one imaginary opponent then striking with his open palm at another. It was times like this when he could practice alone that he felt most connected to the Way. It flowed through him like his breathing, connecting him at once to all that was around him.

When the link to Thera vanished he stumbled, his breath catching. Instantly he knew there was something seriously wrong. Without a thought, he skinned himself in power. His flameskin flashed a sublime purple once, as it hardened for defense, then became invisible to the naked eye. He then moved up the walkway leading from his training area to the outer hall.

Whatever was happening, he reasoned, must be near where he last felt Thera, to the north of the school. He meant to head in that direction and see if he could find out anything more. Slowly, he continued his way up and to the outer halls. As he moved, his form wavered, then vanished like smoke. No reason to let whatever it is, see him coming. Like a predatory ghost, Dragor made his way out into the darkness.

* * * * *

Kisan remained motionless, then looked at her remaining doppelganger. She knew where they were, but needed a better distraction to accomplish what she wanted. She concentrated, reaching for the Way. As she did so, the form of her doppelganger changed. It morphed, becoming younger, leaner. In moments, an exact copy of Piter crouched next to her, ready to do her bidding.

The effort cost her dearly. It was one thing to create a duplicate of oneself. To create a full duplicate of another took immense concentration and an intimate familiarity with the subject. *Piter*, she thought sadly, *you are the one I remember best. I need you to serve one last, noble purpose tonight.*

She looked past the curve where the two assassins lay hidden, out of her line of sight. "On my command, you will run past the entrance. You will stop for nothing."

The Piter look-alike nodded, then turned to stare straight ahead. Kisan continued to look at her creation, feeling her loss threaten to overcome her composure. *It was unfair her boy did not get the chance that others did,* the thought crawling in like worms through mud. Then her will snapped down, training taking hold. She would only get one chance at this and needed to focus.

She enhanced her vision to include heat and silenced the sounds of her footfalls and clothes. For this next part, she would need stealth and speed.

"Go!" she whispered, and her doppelganger shot off like an arrow.

Kisan followed at a slower pace, keeping her form hidden within the low grass. As the simulacrum rounded the corner and continued its sprint, she heard the sound of at least two darts fire at its retreating back. They were close, but their attention was on the fleeing "boy."

Kisan knew they would have to make a choice soon and hoped they would make the one she knew they must. Less than a moment passed, then like a black streak, one of the assassins sped after the fleeing image of Piter.

She didn't hesitate, but moved with blinding speed silently up and over the stone entryway. Her enhanced vision easily picked out the remaining man, who only now realized his peril. Before he could offer any defense, Kisan struck his sternum with an open palm, her hand vibrating in tune with the man's bones.

A silent detonation occurred within the assassin's body as Kisan's focused strike shattered every bone in a circular pattern from the center of the man's chest outward. His lungs liquefied and he convulsed, then vomited out a gout of black liquid and bone into the grass. The force of the blow knocked his body backward against the hard stone wall with a solid, wet smack, before he rebounded forward and fell into the waiting arms of the master.

His weight surprised Kisan the most, for it was at least three times what a normal person should have been. It took the enhanced strength of the master to move him at all. She steadied herself, quickly pulling the dying man into the side bushes, then ripped the face cover off to look at the person beneath.

The face was square, younger than expected, a boy with blond hair and peach whiskers now speckled with his lifeblood. A whispered gasp escaped his lips and in that moment, his eyes focused on his killer.

Kisan concentrated, then touched the man's forehead. Names and images flooded her mind. A stone fortress, set deep in the Dawnlight Mountains. A black sun surrounded by blue fire, standing like an open maw. A small cat, calico and mewing piteously. A dark cavern, hundreds of glass caskets filled with men like him.

The flood of life, of this boy's life, gushed from his mind into Kisan's like water bursting from a cut sack before slowing to a trickle and finally ... nothing. The memories had transferred and the mindread was complete. The spell was taxing, however, and she would not be able to read much more from anyone else until these memories were purged. Still, she needed information, and one more thing.

She leaned back, looking at her handiwork, noticing the details. Small beginnings of a beard framed the boy's face, and the eyes were pale blue, no longer glowing and still wide in the shock of death. Even as she watched, those pale blue irises were eaten up by the widening black of his pupils. His skin was tan, with a scar on his left cheek, a quick slash that spoke of a misstep against a sharp blade.

Kisan drank in the features, focusing, memorizing. She looked at the mask, the gloves, and the uniform. She inspected the shoes, the belt. She ran her hands over the man's body, feeling the strength and size of the limbs. She had already spent a tremendous amount of energy tonight in creating her doppelgangers and sifting the assassin's mind, but this one last spell had to be perfect. She looked inward, diving deep into the Way, and called upon the little power she had left.

She refocused herself and shaped the Way to do her bidding. A sparkle consumed her form, a quick flash of ethereal starlight vanishing before it even seemed to take substance. Then Kisan stood and moved back up to the entranceway.

As she did so, her form blurred and changed, becoming stronger, thicker, and taller. In moments, a dark-clothed assassin took watch, with features identical to the boy that lay hidden and dead, some feet away. *Tamlin,* the thought came to her. *My name is Tamlin.* With time, more of her victim's memories would become available as the mindread assimilated the dead man's memories.

Kisan, who was now Tamlin, scanned the direction the other assassin had run, watching with eyes glowing the same soft, deadly blue. The time for a reckoning would soon be at hand.

* * * * *

The leader of the team paused in the hallway, presumably leading from the main landing to the lore father's chambers. He held up a hand and one of his men came forward with a small canister. They moved carefully up to the door, fanning out to both sides like black fingers. Another cross talisman was set against the door, negating the wards with its familiar flash, silent detonation, and sparkle. The man readied the canister, then waited for the signal.

The leader made a fist. The door was yanked open, then pushed shut as the man expertly tossed the canister through the small opening his team had made. The detonation of sound and light within was designed to disorient someone, interrupt any spellcasting, and blind those who did not protect their eyes.

Even as the canister exploded, the team yanked the doors back open, dart weapons ready. They quickly identified a man with a staff reeling forward from the blast and did not hesitate. Four darts hit their target, poison surging and locking muscles. The leader looked in and saw that the old man fit the description he had been given of the lore father. He moved into the room cautiously.

The figure of the lore father lay prone on the floor, choking. The leader moved up and stood where the lore father could see him. He waited until their eyes met.

"Themun Dreys, Sovereign commits you to stone and earth." The leader pulled a sharp stiletto from his belt and kneeled next to the dying man.

In a quick motion, the leader stabbed the stiletto through the lore father's eye and into his brain. The body convulsed once, a wet moan emanating from deep within. Then it went limp, except for a small tremor that ran down one leg.

The leader watched this impassively, then motioned to another man who came up and punched the cross shaped dagger into the older man's chest. They had taken great risk to this point and had to be sure their target was dead. He then double-checked the leader's work and nodded.

"Not as dangerous as we were led to believe," whispered the leader to his team. "Bear witness."

The team moved in, staring at the corpse through glowing blue eyes, memorizing and inscribing the details. As each was satisfied the target was dead, they whispered, "Witnessed." The leader watched until all had spoken, then made his way for the door. An Archmage of the Way was dead, he mentally added with satisfaction. Now it was time to get out of here.

The pieces of the destroyed canister could not stay. No evidence could be left behind that could lead anyone back to Sovereign. He motioned to his men and they stowed their weapons and retrieved any of their detritus. Their expertise showed in the thoroughness with which they quickly accomplished their tasks. Then, they made their way out of the chamber and to the edge of the banister that looked down into the spiral well created by the tower's stairs.

Looking down over the edge they again did not hesitate, but leapt over the banister and down the hole of the central stairwell. They jumped headfirst like swimmers for water. Halfway down, they tucked and flipped so their feet pointed at the ground.

All four landed in a crouch, their light exhalation at impact belying the distance from which they had just fallen. The door to the outside stood slightly ajar, just as they had left it. All four moved silently through it and into the night.

* * * * *

Dragor took a deep breath of the night air, trying to sense anything that might be wrong. He sensed someone tapping into the Way not far from him, and by its feel, he knew it was Kisan. Would it make sense for him to mindspeak her now, or wait until he knew the nature of their attackers?

The fact that no other adept had broken mental silence demanded he remain cautious. Furthermore, he couldn't afford to expend the energy right now. Mindspeak, though efficient, could deplete him before he knew what they faced. Waiting would be most prudent, he decided, especially in light of losing contact with Thera. Anyone who could silence her could potentially tap the Way.

He moved quickly from the training hall to the main courtyard. They gathered here for the seasons' festivals, and to relax between classes and training. Tables and lamps adorned the circular forum, creating a natural theater for the island inhabitants. He stayed away from the brightly lit central area, instead flitting from shadow to shadow. Regardless of his cloak of invisibility, Dragor was taking no chances.

As he neared the Hall of Adepts, he stopped, motionless. Ahead was the point where he had sensed Kisan. Though the flash of power was gone, the residue lingered like a scent. She was still about and Dragor felt the need to be even more cautious. He moved quickly up to the wall, taking advantage of the terrain and shadows.

That they were under attack was a certainty in his bones. He did not remember when he came to believe this true, only that every sense told him a mistake now would be deadly. He moved around the wall until he could see the front entrance, then he crouched and waited.

At first, nothing happened. His skin crawled in the cool night air as if at any moment lightning would strike and the battle would be joined. The tension grew and Dragor knew something was about to snap.

Then a single black streak came from the woods to one side of the Hall of Adepts, joining up with another crouching on the stairs, motionless as he was. Those two were soon joined by four more emerging from inside the hall like living shadows. That made six against one. As that thought flitted through his mind he felt a sudden change, like a shifting breeze that brought a sudden chill. Dragor knew his cloak of invisibility did not hide him any longer, and he had been seen.

He didn't hesitate, dropping it to conserve energy. Then he stepped out from the wall, his form lined in power, his flameskin flashing purple as it flared into existence at his command. He could see all six fan out to take positions around him and nodded in satisfaction. This would be no training *kata*. This was real and his life would balance on the keen, deadly edge of his Talent against theirs. He took a deep breath and cleared his mind. He knew he was ready.

The breeze shifted, bringing with it the scent of jasmine, and they attacked.

HOPE

Focus on killing your opponent now.

Tomorrow, it will make today

a good memory.

Today, it will make tomorrow,

a promise of glory.

—*Kensei Tsao, The Book of Blades*

I think it will work." Ash stood facing his commander and the King of Bara'cor in a small room high atop one of the castle towers. Behind him were Niall and Yetteje. "It may be the key to ending this conflict quickly."

"It's a death sentence," answered the king, looking at his young commander. Still, he had to admit the plan was cunning: A small team of handpicked men steal into the nomad camp and assassinate their leader. It would throw the nomads into confusion. If Bara'cor attacked, it was likely they could cause significant losses to the nomad army. Though he doubted being reinforced by Haven, any plan that disrupted the nomad command bought them time, and with it life. Yes, thought Bernal, impressive.

"According to Sergeant Stemmer the honor goes to the Princess of EvenSea, my lord. She had the inspiration," Ash said while motioning to Yetteje, who stood slumped against the back wall.

"Don't call me that," she stated.

"Princess?" asked Ash.

Yetteje looked up, her eyes angry. "Do you intend to mock me, sir?" she snapped. "I am nothing. I have no people, my home lies in ruins. Of what people and lands am I a princess? My name is Tej, at least until I have set things right."

An uncomfortable silence would have followed, but the firstmark stepped in. "Aye, you have the right of it. Maybe you're not heir to anything, but if you snap at my armsmark again you'll be over my knee like the child you're acting."

Dead silence. Then Yetteje's face broke into a hesitant grin. "I guess I deserved that."

The firstmark smiled too, coming over to clap the girl's back lightly. "Yes, you did. Insolence is never a virtue, and sometimes even mules need to kick each other in the head. Still, I'll be taking your advice. 'Tej' it is, till you say different."

He gave her another clap, this one almost knocking Tej off her feet, then turned to take his place by his king's side. He threw a sidelong glance at Yetteje and said, "But it's still 'Firstmark' to you, Tej."

Tej sketched a hasty bow and said, "Of course, Firstmark."

The king smiled, shaking his head. Leave it to Jebida to talk sense into a stubborn girl thirty summers his junior. He then motioned to Ash and said, "Regardless of the plan's origin, it still means death to those who volunteer."

Ash nodded, "I know, but a small number of dead men instead of . . . what is our alternative?"

"Hmm." The king looked at his firstmark, the question plain on his face. Who would go?

"You'll ask for volunteers?" Niall asked, to no one in particular. The question hung in the air without answer.

Finally, the firstmark said, "And risk word getting back to the nomads? Spies may be about, or worse." Jebida moved his large frame over to a water bowl and rinsed his hands. "I'd rather not risk that."

"We don't need to make a general announcement," Ash suggested. "We know who could be useful, less than ten I'd trust. We call them together and ask if they wish to volunteer for something that may mean death, but may also win the lives of those behind these walls. And we pick from there."

The king sighed. It always seemed to come down to choosing who should die and who should live. It didn't matter that these men were "volunteering." Sending someone to his death was not Bernal's desire and the thought sat with him uncomfortably. Still, Ash had asked the right question earlier, what was their alternative? He looked at the armsmark and asked, "Who would you choose?"

Before Ash could answer, Yetteje spoke up. "I'm going."

For a second time, there was silence caused by the princess. Bernal recovered first and said, "No, you are not."

"This nomad had my father *impaled*," Tej said, stepping forward. "He may have murdered my whole family. I am going."

The entire room paused, thinking the princess mad, but the expression on her face showed her mind was set and nothing further was going to be said. Bernal had to remind himself it had only been two days since Yetteje had seen her father killed. The king knew it was unfair to expect the girl to act more mature. Still, he had to temper his advice in a way so Tej would listen. The king tried again in a mollified voice, "You will not endanger yourself. Part of being a ruler is caring for your people. How will you do that if you are dead?"

It took a moment for Yetteje to respond, but once she did, she spat out, "I have no people. The nomads took care of that. Who am I caring for, sir?"

The king was ready to throw something at the girl, but instead clamped down his frustration and said, "Tej, I grieve with you. We have both lost family, but you are all that is left of your noble house. How will I face your father or my sister in the afterlife if I don't protect you now?"

Yetteje looked down, her father's face in her thoughts, perhaps. When she looked up, there was determination in her gaze. She looked at the king and said, "If I am all that's left, then the Tir name is dead and you protect nothing. Let me go, or I will find a way to go on my own." A sudden silence filled the room as the young princess sought to match her will against the king.

The contest of wills was over before it began as the king snapped his fingers and Alyx came in with a guard. He kept his eyes on Yetteje but said, "Sergeant, you will find two more guards. Then you are to take Yetteje Tir to her room. You will place her inside and lock the door. Two of you will stay inside the room, the other two will stay outside. I will be there momentarily to speak with our . . . guest."

He then addressed the young princess, "I will not allow you, in your grief, to end the Tir line. You can choose to be insolent, but you are still my ward. And within these walls, my decisions are final, for *I* am king."

Yetteje looked ready to disagree, but then her shoulders slumped and she broke into sobs, barely stifled. She went to a knee with her hands over her face. The gentle hands of Alyx picked her up and began to guide her from the room.

"May I go with her?" Niall quickly asked. "She shouldn't be alone."

The king's eyes were on Tej's back, sorrow for his niece's loss plain on his face. He nodded to his son without looking, not trusting himself to speak.

Niall fell into step with the sergeant, relieving her of her burden. His arm went around his cousin as they made their way from the tower down to Tej's room.

They couldn't know that in just a few moments, everything they knew would be tested.

CONFLICT

Do not negotiate from a weakened position.

The fearful never grant reprieve

unless threatened.

Be overly aggressive,

dominate to within an inch of their life,

then offer a morsel of hope.

—*Tir Combat Academy, The Tactics of Victory*

A rek! Get up!" Silbane's urgent voice broke through the light sleep that had stolen over the young apprentice.

He cracked an eye open and then asked, "Master? What . . . ?"

"Quiet. Get up, we don't have much time."

Something in his master's tone brought Arek to full alertness. He scrambled awake, scattering the last remnants of whatever dream he had been enjoying into the cold night air.

Snatching up Tempest, he quickly scanned the area. Master Silbane stood looking over his shoulder, as if expecting pursuit. When he looked back at Arek, the boy saw something he had never seen before: fear in his master's eyes.

"What is it?"

Silbane looked at his apprentice as though not sure where to begin. "We are no longer safe here."

"Why, because of the nomads?" Arek could see his master was upset, which worried him more than anything else did. "What has happened?"

"I need your full attention. You will follow my instructions. Understood?"

Arek nodded, his eyes wide. A cold knot of fear coiled in his belly and his palms became clammy. Something told him this was not going to be good.

Then, as he heard his master begin to speak, his vision tunneled and the scene froze in front of him. He looked around, but everything had stopped, even the wind was silent. His master stood in front of him mid-word, like a statue. The air was cloudy and Arek realized it was all the fine particles of sand, their motion frozen in place, which now made them visible.

"You'll want to hear what your master has to say."

Arek turned to see Piter casually walk out of thin air. Along with him came that feeling of malevolence, a barely contained hatred directed at him. "Piter, what's happening?"

"The same thing as when we first spoke." Piter looked at him with an expression that Arek could only interpret as pity. "Our conversation is between heartbeats, imbecile." Piter looked at Arek and added, "You know, he means to kill you."

Arek closed his eyes, willing this nightfright to end. When he opened them, however, Piter was still there and nothing had changed. Arek stammered out the first thing that came to his mind. "Wh-what do you mean?"

"The dragon. This is no mission of information gathering, not after he comes back. Your life ends here, unless you escape."

Arek found his inherent fear and unnerve fading faster than it had during the first encounter with Piter's shade. It was as if he'd grown more accustomed to Piter's presence. His voice came out stronger as he answered Piter's accusation. "I don't believe you. My master is here about a rift near Bara'cor."

"You believe that?" the shade looked out over the moonlit night. He seemed to be listening for something, something Arek couldn't hear. His gaze turned back upon his former classmate and in that moment, Arek felt his soul bared. "Yes! You must go to Bara'cor." The statement surprised Arek, who had not yet seen the shade be anything but insulting to him.

"Bara'cor?" he asked.

"Do not believe what he says," Piter said, pointing at the frozen Silbane.

Arek hesitated. How much of what he felt and saw had been challenged by the actions of the lore father, this "new" power, or the dragon's scrutiny? Nothing seemed to fit. Still, a part of him felt better as they neared the land and Bara'cor. He could feel something pulling at him, like a harmonious note that echoed just below his hearing. It spoke of power, of strength, of *destiny*. He wanted to believe it but his master felt this place was dangerous, and he trusted that too. Master Silbane was the closest thing he had to a father. Still, there was doubt.

Arek shook his head. "I won't listen to you." But it came out with less conviction than he wanted. He knew the masters were not telling him the whole truth, and he had seen it in the lore father's eyes. Now this shade was picking apart the fragile peace he had created within his mind.

"He will sacrifice you for the good of this world," Piter said, "if he believes it."

Arek grew exasperated and shouted, "What do you *want?*"

Piter arched an eyebrow. "Mercy . . . but you're too late to grant that. I'm cursed as a lackey to a dimwitted fool."

What could Arek do? He felt guilt, even remorse for Piter's death. He knew he was to blame. Now it seemed that either Piter's soul was trapped in some horrible servitude, or he was slowly going mad. Perhaps that was it. Was he losing his mind?

Then another part of him, the part that strove to be best in blades, the part that fought to gain respect despite his inability with the Way, remembered something he almost missed . . . *lackey*.

It made sense now. Piter had made a mistake, tiny, but still a mistake. A small smile escaped Arek's lips, his confidence returning as he unraveled the specter's web of lies. His thoughts sharpened and as they did, he noticed a change, a hesitancy. It was almost missed but a caution, a trepidation on the ghost's part became obvious, as if Piter were facing his own . . . *master*.

Arek looked at Piter and said, "You belong to me." His voice brooked no argument. It was strong, for he knew it was true. This shade, for all its malevolence, had no power over him. Instead, it was quite the opposite. His dreams of power suddenly came back to him, the feeling of twisting the blade and killing his opponent. This was the same. This creature's mockery and anger were designed to make Arek frightened. No longer! He would cower to this pathetic creature no more.

"What do you think—?"

"Silence!" Arek stepped forward. "You will answer me."

Piter's shade looked sidelong, an obsequious grin on his face, and slowly the ghost knelt. *"That* didn't take very long . . ."

Arek ignored him, looking about. "What's happening right now? Has time actually stopped?"

"No. We stand within the blink of an eye. When it ends, you will be right where we first started." A sly grin appeared on Piter's face and he added, "Of course, I'll still be dead."

"I don't remember killing you, Piter. I don't even know if you're telling the truth about any of this."

"I made this up? Then I appeared to you in the desert? How stupid are you?"

Arek sat down in the sand, trying to piece together what to do. His logical mind took over where his conscious thoughts had given up. "You said earlier the dragon means to kill me . . . why?"

Piter's shade moved over in front of the young apprentice, his form and his demeanor subservient. "Let me prove my worth. I will tell you a truth only your masters know." The shade looked at Arek conspiratorially and said, "You have a great destiny ahead. You can *feel* it. The dragon sees a lie, he sees an end, but he is *wrong*. He does not see truth, yet believes it true."

"What is my master's mission?" he asked again, his patience wearing thin with the roundabout way the shade answered.

"The fact you mask the scent of magic is useful, but not the reason you were sent here. Your particular Talent for destroying enchantments is not a side effect." Piter trailed off, waiting for something.

"Piter, I'm losing my patience," Arek said. "Answer me!"

Then the shade smiled, and in that smile Arek could see true evil. It seemed to relish having this information. Slowly, like a snake unwinding, Piter whispered, "Sacrifice."

Arek stood up, shocked. "What do you mean?"

"They would need someone," smiled the shade, "whose touch disrupts magic." Piter stood and paced around the apprentice, his arms folded within his dark uniform. "Ask yourself, what happens to this person? It is quite a masterful plan."

Then, with perfect clarity, Master Silbane's words came to mind, Your Talent to disrupt magic makes you important for this mission. I wish it were different, but you and I are the best choice to go.

Arek shook his head and said weakly, "I don't believe you."

"How do you think you'll survive once your master finds the Gate? How will he protect you and accomplish what he must? You are the key to his success." Piter smiled and shrugged, then whispered, "You are *expendable.*"

Arek thought about it, slowly nodding, the shade's information filling the missing gaps, fitting things into place. Would the lore father hesitate to use Arek's power to safeguard the land? Would he balance the world's need against Arek's life?

He remembered Adept Giridian's gift of Tempest, and realized it wasn't worry or disappointment he had seen in everyone's eyes, it was *shame*. A cold anger settled into place at being used by those he trusted.

Piter leaned in and said, "It matters not. What matters now is you listen to your master's tale." The shade smiled again. "There is real danger coming. If you hesitate, you will die."

"What do I do?" he asked. A sudden chill ran through him, a cold feeling that spread out from the pit of his stomach. Where it went, a mindless worry began to grow.

Piter looked sidelong at Arek and whispered, "You must flee to Bara'cor. It is your only hope."

The reality of the danger he faced suddenly hit him so he did not question the obvious contradiction in Piter's advice, blurting instead, "How can I?" The shade prepared to leave and Arek was not ready for that just yet. As much as he hated him, Piter was someone he knew.

The shade replied, "Strike the Far'anthi Stone with a stone. It must shatter and when it does, the stone will glow blue." He paused, then fixed his gaze on Arek until he was sure the boy was listening, "It is very important you go through first. Your master must come second, so he may close the portal."

Piter's form started to fade, and Arek felt his vision begin to tunnel again. For an instant, he thought he heard the shade laugh. Then a final whisper, "Do not forget the Far'anthi Stone. You will need a rock to speak to a rock," and then he found himself snapped back, facing his master.

"—I'm going to try to activate the Far'anthi Stone. Once I do, we take our provisions and send you to the Isle."

Arek looked around, confused. His master stood in front of him, speaking. Of Piter, there was no sign.

"Pay attention, Apprentice! Your life rests in the balance!" the mage said.

Startled, Arek looked back at his master. "Home?" The fear still ran through him, making his master's words difficult to understand.

"Yes, Apprentice. You are going home. Do not talk to anyone upon your return. Wait for me, stay out of sight, and trust no one." He met his apprentice's eyes, to emphasize one last point. "If we do not meet within a day, gather supplies and leave the Isle."

"How will you get there?" Arek asked.

Silbane turned and grasped his young apprentice by both shoulders, but not unkindly. "Remember, I have Themun's Finder. Use your knowledge of the Isle and stay hidden. I will come for you after I finish this mission."

"What mission?"

"Arek, please, there is little time. The council made a mistake in sending you. You know our mission is to investigate Bara'cor. Before I do that, I would see you returned to a place safer than here."

Arek watched, unable to reconcile what he had just heard from Piter with his master's actions now. Someone was lying and Arek thought it was likely Piter. Still, something the shade said had sounded right, something deeper than logic.

Without another word, Silbane moved past his apprentice and made his way to the Far'anthi Stone. It sat there, dull and lifeless, a gray sphere of rock and granite. He motioned to Arek to gather his things.

Arek quickly secured Tempest on his back and grabbed some supplies. He then joined his master at the small tower's base. "Master, wait." He wanted to tell him of Piter's appearance, but something made him stop.

Silbane closed his eyes and held a hand over the Far'anthi Stone. Though Arek had never heard of one activated before, the principle of all magic was the same, intention bred action. Like reaching for a falling object, his intention bred action and stopped that fall.

Now Silbane reached for the Way, concentrating his considerable power on the Stone that could open the portal. Arek watched as his master focused his inner strength, his *chi,* into a tight knot of energy. He then let it flow from the Way to his inner body and through his arms, into his palms. As he did so, they began to glow a soft yellow. He then channeled his power into a tight point and struck the Far'anthi Stone.

Nothing happened, no sound, no outward indication that his master's strike had accomplished anything. The Stone looked the same, as dull gray and lifeless as ever. Arek was not sure what to do, but knew it was imperative he tell his master about the shade. He stepped closer and said, "Master, Piter appeared again." He nervously licked his lips, the fear in him growing.

Silbane whirled to face his apprentice, stunned. "What?" He looked around, afraid. "What did he say?"

"He told me a rock would speak to a rock . . . he told me to strike the Stone with a rock."

Silbane did not interrupt, a dumbfounded look on his face, so Arek continued, "He said the dragon would try to kill me, and that you . . . that I would be used to close the Gate."

Arek didn't know what else to say. He felt guilty saying anything at all but then saw the look on his master's face, like Adept Giridian's when he handed over Tempest. He suddenly knew what Piter told him might be true. "You planned this?" Arek asked, his voice a whisper.

"My boy," his master's voice fell, leaden with regret, "I would never let you come to harm. You must return to the Isle."

Arek met his master's eyes, but belief was far from truth. He wanted to believe the best, but saw something else. Piter claimed they intended to sacrifice him. As he thought back to the council and his master's actions he could see something underneath it all, an undercurrent of the same shame and guilt. He believed his master, but doubted him in the same breath.

Silbane stepped back, then spun around, his face to the sky. "Arek, get behind me and do not move!"

The boy scrambled over and drew Tempest, then stood between his master and the Far'anthi Stone. "I can fight with you!"

"Even with Tempest, you are not ready to face a dragon," Silbane warned him. "Stay back!"

Angry, Arek shook his head and insisted, "I can help!"

Just then, the great dragon appeared, a wing-shaped speck that quickly grew larger, and anything either Arek or Silbane might have said was forgotten.

Both stood alone next to the rocky outcropping of the desolate Far'anthi ruins, whose towers rose like stone fingers from the dunes, dead sentinels of a forgotten age.

* * * * *

Rai'stahn spread his great wings, riding the warm air with a mixture of anticipation and dread, emotions he seldom felt when thinking about the people of Edyn. For over a millennium he had lived amongst them, sometimes as hunter, sometimes as prey. He had served the role of guardian, tyrant, and god.

They lived eye blinks in time. They were physically and mentally weak. They warred amongst each other. In fact, he believed their only strength to be they bred like insects, covering the great Garden like a plague. Still, he chided himself, at times they had their uses.

Over the centuries, Rai'stahn had come to respect their bravery and their willingness to sacrifice themselves to a cause. Always trust one to pick the wrong side of an argument and gladly pay for it with his life, as Valarius had.

It was this fact that concerned him, for Silbane, a man he had come to respect more than most, was not likely to agree with what they must do next. Still, thought Rai'stahn with regret, even Silbane did not matter, regardless of how important he was to bringing about *unity.* The Conclave had made that clear.

The great dragon spotted the Far'anthi Tower below and spiraled down, changing in mid-flight into his knight form just before landing in the soft sand in a cloud of yellow and white grit. His great black wings, now man-sized, flapped the annoyance away, then folded closely along his armored back. He had tried his best to convince the adept his was the right course of action ... now, nothing would stop him from doing what he must.

He had landed near Silbane and hailed the master, who stood a few feet away, saying, "This is thy last chance to parley. Dost thou join me?"

Silbane walked over to stand beside the great dragon-knight, then looked at the tower. A small sigh escaped his lips, words unformed and unneeded.

Rai'stahn's golden gaze swept the tower's base, drinking in the smells and sights of this ancient place. There was no sign of the boy to the dragon's sensitive sight, but that was no surprise due to his peculiar masking. However, Rai'stahn had learned to look for him using his heat, and even *that* did not register. The fading warmth from the lee of the rocks near the sun side of the tower's base was the only thing to shine with a dull orange glow. Only then did he notice the slight shimmer in the air, which could only be an illusion blocking his heat sight.

The dragon spun, already knowing he had miscalculated the master's intentions. He felt rather than saw the three quick strikes to deep, vital points. With those strikes a numbness spread, but not to his limbs. His great fist lashed out, catching Silbane across the jaw and sending him spinning and tumbling away, but the damage had already been done. The numbness spread magically, and deadened his ability to change form. Such a strike would normally never have hurt Rai'stahn, except for the accursed drain he felt in the boy's presence.

Silbane slowly rose, shaking his head. He stumbled to his feet, his hands up in defense. "I would parley with thee, Rai'stahn."

"Parley, *after* thou attacks!" roared the dragon, more furious at himself for letting this man dupe him.

"Nay ... I only sought to level the field. You cannot change form, my lord. I have bound your *prana* points. While trapped in this form you have the same weaknesses that any man does."

"Thou underestimates me, Adept. I am still many times stronger than one of thy pathetic race." The dragon flexed his armored body, promising, "Thou art nothing but prey, and I hath hunted for centuries longer than thee hast lived."

"I have the Way," Silbane said to the great dragon-knight. "I do not wish to combat you, my lord, but I cannot allow you to bring harm to my apprentice." As he said this, the illusion between him and the Far'anthi vanished, and Rai'stahn could see the boy with his sword drawn, standing near the stones.

"Thou wouldst send him to Bara'cor?" the dragon gestured at the gray sphere, knowing it was keyed to only one destination. "Dost thou think this saves him? I can destroy the fortress as easily as I can kill the boy."

Silbane appeared confused, and said simply, "Not in this form." The effect on the dragon was instantaneous.

Rai'stahn took a step back, the master's plan coming to full clarity. He was correct ... in this form, the dragon's great powers were extremely limited. He *was* stronger and faster than a man, but his ability to breathe fire was much less powerful, and he could not destroy the walls with his crushing talons and whipping tail.

A smoldering hate began to grow, an anger that took the place of any regret or pity he might have had earlier. First, he would have to lull Silbane into trusting him.

"Wouldst thou measure the fate of the world against this one boy?" the dragon said softly, his tone soothing. "Before, this was not so."

Understand us, said a voice in Silbane's head. The master began to nod in agreement.

"Remember what thou witnessed," said Rai'stahn softly, and Silbane recalled the vision given to him by the dragon with perfect clarity.

Believe us.

Silbane shook his head, then looked at the dragon-knight. "Valarius is dead. That vision was from two hundred years ago."

"Thou did not See!" the dragon-knight exclaimed. "Thou saw only what thou wished, but thou did not *See.*" The dragon slowly circled the master. "Valarius meant to create something. What?"

"Valarius is dead!" His form outlined in yellow fire, and in an instant, the dragonlust was gone. Silbane said, "You said, 'stand steady.' Do the same."

Rai'stahn retreated a step, knowing the spell was broken. His eyes narrowed to slits and he took a different tact. "Thou came here willing to sacrifice the boy to finish thy mission. The lore father saw the danger. Even the council thought he would surely die."

"My mission includes preserving my apprentice," Silbane countered.

"There was never a mission!" The dragon now stood before the mage, his entire stance imploring the adept to listen. "Do not choose such a narrow path. Thou canst accomplish much with less bloodshed. Remember the vision."

Silbane looked at the dragon and knew he could not agree. Nothing the dragon said would change his mind. "I will not do that."

"Thou art a fool." Rai'stahn looked sidelong at Arek, his golden gaze calculating. "There is another way my *prana* can be released," he let out with a hiss.

"If you mean by my death, then you are correct." Silbane looked at the dragon-knight, then shook his head. "But now it is you who underestimates me, my lord. In this form, you may not prevail."

Rai'stahn began circling the mage, the power within him curling, yearning for release. "Thou dost not understand the nature of death. After my release, I will destroy this abomination *and* Bara'cor. It will ensure this land's safety. I will do what thou dost not have the courage to do."

"Be that as it may, you have not won yet."

Journal Entry 8

It is clear now I never understood Thoth. He spoke of these tiny motes, infinitesimal particles, and other fanciful things. It is a fact these particles exist, but they are not Aeris. They are the substance upon which Aeris are made.

What of us? Are we made of these things? I do not know, but our will seems to Shape them into purpose. In that manner, we are the impetus upon which these Aeris lords gain substance.

However, it is more than that. We bring them into being, incoherent at first, wisplike. They are like wishes or feelings, trapped on the psychic wind between worlds. They surround us at all times, ready to be shaped by our will.

Ritual, myth, ceremony, sacrifice, these seem to give them purpose, life. I walk in a world filled with the promise of the mythology of my people and the legends of all who ever lived.

It is a dangerous place, for I walk amongst Titans, and sometimes it seems, even ghosts.

A FINAL ILLUSION

When facing multiple opponents,

engage each briefly and move onto the next.

Do not linger, or the contest will become you

against many, instead of you fighting many

single engagements.

It is vital to understand the difference.

—Tir Combat Academy, *The Tactics of Victory*

Dragor moved quickly to his right and felt the strike pass inches from his head. He ducked low, tumbling effortlessly in a circle as kicks and punches flew around him, striking the empty air where he had just been or flashing harmlessly off his flameskin in a burst of amethyst. He blocked a strike to his midsection, his hand stinging as if he struck stone and moved into the attacker, preparing to inflict a shattering strike that would pierce armor and cripple the body beneath.

However, the team he faced had endlessly trained and fought together. They moved in unison, keeping him off balance so none faced the full brunt of his attack alone. For every one of his strikes, he had to deal with multiple attacks. As his counter was interrupted by another, he realized they would eventually win. Each had to expend less effort to engage him and eventually he would make a mistake. It was only a matter of time, and they knew it.

Still, they didn't act in *perfect* unison. One of them moved out of sync with the others. His speed and skill were not in doubt, but he moved like a professional just learning his part, a fraction of a moment behind the rest. Dragor worked himself carefully toward that man, the weak link, feinting a kick high then spinning around a counter strike.

Now! He aimed three strikes in rapid succession to the men to either side of the man out of step, then struck with full force as they were recovering. His opponent reacted as he should, moving into the strike and meeting it early rather than at the end where Dragor's power would be greatest. Their hands met in strike and block, like thunder and lightning, and Dragor's flameskin flashed purple in response.

Kisan! The shock of realization hit him and he fell back, stunned. The assassin he was facing was Kisan, disguised as one of them! His body went into defending himself almost automatically. Without realizing it, he began to move back to the wall, his mind racing to understand what was happening.

Kisan was disguised as one of them, but her strikes and blocks to Dragor were not aimed to cripple or damage. None of the others could see the difference, but Dragor knew Kisan's skill. Clearly, she was putting on a show to keep her identity secret from these men.

Infiltration! She must have disposed of one of these men and now sought to infiltrate them. To do that would take almost all of her power. She would need help, without giving away her disguise. Furthermore, mindspeaking would possibly alert them, if they could hear it, and waste valuable energy, something the adept could not afford.

Dragor spun in a circle and struck one of the six with a glancing blow using the outside of his wrist. Following that motion, he trapped that man's arm and pushed him into another. This opened a hole through which Kisan would have to come.

Sure enough, the master vaulted through like a black snake, striking with claws to Dragor's chest.

For Dragor's part, he let Kisan's strike through his flameskin, then pushed power through the physical contact created. Energy suffused the depleted master, and Dragor could almost hear her sigh of relief.

It was but a heartbeat between contact and counter-strike to break it, but it was enough. Dragor had given Kisan all the power he had remaining, enough to replenish her until she could regenerate on her own.

But there would be consequences.

Dragor now had nothing to draw upon, his reserves nearly gone. His flameskin guttered then failed, its purple flames dissipating into the night air, no longer able to tap his depleted stores enough to protect him. His training took hold and he continued to block and dodge the blows, but the end was coming more quickly. As if sensing it, the group pulled back, pausing as Dragor slumped against the stone wall at his back, his breath heaving.

"You've fought well," the leader said. "What is the point in throwing your life away?"

"You'll let me live if I surrender?" asked the dark-skinned adept between huge gulps of air he wished were part of his act.

"Perhaps." The leader looked to his left and nodded, but his hands quickly signaled a coded message to everyone.

"Try again," the adept challenged.

The leader shook his head, about to signal, when Dragor spoke again.

"Try again," he repeated and lurched forward in a clumsy, exhausted attack.

The leader cocked his head quizzically at this, but didn't signal. Four darts sprouted from Dragor's chest, their impact soundless. Dragor's body convulsed once, turning his attack into a spasm. His eyes rolled up to show whites and he bit through his tongue. As with the others, he fell to the ground, nerve toxin racing through his convulsing body, bringing with it tortured spasms and death.

* * * * *

The team watched this impassively, then one moved forward and punched a cross-shaped dagger into the base of Dragor's skull, severing the spine. He yanked the dagger out, while another inspected the body. Satisfied he was dead, they moved back.

The leader spun and kicked Tamlin in the chest, knocking him to the ground in a *whuff* of exhaled breath. "Explain," he said, his voice curt and demanding.

Kisan let the kick hit, barely feeling it, while she fought to assimilate Tamlin's memories. It was happening, but too slowly. She raised her eyes and came face to face with Dragor's dead gaze. He had saved her life at the cost of his own, and Kisan would not let that sacrifice be in vain.

She stood up slowly, shaking her head, hoping the leader would not choose now to review their combat protocol. They were still in enemy territory and it would be more prudent to make their exfiltration. This mission, regardless of any mistakes, had been carried out by professionals. He would know this was neither the time nor the place.

Kisan was right. The leader cursed in disgust, but motioned for them to move. They had achieved their objective and Themun Dreys was dead.

"We'll deal with this on the ship," he whispered.

Then he and the team took off at a sprint a normal man would have found impossible to follow. For Kisan it was easy and every moment that went by gave her more memories from Tamlin, more information about these men and their mission, and more reasons to kill them all.

* * * * *

Silence fell around Dragor's dead form. A light breeze blew, yet nothing stirred behind the fleeing forms. Then, as the assassins disappeared into the night, the very air rippled like the surface of a pond and the scene shifted. From the ripple stepped Themun Dreys, his staff glowing blue and white with power. Behind him came Giridian, Dragor, and the students, servants, and teachers of the Isle, a courtyard full of people who had been "killed."

Themun staggered forward as the illusion finally ended, only to be caught and lowered gently to the ground by the two other adepts. Never before had he pushed himself to such a breaking point and the price he knew would be great. Already he could feel his life-force ebbing as the Way consumed him. He knew he had little time. Unnoticed next to him, his runestaff dimmed and dissolved, flowing into the air and ground like smoke from a fire.

"Lore Father, it is enough," Giridian said. He looked about, hoping against all hope that it was not too late. The power necessary to cloud everyone's mind, to make the attackers believe they had been successful, was staggering. He surely had never known such a thing could even be done. Even now, seeing everyone safe and whole, he didn't seem to believe it. A gentle hand on his arm interrupted his thoughts.

Themun looked at him and said, "What of Kisan?"

"She was with them, in disguise," Dragor replied. "She means to infiltrate them, but she will need our help."

Giridian motioned to a servant and commanded, "Search the area. If Kisan is with them, she took the place of someone she either killed or incapacitated. *That* person is still here." The man nodded and raced off with two others.

Dragor looked at the lore father, his face screwed into a mask of misery. "Had you not cloaked me into the spell while I stood against the wall, what they saw would have been the truth."

"It was sloppy work," countered Themun, his voice growing fainter. "I had you repeating what you said."

Giridian knelt and laid a gentle hand on Themun's brow. "None were the wiser. Dragor speaks true. You felt the attack on Thera and acted to save us all. Can we not now do the same for you?"

Themun shook his head and replied, "Not Thera. Not the children with her. Their deaths saved us and she knew it not. What do you think she would think of my final solution?" His eyes closed and a tear crept its way down his face. "I wish I could have said goodbye to her."

Giridian shook his head, unable to speak.

Themun looked at the bear-like adept with a sad smile and said, "The damage done to me is too deep. When used like this, the Way exacts its toll. You must continue my work. It falls to you to lead these people now."

Giridian stared in shock. Then he shook his head. "You cannot be serious! It should be Silbane."

Themun only nodded, then leaned more heavily into Dragor's arms. "It should." The lore father smiled, then said, "But we don't always get to choose." He reached out his hand and took Giridian's own.

A small flash of blue passed between them and Giridian staggered back, as if struck a physical blow. His eyes widened in surprise and he whispered, "I never dreamed..." He sank to his haunches as the lore of the council and its knowledge passed from Themun to him. Though he could not use it yet, the lore would not die with Themun. It was the only thing the lore father cared about.

More of the Isle's inhabitants clustered around, some reaching out to touch him, as if they sensed the inevitable was coming. Dragor suppressed a sob and then implored, "You ... don't leave."

Themun's eyes cracked open and the barest of smiles showed through. "I will live, as long as I am remembered." The words came out as a whisper. The lore father reached up slowly and grasped Giridian's hand, pulling him close. He put his mouth directly next to the new lore father's ear and whispered, then his head fell back, exhausted by this last effort. His gaze locked onto Giridian's own, as if trying to convey the importance of what he had just said.

Then a single breath washed out of his broken body and turned into a soft breeze in the still night air. It caressed everyone standing there, lifting tired spirits, cleansing souls, drying tear-filled eyes, and bringing with it the smell of honeysuckle and pine. It swirled about them gently, then slowly faded away. Themun Dreys, Lore Father of the Council of Adepts, passed on.

* * * * *

Giridian sat back, unable to believe it. He looked at Dragor, who knelt beside him, speechless.

The servants sent to retrieve the assassin's body stood some distance away. Then one came forward hesitantly and tapped Dragor on the shoulder, not wanting to interrupt. Though they were shaken by the death of their leader, something still compelled them to act.

Dragor looked up and the man pointed to the body left by Kisan. "You need to look at this."

Dragor stood slowly, carefully shifting the lore father's body to Giridian. The picture of Themun's head cupped on Giridian's lap would be forever burned into his mind. He then turned and made his way numbly over to the still form of the dead assassin. It had taken six men to drag the body over to them.

Behind him, Giridian looked down at the lore father and said, "What do I do?"

He was interrupted a moment later when Dragor came to stand near him. His eyes, red-rimmed, met the new lore father's gaze. "I cannot believe it."

"I know," Giridian replied. "How can he be gone?"

Dragor laid a gentle hand on Giridian's shoulder and said, "No, the man ... the assassin ..." He took a deep breath and said, "He's dwarven."

Duel in the Wastes

Strike your opponent's face,

and he remembers you

only when he looks in a mirror.

Break his ribs, and he remembers you

every time he breathes.

—*Davyd Dreys, Notes to my Sons*

Silbane saw his opening, and in the space between heartbeats he shot forward, his hand straight and rigid, aimed at a small point on the dragon's neck. It was a chink in the armor, no more than a finger's width across. Given the form Rai'stahn was trapped in, Silbane hoped a strike to this spot would be deadly. He knew he only had a few chances before the dragon's natural strength and speed overcame him, so he struck to kill.

But Rai'stahn was not fooled. He had battled creatures great and small over the centuries and his instincts were those of a true predator. He shifted imperceptibly to his right so Silbane's attack went just over his left shoulder, then struck with an armored fist to the master's midsection.

The strike detonated against Silbane's magical shielding, the impact a flash of pure yellow and white. Silbane was hurled backward, digging a long, straight furrow into the soft sand. The flameskin had taken the brunt of the blow, but the mage could feel pain where some of its power had bled through. He levered himself up, knowing he'd have to rise quickly and move if he was to survive.

* * * * *

Arek couldn't believe what he was seeing and hearing. He could feel the dragon's power as if it were a tangible thing. A strange hunger rose within him, a blackness that seemed to leak from his soul. He stood frozen, unable to move, but when the dragon spun and breathed fire at him, he reacted instantly. A wave of red-orange flame lit the night, painting the sand in front of the dragon yellow. It billowed forth, enveloping the young mage.

Arek crossed his arms and leaned into the fire, bringing Tempest to bear. The sword, still quiescent, did nothing. It stood dull and lifeless, yet the dragon's fire parted before Arek. It washed around him like a stream around a rock. He leaned into the blast, hoping to withstand it, but the air around him detonated with force, and he felt himself thrown backward.

He rolled, scrambling on all fours to get back into a tactical position, unable to believe the flames had not touched him. He could feel hot breath on his neck, could almost sense the claws about to rend his throat and rip the flesh from his back. A mindless urgency filled him and without thinking, he spun and struck with Tempest, but his sword cut through empty air. The dragon was nowhere near him.

Confusion ran across his features, for he was sure the dragon had been right behind him, and he began to suspect something more was happening. He had never misjudged things in combat before. What power did the dragon use? Then he saw Rai'stahn, still some distance away, coming toward him.

The dragon-knight hunched forward like an animal stalking his prey. "Thou art outclassed in this contest, boy. Stop fighting and I will make thine end quick and painless." On those words Rai'stahn moved in a blur, his fanged teeth bared.

Arek didn't hesitate, but moved quickly to his left, sword to his opponent. He circled till the Far'anthi Stone lay behind him, some few feet away. He would make his stand here, he thought, bolstering himself for the inevitable clash.

* * * * *

Silbane watched Arek circle and did not waste another moment. He leapt up and over the dragon, landing lightly between Rai'stahn and his apprentice. He struck twice. He could see the resulting grunt of pain, but had no time to enjoy it.

The dragon swatted the mage with the edge of an outstretched wing, sweeping through him like an enormous black blade.

Again, Silbane's flameskin saved him, flashing like sunlight with the force of the blow it turned. Silbane found himself on his back. *The power!* Even the small portion of what blasted through his protective spell damaged him greatly. He could feel his strength ebbing and tasted salty blood in his mouth. If this was Rai'stahn "weakened," Silbane couldn't imagine facing him at full strength.

Before he could rise, Silbane felt the dragon grab him by his head and pick him up. An armored fist struck his flameskin again, right in front of his face, and the force of the blow staggered him. His vision went gray, then slowly began to return, along with a ringing in his ears. He found himself sitting up some ten feet away and didn't remember how he got there.

* * * * *

For his part, Arek could think of nothing but what the shade of Piter had said. He spun and snatched up a rock as Silbane fell. With a preternatural burst of speed, Arek ran the few steps left to the Far'anthi. He thought he heard laughter again, but focused completely on the Stone. Activating it was their only chance.

Before Rai'stahn or Silbane could intervene, Arek took the rock and swung it in a tight arc, striking the Stone. To his astonishment, it gonged like a bell and began to glow a soft blue. Piter had told the truth, he realized with dismay. He had also said that Arek must be first through the portal.

Its surface became smooth, lit from within like a blue-white star. Arek could see scenes shift beneath, those of a fortress in the desert, its black and gold pennons snapping from the castle walls in the breeze. Some of the images were of outer walls, others of what looked to be the interior of a chamber, dark and unoccupied. It was Bara'cor, and he knew this portal was their only hope.

* * * * *

Silbane bolted forward, again into the dragon's path. He struck out, his aim guided by years of experience. Though half blinded, he used the small nuances of position and breathing to target the vital areas on the armored body of the knight. His fist hit Rai'stahn's chest, knocking him backward and up. Silbane vaulted quickly to his feet and leapt past the dragon, reaching for his apprentice.

"Arek, wait!"

The boy never looked back. He stood transfixed by the glowing blue orb, and before Silbane could do anything, Arek reached out with his gloved hand and touched it. In a black and blue flash, he disappeared. Silbane fell inches from where his apprentice had been, his hand closing on nothing but sand.

As Arek's form vanished, the stone seemed to collapse in his passing. A black hole appeared within, spreading cracks of power. The ground shuddered, as if protesting something unnatural. Before either the dragon or the master could react, the stone imploded, drawing into itself and disintegrating into dust.

"Fool!" Rai'stahn roared. "Dost thee see his power now?"

Silbane ignored him and fumbled for the Finder around his neck, preparing to crush it.

The dragon knew what the master planned and moved with blurring speed. He billowed out fire to hide his attack, then emerged from the flames, catching Silbane with an armored foot to the head.

The kick overcame Silbane's flameskin, which dissipated in a flash of argent fire. The force of the blow knocked him away from the dragon like a puppet. The Finder fell from his limp grasp.

His protection was gone, destroyed, having absorbed most of the dragon's blow. It was the only reason Silbane still lived. The next strike would kill him and both he and Rai'stahn knew it.

"Thou art beaten. Remove the locks on my *prana* and I wilt allow thee to live." The dragon moved forward and stood over the prone master, within easy killing distance. Nothing Silbane did would stop the dragon now.

"And what of my apprentice? Do you still intend on killing him?" the mage spat, blood dripping from his nose and ears. If he could just clear his head, if he could just stand up . . .

"I wilt agree—"

The dragon stopped, his eyes widening in shock. Silbane looked up through bruised eyes to see the dragon-knight caught in mid-sentence, trying to say something.

The knight's mouth moved, but only a strange gurgling sound issued forth. A trembling hand rose, picking at the air as if trying to grasp something from behind his massive head. He took a staggering step forward, then fell face down into the desert dune, next to the surprised master.

An arrow protruded from the base of the dragon-knight's skull, its dark fletching and shaft almost invisible in the night. A pool of blood, almost black under the moonlight, began soaking into the sand below Rai'stahn's head.

"This one's alive," a voice said in guttural Altanese.

Silbane turned to look in the direction of the voice. A booted foot smashed into his face, breaking his nose and burying his head halfway into the sand.

"The u'zar wants prisoners," said another, without much interest. Silbane tried feebly to move, but the heel of that boot came down again, twice, and a third time. Each strike smashing into his face and head, breaking bone and cutting flesh.

The last thought Silbane had was that it wasn't fair, a master of combat beaten to death, then his world went mercifully black.

INTO BARA'COR

Know your weapon intimately:

the feel of the grip in your hands,

the press of the guard to your thumb,

the back of the blade to block,

the keen edge at the cut,

and the point that ends your opponent's life.

You and your weapon are one.

—*Kensei Tsao, The Book of Blades*

Yetteje shrugged off Niall's hand as they walked down the stairwell.

Fairly certain he knew what she was thinking, Niall said, "I know I can't understand."

"No, you can't," Yetteje cut him off. "Just drop it. I don't feel like talking."

"You can't have been serious about going into the camp," said Niall, ignoring his friend's request. "I mean, my father wouldn't even let *me* serve on the wall." This last part came out with a trace of annoyance.

Tej spun and shoved Niall against a wall. "Do you think playing soldier is what's important? Is that what you really want to say right now?" She met his eyes with anger in her own. "Imagine your whole family dead." She pushed him against the wall again and stepped back, shaking her head. "It's my choice."

Niall stood, stunned a bit by Yetteje's response, but a part of him realized he must have sounded selfish talking about himself. He put up a hand to mollify her and said, "Going into that camp with Ash is certain death."

"You think I care?" Tej asked in a small voice. She looked her cousin in the eye, then turned and continued down the stairwell.

Alyx moved forward and put a restraining hand on the prince's shoulder. "Leave it. You won't convince her of anything right now."

The stairwell descended back into the fortress proper, away from the main walls and combat areas. As they made their way to the interior, they saw fewer and fewer people, the majority of Bara'cor shuttling between the inner wall and the forward stations.

This hallway led straight down into the lower halls, then over to the guest rooms. Between them and their destination lay an adjunct council chamber, used for meetings with lesser dignitaries.

Their hallway spilled out onto a large circular platform, with an octagonal opening to the council chamber on one side. On the other side was an opening in the floor, the stairwell that continued down to the lower halls.

Niall and Tej had just exited the hallway when a blue flash erupted from the council chamber. Because of the siege and with no council in session, this level was deserted, and they both realized just how empty this part of the castle was.

Alyx motioned for Tej and Niall to stop and made a silencing gesture. That flash had been intense and very real. She leaned in close to the guard behind her and told him to get help. A signal with her eyes gave the other guard his orders: flank left. She then met the prince and Tej's wide-eyed stare and whispered, "Stay behind me."

They nodded in answer, then silently, the remaining three drew their swords. The guard still with them moved around and to the left of the entrance.

Niall watched him, then began to do the same, his eyes wide. Cold fear made his grasp weak and his palms clammy. He couldn't get a good grip on his blade. Then something sounded like it was coming toward the entrance they now surrounded.

They didn't have long to wait. From inside the great octagonal doors poked a blond-haired head. The face was intense, with pale blue eyes that shone with intelligence. He was dressed in a dark, armored leather jerkin and breeches, functional without adding bulk. With a start, Niall realized this intruder was close to the same age as himself or Yetteje.

Alyx was the first to move. "Stay where you are," she said, with her sword pointed directly at the boy's face.

The boy's eyes tracked the weapon for a moment, then drank in the rest of his surroundings as if dismissing her as a threat. That, Niall thought, was his first mistake. Emboldened by the sergeant's courage, he moved into view and flanked the doorway, his weapon held low and in front of him.

"You'd be wise to listen . . . Who are you?" Niall asked.

"Intruder!" the guard flanking the door yelled.

Before the word had echoed up the hallway, the boy exploded into action. A liquid silver sword appeared in his hands and he moved with blurring speed. He crossed the distance to the guard before he could draw another breath.

The guard brought his weapon up, but the boy slapped it aside like an afterthought and slammed the pommel of his weapon into the man's face. A heartbeat later he struck with an elbow followed by an open palm to the guard's stomach. The air whooshed out of him and the guard sank unconscious to the floor. Niall had never seen anyone move so fast.

The sergeant was already in motion, moving quickly to counter any killing stroke the boy might level at the unconscious guard. She struck at the back of the boy's head, her blade almost whistling as it cut through the air.

The boy ducked under the blade and punched her in the face, then spun and caught her in the forehead with the flat of his blade. The blade made a dull *thwack* and snapped Alyx's head back. She staggered from the blow, her equilibrium gone.

As Niall watched, dumbfounded, the boy stepped in and took the sword out of the sergeant's dazed grasp, then almost nonchalantly punched her in her helm with her own sword's pommel.

Alyx dropped as if poleaxed and the boy tossed her own sword onto her unconscious body before turning to face Tej, who yelled back to Niall, "Attack at the same time!"

She launched herself at the intruder, attacking with a flurry of strikes aimed at his head and midsection. Tej had been well trained; her strikes came out fast and true, a dance of steel that should have scored more than once with first blood. To her detriment she attacked alone, as Niall stood by and watched, paralyzed.

To Niall's amazement, the boy blocked everything thrown at him, his breathing even. On the last strike, the boy countered with a sharp knee to Yetteje's stomach, then a ridge hand to her forehead.

Before she could recover, the boy spun in place and kicked her with a booted heel to her jaw. Niall watched Tej knocked senseless. She fell like a ragdoll, her eyes rolling into the back of her head.

The boy continued his spin, landing and facing Niall with his weapon pointed on a spot directly between the young prince's eyes. As their gazes met, Niall knew he had hesitated too long and lost a critical advantage. Worse, one look at Tej's crumpled form and he knew he had also failed his cousin.

Niall started to back up, but the boy moved again with that blurring speed. He raised his weapon, hoping to block, but met empty air. He then felt the stiff steel side of the boy's weapon batter him across the chest. He lurched forward and felt a sharp blow and an explosion of pain to the back of his head.

His vision blackened and he fell forward, but strangely, could still hear. He heard running feet in the hallway and Ash's voice yelling, "Halt!" Then a final strike with what felt like a booted heel crashed into his head and he felt no more.

* * * * *

Ash surveyed the scene before him. The guard had reached them even as he heard the cry for help. They had immediately raced down the stairwell and into the hallway, only to find Alyx, Niall, Tej, and the remaining guard down, perhaps dead. The intruder didn't look like a nomad, but that meant nothing. They could have hired an assassin to enter the fortress and Ash was taking no chances.

He moved forward, his sword held in a relaxed grip. Yetteje was nearest, so Ash moved slowly over to the princess. Without taking his eyes off the intruder, he listened and heard the faint sound of Tej's breathing. At least the girl's alive, he thought with relief. He turned his full attention to the would-be assassin and realized for the first time that he was a boy, no older than Niall himself.

"Who are you?" Ash demanded. He raised an open hand and said, "Put down your weapon and we can talk."

The boy put his sword point on the back of Niall's unconscious head. The meaning was clear.

"Spill the blood of the crowned prince and yours will surely follow," promised the armsmark.

The boy looked down at Niall's prostrate form in shock, and Ash used that moment of distraction to attack.

He moved in, aiming for the boy's sword arm, hoping to disarm him quickly. But the boy reacted with the reflexes of a snake. Instead of jerking his hand away, he lowered his shoulder and moved into Ash, getting under the blow and striking the armsmark in the chest. The boy was good, thought Ash, *very good.*

The blow wasn't strong, but it knocked the armsmark back and off balance. The boy followed with a short heel kick to the armsmark's forward shin. This locked Ash's knee backward painfully, but Ash knew what was coming next.

He aimed three lightning-quick strikes to the boy's head, only to see all three blocked and turned. Before the boy could complete his counter attack with a finishing strike, the armsmark went with the pain in his forward knee and twisted to one side, falling to the ground and rolling.

The liquid silver blade of the boy swished through empty air and then turned, point down. As he rolled, he saw the boy's sword point bury itself into the space his head had just occupied.

Ash continued his motion and used his legs to trap the boy's in a scissor hold. The boy fell facedown to the floor, pinned under Ash's weight and immobilized by his crisscrossed legs. Ash never hesitated, bringing his elbow into a short, brutal arc that came down hard on the back of the boy's head, smashing it to the stone floor.

He felt the boy go limp and quickly pushed his sword away, then moved over to check the prince. Praise the Lady, he thought, Niall was alive. He then made his way over to Alyx. She, too, lived. Something was strange. An assassin who did not kill? Ash was struck by the odds of having all of them survive an encounter with someone of this boy's skill.

He turned his attention back to the intruder, who was unconscious and except for the painful bruise he'd likely have on his head, unharmed. This boy had training—real training from someone who knew how to fight and how to kill. He remembered the boy's concentration, his breathing. So why were they still alive? Something didn't fit, and Ash didn't like unsolved puzzles, especially those that pointed to luck as the answer.

Ash looked at the clothes and . . . the weapon. It was silver, with a green gem set in the pommel. Silver runes danced down its keen edges. For a moment, time seemed to slow and Ash felt a strange stirring within him. The sword was beautiful, more beautiful than any he had ever seen. Then, almost as a whisper, Ash thought he heard the word, *beloved.*

He stood transfixed, the echo of her voice in his head. Then a guard came and placed a hand on his arm, and he snapped back to the here and now, the voice and the stirring forgotten.

"Are you injured, sir?" the guard inquired, concerned. Many men didn't notice wounds in battle that later proved deadly.

Ash ignored him, his mind turning over the facts. With that training, the boy could be a very highly paid agent. The question was, whose? Still, doubt surfaced when Ash considered his age. Who would train a child to this level of expertise, and more importantly, why? Most of what the boy wore seemed to be close-fitting armor designed for unimpaired movement. It was of a style Ash didn't recognize, but it was definitely *not* nomadic.

Motioning to the guards he said, "Search him and secure his items, then take him to a cell. Bind him there and report to the Firstmark." The guard gestured to his compatriots, who moved quickly to obey the order. Ash winced as he put weight on his injured knee and added, "And send a medic. We're all going to need one."

Journal Entry 9

My sense of time is gone. I may have been here for weeks, or months, it makes no difference, for it all feels like an eternity. I cannot return through the Gate. Betrayed by dragons is the same as forgotten. What can I do, except endure?

The young Aeris (I have given up on calling them "infinitesimal particles" it is too much to write, forgive me) permeate the planes and do not need the rifts. They suffuse all things, incoherent power from undirected thoughts and dreams. I envy their freedom.

I know I create them, but what if everyone does? They do not seem to be able to manifest themselves except through the will of others. They are easy fodder for use by our Way, but in that action lies our undoing. I burn through them easily to create fire, home, and hearth. A part of me enjoys it. In my own way, I free them too.

I have come to understand another truth, something I did not understand when I stood before Rai'kesh. There exist other beings, Aeris already given shape, not by one person's vision or will, but instead by our entire people's beliefs.

Given no impedance, these Aeris Lords will run amok, for they are nothing less than children demanding whatever they want, with the power to enforce it. Lilyth is one of these, and our world suffers from her attention. I cannot afford to open more rifts, they are already too numerous. In fact, I wonder if I even have the power to open a rift from here.

If every belief from our world has given life to a god or goddess, I wonder how, or even if, these Aeris Lords can be defeated . . .

THE SCYTHE

When your opponent's intention is in doubt,

watch his eyes,

for the eyes are the windows to his soul.

—*Kensei Shun, The Book of Shields*

Silbane awoke suffocating, his nostrils clogged. Blowing hard caused chunks of dried blood to come free, but with that came a gush of warm, fresh blood and pain. Still, his breathing became easier. He spat coppery blood out, imagining how gruesome he must look, but thankful to be alive to feel anything at all. Then, he took stock of his surroundings and realized he sat, secured to a pole in a tent, on hard earth. Around him were various instruments of war, razor spears and barbed whips, coiled and ready, offering any willing hand the release of their deadly intent.

"You look rested."

Silbane started at the voice, coming from just outside of his field of view. Straining, he turned to identify the speaker, then cursed with pain as his neck and jaw protested. It was clear his face had borne the brunt of that last nomad's attack, and it was likely the damage was not just superficial. Silbane centered his thoughts, reaching for the Way to heal himself. Nothing happened.

"That won't work." Soft footsteps followed and red robes slowly came into view. They belonged to a tall man, striking because of his calm demeanor and confidence. Most of all, the man projected *power*. "I've blocked you. Surprisingly, not very difficult," the man continued. He stooped to come eye to eye with his captive and his pale gaze narrowed, but he said nothing else.

Silbane croaked through a bruised and parched throat, "Who . . . ?"

The man moved forward and offered a few drops of water from a small skin. Then, as the mage drank, he carefully offered more. Silbane could feel strength flow back into him as the cool water eased his wounded throat, but that moisture brought with it a fit of coughing that wracked his chest. Fresh blood flowed again, and with it more chunks of dried grit and blood. Silbane spat again, clearing his mouth, then he looked back up.

For his part, the man looked unperturbed. He smiled and offered a bit more water, then said in a soft voice, "I am the Scythe. Like the reaper's tool, I ascend those found worthy, or wanting." His head tilted to one side, as if he looked past Silbane and at something else. "I judge you worthy, but I am curious."

Silbane winced at the new pains he felt from renewed circulation, but his voice was stronger with the water. "I owe you my life." It was not a question, but a statement of fact mixed with an involuntary undercurrent of thanks.

The man nodded, settling back onto a waiting stool. "I would speak with you plainly. I have ways of finding out what I want, but if you cooperate, I promise things will go more comfortably." When Silbane did not respond, the man continued, "I will tell you I side with the Way."

The man settled back, as if they sat across from each other in the comfort of a home. "Shall we begin?" he said simply. "You are Silbane Darius Petracles, noble born of House Petracles, now a master in an order of monks residing on an isle in the Shattered Sea. I won't go into all the boring details, but I know where you're from and all the inconsequential shames anyone has after a life as long as yours." The man paused, then added, "You are a *good* man. What I don't know is, why?"

Silbane did not say a word, not trusting himself to speak. This man seemed to know too much already.

"You see, my knowledge is incomplete. For the past century, the people of Edyn, people of *power*, have been preparing for the Gate of Lilyth to appear. Why do you come only now, and who are your companions?"

"Companions?" Silbane asked innocently, spitting out more blood.

The man leaned forward and smiled, but the smile never reached his eyes. "Really? The camp you made was for two people. I could assume it was for you and your unfortunate friend." The man gestured to the left and when Silbane turned his head, he was shocked to silence. "Except that while I healed you, in your delirium you emphatically mentioned someone named Arek. You were quite insistent he needed protection. You seemed almost . . . ashamed."

Silbane's eyes were locked on the space behind the red-robed man. There was Rai'stahn, upright, nailed to a circle of iron and crucified. He hung limp, the arrow still sticking out from the back of his head. Silbane drew a shuddering breath and quickly looked away.

From the way his head lay canted at an unnatural angle, he could tell Rai'stahn's neck was broken. Despair washed through him at the great dragon's death, if for no other reason than the loss it implied. Rai'stahn and his kind were ancient, representing a knowledge of the world most races had yet to learn.

It was true they had faced each other in combat and he knew death would have been the outcome for one of them. Still, he believed Rai'stahn had withheld for the same reasons he had, because death may not have been the only answer.

Now the great dragon had been felled by a nomad arrow, an injury impossible except for the weakening he claimed resulted from his apprentice. Another testament to the idea that Arek's magical nullification was more powerful than he had suspected.

Could Rai'stahn have been right? Could the world really lie in the balance over Arek? He was stuck here now, and his apprentice was gone, lost to whatever destination the Far'anthi had sent him, likely Bara'cor.

Further complicating things was this person, who seemed connected to the Way. Likely this was the person the lore father had sensed, the helper of the nomads. Silbane had found him, but now sat helpless and captured. The master felt his mission slipping to failure, before it even started.

"It's quite simple," Scythe said, interrupting Silbane's thoughts. He leaned in, his dark red robes closing about him like wings, and asked in a soft voice, "Who is Arek?"

CAPTURED

Fear is the eager substitute

for inexperience,

and safety the forgiving mother it runs to.

—*Altan proverb*

H e's been trained, of that there's no doubt," remarked the armsmark. "Whoever did it knew what they were doing."

Jebida looked at his second-in-command. He didn't need to ask again to know Ash was sure. "How did he get in?"

Ash shook his head and replied, "No idea. Alyx sent one of the guards with Niall and the princess to come for help. We also heard their cries from outside the chambers in the west hallway, but how this boy entered is a mystery."

"What did he have on him?"

Ash motioned to a desk where all of the intruder's belongings lay. "Aside from the sword, some supplies and food . . . the kinds of things I'd take on a scouting mission." Ash looked at the cell where the prisoner now lay, chained and unconscious. "I'm still trying to figure out why."

"Why he's here?" asked the firstmark.

"Why any of them are still alive."

"You're serious?" the firstmark asked. "Clearly you arrived in time."

"No," Ash stated, "I didn't. He could have killed all of them and still faced me. He's *that* good."

The firstmark moved closer to the bars and looked in on their occupant. "How old do you think he his? Can't be over sixteen or seventeen summers."

Ash joined his firstmark and said, "Yes, and that is even more peculiar. For someone to have his level of skill, he would have had to begin training as soon as he could hold a blade." The armsmark looked sidelong at his commander. "Who trains like *that* anymore?"

The firstmark gave a short laugh. "You ask that with a straight face? As I recall, you started your training in much the same way."

"Yes, but there are very few in the world who grew up as I did." He looked back at the unconscious form, a hint of sadness in his eyes. "Very few."

Behind them, the guards came smartly to attention as the king entered. He acknowledged them and moved over to his two senior commanders. "This is the assassin?"

"We're not sure who he is, sire," replied Ash, carefully. There was more here than met the eye, in his opinion. In that moment he felt something familiar, like a smell that elicited a memory, but it did not linger long enough to recall. The colors silver and green seemed important, somehow.

"He almost took my son, if it were not for you . . ." the king began, startling the armsmark out of his reverie.

Ash held up a forestalling hand. "I didn't save Niall. This kid just didn't kill him. Frankly, when he realized his blade rested on the prince, he looked shocked. What assassin doesn't know his own target?"

The king moved closer to the bars and looked in on the unconscious form for the first time. The king drew a sharp breath, "Jebida, look at him."

The two commanders moved up and peered in with the king. "What do you want us to look at?" asked Ash.

The king whispered, "At *him.*"

The armsmark shook his head and looked at the firstmark. Jebida looked at the face, youthful, his visage line free, with blond hair—"By the Lady!" he said.

"You see it too?" the king asked.

Jebida nodded, his eyes never leaving the boy's face. He had not taken a close look at the prisoner until the king mentioned it. "He's almost exact..." His voice trailed off as his eyes went back years.

Ash turned now in confusion to the king. "Exact what? What are you two talking about?"

The king stepped back from the bars, his mind in deep contemplation. He held up a hand to forestall more questions and paced away from the cell. Motioning to the other two to join him, he looked at the armsmark and said, "Ash, you are too young to remember, but that boy looks like someone we know. Someone we know very well."

"Who?" asked the armsmark, more curious now than ever.

Bernal turned is gaze to Jebida and a moment passed as the firstmark silently confirmed the king's observation. Then he turned back to Ash and said in a low voice, "He looks like me at that age."

Ash looked at both men, then smiled at what he thought was a joke. "You are jesting. I'm not—"

"That boy looks like Bernal," Jebida interrupted, "as if they were brothers."

Ash spread his arms. "To what purpose? Are you saying he's actually *related* to you?"

The king's eyes remained hard as slate. "Perhaps Niall wasn't the target." He looked at both his men and the next words that came from his mouth sounded forced. "I need to know who he is and why he's here. And if there's a way for the nomads to get in, we need to know that too." Though he didn't say it, the words seemed to carry another message, one the firstmark immediately understood.

"Are you sure? It will likely kill him," Jebida said.

"I can't wager the safety of everyone in the fortress for this one boy. Do what's necessary."

Ash realized what the king meant and stepped forward, hoping to intervene. "Sire, perhaps if I spoke with him?"

"And said what? 'Please tell us the truth?' You and I know there is only one way, and he chose this possibility for himself when he chose to sneak in here. We must know everything he knows." Bernal looked away from the two, clearly not liking his decision, but in this his will was firm.

Jebida said, "I will see to it and report back to you, sire."

The king nodded woodenly then excused himself. As he left, the firstmark looked to his second and said, "I don't know whom to feel worse for, the king or this boy."

Ash motioned to the pale blond head of their prisoner and said, "Feel worse for him . . . definitely for him."

DEBRIEFING

Do not concern yourself with the style

of fighting you face.

Masters rely on the same techniques,

forged and tested in the crucible of combat.

But men vary greatly in skill.

—*Tir Combat Academy, The Tactics of Victory*

A fist smacked into the oak table, the broad knuckles leaving dents in the hard wood. "Five darts should have gone into that last adept! I counted four. You know the drill, no mistakes, and no excuses." The leader did not look happy, nor did the others on the team. "Any answer?"

Kisan looked at the leader, her disguise as Tamlin complete, the language of these men assimilated from the memories of the man she had killed. She bent her tongue around the strange speech, but found it easier to do if she didn't think about it. "Something . . . that last fighter did . . ." She let her voice trail off lamely, hoping they would complete the thought.

The leader backhanded her, the shock of the strike more surprising than painful. Kisan reeled back convincingly, falling over her chair and onto the pitching deck of the small ready room.

They had assembled here after a retreat that took them through woods to a cliff overlooking water. There Kisan watched as the leader signaled with a small white gem, answered by a similar flash from the prow of a long, black shape, just offshore.

Having fixed their destination, all dived off the cliff and into the inky waters below. They had made it to the waiting boat quickly and shed their masks. Kisan realized with a start that the glowing "eyes" were actually cleverly placed lenses within each mask. She assumed they worked much the same as using the Way to enhance her own vision. She adjusted her illusion to compensate, happy to discover these men were less magical than she had feared, but remained vigilant. They had already proven capable and deadly.

She followed the team into the ship, trying desperately to understand more of Tamlin and these men. She knew enough now to know they referred to each other by number, not name, in case of capture. In fact, she doubted if Tamlin had known their real names. The only exception was the leader, whom they called, Prime instead of One.

"Slug-brained and pitiful," Prime accused with a jab of a finger. "Get your act together, *mudknife.*" He turned away in disgust and left the small cabin, slamming the door shut behind him, though Kisan wasn't sure if it was due to the man's anger or the natural back and forth of the boat's motion.

"Good job," laughed one of the men sarcastically. "Lucky we drew you for this rotation."

Kisan picked her way to her feet carefully and righted the chair. She didn't quite understand what he meant so instead said, "You saw those adepts. That last one did something."

Another, *Two,* Tamlin's memory furnished, stepped up and said, "That why your voice sounds funny?" The man's eyes narrowed, "Or maybe that's why you can't follow signals a cadet would know?"

Kisan realized she had never heard Tamlin's natural voice. Quickly she fished through the memories, which were coming more easily to her and listened to the man whose life she had taken and now imitated. A small exertion of the Way fixed that last detail and Kisan now spoke with the lower pitched voice she had heard in Tamlin's mind. "More like the backhand I just took to the throat."

Two's eyes bored into Kisan's, then he let loose a harrumph of disgust. They had accomplished their mission and their target was dead. He shook his head though at the ineptitude, then addressed Three with a jerk of his thumb in Kisan's direction, "Get him squared away." Not waiting for a reply, Two made his way out, following his leader.

There was a silent pause, then the entire room seemed to take a collective sigh of relief. Kisan realized the rest had not shared their leader's ire, and frankly had only been worried the anger at her would spill over to them, resulting in extra duties or worse.

As if to confirm this, the one she knew as Three came forward and clapped her on the shoulder saying, "First couple of times out is always tough, but you know the signal if you're not steady and ready."

And suddenly she did, a quick slash through her wrist. Her body mimicked the motion automatically as another of Tamlin's memories fell into place. Tamlin would have made that sign the moment the leader signaled for everyone's status, standard practice for this team.

As memories began to assimilate, Kisan constructed a more complete perspective on the discipline of these men, which rivaled that of her own training on the Isle. At first, she assumed they had gained their abilities through the Way. She could have accepted that.

It was more difficult to admit that while they *were* magically imbued, much of their profound lethality grew from simple hard training and their enormous strength, which seemed a natural part of their bodies. Clearly, if someone desired to hire highly trained assassins, they could do no better than this group.

Her mind wandered back to the fight with Dragor. Had Kisan answered Prime correctly during that engagement, she'd have been ordered to a support role. Prime had reacted to the simple fact that "Tamlin" had endangered the team. Not only did he not signal his inability to help, but by continuing to fight, had hindered everyone else.

In truth, Kisan did not care. She had intentionally tried to thwart their efforts to kill Dragor without giving herself away. However, as Tamlin's memories became more available, she saw the leader would not allow this again. Prime would kill Tamlin, a fact that neither she nor the team doubted.

Still, she grieved the loss of Dragor. She had not felt his death the way she had Thera's, but this was not surprising. Dragor was comparatively young in the Way, certainly not as powerful. Still, her friend had given his life so Kisan could be here, now. She meant to make herself worthy of that sacrifice.

Frankly, despite their discipline and training, she knew she had little to fear from these men physically. Her only fear was she would expose herself and lose the opportunity to trace them back to the person who gave the order to attack the Isle. Whoever *that* was, would pay with their life for Dragor, Thera, and any others who had died on the Isle.

Three nodded, interrupting her thoughts and echoing Kisan's certainty about Prime, "Get it right though, or there won't be a next time."

As he spoke, Four and Five went to their lockers and began taking off their equipment, expertly storing them with practiced ease. As they stripped off weapons and small pieces of ingeniously placed armor, Kisan could see muscles and sinew ripple. She also noticed something else, something significant. These men were not *normal.*

They were too big and disproportioned to be of her race. They stood taller, their torsos wider, with forearms and legs as thick as logs, and hands that looked suitable to crush stone. She was too pragmatic to be embarrassed by their nakedness. Instead, she drank in the details, unconsciously fixing her own illusion to match their physical features. Kisan didn't recognize them, but searched Tamlin's memories.

The answer stunned her . . . *builders.* Her people called them "dwarven," but that was impossible. Her first thought was rather absurd. Wouldn't they be smaller than us? Further delving into Tamlin's memories supplied the reason. The builders were the smallest of the Elder Races, referred to affectionately by those as "dwarves." Her race, though physically smaller, were not an Elder Race, so the name for the dwarves stuck. Indeed, dwarves referred to Kisan's people derogatorily as "halfmen," or "halflings."

The dwarves disappeared some centuries ago, shortly after the battle against Lilyth. No one Kisan knew had ever seen one and nothing but stories of their existence remained. The possible exception would have been the lore father or Silbane, but neither had mentioned it to her.

Still, their strength matched those told in the legends. Moreover, they fought with a cunning tenacity they became known for during the Demon Wars. It lent credibility to the fact that these may indeed be dwarven men. Now the question was, what were they doing attacking the Isle?

They were highly trained and well conditioned. Another memory flashed by, of endless combat drills with one man, then two, all the way up to six-man fighting teams. They were experts in hand-to-hand combat and trained to fight as a synchronous group. Their strength and exactness stemmed from their repetitious training and their ability to coordinate and cooperate without speaking, using hand signals. Kisan would have to be extra careful to mesh perfectly with them if she were to maintain her cover.

Four stood and motioned to Kisan. "Get cleaned up, then stow the gear. Two will be by for inspection shortly, you know the drill." He tossed a grimy towel into a bin without looking. He tapped Three on the shoulder and motioned to the table near the back that glowed with magic.

A large map was displayed upon it. It looked much like Themun's conjuration, except flat and less detailed. Without another word, they both went to the table and began discussing points on the map in low tones.

Kisan watched them for a moment, knowing even as they walked away that everyone was following a strict protocol. Tamlin's memories supplied that Three and Four's duty was to evaluate their performance on this last mission and to provide tactical training on bettering them for the next. Prime and Two would be contacting their leaders and reporting on the mission outcome. Five and Six were to stow and set up all gear, then prep the area for the mission debriefing.

This had gone on for as long as this group had been in existence, no matter who fulfilled the roles. When Two felt Prime's leadership endangered the team, and Prime concurred, he would retire back to train new cadets and Two would take his place as the new Prime. If they did not, command would pass through trial by combat. She assumed the current Five, whom she had been paired with, had been the old Six, but really had no idea.

The name of the place, the Core, rose unbidden from Tamlin's memories, the training academy Tamlin had graduated from. A new graduate of the Core would become Six and he would move up to the Five position and rank, either here or on another team. Still, there was something strange about Tamlin's memories. There were none from before this time of training, as if he suddenly came into being fully formed for his role. It didn't make sense.

Also strange, Tamlin's memories did not include whose place he had taken, but he knew who led their people. Someone named Sovereign. Kisan knew the ancient legends of King Bara leaving to search for someone named Sovereign. Perhaps this person and that were the same?

More information from Tamlin's memories surfaced, but all of it recent. The team to which he was a member was akin to many elite fighting forces in the world, but focused on one primary service: kill any who used the Way.

To accomplish this, they trained endlessly in infiltration, information gathering, and sabotage. Tamlin believed they acted directly on behalf of their leader, divine in both right and judgment, but didn't know for sure. Did their Sovereign order the strike on the Isle? And to what purpose?

Kisan could tell Tamlin had been on the verge of religious zeal in his love for this team. The circumstances were too coincidental, however, with the Gate, for this strike to be merely random. The timing was too precise and the targets too specific. Kisan intended to find out what was going on. Of what strategic importance could the Isle have been?

Unfortunately, the memories she had siphoned from Tamlin's dying mind only contained a single-minded determination to qualify for the team, and none of the surrounding geopolitical information necessary to put context around their existence, or who specifically would have ordered the attack. Tamlin simply had not "needed to know."

The problem was two-fold: First, she had not yet assimilated many of Tamlin's memories and would probably never be able to, and the boy had died before anything but the most recent memories could be extracted. It was enough for Kisan to get by, but contained no real depth.

Second, What could cause that strange blank area where no memories seemed to be, just before Tamlin's training and qualification started? How could someone have no childhood? From what Kisan could now discern, there seemed to be nothing before the Core. She realized that if she were to solve this mystery, it would be from listening to these others and drawing conclusions for herself.

The team had moved to their assigned tasks and Kisan followed suit. The label of laggard would not help her situation, and she didn't need any more attention from Prime or Two. She marveled at the simplicity of bringing new team members in as Six's created, the kind designed to insure any senior members knew the role of all subordinates.

Since she was Six, there was technically no one below her. The expectation was she learned how to interface with this team from the ground up. According to Tamlin's limited memories, this was standard for all the tactical teams of the Core, a deadly sort of one-the-job-training.

Kisan breathed a sigh of relief that she hadn't taken the place of anyone above Tamlin's station. As luck would have it, her combat skills far surpassed them individually, and she had taken the place of one low enough in rank that she could maintain this deception indefinitely. That was as long as nothing else taxed her beleaguered stores of energy, she cautioned herself, not wanting to grow overconfident.

"Weapons or equipment?" Five asked in a disinterested way.

Kisan knew Tamlin had preferred weapons, but shrugged, "Don't care. You?"

Five motioned to the blades and dart weapons, "I'll start here." He moved with a steadiness that did not hint at disappointment or eagerness, just purposefulness. Another measure of the discipline these dwarves forged for themselves.

Kisan took a moment to inspect the strange tubes that fired the darts and Tamlin's mindread filled in some of the details, though even they were hard to interpret. The weapon had a handle she could grip easily, with a square hole cut out at the bottom. She could see that a small metal box filled with darts, like some sort of quiver, was inserted there. A lever sat below the tube, conveniently placed for her finger to pull and this action fired the darts through the tube, though even the dead assassin's memories didn't provide an understanding of the magic by which it did so. It was, however, compact and lethal. Ingenious.

She put the dart weapon down and let Tamlin's memories guide her on her tasks. As she did so, she thought about how to get a clue or hint to their destination.

"You think I should talk to Prime?" she asked carefully, while coiling a thin climbing rope.

Five looked at Tamlin with a raised eyebrow. "Only if you're looking to die. Leave it, mudknife, or we'll be cleaning up what's left of you and I'll be stuck doing twice the work."

Mudknife ... that word again, and with sudden comprehension Kisan realized this was their term for any new member of the team. Tamlin was the newest in the group and therefore considered the least trained and the least useful.

She nodded in return and shrugged an apology to what Five thought was an obviously stupid idea. No sense confirming that by talking more. She looked down, concentrating on the task at hand. Soon, Kisan knew, they would make a mistake and she would be there to make them pay for it.

Journal Entry 10

Spells are singular, commanding power only insomuch as the strength of a person's will. In my case, this can be considerable. However, ritual is the key! It is the systematic creation of ritual that gives the formless meaning.

Ritualized prayer, prayer of the masses, holds real power. It breathes life into these Aeris and Shapes them. It gives them substance and meaning. And what do gods want, once alive? What do they thirst for, but worship? What power do they have, except for what we grant them? I know now what we are capable of. I will command the weakness that surrounds me.

But a more deadly test faces me, first. Tonight, I face the guardian of my castle. I have long suspected something lies deep within, something alive. I know my fears feed it. If I can't destroy a simple product of my own imagination, how will I save our kind from beings far more powerful than that thing below?

I have tried to control these thoughts, I know where they will lead, but it is an impossible task. How do you *not* think about something? A part of my mind believes something lives below, an insidious part that will be my undoing. It will tear me apart, but I must face it.

Tonight, I fear, will be dangerous.

TORTURE

When facing certain death,

one will yearn for even

the worst moments in life.

—Altan proverb

A rek awoke to the icy splash of cold water across his naked body. He struggled, but his hands were tied to a crossbeam. When he looked down, he saw his feet secured on top of stone blocks. He stood, taking weight off his painfully stretched shoulders. "Where am I?" he asked in a voice suddenly filling with fear.

A man stepped forward and said, "I am Sargin. You will refer to me as that, if anything. His Majesty's forces have captured you as an intruder into Bara'cor. We are under siege and therefore you are the enemy, by the king's decree. We have questions."

Arek looked around, confused. What was he doing here? He remembered jumping through the portal, the freezing cold of *in between.* Then he flashed into that chamber. Beyond that he had no memory, but knew he'd been in a fight. His forehead throbbed with that familiar ache of having been hit, pulsing in time with his heartbeat.

He looked down at the man in front of him and asked, "What's going on? Where am I?"

Sargin held up a hammer, balled on one side, flat on the other. "I'm sorry, sir, we aren't interested in answering *your* questions, but understand what will happen if I think you are lying."

Arek looked wide-eyed at the hammer, understanding its purpose. "You, no . . . you don't need to—"

The moment froze and there stood Piter. "Oh, this is too perfect," he said with a smile.

"Piter! You have to get me out of here. I order you!" Arek screamed.

"Get you out? And how would I do that, Master?" Piter crossed his arms and seemed genuinely happy. "You keep forgetting that because of you, I'm dead. Forsaken. Committed to wander the realm as a ghost beholden to serve you. Silbane sent you into this mess, so ask him."

Arek quickly looked down for the Finder and realized with dismay that he was stripped bare. He had nothing. He fought to free his wrists, bound tightly to the crossbeam. "You told me to come here. You said I'd be safe!"

"If I were you," Piter said, "I'd get used to the idea that they are going to hurt you."

"What? Why? I don't know anything. Please," he begged. "I'll do anything! I'll release you . . . anything! Please don't let them do this!"

Piter laughed and said, "You are truly pathetic." Then the shade leaned in and said conspiratorially, "I love this next part, a lot." With that, he leaned back with a smile on his face and disappeared, and time continued its normal flow.

Sargin nodded, continuing to answer Arek's last plea, "Yes, sir. I do. This way, anything you tell me after this, I will be inclined to believe is true. You will do your best to convince me, because you will do anything to avoid the pain you are about to feel."

"Piter! Please, come back! I'll do whatever you want!" sobbed Arek.

Sargin looked at the boy with some confusion then said, "In due time, you'll tell us everything." He moved forward and put a foot over Arek's own, exposing just his toes on the hard stone.

The round end of the hammer came up, "I will start by shattering your little toe." He looked up at the boy, who started to whimper, "and then we will talk about what you know."

Arek tried to concentrate on his training, repeating in his mind, *The body is just a tool, the mind is in control, the body is ju—*

"No!" Arek screamed as the hammer came down. Terror turned into a cry of pure pain as the hammer smashed his toe into a pulp. A lightning stroke of pain lanced up his body and exploded in his brain. He saw purple and realized he had bitten his tongue.

He gagged and his throat closed on the coppery taste of blood mixed with mucus and spittle. It fell, drooling pink and red from his mouth as he hung paralyzed, his face frozen in a silent scream. His lungs didn't work, he couldn't draw a breath or stop the pain. Nothing, no martial training or litanies on discipline, stopped him from begging with anguished cries for Sargin to stop. The cries became sobs, then dry heaves.

Sargin stepped back as Arek soiled himself. Shame now mixed in with fear. He continued in a calm voice, "What is your name?"

Outside the room, the screams of Arek's questioning echoed throughout the hallways. Some even said they heard amongst the screams that day the sound of someone laughing.

THE TEAM

In combat, winning is preferable to losing.

Sacrifice anything and hold nothing dear,

if it gives you the killing stroke.

—*Kensei Shun, The Book of Shields*

The war chamber was an octagonal room cut from the very rock of Bara'cor. It was large, easily able to accommodate fifty men and featured a huge table in its center.

The table had carved on it a relief map of the known world, one that always stayed current with features of the land. When the rivers of two summers past had flooded from EvenSea and almost reached Last Reach, this map had changed. It was as if Edyn itself spoke to the table, which shifted in response to remain true.

One could almost imagine a time when military strategists planned tactics upon its surface. Now, despite its strange and peculiar powers, it was nothing but a relic of the past. Large braziers and torches along the wall lit the chamber, giving it a warm and ruddy glow.

Seven statues of female figures sat arranged around the room. They were each different and of indeterminable race. Some were normal, others not. Some were taller, some wider, others bigger. One female figure had horns, another had wings. What each statue did have in common was a large, gray, rounded stone clutched in its arms. In front of each statue was a raised dais with dwarven script.

Ash saluted the king as he entered the chamber. Behind him came three others, each a final candidate for the attempt on the nomad's camp. The king had been inspecting these statues, their workmanship still a marvel to him. As his armsmark came in, he turned his attention to Ash.

"Report."

"Something curious happened. Our scouts reported a fire last night, about a day's ride to the east."

"What was it?" asked the king.

"We don't know, but what burns in the desert?"

The king pursed his lips and said, "Have our teams watch the camps. See if anything strange happens." He watched as Ash nodded, then turned his attention to the team that had followed his armsmark in.

The first was Sevel, Captain of Second Company. He and Ash had advanced together, training in the same academy and posting under Jebida when they had been commissioned officers. They were fast friends and could count on one another. He acknowledged both with, "Good to see you, Armsmark, Captain." He then motioned to the others and said, "I trust all of you are curious about what we've asked you to volunteer for?"

Captain Sevel nodded smartly, his action almost a salute rather than an acknowledgment. Ash knew from the moment he'd said he needed volunteers that Sevel was going. Even after Ash told them it was a suicide mission, it had not deterred him. In fact, Sevel had decided then and there to make it back, *with* his friend. Now, they were going to find out the details of the mission and the prospect obviously excited him.

Ash gestured to the second candidate and said, "This is Sergeant Chandra, sire. She served under Captain Durbin. She is one of our finest archers and especially good at getting in and out of places unseen. She's also quite handy with a dagger." The sergeant stepped forward and saluted smartly to the king. Her lithe form seemed to hold a barely contained energy, like a coiled spring about to release.

The king nodded and looked at the third candidate, a wiry man with a ready smile. His name was Talis and it was clear the king knew him with an intimacy that came only from firsthand experience. He clasped the old warrior's hand, and with a laugh said, "Talis, you old dog! I thought you had transferred to Haven, 'something easy' as I recall."

"Aye, I did at that," Talis replied. "But when word came that the queen was evacuating, I thought it best I come see what trouble you've stirred up. Plus, you know the politics at Haven."

"He has direct experience with just this sort of thing," Ash said.

Talis stepped forward and bowed. "Ah ... speakin' of that. You were about to tell us what we've volunteered for, sire. Besides dyin' that is." He smiled again and stepped back. His easy demeanor and familiarity in the face of rank came because of his long service to the king and his family. He had been the unarmed combat instructor for three generations of Galadines, and though near his fiftieth summer, he still held a dangerous glint in his eye. Many had wagered and lost a week's pay making the mistake of measuring Talis's worth by his age.

The king looked at each of the candidates, then began, "I'm sorry it has come to this, but we have little choice. I asked the armsmark to select the best qualified and from there take only volunteers. The chance for success is good, but the chance of surviving that success ... slim.

"However, if you succeed, the people of Bara'cor will owe you their lives." The king paused, then looked at the group meaningfully. "I'll not mince words. We are asking you to infiltrate the nomad camp and kill their leader."

Discipline reigned. None of the candidates moved, nor spoke. Each absorbed the information and processed it in their own way—another confirmation that Ash had picked them well.

"Questions?" the king asked.

Captain Sevel stepped forward, his eyes straight ahead. "Sir, how will we know our target?"

The king nodded to Ash, who answered, "We all saw him, the day Durbin let his arrow fly from the walls. He is a massive warrior, clearly born and bred for battle. I doubt there are many that look like him in the camp. We may have new information shortly. If not, we'll need to capture someone once we get in and extract the information."

"Justice for Captain Durbin's last stand," Sergeant Chandra said. She had followed her captain through the thickest of fighting and respected his strength and honor. Losing him had been a blow to the entire Company and Ash knew that Chandra saw a chance to even things with the nomads.

The sergeant stepped back and Talis stepped forward. "Beggin' your pardon, sir, but new information? What does that mean?"

"Last night we captured a spy within our walls," the king said. "He's being interrogated now. If he knows anything, I'll share it with you immediately. Until then, prepare yourselves. You'll leave tonight at dusk."

Chandra stepped forward and asked, "Sir, does anyone have a plan yet on how we're to get into the camp?"

"I have an idea," Ash replied, "but I need to first discuss it with the king. You three are to prepare for single entry . . . we'll split up and rejoin each other behind enemy lines. Select your gear as if you were the only person going in and select clothes from some of the slain nomads. I'll drop by and discuss the mission details shortly." Ash looked to the king for permission, then said, "Dismissed."

The group snapped to attention, then with a signal from the armsmark filed out of the room. Ash watched their retreat with a mixture of pride and trepidation, so few to try to accomplish the impossible. He hoped his sacrifice would not be in vain.

The king interrupted the armsmark's thoughts with, "Small group. Will they be enough?"

Ash turned to face the king. "Too big a group will attract attention, especially if one is captured and forced to talk. That will alert the camp and it will be impossible to get to the chieftain. I thought three was a good number."

"There are four of you, counting yourself," the king corrected.

Ash's eyes never left his king's. "It's something I've been meaning to discuss with you. One of us will have to create a diversion, something to allow the other three to get by the nomad sentry line."

The king didn't seem to understand the implication at first. When the simple fact hit him his eyes betrayed his thoughts.

"We knew this was the only choice," Ash said. "We have to get into the camp somehow. We can't just walk in."

"You would be wasting all you could bring to the attempt against the nomad chieftain, dying needlessly."

"It's not needless if the others manage to slip into the camp unseen," offered the armsmark. "Besides, should I order one of them to do this? I couldn't live with myself."

The king turned his gray eyes on the young armsmark and laid his battle-scarred hand on his shoulder. "It is difficult to order others to their deaths, but good leaders know this. You cannot sacrifice yourself, as you are the one with the best chance of finding and killing the nomad chieftain."

Ash opened his mouth to argue, but the king's hand squeezed his shoulder like a vise.

"Hear me out," the king persisted. "Firing Bara'cor's catapults and performing a mock charge on their lines will force them to hold their line. At the clash, we pull back and retreat. Many will fall, but the nomad line will push forward on our retreat. Dressed as nomads, the four of you, fallen amongst the many slain, will go unnoticed. When their line passes, you will be behind it and able to rise and blend in with the enemy."

"That will mean the deaths of many of our men, just to cover our infiltration."

The king nodded and said, "And if you fail, it will mean the deaths of all of us. I am king, and these are my orders."

Ash did not meet the king's gaze when he said, "I should be happy with this alternative, but I am not."

Bernal looked grim, his men's choices weighing heavily on his conscience. He looked down, as though doubt threatened his composure, but when he looked up, steel flashed in his eyes. "Nevertheless, the soldiers who fall in this charge are heroes, insuring you and your team get past the nomad line. I wish the Lady's fortune on you, Armsmark. Do not waste *their* sacrifice."

Ash's voice was solemn as he replied, "Yes, my king."

OBSESSION

An opponent is weakest

when he breathes in,

and strongest when he exhales.

A Bladesman knows this and times

his strikes with the indrawn breath.

He shocks the body, promotes fear,

and inflicts damage.

—*Davyd Dreys, Notes to my Sons*

W hy would a dragon need a camp and supplies?" Scythe asked. When he saw his prisoner's surprised look he added, "Silbane, I know much more than you think. You can see the dragon, Rai'stahn. I know you trapped him in his knight form." He gestured at the crucified figure then, adjusted his seat on his small stool and finished, "I did say, 'let us speak plainly.' "

Silbane hesitantly nodded, at which point Scythe continued, "You know of the ability to read someone's memories. I know this because while I healed you, I mindread some of what you know. I know of your mission, of the Isle, and of your lore father."

He paused, looking about the tent as if wondering how to continue. He then met Silbane's surprised gaze and asked, "But who is Arek? You refer to him as your apprentice, as does Lore Father Themun, but of this apprentice there is no record in *your* memory. I find that most curious." Scythe leaned back again, finger to lips as if deep in thought. "How can someone you believe exists not be in your memory?" Scythe seemed genuinely confused.

For his part, Silbane sat stunned. If this Scythe had mindread him, nothing he did now was secret. He gathered his wits and decided it would be better to delay things until he could understand the situation he found himself in and who Scythe was.

"If you know all this, why do you need me?" Silbane rasped, his voice almost back to normal.

Scythe took a deep breath then said, "There is a divergence." He paused, then added, "Don't mistake me . . . you believe what you say and it is clear you and the dragon fought over the life of this 'Arek' . . . but there is not a single memory within your head of him. Or, to be more clear, no memories I can read. Again, why?"

Silbane didn't know what to say. He clearly remembered his apprentice, and if in fact this person was telling the truth, there was no reason for him to provide any more information.

Something in his demeanor must have shown through, for the man let out a sigh that seemed to be both tired and sad at the same time. "I had hoped this would be a conversation and not an interrogation. I hesitate to hurt you, seeing we are both practitioners of the Way, but I will do what I must."

Silbane laughed. "Clearly you wield some sort of magic . . . but what do you know of the Way?"

The man stood up and walked over to the corpse of Rai'stahn. He cupped the great dragon's chin and raised his large head. "Do you think you and those few pathetic adepts you left on your Isle are the last essence of magic in this world?" He let Rai'stahn's head drop with a dull thud, its face coming to rest upside down on its armored chest, the spine severed.

"Much has transpired since your self-imposed exile." Scythe's eyes narrowed as he looked back at Silbane. "I am also curious as to why you have allowed yourselves to be so isolated."

He paused, again looking at the dragon-knight's head with obvious remorse. "These blank areas of your memory are very regular, happening at almost precisely the same time everyday ... as if they are scheduled. How are you unaware of it?" Scythe stopped, then looked at Silbane and asked, "How could such a thing occur?"

Silbane found himself wondering the same thing ... a regular pattern of blankness? Then, with sudden dismay, he knew how, but he was careful not to let this knowledge show on his face.

Arek and his training schedule.

Those blank areas were when Arek came within close proximity of Silbane, at class, or lectures. Arek's power to mask magic caused the blank spots. Strangely, the recognition left Silbane feeling somehow better about himself, as if he had solved something. It was as if an unspoken nag had been lifted away.

"Have you come to an understanding? If so—" Scythe pulled the rawhide stool closer to Silbane and sat back down—"please share it with me."

Silbane looked at the man, his eyes turning cold and hard. It was clear this man was a danger to Silbane, and by extension to Arek. He was not about to say anything.

Seeing no response from his captive, Scythe continued, "Do you know what else is strange? I could not see your aura till you were discovered here. That *thing*—" he motioned to something around Silbane's neck with obvious distaste—"accomplishes the same purpose. But what blocked you from my Sight before?"

Silbane tried to crane his head down but couldn't move. He caught a glimpse of something coppery, but was unable to focus on it. Whatever it was, Scythe seemed to be implying it was the reason for his inability to connect with the Way.

He waited for Silbane to answer, a contemplative look on his face. When again no word was forthcoming, he continued, "You wear a torc fashioned by the Magehunters, a device with only one purpose—" his gaze grew thoughtful, as though reliving old memories—"to kill us all."

"It blocks my aura?" Silbane ventured this, hoping to keep the man talking. As long as he did so, the conversation stayed away from Arek and their mission.

Scythe blinked twice, his attention coming back to the captured master. "Yes, but what blocked your entire Isle? You disappear for over two score years then suddenly appear like a distant fire in the night. It explains the attack, for your brethren now sparkle like a shining star in the middle of the Shattered Sea. But why now?"

A cool breeze drifted in through the tent flaps, jingling hanging bells and swirling loose pieces of debris. The scent of jasmine wafted through, filling Silbane with a sense of peace and relaxation.

"Even more curious; how do you hide a dragon's aura, which should outshine yours like a bonfire next to a candle flame?"

Something was wrong. Silbane could barely touch it, his dazed mind trying, then it hit him with a start.

Scythe had said "attack." Did he mean others who were sensitive to the Way knew their location and had attacked them? A part of Silbane's mind reacted to the knowledge with alarm, but before he could do anything, a gentle coaxing set in, a reminder that all was safe and he should not worry.

Silbane found himself preoccupied with the passing time measured by his heartbeat. It seemed so natural, so soothing. A question formed in his mind and his voice uttered it almost automatically, "How long have I been here?"

Scythe rose and let out a deep breath he had been holding. "The better part of a day, not counting time at your camp. You were in sorry shape. My scouts were a bit too ... enthusiastic." He gestured to the other side of the tent absentmindedly and Silbane saw two men hung on hooks. Actually, they weren't men, but the *skins* of men, he realized through his fogged mind.

"I had them staked out in the sun and then skinned alive. Discipline must be maintained, no?" Scythe said seriously. "I had to do quite a bit of healing to fix you."

Silbane worked his jaw, which painfully clicked in protest. "Could have done better."

Scythe laughed. "You are quite a man, and dangerously accomplished for one who knows so little of the Way. You brush off my Talent as an afterthought, then jump directly back into it like a fish for water. It is as if you harness the Way differently than most. Perhaps a side effect of your training?

"Still ..." The red-robed man came closer and sat down. His tone became serious, almost menacing. "I have planned too long for the Gate's appearance. Now you show up with a dragon and a mission to close this very same Gate. I cannot let that happen."

The man gestured and Silbane found he could use his right arm. He realized the man had held his arms immobile with magic, an overt use of power that surprised him. The Way he knew was mostly internal and rarely manifested itself as direct control over another. Even illusion happened by fooling a person's senses, rarely forcing any *real* change to something.

Scythe leaned forward and handed the water skin to the captured master, then leaned back and began to speak. "For all our advances in magic, few have achieved what you monks have with regards to our bodies. In fact, I am not surprised by the sheer ingenuity of Dreys's family. Unfortunately, my chance to tell Themun just how much I respect him will have to wait."

To Silbane's puzzled look Scythe replied, "Lore Father Themun Dreys has passed on to the next world. I felt it, earlier this evening. The moment your people became visible, forces took direct and lethal action." He looked down, genuine regret in his voice. "Now it is too late."

The red-robed mage leaned back on his small stool and sighed, then met Silbane's eyes and said, "Did you know I saw him once, when he was much younger? He did not know this, though even then he was strong in the Way, and cunning. He saved a girl who had been captured by the king's men. Her name was Thera."

Silbane knew how the lore father and Thera had met, but nothing came out. He was stunned by what the man had just said. The Isle had been attacked?

"She, too, has passed, as if their journey in this world was meant to both start and end together." Scythe sat there for a moment, reliving another distant memory. His head shook then, an involuntary gesture, as if he struggled with himself on an unspoken level to remain in the here and now. When he spoke next, he did not meet Silbane's gaze and whispered, "Have you ever lost someone? Someone important to you?"

Silbane watched him, the fog momentarily clearing. His first thought was Arek, but instead he simply said, "No."

Scythe did not move, but his eyes closed. "You cannot understand then, what it's like." His voice grew stronger and he stood and faced the captured master. "You are a very small part of the story of this world, and your chapter is ending."

Silbane sat, looking up at Scythe in silence. The lore father *and* Thera, dead? That was impossible. He would have felt it, wouldn't he? Could Arek somehow have blocked his senses? What of Scythe, could he be responsible?

Silbane mentally berated himself, nothing could kill them that easily, and they had the Vault. Tempest was only one of many items of power that could save them should anyone be seriously injured. Scythe sought to throw him off balance and Silbane refused to let himself be baited.

Scythe cocked his head, as if listening, then said, "Your memories of the Vault are most interesting. Many of the artifacts I thought lost are there. They are wasted with you and will be put to better use. But I digress."

Scythe motioned to the water skin, which Silbane held in shocked silence. *He reads my thoughts, even now?* Then a gentle caress eased his shock and worry, and he struggled to remember what had upset him so much a few moments ago as the fog once again wrapped him in its warm embrace. They were talking about someone and the history of the world, were they not?

Scythe grabbed the water skin from Silbane's nerveless fingers and took a swig, clearing his throat. "Have you noticed something?"

When the mage did not answer, Scythe continued, "The rifts between our plane and Lilyth's are getting more numerous and unpredictable. Things aren't getting better."

Silbane still did not respond, his mind in a fugue of memories and thoughts, as if someone were rifling through them at high speed.

"We've managed to stop the larger ones," Scythe continued, "but dozens appear each year, and who are the casualties?"

"Children," croaked Silbane. "Always, the children."

Scythe nodded. "Always, and usually those strongest in the Way. They disappear as if they never existed. Have you asked yourself, where do they go?"

"They're killed by the demons that emerge from the rifts. Families speak of it, of their loss." This came out as a mumble, but there was still strong emotion behind it. Much of the council's efforts had been to recover children born of Talent before they fell to the king's Magehunters, and now these demons.

Scythe cocked his head, a puzzled look on his face. "Killed? Nothing really dies. You know that."

It was Silbane's turn to look confused as his fog again lifted and he found he could answer with perfect clarity. "What are you talking about? Things die all the time. Your men over there, the dragon, the people of EvenSea!" He spat these out, laying each death at Scythe's feet.

The red-robed mage smiled and caught Silbane's gaze and held it, a feverish glint showing in his eyes. "Nothing *really* dies. I will answer to them still, for my part in their passing.

"Are you comfortable? I mean, I cannot let you go, but I can allow you to adjust your position."

Silbane thought about it and was happy the conversation stayed away from Arek. His apprentice's ability to mask magic was clearly important to this man, and it made sense for him to keep Scythe talking. The longer he did so, the farther from the truth they went. When the chance presented itself, he would use his Finder and escape this location to wherever his apprentice was. Then they would make their way back to the Isle and warn the others of Scythe and everything else he had learned.

Silbane said, "Yes, some water, and please, continue . . ."

"There's not much more to say. These rifts are passageways to Lilyth's plane, a fact you already know or you wouldn't be here. You wouldn't be trying to destroy my life's work."

Silbane shook his head. "You can't let that Gate reopen. It would mean—"

"Silence!" roared Scythe. He kicked Silbane in the chest. The suddenness and violence of the move caught the master by surprise as the air whooshed from his lungs.

Silbane looked up through pain-dazed eyes and came face to face with a lunatic, nose inches from his own. His captor's eyes were wide, the whites showing. His mouth stretched over teeth into a grin that looked like a feral animal's.

In that moment of clarity, Silbane realized that Scythe was unpredictable and violent. His life hung on the edge of a blade balanced on the tip of this lunatic's finger. He froze, knowing the slightest movement could overturn this man's carefully crafted semblance of sanity.

At first, he didn't think he would survive. His captor seemed to be watching a different scene, his eyes jerking back and forth, looking through and past Silbane. Then the lids drooped slightly, a breath escaped, nostrils flared as another breath was taken, and Scythe leaned back. His eyes closed and his head tilted back as he sat on his haunches.

He raised his hands together in front of his face, palm to palm, and spoke through them, "Nothing really dies, Silbane. You need to understand this. Tell me about Arek. If he has the power to interfere, I *must* know."

Silbane closed his eyes and shook his head. He would not give up one more piece of information that would lead Scythe anywhere near his apprentice.

"Look at me."

At first Silbane considered ignoring him, but after witnessing Scythe's mercurial violence firsthand, he realized the inherent danger of such an infantile gesture. Staying alive was their best hope so he opened his eyes and found himself across from a man who was calm and composed. The transformation was unnerving and hinted at a deep psychosis, with triggers to extreme violence at any given word. Silbane kept his mouth shut, watching with the same care and utter stillness he would exhibit had Scythe pressed a real blade to his throat.

"You see this as a nomad's tent, with all the expected trappings and furnishings. However..." The red-robed mage snapped his fingers and the entire room darkened, changed, cleared, then solidified.

It was basically the same tent, but now the acrid stench of waste filtered in, mixed with the cloying sweet smell of *hazish*. Behind Scythe stood a gargantuan Altan warrior, clearly pleased with something. Elsewhere in the tent, Silbane could see moving forms that hinted at bare flesh and oil. "Not everything is as it seems."

Silbane dropped his head to his chest, knowing now he had been part of a grand illusion, an exhibit of power far beyond anything he could accomplish easily. He coughed once and spit blood, then said, "I am not giving you Arek."

Something Scythe must have read in Silbane's mind showed him the futility of pursuing this line of questioning. He backed away, staring at the master and thinking. Then he motioned to the warrior and said, "U'Zar, I am not finished with him."

He looked at Silbane and said in a conspiratorial voice, "No escapes." The smile that followed was bright and clean, free of anger or worry, a far cry from the man who looked about to kill him a moment earlier. To Silbane, it was like looking at a door that sat unevenly on its hinge when open, yet where no defect could be seen when closed.

Scythe moved closer and Silbane felt his right arm go numb again. "I also know about Themun's Finder." Scythe reached in and in one motion ripped the charm from around Silbane's neck. "If you won't help me find Arek, this will."

Silbane sat stunned, his mind dazed again. It was clear to him now that with the torc on he felt nothing, no connection to the Way. Without that, he was effectively blind. Everyone on the Isle *could* be dead. Then he found himself thinking about beautiful summer days, where the sun set with its warm, orange glow. Something whispered in his mind, *you need to rest.*

"What will you do with that?" asked the giant, referring to the charm.

Scythe looped it around a nail above Silbane's head. "I will create a portal web on this side, should the boy be foolish enough to use it to get to his master. Post additional guards outside this tent. If we are lucky, we won't have to do anything. He'll join us on his own and open a door for me into Bara'cor."

The nomad shook his head and grumbled, "You have made it clear that Bara'cor's dwarven stone is proof against your magic, so we throw our men at her walls. Why not use this charm to enter?"

"We will, in due time," Scythe answered, his eyes resting on Silbane. "Once the Finder is used, the portal opening cannot be moved. We do not know the whereabouts of his apprentice. What if he has been captured by Bara'cor's forces? What if the other end opens to an iron and granite cell?"

Scythe turned to the leader of the nomads and said, "Let us both be patient for a day and see what transpires. You want the fortress and I want to achieve the Gate within. Our interests are still aligned, but we must be sure no one can stop us." He looked back at the dazed master. "I suspect his apprentice will come to us at his first opportunity."

Then he put a hand on the u'zar's massive forearm and added, "Prepare an assault team to enter Bara'cor. It is a good suggestion."

Silbane shook his head, and his eyes flamed in anger. "Lies! I would have felt the death of Themun." The words tore from his mouth.

Scythe moved over and sat back down across from Silbane. He grabbed the water skin from the ground and took a long swig, then said, "I would consider sparing *you*, though. Losing any practitioners of the Way is tragic, and as I said before, you are a good man."

Silbane looked at Scythe, hatred smoldering in his eyes. He did not believe anyone on the Isle was dead. The thought was inconceivable, and he knew they were the land's last hope.

Scythe looked at Silbane, his head cocked to one side. "The land's last hope? You still don't understand, do you?"

Scythe stood. Smiling down on the master he said, "You are not the land's last hope. *I am.*"

With that, he turned and motioned to his guards who formed up on either side. He looked at the clanchief and said, "I go to prepare the portal web. Wait here and guard him carefully."

He looked at Silbane and gestured. At once Silbane felt lethargy come over him, a quiet lassitude that offered him the luxury of sleep. It seemed so natural to him, to be tired now. After his apprentice arrived, he knew everything would be all right.

Scythe said to the nomad chieftain, "Keep him alive until I give the order. He shrugs off my enchantments too quickly ... some side effect of his training. It only invites trouble, but I want his apprentice. If what he thinks is true, the boy is dangerous, to both of us."

"What of that collar?" the nomad asked. "Can he not just remove it?"

"No, Hemendra. I have seen to that."

Silbane came more awake, watching as a gap of light appeared from the departure of the insane mage. Into the gap stepped Hemendra, who looked at the master with a strange expression on his face. Contempt mixed with something that Silbane in his addled state could not identify. He realized he could now move his head and speak.

His mind cleared, as if a fog had been blown away by a clean spring breeze. With his newfound clarity he looked at the clanchief and said, "My apprentice will never come here. You and I are soldiers. It would be better to get this over with now."

Hemendra tilted his massive head to one side and said, "Redrobe has requested you be kept alive until your apprentice arrives." The big man leaned forward and said, "I will follow his suggestion." With a smile, he turned and left the tent.

As Silbane watched him leave, a crushing sense of failure closed in around him. Worst of all was the fear that Scythe was right and everyone on the Isle was truly dead. With the torc blocking his path to the Way, he had no way of truly knowing. He closed his eyes and leaned his head back. All hope was not yet lost, he reassured himself.

Something tickled the back of his mind. In addition to the physical training they endured on the Isle, much of their learning went into understanding an opponent's mental state. The nomad chieftain, Hemendra, had said something ... something that didn't fit well with his demeanor around Scythe.

Then it struck him, the clanchief had used the word "suggestion." Perhaps the mage's help was not as welcome as he thought. Here was a potential weakness, and Silbane prepared himself for any opening that might show itself, however small. For now, all he could do was sit and wait, the heat of the day soaking in through the very air itself.

A hot breeze blew into the tent, stirring the various trappings. As he sat and waited, he thought again about the torc, the Isle, and about his friend Themun. Could he be dead, as Scythe had said? He took a deep breath. If so, the loss hit him deeply. He rested his head back and his mind flew to the first time he and Themun had met....

Journal Entry ... unsure

victorious
   healing
   I am tired, too tired to write this morning. Facing it was the key ... courage, faith in oneself.
   I do not know how long I slept. The world here is similar to our own, yet vastly different. It is the reflection of our dreams and hopes, so the fact that it is mostly beautiful speaks to our secret wish for a better place, some sort of heavenly abode for the afterlife. It is where we all end, hence the dragon's question about "who has died?" I didn't understand, but regardless, enslavement is not an option. It is the only choice left to us if we continue as the dreamers.
   As I have written, here our thoughts are as dangerous as reality, for our thoughts bring the Aeris into focus. But my encounter with the dark thing below the castle has taught me my first valuable lesson. Though I dream it, I can still destroy it. In fact, I know I am destined to do exactly this.
   I am surrounded now by little helpers. I cannot explain what they are ... Imps? Sprites? They are tiny beings that seem to know what I want and fetch it for me, whether it be food, paper, ink, water ... I know my mind is creating these supplies, but why small creatures to fetch them? I must research this more.
   They are, however, a pleasant distraction.

HISTORIES: SILBANE

Teaching children the Way of Making

reveals the core of your being.

A child will show you,

through deed and action,

more truthfully than any mirror,

who you really are.

—*Lore Father Argus Rillaran, The Way*

Silbane felt rough hands push him forward, not unkindly. "He's ready."

The older man standing in front of him nodded to Silbane's father and said, "Yes, my lord. We'll see." A wry smile flashed across his face and he stooped, coming eye to eye with the eight year old. "Are you ready, son of Petracles?"

"Of course," Silbane piped. "Been ready forever." The latter came out matter-of-factly.

Themun stood up, a smile still dancing in his eyes. "Really?"

The boy nodded. *"Really."*

"All right," Themun said, laughing, holding up a hand in mock protection from the boy's confidence. "Give us a moment."

Silbane shrugged, looking expectantly at the stone dais and the concentric circles inscribed upon it.

Themun looked at the other man and said, "He won't be harmed. If he shows Talent, we will provide him, and you, refuge."

"Doubtful, but the king's law requires I turn him over to Deft."

Themun raised an eyebrow. "She lives?" It was rumored that Alion Deft had died, many years ago.

"She's dead, but others of her line continue her work, much to the land's ill. We won't risk Sil," the man said, squeezing his son's shoulders again. He stared meaningfully at the other man, then turned the boy around and hugged him, saying, "Remember all your puzzles ... you were always good at figuring things out."

Out of his father's view, Silbane rolled his eyes, but hugged him back. They were so concerned all the time. He didn't know how to explain it, but he knew he'd be fine. He wished, with the exasperation only children have, for his parents to stop worrying. *And how long would this hug last?*

"He won't be harmed," Themun reassured his father.

The man let go, reluctantly, then stood up, looking around. "You've done well for yourself here. Your services are still in demand?"

Themun inclined his head and answered, "Only when a subtle hand is needed."

"Seems that will always be the case, King's Law or not." Then he cast his eyes about the Testing area and asked, "Where do you want us?"

The lore father gestured to the left, a path that led to a small garden. There, the Lord and Lady Petracles could wait for the outcome of their son's test.

Few knew of this place, and fewer still dared the journey. It took real coin and not an inconsiderable amount of luck for his father to find the Isle. And though Silbane and his father were lords of the land, they still defied the King's Law. Should they be discovered, it would mean a quick and harsh end to House Petracles. They risked much on the off chance Silbane showed some Talent.

Most parents worried about their child passing the test, but Lord Petracles was different. He acted as if Silbane's power was a foregone conclusion and seemed more worried about what would happen once he passed.

"What do you know of this test?" Themun asked.

Silbane looked up, meeting the lore father's eyes without waver. "Nothing, sir. Can't be that hard, though."

"Why?"

"Nothing is for me."

Themun laughed. "What if you don't pass?"

Silbane shook his head and a seriousness encompassed him like a cloak. "That won't happen."

"We normally give this test to more advanced students," the lore father explained. "But your parents have come here at great expense."

Silbane looked around, then said, "Things attacked our land. We escaped."

"If you're accepted, your parents will have a home here."

The boy didn't respond. The man hadn't asked him a question. He just stood still, looking at the circle. Eventually, his curious mind blurted, "I stand there?" It was less a question and more a deduction. He just wanted to get started.

Themun's mouth tugged up on one end. "Yes."

The boy didn't wait for leave, but scampered to the central octagon tile, jumping at the last moment to land in its center. Everything to him, it seemed, was a game.

"Fine. Stand ready. Four walls, each based on one element, will rise. Your task is to get through them. If you can't, I'll drop the walls and come get you. Don't be afraid."

Silbane rolled his eyes again. Everyone sounded like his parents.

Before he could finish the thought, four concentric circles sprang up. The closest was made of water and behind that, earth. Beyond that, he could see nothing else.

He looked at the swirling wall of water before him. It rushed by with a dull roar, echoing through the small, circular chamber it created. He pushed a finger into the wall and felt his hand swept aside by the current. How many had tried to defeat it by pushing through? That would never work.

Stepping into the current would mean his death, either by drowning or damage, as the wall of water smashed him into the wall of earth. Since this was not a desirable outcome, his mind continued its analysis. Silbane had always been accused of thinking too deeply, but here it served him well.

Wait . . . the wall of earth? his thoughts narrowed, his young mind flitting through possibilities, discarding each quickly when it did not suit his means. The older man had mentioned *four* walls, so he assumed air and fire would be the last elements. The order might matter, he thought at first. He turned that over in his mind, running through the combinations and quickly came to the realization that it wouldn't. A slow smile broke out on his face as the answer came to him.

He positioned his hand, knife edged, into the water. It cut a line within the stream and threatened to pull him in, but he resisted. He pushed hard, making the gush of water obey his simple redirection. He kept his hand open and still, then angled it, *just so.*

Water, hitting the flat blade of his palm, flowed in the direction of his choosing. He tilted his palm more and the stream of water hit the wall of earth. Slowly, the earth became mud. Soaked into submission, it fell away in a mix of brown sludge and dirt. As the hole widened, he continued until there was an arch in the wall of earth that was large enough for him to stand in. Beyond it, he could see the wall of air.

Then, without hesitation, he pushed both hands against the wall of water and jumped through the momentary gap he'd created in the current. He stumbled and fell inside the arch in the wall of earth.

"Should I keep going?"

There was no answer.

The boy added, "I will do the same, bending earth into air, and pushing air into fire."

There was still no answer, so Silbane heaved a sigh. "Either the fire will eat the air, or the air will move the fire out of the way. If fire wins, I'll use water, and you know how that will end." He made a calculated guess, but his conviction never wavered. He smiled. "You know I'm right!"

A moment passed, then two. Then the walls collapsed. Outside the circle stood Themun, smiling. "You are an insolent child." He paused, then added, "But there seems no point in continuing your test."

Silbane didn't know what that meant, so he asked, "I'm accepted?"

"Would it matter if I said no?"

Silbane looked down, not sure if the lore father was kidding. "I want to be here. I won't give up," he said most seriously.

The lore father moved forward and clapped a hand on the boy's shoulder. "You are accepted. Don't worry, your parents are also free to live here, should they choose to do so. Tell them of your success." Themun gestured to the path on his left.

"Yes!" Silbane smiled, a beam of sunshine the lore father couldn't help but return.

"There are many rules to living here. See Adept Thera and she will answer any questions you or your family have."

The boy looked at the older man and asked, sheepishly, "Is it true that only one in a hundred are accepted?"

"No." Themun's mock sternness put Silbane in his place. "Go find your parents."

The boy nodded, a gesture that included his whole body in a miniature bow, and ran off.

He shrugged, mentally correcting Silbane's guess. It was closer to one in ten thousand.

Part II

THE NEXT MISSION

When your stance is comfortable,

you are vulnerable.

Check your legs, maintain your discipline,

master your body.

With repetition, discomfort will feel safe,

and you will begin to see

weakness in others.

—*Tir Combat Academy, Basic Forms & Stances*

Prime and Two returned to the cabin, but neither looked happy. They moved over to where Three stood quietly conferring with Four. The group spoke softly in turns, each nodding as their leader explained something. Then the four turned and made their way back to where Kisan stood with Five.

"That last adept was stalking us." Prime said this as a statement of fact. "When we saw him, he was making his way toward you two."

Three then added, "He certainly seemed to know we were there. Once the rest of us detected him, he dropped his visual cloak."

"Conserving energy for battle," Prime replied softly. He seemed deep in thought. Then he looked at the group and asked, "If he knew, then the others might have also. Give me the best scenario."

They went in order and based on Tamlin's memory, Kisan knew this exercise had a very strict protocol. The newest member spoke first, then each spoke after moving up in rank. This way the more experienced members received the benefit of the other's observations. Kisan knew she only had a heartbeat to answer. "He followed us, but meant to attack earlier. When he became visible, it was six against one. Not good planning for as good a fighter as he was."

"Separated us with a decoy," said Five. "Thought we chased a boy."

"He was following us. He could have been out, seen what happened, and waited for the perfect moment, but that never came, huh?" Four added with a laugh.

Three said, "Something warned him. Maybe the area was protected by countermeasures we're not familiar with."

Two thought for a moment, his mind moving through the various scenarios. He then said, "I agree with Four. He was already out, heard something. We would have heard him, if our positions were reversed."

Kisan seriously doubted this last statement, given their abilities, but remained silent. Now was not the time for her to come to anyone's attention.

Prime bowed his head, assimilating everything he'd heard. "Three, you think something warned him? What?"

Three stepped up. "We don't know their complete capabilities. Maybe the woman managed to send out a warning. Those damn halfling kids were squealers."

Kisan closed her eyes, keeping her emotions in check.

Prime nodded, then looked at Five and asked, "You said decoy . . . ?"

Five stepped forward, saying, "Just before he showed up a young boy ran past us, heading for the woods. We each fired a dart, but the boy kept running. We followed standard procedure."

Standard procedure meant Six would hold position while Five took the target. Prime looked at Six and asked, "How long was Five gone?"

"No more than twenty beats," Kisan answered. She realized now, with great relief, that they could not mindspeak. Had that been part of their repertoire, this sort of mission debriefing would never occur. They would simply have shared thoughts and seen what each other saw, but her identity would immediately have been uncovered.

Her thoughts were interrupted when she realized that everyone was staring at her. No one moved, but it was clear something she had just said caused this.

Then Two snarled, "What the hell is a *beat?*"

Kisan's mind scrambled ... *hell?* She didn't know what that word meant, but how could they not know the rhythm of their own hearts? She dived into Tamlin's memories and realized that timekeeping for these dwarves was much more sophisticated, more precise. She searched, then dredged up the correct unit of measure, sounding out the word, "I meant, *sekunds.*"

It sounded strange to her, but it was roughly equivalent to a heartbeat, so she hoped Prime would accept it.

It seemed to work. With the exception of Two, the rest had gone back to looking at their leader. Two continued to stare at her, though, shaking his head in disgust.

Prime looked at the group, silent and thoughtful. After a moment, he offered, "The boy was likely a student. However, the profile of these adepts shows they would not use students as bait. The boy you saw probably spooked and ran. The adept unshielded himself in an effort to misdirect us from him, not knowing that Five had already taken the boy ... Where are my holes?"

The group stood silent. Then Five hesitantly said, "We never found the boy. He made it to the edge of the woods and disappeared."

Prime looked at the two of them with disgust. "You *both* missed?" Behind him, Two, who was in charge of their continued training, shifted his weight, an unspoken promise of endless drills after this debriefing concluded. Five and Six were officially on his list.

"Or he is dead," Three offered, "hit by one or both darts just as he made it to the wood's edge. Five wouldn't have been able to find him in that undergrowth. The signal to regroup came just as the boy raced past them."

"I have our orders," Prime told the group, thankfully choosing to focus on the next phase of their orders. "We are to proceed to the port of Haven where we will drop the boat off with Arsenal, then make our way to the fortress of Bara'cor."

"Target?" Three asked.

"Our secondary target is the entire Galadine line. The king has gone soft on those that use the Way, and is a target of opportunity."

"The royal family?" Four shook his head. "Heavy prep. Lots of variables."

"That's what we live for," Prime semi-chastised, then said, "Our primary is more complicated. Two."

At his command, Two stepped forward and outlined the facts. "The Isle was sanctioned because of two events. One, the dragon, Rai'stahn and a master left shortly before our attack; and two, they both disappeared, as if their connection to the Way had been cut off."

Prime looked at his team and said, "Another null has appeared."

Silence reigned as each team member instantly understood what Prime was saying. Only Kisan felt left out, but waited so she could put more context to what she'd just heard.

"We've never faced a null before." This was from Five, doubt clear in his voice.

Two reacted immediately and said, "Stow that! Every team has their first and this is our job. Plain steel is all you need."

The others nodded, then Four stepped forward. "Which master was it?"

"We don't know, the null field hides him," Prime said, "but given the body count at the Isle, we can assume it's either Silbane Petracles or Kisan Talaris. Calling them dangerous is an understatement, so stay sharp. If either or both are protecting this null, we have a lethal situation on our hands, and I'd like to see everyone come back alive."

Kisan didn't have to ask what a "null" was. The answer was obvious. It could only be Arek, with his unique ability to mask the Way.

"The queen is in Haven, and outside of mission parameters. She's not a target, yet." Prime grabbed a sheaf of papers with detailed drawings of people and handed them out. Kisan had never seen anything like this before, the drawings were so real, they looked almost lifelike. She stared at them, mesmerized by the detail. In addition to images, the papers contained habits, training, and other vital information on each target. "Memorize these, then destroy them."

"What are our orders?" Kisan asked, leafing through the papers until she came to her own sheet. It was extraordinary. Her mouth suddenly felt dry. How had they gathered such information about them and their Isle, supposedly a guarded secret? The question begged for hints of betrayal, but she could not think of an obvious answer. If not that, then this Sovereign was better equipped and informed than they suspected.

"Intelligence from Arsenal reports a new prisoner in Bara'cor, a boy named Arek. We carry out our secondary objective and then seek out the prisoner. If he's the null, no misses," said Two, locking eyes first with Five and Six, then the rest of the team. "We kill him."

"And if he's not?" asked Kisan.

Two smiled, though the humor didn't reach his eyes. "They are getting lax at the Core, decanting anyone with a pulse. The answer is always the same, mudknife, every time." He looked at Three.

Three laughed and said, "We *always* kill them."

A CHANGE IN PLANS

Bladesmen create their own openings,

but until you achieve such exalted heights,

remain humble.

If an opening presents itself, strike.

—*Davyd Dreys, Notes to my Sons*

H is name is Arek Winterthorn. It was the name given to him when he was found by a group of monks. They reside on an island southeast of here, somewhere in the Shattered Sea." Jebida read from the report, but shook his head. "My king, you're not going to believe half of what's in here. Mages, dragons, ghosts; something about a rift within Bara'cor, which out of this entire report is the most alarming. It reads like our own myths and legends, only according to this boy it's true, and he's in the middle of it."

The king asked for the report, looking it over. With him and Jebida were the armsmark, his son Niall, and Yetteje. Although they had mostly recovered from their encounter, Sergeant Stemmer still had headaches from the blow she'd received and was under the careful eye of the healers. The rest, except for their wounded pride, were not too badly hurt.

"It says he arrived here by a Far'anthi Stone," remarked the king.

"Yes, whatever that is," muttered the firstmark.

"They were stones used to travel between these fortresses," said the king almost to himself, "made by the dwarves." His thoughts turned to the stone statues and spheres in the main council chamber, where the boy had emerged. He knew similar statues stood all over the fortress of Bara'cor, and a sudden dread filled him at their vulnerability.

"Place guards at every stone sphere statue within Bara'cor and inside and outside the main council chamber. Station them in pairs within sight of one another. Rotate them at regular intervals. If the boy is telling the truth, those stones may offer a hundred ways into this fortress," said the king.

Jebida laughed. "And you believe him? This is no boy, however innocent he may look. He could have killed Sergeant Stemmer, Princess Tir, or even your son. He faced my armsmark in *single* combat and held his own. He weaves a storybook tale under physical interrogation. He has clearly been conditioned and definitely has special military training. It's worth repeating ... he could have *killed* your son," the firstmark said gruffly, looking at the king.

"He could have, but he didn't kill anyone," Ash said. "Maybe he's sticking to his story because it's true. Did you see him? He didn't look 'conditioned' after our man finished with him."

"What do you mean?" Niall asked in a small voice. "What did we do?"

The firstmark looked at the young prince and said, "We're at war. He somehow evaded all our guards, entered here and attempted to kill you..." Jebida looked exasperated. "We did what we had to do."

Yetteje looked at Niall and said, "They tortured him." The idea didn't bother her in the least. Her only regret was that it hadn't been the nomad leader instead.

Niall turned back to the king, shaking his head. "Father?"

The king ignored his son and looked to the firstmark, saying, "Carry out my orders. Station the guards." Bernal looked down, contemplating, then asked, "How is the prisoner?"

The commander of Bara'cor's defenses shrugged and replied, "He'll not walk normally again. There's not much left of his foot." He paused, then added, "Our man was thorough." He seemed to understand the necessity of the king's actions, but with the exception of Yetteje, the torture didn't sit well with anyone else in the room.

The king nodded, his disciplined mind neither reviewing nor regretting the actions this boy's appearance required of him. His only concern was the safety of Bara'cor, and the possibility there was a way into the fortress they didn't know about. It was something his son would have to grow to understand: the weight of everyone's safety over one person's life or comfort.

"Does your man think he was telling the truth?" asked the king.

The firstmark and armsmark looked at each other, their long service together a common bond, allowing the unspoken disagreement to hang in the air between them without detracting from their duties. Then with a sigh, Jebida turned to the king and said, "Aye, my lord. I think he believes what's in the report."

The king scanned the pages again. "This boy is from an order of monks who still use magic. They call themselves 'adepts', and their leader is known as a 'lore father.' The boy himself is under the training of someone named Silbane, his master. Last he saw him, his master battled a dragon in the form of a knight, in the desert—a contest of flame and fire."

At the mention of the title "lore father," Ash looked up. His jaw clenched and he asked hesitantly, "You're sure he's called a lore father?"

The king nodded, not looking up from the notes. "Yes," he acknowledged, "evidently this group has been around since the battle against Lilyth, centuries ago."

A strange look came over the armsmark, one missed by the rest of the room.

"Why was he brought along?" Niall asked. "Why include him in something so dangerous," the prince added hastily by way of explanation.

The king nodded and said, "Strange . . . but who knows what this group considers dangerous? He seems to be on a scouting mission. Ash did say he was well trained."

Ash looked up from his thoughts with a start. "What?"

"The boy is well trained?" the king asked.

Ash looked at the king for a moment, catching up, then nodded. "Apprentice or not, he's not in any danger in single combat. One of the best swordsmen I've ever faced." He missed the resentful look he received from Niall. "There was a report of something involving fire in the desert . . . a battle?"

"A contest of fire and . . ." the king replied. "Perhaps the same reported from last night. Tell the others what you told me this morning."

Ash looked at the group and said, "Last night, a fireball was seen, a day's ride to the east."

"I've seen the report," Jebida said. "What else?"

The armsmark continued, "The king ordered me to deploy scouts, to reconnoiter the area for anything strange. I stationed four teams in a line between the reported fireball and the nomad encampment. Early this morning one team reported a small group of nomads hauling two figures back to camp. One was a gargantuan black knight."

The king looked at everyone and said, "Arek claims his master and a dragon in the form of a *knight* fought. Now two prisoners matching this description are being taken to the nomad camp?"

Jebida scoffed, "What does that mean? They are likely dead. What good is that?"

The king's eyes narrowed. "Did you see this entry about a Finder?"

The firstmark nodded and replied, "Of course."

"Two men, described just as Arek says," the king added. "An amazing coincidence."

"So you think his master is captured?" retorted Jebida. "An apprentice nearly bests you and his master falls to simple nomad barbarians? What sense does that—?"

"The Finder is the key," the king interrupted. "When broken, it can transport the user through a portal to the location of the other half. The boy has one half, his master the other." The meaning was instantly clear to everyone in the room, but could it be that simple?

The king locked eyes with Ash, this last bit of news welcome in light of the dozens who would die in a frontal charge to cover their infiltration. Bernal continued, "If Silbane has been captured and taken to the camp, he may be very close to your target already."

"Or you may appear in Bara'cor," remarked Jebida, clearly frustrated. "His capture is doubtful, and he may have continued here trying to save his apprentice. Did you think of that?"

The king held up a hand and said, "According to Arek, his master was trying to send him back to their island when they were attacked by the dragon-knight. Arek managed to escape and thought his master was right behind him. Because we have the scouting report, I think it fairly certain the two taken to the nomad camp are Silbane and this dragon-knight."

Yetteje piped in, "So he fell to a dragon and it's just a matter of using the Finder."

"Perhaps, if the Finder works at all," huffed the firstmark, still clearly not liking the idea of trusting magic, Arek, or anything that had to do with him.

Yetteje looked up from her thoughts and said, "Will it work for us? I mean, what if only he can use it?"

"How would we even know how to activate it?" Niall asked. "Do we break it again, or maybe there's a key word or phrase?" The prince looked around the room. "We don't really know it can take more than one person, either. Do we?"

The king shook his head, reading from the report. "It says the Finder works by breaking it again, and so long as Silbane lives, it will continue to glow." He held up the charm, which clearly sparkled with its own light. "I think he's alive, but you are right, it may be tied to this boy. If so, we cannot take the chance of losing it." He shook the sheaf of papers. "Nothing else is mentioned. If there's some detail we still need beyond this, we'll have to ask Arek."

The group realized with dismay that they would still need the cooperation of their prisoner, something he would not be favorably inclined to give, given his recent treatment.

Ash thought about it, then offered, "The only thing of value we can offer him is freedom."

"He can't be happy in his current situation," the king agreed. "If we let him go to his master with the agreement he must take us with him, it could work. If I were him, I'd want to get as far away from us as possible."

"And just how would we enforce such an agreement? He could just as easily make himself disappear without Ash and his team," Jebida grumbled. "This is a fool's quest."

"Perhaps..." Ash countered, "but his master would not have left him something too complicated. From what the king described, this charm is easily activated." Ash paused for a moment, thinking. "With regards to him just disappearing, how would such a charm determine that? The report says it creates a portal? Perhaps the portal stays open until the charm holder goes through. If that's the case we could take an entire division through, so long as Arek went last."

"What about his foot?" asked the firstmark. "He can't walk."

The king gestured again to the notes they had bought with Arek's pain. "The sword he carries, Tempest. He says it can heal. We could offer him the chance to let his master use it to heal him, *if* he takes our team in with him."

"If I held onto the sword," Ash added, "then he would have to take me along. It's the best insurance I can think of, since his healing would require it."

"And give up a weapon just like that?" The firstmark snapped his meaty fingers. "Why don't we just give him some of our rations as well?" Jebida looked to the king and said, "Bernal, think about what you're suggesting. Even if our team gets to Silbane, he has certainly been captured and may have been killed. How do we even know what it glowed like when he was alive? Ash's team could appear in whatever serves as their prison," Jebida turned to Ash, "or a fire pit, where they dispose of their dead."

He paced around the table coming to stand before his king. "You understand that anyone might see this portal? It could attract their entire army down on Ash and his team. You cannot be taking this seriously."

The king measured the firstmark's words. He was right, they were making many assumptions without enough information. Still, what was their alternative?

After a moment, he asked just that. "The Firstmark speaks the truth. However, I believe his master still lives or, according to our prisoner, the charm would not glow at all. What other choice do we have? We have a chance to surprise the nomads with a small"—and he looked meaningfully at Ash—"but deadly team. They have the chance to kill the nomad chieftain and end this siege."

The king then asked Ash, "Do you think your chances are better trying to sneak past the nomad lines?"

Ash thought about it, then said, "I think his master is captured and they will not be expecting our arrival. It could be an easier way in, regardless of where we appear. Remember, we will be dressed as them."

The firstmark stepped forward and faced Ash. "Forget betting your life. Are you willing to bet Bara'cor's life? If you are wrong, the mission and our best chance, ends with you."

Ash met the firstmark's eyes, his mind clearly in turmoil. He drew a breath, then ticked off with his fingers his reasons. "This talisman seems designed to bring Arek and his master together in an emergency, which would be done with little noise and fanfare or the idea of maintaining a stealthy mission would be lost. If Arek thinks his master can heal his foot and that requires the sword, then he will have no choice. I go first through this 'portal' with the sword, then the team follows. The boy stays here till our return." Ash paused then added, "It gives us a way to get back here without going through the nomad lines."

"You're suggesting leaving the portal open?" the king asked the armsmark.

"Only if we can adequately guard it from this end," answered the armsmark. "I think Stemmer can hold that line until our return, assuming she recovers."

"Girl has a hard head," remarked the firstmark, "she'll be fine."

Ash nodded, then added, "Of course, we might be able to close it by tossing the charm through without Arek."

"And once you're in, you'll be wherever this Silbane is. Jebida is right, what is your plan?" asked the king.

"Remember, if he is one of those seen by our scouts, he was captured while trying to defend his apprentice. He'll no doubt recognize Tempest, proof we have Arek. I think he'll help us, if for no other reason than that. Furthermore, if Arek is this formidable, imagine what his master must be like."

"Even better," Jebida retorted, "now there'll be two of them." The firstmark moved over to the table, looking at the relief map and thinking. "And what if he refuses to help, but instead wants to return here, to see to his apprentice?"

"I suppose I'll let him return, Ash replied. "I never expected to have his help in the first place, but getting in without daring the nomad line is help enough, right? Besides," Ash added with a smile, "why would Silbane abandon us? Aren't I charming?"

"Not funny," retorted the firstmark. "Clearly I'd have better luck talking sense to Bara'cor's walls." After a moment he shook his head and said, "At least this plan is better than the one that had men dying to get you in."

"I agree," Ash replied.

The firstmark shifted his feet uncomfortably, then looked to the king. "I am not against this plan, it's just . . ."

When the firstmark trailed off, the king asked, "What? You may speak freely here."

Jebida shook his head, then threw his arms open and said, "Trusting magic is forbidden, by your very own forefathers! It was a decree that held our people safe, and now you would flaunt that. I say we're better off without the boy or his master. Nothing good will come of it."

The king faced his firstmark and said, "I rescinded that decree years ago, Jeb. The Magehunters are disbanded. If they operate, they do so outside my law. Persecuting an entire class of people because of how they are born is wrong. Who are we to judge the good or ill a man may bring to this life?"

Ash stepped to the firstmark's side and said, "Dead is not better off. Not for us. Not for the people of Bara'cor." The armsmark laid a hand on his commander's arm, "Many will be taken again by these demons."

The firstmark shrugged off his second's hand, "You presume too much, armsmark," he said, knowing Ash referred to what had happened to his daughter and wife.

He looked back to the king and said, "You may have chosen to overturn your family's law and I do not question that. You are correct, it is your law and your judgment and I will always follow. I just don't have to like it." He paused, about to say something else, then instead said, "If I may be excused, sir? We'll need to get the boy bandaged and cleaned up."

The king nodded, understanding. "Yes, see to it. I'll finish up here with the others."

With a nod and salute, Jebida left the room and an uncomfortable silence followed. Finally, Yetteje, said in a quiet voice, "So, where does this leave us?"

The king watched the back of his retreating commander and said, "We need to speak with Arek."

Journal Entry 12

Of the Titans and gods I know to walk this world, I have seen a few. I thought I saw Lilyth in the distance, the Lady of Flame in all her splendor. I've seen Petra, and mighty Heraclyes. Each ignore me as if I do not exist. Am I too inconsequential? If they are the creation of our legends, truly powerful in the Way, perhaps it is better not to come to their attention. Still, what kills a god?

We cannot stop the creation of new Aeris, but they are not the true danger. They are consumed by incantation or spell. They are fuel, and while they create problems in diplomacy with the Aeris Lords, they are not the true reason for our downfall.

It is these Aeris Lords, who have been given life by our thoughts, who concern me. We cannot stop their Shaping so long as we believe higher powers are at work and a god heeds our prayers. It is a difficult problem to solve, especially in the face of the masses who sit cow-like, chewing their mental cud and praying for divine intervention. I "sigh" when writing this.

It will only be a matter of time before these Aeris Lords enslave us. It is inevitable. Once given life, they begin to dream. Their dreams span the entire heart of our kind, from the basest treacheries to the highest ideals. They are our gods and our demons and demand our fealty. It is their nature.

In their place, what lesser station would you accept?

TEMPEST

Attend an ancient wisdom;

If your woman runs away

with another man,

there is no better revenge

than to let him keep her.

—*Altan proverb*

King Galadine waited in the council chamber, joined by the armsmark, his team, Yetteje, Niall, and the royal guards. He expected the firstmark shortly, with their prisoner. Bernal reflected on his choices.

The torture was unavoidable and he would not regret that. Frankly, Arek's injured foot was their key bargaining chip now, and though he had not anticipated it, a powerful advantage for them.

He'll want to be reunited with his master. It won't take much for him to decide to leave Bara'cor's hospitality. It occurred to the king that Ash was correct. Arek's master had real reason to cooperate, mainly because he could depart with his apprentice. He would try to reason with the boy first and leave intimidation as a last resort. Satisfied, he waited for the firstmark to arrive. He did not have long to wait. A few moments later, Jebida entered the council chamber with their prisoner in tow.

The boy hobbled in supported on crutches, escorted on either side by guards. He clearly could put no weight on his injured leg, which now ended in a stump. He looked haggard, devastated, and in pain. Dark circles stood like half-moon bruises under each eye, and to the king the boy looked young and frail. It was hard to believe this was the same person whom Ash held in such high regard.

Behind him came Sargin, the man who had led the interrogation of their prisoner. As the group slowed, Sargin moved around the boy and came to stand next to the king. They had agreed on this tactic earlier, a way to apply added pressure to the boy during these critical negotiations.

The king acknowledged Sargin with a nod, accepting that men like him were unavoidable in times of war. When the king looked back, the boy was looking at his interrogator with a gaze of hatred so pure that for a moment it startled him.

Perhaps this boy has more steel than I thought...

Still, Sargin's presence would serve to remind the boy of the horror he had endured and make Bernal's offer even more enticing.

The firstmark and king had chosen to introduce Arek as if he were a guest, hoping it would set the tone of the meeting correctly. The king couldn't tell if it worked, for the boy stood still, his face unreadable and his faded blue eyes distant. Bernal marveled again at how similar the boy looked to himself, years ago. For him, it was like looking into a mirror dimmed only by time.

"Your Majesty, may I present Arek Winterthorn, apprentice to Master Silbane Petracles."

* * * * *

The king bowed and said, "I won't waste your time with apologies or false platitudes of friendship. We caught you within our fortress during a time of war and could not hazard those inside. I did what I felt necessary to ensure our safety. Even if you cannot forgive this, I hope you can understand the position you put us in."

Arek slowly looked up at the king, his mind numb. His foot throbbed with every beat of his heart, but when he looked down, there was no foot there. He only glimpsed it once after his interrogation, not willing to look again. Given his training on the Isle, he knew it was not repairable, for there was no foot left to repair. He felt pain in a phantom appendage that no longer existed, and with its disappearance he had lost the rest of his life. Gone, he knew, were his chances of ever being an adept.

He didn't know this "king." He couldn't place him in the same reality as the pain he felt, though a detached part of him understood that someone who claimed the title was ultimately responsible. That was not so for the man standing by the king's side.

Arek knew *him,* and both hated and feared the sight of Sargin. If he could have wished his pain on someone, it was the man who stood emotionless to the king's left. He would find a way to make him pay.

For now, though, the apprentice looked at the king numbly, not really knowing what to say. In the end, he decided there was no point in speaking. They knew everything he did and speaking freely now felt like a betrayal to the loss he had suffered. It made no sense, but it was how he felt.

"I cannot fault you for remaining silent, but I have reason to bring you before me." The king looked to another man and motioned for a written report. Scanning the pages, the king looked back at Arek and said, "I've read your confession and I believe you. I am willing to offer you a chance to rejoin your master. Though you claim no ability with magic, perhaps with this sword, Tempest, your foot may yet be restored."

Arek was shaken by what the king had just said. He looked around, his mind latching onto this possibility the way a drowning man will clutch at anything. This was something he had all but discounted, given the treatment by his captors. Rejoin his master?

He was *sure* Master Silbane could restore his foot, he had said as much when Arek had been given Tempest. He would be healed and he would be rid of these people forever.

No, he vowed silently, I'll be rid of these people until I have real power. Then I will return, and there will be a reckoning.

Then it occurred to Arek, this king wouldn't just let him go free. That made no sense. Something else was going on and though pain dulled his thinking, he knew a bargain was about to be offered. He took a breath, then said in a timorous voice, "You know my master will come for me."

The king nodded, acknowledging Arek's ability to discern what had remained unsaid. He then handed the report back and drew forth Arek's Finder. It hung from its thin chain, sparkling and glowing with its own light.

The king said, "We know your master still lives. We also know he's been captured by the nomads, so he won't be coming for you any time soon. We want to insert a team into their camp. Their job will be to kill the nomad chieftain. Your Finder—"

"I don't believe you," Arek interrupted. He understood the king's plan. They wanted entry into the camp. He wanted to sound sure, but couldn't help it when his voice cracked as he caught the emotionless eyes of Sargin.

The king shrugged, then said, "We *know* he was taken by the nomads, along with an armored knight. I offer you a chance to rejoin him, and so long as you do not seek retribution, we will give you Tempest. I will have my men . . ."

Arek's awareness tunneled in what he now recognized preceded the appearance of Piter. He was not surprised when he turned and saw the shade standing there, but there seemed to be something different about him.

"Revenge!" Piter looked at the frozen scene, his eyes finally coming to rest on Sargin's form. "Retribution for what he did."

"What do you mean?" In a way, Arek found himself happy for Piter's appearance. Despite his abandonment before the torture, Piter was the only familiar face in the room, and Arek felt very much alone.

Piter moved closer, his countenance reflecting barely contained fury. "Revenge for daring to attack an Adept of the Isle, and but for Ascension, you are that already! Make no mistake, you have the bargaining power here." He looked around again then nodded at the figure of the king. "He will do *anything* to get into that nomad camp."

Arek thought Piter's anger strange, but said, "I know that already. What do you suggest?"

Piter nodded, coming conspiratorially close, but careful not to touch the apprentice. "I know a way." Then Piter leaned forward and whispered, and a slow smile spread on Arek's face.

* * * * *

". . . watching. So long as you make your way from this fortress peacefully, I will vow to let you go in peace," the king finished. The boy looked like he hadn't heard the last part, but before he could repeat it, Arek hobbled forward on his crutches.

"I am the only one keyed to use the Finder," Arek said. "And I can transport you and your men to where my master is. What is your plan?"

The king looked at his assembled men, his gaze finally falling on his son. It was for Niall he even considered this. His survival was more important to the king than any other, and sending Ash and his men into harm's way ensured that. He cleared his throat and looked back at Arek saying, "I will give the blade to Armsmark Rillaran for safekeeping during transport."

Ash stepped forward so Arek could identify him.

"If Ash and his team appear where your master is, the team will free him," the king continued. "And Ash will request his help in killing the leader of these nomads. If Master Silbane agrees, they will carry out that mission. Once accomplished, the armsmark will turn the sword over to your master, who can come back through the portal and collect you. From there, what you and your master do is of no concern to me, so long as you do not interfere with our efforts against the nomads."

"If Silbane refuses, he may take the sword and return here to collect you." The king licked his lips, then added carefully, "Transporting our team into the nomad camp will be considered payment in full for your release. You may depart, but we hope you both will join our cause."

Before Arek could reply, Bernal held up a forestalling hand and said, "Should you alone disappear when the Finder is used, we will consider Tempest held as fair ransom. However, if you wish your master to heal your injuries, you will do your best to make sure Ash and his team make it through the portal, or you will not have the means with which to heal yourself."

Arek was silent for a moment, thinking. He then said, "You assume my master can't heal me without Tempest."

The king nodded, looking at his men. "We are all making assumptions, but these are desperate times for Bara'cor." The king met Arek's look with a direct stare and said, "I saw the look on your face when I mentioned your master and the sword, so I believe *you* believe this could work. Am I mistaken?"

"No, you are not, King Galadine," Arek said with a sigh. "Tempest, it seems, is my best chance of ever being normal again." Arek hobbled forward a little more. "I can transport your men to my master's location and with that you will have a good chance of ending this siege. That means saving many lives, including those you hold most dear." He looked pointedly at Niall, who stood next to the king, so clearly his son and heir.

"I, however, have one demand, or I will not help you." Arek's eyes left the prince, meeting the king's in a dead stare.

Bernal too stepped forward. "You are not in a position to bargain. I could have you thrown into a cell to await the inevitable fall of Bara'cor to the nomad army, or perhaps there is more information we might extract." With that Sargin stepped forward and Bernal noted the boy visibly paled, but held his ground.

"Do that and you will never have my help. This fortress will fall and your future will die with you." Arek nodded to Niall with that last statement, his meaning clear.

In that instant, Bernal knew the boy understood his predicament, and what was dearest to the king's heart. It was a moment of clarity, the knowledge that this boy had insight and cunning. If for no other reason than this, Bernal began to believe the boy might in fact be more than he claimed. A grave trepidation began to grow in the king's heart, a fear he was about to make a terrible error in letting Arek live. Still, if he hoped for his line to continue, the hope rested on receiving his prisoner's help.

The feeling of dread grew at Arek's unasked demand, but the king used that feeling, the dread that had grown inside him, to lend steel to his voice., "I could just have you killed."

Arek met his eyes and their gazes locked, each measuring the other.

"King Galadine, I am trained in the ways of combat. With what has been done to my body by Bara'cor's hands, I am already dead. Without my foot, and my master, there is nothing for me to live for. You have nothing to compel me with and we both know it."

Arek's pale eyes never wavered. Bernal saw that he spoke the truth. He believed all he was or could be required his body to be whole, and his eyes reflected his belief and brooked no argument.

The king bowed his head and nodded. "What do you want?"

"I want the life of that man," Arek said, pointing to Sargin, his interrogator. "I want him to be executed now, in front of me."

Stunned silence followed Arek's request. It was as if he had spoken in a different language, one that none in the room wanted to understand. The king was the first to recover, "I . . . you can't be serious."

"I am."

Ash stepped forward, looking at the king, then at Arek. "We'll not kill someone acting on orders, against an intruder. Why not ask for my head as well? I'm the reason you were captured in the first place."

Arek drew a breath then shook his head, saying, "You faced me across live blades, sir, and wagered your life against mine. I accept that, because it was done with honor." Arek turned his attention back to Sargin with a look of contempt. "*He* tortured a bound prisoner and never wagered his own safety."

The firstmark shoved himself forward and retorted hotly, "He was following orders!"

Arek faced the giant firstmark and shot back, "And should all orders be followed, sir?"

When Jebida said nothing, Arek turned his attention back to the king and said, "My master taught me that the measure of a man's worth is in his actions. They define *character*. This man deserves to die, and I will have his life else we are done talking." Arek gingerly stepped back, carefully balancing on one leg, his armpits on the crutches.

"Where is the honor in what you request? How is your character being defined now?" asked the king.

Arek retorted, "Do not parry words with me, King. You had me tortured and never asked for my help, which I would have freely given. You assumed I was the enemy, without ever speaking to me. You cut off my *foot!*" he screamed.

"You—"

"When Bara'cor's safety hung in the balance against mine, you chose Bara'cor," Arek interrupted. "Why is the choice difficult now, because you can't hide somewhere and order the deed done? Did he not pledge his life, knowing it could be forfeit for crown and country? The decision is easy, but you are a coward."

The king shrank in on himself, Arek's words acting as stones slung at the carefully crafted panes of his moral life. Yet his duty was to Bara'cor, and he could not release his obligations, even if they were spurred on by the rantings of a possible spy.

He dropped his gaze, unable to meet the pale stare of Arek's, and put a hand to his head. A moment passed, a silence that stretched as the king took three deep, measured breaths. Then he looked up and said, "Ash, take the blade."

The firstmark hesitated, thinking the king meant to do as Arek asked. While they did not agree, Sargin had followed his orders and Ash had no issues with that. He was, however, sorely wrong in the judgment of this king's character.

"I will not order the execution of one of my men," Bernal said. "He is of Bara'cor too, and falls under my aegis." He sighed, his eyes searching the ground in front of him as if the answer lay at his feet, but when he looked up there was nothing but sadness in his eyes. "I accept there were mistakes made, perhaps in my rush to judgment. But I will not repeat those mistakes. Your master is right, character shows in one's actions."

* * * * *

Ash moved to obey the king's order. He picked up Tempest and turned. As he did so, he heard a voice echo in his head.

Beloved.

Ash looked around, confused. The voice seemed to come from behind him, but there was no one there.

I have waited an eternity.

He looked down at the green-gemmed hilt of Tempest and the image of a beautiful woman came to his mind. *What?* he thought.

I have chosen you.

Ash shook his head, not understanding what Tempest meant. *What?* he asked again.

I am all you wished.

Ash felt the hilt grow warm, an almost living thing in his hand. A tingle started in his palms, then moved through his body. Wherever it went, pleasure followed. His eyes closed, and he could almost see the spirit of the sword floating before him.

Beloved? I must first set things right.

Ash's eyes snapped open. For him, it seemed an eternity had passed, but he could see that only a moment separated the time between when he picked up the blade and now.

"Wait," he began.

The sword brightened, then hummed, glowing green. Ash didn't remember having drawn it from its sheath, but it now shone like a green star in his hand. Silver runes appeared running up and down the mirror-like blade and he could see a quicksilver light flash along its keen, bright edges.

Arek screamed, clutching his leg. The scream wasn't one of pain, but of astonishment. Next to the king, Sargin also screamed, but different, guttural, like an animal being butchered while still alive.

Ash turned and saw the interrogator collapse, clutching his chest and reaching out with one hand in the boy's direction. "No!" the torturer screamed, but his plea had no effect.

Ash watched as an unseen force pummeled Sargin's body until his ribs were crushed, caved in. The force then turned its attention to Sargin's skin, shredding it away in a bloody mist. That mist seemed to flow and weave, a red swathe that made its way directly to the stump of Arek's lost foot, as if the gore were being sucked in by the appendage.

The body of Sargin was stomped, spattering pink gobbets of flesh mixed with shards of pulverized white bone, until nothing resembling a person remained. More of the mist followed the first, joining with Arek's body. In the end, Sargin's body lay smashed into an unrecognizable bloody pulp, the hand that held the hammer, still curiously whole, reaching for Arek.

Ash turned a stunned gaze to their prisoner, who stood without crutches. He watched as Arek looked down, and noticed a foot poking out from where the stump used to be. The boy put weight on it, testing it. A lance of pain shot through his mien, but a look of unabashed joy flashed across his face. His eyes said he had not expected any of this.

What have you done? Ash demanded.

Less than what Arek wanted, and what Sargin deserves. Arek carried me faithfully to you, and I promised him my protection, but I did not heal him.

You did this? You killed a man? the armsmark asked in horror.

Killed, beloved?

What are you? How can you just kill a man?

I am a sword. Is my purpose not clear? she retorted.

Ash didn't answer, but in a moment of clarity knew what this weapon would do. Its nature was to cause harm, to relish in pain. He began to drop it, but Tempest held his fingers fast. Then another wave of pleasure rocked him and that last thought, along with his worries, disappeared.

We are meant for each other.

* * * * *

Arek looked at the warrior he had faced before, the one the king had called Ash. Tempest had grown dimmer, but still glowed an unearthly emerald green. The man's eyes were wide, his gaze locked on the blade.

Arek then looked at his foot, which was now partially re-grown. It had bones covered by muscle and tendon, as though his foot had been skinned, but it was full-sized. He flexed his toes and reveled in the shock of pain. It wasn't entirely healed, but it was a *foot!* He felt giddy with happiness.

* * * * *

The king stepped forward. None of this had gone as he'd planned, and now men clustered behind him looking at the pool of blood, meat, and bone that had once been Sargin. The boy's foot had somehow re-grown and with that Ash knew that all of Bernal's bargaining power had slipped away. What would compel Arek to help them now?

Strangely enough, the king paid little heed to the piteous end of his man, Sargin, though he had died in front of him, destroyed by some force, some exhibition of magic. It should have stunned him, should have left him without the ability to think, but the king was made of sterner stuff.

Ash looked at the boy and said, "You are healed?"

Arek looked down in a daze. *"You* did this?"

"It was not me, but I think the blade itself." Ash stood dumbfounded, not sure what to do next. In the back of his head, he thought he heard a lilting laugh.

Her voice then whispered to him, *I didn't do anything, beloved. Arek healed himself by taking another. That is his nature,* she said in a strange parody of his last thoughts about her.

* * * * *

Arek looked around the room, his eyes settling on the broken form of what had once been his torturer. He couldn't help grinning as he remembered Sargin writhing in pain. A feeling came over him, a satisfaction he hadn't felt since being on the Isle. Seeing this man suffer meant there was still justice in the world.

The king's eyes narrowed and he addressed the boy. "Are you happy, then? Your wish is granted, my man lies dead." The king paused for a moment, then said, "Honor? You have none, sir, but what I must do is worse, for I must still treaty with you."

He shifted, his eyes flicking again to the pulverized form of Sargin and a deep regret began to worm its way into his face. He looked back at Arek and reminded him, "You said we but needed to ask and you would lend your aid. Well, I ask now, will you aid us with your charm?"

Arek looked around the room. He still felt anger and shame at having been tortured, but the pain he felt when flexing his new foot left him feeling a strange glee. He couldn't walk yet, but he no longer had a stump. He wondered what had happened and if the healing would continue.

The torturer lay to one side, mangled into something unrecognizable, but where the king radiated remorse, Arek felt pride. That man had paid for hurting him and he did not regret it in the least. He also reminded himself that the ruler of Bara'cor had chosen to torture him first and ask for help only when no other choice presented itself. Maybe he, too, should pay for that decision. Still, to rejoin his master...

Before Arek could answer, a wave of lethargy washed through his body. The world grew dim and tilted to one side. He heard rather than saw the clatter of his crutches. With a small sigh, his body crumpled to the floor and into oblivion.

A NEW LORE FATHER

True skill needs no voice,

it is evident in every movement,

every thrust.

Though the scabbard is dull,

the blade gleams.

—*The Bladesman Codex*

Giridian rested his head on weary hands. The deaths of Themun, Thera, and the children had affected every family deeply. The Isle itself felt covered in a palpable sense of mourning. The attack was a strike to the very heart of their lives and cost them those that were held most dear, the children. Many did not have the strength to continue and just stroked the ground where their child had fallen, as if to caress them to sleep one last time.

Giridian felt the loss even more keenly. It was because of the lore father's sacrifice that the majority had survived at all. Had he not used every ounce of his life-force, it was doubtful they would have escaped without more carnage and death.

Now *he* was lore father. The simple thought belied the power that came with the title, the magic of his Ascension still changing him from the inside out. He could *feel* it and marveled at the sheer energy coursing through his veins. With it, he felt he could swim to Bara'cor and topple her walls himself. However, even if this were true, it was not the path he would choose.

Kisan. That was the problem he set his mind to now. How could they help Kisan, who had managed to infiltrate the assassins by taking the place of one of their own? Further investigation of the dwarf's body shed little light on his identity. He carried with him no papers, only an assorted set of strange items and things that *could* have been weapons. His death had made it impossible to mindread him, and contacting Kisan was out of the question.

Giridian knew he could do it, for he now had the strength to mindspeak with the other adepts with as much effort as it took to utter a sentence, no matter their location. However, he did not know if that would alert anyone else to Kisan's presence. Given these assassins seemed to command magic of some sort, he did not want to take the chance of ruining her cover.

Therefore, he did the next best thing. He opened a path to the Way and left it open for Kisan. Perhaps the young master would try to contact him when she could. Once she found she could not reach Lore Father Themun, it was inevitable she would move down the line, until she reached Giridian.

Next was Silbane, from whom he'd had no contact and no word. Giridian had stretched forth his mind and found nothing, not even an aura that would tell him that Silbane was alive. Nothing could get rid of that aura, short of death, or close proximity to Arek.

Giridian desperately hoped it was the latter, but prepared himself that there may yet be a third adept who had perished. Had Themun not passed on his knowledge to Giridian, losing the lore father and Master Silbane would have been a blow the council could not have survived.

Dwarves? he thought. Where did they come from? They had left the land, never to be heard from again. Only their great feats of architecture, the massive works and fortresses that dotted the known world, gave evidence that they had ever existed.

"Builders," they had been called in ages past, creating the marvel of stone and steel that many took for granted. Now a team attacked them, killing Thera and the lore father, and worse, the children? Who would care enough to specifically target the Isle and to what purpose?

A knock on his chamber door surprised him, but the aura brought a smile to his lips. "Enter, Dragor."

Dragor made his way into the chambers of the new lore father and bowed, then took a seat in a nearby chair. "How are you doing?"

Giridian's smile wavered as he replied, "Been better."

"I've seen to posting guards. They're instructed not to engage these men, should they return. Everyone else is preparing for the Rites, tonight. You will administer them?"

Giridian looked down and nodded, the Rites of Last Passage, a well-known and necessary part of saying goodbye to those loved ones who had fallen. "I will, though I wish we did not need them."

He put a hand over his face and rubbed his skin until he felt it turn red, his mind a cauldron of confusion. Why had these dwarves attacked, he asked himself again. They were after something, and it could not have been to kill children. Something just didn't feel right and this brought about another realization, the aura of the demon Lilyth was not all he sensed at Bara'cor. His heightened senses could now feel what Themun had, but *what* he felt was somehow different.

In truth, he could feel something powerful in the process of awakening, but when he searched the currents of the Way, the scent of Lilyth was subtly combined with something else.

It recalled Lilyth, but in the way that an acrid rind recalls the fruit inside. The two were parts of the same whole, but different. Themun may have confused the two, but Giridian now knew that what was somehow connected to the Gate was not necessarily connected to Lilyth.

Giridian meant to unravel this mystery before more of his people died. He looked at Dragor and said, "We need to search the Vaults."

"For what?" replied the adept in shocked surprise.

"Follow," Giridian replied. "I will explain."

They made their way out of the tower as Giridian shared his feelings of unease with Dragor. He spoke of the fact that he could potentially sift through memories of the previous lore fathers and see which did not fit cleanly with the history he and Dragor knew.

Dragor held up a hand and interrupted, "You say you have the other lore fathers' memories?"

"I think so, for the most part."

"And this stretches back to the first?" Dragor continued. "You can sift through centuries of learning?"

Giridian looked at his friend and hesitated before saying, "Maybe, the same way you could in our library, and just as inefficiently. It is not as if the correct answer pops into my head. I have to find it by watching their lives, their interactions. Unless I know specifically where to look, I would spend more time than I had in this life searching."

They made their way around another turn when Dragor's hand clamped onto his shoulder. The dark-skinned adept looked down, then back up again at the lore father and whispered, "If it is the Gate we must gain knowledge of, then why not look at *his* memories?"

Giridian shook his head, not understanding.

Dragor licked his lips, his eyes darting between the lore father's and the ground, then he said, "Valarius," with obvious distaste. The knowledge of how close this archmage had brought their world to destruction was still difficult to put aside.

Giridian took a deep breath and stepped back, his mind racing. General Valarius Galadine, Edyn's worst enemy and harbinger of the last devastation. He had been everything the council had stood against, but at one time, he had also been a lore father. Looking into his memories could help shed light on the riddle of the Gate.

He put a hand on Dragor's shoulder and squeezed. "Thank you. Let us get to the Vaults, then we will see."

By the time they reached the underground doors, Dragor seemed to have grown to regret his suggestion. "Forgive me, I did not mean for you to try something foolish."

Giridian nodded, touching the cool metal doors that barred the way to the chamber behind. His eyes closed and a faint click sounded as the doors magically unsealed. He pushed them open, but turned to Dragor. "The lore father sacrificed himself to save us and for that I am grateful. Nevertheless, there *is* a divergence in the Way, and I mean to find out why. How could I do any less than those who came before me to protect my own?"

Dragor sighed, still worried. Then the majesty of the chamber took hold and he drew an involuntary breath. The chamber was vast; two hundred paces from end to end. Along the eight walls that circumscribed the perimeter stood bookshelves stacked more than three men in height and lined from top to bottom in books on lore, magic, and the Way.

The middle of the floor stood cases and displays, each holding a category of items. One section dedicated itself to armor, another to bladed weapons, and still a dozen more to a myriad of other items. The adepts of the Isle had not been idle in their seclusion and the Vault held a great many powerful and wondrous artifacts from a lost age.

Giridian, as the former Keeper of the Vault, was less dazzled by the objects within, but nonetheless the sheer amount of effort it took to find and catalog all these things gave him pause. This was the result of over a century of work and it showed. If nothing else in the chamber awed him, this fact did.

He motioned to a particular set of manuscripts and they made their way to that section. As he walked, he talked over his shoulder to the trailing adept. "Something was not right at the final battle at Sovereign's Fall."

Dragor looked about, wide-eyed at the items within the vault, and he absentmindedly replied, "So you have said."

"There should be historical texts that speak in detail of that time and of the events leading up to it," Giridian continued, "and yet, few manuscripts have been found. We have some, but not nearly the number that should exist."

"And where might those be?" Dragor had stopped near a shield, mirror bright and etched with a sigil reminiscent of a hawk with outstretched wings. As he neared it, Giridian could hear the shield start to hum, as if it vibrated to the same song as his heart. Dragor's hand reached out slowly and the air shimmered in response.

"Dragor..." Giridian grabbed the adept's arm and pulled him away, a smile on his face.

Dragor shook his head and looked about in confusion. "What happened?"

"That shield seeks a wielder, but will always put you in harm's way to prove its worth. Not the best companion," the lore father said with a chuckle. "We're here to do research. Come, shiny things later, my friend."

The two made their way to a section of the bookshelf that held histories from the time of Lilyth. Giridian found the few books that were germane to the subject and pulled them down. These he split into two small, even piles. One contained information on demons, the other on the final battle at Sovereign's Fall.

"I will read on the way of demons. You can re-read what happened at Sovereign's Fall," the lore father said. "Look specifically for what happened to the dwarves following the battle. I don't understand why they would reappear now, or for that matter here on the Isle."

With a sigh, Dragor picked up the stack indicated, then motioned to a young page who stood innocuously to one side. "Please bring us something to eat."

The page nodded, then scampered off through one of the many backdoor passages that connected the various chambers to the kitchen.

For the next few hours the two read in silence, the bits of leftover food and drink littering a serving tray placed on a nearby stand. Giridian finally broke the silence, standing and stretching as his back cracked in protest. He then looked at the adept and said, "I think I've found something interesting."

Dragor's voice echoed the boredom Giridian felt when he answered, "That makes one of us." He shut the book he had been reading and leaned back. "Nothing on the dwarves. Once they left Bara'cor, they disappeared as if they were nothing but myth."

"Do you know where demons, or for that matter, angels, come from?" Giridian asked.

The other shrugged. "From the left and right hand of the gods."

Giridian shook his head. "They are now our myths and legends. We call them angels or demons, but it says here they are actually a race known as the Aeris. It claims that in the distant past they came upon this world and were emissaries to the people of Edyn."

"Emissaries? To what purpose?" Dragor asked. "And if they sought us out, what happened? Demons are vastly powerful and dangerous. I have never heard they were emissaries, or they would seek some sort of peace with us. They are disembodied and cannot exist on the corporeal plane, so why treaty with us?"

Giridian nodded, then pointed to a manuscript that looked truly ancient. "The author of that tome didn't think so. He seems convinced of what I just told you." The lore father picked the book up and flipped to the first page so Dragor could read what was written in clear script on the inside cover.

Dragor leaned in and his eyes widened in shock. "It cannot be!"

Giridian read aloud, " 'In hopes of rectifying our mistakes, *Valarius Galadine.*' " He looked at his friend and said, "Your idea to look through the memories of Valarius is a sound one. We will try and see what memories he has of the battle that cost him his life."

Dragor laid a cautionary hand on his friend's arm and said, "Can I help in any way?"

Giridian looked at the younger adept and smiled. "Keep your hand in contact with me, so I can draw upon your strength, should I need it. The visions are seen by lore fathers only, but your presence fills me with confidence."

Dragor answered with a small smile, though Giridian could see he feared to be near even the memory of one who had caused so much pain and anguish.

Giridian closed his eyes and sank into blackness, a space with stars of light. These would be the memories of the lore fathers who had come before. He took a mental breath, then dived into the stars and back through the memories of the lore fathers who had preceded him.

His mind swept past Themun's to Duncan Illrys, who was lore father for only a moment before dying on the slopes of the Fall. His memories then flew past him to his wife, Sonya, lore mother before Duncan. Her reign was singular in her stalwart defense of their world against Lilyth. He then slowed his thoughts, for before Sonya's time came Valarius Galadine. His memories occupied a space, here . . . but there was *nothing.*

His mind searched, carefully sifting back through Sonya's memories. Her mind went from her ceremony where she became lore mother through her reign. Giridian shook his head, not understanding. Declaring Valarius an enemy of the land conferred his seat as lore father to Sonya. The ceremony, now known to him, should have resulted with Valarius's memories *here.*

Wait, he told himself, if the ritual of transference was not carried out willingly, a lore father's memory transferred to the Way upon death. Valarius did not die when they stripped him of his title. He had died on the slopes of Sovereign's Fall. Giridian moved forward again with renewed energy. The answer would be somewhere before Duncan or Sonya's passing. Nothing else made sense.

Giridian opened Duncan's last thoughts, but where there should have been a lifetime of learning and lore, he also found . . . nothing. He backed up mentally and felt the reassuring presence of Dragor. Taking a deep breath, he opened the memories of Sonya Illrys and found them to be intact. He could see her life, her teachings, and her last stand against Lilyth. He could see everything up till the moment she let her spark jump to Duncan, when transference had occurred.

He went back to search for Duncan again and still found nothing, no memories, no transference. The same was true for Valarius, nothing but a blank space between Sonya and Themun's lives. A disturbing thought began to grow in his mind.

There was no situation where the lore did not transfer from father to father. It was the single thing that kept their teachings intact, or at least accessible for later generations. Furthermore, there was no way Themun would not have known this. Now his dying message seemed all the more cryptic.

He opened his eyes and looked again at Dragor.

"What?" asked the adept.

"The lore father said something to me before he died," Giridian said, looking at Dragor.

The younger adept asked, "What did he say?"

"It doesn't make sense." Giridian looked about as if trying to find an answer in the air around him. He stopped when Dragor laid a gentle hand on his arm.

"Share it."

Giridian paused, then said, "Armun." He looked at Dragor again and continued, "It makes no sense. Who is Armun?"

"I don't know," whispered Dragor. "What about the memories of the other lore fathers?"

"There's nothing," he replied woodenly. "What I mean is, they are missing." Giridian closed his eyes again, searching, "They do not exist. No memories from Lore Father Duncan. None from General Valarius Galadine."

Dragor shrugged. "Is that so strange? They died. Perhaps they never carried out the ritual and their memories didn't transfer, or Themun rejected their learning. Duncan wasn't even lore father for more than a few moments before the king killed him."

Giridian shook his head and said, "Any lore father can unlock them."

He paused, looking at Dragor's confused expression, then explained, "They don't need to carry out the ritual, for their lives are contained in the Way. The spark of transference is not knowledge, but *access* to knowledge, which is recorded and contained within the Way, forever. Even Lore Father Themun, who was largely self-taught, gained access to the collective memories of those who came before him in this manner."

He stood, shaking his head. "For countless centuries the tradition has been followed, even when the lore father was petty or misguided. Knowledge of weakness and mistakes is more valuable than lessons from success, and we cannot count on every lore father choosing to pass on his knowledge. It is impossible that Duncan's and Valarius's memories are not here."

Dragor locked gazes with his friend and said, "Unless . . ."

"Unless they never died."

Journal Entry 14

When you read this, you make yourself stronger. You survive, against all odds, and your belief will suffuse you with strength. Doubt is your enemy, your faith is the key.

My area is not safe, and it is this continued belief that I am in danger that fuels these raids. Ritual is key, faith is power. I will keep writing it again and again to commit it to memory and heart. Ritual is key, faith is power.

My mind, like any man's, must perform a system of actions that result in the conviction that I am safe.

It is the same for the mother that hangs hollyroot above her baby's bed, or when one consumes sunbeam for fever. It is our nature to believe these remedies work, therefore they do.

Now I must do the same, but on a grander scale. I must create a system of faith that is impervious to doubt, and it starts with me.

I know many spells of warding. I believe here, in this place, they will have greater power. I know this to be true, I feel it. I believe it. It is my will that is master here.

Ritual is key, faith is power. Nothing can stop me. I must believe. My life depends upon it.

FALLS OF SHIMMERENE

You cannot know a person's heart

until you have crossed blades.

Once done, their character lies open to you.

They will always act as they did

when trying to survive.

—Davyd Dreys, Notes to my Sons

A rek awoke to the sound of birds ... a sound more incongruous because of its source. Was he not in the Altan Wastes? As his eyes cracked open, he found himself lying in a bed, with a canopy of fine silk above. Flitting about in a small, golden cage were a pair of black and yellow songbirds singing to each other. He was dressed in soft clothes that made him uncomfortable, but only for their fineness. Then he looked down and two shapes pushed up the fine blankets, his *feet*.

He choked out a small laugh ... it was not a dream! Then, with a trepidation he had not felt since he was a child, he wiggled the toes of the foot he had thought lost.

Pain shot up his leg and exploded in his brain. Yet instead of feeling bad, he could not help but laugh. To feel anything at all was better than feeling nothing but a stump ... and with that exhausting effort, a world of new hope opened. Tears sprang unbidden down his cheeks. His foot and therefore his future might once again be his.

"Nice."

Arek started, then turned to the voice, hastily wiping his face. Piter, he thought at first.

"Sorry, didn't mean to surprise you. Honestly."

Arek finished wiping his eyes and realized the voice came not from the shade that had recently become a part of his life, but rather from a girl. "Your name?" he managed to croak, sleep still in his voice.

"Tej," she answered simply. "I'm the Princess of EvenSea."

Arek's eyes focused on his guest and his breath caught. Not just any girl, he corrected himself. She was one of the most beautiful he had ever seen. Her hair flowed from her head like an ocean wave and framed a face that was exotic, but burdened by a deep pain, a pain that made her seem more vulnerable.

"I ... your name?" he asked again, his voice sounding stupid to his own ears.

She laughed, then looked past his bed to the window. Her amber eyes caught the sweep of the desert sun and seemed to soak it in, then intensify it, until her gaze almost glowed. When those eyes looked back to him, his heart fluttered.

"I already told you ... Tej," she answered again, just as simply. "For someone so handy with a weapon, you're not very good with faces," she said with a faint smile, pointing to a small bruise on her temple where Arek's foot had connected.

Arek realized with a shock where he had seen her before, in the hallway outside that chamber. That seemed an eternity ago. She was a princess? The look on his face must have betrayed his thoughts, for he saw the girl's smile grow and she moved closer.

"You fight well. Ash says you're better than anyone he's ever faced."

Arek looked around, then asked, "No guards? What do you want?"

"A favor."

At that moment, Arek's vision tunneled and the world froze and he felt the familiar space of time that portended Piter's arrival. It didn't take long until the familiar dark-robed figure strode into view, appearing from thin air. The shade paused, looking at Tej. "Pretty, but useless."

"You tricked me!" Arek accused. The anger of the torture and treatment by the king, the fear of having been abandoned here amongst strangers, it all came together now, then burst out at the shade of Piter.

"I *saved* you. If I had not come, you would be dead now!" Piter moved past the frozen figure of the princess and faced Arek, standing his ground. "It's more than you *ever* did for me!"

"What are you talking about?" Arek asked. Something in the tone of Piter's voice broke the turbulent anger that had boiled in him a moment ago. Rather than escalating into a yelling match, his outburst left him feeling drained and somehow melancholic.

Piter looked down, but when he looked up again, there seemed to be a change in the shade's eyes and a question came out in earnest: "Why did you hate me?"

Arek stopped, dumbfounded. "What?"

"You were always cruel, letting your friends poke fun. When did you include me? You fall in with them and I am left behind, the odd one?"

Arek took a breath, then asked, "When did I hate you?"

"It wasn't always like that. We grew up together and were friends, brothers." Piter looked away, then said, "It's hard to be an orphan, but you made my life on the Isle miserable."

A heartbeat passed, then two, and Arek dropped his gaze. He hadn't thought of it like that, it had always seemed that Piter was annoying, or somehow just in the way. He answered, softly, "We . . . I didn't mean anything."

"No?" The shade looked on a bit longer, then said, "Forget it, *Master.* It doesn't matter now. All you should care about is your own life, your own friends, as usual."

Arek didn't have an answer. His treatment of his classmate hadn't felt particularly mean or base. Neither Tomas nor Jesyn liked Piter and therefore he became an easy target. But it was just jokes, Arek told himself, no harm had really been meant.

Now the shade forced him to think about his actions from his name-brother's point of view. By that measure, he was less sure he had acted so kindly.

Silence hung between them, stretching out for a few heartbeats before Piter said, "Your destiny lies deep below this fortress. Don't be foolish and open a portal for the king. You'll be killing me twice."

Arek shook his head to clear it, not hearing Piter completely. "What?"

Piter rolled his eyes and said, "Fool, you need to head downward. The Gate you seek is there. It is a place of power. Your will is the key, and achieving this Gate will set things right."

"You mean, free you? You can still be saved?"

The shade looked around, as if sensing its own departure, and said, "Perhaps, but you are likely too stupid."

Arek felt a flash snap as time resumed its normal pace—the jolt of connection and the shade of Piter was gone.

In that moment, he heard Tej finish her request, "Take me with you when Ash's team goes to the nomad camp."

Arek looked at the girl with a faraway stare, the last conversation still filling his brain. He knew he needed to think about how he had treated Piter, but the direction the shade had given him burned its way into the forefront of his mind. The Gate lay below Bara'cor? Then he looked at Tej and blinked, her question registering for the first time. "What do you mean, take you?"

Tej cocked her head to the side and looked at the songbirds, not seeing the effect it had on Arek. "I feel like one of those birds."

Arek looked up and knew what she meant. "So do I, but in my cage, there always seem to be cats." He smiled and when he looked back at her, he was surprised to see she was smiling too.

Then her gaze grew serious and she said, "The nomad chieftain killed my father, he impaled him in front of me. I want to end his life."

"I am sorry." Arek's mind raced and he added, "But how can I help?"

Tej gestured with her chin to the blank spot on his chest where his Finder had been. "Your charm. Take me with you. I'll be ready."

"First, I'm not going with them, and even if I was . . . be accused of kidnapping you? Not likely," he retorted, then let out a small laugh at the absurdity of her request.

Tej pushed past the boy and plopped herself onto the bed next to him, sullen on the edge of angry. "So you're scared?"

"Yes, very," Arek nodded vigorously, not caring what she thought of that.

"The king won't do anything. I'll already be on the other side and Ash will still parley with your master for your release."

Arek stared at her, startled at how close she was and that she seemed wholly unaware of her own beauty. As to her question, he also began to think she was slightly crazy. "I don't even have the charm."

Tej looked up, her amber eyes glinting. "What if I stole it for you?"

Arek laughed. "Use the charm and ruin your king's one chance at breaking the siege? What part of my body do you think he'll cut off for that?"

"Cowards always find reasons why something is too difficult. Heroes don't." Her quirked lips and crossed arms made it clear which part she thought he was acting now. The accusation was plain on her face and stance.

Arek leaned back into the soft pillows, thinking. This was not at all what he had expected and in front of her, his ability to reason fled. He closed his eyes and took a deep, steadying breath, focusing. As he did so, his thoughts cleared and he said, "Going into the nomad camp is the job of trained warriors. No offense, but your skills aren't good enough. At best, you'll hinder any attempt to achieve your own goal."

He hated being so direct and worried she would leave right then and there. Instead, her face took on a thoughtful look.

"What do you think I should do?" she asked in a small voice.

Arek shook his head, not wanting to mention that anyone could open the portal by breaking the Finder. That fact would likely send Tej on a fool's mission. "I don't know. I can create the portal. Assuming you could sneak past the guards, you could go in after the king's men, but for what? It won't be easy to find who you want. There are thousands of nomads in that camp. Furthermore, the team won't stick around once they're done, and there's almost no way you can be there right when it happens."

"That's easy," replied Tej, "we go where all the yelling is."

Arek looked at her incredulously. "You're assuming the king's men can do the job. What if this nomad chieftain is tougher than they think?" He looked directly at the girl and met her amber gaze, adding softly, "I'm sorry, but if your training is an example of the skill of Bara'cor, they are all going to get killed."

He looked down, not wanting to disappoint this girl. No, this *lady,* he corrected. Then his mind latched onto what the shade said just before leaving and he decided to redirect her and get some of his own questions answered. "Tej, what's below Bara'cor?"

Tej stared back at him, a strange look on her face. It was as if he had some how acquitted himself well in her eyes, or at least he imagined that's what she was thinking. Then she shrugged, "Lots of things. The fortress is pretty extensive."

"But do you know your way around down there?" What Piter had said planted the seed of a plan, but it required someone who knew the fortress intimately.

"I guess so. Why?" She plopped back down, rolling onto her back to stare again at the canopy and the songbirds.

"I think there's something down there, something that might help us defeat the nomads. If we could find it, you may get what you want," he said. It was mostly true, but he had tweaked it a bit to appeal more to her need for revenge.

Tej sat up and her eyes filled with hope. "A weapon?"

Arek shrugged, "I'm not sure."

Tej nodded, then tilted her head to one side with that strange look she had earlier. "You don't care what I think, do you?"

"No. . ." Arek stated truthfully. He found her alluring, and outright lying to her seemed somehow wrong.

The princess continued to stare a bit longer, then smiled and stood up. "Refreshing." She stooped to grab a pair of boots sitting unnoticed at the foot of his bed. "Put these on. They look like something from the medics, probably soft."

Arek caught one, the other smacking him in the face. He almost yelled, but her laughter gave him pause. Plus, the boots *were* soft and filled with a cotton fluff that when laced tight would serve as a nice bandage.

"What happens when I have to change these?"

"Like I'm going to know you that long," she replied. "All right. I don't know the fortress *that* well, but I know someone who might."

"Who would that be?" asked Arek.

A voice from a shadow near the door spoke then, startling them both.

"Me," said Niall as he stepped into view.

REBORN

You must give away

any thought of surviving.

Enter each battle as if you have

already died, and your time here

is merely borrowed.

Embrace this, and you will act without fear.

—*Kensei Shun, The Book of Shields*

S cythe watched the image of Silbane in a small water bowl. Beside him stood Hemendra, not at all happy to be in the Redrobe's tent. The watery image showed their captive, still secured to the pole in the tent where they had left him.

"You take a great chance leaving him alive," stated Hemendra.

"I would hazard the world, this army, your life, even the pathetic lice on your skin, to ensure my plan's success. I leave nothing to chance."

The words came out almost normal, betrayed only by a slight tremble at the end. The nomad chieftain had spent enough time with Scythe to tell when he was teetering on the edge of a violent outburst. Usually these ended in the death of a nomad or two, like the skinning of the two scouts.

Hemendra didn't think too deeply over this. The mage instilled fear, and Hemendra gained respect as a result. Still, the man *was* dangerous and in Hemendra's opinion, only the Redrobe's power and promise to help breach Bara'cor's walls had kept him alive this long. He scowled, but said nothing. Gutting him would be simple, when the time came.

"Patience, Mighty U'Zar," said Scythe, smiling.

The chieftain gave a mental start, knowing this man could read thoughts. He cursed his lapse. Scythe's voice reverberated in his head, echoing, *This man is dangerous.*

He let out a forceful sigh, then said the only thing he could, "We both still have our uses."

Scythe locked eyes with the nomad chieftain and a small twitter escaped his lips. "Indeed." Then he looked away and back at the watery image of Silbane.

The voice that came next out of Scythe's mouth had a different tone, one now filled with tactical confidence and military demeanor. "Only two things can happen at this point. Either Silbane uses his Finder, or his apprentice does. I have set the portal web in place."

"And you think this unseen web will work?"

Scythe flicked the water's surface and the image collapsed in a dozen ripples. They quickly died, as if the water were made out of something thicker, and the image returned. Now Hemendra could see purple lines crisscrossing the tent, filling the air around Silbane like a strange spider's web. "If the portal opens, it touches one of these lines. That will not only summon me, but lock the portal open until I can decide what to do."

Hemendra smiled and said, "Giving us a way into Bara'cor." The massive warrior looked at the Redrobe with a grudging respect. "A good plan."

Scythe ignored the chieftain's compliment and said, "I attend to the great dragon. See I am not disturbed."

Hemendra nodded, backing out of the tent along with a small contingent of guards. He went to choose a small group of elite warriors for the difficult task of entering Bara'cor. In case the Redrobe's plan worked, he intended to have a team ready to enter the great fortress and take her from the inside.

* * * * *

Scythe went outside and then to a tent near his own, moving with purpose. He had had the warriors transfer the body of the dragon to this place. It afforded more privacy for what was to come next. He entered the tent, his eyes quickly adjusting to the gloom, and made his way over to the iron circle upon which the great dragon-knight's body lay.

He walked close, inspecting it with a clinical eye. The warriors had left the circle resting upon a table at waist height, making his inspection easy. Satisfied there was no other injury, the mage straightened the dragon-knight's head and neck, then reached behind and in one fluid motion, ripped the arrow from the base of the skull.

It released itself with a wet *pop,* the arrowhead covered in a black, oily liquid that stank of sulfur. The mage dropped the arrow and waited, but not long.

A sudden gasp tore through the dragon-knight and his eyes opened wide, glowing with yellow light like two miniature suns. Scythe could hear bones snapping back into place, muscle and sinew repairing itself. Dragons, he knew, were notoriously difficult to kill.

Smiling, he motioned and the great iron circle lifted into the air, suspended by his power alone. He turned it so the dragon-knight faced him and said, "I welcome you, Lord Rai'stahn."

Rai'stahn looked at the mage, golden eyes calculating. Scythe knew the strength was returning to his limbs, but Silbane's prana locks were still in place, limiting his power.

"Mortal, thou are not my equal. Release me, or suffer."

Scythe held up a forestalling hand. "All in good time, my lord. First, I would know the purpose of your visit."

The dragon-knight strained against his bonds, but was held tight, his armor and scales fused to the metal circle behind him. With his prana locks in place, breaking free would be impossible. He turned his full attention to the mage and recognition dawned on him.

"It has been some time, my lord," Scythe said, "but my quest remains the same."

Scythe felt understanding flood Rai'stahn's mind. "Bara'cor, then, is still thine objective."

"Yes, though your presence and, Silbane's, bodes ill. The timing is not ideal." A smile tugged at the corners of his mouth. "And as *you* know, timing is everything, is it not?"

The dragon-knight ignored the bait and simply replied, "We do what we must."

"We do indeed, my lord. We act when our actions will have the most effect." He paused at that, then added delicately, "The Isle came under attack."

* * * * *

Rai'stahn felt a sudden panic for his hatchling and closed his eyes, searching. He easily located the Isle and the multitudes of bright sparks that existed there, the brightest being his child. The Isle seemed untouched, but the great dragon knew his demesne as only a lord of his people would. While many lived, many had passed on, their sparks extinguished. With shock, he realized the mortal spoke truly. "More than just Themun."

"Why did you hazard their safety?" asked Scythe.

The dragon ignored him, still searching the vast world. He then saw the spark he was looking for and sent out a silent call.

"You left them undefended, to escort a mage and his apprentice here. None would have dared move against you, but you left an opening. Why?"

He felt Scythe try to reach into the his mind, but set a wall of psychic energy to slam closed, shutting him out. Frustration washed across Scythe's features and he said, "Must you insist on plain speech? Can we not parley directly?"

"Sharing thoughts with thee hath not been earned, *mortal.*" He put emphasis on the last word, the entire situation serving to frustrate him to greater degrees. First Silbane, now this. He also cursed Sovereign, who had caused harm to his people. He, too, would pay most dearly.

Scythe looked away, then pulled up a stool and sat down. Perhaps a wisp of the dragon's anger leaked out, for he said, "Silbane lives."

"Until I am released."

"Why?" Scythe asked. "Why did you attack Arek?" As he spoke, a kind of hunger seemed to take over, his questions spilling into one another as if they fought to get out and be heard. "Can he truly disrupt the Gate? Is my quest in danger?"

Rai'stahn said simply, "Release me and thou wilt see."

Scythe shook his head. "Not until I know exactly what is going on." He pulled out a short knife, wickedly sharp and curved, designed to butcher an animal. "I cannot compel you, my lord. We both know this." He looked down and another voice from him hissed, "Nothing really dies."

His head stuck there, reliving a memory, but then with a start he looked up, his pale eyes going from a distant stare to the here and now with an almost audible *snap.* "It took you only a few moments to heal from the arrow wound."

Rai'stahn did not answer, merely looking at the man with his golden gaze. Mayhap achieving his quest would be best for all the worlds, he mused.

"How long would it take if I cut you apart, burned you to ashes, and spread those to the four corners of Edyn?"

When the dragon-knight didn't respond, Scythe smiled and said, "It could be hundreds of years before you revived. What will happen to your daughter who nests on the Isle? Perhaps, someone will pay her a visit, too?"

At the threat to his hatchling, Rai'stahn surged forward and an animal roar tore from his throat, "Thou *dares!*"

* * * * *

For his part, Scythe did not move, his face inches from Rai'stahn's fanged teeth. The events over the many years of his long life had slowly deadened him to most things. He saw the dragon's outburst in a detached way, as if someone else watched through his own eyes.

No, not deadened, a voice gently reminded. *Your suffering has shielded you*. Even the dragonfear washed over him like a cool breeze.

He exhaled once through his nose, then said, "Tell me what I wish to know or I will do as I say and see if your hatchling can be forced to mate with dogs. She will suffer every single day, *for years,* just as I have. I promise you." He kept his gaze locked on the golden eyes of Rai'stahn. "Test my word."

In a contest of wills, one did not attempt a dragon. They were implacable creatures suffused with power, their very essence made from the Way. They were power incarnate, living gods who still walked this world. Normally, a single man would be devoured both mentally and physically for daring such an affront.

However, there was nothing normal about Scythe. He had suffered, lost, and fallen far from a place where any semblance of normalcy still reigned. Fear required one to have something to lose, and Scythe had nothing. He would make good on his threat and the great dragon was too weakened to stop him.

Scythe did not say anything more, holding the dragon's molten gaze in his own pale one, his eyes never wavering. In the end, the conclusion was inevitable. He would win and they both knew it.

The dragon-knight stared, but a sulfurous sigh escaped from his lips. A moment later, Rai'stahn was the first to look away. "Do not believe thy threat will go unanswered."

Scythe could almost feel the dragon's will collapse. "To do so would be foolish." He stood, waiting, the dagger slowly tapping on his thigh.

Rai'stahn's lip curled, revealing his fanged teeth. His golden eyes narrowed. "Very well. The boy is more than he seems."

"Obviously," Scythe said curtly, then asked, "but can he truly disrupt the Way?"

The dragon-knight shook his head. "He doth not disrupt it. He *consumes* it. He draws the Way unto himself, depleting all around him. I felt mine own strength ebb as we flew here. Worse, he continues to absorb power from the very air. He must be eradicated, or he will be the death of us all."

"The Gate cannot be threatened!" Scythe's jaw worked, his teeth grinding as he felt the panic begin to build again at the idea of his life's work at harm. It was his only chance. He could feel his emotions well up, threatening to spill over again into that place where he could do nothing but watch. He did not like that person, it was not who he really was.

Just when the force of memory became almost too much to bear, he heard the dragon say, "Release me and thy Gate will be safe. I will kill the boy."

Scythe spun and faced Rai'stahn, a blanket of calm serenity stretched tightly over his mental conflagration. He took a careful step forward, as if treading lightly to avoid breaking his precarious hold, "Why?"

"The boy cannot be suffered to live. He will eventually destroy any who harness the Way."

The simple statement hit Scythe with an almost physical force. His mind whirled through the logic, like a game of planks, toppling each fact in a quick line. That would include all the Elder Races: dragons, dwarves, even those who were born with Talent. It would make everything, Scythe involuntarily gasped, *mundane.*

"Thou sees the danger."

The calmness continued its hold, as the analytical part of Scythe's fractured mind now turned its attention to the problem of the great dragon. "If I release you, you will kill me." He said this with no emotion, a simple statement of fact.

"Will that not help your life's work?" asked the dragon, seemingly mocking the mage.

"If I am to recover *them,* I must pass through alive, else I would have ended this accursed existence long ago."

The dragon-knight shifted, then said, "My hatchling cannot live in a world where this boy lives. Our interests are aligned, and I can put aside thy words."

"You'll understand if I say I don't believe you, my lord." Scythe looked at the dragon for a moment, noting that most of the creature's visible wounds had healed, then said, "Take the Blood Oath."

Rai'stahn laughed. "Oath-forged, with thee? Thou art truly mad."

"Then you are of no use to me," Scythe replied. He moved forward with the knife.

"Wait." The dragon met the archmage's pale gaze, then let loose a volcanic growl, emanating from deep within his armored chest. Anyone else who faced the dragon's anger would have fled, but Scythe was not just any man. The dragon dropped his head in defeat and said simply, "I agree."

* * * * *

Rai'stahn felt one arm come free. He pulled it close, his hand tightening into a fist. He could feel power course through those veins, but held back by the bonds of Scythe and the locks Silbane had placed. He cursed himself again for trusting that particular mortal, and frankly, he corrected himself, mortals in general. His eyes narrowed into golden slits and he asked, "Thou wilt seek out the boy?"

"No, my lord. I have reason to believe that Silbane's apprentice will come here using a Finder. I have arranged for that portal to remain open, leading me back into Bara'cor. You can do what you want with the boy and leave me to my purposes."

Rai'stahn nodded, thankful Themun had followed his orders regarding his talisman. Now that offered him a chance to retrieve the boy before it was too late.

Scythe continued, "Do you take this oath with me?"

"Very well, Lore Father," Rai'stahn intoned. "By the blood of my people, I bind myself to thee as ally. I wilt cause no harm to befall thee from my action or inaction." In one fluid motion, he bent his finger forward and sliced a razor sharp nail across his palm. Black blood seeped from the cut.

Scythe bowed and said, "By the blood of my forefathers, I bind myself to you as ally. My oath as Keeper of the Old Lore, I will cause no harm to befall you from my action or inaction." He tapped the gutting knife against his temple, smiled at the dragon, then cut his own palm open. Red blood gushed from the wound and he quickly clamped his hand with the dragon's so their wounds touched.

A golden flash occurred at the point of contact, then grew to encompass them both. Then, just as quickly as it appeared, it disappeared in a flash of white. Scythe removed his hand and his wound had healed, leaving only a thin white scar where the Oath Cut had been. A similar scar ran across the dragon's palm, but even that was quickly fading.

Scythe stepped back, then gestured. The dragon-knight felt all the bonds holding him to the circle disappear. He slipped off the circle and landed with a grace that belied his great size.

The mage moved to the dragon and looked up at him, then closed his eyes. Rai'stahn could feel the binding knots that sealed him from channeling his full might. While Silbane may not have the skills of a Lord of the Old Lore, what he did he did well. Still, it only took a moment for Scythe to unbind Rai'stahn, and when he finished, the mage stepped back and said, "It is done."

Rai'stahn could feel it! His power was free, coursing through his veins, healing and strengthening his body. He could feel it bunch and flex, like lightning aching to strike. He breathed in deeply, then stretched his wings to their full span, reveling in the sheer power of the earth and air around him.

His wings snapped back into place and the dragon-knight looked at the red-robed mage and said, "I wish to kill thee, mortal, but that can wait."

Scythe smiled and said, "Kill Arek and leave me to my purposes. If I succeed, you will still get your wish."

Journal Entry 15

Failure and success of sorts. I find it hard to write "failure," so will call it, "an experiment whose outcome I could not predict."

The fact I am still writing means I survive, though barely. I have tried every version of the wards I know, yet after a time, they all fail. It is as if deep inside I know they are not enough, and I erode them. Ritual is key, but faith is the power.

I look at the last sentence and realize something. I have written that before, but not exactly in the same way. The word "but" creeps into the writing and therefore must also exist in my thoughts. Doubt fills my very journal and condemns me, yet I must keep this as a testament.

I need something else, something here that is unassailable in building my faith. I need to find something to believe in. Perhaps something that is a part of me . . .

My imps are becoming smarter. Today one watched me for what seemed the entire day. So I decided to speak to it. Strange to hear my own voice in all this desolation. Of course, the mere utterance of any sound scared it away. Hopefully, it will return and we can continue the lesson.

FIRST COUNCIL

In mastering yourself,

give away all that one can use against you.

Share your weakest moment willingly,

tell your deepest fears.

Once uttered, these things lose

power over you.

You become a wall

that no doubt can cling to.

—*Kensei Shun, The Book of Shields*

The Last Passage for Lore Father Themun Dreys was a solemn affair and held at the time of the setting sun. The body rested inside a wooden boat as mourners gathered along the beach. The repetitive sound of the waves breaking along the surf was in its own way welcome. It was far off, a building rumble, crash, then bubbling hiss that gave the assembled a sense of peace, as if the entire world waited for the lore father to be put to rest.

Along with the adepts came those elders of the Isle who sought to mourn their loss, these orphans having become part of their family as much as any child born to them. Each carried a small candle set upon a wooden plate. These would be set to float alongside the funeral boat of the lore father. They had chosen a secluded spot on the shore where currents flowed quickly out past the breakers and into the wide, blue expanse of the ocean.

Lore Father Giridian spoke of the life of Themun Dreys, his single-minded vision that kept his people alive and protected. He paid homage to a man who had spent the better part of two centuries protecting those he loved and in his final act, saving the Isle from unknown assailants.

At the proper moment, the boat was launched and set afire. Along with it floated dozens of candles, individual flames of tribute to those who had fallen. The boat blazed orange and yellow, like a sun brought to earth, reflecting its light in the deep blue waters. It made its way out to sea, a shining beacon that illuminated the dark, much as the lore father had done during his long life.

Once concluded, some mourners remained, seating themselves on the beach and gazing out at the sea and the stars as they slowly winked into existence. Others wandered back toward the main halls, their purpose lost with the death of those they cherished. It would be some time before those on the Isle who survived would heal, but they would never forget.

Lore Father Giridian watched everyone, his concern plainly evident. They needed answers, a reason why this tragedy had occurred, or else there would be no closure. He motioned to Dragor, who came and stood beside him.

"We need to delve deeper into the lore fathers' memories. The answer to this attack is somewhere in our past," he said.

Dragor looked out across the sea and asked, "To what end? You said the memories of Valarius and Duncan are missing. Even if we find an answer, what will we do about it?"

"Come," the lore father said, moving off the beach and to the Halls, "there is still a lot to be answered for."

They made their way back to the Vault and settled into the chairs they had occupied earlier that day. One of the pages had neatly arranged the books they had found so they could easily continue from where they had left off. Giridian picked up Valarius's tome and said, "He wrote of demons as emissaries. Why?"

Dragor shrugged, "You know I don't believe that. We know demons exist on other planes and seek entry into this one. It's the reason for these periodic incursions by Lilyth and its forces. Families lose loved ones, but we stand guard against them. They are ethereal and need a corporeal body to exist." He looked at the lore father, then grabbed his hand and squeezed the flesh, saying, "It is this existence they crave, for with it they experience the physical pleasures of the body. We are *life* to them."

"What if that is wrong? I have heard it said that demons are more like moths drawn to a flame. They don't wish it, just as a moth has no desire to be consumed by fire."

"That is absurd. How many died in the last war against Lilyth? Families watched as their children were torn from them and taken through the Gate. This was no involuntary, 'moth to a flame,' impulse but true, sinister aggression."

Dragor took the book from Giridian's hand and flipped through it, stopping on a paragraph that had a few marks in the margin. "Did you make these?"

Giridian looked, and shook his head.

"Listen to this then," Dragor continued. " 'I have concluded the Aeris suffuse our world. Upon creation, they are helpless, existing for no other reason than to bring our focus on the Way into clarity, to breathe life into our spells. They are used, subsumed by the spirit and lost forever. They are the basis of our magic.' "

"The basis of our magic . . ." Giridian shook his head. "If that were true, then we, by using the Way, are using the demonkind?"

Dragor simply said, "Aeris. He names the demonkind: Aeris."

"So these 'Aeris' are used by us, unknowingly? They then become a power source by which we are able to exercise our spells?"

"Simply not true," Dragor said. "Think about it. Centuries of lore fathers would be hiding this truth from everyone else. To what end?"

Giridian looked at his friend, thinking, then said softly, "Not if they didn't know, or to keep things as they are." To Dragor's confused expression, Giridian said, "Freeing the Aeris would mean changing the very fabric of our society. In whose interest is that?"

"No one, least of all Valarius," Dragor admitted. "His thirst for power brought the last Demon War upon us."

The lore father leaned forward in his chair. "Exactly. I think there is some information missing, and I need to see for myself."

Dragor leaned back, his offer to help plainly written on his face. He held out a hand and said, "Do you wish me to . . . ?"

"No, my friend." Giridian smiled, but after the first attempt realized he could do this alone, as clearly every lore father before him had. While he did not believe they would hide something so important, neither did he wish to break the sacrosanctity of his office.

"Perhaps, then, I can wander around and look at things?" Dragor inquired.

"Of course, though try not to touch anything," Giridian replied with a smile. "Nothing will harm you, but you never know what might happen. And keep in mind—" he smiled at the younger adept—"the job of Keeper of the Vault is open now."

Dragor nodded, smiling in return, then made his way into the main Vault, his eagerness hard to hide.

Giridian sat back, closed his eyes, and concentrated on the Way. It opened before him easily, a liquid silver flow that brought him dizzyingly to a central point of stars. Each of those stars, he knew, would be one of the lore fathers who preceded him. Now, the key was to find the right one. Part of him wondered why whomever had created this method of archiving their knowledge had made searching it so absurdly difficult. It was unnecessary and spoke either to a cruel architect, or a clumsy mistake. Regardless, it was something he would look into later.

Now, he needed to focus his attention and look past Themun Dreys to Sonya Illrys, the woman most connected with the time of Valarius's dismissal. Her knowledge may shed light on his current predicament.

He chose a moment closest to the time when Valarius was still an adept and not yet lore father, hoping to see what events led to his elevation. The search brought his vision to a council in session, over two hundred and fifty years ago.

* * * * *

"He continues his research, though forbidden." A young woman reported, her eyes flashing in anger. Giridian didn't recognize her, but Sonya's memory supplied a name: Finnow.

"I trust him, Fin ... don't you?" asked a man Sonya knew as Dale. "He may be reckless, but never has there been one of his power before. Perhaps he sees what we cannot. What if he's right?"

Finnow spread her arms, clearly exasperated. "That we need to stop these encroachments by going to their side? That is absurd, but more dangerous is that he seeks to open a new gate for them, one through which they could enter our world!"

Dale shook his head placatingly and said, "You misunderstand him. He wishes to journey through a gate of his Making and find a way to stop them from the other side. He does not wish their entry to this world."

Finnow said to Dale, with acid in her voice, "You believe his claim they are here now, amongst us, silent and watching?" She laughed, turning to her brethren. "Angels and demons, necessary to give us the commands of our gods?"

"Watch yourself!" admonished Dale. "You presume much, for one so young." The older man looked at the council members and said, "It is easy to say inflammatory things, but Valarius has never claimed these creatures speak for our gods."

"Then where is he to explain this?" retorted Finnow. She stepped up to the older man, her withering gaze filled with ire. "Why do you speak for him? The *prince* mocks us, even now."

"Are you so sure of that, Finnow?"

The deep voice came from the entrance to the council chamber, where a man stood. A palpable power emanated from him and Giridian knew instantly this could only be Valarius Galadine, brother to the king, and crowned prince. All eyes turned to him as he strode into the chamber and claimed the speaking floor.

Finnow backed away, her eyes downcast. The rest of the council waited to hear what Prince Valarius had to say.

"I apologize for my late arrival. There were matters to tend to that necessarily delayed me." He looked around the room, and where his gaze fell people shrank back, but not in fear. This man radiated power, the kind that made one uncomfortable because of its intensity.

"It is true, there are Aeris amongst us, unseen, unheard." He took measure of the room and the people within it, then looked pointedly at Finnow.

Finnow stood defiantly, her back ramrod straight, and said, "So *you* say. Only you." She nodded to another man seated at the head of the chamber, "Lore Father Damian does not feel their presence, nor do I. *None* of us see what you claim."

Valarius outwardly remained calm, but one could almost feel the storm that brewed within, barely contained. "Must you see something to know it is real?" he challenged. "What of the Way? How does your will, unseen, move the earth?"

Finnow paused, her eyes calculating. Then she said, "Our gods give us the Way. It is blasphemy to deny this, a fact you are well aware of, *prince.*" She then looked to the assembled council and said, "It is absurd to believe these Aeris are the source of our power. You make us to be nothing but siphons, leeches?" Her gaze turned stern and she shouted, "Our power stems from the most divine of sources, the power of the *gods,* channeled through us!"

Valarius laughed. "Gods? You believe in unseen gods over unseen Aeris? It is a fine hair you split."

The force of Valarius's presence made Finnow retreat again, despite herself. Giridian saw her visibly gather her courage, then haltingly reply, "Divine Right. It is our destiny to have the Way, else we would not have it."

"Your argument is at best circular. Our gods do not grant us these rights—"

"It is now you, who blaspheme! The gods do not forsake us! It is we who are their servants and it is our burden to spread their kindness upon our world."

Though Finnow's retort had a tint of fanaticism, Giridian could see quite a few assembled adepts murmur their support. The crowd, it seemed, believed her more than they respected Valarius's power.

Giridian had no idea that religious zeal so permeated the Old Lords. How had they believed their powers emanated from some divine source? He shook his head, his opinion of his ancestors changing radically from the wise and learned, to the realistic view that they too had their flaws. Still, he had never expected them to be so steeped in religious mysticism. The Way required no gods, only discipline and control.

He saw Valarius sigh, a weary look upon his face, "Over the ages, these Aeris may have been responsible for the incursions to our world. If true, there is a reason for their attacks and we need to find it, or we risk our own annihilation."

Lore Father Damian stood and asked, "And if we believe you? Rather than speak through your various agents—" he motioned to Dale, who bowed, with a chagrined look on his face—"I would hear from you. What do you propose we do?"

Valarius looked down, his expression one of consideration. Then he met the lore father's gaze and said, "We journey to their plane, find the reason for their incursions. We parley."

The murmurs surrounding the chamber broke into cries of shock and horror. Even the lore father looked at the archmage as if he had lost his mind. He motioned for the room to quiet, then said, "Open a planar gate? Once done, it cannot be undone. Our time has been spent sealing the rifts we know of and still new ones appear. Whole villages disappear as a result, every living person within taken by these demons. Yet you say the Aeris are peaceful and would have us open yet another path for their invasion."

Valarius shook his head. "They are already among us. I feel their presence, like a hand upon my own."

Lore Father Damian's gaze became steely. "You do not know that," and before Valarius could reply, he continued, "and neither do we. But we will not chance another gate."

Valarius met the lore father's eyes and something unseen passed between them, an understanding of their positions. "I will do what I think is best for this land and her people."

Giridian listened as murmured shock whispered again through the crowd of assembled adepts. Shouts of "Usurper!" and "Traitor!" blurted out, echoing in the chamber, though whoever uttered them quickly hid amongst unfriendly faces. He saw the lore father raise his arms for silence, which slowly came at his request.

"What *you* deem best, Prince Valarius? Your oath precludes that. What you deem best . . . is for *us* to decide," said the lore father. He had added Valarius's title as a reminder of the crown he had voluntarily relinquished. "Surely you intend to stay within the restrictions of this council's orders."

Valarius's eyes scanned the assembled council, the torchlight reflected in dozens of unfriendly eyes, waiting for his next words.

To Giridian it looked like a mob, ready to attack, but held back by the power of this man. He shook his head at the sight of it and his attention returned to the tall archmage as he bowed, "As a Galadine, I remind you that these are my people too. Yet, I will abide by your restrictions." He slowly looked around the chamber till his eyes came to rest on the one called Finnow. To her he said, "My name, my true name heard upon the day I Ascended, is *Azrael.*"

Stunned silence followed Valarius's revelation of the most sacrosanct information a mage could ever share. It was never to be uttered, held only between the master and the wind that gave it voice. To tell others was unheard of. It gave those who knew power over him.

Valarius smiled and looked down, nodding, "If you believe me to be a danger, Finnow, you now have the means to stop me." He paused for a moment, his face solemn,. "We have no Divine Right, and knowing my name gives you no power over me or the Aeris. Delay in acting, however, and I will join you in wishing it did."

* * * * *

The vision went dim, then faded to black.

He gave them his true name? Was Valarius mad? Then a cold logic settled over Giridian, the analytical part of his mind asking the next most logical question. If they knew his true name, why were they unable to stop him?

Could their true names really be unconnected to their power? If so, what did it mean? He had grown up believing the name he heard upon Ascension, Artorius, had been his birthright, a sign he had achieved something. Now that had been cast in doubt. How was he to find the truth?

Giridian needed more information, more facts to put the conversation he had witnessed into context. He decided to skip ahead to the time closer to the War, where Lilyth and her forces had attacked.

He plunged back into the void. At first, he flew as if he were the wind itself, the stars streaking past. Then slowly, his feeling of immense speed faded and he became mired in blackness. Each movement slowed as if he were submerged in a viscous fluid and the tiny stars sat steadily twinkling around him, as if bearing witness. His path forward had effectively been blocked by this unending blackness.

Then, in the distance, Giridian could see . . . *something*. It was a tiny point of light at first, flickering and wavering. It was so indistinct he blinked a few times to make sure it was no trick of his eyes, but it did not disappear. Instead, slowly the light grew.

Soon he could tell it was a figure, either walking toward him or he toward it. Then they were in front of each other. He stood looking up at a being made entirely of light. Its form was indistinct and though it did not shine brightly, Giridian found himself shielding his eyes.

The figure held up a hand and a chime sounded that seemed to pierce his mind, a spear of sound that stabbed through his entire being. The chime began almost harmoniously, but ended in a harsh double chirp.

Slowly, the being of light condensed until it took on the form of a large man in robes. He smiled and said, "Lore Father Giridian Alacar, be well come. It is with joy we greet this meshing."

Giridian stepped back, not knowing quite what to say.

GUARDIAN OF THE WAY

Do not teach a student before he is ready;

train him until his body no longer fails,

till discomfort is ignored.

Train him until he resists no more.

Only then can he accept the Way.

—Davyd Dreys, Notes to my Sons

Meshing?"
"Ahh ... our lexicon is incomplete and I am using the word in our language that is closest to yours. You are hearing the translation."

"But you are speaking my language."

The man smiled again. "You are *hearing* your language. There is a difference. Still, our hope is it will suffice." He looked away for a moment, then back at Giridian before continuing, "You have entered a library of sorts, an archive of knowledge. It was placed here to safeguard all learning."

"I know. The lore fathers' memories and lives are here."

"Indeed, and much more." The area around them changed and Giridian found himself back in his Vaults, where he and Dragor had just been. Except now it was empty save for the two of them. The man gestured to a chair and took a seat himself. "Your journey here was not anticipated."

"Why?"

"You were not considered vital for unity, but as in many things of late, we predicted wrongly." The man smiled again, not unkindly.

Giridian took his seat slowly, the transformation of the black emptiness into his Vault so complete, the illusion so real, he could smell the leather and see dust in the air. This was power above anything he had seen done, except by Themun in saving the Isle. He cleared his throat and asked, "Your name, sir?"

"I am known as Thoth. I maintain these archives," he said, looking around him.

"Seems like a big job for one with so short a name," Giridian said warily, though a smile hid behind his eyes.

The man smiled back. "I believe you are making fun of me, Lore Father. We are both responsible for much the same thing."

Giridian let the surprise show on his face, "You are a lore father?"

"Similar, but closer in spirit to your duties as Keeper of the Vaults. You collect and preserve this storehouse of knowledge—" he took in the area in which they sat with a gesture—"I do much the same, but on a far vaster scale. I am Thoth, the Keeper."

"And you greet every new lore father who enters the Way?"

Thoth gave a friendly laugh, his hand clapping his knee. "I wish we had. If so, we may have avoided much difficulty. Unfortunately, we have jealously guarded much, kept information to ourselves, and now face the consequences." His face grew contemplative, then he leaned forward and said, "You understand the world faces grave danger."

Giridian nodded. "Is there ever another type?"

The man's eyes seemed to glint with humor at that, and Giridian found himself again marveling at the detail of the vision.

"Well said. Do you recognize this?" In the air floating next to the man appeared an intricately carved runestaff. It was black and made of a polished metal that was both strong and light. Giridian knew it immediately.

"It is Lore Father Themun's runestaff. We could not find it after his passing..." His voice trailed off as the losses to the Isle came unbidden to the forefront of his mind.

"Be at ease, Lore Father. You can forestall much hardship by keeping an open mind. You see, you are the first to be invited into our Conclave, a group whose stewardship is the safety of this world."

"How is this different from our council?" Giridian scoffed.

"Our Conclave includes many who have been created for specific purposes. They are better suited to deal with certain situations, just as a bull is better than a hawk for certain things."

"And you want me to be a bull?"

The Keeper smiled again. "We want you to be both." When the lore father didn't interrupt with another question, he continued, "You see, something important has changed. But we cannot act in your world. That falls to your people, for you are the Will of the Way."

"So you want me to fix your mistake?" Giridian couldn't help the frustration that came through in his voice.

Thoth shook his head. "You misunderstand me, so it is apparent I need to be more clear." He sat back, his gaze narrowing. "Our people are explorers. Ages ago we came to your shores, but an accident made our vessel unable to sail again, so we used it to build ourselves a new home, a new life."

"Not surprising. Much of the Shattered Sea was settled in this manner."

"Indeed, but our people brought something special and unique to your lands, something so wondrous the world would never be the same again. We brought the Way and it infused every part of life with its energy and power."

Now Giridian found himself growing interested, for the emergence of the Way was still subject to myth and speculation.

"Much was lost in our escape—tools, tomes of knowledge—but we as a people survived. The Way saved us, it helped us shape the land to our needs, and hid us from our enemies. As we grew and multiplied, so too did it grow in power."

Giridian nodded. "I think I understand."

The Keeper shook his head. "You do not. Untold millennia passed and the world moved on. We are today what the Way has made us, shaped by it and our beliefs into everything you see. Nothing will change that. We are also inextricably linked to the Way, so much so that our existence depends upon it. It gives rise to your powers, to every creature that lives on, above, or inside this world. It is the stuff everything you see is made of, save your people. You are still flesh, unchanged, *inviolate.*"

"You seem real enough," Giridian said, confused. "Are you, then, made of magic?"

"I am real, but only in here. This is Will of the Way. It is a kind of magic, one with a purpose, but certain things were allowed in the name of expediency."

The man paused, then said softly, "Normally, it would never have been so. When we first arrived, Guardians were in place to protect the Way from corruption, but we were so few. Hurt, sickened, dying, our survival was deemed most important. The Guardians were removed, put to sleep, and dispensation was given. Now, ages later, this is the result." He looked around the room, but his expression seemed to include the entire world.

"Why are you telling me this? Did Themun know?"

"The Conclave cannot sit idly by any longer, nor can cryptic direction suffice. We made a feeble attempt with Valarius, and frankly, made things worse. With Themun we also said too little, and he focused on bringing order to the chaos that reigned after the last war."

"The Aeris? Why do they attack us? Are they demons, truly?"

Thoth looked uncomfortable, his gaze dropping to the floor as if searching for an answer. Then he looked up at Giridian and said, "You are one of very few to be entrusted with this knowledge. It is not because you will misuse it, but because the knowing will intrinsically change you. We cannot predict the result, and that makes us wary."

"You'll have to trust me if you expect my help."

Thoth nodded, thoughtful. Then he said carefully, "The Aeris *are* the Way. They are your dreams, hopes, and fears. They were a necessary part of your survival, but without the Guardians, they remain unchecked. The Conclave acted and sealed them within their own plane of existence. But . . ."

Giridian waited, then urged, "What? They seek to possess us?"

"No, they seek *life*, Lore Father. They are formed for a purpose, given meaning by every life in this world, but what then? You cannot banish them for they are necessarily a part of you. Valarius Galadine was the greatest archmage to have ever lived, and we thought by giving him insight, he could solve the problem. He did much worse."

Thoth sighed, then shook his head. "Themun did not understand what was at stake, instead focusing single-mindedly on these rifts and gates. Now it falls to you and your brethren and for that we must be more clear."

Giridian swallowed, his mouth dry. "What did Valarius do?"

"Something was created, a creature that feeds on the Way. Wherever it goes, magic dies. For now, the effect is small and contained. It can absorb those that exist as shades and the weaker Aeris. But if the creature is allowed to continue, beings whose nature exists on the Way, beings like *us*, will be eradicated. Soon, it will consume everything."

Giridian looked at the man, his analytical mind already skipping forward to the logical conclusion, and the implication stunned him. He took a deep breath then said, "Arek."

"Because of the decisions made so long ago, we foresaw that something like this could occur. We have always stood vigil throughout the world, watching for signs. We call them 'nulls' and have stopped them in the past, but each time one appears it grows stronger more quickly. We need to fix things at the source. We cannot continue to bandage these points of injury. There are too many."

"Me, the bull and hawk?"

"You are astute. The runestaff is more than just a badge of your office. It is an ancient artifact. With it you can see far places, create form and substance from nothing, locate things, even heal."

"Heal? I can do that now."

"Not people, Lore Father. The runestaff was designed to heal the Way, but it needs a wielder. Only your kind's will shapes the Way. This is why you are necessary. You are the Will of the Way. You must do what Valarius did not."

Giridian sat back, more than a little stunned. "How?"

For the first time, Thoth looked sheepish, as if he did not want to admit his next words, but they came out, haltingly, nonetheless. "We are not sure."

"What do you mean?"

The Keeper hesitated, then said, "Much information was lost when we came here, but we are searching for how the runestaff should be used. Until then, know the Way can be destroyed by one such as Arek, but it can also be saved, restored." Before Giridian could say anything, Thoth held up a hand. "You must destroy Arek, but he is immune to anything that comes from the Way. He absorbs its power and uses it. This means—"

"Spells, magic, even magical weapons?"

"Indeed. He cannot be killed except by unaltered steel, but can command the Way against you. Once he realizes what he is, he will do just that. Tell your adepts, all of them, for they are uniquely gifted to stop him. Explain things however you wish, but be judicious. You are part of the Conclave now."

"How can Arek use the Way if he destroys it?"

Thoth looked at the lore father with respect in his eyes. "Arek is the unification of both magic *and* flesh. He is a combination of these things, neither wholly flesh, nor purely the Way. As such, he can command the Way even as he alters and destroys it. Think of it like a sponge that soaks in water and when squeezed, expels it. The danger lies with the Aeris Lords, who will safeguard Arek until they can understand how he achieved unity when they themselves cannot. Our worry is they use him to try to breathe life into themselves."

Giridian sat back, thoughtful., "Can they do this?"

"We do not know, but they risk their own destruction and the destruction of this world in their attempt."

"What of these archives, of seeing the lore fathers' memories?"

"Even if the archives were not failing, would you sit watching lifetimes of unending daily routine and drama to find what you already know? It would be a sad existence." He looked at Giridian for a moment, his gaze measuring. Then he hesitantly added, "There . . . is one more thing."

"There usually is."

Thoth chuckled. "It was thought that things could be fixed within the boundaries of the laws of this world. However, another believes differently and has left the Conclave to pursue its solution independently. It is the Sovereign, and at one time ruled us all."

"What does it want?" Giridian asked.

"It wants to eradicate this, all of it, and start over." He took a deep breath, then continued, "You have faced its assassins."

Giridian nodded, the shock difficult to hide from his face. "They killed children . . ."

"Sovereign will kill *everything*, if left to its own will."

"This seems to be a bigger problem than Arek," Giridian countered, angry, the deaths of those on the Isle still raw and near the surface.

"For now, your interests in stopping Arek are aligned. He endangers the Sovereign, too. However, do not hesitate to protect yourselves."

"That's it? You said you would share information, but this tells me nothing."

Thoth smiled a small, sad smile. "The Conclave, *your* Conclave, is working on a solution to the runestaff. We have shared with you all that you can comprehend. Have patience, for you are not our only herald in this world. "Focus on Arek. He is a greater danger than you realize, even with the knowledge we have granted."

He looked around the room and added, "You have some of the ancient lore here, and now understand the Way better than any who came before you. Do something better than they did with that knowledge. Forge something new, Lore Father."

Thoth stood. Looking down on Giridian, he said, "I will always be here to answer your questions, as will the Conclave. You may also continue to See any lore father's memories provided you know where to look. Our ability to search them for you is now limited by the energy it consumes. Perhaps you wondered why your ability to search the memories is so linear?"

Giridian arched an eyebrow. "I had wondered, but let myself become content that it was plain cruelty."

"No," Thoth said with a smile, "true searching would consume us and leave you without aid. I warn you again that time is precious. You may trust the dragons, who were and continue to be defenders of the Way and hold this world's protection under their wings. However, maintaining this meshing also tasks us greatly. Use it sparingly."

Giridian paused, then asked carefully, "Why is your energy limited?"

Thoth smiled, but there was a sad inevitability in his gaze. "Sovereign. It draws our sustenance away and will eradicate us if we do not learn how to use the runestaff."

"How will I find the staff?" Giridian asked as he also stood. He sensed the guardian was about to leave and felt a sudden panic, his mind still trying to assimilate all of this.

"Come forward." Thoth raised a finger and from its tip a blue star appeared. It was blinding, so intense that Giridian had to shield his eyes.

He extended that finger and touched Giridian on the forehead. A deluge of visions washed into the lore father's mind faster than he could perceive. His vision became blurry and his head tingled, as if ants crawled across his scalp. "Ascend and become part of this Conclave," echoed Thoth's voice with a reverberating boom.

Giridian's body arched in shock, his eyes shut and his mouth opened in a silent scream. His form stood outlined in white power, blazing incarnate as the process of Ascension took hold. He could not feel, see, or hear anything, except the rush of energy and strength that suffused his body and washed through his soul. The Way infused him with power, remaking him from the inside out.

Another form appeared, superimposed on the lore father: a winged creature armored in black and green, and carrying a warhammer that blazed with green fire. Enormous wings stretched from its sides, black blades made of pure ebonite, one of the hardest substances known in the world. It stood above the lore father, but held him protectively within its form.

Thoth stepped forward and raised a hand. "Hail, Artorius. It has been too long."

The Aeris Lord smiled and said, "It has, Keeper, and yet you look the same."

"As do you." Thoth's attention turned to Giridian, held in stasis by the Ascension and oblivious to this conversation. "He was not what we expected or prepared for."

"Neither was I, if you recall. Yet I achieved the right to ascend, and have served him faithfully since." Artorius turned his massive head to look down on his bonded partner. "Do not judge one from their meager beginnings, for none can trump such scrutiny. He is true to the Way, and has more strength than you know."

Thoth stood deep in thought, weighing the Aeris Lord's words. "You stand with him then, through this life and the next?"

"I do, Keeper. He will need my strength to stand against Sovereign. Permit the Ascension to continue."

"And what of Azrael?"

Artorius paused, his armored form towering over both Giridian and Thoth. "After Valarius fell he chose another, but none know who. Mayhap it is a boon, for Sovereign would surely move against Azrael were his whereabouts known."

"I wish there were more of us, more like you," said Thoth.

"There are enough to do what must be done, and Azrael is not lost." Artorius bowed his armored head in thanks and settled his form over Giridian's own, covering him protectively in his black-bladed wings.

A sphere of power exploded from within the two, brightening to an incandescent white as the raw energy of the Way consumed both the Aeris Lord and Giridian. It poured through them and as it did so, Artorius grew larger.

His armor darkened and changed, becoming more splendid and dangerous. His wings grew longer, bladed and sharp, lethal and potent, a visible testament to the power that was now Giridian's to command. Then a silent detonation and Artorius disappeared in an emerald flash of power and light.

"It is done," Thoth announced. "You have the knowledge necessary to forge a new runestaff, Archmage Giridian Alacar."

Giridian staggered back, his hand to his head. The scope of the Ascension flooding his senses beyond what he thought he could take. Just as he sank to one knee and could take no more, he found himself supported by strong arms, helping him up.

"Sit here."

He opened his eyes to the concerned look of Dragor, kneeling in front of him. He had no memory of anything after Thoth touched his forehead. He was in the Vault still and nothing had changed except instead of Thoth, it was now Dragor who sat next to him.

In a whisper that was almost to himself, he said, "By the Lady . . ."

Dragor looked confused. "What?"

Giridian looked at Dragor with a start, as if seeing him for the first time. Then he shook his head and said, "We were wrong."

"About what?" Dragor looked at the lore father, concern plainly written on his features.

Giridian's face was ashen. "About everything." He looked around the room, seeing it now with eyes opened by his newfound powers, and took a deep breath. The Way flooded into him, healing and restoring him just as breathing air did for his lungs. He held out his hand and could almost see the Way as it flowed. He concentrated, then clenched his fist, knowing what would happen next.

The air brightened at his grasp, a flash of green energy that elongated into a spear of blinding light. Within it, he could see an infinite sea of particles, all converging at his command. From his fist outward, the air itself solidified and turned dark, growing into a shiny black spear of metal. It shone with a green lightning flashing across black metal, the new runestaff of the lore father, remade by the new Archmage of the Conclave. In a moment, it was done.

Giridian looked at Dragor, who watched him with a stunned expression. He took another deep breath and could feel the Way enter him again, silent and strong, his to command. He thought about what Thoth had revealed, then in a voice that came out almost a whisper, he said, "We must kill Arek."

Journal Entry 16

My failure to protect myself from these strange raids, none of which are distinct or identifiable, is a critical piece of information. I understand it now, for these are the formless fears I have that every man has, and they find life through the younger Aeris.

When enough time passes and I feel insecure or exposed, a raid is inevitable. These cannot simply be banished. To do that, I would have to banish my fears completely and what man can truly do that?

It is clear now that defeating the Aeris is a much more complex issue than I first thought. Perhaps this is what the dragons meant? Still, they did not understand who I am. I must get everyone to believe against the Aeris, but how to disbelieve an entire pantheon of gods?

If I cannot control my own subconscious, how can I expect an entire society to accomplish the same? Our will and belief give these Aeris life. To destroy them, every man, woman, and child would have to stop believing in the things they cherish or fear.

That will never happen. I must do something else. I must give our people something else to believe in, something better.

THE CATACOMBS

In a grappling contest,

hold your opponent tightly and do not release

him when you are thrown.

This will force him to hold you up,

and lessen any damage you may suffer.

—*Tir Combat Academy, Basic Forms & Stances*

Why would you want to help?" Arek asked, surprise registering at Niall's sudden appearance.

The young prince shrugged and moved into the room. "You've offered to help *us,* and we..." he moved closer to the other two, a look of guilt washing over his features, "do not believe that torturing you was the right decision."

In truth, his answer had little to do with his actual reason. After listening to their exchange from the door, Niall knew his cousin was just stubborn enough to get herself into real trouble. He knew the underground passageways led to nothing but empty corridors and tunnels.

Letting Tej waste her time down there was a choice more likely to keep her from doing anything stupid, and satisfied her desire to be doing *something* to exact revenge. Plus, a small part of him liked the idea of leading an adventure into the catacombs, even if it was a fool's errand. Besides, with things going the way they were, he was never getting on the wall.

Arek looked at Tej, an unspoken question on his face. He didn't know Niall other than that they had fought each other. "I'd like you to answer a question."

Niall, nodded, knowing it would take some amount of trust before Arek would accept him.

"When we faced each other, she expected your help," he said, indicating Yetteje. "Why did you abandon her?"

Niall felt a flush of shame color his face red, followed by hot anger. How dare this intruder accuse him of cowardice? Perhaps this was a stupid idea, and allowing a so-called "guest" to walk about the fortress was madness. Then he thought of what Ash would have said. His instructor often told him his best lessons would come from the hardest tests: the ones that made you face things about yourself that you didn't like. It was in these moments that you grew the most. At least that's what *he* would have said.

Niall faced Arek and said, "You were my first real opponent, and I hesitated."

Arek's eyes narrowed, but a small smile escaped, "So did I, the first time I crossed blades with my master. I asked because I wanted to know if you would lie to me or not."

Niall shook his head and looked at Yetteje. "Tej, I'm sorry." A steel came to his eyes and voice, then he said, "That won't happen again."

Yetteje looked confused. "Wait, you didn't attack when I did?"

The two boys looked at each other, then burst out laughing.

She looked annoyed. "It's not funny."

More laughter erupted and Yetteje continued, "Seriously, I thought you were right behind me."

Arek looked at Tej, a smile in his eyes, and he said, "Well, in a manner of speaking, he was."

The laughter continued for a moment longer from the two and Yetteje sat back annoyed. That emotion slowly seeped away in the presence of these two imbeciles and she started to smile, too, though her amusement lay in the obvious stupidity of boys.

"Happy?" she finally asked. "Are the two of you friends now?"

Niall looked at Yetteje with a smile in his eyes. "I really am sorry, but if it's any conciliation, you did much better than I against him. I didn't even get a strike off."

"I don't care," Tej said with a sigh. "How are we going to get to where Arek needs to go? And by the way," she said, turning to Arek, "where is that?"

"The thing I seek is below the fortress somewhere. As we get nearer to it, I'll know."

Yetteje scratched her head. "So you don't know what you're looking for?"

Arek stood up gingerly and stepped forward, careful to put as little weight as possible on his partially healed foot. "No, not exactly, but I know it exists. Think of this as an adventure."

Niall stepped around the large bed and plopped himself into a chair, happy Arek used the very word he would have used. "All right, an adventure it is, but we just wander about down there?"

* * * * *

Time slowed and stopped, and the scene froze. Arek looked around and saw the shade of Piter appear again. He moved over to the group and looked at Arek, "A new group to torment me?"

"Piter, I'm sorry about that . . ."

Piter held up a hand, stopping Arek from talking further and said, "Tell them you seek a place where Shimmerene falls, a place below the fortress."

"Shimmerene? The lake?" he replied, not quite understanding.

The shade of Piter nodded. "I will guide you from there."

The scene snapped back and Arek blinked a few times, shaking his head.

"You all right?" asked Tej.

"Yes, but," Arek hesitated. He had grown accustomed to the sight of the shade, its appearance familiar and somehow welcome. Still, when he thought about how he, Tomas, and Jesyn had acted, it left him with a pit of guilt in his stomach. He could only hope that Piter wasn't trying to exact some revenge for this, or for Arek's part in his death. The thought filled him with a nameless dread. "Sorry, yes, I'm fine. May I ask, does Shimmerene fall anywhere below?"

Yetteje looked at Niall, who became thoughtful. Then he said, "Inside Bara'cor? Doubtful. I've never heard of that, but I do know the entrance to the underground cisterns, which are fed by Shimmerene. From there we may find something."

"Can you take us there?" Arek asked Niall.

Niall nodded and said, "We should outfit ourselves first, though. Believe it or not, it gets pretty cold down there."

Led by Niall the three went to the door, slowed by Arek, who could manage nothing more than a hobble. Niall addressed the guards stationed outside. "I'm taking Arek to the Healers Ward. He's complaining about his foot."

"Your father didn't leave specific orders, my prince, but I was under the impression he was not to leave this room," the guard said nodding to Arek.

"My father named him 'guest,' during our last meeting, and retracted his status as prisoner. I wish to take our guest to the Healers Ward. Stand aside." Niall met the guard's gaze with his own, his eyes not flinching.

A few heartbeats passed before the guard bowed and stepped back. "Of course, my prince."

Niall motioned to the other two and the three of them made their way out of the room and to the nearest stairwell spiraling down into the great keep's bowels. Ahead of them lay a small storeroom, into which Niall ducked.

"Grab something warm to put on and something to eat. Not sure how long we'll be down there," he said, stuffing his mouth with dried fruit.

Arek stood at the doorway to the storeroom, his foot throbbing. Then his eyes widened in disbelief. "Why is everything so big?"

"Huh?" Niall looked about, then asked between chews, "What do you mean?"

"Everything. The halls, this room, even the door. Everything is so *big.*"

Yetteje laughed. "I thought so too, when I first arrived here. I don't even notice it now."

"The whole fortress is like that," Niall said, "like it was made for people bigger than us." He swallowed one last mouthful, then grabbed a canteen of water. "Like Tej said, you get used to it." He handed both of them something to eat, then began rummaging through the shelves for anything useful he might have missed.

Arek looked at Niall, disbelief in his expression, but didn't comment. How could someone get used to a place where everything made you feel small?

Instead, his mouth crooked into a smile and he said to Niall's back, "That was impressive, with the guard." He knew a prince was important, but to bluff your way past your own father's orders? For someone raised in an environment based on a strict adherence to rank and protocol, the feat was impressive.

Niall shrugged. "If you act like you're in charge, nine times out of ten, people believe it."

"Or if your last name is Galadine," Yetteje offered with a smile. "Grab the gear and torches and let's go. Whether they believed you or not, someone will be sent to inform the king and the Healers Ward. When we don't show up, we'll pay the Lady's price."

"He *was* named guest, you know," retorted Niall over his shoulder to Tej's retreating back. Her answer was a quick spin with an eye-roll and a laugh.

Arek focused on grabbing items he thought would be useful. He checked his foot again, thankful once more for the soft boot that held it safe. Niall, had his sword, but neither Yetteje nor Arek had a weapon.

As if she read Niall's thoughts, Yetteje grabbed a short blade and looked at Arek. "You need something?"

Arek shook his head. "No. I'm all right." They knew he was good with a blade, but even unarmed he was far deadlier than either of them could imagine. Given his injured foot, he was loathed to weigh himself down with anything more than he needed.

Satisfied they had packed lightly, but enough to make their way to the cisterns, the three left the storeroom and continued slowly down the passageway, turning and descending more than enough times through cavernous hallways to completely confuse Arek.

They passed occasional soldiers and the odd servant or two, causing Arek to comment on the lack of people.

"You really don't understand how a siege works, do you?" Niall asked with a raised eyebrow.

"Just seems strange not to run into more guards."

Yetteje answered with a small laugh, "It would help him to know that we're deep in the interior. Almost everyone concerned with Bara'cor's defense is on duty, near the outer walls."

Niall nodded, mirth in his eyes. "Would you rather we ran into more sentries, ones who would want to know what we're doing?"

Yetteje leaned in conspiratorially and said, "Be thankful, we're with a *Galadine.*"

"Shut up, Tej. You know we couldn't have gotten past that guard without me."

"True." Yetteje smiled, then winked at Arek and shook her head, mouthing, *not true.*

Eventually, they stopped at a large iron door. The only thing Arek knew for certain was that they were far below the sands of the desert. He shook his foot to relieve the pins and needles. It continued to throb and feel twice its size. Still, he thought thankfully, it was better than a stump.

"This is it," Niall said, "the entrance to the lower catacombs. They'll eventually lead us to the water cisterns." He looked at Arek and asked, "Are you sure?"

Arek nodded. "I know we have to go where Shimmerene falls."

Niall took a deep breath and opened the door. The passageway beyond was black. Lighting a torch from the wall sconce, Niall made his way in, followed by Arek. Yetteje came in last and secured the iron door behind them.

Ahead stretched the catacombs, and beyond that, a place where Arek felt he would soon meet his destiny.

HISTORIES: FORGING THE ISLE

Just as one cannot fill an already full cup,

one cannot teach the Way of Making

to those who believe they already know.

To learn, they must first empty their cup.

—*Lore Father Argus Rillaran, The Way*

D ragor grabbed another book, hefting it onto their table. "This is a list of the known Lore Fathers and Mothers. There are many pages missing, but in what's there, the name 'Armun' doesn't appear."

"Not surprising. Who knows how many were lost during the heyday of the Galadine purging," Giridian said softly.

Dragor sighed. "Did anyone mention the name?"

The lore father shook his head. "Not exactly. I remember Themun arguing more than once with Thera, who wanted to go to Dawnlight. She might have said something that sounded like the name 'Armun,' but I could never be sure."

"Wasn't Thera found at Dawnlight?" Dragor asked.

"By Themun," Giridian replied. They were at a dead end. There was no way to move forward without understanding the lore father's reason for mentioning Armun, and that left only one solution. Given what Thoth had said, though, he now felt like this was a waste of time. Still, something about Themun's dying words spurred him on. He turned around and said haltingly, "I . . . I will search his memories."

Dragor arched an eyebrow. "Two hundred years of it? For what, exactly? You said earlier the right vision doesn't just pop into your head. Where do you look?"

Giridian leaned against a shelf, turning over Dragor's question in his mind. What did he look for? Then, the solution came to him in a moment of clarity. "Maybe Themun said the name because that would be enough. Maybe I just need to focus on his name and let Themun's memories guide me."

"You think it will work?"

"We shall see." He closed his eyes then and opened his mind to Themun's thoughts. They were available, a lifetime of learning at his mental fingertips, only he would have to go through them in real time, unless he knew where to look.

He thought about the name, *Armun.* Somewhere, he hoped the memories of Themun Dreys would help him solve the mystery of who this person really was. He had to trust his desire would lead him to the right memory to watch.

Slowly, Giridian's vision went black, then he saw Themun, much younger, standing on a rocky outcropping. Beside him stood Thera and another man who looked similar to Themun except slightly older. They had outfitted themselves for combat, with tight fitting clothes and swords across their backs. Giridian marveled again at their appearance, for he had never imagined Themun quite so young.

The young Themun here did not look much older than Tomas or Arek, but Giridian knew appearances were deceiving. In this memory, Themun was close to his thirtieth summer. His aging had already slowed, though he was clearly not a lore father yet.

The trio looked over a green expanse and the mountain that struck upward from it like a giant granite fist of stone and snow. This was Dawnlight, the first place the light of the sun touched their land. It stood on the horizon, its icy peaks sparkling. Giridian heard the older man heave a sigh.

"You sure?" he asked, looking at Themun pointedly, his expression clearly reflecting he did not relish the idea of scaling something so big. "It could just be something natural."

Then his name—*Armun*—became one with Giridian's own knowledge, along with the stunning realization that Armun was Themun's older brother. Neither Themun nor Thera had ever mentioned him before. Another thought occurred then, bringing a small smile to his lips. Interesting that even then, Themun was clearly the leader.

Themun nodded and answered, "Nothing natural is that powerful, and there is the disappearance of the dwarves. They journeyed to this spot as well. The two may be connected."

Armun leaned forward and squinted. "The power of whatever lies there is incredible. I couldn't sense it before, but from here it shines like a star."

With his new power, Giridian knew he could now do more with his visions. He bent his will and felt his perspective shift, then swoop down until he could feel, see, hear, and sense everything Themun thought or felt. It did not give him all of Themun's knowledge, just his state of mind during these events. For these next moments he *was* Themun, and saw the world through his eyes.

* * * * *

Themun knew he was strongest in sensing these sparks of Talent, but this was something completely different. It seemed inconceivable a single person could radiate such power. But the only way they could know for sure would be to investigate. He looked at the other two, catching for a moment the strange look that had been passing between them more often as they journeyed together.

"Something is inside that mountain and if we can sense it, so can the king's Magehunters," Themun said. "We need to get there first."

Just then, an earsplitting shriek sounded. It came from below the ridge they stood upon, from a small clearing that led to a ravine. As they turned their attention there, the shriek sounded again, forcing them to cover their ears. They looked down and saw a black, reptilian shape quickly circle up a rocky outcropping, clearly evading something coming out of the brush.

It was a young dragon, its black scales scintillating in the dappled sunlight that filtered down through the canopy of leaves above. It circled itself at the top of the outcropping, hissing at something yet unseen from its makeshift perch. The brush shook, but the trio above could not yet see what hunted this creature through the undergrowth below.

Then the crack of breaking limbs echoed across the clearing and the trees and underbrush gave way to three lizard-like shapes, similar to the dragonling, but clearly not dragons. Each stood a man's height at the shoulder, but unlike the dragonling these had massive forelimbs and walked almost upright. They had heads like crocodiles' and looked to be full-grown adults of a different species all together.

Giridian quickly recognized them as basilisks. They had gray, dry scales, with neck frills that expanded as they hissed. Their nictitating eyes shone silver, affording them protection against their own petrifying gaze.

Themun asked the other two, "What do you think?"

Armun was first to respond. "Animals fighting is not our concern. Plus, we cannot prevail against a dragon, even with three basilisks to help."

Thera looked wide-eyed at him. "You *are* joking . . ."

Armun nodded, rolling his eyes and flashing a smile, and Themun felt a flush of relief. His brother was not as callous as he sometimes acted. Still, he couldn't help but be annoyed at the joke. His intent to come to the dragon's aid was predictable, and Armun was poking fun at him, even now.

"All right, what do we do?" Themun looked about the clearing, starting to formulate a plan.

Armun clapped him on the shoulder. "It's four against three . . . stop thinking." With that, he stood up and stepped off the ledge, dropping from sight.

"Assuming the dragon helps *us*," said Themun, in a voice that sounded more resigned than angry.

"It's not so bad," Thera replied, her eyes on Armun. Without another word, she stepped off the ledge and fell to join him.

Themun stood by himself, shaking his head, then surveyed the scene, his mind automatically assessing the strategic situation. In this, he was much like his father, who had taught him the importance of tactics and position. Seeing where the conflict would likely end up, he ran to his right and jumped, landing near the dragonling.

Armun fell an easy fifteen man lengths down, but his landing demonstrated his training, as he did so with barely a sound, exhaling softly. He took stock of the situation, then ran up to the closest basilisk.

The creature was fixated on its most dangerous prey, the young dragonling, and did not notice his approach. Armun leapt up into the air and drew his sword in one fluid motion. The blade flashed white and silver, potent with power. He descended and cut, severing the monster's head from its torso. The detached head tumbled forward some distance, coming to rest at the base of the dragonling's perch.

The basilisk next to the unfortunate first kill looked up and focused its baleful glare on Thera. Had it been turned upon those without Talent, it would first paralyze, then char them into a statue of ash within heartbeats.

Thera was far from untrained, however, having spent the past fifteen years under the Dreys family's tutelage. She called upon the Way and the very air around her became a reflective shield, one that let her see out, but did not let the basilisk's gaze penetrate. Then she moved forward in a blur.

Her sword licked out, even as she called upon the Way again, her very being speaking to the earth and trees. Grass, caressed by the Way, grew at an impossible rate, encompassing the basilisk in a web of woven fibers, pinning the man-like reptile in place. It tried to escape, but Thera's sword was unerring. Within a heartbeat, another lay pierced through the back of the neck and impaled to the ground, its legs twitching in death.

The third creature seemed intent on the dragonling, a strange sight as by now it should have tried to escape. Basilisks were at least intelligent enough to know when the odds were against them, yet this one did not run. The thought crossed Themun's mind that something may in fact be controlling these creatures.

Its single-minded attention on its prey proved to be its undoing. A wing-shaped shadow crossed it, and a clawed foot smashed into its skull and obliterated the head in a wet explosion of gray matter, bone, and blood. To the surprise of Themun and his companions, there stood atop the ruined skull of the third dead basilisk a full-grown dragon with black wings encompassing the entire clearing.

Themun landed in time to realize his leap had been perfect, bringing him within a sword's length of the dragonling, which still stood curled upon its perch. Somehow, it looked smaller now that the full-grown dragon had appeared, but no less dangerous.

The thought flitted through Themun's head that he now stood close to the young dragon with an unsheathed blade in hand. If the elder believed Themun meant harm to the younger one, he knew they would all die. He decided that straightforwardness was the right approach and sheathed his sword, addressing the elder dragon with a bow. "By your leave, my lord."

The great dragon turned, hissing a challenge and warning. Both Armun and Thera melted back into the brush, ready to help, but Themun stood near the hatchling and in direct view. It was too late for him to retreat and the wrong move would prove his end.

The creature turned its yellow-golden gaze on the mage and said, "Dost thee ransom my brood?"

The voice was deep, like gravel against stone, and Themun found himself kneeling. He opened his arms, showing no weapons, and said, "Nay, my lord. We only offer aid." He knew dragons detested normal speech and his kind in general.

"Thou hast given aid. And now?" The dragon moved forward, taking time to trample the body of one of the basilisks who had threatened the younger dragon's life.

From behind Themun came a girl's voice, young yet strident, "Thy companions intervened, my sire."

The dragon's eyes narrowed and it said, "Nay, no companions of mine. Naught but halfling vermin."

Themun looked behind him and saw a young girl, no more than fifteen summers. She looked normal, except for the two black wings that emerged from her back. They flashed in the shafts of sunlight, iridescent and beautiful. The expression on her face, if readable, seemed vexed.

"Sire, I have not earned thy name yet, but these three came to my defense," she stated. "They hath no need to do so." She narrowed her gaze and Themun felt the distinct impression this young dragon was used to winning arguments.

The great dragon changed, a flash of light that left a dark armored knight that Giridian now recognized as Rai'stahn. The knight approached Themun and said, "Thou know of the Way. By what means?"

"My father," Themun answered, "who taught me that the Way is that which makes us."

Rai'stahn's eyes narrowed. "Thine answer is childish, but that is expected."

While the dragon seemed angry, Giridian sensed it had been impressed with Themun and his openness.

"Wouldst thou live in these times, son of the Way?" Rai'stahn continued, "Thy king's men hunt all with Talent."

"Aye, you have the right of it. But my friends and I seek to stop this." At his gesture, both Armun and Thera emerged. "We three live in the woods and escape the king's long arm. What is your intent, my lord?"

The little girl dragon came up then and said, "Thou wert ever impatient with me. Now I wilt have my say."

The great dragon inclined an armored head, but Themun could see the hint of amusement in the corners of the knight's golden eyes. "Very well, have at it."

"Thee hath spoken of the king's justice. These three are strong in the Way. Wilt thou turn thy back on them in such a craven fashion?" The girl spread her arms, encompassing the clearing with Themun and his small party. "Surely thou wilt offer them thy aegis?"

Rai'stahn stared at the young dragonling, his golden eyes narrowing in a calculating stare. His mien reflected what Themun could only interpret as frustration, but that countenance was mixed with a sense that this exchange was one the great dragon was accustomed to from this particular dragonling.

Before the younger dragon could say more, Rai'stahn turned and addressed Themun, saying, "What is thy business here?"

Themun motioned to his companions, who moved slowly forward. "We seek a plume of power, somewhere near Dawnlight."

Rai'stahn's head swiveled, looking to the great peak. He sighed, then said, "A rift hath opened upon this world. Remember its taint well, for it marks danger to all the land."

Themun stood aghast. "Do you mean like the one through which Lilyth's forces emerged?"

Rai'stahn looked back at the young mage and nodded. "Verily, for I and my hatchling journey to the same place, to ascertain the threat and put an end to it."

"Sire, shall I speak of the Isle?" asked the younger dragon, steering the conversation back to the fate of Themun and his party. "Thou canst grant safe haven, if they so petition." She cocked her head to one side, a small smile escaping from her youthful face. Behind that smile, Themun could see razor sharp teeth, reminding him once again that this was no young girl.

The great dragon drew a deep breath, its eyes never leaving Themun's own. Then, as if coming to a decision, he said, "Thee hath come to the aid of my brood. For that, I offer a boon. I and my kin stand as guardians of the Way. We serve a Conclave and protect the world from those who would desecrate it."

The girl dragon then offered, a bit eagerly, "My sire and I make our home deep in the Shattered Sea, at the end of a chain of islands, southeast of Koorva. It holds upon it enough sustenance for those of thy kind."

The dragon-knight rumbled his displeasure at his daughter's interruption, "Why dost thou seek permission, only to speak regardless?"

When the younger dragon didn't answer, Rai'stahn looked back at Themun and said, "It is named Meridian, and stands as home to my hatchlings, though some may still not survive this journey." He eyed the dragonling meaningfully, but the younger dragon seemed unperturbed, smiling innocently up at her father.

Themun could see the great dragon deflate, accepting his loss to the younger, then heard him growl, "Seek it and I wilt allow thee and thy companions to remain there, safe from the king's justice."

Themun looked at the dragon, questions stumbling in his mind, clamoring to be given voice, but held his tongue. Before insulting anyone, he bowed formally and said, "We stand honored."

"Pay heed, for thy boon comes with a price. Thy petty affairs concern me little, for thy people are short-lived and useless. However—" Rai'stahn held up a taloned hand— "thy current king hath a long reach and seeks to eradicate those gifted with Talent. This I cannot abide. I stand against him and offer thee and thy people safe haven. In return, thou shalt aid me in protecting the Way, in any manner I deem necessary."

"A fair exchange, my lord." Themun bowed again, then stood and stepped back from the great dragon. "If I may ask your name?"

The dragon looked at the young mage, then stepped forward. He raised his armored hand and placed it upon Themun's forehead, as a god would to a supplicant. "I am known as Rai'stahn, Lord of Meridian, and guardian of this world. Dost thee accept me as thy lord?"

Themun did not directly answer, instead saying, "I am Themun Dreys. With me stands my elder brother, Armun, and Thera Dawnlight. We seek to save those born into this land with Talent and would ally ourselves with you."

"Well met," intoned the dragon, Rai'stahn. "Two shall journey back to the Isle with my hatchling and prepare for my return."

"My lord?" Confusion ran across Themun's face. "What of this rift we sense?"

The dragon moved forward, towering over the young mage, and growled, "Mortal, I do not request, I command as your liege."

Themun took a deep breath, then slowly stepped back. The power this creature radiated was palpable and he knew his next words could still condemn them to death. Rai'stahn was an elder dragon, and they would have little hope of defeating him should he suddenly change his mind. He spread his arms and bowed, breaking eye contact. "As you wish, my lord, but you said two. Who remains?"

The great dragon looked at the three, his golden gaze measuring. Then he pointed at Armun and said, "Thou shalt accompany me."

Themun and Armun locked gazes, then Armun said, "It is better I go. You must see to this island and our continued safety."

"No!" Thera blurted. "It may not be safe."

Armun looked at her and smiled. "With a dragon? You were safer with me than I with you. I will see to Dawnlight and this rift. Await my return."

Themun stood speechless. His brother and he had not been apart since their father's death, and a part of him feared their separation.

As if answering his unspoken thought, the younger dragon stepped forward and said, "Thy brother is safe. He stands under the wing of my sire, and that is enough. It is not thy place to question thy lord."

Rai'stahn then turned toward the young Themun and growled, "Do not forget our pact. Upon my return, we shall take the oath and bind your service to mine."

Themun knew what taking the oath would mean, for it would fundamentally change their role in this world. What would it do to those they saved, obligate them to serve whatever agenda the dragon had? He looked at Armun and Thera. "And shall we accept this unquestioned, for service unnamed?"

Armun was first to speak, "You know what father would have said." He moved to stand closer to the great armored knight, "I believe we accomplish much in building a future for our children, just as Rai'stahn does for his. Let us join forces and save who we can today." He smiled. "The future is for an older, better you."

Giridian watched as Rai'stahn changed back into his dragon form, and had Armun climb aboard. Through Themun's eyes, he saw his brother raise a hand in farewell, a small crooked smile playing across his lips.

"Father chose well when he chose you to lead," said Armun. "I will return and follow, no matter what you decide."

Giridian felt the heartache Themun felt, the fear that knotted his stomach as the great dragon moved a bit farther away.

Rai'stahn looked back one more time and locked eyes with the young adept, saying, "It is a fair bargain I offer thee, mortal. Unasked, thou came to the aid of my hatchling and for that, I offer thee this boon. Think on it and we shall speak upon my return." With that, he bunched his great muscles and leapt into the air, departing with Armun aboard, a small streak of black arrowing through the clear blue sky. They quickly turned north to Dawnlight and a rift that seemed eerily similar to the one Giridian now faced at Bara'cor.

Rai'stahn's daughter smiled, revealing again those fanged teeth and said, "Come, I will convey thee back to our lord's demesne."

Giridian watched as the three walked down to the clearing littered with the remains of the basilisks, then, his vision faded to black.

* * * * *

Slowly, the Vault came into focus again, along with the concerned face of Dragor, who now stood to one side, rubbing Giridian's hand to wake him.

He looked at Dragor and smiled. "Did you know Themun had a brother?" He did not yet mention the pact Themun had agreed to. In light of his conversation with Thoth, he had begun to see why these visions were problematic, for they created more questions than they answered.

Dragor shook his head and asked, "Trained in the Way?"

Giridian nodded. "His name is Armun, and when they last saw each other, his brother had begun a journey to—"

"Dawnlight," Dragor finished, guessing correctly. "We need to find Armun, then, if he still lives. He may know much of these rifts and the dwarves."

"There is more," Giridian said. "I think I saw how we came into our service and our oath. It was driven by Rai'stahn."

"A dragon? You know that's not true."

"No, I don't mean that." The lore father looked about the room, as if searching the air for an answer. "What happens when one takes an oath so encompassing, so consuming, it defines the very nature of all who follow? What if it changes the very essence of who we are?"

"I don't know what you mean. We are who we are," Dragor said simply. "Our oath is to serve the land and we have done so since Themun came here."

Giridian stood deep in thought, then came to a decision and said, "Prepare Jesyn for her test. There is no reason to delay her Ascension, and we will have need of another adept. Tomas will have to wait till he fully heals."

He needed to think more about Themun, Rai'stahn, and their role in all this. He had not known Meridian Isle and their beginning stood so inextricably linked to the great dragon, and knowing now gave him new perspective. It explained how so many of Talent found their way here. Rai'stahn brought them for protection by Themun and his council. It also shed light on some of Themun's actions, though their moral rightness still seemed uncertain.

"And what of Armun?" Dragor asked.

Giridian looked at his friend and paused, not relishing the idea of sending yet more adepts into danger, but knowing there was no other choice. Assailants bent on their destruction had attacked them. Only Kisan's quick thinking and the lore father's sacrifice had let them survive. He needed to protect the Isle and contact Kisan and Silbane, which left only Dragor to deal with finding Armun.

Giridian laid a comforting hand on Dragor's shoulder and said, "We must find him."

For his part, Dragor seemed to know what was coming next and asked, "By 'we,' I assume you mean me? You can't use your new powers to just See there?" He didn't expect an answer. "No, I suppose it's not that easy."

The lore father smiled, "It's not the same as *being* there. You will start at Dawnlight."

Journal Entry 17

I wonder who survived the last assault. My thoughts linger on them more, as time crawls along. That Rai'stahn intended the blow that pushed me here is uncontested. I have no doubts of his betrayal, and cherish the sharp focus the memory of it provides. I hope to see him again so I can repay his act of kindness.

Beautiful Sonya, surely, for she was strong in the Way. Perhaps Duncan, though only by someone else's sacrifice. He was always weak-willed so I question Sonya's judgment, but only in her choice of him.

Elsimere, Dale? I hope they lived. Do they know it was my forbearance, my love for them, my intervention on their behalf that bent Lilyth's final blow? Or do they blame me still? Is it foolishness, to want their company, yet be angered by their lack of action, of fortitude? I feel no desire to write anything except how I stood alone in the end, victorious. Curse them all and good riddance to the lot. Perhaps I will see them again, but as conqueror and king.

Did I expect any different? No. I am the greatest. I am the most powerful archmage to have ever existed. Why would anyone stand with me to the very end? In trying, it would mean their lives, for they would have died long before I succumbed.

The imp is speaking now. It whispers things sometimes . . . it asks questions. What is it? Why do we live here? Stupid questions.

Documenting the failure and shortcomings of my so-called friends grows tiresome.

I am weary . . .

HISTORIES: KISAN

Is one style of fighting better than another?

Will you see a different horizon

from the same mountaintop,

as one who arrived by another path?

—*Kensei Tsao, The Book of Blades*

The sky serpent flew through the dense foliage, its senses attuned to the heat of any living thing small enough for it to eat. A forked tongue flickered in and out, tasting the air for a meal. Its blue and silver iridescent scales flashed in the sunlight that pierced through the canopy above. The light pooled in reverse shadows, creating edges that looked like leaves.

Sky serpents were dangerous, something even a child knew. Unlike normal snakes, they hunted in either day or night, usually for small rodents and the like, but two things made them especially deadly.

First, their poison worked quickly and fatally on most warm-blooded creatures. Even the tiniest of these flying snakes could kill a man with one bite. Second, wherever baby sky serpents flew, there were usually one or two adults.

The adults were fearsome to behold, their bodies stretching for several lengths of a man. As they matured, their upper torsos became more man-like and their wings reduced into something similar to arms. They stood on their lower torso, wending their way through their hunting territory in search of larger prey.

It was said that adult sky serpents could speak, but learning their language presented severe challenges, resulting in few success stories. The most likely reasoning: Adult sky serpents seemed unwilling to have a civil conversation with an inquisitive linguist, having the nasty habit of poisoning and eating them instead. As a result, little had been learned of these dangerous creatures, other than to give them a wide berth.

This juvenile still had its wings and now spotted something near the ground, a baby falcon fallen from its nest. Instantly the serpent moved in, its senses alert and watching, both for the chick's parents and for any other dangers that might lurk near so easy a meal.

Sky serpents' nemeses were falcons, one of the few creatures they feared. They would plummet from the wide blue above and kill with their taloned claws. They were fast and unerring, a predator equal to these feared creatures, at least while a sky serpent was still a juvenile.

Satisfied that there was no immediate threat, it wove through the air in a graceful spiral, unerringly at the fallen chick, who sensed the danger and began to cheep.

The serpent came to a stop a hand's span away from the chick, its wings moving in a blur as it hovered. Its forked tongue flicked out, measuring, tasting. Then it shot forward, mouth open and fangs outstretched. The air shimmered and a blade whistled down, slicing the serpent's head from its body in one clean stroke.

Even as the two pieces fell to the ground, the form of a girl appeared from out of thin air. She may have been sixteen or seventeen summers old, but one could already see the nascent beauty she would one day command as a woman. The blade she wielded rested comfortably in one hand, with a small streak of the serpent's blood, bluish-black, dripping from its keen edge.

Her other hand held a string tied to the baby falcon's foot. She pulled that string and grabbed the chick, stuffing it into a small, soft pouch on her belt. The head popped out, complaining in bird cheeps, and she fed it a grub saying, "Stop it. You were never in any *real* danger."

Turning her attention to the serpent's body, she grabbed and stuffed it into another pouch. Later she would skin and eat it. It wasn't the best tasting, but highly nutritious. She straightened to stand and the hairs on the back of her neck stood up. Something was definitely wrong.

She looked around, her eyes bright and keen, searching for whatever was out there. If it was an adult sky serpent, she would need to move quickly to a defensible position. She had never faced one and did not relish the thought, though her heart quickened a bit at the idea of the challenge.

"How long will you continue this?" The voice carried clearly through the trees, and the form of the man attached to it slowly became visible. "You have better options, Kisan."

She let out a sigh and an expletive. "Wasn't 'no' the last three times enough?" She backed up, sheathing her blade in one smooth motion. "At least this time you didn't scare away dinner."

"Snake meat? I heard it tastes like—"

"Snake?" She sighed, then said, "What do you want?"

The man who walked up to her looked to be in his twenties, with faded blue eyes and dark hair that had not yet seen the lightening of the summer sun's kiss. A small smile played on his lips, as if humor lay on the tip of his tongue. The corners of his eyes crinkled, familiar lines of a face used to laughing. "Same as always. You seem determined to live out here."

"And you keep visiting. Who is the bigger fool?"

He bowed, conceding, "The answer is clear."

She snorted and said, "Silbane the Fool. Nice ring to it."

Silbane smiled, taking no offense. He moved over to a log and sat down. "We're not giving up."

"We?" she asked, wary again.

"I brought a friend," he said, nodding to his left.

From thin air stepped a second man, older, perhaps in his thirties. He smiled at Kisan, then said, "I knew your mother, and offer my sorrow at her passing."

"You're a month late," Kisan said through pursed lips. She and father are buried over there, if you want to visit them." She said this while pointing with her chin. "But you can leave me alone."

"Your mother was powerful in the Way and has taught you some of its uses. Come with us and we will complete your training."

She rolled her eyes at that, then looked back at Silbane. "Has everyone become suddenly more stupid? Breaking the King's Law will only get me killed."

"The Magehunters will not spare you, because you have not been trained. You are only making it easier for them."

"How long do you think you can hide out here?" This came from the older man. "Your mother was a gifted initiate, and still she fell."

Kisan moved away from them, taking a deep breath, trying to stay calm. The two men followed her, but kept a respectful distance behind. She walked in silence, knowing they wouldn't give up and running would solve nothing.

"Maybe you think you're like one of these sky serpents. Fast, agile, deadly?" The older man scoffed behind her, "Take a good look at yourself. Calling you 'dirty' would be a compliment to dirt."

"Are you trying to be mean?" she spun and asked in exasperation. When there was no answer, she moved farther along the forest floor. "I've been here since they died. No one's found me."

"No one is looking for you . . . yet."

Silbane stepped in and offered, "Maybe my friend is a bit too direct, but if we can find you, so can they."

She stopped, her shoulders hunched, then turned and faced them both. "Don't you get it? The Magehunters killed *everyone.*"

The older man began to say something but she cut him off, "No! I'm done with this. Leave me alone and don't come back." A small flame appeared then, surrounding her. It was faint, almost invisible to anyone who could not see the Way, but Silbane could not hide his astonishment. Neither could the older man.

"I'm through listening to your childishness, Kisan Talaris," the older man said. "We may not return, but others will. The Galadines have a long arm. Learn everything you can from these serpents you fancy. They are hunters too and yet fall even to your inept blade. What lesson does that teach you?"

The girl looked at them with anger in her eyes, but something else. She had not expected him to give up so easily. Her focus narrowed and she asked, "What's your name?"

"Why do you care?" he replied. "For all your Talent, you're thick-headed and stubborn. You're not a sky serpent, just pathetic and useless, like your pet bird. And within another month, you'll both be dead." With that, the man turned, took two steps, and vanished.

Silbane gave her an apologetic smile, and snapped his fingers. A sparkle flashed then fell to his feet. She could see it still glittering where he stood, as if he left behind bits of ... something. "If you change your mind, you can follow this and join us. We will depart tomorrow at dusk and this trail will disappear." He met her eyes and gave her another small smile. "I do hope to see you before then."

He raised a hand in farewell, then faded into nothingness. But the glittering trail appeared, moving through the woods in a relatively straight line toward the coastal city of Sunhold, a half day's walk away. Most likely to catch a boat, she surmised.

Later that evening she sat, hunched in front of a campfire, chewing absentmindedly on sky serpent meat while her mind seethed. How dare he call her pathetic? Had he ever lived on his own? What had he ever lost? Probably born into wealth, suckling milk from some fat cow of a nurse in some grand castle filled with servants and food. The more she thought about him, the angrier she became.

Behind her stood a small shelter, built out of branches and leaves. In it were the few things she had salvaged, scrounged after the Magehunters had razed her village. She had been safe only because of her timing and luck. She had been gone that day, hunting, as she often did, deep within the forest. Her return had been a harsh end to childhood. Exactly twenty-nine days ago, her life had changed forever.

She looked up and could still see the sparkling trail, winding its way through the trees. The stillness of the forest and the silver moonlight seemed to intensify the effect, showing her a way quite literally to her own future, if she chose to follow it. What lay along that bright path? What happened if she stayed?

She took whatever stock she could of her life, and though it was not with the deep rumination of one with years behind them, the tragic end of her childhood had forced her to grow up faster than most. She accepted she had no family, no home, that everyone she knew was dead. How long could she truly live out here alone?

As the night wore on, her reasons for refusing Silbane's invitation seemed less and less clear. She was still angry, but questioned herself honestly, a habit she had recently found useful to her survival. How long would it be before the Magehunters returned? Was she just being stubborn?

When morning came, it greeted an empty shelter. Anything she valued had been packed up, but one small task remained. She moved over to a dense bush, reached into her pouch, and withdrew the falcon chick, still complaining, and the rest of her grubs. She undid the string from its leg and carefully nestled it in, then scattered the grubs around for it to eat.

"Don't eat it all at once, stupid bird."

She knew it would perish, likely killed by the very serpents it helped her catch. Nothing left alone out here survived for long, a point the older man had made so abundantly clear. The message had sunk in, but she still hated him for it.

The chick sat there with its small beak wide open. When it realized that nothing more was coming from Kisan, it turned its attention to the grubs and grabbed one, swallowing it hungrily before moving to a second. Kisan drew a deep breath and watched in silent thought. Then, with a curse, she moved over and grabbed it, stuffing it back into her pouch amidst a small flurry of flapping wings, cheeping complaints, and a painful peck for her efforts.

Anything soft about her had died with her family, but she still found herself unable to abandon the falcon to its fate. Finding it alone and injured, she had nursed it back to health. Soon it would be able to fly and grow into a deadly raptor of the air. She was not ready to give up on it, not before it had a fair chance. With the obtuseness of youth, she never considered anyone else could feel the same way about her.

Instead, she remembered Silbane's friend calling her helpless and pathetic and let out a small, derisive laugh. He had no idea she had already mastered much of what her mother could do and a few things she couldn't. She looked over her shoulder at the sparkling trail, then grabbed her pack and blade. Securing them, she made her way along its glittering path, listening all the while to her falcon chick continue its complaints.

"You don't know me," she said, addressing the memory of that man.

The one-sided conversation cooled her anger a bit but left her unsatisfied, so she turned her attention back to the forest and the path, winding ahead through the sun-dappled undergrowth. She had to admit starting this journey filled her with a strange excitement, and as the morning crawled on her mood lightened. For the first time in a while, Kisan felt anticipation at what the rest of the day might bring.

Above her, she thought she heard the cry of a falcon making a kill, and the sound brought a faint smile to her lips. Her eyes then flitted down, sparkling as she focused on the scintillating trail once again. Somehow, she knew only she could see it, a path left by the Way for her and her alone.

The chick had settled down in the comfy darkness of the soft pouch. It wasn't completely altruism, she admitted then with a touch of guilt, for Kisan knew bringing her bird along would only infuriate the older man. The thought tugged the corner of her mouth up in an impish grin. The vision of their surprised faces as she appeared in Sunhold only made her smile more.

He thinks I fancy sky serpents, like I actually want to be one? He was stupid and wrong. There were things far deadlier in this world than snakes or birds, evil things living in the hearts of men. She had learned this firsthand when her family had been butchered. They had been hunted and lived their lives in fear till the very end.

I'm going to master everything you have to teach, she vowed silently, *no matter how long it takes. I'll earn the black robes and show you just how powerful I am.* On that day Kisan knew with cold certainty that she would be the hunter, and those with evil in their hearts would become her prey.

HAVEN

When you are the anvil, be patient.

When the hammer, strike.

—Altan proverb

The team waited under cover of night, within sight of the walls of Bara'cor. They had docked in Haven a day before, handing the boat off to waiting dockhands, specially contracted by Arsenal to give them discrete access to the capital city and beyond. These dockhands would also dispose of the boat and any other evidence of their arrival.

From there they had made their way quickly up the Land's Edge pass. Kisan wondered again at the conditioning of these dwarves, who ran for hours at a stretch with the same ease as a normal person breathed.

It was during one of these prolonged runs that she finally attempted contacting the lore father, having regained enough energy for the attempt, and having become comfortable with the conclusion that none of these men could mindspeak themselves.

At first, she heard nothing. Then, strangely, she heard Adept Giridian's voice. The moment they made contact, though, Kisan knew her old friend was an adept no longer, but the new lore father. She could feel the other's newfound might, but what had happened? In an instant, both had conveyed to the other the events that had transpired since their separation.

Giridian confirmed what Kisan already knew, these "men" were in fact dwarves. Upon hearing of Themun's death, however, the master nearly lost step with the others.

Arguments happened, but they were the result of those who felt passionate about their own stance. Kisan held no ill will at their last confrontation at council. The old lore father had been a mentor, a wise teacher skilled in the Way, and he had been a close friend.

She knew they had lost Thera and had feared Dragor dead as well. Her grief was only balanced by the fact that Dragor lived, saved by the lore father's final illusion. Kisan breathed a sigh of relief as the burden of Dragor's last sacrifice lifted from her heart.

The children were a different story. The memory of Piter welled up, and Kisan knew how the parents of those lost felt. A cold anger grew in her heart, a need to exact vengeance upon these assassins who cared nothing for their victims or the families that suffered in the wake of their passing. She would not forgive. They had performed their atrocities on the Isle thinking it had all been real. Despite the lore father's final illusion, not one death, real or not, was removed from their hands.

Giridian shared his vision about Valarius in council and Thoth next, but because of the distance, Kisan could not be given the full immersion of the experience that touch required. She could, however, feel the profound impact it had on the lore father and his beliefs. It was more than enough.

Arek posed a danger and he had committed murder when he took Piter's life. That fact alone condemned him in her eyes, but the needs of the mission had taken precedence. Now, with his denunciation by the Conclave *and* Lore Father Giridian, Kisan was free to act, but what she should do was still unclear.

Kisan related the dwarven team's orders to find and kill Arek and the royal Galadine family inside Bara'cor. Given that fact, were their interests in conflict? Also, what were her *actual* orders? Was she being ordered to help these assassins seek out and kill an apprentice they had trained since he was a child, aid the same men who had killed Lore Father Themun Dreys?

What troubled her more was the knowledge that if this "Conclave" could direct their hand against Arek, why not the Isle itself? That knot of worry she found was more difficult to unravel. Measured against the fate of the world, the lives of Themun, Thera, or of everyone on the Isle would be a small price to the Conclave—a price they would not hesitate to pay if they thought they were right.

Of Silbane, Kisan had heard nothing. What were her orders concerning the other master? Silbane would not allow his apprentice to come to harm and Kisan could not fault him for that. Her doubt and weariness came through the connection to the new lore father, who could empathize, but decisiveness was needed.

Though he had only been lore father for a very short time, he could not be uncertain in the face of the challenges arrayed against them. Giridian felt the Conclave was correct about Arek and if left alive, the boy threatened the very existence of the Way. He knew that Silbane would not allow any harmful action against the boy without significant proof and the question was, did they have time for that luxury? The lore father turned it over in his head and came to the only decision he felt he could. He ordered Kisan to kill Arek at her first opportunity.

As far as sharing information with Silbane, Giridian knew they could not take that chance. If he interfered it endangered the entire land, something the new lore father would not allow. While he shared this with Kisan his heart felt heavy, but once the decision was made he felt it was the correct one, and that confidence bled through the connection to the young master.

He *did* take care of one vital thing and used his newfound powers to replenish Kisan's health and vigor. The master marveled at the wash of energy that came through the connection, easing her muscles, lending clarity to thought and providing much needed succor to her entire being.

Facing Silbane was not something she relished. Despite their argument, Kisan still thought of Silbane as a mentor and friend. Piter's death supported the Conclave's claim and though she did not want to bring harm to one of their own, her orders were clear. Her best chance would be to take Arek alone, when Silbane was not around.

Losing Piter had shaken her to her core and it was clear Arek was to blame. She would not compound that loss by letting the land suffer because of a misplaced sense of family, especially not to one who had already proven lethal by killing her apprentice.

With renewed freshness she let Giridian know she would carry out the lore father's orders. She hoped to accomplish this without injuring Silbane, if possible. These assassins, however, would receive no such quarter. Once she felt she could glean no more information from them, she would kill them all.

Giridian hesitated at that, for they still did not know enough and his caution came through the connection. These dwarven men were highly trained and the fact that Kisan had infiltrated them spoke to her quick thinking and self-sacrifice. Giridian instructed her to keep her cover and first find out more about this Sovereign, who gave them their orders, before taking any action.

The lore father did not stop there. He shared the knowledge about the danger that Sovereign represented to their people. He did not know if the Conclave was behind this and meant to keep his wits about him, regardless of how much he believed the vision given by the enigmatic Thoth, guardian or not.

Giridian did not explicitly tell Kisan how to handle the orders to kill the Galadines. Kisan was there and had to have the freedom to respond in any way she judged best. He knew she was no supporter of Galadine rule, but let her know he hoped current circumstances would outweigh any personal feelings she might have with regards to them. The fact was that *this* king had disbanded the Magehunters and ended the laws that persecuted those with Talent.

The full moon shone overhead, turning the ground between their cover and the base of the walls of Bara'cor an eerie white. Their uniforms had changed color to match the surrounding terrain, a dusky gray and beige. From their vantage point, they could see the rear gates. Bara'cor sat hunched into the recess of Land's Edge, its rear three walls connected to the switchback pass that dropped to the lower plains and Haven two thousand feet below.

Prime didn't seem to think that making it into the fortress would be much of an issue. He gathered his men close. "Let us ask Sovereign to guide our hands," he intoned, and the rest bowed their heads.

Kisan did the same, seeing in Tamlin's memories that this was the benediction they offered before combat.

Prime continued, "We fell, and from ashes rise again. We exact justice in Your name. Blessed be our hands, for they deliver to You the new Way. Blessed be our people, who will regain the sky."

The others intoned, "We are the First, We are the Last, We are the new Way."

Prime made a strange sign, grabbing his fist with his other hand and offering both, then looked up. "We make our way to the Stone and from there into Bara'cor, the fortress of our fathers."

Two looked at everyone and said, "From here we keep silent. Getting in is the easy part. Getting out will be more difficult. Five and Six will secure the room for our egress. The rest of us will carry out our orders, no prisoners, no survivors. If we come in contact, they die. We may be coming back with pursuers, so be ready."

A pit formed in Kisan's stomach. She couldn't be left behind as rearguard. While she didn't particularly care about the king's family, she would not be in a position to insure her orders concerning Arek were carried out. Indeed, she had argued for the destruction of Bara'cor with the lore father, and nothing had changed her mind yet.

Still, she didn't want these assassins to achieve any goal they set themselves to. Perhaps it was because they had attacked and killed those on the Isle, or maybe it was the loss of Piter, more than likely it was just sheer spite. Regardless of the reason, the king had a newfound and unknown ally in Kisan, who knew what it was to lose a son. Not this time, she promised herself.

The team made its way quickly parallel to the great fortress, which used its rear walls to create a protected area that led down Land's Edge. Because of this, the only way to the rear of the fortress was up the same cliff and through the fortress itself. Kisan appreciated the tactically sound strategy the dwarves followed when building this stronghold.

They continued until it came upon a small way station situated in a copse of trees. A pool of clear water bubbled forth, fed by the same underground rivers that fed the lake within Bara'cor's walls. Its gurgling was the only sound that broke the still night air.

Kisan marveled at the beauty of the place, peaceful and clean. The trees gave weary travelers respite from the sun, providing shelter and cool shade. In the center of this way station stood a statue of a female with horns, her arms outstretched and holding a stone sphere roughly two feet in diameter. The sphere was smooth to the touch, the granite polished by an artisan's hand.

Prime moved up to it and picked up a piece of loose stone from the ground. He gripped it in his hand and squeezed. The rock pulverized into fine dust, which he slowly let fall on top of the sphere. He said something under his breath then, something Kisan couldn't make out. At that moment, the sphere began to glow a soft blue. It was not so bright as to alert anyone, more like the soft light one sees in the night sky just before dawn.

He looked at the others meaningfully and whispered, "Keep silent, watch each other's backs. We finish our job and we get out, *all* of us. Remember that tonight, we fight on home ground." At his command, all six touched the stone and vanished.

Journal Entry 18

The raids continue, and I have created a ritual of sorts. I hide, hunker down and put my head in the sand. Truly.

I can feel them now, the hunger of their presence building to a point where I can predict their entry.

I build a cocoon of power, one I know can withstand assault. I cannot ward the entire area, but warding myself seems to be something I believe in enough to be successful.

Of course, I emerge to devastation, my gathered resources taken and the ground scoured. They take everything of value, and while I know it is precisely for this reason . . . I am sick of it.

I took the imp into my cocoon with me. I know it is nothing except a conjuration of my loneliness, but it speaks and I find myself strangely attached. My desire to protect it seems to strengthen my wards and more importantly, my resolve.

Even with the benefit of the dragon's vision, I find it hard to understand how to unravel these Aeris.

INTO THE DARK

To act without knowing is fatal;

to know and not act is cowardice.

—*The Bladesman Codex*

The three made their way into the darker bowels of the great fortress, with Niall in front. The passageway cut roughly into the rock, but merged to join with a smooth floor that strangely had neither seams nor cracks. It was yet another example of the ancient lore of dwarven builders and their skill with stone.

"How far down does this go?" asked Arek.

Niall looked back over his shoulder, his face in the shadow of the torch, and said, "I don't know. Pretty deep, maybe all the way down to the lowlands and Haven. My father once told me that Bara'cor was just the visible part of an entire dwarven city built below it."

Arek looked to his left, where the passageway dropped off into inky blackness. "Can I see your torch?"

Yetteje lit another torch off Niall's and handed it to him. "Here."

Arek looked down using the torch as a guide and saw they stood within a passageway that joined a rock face on their right and opened to empty space on their left. "Pretty far down, by the looks of this." He fought a sudden sense of vertigo and looked at Niall.

The prince answered, "We're not going that deep to reach the place I think you want." He looked down the passageway where it forked and said, "Come on, this way."

They started to move forward, the cold, damp air clinging to them like a second skin, when Arek's vision tunneled and time froze. From the darkness came the shade of Piter.

"Not as stupid as I thought and not as crippled."

"Piter," Arek acknowledged with a nod, ignoring the jibe. "what am I looking for, exactly?"

The shade looked down the passageway, then back at Arek. "This is a rare and potent place. Can you feel it?"

And all of a sudden, he could, as if it had always been there. It felt the same as when sunshine soaked into his skin, but this was not sunlight, it was *power.* "How can this be?" he said, but Piter held up a forestalling hand.

"As you get closer, you will feel and see more. Your powers are only now coming into their own, as your maker intended. Stand ready and pay attention to the world around you." The shade nodded then pointed to the right passageway and said, "Your destiny lies there."

The scene snapped with the dizzying speed Arek had grown accustomed to. Piter was gone and Niall was quickly making his way to the fork. Arek looked around once more, steadying himself against the wet rock wall, then hobbled forward to catch up.

"We need to go right at the fork," he said, his voice echoing strangely through the subterranean space. He stumbled, his injured foot jarring painfully against a rocky outcropping and eliciting a soft curse.

"Got it," said Niall. He motioned for them to slow down and then gathered their small group together. "Listen, we came in through a side passageway. It's never used. However, my father has patrols, even here. Galadine name or not, if they see us, we'll be arrested, so douse the torches." He smothered his.

"How will we see?" Arek asked, wincing a little at the pain he felt from stooping.

Niall nodded to the walls and ceiling and said, "Trust me."

Arek looked at him a moment longer, then smothered his torch as well. They were instantly plunged into blackness. He felt Niall's hand come and squeeze his arm and assumed he had a hold of Tej also.

"See?" he heard Niall say.

As his eyes adjusted to the dark Arek noticed he could see quite a bit better than he expected to be able to, and noticed a sparkling on the slick walls of the passageway.

"It's some sort of byproduct of Shimmerene. They let off light, like starlight," whispered the prince to the others. "It clings to the wetness and grows, and as it does, it gets brighter."

Indeed, as Arek slowly stood he could see quite well as everything was covered in this faintly luminescent growth. "How much farther?"

"And what do you think we'll find?" asked Yetteje. "A weapon?"

"I don't know," Arek whispered, "but it's important."

They made their way down the right passageway, which turned colder and wetter as it angled sharply downward, and followed it for a few hundred paces. As they progressed, a distant roaring sounded in the distance, getting louder. The path doubled back on itself, turning downward again, then ended at a small landing.

From that landing, Arek could see a mist rising. He went to the edge and saw below a white ribbon of water, falling hundreds of feet into the darkness. It sparkled with the same luminescence as the walls, as if the water itself held a light of its very own.

"The Falls of Shimmerene?" asked Arek, to no one in particular.

Niall looked on in awe. "I've never seen this. This wasn't here before."

The pearlescent stream of water fell in a white wash of mist and sound, disappearing into, it seemed, the very bowels of the world.

"How could something like this appear out of nowhere?" Yetteje asked.

"I have no idea, but we'd have known about *this.*" He looked at Yetteje and said, "I've played in these catacombs since I was a child. I know them like my father's face."

One side of the landing abutted against a large, flat stone wall. Carved into the granite face stood a stone door, but there seemed to be no hinge or seam to open it. All three looked at the door pattern, clearly etched and outlined on the wet wall by the sparkling luminescence from Shimmerene, clinging to it like a sparkling and fragile sheet.

"What now?" asked Niall, a bit unnerved by what they had found, a waterfall he had never seen before today. "Maybe we should get back, warn my father ..."

Arek ignored the fear he heard in Niall's voice and looked around, saying, "I'm here, as you asked."

"Who are you talking—?" The scene froze, cutting off Yetteje's question.

Piter's shade appeared, illuminated by his own light. He looked at the door, then at Arek. "Do you remember?"

"Remember?"

"How you killed me?" the shade sneered.

Arek shook his head and said sadly, "I don't remember anything about that day ... but I am sorry." He tried to convey to the shade the guilt he also felt for his treatment of him, but it seemed to fall on deaf ears.

The shade didn't respond at first, staring at him. Then it said, "Do you remember your Test of Potential?"

Arek hesitantly nodded. "Not the details, but I remember preparing."

"This door opens the same way. Prepare as you did and the Way will open."

Reality snapped back into place and Arek heard Yetteje finish, "—to?"

He held up a hand for silence, then moved closer to the door. Now that he was closer, he could feel power in the air, like a vibration just below his senses. It flowed through him, tantalizing and just within reach. His injured foot began to itch.

"I think I can open it," he said.

"Wait," began Niall, but Yetteje took him by the arm and moved a short distance away.

"We'll be here, Arek. Do what you have to," she said.

Arek closed his eyes and willed himself to relax. He took a deep breath and with the exhale let go of the turmoil of the past few days. He took another lungful of the cool, wet air and let go of the fear and anger, felt it bleed out of him. He took another and imagined cool water washing in with each breath and cleaning out the detritus of emotions and peace-robbing conflict within his heart and soul. Arek breathed in peace and exhaled chaos.

There! In the calm waters of his mind, he could almost see something bound to the door. It was a woman. No, something *like* a woman. She hung suspended, with her arms outstretched to either side. Her body was covered in a fine gossamer gown, falling in straight white lines as if frozen in time. Feathered wings flared out, rising above her head, the tips almost meeting in the air above. Her head was down, as if she were lifeless or slept. To Arek, she looked like an angel.

He whispered, "Who are you?"

Her head slowly lifted and she opened her eyes. A cerulean light shone from them, power incarnate. Silver flashed down her length, as if awakening her also brought to life some eldritch power within. She looked around, questing with her ears, seemingly unable to see. "Where are you?" she countered.

"My name is Arek. What are you doing here?" he asked, unable to see where the door ended and she began. The air began to shine, as if infused with an energy all its own.

"My name is Dvarin." Her form strained forward, but still she could not see Arek.

Arek took a mental step closer, unable to understand how she had gotten here. As he did so, he felt something change within him. Something grew, a hunger he could feel gurgling up from deep within himself. The itching in his foot grew worse.

As if in response, Dvarin pulled back. "No! You cannot mean to do this!"

Arek took a deep breath, then stepped closer. He could feel his body hunger for the energy that surrounded her. It flowed cleanly through the very air, infusing her with an almost holy light. He could not resist it. It was meant for him, it was *sustenance.*

"No, I beg you. You cannot!" She tried to withstand the onslaught, but the power within Arek was too much. She bucked once, desperately trying to free herself, but the black tunnel had formed, and in the blink of an eye it tore her very soul. Her psychic scream of death echoed across a vast, ethereal plane, before fading into nothingness.

Arek's eyes opened, liquid pools of darkness, and his form flashed, outlined in a luminous black fire. Power coursed through his body, healing and regenerating. The stone door responded, itself burning silver in protest, flashing brighter for a moment than the sun itself. Then, with a silent implosion, it lost its struggle against Arek's fire and disappeared, leaving behind only a square afterimage floating purple in both Niall and Yetteje's eyes.

Niall looked in wonder at the door, now a blank opening before them, then at Yetteje. Neither could believe what they saw. Then they heard a small sigh and saw Arek crumple to the floor, his black fire extinguished.

Before either could move, the luminescence surrounding the entire area faded as if drained, and they were plunged into a complete and utter darkness.

Journal Entry 19

I have been watching my imps more. It is another piece of the puzzle. They were formed from nothing but my need, my need for company, for help in scavenging.

As my need for companionship grew, they have slowly begun to speak. My will is evolving them, but to what purpose? It satisfies me, yet could something like this be created with a different purpose?

My little imp, the first one to speak, has become inquisitive, almost childlike. It whispers the word, "self," as it points to its tiny chest. I find myself taken aback, for it had not occurred to me it could understand its own existence.

Its innocence and desire to help can only be described as adoration. More surprising, it adores me as if it knows I am its . . . father.

FIND AND KILL

When blades meet,

the distance between you is equal.

Execute your strategy without hesitation.

Make your opponent respond to you.

Lead him down the keen-edged path.

Your focus should always be victory.

—*Kensei Tsao, The Book of Blades*

The team appeared with a blue flash within a war room of Bara'cor. The chamber had two guards stationed within and two more outside, per the king's orders. Their job was not to fight, but to send the alarm should intruders appear. Had they been facing normal foes they may have succeeded, but the six who appeared were no ordinary men.

Kisan exploded into action, moving with blurring speed at the nearest of the guards inside the room. She knew that if she did not act quickly, the defenders of Bara'cor would pay with their lives. She kicked one in the temple, then spun and elbowed the other in the sternum. She moved back to the first, a quick chop to the throat, then back to the second with a knee to the head. Both sank to the floor, unconscious.

Neither had had time to cry out to their compatriots stationed outside, but the muffled sounds of a scuffle drew the other two in to investigate, to their misfortune.

Five had moved with Kisan and continued through the doorway just as the two guards appeared. Thin stilettos appeared in each hand and he drove them quickly through the front of each man's throat, severing their spines. Letting go of the daggers still lodged in their throats, he grabbed the two dying guards and pulled them fully into the room, dumping them in a heap and retrieving his weapons.

Prime moved in and signaled, *Clear?*

Kisan looked out into the hallway and saw no one. She signaled, *All clear,* then turned and was greeted with the sight of Five sinking his stilettos into the chest of each of the men she had just rendered unconscious.

One of the guard's eyes opened, shock registering on his face, but Five clamped a hand down over his mouth and nose. He struggled for a moment, then died without uttering a sound, nothing but a small sigh escaping from between the assassin's fingers. Kisan felt anger welling up inside her, but quickly held it in check. It was not yet time to act.

* * * * *

Clear, signaled Five. All the guards were dead. Except for the night watch and the soldiers patrolling the walls and corridors, most of Bara'cor would be sleeping.

Prime pulled off a glove and knelt, touching his hand to the bare stone. His eyes closed and his stonesense opened. Then, as he and the stone of Bara'cor became one, he could see what the fortress could see.

People throughout the fortress became visible to his mind's eye, each where they touched or slept upon the stone. These were the ones who soiled the granite of his forefathers but today was not the day to exact justice on all of them, just three. He searched them quickly, and saw the king gathered with a few others in a ready room, not far from here. But where was his son and the null?

Prime's stonesense spread, searching. There! He saw the prince now, but he was far from his father and deep within the fortress. Why would he go there?

The king's son stood with a girl. There was also a strange black spot that moved along with them, blurred and indistinct. This was the null, he realized with a start, and so long as he was within Bara'cor's walls, he could be tracked by his stonesense. Whether or not the null was the prisoner was irrelevant now, but why were they so far below the fortress proper?

As he struggled to understand the logic of this, another fact punched him in the gut and he almost lost his composure. He focused on his training and protocol, then made the necessary changes. With multiple targets and the need to protect their egress point, he would have to split up his team. Killing the null was the primary mission, and therefore it fell to him. His team would have to take care of the rest.

He gathered his group, signaling their change in strategy. He would send the majority against the king. Their orders were to terminate their targets, confirm using Bara'cor's stone, then exfiltrate.

He knew the null was with the king's son, and this allowed him to finish both primary and secondary missions in one place. He wished he could take more men with him, but given what he knew now, plans had to adapt and a more immediate problem had to be dealt with.

Five, Six, remain, protect our exit. Two, take Three and Four. I will proceed alone.

He finished his hand signals, then motioned for the team to touch Bara'cor's rock and see what he saw. In a moment, the entire team saw the situation and knew what their leader wanted.

Prime signaled to Two, *Execute*, then stood and moved out into the hallway. In an instant, he was gone.

* * * * *

Two shot a quick glance to Five, nodding once. Whatever he saw must have satisfied him, for he oriented his team and shot out of the room in the opposite direction, followed by Three and Four. They left like a small wing of lethal predators hunting Bara'cor's halls.

Kisan, for her part, had played along, but did not understand what had just happened. At first, she thought the touching of the stone had been some sort of ritual, another homage paid by the dwarves to Bara'cor.

But something had been communicated when they touched the stone, something lethal and deadly. Prime had signaled, *Execute,* and separated from the group. That could only mean that their targets were in two or more places, but who was Prime going after?

A sudden sickening realization hit her that they had not been performing a ritual. They somehow used the stone to determine their targets' locations. They were dwarves and had an affinity to the very rock itself, hewn from the earth and shaped by their people. Had they used this rock to find the king, his son, and possibly Arek?

Kisan knew she couldn't wait here with Five, and was going to have to make a difficult choice on who to follow. She closed her eyes and increased her awareness, bringing herself up to full combat readiness, preparing for battle. She shot a quick glance at Five, then crouched against the wall. That act saved her life.

A stiletto buried itself where Kisan's head had just been. Before she could react, a booted foot struck her in the ribs, flipping her over and backward. Five advanced on her, his eyes burning blue and his intent clear.

Five stopped a few feet away from the prostrated form of Six and said, "We know you're not one of us. Tell me who you are and I will make this quick and painless."

Kisan flipped up to her feet and stood facing the dwarf. It was clear she had lost her cover, but did not understand how. Then with sudden clarity she knew, *the stone.* The fortress itself had shown Prime and the others that one of their team wasn't a stone maker.

Her flameskin blossomed around her in an ignition of orange fire. Kisan's subterfuge no longer mattered, and she felt an icy cold anger settle into place.

"Six is dead," she admitted. "I killed him back on the Isle. Tell me, which target does Prime pursue?"

Nothing but silence came from Five. In a blur of motion, he attacked. His granite-like fists struck quickly and unerringly at Kisan's body in multiple double punches and kicks, followed by knees and elbows.

To Kisan, however, the dwarven assassin moved in slow motion. On the Isle, when they had faced Thera, they had used poison and surprise to best her in combat. She had paid with her life, trying to protect so many children around her.

This time, Kisan wasn't surprised, and there were no children to protect. This assassin faced a master who wasn't outnumbered and knew her opponent. Whether he knew it or not, this assassin faced death.

Kisan moved into the attacks, instantly reading the timing and style of everything thrown at her. Her arms moved in a motion that was both economical and brutal, inflicting damage at every block. Orange fire blossomed to white as her power grew. She countered with elbows, then used the assassin's momentum and weight against him, striking with short arced knees to his upper thighs, and forearms to her opponent's collarbone and neck.

Each blow hammered into the dwarf like the maul of a titan, battering him backward. When the assassin, in desperation, threw two punches at Kisan's head and midsection, the master stepped in with her arms circling, blocking both. She continued her motion, pushing the assassin's arms away from her body. Then, her head slammed into the dwarf's nose, splattering it in a detonation of orange-silver fire and pain.

Before the assassin could recover, Kisan hit him with a spinning back kick to the chest. The force of the blow threw the dwarf against the back wall, where he crumbled to a heap. Kisan moved up and grabbed the assassin by the hair.

Just as she pulled his head up, he punched upward like a snake. Her hand stopped the punch in mid-air, caught in her vise-like grip. Then, consumed with rage, she released the illusion and was Kisan once more.

"I want you to know who killed you,": she said. "This is for my friends on the Isle, and for the lore father."

The bones in his wrist snapped and broke as Kisan crushed them in her grip, the pain flashing in his eyes like lightning. The stiletto turned slowly until it pointed at his eye.

"And this is for the children."

The stiletto punched into the assassin's eye, the poison taking hold even as the brain registered shock and confusion. Five fell back, his one remaining eye focused on the adept as his muscles clenched and tightened, a gift from the poisoned blade. Kisan pulled her hand back, delivering a strike that crushed his neck and spine, ending his life.

She stood, looking down at the dead assassin, breathing in gulps. Incandescent anger flamed within her, a blinding rage that reflected in the orange-white intensity of her flameskin. Slowly, the fire along with the anger within her ebbed as she saw the dead man at her feet.

There was no pity in her, but she didn't feel any better. She wouldn't until every one of Prime's team was dead, but a mistake she had just made needed to be addressed. She quickly knelt and put a hand to the assassin's forehead, cursing her own rashness.

She had to act quickly if there were any chance to mindread this one and gain critical insight into Prime's plan. Slowly, her vision went black and she dived into Five's fading memories.

Prime went after the null, which could only be Arek. Two led the team to the king himself, but the details were jumbled and difficult to understand and getting worse. Unlike Tamlin, who had still been alive, Five was already dead because of the virulence of the poison and Kisan's anger. She should have kept this assassin alive and incapacitated, and cursed herself again. She knew Silbane would never have made such a mistake. Now she was forced to make a few educated guesses.

She moved over to the doorway and took a moment to think. It was no surprise that Prime would go after the primary target. Their orders were to kill him, and Prime would not chance that to anyone else. Kisan didn't hesitate in coming to a decision, for her mind had been turning it over ever since her contact with Lore Father Giridian. Arek made his choice when he killed Piter, but she would not let another family die if she could prevent it.

Kisan decided not to change back to look like Tamlin. Prime knew and had left Five to finish her. The disguise was a waste of valuable energy, something she was using quickly, and the team would be suspicious of any dwarf that showed up at their location.

She decided instead to conserve her strength and track the larger team led by Two. She moved out into the corridor and looked in both directions.

Prime had been smart. He followed mission protocols and hadn't shared anything with Five that could lead to him, except his target. That made tracking him impossible through the jumble of memories, but Four hadn't been so careful. He and Five were friends, and he had shared their path.

Kisan smiled, then set off at a fast but silent run, her form fading from sight like a shimmer of heat. She would find and kill this team, extract whatever information she needed to put an end to Prime, and find out what she could about Sovereign.

FALCON'S PREY

A Bladesman never interrupts

while his enemy is making a mistake.

—*Davyd Dreys, Notes to my Sons*

A sh and his men were assembled in a ready room, a smaller octagonal room that resembled the great council chamber, except there was only one statue and sphere here. The room was dominated by a table like the one in its larger counterpart, around which clustered soldiers of Bara'cor, each with varying expressions of awe.

They looked upon an enchantment that had suddenly sprung to life, causing this table to display images of a miniature map of Bara'cor and the surrounding area. The enchantment seemed to change the map as necessary, so as features changed in the land around Bara'cor, so too did the table. It was as if the rock itself knew what was happening around it. However, unlike the table in the larger war room, this displayed the images hanging in the space above the table in three dimensions.

Another aspect of the table was that it showed the nomad army like a red stain of blood spread before the fortress walls. This had begun not too long ago, and clearly not in time with any attack launched by the nomads. Still, whatever magic allowed the table to mimic the landscape of the terrain, also considered the nomads an enemy. Though it was not detailed enough for small scale tactics, it was useful to understand quickly the disposition and concentration of the enemy forces. Talis looked at it now, while Ash flipped a small leather belt to Chandra.

"This will be good for your knives," he said. "The king will be here shortly."

True to his word, King Bernal Galadine came into the room, followed by his firstmark. He reached into a small pocket and retrieved the Finder, which he placed on the table as he came up to stand next to Talis, his eyes on the map. "Anyone come up with a reason for the table to start doing this?"

"No, my king," answered Talis. The older warrior turned his attention to the map, interpreting it for the king. "Their forces are still groupin' here, sir," he indicated with a cracked fingernail to a spot just outside of arrow and catapult range. "It seems the darker areas mean more troops, though I can't say I understand how this blasted table knows that."

"Have you ever seen the likes of this?" asked the king. He looked askance at the firstmark and the armsmark.

Jebida moved a bit closer, displeasure in his eyes. "The damn thing has been a simple table through countless military encounters and now lights up like the Spring Festival. It's clearly magical and not to be trusted. Probably misinformation from someone who means Bara'cor harm. Perhaps even that kid."

"To what end?" asked Ash. "More likely this is some dwarven enchantment that has recently come to life."

The king asked the armsmark, "Why now?"

"Who knows?" Ash replied. "It hasn't been doing this for very long. King Bara might have created it as an aid if it looked like the fortress would be breached."

"Waiting till breach does not make military sense, whether you be dwarven or not," the firstmark huffed. "No, something else is causing this."

Seeing the enemy in this fashion did allow him some measure of comfort, so long as he trusted the information was true. *That* worm of doubt still had not receded. Ash then looked at the assembled men and motioned to the king. "With your permission, I'd like to go over the final preparations before we infiltrate the camp."

The king nodded, but then looked around. "Where's the boy, Arek? We'll need him to activate the Finder." He motioned to a waiting runner and ordered, "Fetch him . . . and my son for that matter." Looking back at the armsmark he said, "A moment, no sense in repeating yourself."

As the runner took off, Talis bent over, inspecting something on the section that showed the translucent image of Bara'cor's interior. "Now . . . what's this?"

Three small blue dots moved through the fortress. They followed the hallways and corridors and moved with alarming speed.

The king and his men came closer to look. "What *is* that?"

Ash took a look and his eyes narrowed. "Whatever it is, it's coming toward us." He turned to the door and drew Tempest. His team, the king, and Jebida followed suit. "Prepare yourselves."

Talis drew his short blade and kept his eyes glued on the map. "It's coming down our passageway." A few heartbeats went by and then he whispered, "It's right outside the door."

With a deafening crash and a flash of blinding light, the door burst inward and chaos ensued. The king and Jebida fell back as Ash and his team moved forward out of instinct, the party able to act only because of the warning they had gotten from Talis and the table. However, the explosive entry had served its purpose and disoriented the defenders, who still moved without coordination.

Their disarray cost them, and Sevel took the brunt of the first attack. A black shape slammed into him. Three punches that looked like they came from a granite hammer sent him flying backward across the table. He landed in a crumpled heap on the far side, unmoving.

Two knives flashed past Ash ear as Chandra whipped them at her attacker. Both scored a hit, sticking into the chest of the man, but not as deeply as Ash expected. The man slapped them out of his body, then threw his stiletto at Chandra, who ducked and rolled at the last instant. The knife stuck halfway to its hilt in the stone behind her.

Behind the leader came two more black shapes, fast as lightning. They arced over the point man, landing lightly on either side of the table, engaging the defenders, who had fallen back to the sides.

Talis moved forward, slamming into the man on his side, and put him into a wrestler's hug. It wasn't until he tried to get his arms around his opponent that he seemed to realize his mistake. The man was bigger than he looked and his body did not give at all.

Ash wondered if the intruders wore armor under those black clothes, but what kind of armor fits under clothes? Two crushing blows slammed down on Talis's shoulders as the attacker's elbows smashed into his back. His grip loosened. Then a fist cracked into his skull and he fell back, half unconscious.

Ash held Tempest, who pulsed green. He drove his attack forward, spinning a deadly web of steel around the attacker facing him. The man used his forearms to block the blade, and Ash was surprised to see Tempest spark and skitter off. Then his foot caught. The very stone of the room seemed to trip him.

Shieldrock! she cried. These aren't men, beloved.

Ash didn't reply, recovering from the trip and continuing his deadly dance with his attacker, who moved with the fluidity and grace of one borne to combat. Each of his cuts and strikes met a forearm block or an ingenious dodge, leaving the armsmark tired and frustrated.

The king had only his short sword, but knew its use intimately. He started to move forward, but a meaty hand closed on his shoulder, pulling him back. Jebida stepped in front, armed with his blade, a dangerous glint in his eyes. "You'll be fed to the dogs tonight."

Jebida swung the blade, but the man was incredibly fast, moving in with a kick, then dancing back out of reach. The firstmark let the kick hit him, obviously expecting his greater size and bulk to protect him, but would regret that decision—the kick sounded like a stone maul. Jebida was picked up and slammed into the wall on his left.

Ash pivoted around a punch-kick combination, then aimed a strike for the intruder's head. As he did so, he felt a sting in his neck and saw the man who stood behind the others firing some sort of metal tube. He started to raise his hand, but his muscles involuntarily tightened and he hit the floor, paralyzed. As the poison worked its way into his body, Ash began to convulse and his vision dimmed.

Poison! Tempest cursed through her connection to Ash, but he could feel nothing. He sensed the sword desperately searching the room for something.

The man turned and shot another dart at the king, who couldn't move fast enough. But Jebida's arm pushed him down at the same moment Talis stepped in, putting himself in the way. The dart hit him in the neck and the gruff old warrior clutched at it, his features locking into a grimace of pain, his hands becoming claws. He fell back, gurgling, even as the life left him. Talis fell, dead before his body hit the ground.

The assassin flipped himself up over the table, then jumped and rolled as two more knives from Chandra flashed past him. He threw a stiletto, catching her in the midsection, and Ash heard her gasp as it drove through her stomach and out her back. The assassin continued his roll across the table and landed lightly in front of her. Then his fist crushed her sternum before she could draw another breath and she hit the back wall with a wet thud. He could hear her bones snap under the assassin's fist, and knew she would soon be dead. Then the man pivoted, flipping back to land near the king and his final bodyguard, the firstmark. Another held his position while the third circled around until they faced the last men standing in the room.

"Surrender and I will let the others live." the lead assassin said, indicating the firstmark and the fallen. He looked at the king with glowing blue eyes. "They have no need to die here, King Galadine." Then he flashed some kind of sign to his men.

Ash lay on the ground, his vision nearly gone, his body wracked in pain. Then something happened and the pain began to lessen. He saw a clean green light in his mind's eye, suffusing his body with energy, beneficent and healing. It neutralized the toxins and drove it from his blood. The tiny dart fell out with a small sound, like a glass shard hitting the floor. Ash looked to his left, where the sound of labored breathing ceased. It was Sevel, his eyes frozen open in death. Ash carefully levered himself over and was about to stand when a voice from the door stopped him.

"Two."

There in the doorway stood a woman, dressed in the same style of clothes that Arek had been wearing, but darker. Her lean frame hinted at violence, but controlled and focused. She was younger than Ash by his reckoning and spoke with authority. Her voice cut into the room like the keen edge of a blade.

"I know death means little to you, but *failure* . . . that's different." The woman walked slowly into the room. "You failed to kill the Adepts of the Isle, you failed to protect your team, and you will not kill another child."

At first, the man didn't appear to know who this woman was. He signaled his men, again, though Ash had no way of understanding the meaning of the gesture, though by the smile on the woman's face, she did. The assassin faced the woman in the doorway.

The strange man looked at his new adversary and snarled, "You halflings are vermin." He signaled again, but the woman was faster than Ash—or the assassin—imagined. Even as all three brought up their dart weapons and fired, she was in motion, bringing her hands together in front of herself.

The darts sped at her, their glass bulbs filled with the toxin that had nearly killed Ash, but they never reached their target. The woman's hands came together in a single clap that detonated in the room like thunder.

The sound was frightening in its intensity and the very air seemed to bend and flex, then every piece of glass and crystal in the room shattered. The darts, lethal messengers of death, exploded into tiny fragments, as did every dart on the assassins' belts. So too, did every pitcher, glass, and plate in the room.

The woman waited for the carnage she had wrought to end, then looked at the assassin. Her form burst in a flash of orange-yellow fire, surrounding her in its ethereal, protective flames.

"My turn," she sneered.

The man she'd called "Two" didn't wait and neither did one of his comrades. Both moved forward with a speed that belied their bulk. Again, their adversary proved even faster than they anticipated. She met their attack with her own, a series of striking blocks that looked strong enough to break bone and shatter stone.

Two moved to his left and tried to come up from behind her, but she grabbed the other man and flung him as if he weighed nothing at all. Both assassins went down in a tangled heap.

The third man started to move, but reacted to a sharp pain in his back. He looked down and saw the point of a sword emerge from his chest. Then he was spun around to face the man he had seen die with a dart in his neck.

Ash yanked his sword out, then in one fluid motion swung it in a short, deadly arc. The sword flashed emerald as it decapitated the man where he stood. The head flew off, but the body remained standing a moment longer before dropping to its knees then falling forward.

Ash saw the woman at the door had begin her attacks in earnest now, moving through her opponents as one would when fighting children, her aim sure and true. Occasionally her flaming aura would flash orange or yellow as one or the other managed to get in a strike, but nothing actually touched her. She and these assassins dueled in a deadly dance of strike and counter-strike, something that Ash knew well. It only continued for a heartbeat or two, then Ash heard the sound like a branch breaking and the leader fell back, his arm hanging at an unnatural angle and useless.

In the blink of an eye, the woman spun into the opening created by the leader's misstep. She swept aside two punches from the second assassin and struck with the tips of her fingers through the assassin's neck, crushing his throat and spine. That one fell to his knees, gurgling at the leader's feet, unable to breathe through his pulverized windpipe. She didn't wait for him to die. She slammed her elbow into the crown of his head, driving it down and crushing his neck. The assassin died instantly.

The woman took a breath, her form brightening with fire, then she exhaled. Only Two was left alive, his arm broken, his options limited. Without moving, she addressed the last remaining assassin, "Two, who is your Sovereign?"

Beloved, shall we kill this one? implored Tempest in a girlish voice.

No, Ash replied, we must have answers.

* * * * *

Two stared at Kisan with hate and said, "How do you know my designation?" Then it seemed to dawn on him.

Kisan came eye to eye with the assassin and said, "I killed your men—" she making a slight motion to encompassed the room—"all of them."

Two met the master's gaze, a small smile on his lips. "Then they deserved it. What of Prime and the king's son? Will you bargain for that information?" He began reaching with his good arm for something on his belt.

"Stop." Kisan saw the dwarf begin the almost imperceptible motion and froze him with her voice. She knew what Two intended. There was a small point on his belt, behind which lay a sharp needle coated with the same poison as in the darts. One touch and the needle would scratch him, bringing instant death. "You know I can stop you before you kill yourself."

"Then why haven't you?"

"Wait!" said the king, holding up both his hands to prevent any ill-conceived attack. He looked at the woman who had dispatched these assassins so easily and asked, "He spoke of my son. Where is he?"

Kisan never took her eyes off Two, but nodded in response to the king's question. If there was a chance to save the prince, she wanted to hear it. "Where is Prime? Give me his location and I will let you use your poison."

Two looked at the king and said, "By now, your son is dead." Then he looked at Kisan and said, "It's always a pleasure killing halfling kids."

She locked eyes with Two for a heartbeat, then said simply, "Fine." Before anyone could move, she shot forward, her hands a blur. Even as Two began to push his finger against the needle, Kisan had touched his forehead and dived into the man's mind. She could see Two's life before her, but knew she could not absorb it until she purged the jumbled life and death of Tamlin and Five. Her goal, however, had not been to assimilate Two. That would take too long and she didn't need to. She only needed three things.

First, she paralyzed Two by locking points along his spine at the neck and waist, then found the entry point of the poison and collapsed the blood vessels around the upper arm, trapping it and slowing its spread. She couldn't stop the poison from working, but would gain the few precious moments needed for what was to come next.

Second, she searched for Prime's location. As she suspected, he had been careful with that information. All Two knew was the egress point where Five now lay dead. He had offered the boy when bargaining, though it now was clearly a tactic to buy time for Prime. Whether or not the king's son was truly with Arek could not be confirmed, and Kisan suspected that Two simply did not know.

Finally, she searched for any information about Sovereign, but what she saw made no sense. She saw a being made of pure light, standing in a cavernous opening. Around it opened hundreds of tunnels, as if this Sovereign stood within a network of caves or a vast subterranean space. The space was filled with what looked to be worms covered in tiny glowing points. Around those worms moved creatures that looked like dwarves, but that Two called, *yewmins.* Kisan knew she didn't have much time and couldn't risk following this assassin into death. She pulled out of Two's subconscious, leaving the paralysis in place.

She opened her eyes and made sure Two could see her, then said, "Six's memories showed me you can be rebirthed. I'm not going to leave your Sovereign with much to work with."

Her hands whipped out to either side of Two's head and struck, shattering every bone in his skull. The pressure wave from the blow destroyed Two's brain, liquefying everything inside. Kisan didn't even look at him as she kicked the body back. It slammed into a wall with a wet smack, before sliding down in a lifeless heap. She then turned to face the king.

Bernal moved out from behind his men and said, "How will we find Niall? You killed the only man who could tell us!"

Kisan held up her hand and said, "King Galadine, I searched his memories and there is nothing there. They do not share information that can lead to each other. We need to find your son and Initiate Arek on our own. Are you saying they were together?"

"Yes..." the king stammered. "I mean ... I don't know." He took a deep breath, his warrior instinct telling him this woman spoke truly, but the father's heart in him clearly searching for a way to save his son.

Then, he seemed to realize his best chance stood right before him. "We had assumed Arek's master a man, but you must be Silbane. Arek said you were with the nomads. Defeating these men speaks to your skill. We are well met, though your presence here destroys our own plans."

Kisan shook her head, looking about the scene of carnage until her eyes came to rest on the Finder, still on the tabletop. "I see the men of Bara'cor are just as insightful as those found elsewhere in the world." She met their confused stares with a small smile, then made her way over to the Finder and inspected it, noting it still sparkled with its own light. Satisfied the other master was alive, Kisan turned back to the three men and said, "Be happy that I am not Silbane. He's far more dangerous and less merciful than me."

Journal Entry 20

My excitement grows, for I have yet another idea to keep me safe from these raids. The cocoon, but bigger. I know the ritual of setting wards and will follow it to the letter. I will not doubt this place, nor myself as I have in the past. Not this time . . .

With the help of the numerous imps surrounding me, I have Shaped four wards and spent hours infusing them with power, drawn from blood (mine). This may be the secret I was missing before.

These blood Marks will be the foci for my barrier. The imps watch me wide-eyed, their attention transfixed by my efforts. The Marks I fashion resemble shields, but I have inscribed runes of defense on their surface. My blood is a part of this ritual now, for I have neglected the might that my name holds, an ancient name with the promise of power and protection.

I have planted one Mark at each corner of my castle's outer wall. Together, they should create an impenetrable barrier, starting with my firstmark.

Perhaps tonight, I shall finally sleep in peace.

THROUGH THE DOOR

The thought of enemies should not

bring fear to one's heart;

it is the plight of friends

that keeps one pacing at night.

—*Altan proverb*

Arek heard a voice, filled with urgency, pushing and prodding him from his sleep. *Get up! Arek, you must get up!* He shook his head, trying to clear it and felt helping hands below his arms. "What happened?"

Niall's voice whispered, "Shssh! You collapsed, but not before opening the door."

Arek opened his eyes cautiously and saw the open portal. Beyond it seemed to be a great hall, lit with an unearthly blue light. "I don't remember what I did."

Tej came up and kneeled at Arek's other side and said, "It was pretty amazing. You lit up like you were on fire, and the door did too! Then it opened."

"That's impossible," Arek said. "I can't do magic."

"What?" asked Niall. "You're apprenticed to a mage."

Arek rose to his feet with their help and said, "Tell me something I don't know." Then he realized his foot had not shocked him with debilitating pain. In fact, each time he went through one of these "events," he seemed to be getting better. He was reluctant to take off the boot to check, but could feel his body healing. It occurred to him then that he was also recovering faster than usual from these various blackouts. He had been in bed for weeks after his Test of Potential, maybe a day after his fight with Piter, and now only moments after this encounter with the door. It was as if he was getting used to ... what? *That* he didn't know and it scared him just a little.

"What happened to the glow on the walls?" he asked, looking around.

"I don't know," Niall said. "After you opened the door, it all went dark."

The only light came from the opening to the room, streaming out in silver and blue. The portion of the room he could see through the door seemed huge, almost like a cathedral. He moved forward cautiously at first, expecting his foot to cry out in pain. The only thing he felt was a twinge of pain and sluggishness that spoke of lax reactions, as if these new muscles needed training. A small smile escaped his lips as he was followed by his companions through the door.

His earlier guess had been correct. The room was a vast columned cathedral with a small pyramid at its center, stepped and four-sided, leading up to an azure radiance that came from a dark sphere hanging in the air above the pyramid's flat apex. This sphere was surrounded by a blue fire, filling the chamber with its radiance, like a strange, second sun.

Niall took in the room, then said to Yetteje, "This can't be here. It's just like the waterfall. Patrols would have run into it long ago."

"Through a blocked stone door? Who knows how far we've actually walked," said Arek over his shoulder. "We don't even know for certain that we're still under Bara'cor."

"Why?" Yetteje asked said.

"Because Niall is right, at least about that waterfall. No way something that big stays hidden. I think this chamber, and the path to it, opened only recently."

"How can a path 'open'?" asked Niall. "It's not as if this fortress is alive."

Arek turned and faced the other two. He swiped his foot along the dry ground and said, "No water, not a drop. Taste the air. It's dry, yet there's a waterfall not a hundred paces from here. This room has been sealed for a very long time."

He turned away from the other two's wide-eyed stares and moved to the pyramid.

"Arek, wait." Niall came and laid a hand on his shoulder, a look of dread in his eyes. "What do you mean to do?"

Arek looked up at the pyramid and the scene refracted then froze. Everything was still, except the scintillation from the sapphire-colored sun. It still burned brightly, painting the cathedral in contrasting light and columned shadows. Out of this stepped Piter, smiling.

"I doubted your ability to get this far."

"What is this place?" Arek asked, ignoring the phantasm's usual ire. His foot felt better and he began to think about what more could heal him fully.

Piter's expression grew thoughtful and he said, "There are a multiverse of planes that intersect our world. This is one of those intersection points."

Arek nodded, familiar with the idea from the teachings of the Isle and asked, "What do you want?"

"That depends on whether you want to live or die. Something pursues you," the shade said, his smile growing wicked. "Your only escape is to go up there." It pointed to the blue-black sun flaring at the apex of the pyramid.

Arek looked at the shade, his anger balanced by a new fear. What would be chasing him? The only thing he could think of was the great dragon, who seemed bent on his destruction. He looked at Piter and stammered, "W-what is it . . . Rai'stahn?"

"Something has been unleashed, and it hunts you." Piter smiled, looking immensely pleased with himself. "Run, Apprentice, run . . . or die."

The scene shifted and snapped back. Arek stood with Niall's hand still on his shoulder. Piter's voice was gone. He blinked once, orienting himself, then turned around and said, "Something is coming."

"My father's men?" Niall asked.

"I don't think so. Something more dangerous. We'd better get ready." He shook off his gloves and prepared for real combat, his magical disruption too important an advantage to ignore if he was about to face a dragon alone. But still, part of him doubted the shade's warning.

Tej came up, drawing her short blade. "Who's coming?"

"I don't know, only that whatever it is, it's after us," Arek replied.

"How do you know that?" she asked, looking at the entrance to the chamber.

"The same way I knew about this place." Arek moved between his friends, then closed his eyes, calming himself. He wasn't about to leave them, especially if that's what Piter wanted.

He breathed in evenly, then out again, his mind clearing. He relaxed his body and mentally prepared himself for combat. His combat sense expanded and the world slowed. At least here he felt comfortable, in his element. Whether or not it was Rai'stahn, it would face a Brown ready to test for Ascension, and weren't they the most dangerous?

"There!" Niall pointed, his voice etched with barely controlled fear.

They both looked to where Niall pointed and saw a man dressed in black stride into the room. He didn't seem concerned with hiding himself, but stopped short when he saw them. Something in his stance hinted at uncertainty. He kneeled and placed a hand on the floor.

"What's he doing?" Tej asked.

Arek ignored her and whispered, "We have to attack so he doesn't have time to focus on any one of us. Attack together, unless you have an opening." He then moved forward slowly, motioning for the other two to fan out to his left and right.

* * * * *

Prime looked at the three people in the room. His stone sense pointed out three figures, but one was different. The boy in the middle seemed to absorb the senses of the fortress and a blackness surrounded him. This was the one he had sensed earlier, the indistinct shape that seemed to suck at his senses. This was the null.

His appearance fitted the description of the prisoner, Arek, but the boy did not act like a prisoner. It looked as if he led the other two, and that made the situation harder to predict or control. Furthermore, Prime's ability to sense anything through the stone seemed somehow diminished, likely because of his proximity to the null. Better to end things quickly, he thought. Kill them all, then get back to the egress point. Leave no loose ends.

Prime slowly came to his feet, his skin turning harder as Bara'cor itself lent him the obduracy of the stone he stood upon. His confidence was justified. They had faced and killed the overrated Adepts of the Isle with relative ease. The king would die, as would the infiltrator, and no one was going to stop him from terminating the null, especially not a group of halfling kids. As he had reminded his men, they now fought on home ground.

They had started to move on the boy's orders, spreading out, trying to take tactical advantage. That confirmed Prime's suspicion that this boy was in charge, and that made him his primary tactical target. He slipped two poisoned stilettos into his hands, then moved forward like a hunting cat, directly for the null named Arek.

THE MEASURE OF A MAN

You cannot know when

your final day will come,

so seize greatness in all things;

prepare as if every moment

will be your last.

—Davyd Dreys, Notes to my Sons

Kisan looked at the king, her eyes taking in the man who stood before her. The warrior in him was plain to see, but she also noticed he spoke carefully, measuring his emotions against the greater good of their situation. Perhaps her initial impression of him was wrong. His care meant he had some wisdom.

"What we do next determines who lives and who dies," she said.

The king nodded slowly, answering, "Your name? I would speak with you plainly."

The master smiled and said, "Kisan. I am here to recover Arek and Silbane." Kisan sensed a nobility of character, but did not volunteer any other information. Instead, she waited to gauge the man by his actions.

"My son is somewhere in Bara'cor, with your apprentice, Arek. They are missing, but I have sent runners to find them. These men attacked me, but that one spoke of another going after my son."

Kisan ignored the king's repeated mistake of assigning Arek's apprenticeship to her and gestured instead to the assassins, saying, "These are dwarves, not men. They were sent here to kill you." She had guessed correctly in following Two, but now regretted that Arek was not alone. Her decision to come to the king's aid had put the man's son in danger. She found she couldn't hold his gaze then, the loss of Piter bubbling up fresh in her mind. Instead, she offered, "I am sorry, but the leader, Prime, goes after the boys."

"Then we have a common interest in saving Niall and your apprentice," the king stepped forward and offered his hand.

Kisan took his hand in a firm grip. While saving Arek was not her objective, she could empathize with the king. Her attention went back to Silbane's charm on the table top and she changed the subject, asking, "What did you intend to do with the Finder?"

In response, one of the soldiers stepped forward and said, "My team and I were going to use it to enter the nomad camp and find your friend. Then, we were to attempt to assassinate the chieftain of the nomads. But this attack..."

That plan required knowledge of how to use the Finder. "How did you come to know of its use?" she asked.

An uncomfortable silence followed as the men looked to their king. But it was the older of the two officers who stepped forward and to the rescue.

"You consider yourself a warrior?" he asked.

Kisan shrugged. "Do you consider yourself intelligent?"

The soldiers stopped as if unsure of how to respond, then said, "Understand that your apprentice nearly killed the Prince of Bara'cor and the Princess of EvenSea. Our armsmark—" he gestured to indicate the younger officer— "stopped him. He entered by unknown means and posed a threat to our security. When it was over, we needed information, and we extracted it. We tortured him for it."

The armsmark stepped forward then and said, "But this sword, Tempest. It *healed* him. His injuries are gone."

Kisan stepped around and picked up the Finder. She spent a moment deep in thought, looking at the circumstances from their eyes. An intruder during a siege would indicate a weakness in the fortress's defenses, potentially a deadly one for those inside.

"The sword cannot heal him unless it's held by someone attuned to it. Who did that?" Kisan knew the answer, but addressed the armsmark.

The armsmark bowed and said, "It was held by me. She . . . *spoke* to me."

"Really?" Kisan took that in with a bit of surprise. The sword had been quiescent on the Isle. What was it about this man that brought the sword to life? "We should talk about this later. Your name, sir?" Kisan asked.

"Ash Rillaran," he offered.

"Rillaran?" Kisan inquired, the picture becoming more interesting in her eyes. If the Rillaran line lived, it may explain the actions of Tempest. She determined to follow up on this later and turned her attention to the firstmark. "I appreciate your honesty."

"Firstmark Jebida Naserith," he replied with a bow as sarcastic as his tone, "and your apprentice left us no choice."

She returned the curt salute, and a moment went by as she weighed the facts, then she made her way around to the front of the table and faced the king. "Arek is not my apprentice. He is Silbane's, and you will have to answer to him for the treatment of his ward."

She paused again, thinking. Few choices were left: either go after Arek, or Silbane. Kisan knew how lethal Prime was. While Arek was well-trained, he would be no match for the leader of the assassins, who would unknowingly carry out the lore father's orders for her. This freed her to rescue Silbane and give Bara'cor a chance at life. However, it also meant collateral damage. Prime would not leave the king's son alive.

Kisan did the quick calculus then turned her attention to the king and said, "Your team is dead. Finding Arek and Niall in this fortress before the leader of the assassins does is doubtful. Rescuing Silbane and giving your man a chance at the nomad leader is the only choice."

"What of my son?" asked the king. "He is here, with Silbane's apprentice. Surely they are still in danger?"

Kisan agreed, replying, "Yes, but recovering Silbane is the best way to find Arek and your son." She hated how the lie fell so easily from her lips, but as distasteful as this made her feel, buying Prime an opportunity to carry out his mission was the simplest way to ensure that the lore father's orders were followed. She would deal with Prime regardless, or let Silbane do it. None would be the wiser. "And if the nomad chieftain is left alive, Bara'cor hangs in the balance."

The king wasn't listening. His arms out wide, he said, "I can send out patrols, runners. We will have a hundred eyes looking for the boys." He desperately searched for an answer, then his eyes lit upon the table and its enchantment. He looked at Kisan and said with a hint of desperation, "Wait! A few moments before these assassins arrived, this table—" the king pointed to the glowing images—"showed three blue marks coming toward us. What do you know of that?"

The master nodded, not entirely surprised. "These assassins are dwarven. Bara'cor was built to serve them and responded to their presence, just as it shows the enemy forces now arrayed against it."

The king seemed to ignore her, instead pointing to the table and to one small blue dot standing stationary, deep in the bowels of the fortress. "And is this their leader, Prime? He goes after my son?"

Kisan looked closely, then carefully offered, "Perhaps . . ." She thought it likely, but did not want to offer any hope, real or false. The fate of the land rested in the balance that Arek did not survive.

Even as they watched, the blue dot moved forward, flickered, and vanished as if swallowed by something. The king looked at it with wide eyes. "What? What just happened?"

Kisan took a deep breath and said, "I do not know, and regardless, I cannot reach there in time. Even with this brief glimpse, he is in motion and I have not the stonesense that dwarves do, to tap into and readjust my course."

"No! I beseech you, save Niall *and* your student. Save our boys." At this point, the king didn't seem to care about the needs of his fortress or his men. His only thought was for his son's safety.

Kisan held her breath, knowing they were wasting valuable time. Nothing the king had said had changed her mind. She breathed out, a heavy sigh that seemed to carry the weight of her decision with it, but before she could say anything, the table images flickered, then dimmed. Then, to everyone's astonishment, they vanished completely.

Ash looked to Kisan and asked, "What happened?"

She looked at the dead table, her expression thoughtful. "Perhaps Bara'cor no longer wishes to aid us against its Makers." She realized this also gave her the perfect excuse.

"How will we find them before . . ." the king said as he fell back on his haunches, dejected, slamming his fist into an open palm in anger.

"Bernal, we *will* find Niall," Jebida vowed. "I will order patrols of that area, we know the catacombs and cisterns. Do not give up hope."

"Aye, your Firstmark speaks true. Do that." Kisan stepped forward and laid a hand on the king's arm. "I have a chance to save Silbane and help your man accomplish his mission. Do you waste this?"

The king looked down, but when his eyes met Kisan's they had steel in them. "No, we attempt the nomad camp."

"I'm going with you," said Jebida, suddenly stepping forward. "Ash has lost his entire team and I can provide another strong arm. We will only get one chance to kill the leader of these nomads, or Bara'cor falls to ruin."

A moment passed as the king composed himself, something in what Jebida had said striking a chord. He stood then, addressing the people in the room, "Forgive me. I should be thinking of the welfare of all of us, rather than just my son. It is difficult . . ."

His voice trailed off, but then he stepped forward and faced the firstmark, "No Jeb, I cannot allow you to go. If Ash is successful, it's still doubtful he'll return. Bara'cor needs one of you to survive and I can't lose both of you on this mission." The king looked down, then at his second-in-command. "I am sorry, Ash."

"Do not apologize, my king. This was always the plan." Ash looked around the room and said, "I'll kill their u'zar, and cause as much trouble as possible." He delivered this last statement with a smile, but it fell flat. He then looked at Kisan and added, "I wish we'd had more time. There's something I wish to speak with you about."

"Perhaps, with Tempest, you may yet survive," she said with a smile, "then, we can talk."

She looked at the trio and stepped back. Though the mission called for urgency, every moment wasted here brought Prime one step closer to Arek and the chance he would finish Kisan's unpleasant task for her.

Ash grabbed a few extra weapons and adjusted his armor. He then looked at the king and bowed. "I wish you well. Find Niall, protect him."

The king stepped forward and embraced the armsmark. "You are family to me. Try to survive."

Ash nodded. "You know I will." He seemed to find it difficult to meet the king's gaze. "I ... want to thank you, sir, for everything."

The firstmark cleared his throat in a noisy cough and said loudly, "By the Lady of Flame, this is like the goodbyes of a mother to her child! I can't take any more." He grabbed the armsmark and spun him around so they were face to face. "I promote you to Firstmark, Ash Rillaran. Defend Bara'cor with your life."

He then looked at Kisan and said gruffly, "Will that portal be big enough to take me with you?"

Before the startled master could answer, Ash said, "What? You can't go. I—"

Jebida looked at him and said, "You what? You stand a better chance of finding Niall, and what if he needs healing? Your pretty blade insures that. Better you go after the king's son than me. You are Bara'cor's future. And," he added with a twinkle in his eye, "I know you've been itching for the job."

He then turned to his long-time friend, King Bernal Galadine. The giant firstmark said, "By your leave?"

Perhaps not trusting himself to speak, the king nodded. They clasped forearms in a warrior's embrace.

Kisan evaluated the change with an eye toward complications. Could Tempest heal Arek, as these men claimed she had done once before? She had thought magic didn't work on the boy, but their claim made it an open issue. Still, what choice did she have? She knew there was no chance of Ash finding Arek or the king's son before Prime did. She had not been joking about the difficulty and now needed to let things unfold according to her improvised plan. The leader of these assassins would pay, regardless. Silbane would see to that, and if he didn't, Kisan would gladly finish the job.

She thought about it, then offered carefully, "Ash, if you find them, save the king's son first. We know and accept danger as part of our service. This includes Arek."

She then looked at the team and said, "The portal will remain open until Silbane comes through. You'll know him because he's dressed like me, short hair, beard, ugly." Kisan smiled then continued, "Until then, guard it, for anyone can enter the fortress until it's closed." She looked back at Ash, emphasis in her voice, "Do you understand what I mean, Firstmark?"

Ash nodded.

Kisan crushed the Finder and a black portal opened before her with a sucking in of air and a *pop*. She then looked at the king and said, "Four guards were slain by these assassins in the room with the Far'anthi Stones. I could not stop them, but I killed the one who took their lives." She nodded to the king, an unspoken apology, then entered the darkness without looking back.

Jebida checked to be sure he had his black-boned fighting knife, then went to an arms rack and grabbed a larger axe. He motioned to the king and the newly appointed firstmark, and said, "Always loved fighting with an axe." He smiled at both, then also took a step into the blackness and disappeared.

Journal Entry 21

There is a place within us, unassailable by our bravado. It sits and watches our actions through our own eyes, and judges. For most, it is in our own voice that it whispers back to us.

It is what I hear when I have been mean or base. It is the small voice that tells me I did not give true thanks, benefitted through luck, or knew I had been purposely more hurtful than needed.

It knows the truth and does not let me hide behind my lies.

It is in this place that I now sit, my shields above and the raid upon me. I know they take everything and I cannot help the fear that grips me.

I write, thinking you should at least have my last thoughts, in case my defenses prove inadequate.

ASCENSION

When fighting at morning and afternoon, keep

the sun on your back, and on your sword arm

side at midday.

In water, be mindful of reflections,

and tread carefully. Remember that even the

wind can hide sounds.

Use everything to your advantage.

—*Tir Combat Academy, The Tactics of Victory*

Initiate Jesyn, advance." Lore Father Giridian looked at the young girl, controlling his face and his fears. This was the first time he had tested anyone for Ascension. If Jesyn passed, she would be the first adept made under his rule as lore father. His hopes for her ran high, as did his fear she would fail. His face was inscrutable, however, as he put particular effort into masking his inner turmoil.

Jesyn had healed quickly from her bout with Piter, for two main reasons. The first was that at her level of training, her healing had already begun to accelerate, and the *rhan'dori* was specifically designed to minimize a chance of injury. The only visible sign of the fight was a slight bruise on her cheek where Piter's *bohkir* had struck. She didn't feel discomfort from it any longer, only shame for having been bested, and regret for what had happened to Piter. Her worry encompassed Arek, whom she knew was a kind person who would not willingly cause harm.

She moved forward into the stone square inscribed on the floor, her body relaxed and her mind attuned to her surroundings.

"I have come to be tested, Lore Father."

Giridian looked at the girl in front of him for a moment, measuring her readiness, then as ritual demanded asked, "You come of your own free will?"

"I do," she responded without hesitation.

"You know you may not survive the test?" he continued.

"I do," she said again.

"You will face the Truth you bring with you into the Test of Ascension?"

"I will," she intoned, bowing once.

The lore father looked at Dragor and asked, "Who seconds her right to test?"

Dragor stepped forward and answered, "I do, Lore Father. Jesyn Shornhelm has learned all I can teach her and must Ascend to continue."

Lore Father Giridian nodded, then looked back at the initiate and said, "As it has always been, you stand in the crucible of Ascension. You must face what you bring forth and defeat it."

To Jesyn, it seemed the lore father's gaze became more stern, if that was possible, and she heard him say, "You cannot leave the square until all within have acknowledged your worth."

All? she thought . . . what did he mean by that?

"Once the test begins, we cannot interfere. The test is yours and yours alone." Then he clapped his hands and both he and Dragor moved back and away from the square. He raised his hand and waited until Jesyn nodded she was ready and said, "Begin."

Instantly, the square was surrounded on all four sides by a different element. One side ignited in a wall of fire, another filled with water. The third stood unmarked, but she knew it was blocked by unseen winds, and the fourth erupted in stone and earth.

"You cannot leave until you have defeated that which you bring forth," the lore father said. "You will have two periods of rest during the test. Use them well."

Jesyn nodded at that, then turned her attention back to the square ring the four elements had created.

At first, nothing seemed to be happening. Then she thought she saw movement and a figure appeared in the wall of fire, hazy at first, but solidifying. It coalesced and stepped forward and Jesyn recoiled in shock. The being made of fire was an exact duplicate of her!

"We are here to test you," the fire Jesyn said.

She heard the same proclamation echo around her and she spun. She was surrounded by four duplicate Jesyns, except each was made of the same element as their wall counterpart: fire, water, earth, and air.

The four duplicates eased into combat stances, ones she was intimately familiar with, because they were identical to hers. These doppelgangers looked to be more dangerous versions of normal elementals, as they clearly had her combat knowledge. The one made of fire acted as leader. It said, "Defend yourself." And then the four attacked, jumping and spinning with kicks and punches thrown with deadly intent.

Jesyn's training took over and she moved with lightning speed. She intercepted the fire elemental first, but the moment her arm made contact she felt a sudden shock of pain and smelled her flesh burning. She disengaged and tried to punch her opponent, but her fist went completely through the fiery body without harming it. A kick to her chest from the water elemental sent her skidding back into the wall made of earth.

She flipped to her feet and took stock of the combat situation. Her opponents were arrayed in front of her in a loose semicircle with her back to a wall of earth. She breathed out, relaxing her muscles and her mind, and opened herself to the Way.

Time slowed and she could see all four shift imperceptibly, making room for the earth elemental, which moved in quickly. She braced herself, knowing the impact would give her an opening, but was shocked when nothing happened. Then she felt a blow to her head that shot purple stars across her vision.

The earth elemental had flowed around her, then under the stone, and reappeared on the earthen wall behind her. One hammer-like fist had smashed into her skull, sending her reeling forward and into the midst of the other three. She fell at the feet of the air elemental, who picked her up and threw her back against the stone and earth wall. Her breath left her in a whoosh and she slid down the wall, barely conscious.

"Hold!" the lore father commanded. The four elementals bowed and moved back, allowing Jesyn her first moment of proscribed rest. She hacked up something and realized it was blood, but couldn't tell if it was from something broken inside her body, or just her mouth.

She eased her way up, then staggered over to the wall of air. Dragor stood behind it, concern written plainly on his face.

"How am I doing?" she asked, smiling, then spitting more blood.

"No better than any of us did," her teacher replied. "And no worse."

Jesyn nodded, then reached for the Way. Power flowed into her, but she was only an initiate and her ability to heal herself was limited. She would have to pass this test of her skills alone, such as they may be. She slowly rose to her feet.

The lore father looked at her and said, "Do you wish to continue?"

Though he sounded concerned, Jesyn knew this was part of the ritual and she only had two responses. She wiped blood from the corner of her mouth and nodded, "I do."

"Very well. Begin," he commanded and the elementals exploded into action again.

The water elemental sank to the stone floor and flooded toward her like a liquid snake. She leapt up, over it, only to be intercepted by the air elemental, who threw her back to the ground. Instantly the water elemental flowed up over her, covering her nose and mouth, intending to drown her.

Jesyn rolled and jumped to her feet, her head and face still encased in water. She looked about, her mind racing. How could she stop a creature that had command of the elements? She pushed at the water, but her hands went through it. Before she could try again, the earth elemental kicked her and she felt bones snap in her ribs as she was hurled back against the wall of fire.

She could feel the burning again as she bounced off and landed on her face. The water elemental released her in an explosion of steam from contact with the fire wall and she fell on all fours, gasping for air. She could tell her ribs were broken. She pushed herself up, wincing at the pain and clutching her side. The elementals began to close in and she knew she would not be able to survive the next encounter.

Then the lore father shouted, "Hold!" The four elementals bowed and moved back, allowing Jesyn her second and last moment of rest. She fell in a heap, her broken ribs leaving sharp stabs of pain at every breath, her head still reeling from the earth elemental's kick.

Jesyn knew she could not continue to fight them this way. She was missing something, something important. The test was designed so initiates could pass with their skills, so she needed to think.

Dragor moved over to the wall closest to her and said through it, "If you cannot prevail, it is better you do not continue."

"You're telling me to quit?" she said, incredulous.

"No, but if you have no inkling how to defeat them, you should not continue. If you go past this point, neither the lore father nor I can stop the test. These elementals *will* kill you."

Jesyn pulled herself together, anger giving her strength, and pushed herself up to her feet. "I'm going to pass this test, Master."

Dragor looked at the young initiate, then said, "Pay attention, then." He backed away, then nodded to the lore father.

The lore father looked at her and intoned, "Jesyn Shornhelm, do you wish to continue?"

Jesyn took a deep breath, her mind racing. What was she missing? Something nagged at her, a detail, something small. Then, a moment of their fight sparked her memory. The water elemental! It had her at its mercy. Why then, did it release her? The lore father had not yet called time for rest, so why had it given her respite?

Then she asked herself, had it *given* her a chance, or had it been forced? Her mind narrowed the possibilities and she looked at the lore father and said, "I do."

Giridian locked eyes with Jesyn, assessing her will, then said, "I cannot stop the test from here out, so I must ask again, do you wish to continue?"

Jesyn took another deep breath, exhaling out her fear, and replied, "I do, Lore Father. Let them bring their best."

The lore father sighed then said, "Continue."

The elementals moved into action, but something in Jesyn's manner was subtly different. She didn't move forward to engage the first that moved, but instead tapped the Way and used it to focus her senses, watching.

The earth elemental moved in, its earth and stone fists ready to finish the dance of pain they had started on her body, but Jesyn shifted. As the earth elemental struck, she pivoted under the strike, then used the creature's great strength against it. She pulled it toward her, spinning in place, then added a shove from behind.

This sent the creature made of earth stumbling forward and into the target Jesyn had chosen, but it was not another elemental. Jesyn had cleverly pivoted and pushed the earth elemental into the boundary wall made of water! The elemental struck it, then stood upright, trapped by the current of the wall. Slowly its body began to dissolve into a sludge as the wall of water ripped its earthen skin away.

Jesyn didn't stop to gloat over her victory. Her match with Piter had taught her a valuable lesson, and she did not hesitate. Biting down on the pain that shot from her ribs, she charged the water elemental that had nearly choked her to death.

The creature moved to encompass her, but Jesyn struck with open palms on the creature's body. The elemental relaxed, making its body less dense to absorb the blow, something Jesyn had counted on.

She slapped her hands together inside the creature, creating a shockwave of force throughout the elemental's body. The double shattered into tiny droplets, but Jesyn's strike directed it to rain on the wall made of fire. An explosion of steam billowed out and the water elemental disappeared with a scream.

Jesyn moved quickly and put her back to the wall of earth. She could see the air elemental moving toward her, but in order for it to cause harm, it had to find purchase. With her back to the wall, the elemental could only try to dislodge her. She smiled and waited. It would have to close, then she would have the advantage.

The air elemental looked at her and paused, as if understanding her strategy, then dived at her like a dart of wind. Before Jesyn could move, it had surrounded her completely, whirling about her limbs and pulling her away from the safety of the earthen wall. Every time Jesyn tried to breathe, it sucked the air from her lungs. She had not expected this and as a result found herself gasping. Her vision began to dim and she heard a mocking version of her own laugh as she fought desperately to breathe.

Her eyes cast frantically about, looking for something, anything that could help. Then her gaze fell upon the fire elemental, still standing with its arms crossed. Why did it not attack?

The edges of her vision were now going from gray to black. Tunnel vision: a sure sign she was losing consciousness. She sucked in a little air stolen from the winds surrounding her, as her mind kept turning the question over with lightning rapidity. Why had the fire elemental stayed back?

Then she had it and forced herself to remain calm. Her battle-sense took over and time for her slowed in response. She knew what the fire elemental feared, and with supreme effort, she twisted herself in mid-air so one foot came briefly in contact with the stone wall behind her. Before the air elemental could react, Jesyn pushed with all her might and threw herself and the air elemental into the fire elemental.

The three collided, surrounding her in a fiery maelstrom.

She could breathe again. The air elemental fought to disengage with her. It knew what she attempted, pitting wind against flame. Jesyn shook her head. They would not escape so easily.

Her push had positioned them against the corner of the walls made of water and earth, leaving no direction for fire to escape. It forced them into the same space, and in doing so, made each choose. Would fire burn brighter, sucking in air? Would air blow harder, dissipating fire? Her strategy worked, as both elementals sought to protect themselves from the other.

The conflagration surrounding her brightened and the heat grew in intensity until it shone like the sun, surrounding her in a whirlwind of fire and air. Jesyn felt the pain but remained calm, ignoring it. Her training and mental discipline offered her that focus and she used it to center herself on the Way.

The heat became greater and she could feel her skin burning, blistering along her back. She could smell her hair burning away, but closed her eyes and kept her focus. She was the master of her body, not the other way around. The elementals would destroy each other before she would let them go, and this further strengthened her resolve.

"You will die, Jesyn." She heard the fire elemental say in her own voice. "You will throw your life away, needlessly."

Jesyn tightened further on the two, feeling the skin on her arms blacken and burn. Still, she did not let go. She knew they could not kill her. The Way was everything. All they could do was return her to it, in one form or another, but the price for their victory would be their destruction. She could no longer see and knew much of her face must be burned away. A small laugh escaped her then, a protest at the absurdity, but she still said nothing.

"No!" screamed the air elemental. "I acknowledge your worth, you may relent!" She could feel the air elemental stop fighting her, but she did not let go nor drop her guard. She would not fall to trickery, again remembering her duel with Piter and the lesson the masters insisted on in *rhan'dori*. You never stop until victory is achieved. She understood that now.

"What of you, fire-born?" she croaked blindly, her eyes having been burned away entirely. Though she could not see anything, she could feel its gaze upon her and continued in a hoarse whisper, "Do you . . . yield?"

Slowly the heat reduced in intensity and she could feel the fire elemental acquiesce. "I acknowledge your mastery, Adept Jesyn. We submit." They dimmed themselves and waited to be released. When Jesyn did so, both coalesced back into strange elemental versions of her, uncanny in their likeness, more because their movements were so similar to her own.

As soon as they retreated, Jesyn collapsed into a smoking heap, barely conscious. Her body lay blackened and burned, without hair, eyes, or other recognizable features. She did not move, but whispered, "Then I prevail." A small smile escaped through charred lips, then the barest of sighs, before Jesyn sank into oblivion.

The two remaining elementals were joined by earth and water, reformed by their walls. All four elementals bowed to her then, palms to foreheads, and intoned into the air, "Anala, come forth and be bonded in Ascension."

From behind Jesyn's crumpled form came a light, shining pure and silver. It flared like the moon, bathing her in its argent brilliance. Out of that light stepped the winged figure of a female warrior, an angel who looked born and bred for battle.

It was immense, powerful, armored in silver and blue. Its wings stretched to each side, each feather a blade made for killing. Its visored helm sat across glowing eyes, eyes that demanded nothing less than fealty. The dazzling light receded and Anala of the Fire stood above the still form of the adept-to-be, called forth by the elementals of the test.

"Do you accept the bonding, Lady Anala?" intoned the fire elemental with deference.

The angel tilted its massive head, looking down on the smoking ruin that was Jesyn's frail form. "It hath strength and nobility, and most of all, perseverance." The voice was soft, but held the edge of a finely forged weapon. She seemed to smile, then completed the ritual, "I accept the bonding."

The fire elemental stepped forward. "Welcome, and rejoice. You ascend to a new life." It spread its arms wide and stepped back and all four elementals went to one knee, waiting.

Slowly, as if sinking into the ground itself, Anala gathered Jesyn into her powerful arms. She pulled the young girl to a kneeling position and then held her unconscious form from behind. Her armored wings embraced Jesyn, enclosing her in a cone of feathered steel and pure light.

Anala's form became potent with power, glowing softly at first, but quickly becoming a dazzling star of white, silver, and blue. She gave her the life-force that flowed so strongly and deeply within her, within the Way. The incandescent star that was Anala became part of Jesyn, who still knelt on the floor, head bowed and lifeless. As the elementals knelt in reverence, Anala became one with Jesyn and that light faded like a song's last note.

A moment passed, then two. Something happened then, a change that snapped Jesyn into the here and now, a change she could feel deep in her very bones. She arched up and a gasp tore out of her. She drew in air as if she could gain sustenance from the entire room in one lungful, her form blazing blue and white.

She could feel her strength magnify. It was as if something had settled over her and become part of her, a feeling of comfort and strength. It wrapped around her, holding her within its ethereal arms. Liquid power incarnate, a pure note of the Way sounded and she felt the cool wash of healing and rejuvenation flood through her entire body.

Her wounds began to heal, burns disappeared, ribs and bones reknit, hair and skin re-grew, and her fears vanished. She breathed in a lungful of cool, clean air, and could feel the Way permeate every part of her being.

She had heard the name, Anala. Was that her true name, whispered on the wind? Before she could ask, the water elemental stepped forward and bowed to her, saying, "We cannot be destroyed, for we are the Way, as are you." The elemental looked to its brethren and nodded.

Earth then stepped forward and said, "There are more worlds than this and you are a defender of the Way, in all its forms. Do not forsake your duty."

"You have earned your flameskin," the fire elemental continued. "You may bring it forth whenever needed. Become one with the Way and it will shine with light as unblemished as the sun. Its purity will reflect your mastery. We pledge you shall never be without it, or us."

The air elemental stepped forward and said, "None outside this square can hear us. They are not privy to your Ascension, only the outcome. Do not share what you learn here with anyone. Mastery must always be earned through sacrifice."

All four elementals bowed again, palms to foreheads, and said, "Welcome and rejoice. You Ascend to a new life." With that, they vanished and the four elemental walls disappeared in a flash of power and sound.

At first, the room seemed black, pitched in darkness. Then Jesyn realized she still knelt with her head in her hands. What had just happened? She looked up, a stunned expression on her face. She remembered fighting, and the feeling of being raised up, but what happened between? How had she been healed? Her fingers ran nervously up, touching her face and hair as if to confirm what she already knew. She had been healed and was truly whole. The act left her smiling and shaking.

Dragor stood before her, looking at his former student with pride. Her face was clear of pain, her wounds healed. She radiated strength and might. Even so, he knew there was still something missing, something incomplete. He could see she was now connected to the Way more deeply than ever before, save for one final detail, the oath.

He moved forward, picked her up and hugged her, saying what was in his heart. "You are well met, Jesyn Shornhelm. I am so proud of you."

Lore Father Giridian also stepped forward and bowed. "Welcome to a new life. You have succeeded where many fail, but I never doubted your resolve." His face became a little harder when he said, "You understand now why we cannot tell you of the test?"

"If you had, I would never have passed," Jesyn replied. "I had to truly believe in myself." Something in her knew this to be true, just as she would have failed if she had given up and succumbed to the pain.

"If you had known you would be healed in the end, would you have hesitated?" asked Giridian. "Would your *sacrifice* have been honestly and truly given?"

She shook her head, no, though the details of her healing were still unclear. The *only* way to become a true adept was to triumph without assistance, on her own merits, with her own hard-earned skills. One had to be willing to sacrifice everything and understand their place within and as a part of the Way. Defeating the elementals did not matter. Giving up, not fighting till the very end, did.

Now she felt the benevolence, the embrace of something far more powerful than herself. It conveyed a sense of pride in her perseverance, an acknowledgment that she had offered every last breath and in return had risen whole and new. She knew her spirit had truly been tested and like a blade forged in an incandescent fire, she had emerged stronger, tempered.

She lived because she had been willing to die, and her conviction in herself never wavered. She walked through death's door as Jesyn Shornhelm and returned as something more. She sighed, a happy sound this time, one the others could appreciate, for they too, had given everything of themselves to stand here with her.

Lore Father Giridian nodded and said, "Then let us complete your Ascension and take the oath, so you may add your voice to our council as a true Adept of the Way." He said this with a smile, but behind it ran a discordant tenor.

Jesyn stepped forward and took a knee. She knew the words of the oath by heart, something every initiate memorized as they dreamed of one day earning the Black.

She looked up at the lore father and said, "By the blood of my forefathers, I take this Binding Oath of Fealty to the land and her people. I will not cause harm, either through my action or inaction, for I am the shield of the weak, the blade of the helpless, the healer of the sick, and the spirit of the Way. I pledge myself to the service of these duties and obedience to the Will of this council."

Lore Father Giridian's tone became more serious as he spoke. "As lore father of this council, I hear and accept your Oath of Fealty. Arise, Jesyn Shornhelm, for thou art now a full and true Adept of the Way."

An intense yellow flash occurred then, Binding Jesyn to the words she had just spoken. She could feel her body begin to attune itself to the land and its need. It was a feeling of oneness she would soon share with every other adept and master on the Isle and suddenly whatever had been missing, whatever felt somehow amiss, was gone.

The Way cleared her senses, and for the first time, she saw the world the way the other adepts did. Every motion, every detail, was magnified. She drank it in, reveling in the newfound precision that coursed through her body and mind. By comparison, her earlier skills now seemed ungainly and rough, like a child's drawing. Upon completing the oath, she had truly Ascended, her potential had been realized, and her options were limitless.

"Your training and discipline gives you faith in yourself. Never forget, this is the basis of your power," said the lore father. He looked at her for a moment then laid a gentle hand on her shoulder and said, "I hate to greet you with this, Adept Jesyn, but you Ascend at a perilous time. Come, we have much to speak of regarding this council, events in the world, and your friend Arek."

BLACKFIRE

Perception comes from an open mind,

power from focus,

and speed from a relaxed body.

Perception, power, and speed

when applied properly, cause damage.

—The Bladesman Codex

Arek moved quickly to intercept the assassin, his mind clear and his breathing even. Unlike facing the dragon, Rai'stahn, he felt no fear this time, nor had he for the entire time he'd been within Bara'cor. It was as if his very proximity to the Gate had infused him with a kind of preternatural strength and confidence. That or the dragon's aura had somehow negatively influenced him. Arek doubted it, but whatever the cause, every detail seemed magnified and slowed. He could dissect the combat in pieces, feel each heartbeat pass by in detail, and see *everything*.

On his left, Niall had imperceptibly shifted his weight back, giving their attacker a slight advantage. On his right, he saw Tej's fingers tighten on her grip, readying herself for the point of engagement. He could feel the air shift as his attacker moved toward Niall, lengthening his distance from Tej.

Arek knew a small increase in speed and a slight shift to his left would bring him to the assassin before the assassin could reach Niall. The problem was his foot. Though almost healed, it still felt like a piece of meat tied to his ankle. It was sluggish and did not move with the training and efficiency the rest of his body enjoyed.

To his right ran Tej, her short sword ready. She had chosen a path to bring her up and beside the man. Perfect, thought Arek. She, at least, seemed to know what she was doing.

When the assassin turned and charged, Arek was not at all surprised. It was smart, as the assassin would face two of them, instead of all three. Niall would have to scramble forward to attack at the same time and would never make it, his inexperience hard to hide. Arek appreciated the speed in which the assassin had discarded any idea of attacking a lone victim, dropping it as soon as the strategy proved untenable.

Arek anticipated the assassin's moves like a player at Kings and smiled at the man's overconfidence. He decreased his speed toward the man in black, easing the pressure on his lame foot. The move caused a gap large enough that his attacker would have to choose one of the three, instead of two. Arek knew that momentum mattered and the assassin's instincts would drive him to continue his assault directly toward him. No doubt, by now the man had identified him as the leader. Killing him would make the other two easy prey.

He was not wrong. The man in black did not hesitate, nor try to accommodate the shift in targets. It was a true testament to his training, but an error nonetheless. Arek had counted on it to pull the attacker into a one-on-one confrontation with him, keeping both Tej and Niall safe.

At the very last possible moment, Arek jumped and tucked, somersaulting over the head of his surprised assailant. As he did, he punched downward, striking his opponent's head. His fist exploded in pain. By the Lady, he thought, the man feels like stone! He landed in a heap, his injured foot unable to manage the impact and weight.

* * * * *

Prime watched, more than a little impressed when the kid shifted the engagement to his own terms. *So, he's had some training.* He spun in place and moved toward his prone opponent when he felt a searing pain in his head. His stone skin began to dissolve from the strike, leaving it unprotected. Something in the *null's* touch, something he hadn't been warned about. He cursed the lack of information on these abominations, then turned his attention back to Arek.

* * * * *

It was a mistake.

Yetteje had seen the man spin and realized he had dismissed her. She first thought Arek had been showing off, but now realized the purpose behind his vault. He had taken the assassin's attention off of her.

Arek had said not to attack singly unless they had an opening, and this was a *big* opening. She ran forward and braced her hand behind the pommel of her blade, the other on the hilt, and stabbed the man in his open back.

The blade sparked and began to skitter, but she clenched her teeth and focused. There was a sudden flash of light and it sank halfway in. Her hands and wrists exploded in pain and shock and she lost her grip, stumbling painfully against the man's granite skin. Like Arek, she had not expected it to be so hard. She pushed off, remembering that sudden flash and suddenly felt drained, as if her body had given something of itself to the strike.

The man spun with an open backhand that blurred as it traveled, striking Yetteje in the jaw and flinging her backward. She had managed to begin a duck and roll so the force of the blow did not kill her. Instead, she hit the ground hard, barely able to focus her eyes. Her jaw made a strange clicking sound when she tried to move it, bringing tears of pain to her eyes.

* * * * *

As Prime turned on the fallen girl, he felt three sharp impacts on his head and neck. The null was attacking again, and at each point of impact he saw his stone armor fall away, shedding at the boy's touch like bark from a rotted log. *Impossible!*

He pivoted in place and blocked two of the punches, satisfied by the look of pain that flashed across the boy's eyes, then struck the boy once in the midsection, then twice to the head and chest. The kid flew backward and landed near the prince's feet, rolling and coming to his knees smoothly.

Prime knew the boy would have been killed had his hands still been gloved in granite, but the shieldrock had fallen away at the null's touch. Bara'cor then came back to his aid and his armor began to reform. Under his mask, his face broke into a smile. The Galadine whelp had still not moved. Time for him to die.

* * * * *

Niall stood transfixed by the scene, still unable to attack. They moved so *fast*—and now the assassin advanced on him. He backed up, holding out a hand, and shouted, "Wait, stop! Why?" He meant to sound authoritative, but the words came out in a high, gibbering rush combined with a healthy note of fear. The sound of his own voice disgusted him.

The assassin didn't answer, instead raising two thin blades. He drew his arms back and in a lightning motion, slung the daggers at the Galadine heir.

* * * * *

A very different thing happened to Arek with each strike he landed. His body felt a kick of energy, a surge of power that brought him unsteadily to his knees, feeling light-headed but still stronger than before.

Arek could see the blades flying at Niall with deadly accuracy, but didn't know what to do. Because of his combat sense, the scene played out in agonizing slow motion. Still, he thought, he might be able to intercept *one* of the blades. He snapped himself from his knees to a wobbling stand, putting himself in the path of the lead blade, his hands moving to block the assassin's knife.

The scene froze, with Arek's hand not an inch from one dagger. The other dagger was only a foot behind the first, both hanging in the air with death glinting on their points.

"You'll die, dimwit."

The voice was angry and familiar. It came from behind Arek, near the pyramid steps. He turned and saw Piter standing some feet away, looking at the scene with the same sneer on his face and obvious disapproval.

"This is Sovereign's hand." The shade took in the assassin and stilettos hanging motionless in the air with a gesture and continued, "Poisoned. A touch incapacitates. A cut and you're dead."

Arek looked at Piter, anger and fear filling his mind with so many questions, but he blurted, "Just tell me what to do!" It was the only thing he needed to know at the moment.

He heard Piter sigh, then move closer. "You're going to protect these two? Really?"

"Piter, please!"

The shade shrugged. "Perhaps your strength comes from the same way you opened the door. The same way you gave me what I 'deserved.' Look to what you yearn. Look for *sustenance.*"

Confusion set in. Could the shade be telling the truth? He *had* opened the door, had he not? Piter had died against his magic, hadn't he? Arek wanted to believe, but realized that in both cases, he had no idea what he'd done. He needed to focus and closed his eyes. He took in a breath, his mind centering and calming. He took in another, then opened his eyes, looking about.

At first, he saw nothing, but then something moved in the corner of his eye. He turned but it disappeared. He forced himself to relax, taking deeper, calming breaths that brought with them a strange sense of purpose. He was meant to do this, he told himself, he was meant to understand.

Slowly, shapes and objects came into view, ghostly shadows superimposed on what he could see in the real world. Vague forms moved about on the very edge of his vision. They were hardly there, almost a shadow or a ripple, but they gave the impression of an infinite sea of tiny motes or particles hanging in the air.

He narrowed his concentration, then a glint of something caught his eye. He looked up and while his eyes saw nothing, his mind felt the presence of something gargantuan, a winged warrior armed and armored. The creature's power was palpable, emanating in waves that threatened to drive Arek to his knees. It stood armed with a spear of orange and red fire, and horns curled down from its visored helm. The figure stretched forth a hand, as if imploring Arek to accept.

His mind jumped back, flooding with memories he had not known existed. He remembered facing Piter now and the creature that had superimposed itself around his name-brother. He remembered the wings and the armor, and its name, *Kaliban*. This creature was the same, but also different! What was it?

Then he heard a deep voice intone, "I offer myself. Our powers will be limitless through Ascension. Wilt thou accept?"

Arek's eyes narrowed. *Ascension*? He could feel the hunger grow again within him, the same hunger he had felt when he had faced Piter and the doorkeeper he now remembered was named Dvarin. Was this what it meant to be Ascended?

It did not matter, for Arek began to realize something more. His body hungered for this creature, a hunger he felt down in the very pores of his skin, a black hunger emanating from deep within himself. A small smile played on his lips. He remembered what taking Piter's creature felt like, the power, the ecstasy. He knew now he did not need to Ascend with this armored knight, whatever it was. He would get salvation another way.

He inclined his head in a slight nod of assent and said, "Of course." He slowly extended his hand, inviting the being to join with him. So easy to touch, he thought, so close. Just reach for it.

The creature took his hand in its grasp and completed the bond necessary for Ascension, offering its own true name whispered on the wind: Adramelek.

Arek smiled, for he now understood that for him, Ascension was a lie. It was a misunderstanding of where his power came from. It was not one's true name that was heard, but that of the creature who offered power by bonding with its host, like some sort of sick parasite. *Adramelek, indeed, for you it is too late.* Arek would not play host to this thing, he had other plans.

The creature looked at first with satisfaction upon the boy, the ritual bond forming and growing, promising power beyond his dreams. With this, he would gain life. The power multiplied and a giddy wave of energy shuddered throughout his armored body. Who knew what he could do, what he would become, once Ascended?

Then something changed. Adramelek looked down at the boy, still grasping his ethereal hand with a strange look on his face.

Black lines of power appeared as cracks within the creature's armor and skin. Even as Adramelek watched, Arek's eyes became liquid black pools, shining and dead, absorbing what little light there was left around them. The boy's gaze bore into the winged creature's soul and drew it in.

"What are you?" Adramelek screamed in horror. "No! Wait! You are not pure!"

Arek watched the giant winged creature fight him, twisting, bucking, pulling to be free, and smiled more. His grip tightened, though there was nothing it could do now to escape. The dark hunger within Arek welled up, almost too much to control as he opened himself to it fully.

In that instant, the entire form of Adramelek arched backward and another scream tore through him. The black cracks of power widened and he began to fall apart, like a shattered statue. Then, his form imploded in a blinding ethereal flash of black flame, exploding into a sparkle of power and life. Arek absorbed all of it, drawing in every single particle, consuming every last bit.

Power, black and potent, coursed through him now, re-knitting his bones, rejuvenating his body. Any harm he had experienced no longer remained, healed by the deluge of life that had once been Adramelek. His last scream echoed through Arek's body, but nothing else of the Aeris Lord remained.

The shade of Piter laughed, then said, "Well done, Master! You have exceeded depravity and corruption on every level. Rai'stahn would be proud of your use of the Way."

Arek turned his black eyes on Piter and something in his gaze silenced the shade. "I begin to understand my place in this world. *This was my Test.*" He took a breath, feeling the power course within him. His sight magnified, became clearer. The world moved slower and he could discern each moment between heartbeats if he so wished. He felt explicably *precise,* as if his entire being had been reshaped and honed to a keen edge.

He knew he had transcended his master and the other adepts of the Isle. His body was potent with power, but he had accomplished this in a manner never intended. He watched as Piter bowed, a smirk still on his lips, then slowly fade from view. The scene became still and for a moment, nothing happened. Then time snapped back into place.

In the blink of an eye, Arek's form exploded with power, but not light. A dark flame erupted, an ebony wash that licked up his form and surrounded him in a mantle of black fire. It covered him from head to toe, misting off him like hot air on a frozen day. His flameskin had been unleashed and with it, everything in his body had been reborn, reshaped to perfection.

His hand, now protected, shattered the first dagger on impact in a pulse of black fire. The second struck his protective barrier near his shoulder. His flameskin darkened further and the dagger vaporized in a flash, leaving behind only a metallic tang he could taste in the air. Arek took a deep breath and his flameskin expanded until it sucked in the light from the very air around him. It shone potent and black and he felt far stronger than ever before.

In response, Bara'cor itself seemed to lose luster and fade, as if he leeched the very essence of strength from its granite walls. The assassin's armor faded, also drained away by whatever Arek was doing.

The glowing particles or creatures were an endless source of energy, as was everything else around him. He could drain them dry the same way he could draw a breath, without thinking. He could be injured and steal life back into his limbs. A part of him now wondered if he could even *be* killed. This was why magic didn't work around him, this was why he could disrupt things with a touch. He absorbed magic, he fed on it, and now he had unlocked his ability to *use* it.

Niall looked at him in awe and asked, "What is that?"

Arek ignored the prince's uncomprehending stare, keeping his ebony gaze focused on his still living opponent, the assassin. Niall showed his lack of training and discipline by being distracted in the middle of combat. Arek's master would never have tolerated it, and for some reason now, it disgusted him. Then his eyes flashed black with power and a small smile bent the corner of his mouth up. Was Silbane still his master? He laughed at the thought.

The assassin clearly saw that things had gone from bad to worse. The girl had wounded him, and the boy's black aura protected him. Worse, Bara'cor no longer seemed capable of coming to his aid. Arek and the assassin closed on one another. Their strikes came out with the brutal efficiency of trained warriors intent on dealing death as quickly as possible. No flowery kicks, no leaps, just short, savage strikes with elbow and knee, followed by grapple holds designed to choke or break bone.

The assassin repeatedly smashed at Arek with a forearm, trying to drive him to his knees. At each impact, thunder sounded and black fire flashed as Arek's shield protected him from the strikes of the other. The assassin grunted as if in pain.

At first Arek had been cautious, fighting more defensively as he was not used to a flameskin protecting him and favoring his unhurt foot through recent habit. His advantage quickly became clear as his barrier absorbed the impact of the assassin's strikes, and judging from the assassin's face, inflicted more pain every time they connected. In fact, as the fight wore on, Arek grew stronger and the assassin grew weaker.

Then Arek took the fight to the man, grabbing his neck and driving his forehead into the bridge of his opponent's nose. Blood spattered in a flash of black flame and the assassin fell back, driven by a series of knees and punches, each strike cracking like lightning. The assassin reeled, staggering backward in an attempt to block and retreat.

Arek moved in with a double palm strike that exploded in a flash of black flames. Ribs cracked and broke as the assassin's unprotected body absorbed the full power of the thunderous blow. A shockwave coursed through him from the point of impact, detonating within his massive frame, shattering his internal organs and causing irreparable harm.

From behind the assassin appeared a battered Yetteje. "This is for hitting me," she said with acid in her voice. She used the man's lack of shieldrock to her advantage and kicked the pommel of her partially buried blade, slamming it the rest of the way in. He vomited a gout of blood as the point of the short blade exploded out of his stomach. Then she yanked the sword out with both hands, staggering backward to fall on her back.

* * * * *

Prime collapsed to his knees, blood running freely from his mouth. His hand touched the stone, but the boy's proximity still blocked his stonesense. He could not feel his team, or anything else in the fortress. He shook his head, uncomprehending, then turned his attention to the other boy. The Galadine prince still stood transfixed where he had started, having never swung his blade even once.

A smile creased Prime's masked face, revealing itself in his voice. "By now, his father is dead." He began to laugh, but that ended in a gurgle as the last of his life's blood welled up. Then the blue light went out from his eyes and he slumped down, kneeling with his chin to chest, dead.

Journal Entry 22

We all have it, this voice of doubt. It is that part of me that looks upon these Marks and believes they will fail.

It doubts my power in this place and that is deadly. I do not know how I can prevail and my powers are slowly fading because of it. You may think it simple to believe something and perhaps that I am weak-willed.

Do you? I smile at the thought.

If you have no Talent, no connection to the Way, then test it yourself. Believe you can conjure a flame at the snap of your fingers. Put all your faith into it and do something as simple as that, something a child of the Way can do without effort. Something I can do without thought.

Your own doubts, those deep within you and those of the people around you will stop you. The Aeris themselves are Shaped by your doubt to stop your connection to the Way.

No effort on your part will succeed to create a flame, any more than mine to believe I can prevail in this accursed place.

LAST STAND

Fear is contagious, as is courage.

—*Altan proverb*

The king and Ash had called the watch into the room after the two men had departed, each wrapped in his personal feelings over the departure of Jebida. For the king, his right hand was gone, a man with whom he had journeyed with for most of his life. For Ash, it had never occurred to him that he would be the one to stay, and he found himself unsure of what to do next.

It was the king, ever pragmatic, who shook Ash out of his doubt and said, "Assemble the men. We have to protect this portal for Jeb, and find my son." The fact the king seemed so sure the firstmark would return helped Ash keep focused.

Ash turned from the king and addressed the watch through Sergeant Stemmer, who had reported back to duty. They respected her as an experienced soldier and leader, a woman who could defend the ground she stood upon. The men stationed themselves in an arc around the portal entrance, but their movements were slow and disorganized by the site of such magic. Their wonder and awe at an eldritch black door was washed away by their gruff sergeant, who barked out, "I swear by the Lady if you can't hold a single door, I'll push you through myself and you'll do it from the other side!"

That got their attention and soon the squad had created a shield wall with furniture and armed themselves with bow and sword, preparing to defend entry to this room from anyone who emerged. Alyx made sure they understood the firstmark and two others might return from a mission through that doorway. They would be a woman and man, and that missile fire be held to ensure they did not shoot a friendly target. The men picked were some of the best, and she and Ash had confidence they understood. She reported back to Ash that the portal was as secure as they could make it.

The king inspected the men, then motioned to the firstmark to accompany him over to one side. "Good work. Jebida knew you were ready, long before this."

"I never expected..." Ash didn't know how to finish that sentence. He felt the overwhelming responsibility of leadership, more so now that his mentor was gone. It was so easy to lead, he mused, when you had someone above you. Now he had been promoted to firstmark and charged with the defense of Bara'cor. It fell to him and him alone to defend this portal and access to the stronghold. Should they be overrun, they would perish from the inside out.

"I will do my duty," was all he could think to say.

The king clasped the new firstmark on the shoulder and said, "Of that I have no doubt."

Ash began to reply, but stopped in mid thought, his eyes searching the room. "Where are they?"

The king looked at his new firstmark, not comprehending the question. "Who?"

Ash pointed at the ground of the chamber, where the bodies of the assassins had lain. "Our attackers ... where did they go?"

The king then noticed what Ash meant. The bodies of Talis, Sevel, and Chandra were still in the room, now arranged neatly side by side, but of the men who attacked them, there was no sign. "Did anyone clear out the bodies of the attackers?" he said to the assembled room.

Alyx answered, "Sire, when we came in, it was only you two and our fallen. I ordered my team to care for our own."

"We need to find out what's going on," said Ash. Bodies don't just disappear.

The king nodded and made his way to the door, followed by the firstmark. A half dozen more men approached from the hallway, clearly in mid run to this chamber.

"My lord," said the first, "sounds have been heard from below the fortress. We have stationed men at every corridor and told everyone to stay in their quarters."

"Sounds?" the king asked.

"Aye, sire. Like animals, something wild." The guard clearly did not know how to elaborate more and Bernal decided against pushing for details he knew would get them nowhere.

"Wise decision," he said instead, "watch for intruders. And bring me the guards that stood watch at the guest ward, where we held the boy, Arek."

The guard saluted, fist to chest. "At once, sire." He sped off while two more took station at the room's entrance.

The remaining two fell in step behind the king, who looked at Ash And said, "We need to send out patrols to look for Niall."

"And the princess," added Ash. "If Niall went with Arek, you can be sure Yetteje is not far behind."

"That girl has a stubborn streak in her," the king grumbled, "much like her father did."

"As many of royal blood," Ash replied with a smile.

Bernal looked at the new firstmark then broke into a smile that looked more like a grimace. "Aye, probably true." A serious look came to his eyes and he said, "I saw you hit with a dart, like Talis. He fell instantly. I hate to ask this, but why are you still alive?"

Ash looked at his sword, *Why indeed?*

At first, nothing happened. Tempest seemed dead in his hands, though he caught a faint feeling of reluctance. Then her voice sounded in his head, *I intervened, beloved.*

How? Ash questioned.

The sword seemed to hesitate again, then said, I took the lives of those who had fallen, to save yours.

It was said so matter-of-factly, so emotionlessly that Ash felt his body go numb. *What?*

They would have passed anyway, beloved. I only took what they did not need any longer. You must survive.

You killed them! They might have been saved.

They had passed beyond help... Tempest sounded petulant, but then her voice became firm and she said, I would kill everyone in this fortress to keep you safe.

Guilt washed over Ash as he heard these words. He could feel the truth in them, and this horrified him more. He looked at the king, then back at the sword. He had to get rid of her or more would fall.

No, beloved. I am yours now.

Ash held the blade out and said, "Tempest healed me, but she took the lives of our men to do it."

The king's eyes widened and a look of horror washed over his regal features. "She ... what?"

Ash nodded, grief etched in his countenance. "She says they gave their lives to her and they would have died anyway, but ... how can I keep her, knowing this?"

You cannot be rid of me, beloved. I am yours.

Ash tried to drop the blade, but as before in the king's interview with Arek, his hand would not open. He used his other hand, but the blade clung as if it were a part of him. No matter what he tried, he could not let the blade go. He then sheathed her and tried to undo the buckle. It would not budge. "This is impossible." It seemed that so long as his intent was to let her go, she would not allow it.

The king moved forward to assist, but Tempest said, *If he touches me, I will kill him.*

Ash held up a hand. "Wait! She says she will kill you."

The king stopped short, then backed away a step. "What can you do?"

"I don't know. I need to talk to one of the adepts. They may know something."

Why do you hate me? Tempest said, sounding both innocent and hurt.

Just then, the guard returned with the two who had been stationed outside of Arek's room. The king looked sympathetically at Ash, then turned to face the men.

"Our guest left his room. Who was with him?" he asked.

The more senior of the two shifted uncomfortably, then answered, "Your son and the Princess of EvenSea, sire."

"And where did they go?"

The man then stammered out, "B-beggin' your pardon, sire, but the prince ordered us to step aside. He said the prisoner—our *guest*—complained of pain and he was taking him to the Healers Ward."

"Alert the men," the king commanded. "We are looking for my son, Princess Tir, or the boy Arek. I have reason to believe they are in the catacombs that lead under Bara'cor, near the cisterns. If any see them, hold them and send for me. I am going to the cisterns."

"As you command, sire." The guards saluted and ran back to the stairwell that led to the wall. They would meet with the commander of the watch and relate the king's orders.

Just then, the ground shook again, heaving itself up as if something below the fortress stirred. Ash took two steps forward, then another, greater shockwave passed, knocking any unsecured items to the ground, including the king and the firstmark. A sound, like a low groan, came from somewhere deep beneath them.

"We can't wait for Jebida," the king said, "we need to go now."

"You're unarmed..." Ash turned to a guard and motioned, who unbuckled his blade to hand it over.

"No need," said the king. "I'll make a stop on the way. Keep your weapon."

The man held it out for a second longer, but then, with a nod from Ash, withdrew it.

"Are you sure?" asked Ash.

"My father's weapons wait for me." He turned to the guards still in the hallway. "Two of you come with us, the rest hold position here. When Jebida and the team come through, you send them to the Healers Ward."

The king started to turn but stopped, a stricken look by Ash getting his attention. "What is it?"

The new firstmark looked around, then shook his head, the facts clear. "I can't go with you. I have to remain here."

"What?"

"My king, these men do not know these adepts. Only you and I know Kisan's plan or identity. If Jebida does not return, these men will attempt to hold them until one of us can authorize their release. This can lead to ruin."

The king was stunned. He dropped his head in shame, but when he looked back up, there was pride in his eyes. "You are correct, Firstmark. Station our defenders and remain. Make sure that when Jeb returns, he and any others are ushered as quickly as possible to the cisterns." The king's eyes searched his friend's and then he finished, "In this instance, I am a father first, a king second. I *must* go."

"Of course, sire," the firstmark nodded. "I am sorry."

The king shook his head, already turning, "You saw where the assassin was going. Bring reinforcements. We will descend through the left main stairwell." He smiled, then trotted off with three guards in tow.

Ash watched his broad back leave, then made his way back into the room with the Finder's portal. A part of him was secretly relieved. His distrust in Tempest and what she might do to the king or his men should Ash's life be threatened had left him unsure for their safety.

The men crouched behind various impromptu cover, bows ready and blades close by. The black doorway would be the killing ground, a natural choke point to concentrate their fire. He hoped Jebida would return with Kisan and Silbane. If not, it would mean they were dead and no one remained to close the portal against a nomad invasion. Either they would hold them here, or Bara'cor would be overrun from the inside out.

ONE DIES, TWO LIVE

Clean the blade quickly,

wash your hands thoroughly.

Blood sticks, the last gasp of a dying man to

put his failure on your fingers.

—Kensei Tsao, The Book of Blades

S ilbane sat in the tent where Scythe had left him, still bound by the magic of the red-robed mage. Though he had been unable to remove the torc blocking him from the Way, his body had continued to heal at an accelerated rate. Either this was due to some of his innate Talent, or the continuation of Scythe's healing spell. In either case, he could feel most of the broken bones in his face and nose had knitted together correctly and he no longer felt on the verge of passing out.

Now it was clear to him that on his first day of capture, he had been in a mental fugue due to his injuries, Scythe's meddling, or both. It was obvious they had interrogated him, but he had been unable to understand this simple fact with the easy clarity he had now.

He suspected Scythe's spells were responsible, more so than the physical damage he'd suffered at the hands of the nomad warriors. The problem was, with the torc in place, he could not defend himself from more magical interrogation, regardless of his willpower. Getting the torc off was his first priority and to do this he needed to free his hands.

He braced his feet under him and slid up the pole he rested against. He had made it a point to do this at regular intervals to keep his legs limber. Though his arms were secured, nothing prevented him from using his legs. His first thought when clarity had returned had been to kick and break the pole he stood secured to, but one look told him it would be impossible without access to the Way. The beam was just too thick.

As he rose to stretch, he saw a flash come from behind him and the sound of air whooshing. The Finder! Arek must have used it, which would attract Scythe. They didn't have much time.

"I told you to wait in Bara'cor. Now we are in grave danger."

Someone came up behind him and whispered, "It's not Arek, old friend."

* * * * *

Kisan saw Silbane's back stiffen in shock upon hearing her voice. His arms were clasped behind a pole, but there was no rope holding him there. It seemed Silbane just clasped his hands together voluntarily. Suspecting the cause, Kisan turned her Sight upon the other master.

She could see that Silbane's power to control his arms was locked by someone skilled in the Way. She should have been more shocked, but given what the lore father had told her and what she had recently seen, she took in this information matter-of-factly.

Now the priority was releasing the locks upon Silbane. She concentrated and looked at the method used to neutralize the master's control. It was not unlike many of the techniques used on opponents during combat and very similar to what Kisan had done to Two. She could see the points on Silbane's spine where the locks held him immobile and smiled in satisfaction as they dissipated to her touch.

Silbane's arms came free and he spun. Kisan looked at him with a hint of a smile but sadness in her eyes. They clasped forearms in greeting and without wasting a moment Silbane grabbed the torc and pulled. Nothing happened. He looked stunned, then let go as Kisan moved in to inspect the torc.

She pulled at it experimentally, but it seemed to grow warmer as she tugged. She turned her Sight upon it and said, "It responds to the Way and somehow uses our energy to stay locked. Ingenious."

Silbane cursed and said, "How do we get this accursed thing off?"

Kisan looked around, then her eyes fell upon the firstmark. She smiled and said, "Jebida, could you assist us?"

The gruff firstmark came over and looked at the collar. What they wanted slowly dawned on him and he asked, "It's magical?"

Kisan nodded. "But you won't feel a thing," she said with a small smile.

Jebida scowled at the woman, then looked at Silbane. It was clear that much of the world still held a distaste for magic that ran deep, but without Silbane's help they were doomed. Need was the mother of all things. He lightly touched the torc. With a small click, it unlatched!

Jebida pulled the torc from Silbane's neck and handed it to the master. "You'll carry your own weight."

Kisan sensed the Way surround Silbane, flooding his body with healing and awareness.

"A lot has happened," she told Silbane. "You need to know." She closed her eyes and touched Silbane's forehead, imparting in an instant what had happened to her since they saw each other last. However, she kept from him anything she had learned about Arek's true nature, as the lore father had ordered.

Kisan had become comfortable that the boy was dangerous and could not afford to have Silbane try to protect him. Furthermore, she couldn't risk Silbane interfering. Instead, she conveyed her regret at their argument, her flight with the assassins, Giridian's news of the death of the lore father and Thera, the assault on Bara'cor and the plight of Arek, the attack of the assassins on the king, and her defense of the same.

Grief visibly punched Silbane's gut at the news confirming Themun and Thera's deaths. He paused, then gave Kisan all the details of what had happened to him. He started with the journey to the Far'anthi Stone, then his argument with Rai'stahn, the great dragon's death, and his own capture at the hands of Hemendra's men, and finally the details of a red-robed mage called Scythe.

Scythe held onto sanity by a very fragile thread and this made him an unpredictable foe. However, Silbane suspected he knew much about the Gate, his "life's work," as he had called it.

Most importantly, he shared his vision about General Valarius's meeting with the Conclave of Dragons, given to him by Rai'stahn along with the gift of Sight. When he stopped, Kisan looked at him with a mixture of awe and a strange intensity.

"What?" Silbane asked.

Kisan didn't reply. The vision was disturbing because the revelations contained within seemed eerily similar to the ones Giridian had with Thoth. She also realized only she had seen both visions and therefore had a unique perspective on the situation.

Having shared thoughts, she knew where Silbane fell on the matter of Arek. Oh, it was true the master had some doubts about his apprentice, but had already faced grave danger once due to his paternal instinct for the boy.

She, however, couldn't allow him to interfere. The new vision about the blackness Silbane saw filled her with dread. To her, the fact that he destroyed the Way was obvious and every mishap concerning Arek on the Isle supported this conclusion. Rai'stahn's admonition portended to dire consequences should Silbane's apprentice be allowed to live. It firmed her resolve to keep this information to herself until she could sort things out, but also gave her hope that if the order came to share this with Silbane, the information might compel him to lend his aid and not stand against them.

She could not, however, trust Rai'stahn. Though they seemed to have aligned interests, she still did not know if this so-called Conclave had fed Silbane a true vision, or if it had been invented for his benefit. They had their own agenda, something that Lore Father Giridian clearly did not trust, and therefore neither did she.

She looked at her old friend, feigning disbelief at the circumstances at the Far'anthi Stones, and said, "You faced Rai'stahn and lived? Impressive."

She didn't trust herself to say more, afraid Silbane would see through her easily. Still, they had suffered much loss over the past few days and rescuing Silbane felt right. She squeezed the other's hand again, a reaffirmation of their common bond and friendship, based on their years together. She unrealistically hoped the situation with Arek would not come between them, and at the same time knew with certainty it would.

Then Silbane stepped around Kisan, faced the firstmark, and said, "Jebida, we can't leave just yet."

The firstmark was startled when this new mage used his name. "How did you . . . ?"

"I know everything she knows, a tactical advantage of sorts." He missed the chagrined look that flashed momentarily across Kisan's face at the mention of "everything," his unwavering focus on the giant warrior instead. "Even the way you treated my apprentice." It came out detached, but the intensity in his gaze hinted at the anger brewing behind his eyes.

Jebida took it in, then spat once and grunted, "Your skin. Risk it however you will. I'm not Ash and I don't want or need your help. You are welcome to leave."

Silbane shrugged, then continued, "We must capture a man known as Scythe. He's unstable and left unchecked could cause serious harm, both to what I care about and to Bara'cor."

"You both are a strange lot. I say you can leave, and you decide to stay." Jebida moved past the man to grab a sturdy wooden desk. With a heave, he pushed it over on its side, creating a barrier. "I hear you on Scythe, and I don't trust magic." He paused and flashed Silbane a half smile, saying, "But you already know this."

The firstmark continued upending tables, stools, anything that would provide cover, as they heard cries of alarm sounding. He buried the point of a spear into the ground and the butt end into one of the tables to brace it, then grabbed another to do the same, saying, "I hadn't expected help from you, nor do I want it. But, ... one doesn't throw away an advantage."

"You're going to trust us?" Kisan asked.

"You two means two more targets. Simple math, so don't get in my way and stay alive long enough for me to get to their leader."

"Spoken like a true hero," Silbane said, though Kisan knew Jebida's part in Arek's torture would be difficult for the master to put aside. "You can bait the chieftain. It won't be hard. In the treatment of prisoners, you both have a lot in common."

Kisan stepped in on the heels of the jibe. "Arek is alive and perhaps healed. You have to let it go. We will capture Scythe and then get to your apprentice. Let's stay focused." She paused, then looked meaningfully back at the firstmark and said, "Be quick with the chieftain. We need to move fast."

"You'll not be waiting on me," replied the giant warrior from over his shoulder. Another chair crashed into the makeshift barrier.

Silbane looked at the firstmark and said, "You and I are not finished."

Jebida nodded, not missing the meaning. "If we survive, you know where I am."

They continued to stare at each other, then Silbane broke eye contact and muttered, "After this." He shook his head and let loose an explosive sigh, grabbing Kisan's arm. "It's good to see *you* again."

"Likewise," the younger master said, happy the encounter between Silbane and Jebida had not come to blows. "You don't look too worse for the wear, maybe a bit uglier," she said with a slight smile.

Silbane reached up and took his half of the Finder, still hanging from a nail in his tent. He looped it carefully around his neck. "I ended up here by making every mistake possible. You made it here by quick thinking and skill. The lore father was right; you have always been a falcon." He smiled back and did not realize how deeply his praise buoyed Kisan's spirit.

The firstmark looked back at them, having now secured a crossbow and a stack of bolts. "This is all very touching, but the two of you might consider talking less and actually *doing* something."

Kisan was about to say something to Silbane, but nodded instead in thanks, then took position near the firstmark. "Talking is one of our best skills."

"Evidently," muttered the firstmark, "but I understand him." He said this while looking sidelong at Silbane. "Let's hope we live long enough to make amends."

"I hope that for all of us," answered Kisan, but then her attention was caught by a motion at the tent flap.

Just then, two nomads burst into the tent. Jebida didn't hesitate but fired his crossbow, catching the first in the throat. Kisan picked up a bolt and whiplashed it into a throw. It hit the second man as if it had been fired by Jebida himself and took the nomad off his feet.

Both dived for cover as those outside the tent returned fire, with dozens of bolts smacking into the table Jebida had overturned as improvised barriers.

"Hold your fire!" a voice screamed from outside. "Silbane, we can discuss this."

Silbane turned to Kisan and whispered, "Scythe." Then he raised his voice and responded, "If you're ready to surrender, we accept."

Laughter, a bit halting, followed. Then Scythe continued, "Clearly someone has used the Finder. I can sense the portal is open and the presence of at least one other like you. So why haven't you escaped?"

Silbane motioned to Kisan to take a flanking position to his right.

Jebida raised his voice and said, "The U'Zar of the Clans is a *coward*. How many warriors has he brought to help him?"

"Who dares challenge me!" a guttural voice roared. From the sounds of it, half a dozen men were barely holding him back.

"Jebida Naserith, Firstmark of Bara'cor," Jebida replied.

* * * * *

Outside the tent, Scythe put up a restraining hand as Hemendra surged forward again, "Hold, Clanchief. He seeks to bait you. There is no need," he said, indicating the hundreds of men now surrounding the tent, and the thousands behind them.

"No need!" Hemendra growled. "The man insults me on the very sands of my people. Do not speak to me of need."

Contrary to Scythe's belief that he was angry, Hemendra knew the expectations of his brethren. If he said nothing, other warriors may think to challenge him for leadership, and that, he could not tolerate.

Scythe turned to the huge warrior chief and said, "You risk much. It is not important in the grand scheme. Control yourself; he is a coward hiding in a tent, instead of facing you openly."

The Clanchief took a deep breath, letting the Redrobe's words have a seemingly calming effect. He turned a deadly gaze onto the closed tent flap, then nodded. "I can—"

Silbane's voice rang out, "Scythe, give your dog permission to fight. We understand who really leads the clans."

Hemendra screamed, a guttural roar designed to scare the men around him as much as strike fear into this unknown warrior, a sound like an animal charging. He bellowed, "I accept your challenge! Crawl from your hole." The gathered troops quickly formed a circle in the sand outside the tent. "No one touch this man or I will kill you where you stand."

A moment went by, then the tent flap parted and a man emerged. The u'zar appreciated his opponent immediately. The man stood close to his own height, with a great axe held casually in one meaty fist. He squinted as his eyes adjusted to the light, then nodded to the clan chieftain. "You'll be the man whose blood soaks the sands today." Jebida smiled and moved forward.

Hemendra could see the grace with which the man walked. He hefted the axe with an easy familiarity born only through countless hours of training and surviving the fields of battle.

* * * * *

Scythe gave a mental sigh, but realized this combat would have no effect on the outcome of his entry into Bara'cor. He had a far more powerful ally now than Hemendra of the Altans, as everyone was about to see. He smiled, then made his way closer to the tent holding Silbane as the two combatants neared each other.

He was more curious as to why Silbane and this other adept had not left through the portal. His plan had counted on any rescuers taking the quick path back to Bara'cor and dragging in his portal web strands, thereby locking it open. He was also curious because this other was clearly not Arek. Who was she and why had she come to Silbane's rescue?

* * * * *

Hemendra picked up his axe and moved into the circle created by his men. "My axe is called, Blood Drinker." He smiled at his opponent.

Jebida smiled and glanced down at his axe. "Donkey." He looked at the men ranged in the circle around him, his eyes finally coming to rest on the Clanchief. "A better name for my axe than for the dead man standing in front of me."

The Clanchief's confusion turned to a cold, calculating rage when he realized the man mocked the traditions of his people and his ancestors. To offer a weapon an unworthy name? Still, he was too disciplined to let this stone dweller's words affect his fighting style.

"You will die here," he said simply. He measured the space between him and his opponent, his hands gripping his own axe with a strong yet supple caress, the result of years of swinging the killing stroke. "Those who fear, talk."

Jebida nodded with a hint of a smile, then burst forward with lightning speed, his axe blade flashing out for the clan chieftain's eyes.

The sudden attack forced Hemendra to move his head and blink, and Jebida dropped low and stabbed downward with the spear-tipped point of his axe. The point entered the chieftain's shin, but missed the vital bone and instead cut into the massive muscle of the barbarian's calf. He pulled the point out, twisting it expertly to enlarge the wound. The resulting grunt of pain that surely gave the firstmark a sense of satisfaction that, while rewarding, would be short-lived.

Hemendra looked down at the point where his opponent's axe tip had exited his shin and the resulting eruption of blood, already slowing to a trickle. As usual, he felt no pain, just anger that someone had entered his flesh, the holy flesh of a true Warrior of the Sun.

But his anger, along with every other emotion within the giant clanchief's heart, was held in check. He would only show what was necessary to be seen, but had notched his regard of his opponent a bit higher. The man had committed to his attack without hesitation once he realized the stage Hemendra had been setting.

Jebida spun and dodged to his right as the barbarian's great axe whistled down, missing his head by a hair's breadth. The nomad's axe did not bury itself in the sand, but rather spun up and wove a figure eight, attempting two more times to connect with his opponent's neck.

Hemendra never overextended himself and finished the short, deadly circles with his axe where they started, protectively across his own body. Jebida braced himself, then launched a swing that could have sheared a man's head from his shoulders with ease.

Hemendra barreled forward, ducking under the horizontal swing and catching the Bara'corian warrior in the ribs. He swung an elbow around, hammering into the man's collarbone and driving him down to a knee, then brought his own knee up in a short, brutal arc. It caught his opponent under the chin, driving him up again to almost a full standing position. Before he could recover, Hemendra spun and struck with his axe. Only a slight misstep, causing the flat of the blade and not the edge to connect with Jebida's breastplate, saved him.

Jebida was hurled backward in a shower of sparks from steel on steel. The firstmark hit the ground on his back, but curled into a roll, coming to his feet in a moment.

Hemendra stalked forward, his axe held across his body. He raised it as if to strike at Jebida's head, but then switched to a dangerous undercut swing. The axe whistled in, unerringly toward its target.

Jebida moved forward quickly, angling slightly away from the blow, but not too far. While he did so, he raised his arm, bracing himself. Hemendra's axe blade slid up the side of Jebida's body, but missed his groin, the chieftain's intended target. Then Jebida clamped his arm back down over the axe blade, trapping it before it could gain its full deadly momentum. It saved him from certain death and trapped Hemendra's axe against his body, too close for the nomad to use effectively.

The Bara'corian firstmark punched, once, twice, before the clanchief raised his offhand and trapped Jebida's axe. For a moment they stood, axes locked and eye to eye, each straining for leverage. Neither said a word, but then the clanchief punched Jebida in the face with the knuckles of the hand still holding his axe. The strike broke the firstmark's nose. He blinked furiously to clear his eyes. Then he grabbed his axe handle, still held trapped by Jebida's armpit.

They re-engaged, each choosing to keep his opponent as close as possible, looking for any small advantage, taking in each other's measure, concentration, and focus. Nothing needed to be said as they pushed and strained, looking for one mistake. One would survive and one would not, and both accepted this.

* * * * *

Jebida knew he had countered the Chieftain's advantage well, but one of them would have to disengage to use his weapon effectively, so he readied himself. When he let go, his opponent would push forward to build his own momentum for another attack. He had only one choice.

Jebida sucked in and spit blood into the clanchief's face, then heaved his axe up. The axe didn't move, but the sudden spittle combined with his great strength pushed the clanchief off balance. He used this to get his center lower, then spun in place pivoting on his forward foot, the hand holding his opponent's axe hilt and circling down and then up.

The movement looked like a children's dance, but the outcome would be deadly for one of them. It forced his opponent to circle with him or lose his weapon, and this was the trap. The Chieftain would fall out of position and the battle-knife in Jebida's hand would make short work of the Clanchief . . . but the strike never happened.

Even as Jebida spun, he felt a punch to his back. Suddenly his body went numb, the shock traveling up and down his spine. He felt his side go limp, yet strangely, no pain. He looked back at his opponent, both locked in an embrace separating them by mere inches, and had a moment of regret. He couldn't remember why he had wanted to kill this man. The edge of his vision became gray and he looked questioningly at the nomad chieftain.

"Sleep, Firstmark. Better men than you have fallen to my blade." Hemendra pulled the short dagger in his left hand out of his opponent's spine.

Jebida's eyes cleared for a moment and he knew exactly what had happened. He could feel the life gushing out of him. He looked into the nomad chieftain's eyes and saw no remorse and felt shame for dying in his killer's arms.

Still, the bone-hilt of his own knife *had been* in his hand, or had he dreamt that too? His thoughts became jumbled and gray, no longer sure what was true. His mind turned to what he loved above all else, lost so many years ago. He could see them now, waiting for him, just ahead. A smile flitted across his face and he whispered to himself the promise of rejoining them at last, "My family . . ."

One hand outstretched, gripping nothing but hot desert air.

Slowly, with a small sigh, the last breath left Jebida Naserith's body and the light went out from his eyes. His lips, however, were still curled into a small private smile, as if he had at last found a small measure of peace before the walls of his own fortress.

* * * * *

Hemendra pushed the lifeless body of his opponent away from him and raised his dagger in triumph, but the assembled warriors did not cheer. He felt suddenly weak, and stumbled a few steps back. His leg brushed something and he looked down. Jutting out from the inside of his thigh was a black-hilted dagger. Blood flowed freely from the wound and down his leg, quickly pooling at his feet.

The clanchief stumbled again and fell to one knee.

"Healers!" he bellowed.

A haze came over his vision and a figure stepped from the crowd. It was Clanfist Paksen, who cocked his head at the clanchief. "Hemendra, we cannot request a healer for a challenge accepted."

"I am victorious! Call a healer, Paksen." The words came out thick and jumbled, barely above a whisper.

Paksen leaned forward, grasped the black-boned blade, and pulled it out. A sudden warmth of blood spurted out even more quickly, a gush timed with each beat of his heart.

"I am sorry, *U'Zar*, I cannot help you."

Journal Entry 23

I have survived, but not in the way expected. Through my failure, I have learned a truth, and it comes from my imps.

They saw me create the blood Marks and believed these have power. When the raids came, my Marks failed, but their power manifested itself. Each imp unexpectedly took up one of the Marks in my defense, and tasted my blood.

They evolved into frightful behemoths, sentinels who stood watch throughout the night. They are my guardians, my belief lending them power. It is truly amazing to behold, but what have I learned?

The young Aeris cannot affect reality, but they are available for use. Our faith gives them power. I can already feel mine growing as stalwart friends come to my defense.

I have now seen the defense they can muster and fashioned their Marks for wearing on arm, each consecrated with my blood, shields against harm.

Swords will be next, made of birch and pine. It matters not, for they believe if it is touched by my blood, it becomes blessed with power. They believe and are changing the Way for me.

I am becoming a true Shaper.

BROTHERS IN ARMS

In the din of battle,

choose your enemies wisely.

Just as tall trees are known

by the length of the shadows they cast,

your prowess will be defined

by whom you defeat.

—*Kensei Shun, The Book of Shields*

S ilbane and Kisan glimpsed portions of the battle through the slight opening of the tent, watching carefully for any advantage they could take. While it was conceivable they could have just attacked or left the tent in stealth, the portal into Bara'cor sat behind them, wide open for anyone to enter. Leaving it unguarded or calling attention to it before finding Scythe was tantamount to putting out an invitation and killing the men and women who defended the fortress.

Then, before either of them expected it, Jebida fell. Kisan began to move forward but Silbane stopped her with a look. "No heroics, we must find Scythe and escape. The portal will close behind us once the Finder goes through."

"Find him, where? Through thousands of nomads?"

"Scythe is here, close by, and we cannot leave him behind."

"Is he that important?" asked Kisan, though with each heartbeat the chance Prime had taken care of the problem with Arek increased.

"Very," he said. "We need him to close the Gate."

Kisan understood the other master's plan and grudgingly acknowledged its need. She nodded, preparing.

Even as they repositioned themselves, they heard Scythe call out, "We have a mutual friend, Adepts."

Silbane's eyes widened in shock. A sudden explosion of psychic power erupted near the outside of the tent. He said, "We're in real trouble."

Even Kisan, who did not have the sensitivity Silbane did, could feel the incandescent burst of energy. "What was that?"

As if in answer, bladed claws grabbed the tent and pulled it up from its moorings, smashing and tossing it aside like so much tinder and cloth. The sun flashed in, blinding in its brilliance.

Kisan and Silbane stood amongst the wreckage of the tent. Surrounding them were hundreds of nomads, but they held themselves outside a larger circle occupied by an enormous black-scaled creature who took their breath away. It was the great dragon, Rai'stahn.

"Not good," muttered Kisan. "I don't think they're going to give up."

"No," answered Silbane, "nothing is ever easy."

Behind them yawned the portal, open and black, leading back to Bara'cor. Before them towered Rai'stahn, in full dragon form. His great black wings flexed and he growled, "The Scythe and I are oath-forged. Thou wouldst be wise to surrender." The great dragon's eyes then narrowed and he looked meaningfully at Silbane, "But mortal, when wert thou ever wise?"

Kisan's mind raced. Because Silbane had shared the vision granted by the dragon, Kisan knew that Silbane had seen the great dragon killed, his neck broken. Now he stood before them, whole again and *oath-forged?* How had Rai'stahn survived? How had Scythe convinced a dragon as ancient as Rai'stahn to commit himself to such a bond?

She knew, too, that Rai'stahn and she were possibly on the same mission. But Scythe was another story all together, and at best unpredictable. Still, the dragon would choose the most destructive path to Arek, whereas the deed might already be done by her decision to leave Prime unchecked.

Then she paused, thinking back to her youth and those days hiding from the Magehunters in the forests of Sunhold. She had beaten the odds and survived because of her wit and, she reluctantly admitted, her luck. A part of that luck had been meeting Silbane and Themun, who guided a stubborn and willful child to a new purpose, a new life. Was that her role now after losing Piter, no longer the falcon but instead the shepherd?

Something had happened when she had come face to face with King Galadine. He had not been the ruthless warlord intent on killing those of the Way as his forefathers, but instead a father looking for his son. She had heard his sorrow, the fear plain in his voice. It had not been selfish or false, he had not worried about the succession of his royal line, nor matters of the throne. Rather, he had asked as she would have, a simple request to save Niall. The only difference was his son was alive and Piter was lost. Had their positions been reversed, she knew she would have done the same. Now, though she had never met him, Kisan found herself hoping for Niall's survival despite the necessity of abandoning him.

Arek was another story. She had no mercy in her heart for him, but there was little reason to let Rai'stahn carry out the wholesale slaughter of Bara'cor and all the defenders within her walls. Her choices had put the hapless prince directly in danger. A sadness stole over her as she thought, no one should outlive those they love . . . no one should bear her grief. There were still children in Bara'cor, and she could not let them die for no reason.

Kisan looked at Silbane, her eyes glistening with the sudden memory of her apprentice. "No parley," she said, "we hold them here."

Scythe stepped forward. "We can settle this. Leave the portal open and allow me to enter Bara'cor. You two can go free. I have no wish to destroy those who practice the Way, in any form."

Silbane took a moment, then said, "You know of the vision shown to me, that of the Conclave?"

The red-robed mage smiled and said, "I don't need the vision, I stood with them against the demonkind at Sovereign's Fall."

Shock ran through Silbane and Kisan at that, but Scythe was clearly not the man in armor who faced the dragons. That man was General Valarius Galadine. What did this unbalanced mage mean?

Kisan mindspoke Silbane regardless of the waste of energy, her tactic clear. *He's crazy, we kill him.*

No! Silbane kept his eyes on Scythe. Rai'stahn will intercede and we cannot prevail against the two of them.

A new voice interrupted them both, *Escape is your best chance.* Scythe smiled, then nodded.

Rai'stahn drew a deep breath then unleashed dragon fire, blasting the wreckage of the tent and igniting everything around the two masters in a fireball of heat and flame.

Flameskins erupted from both, a detonation of power covering them in protective auras. Orange and yellow, they shone like two stars, bending the dragon fire harmlessly around them. They quickly separated, giving the great dragon and Scythe two targets instead of one.

Kisan knew they had little chance against Rai'stahn in dragon form. She moved quickly toward Scythe, her focus now on keeping herself alive, angling to keep him between her and the dragon's breath. She dodged left, then right, then leapt at the mage, so fast she was no more than a blur. Pivoting in the air, she snapped out a lethal kick targeting the man's head.

Scythe raised a hand and a web of lightning arced out, surrounding the young master. Kisan's orange flameskin flashed multiple times in response as it tried to protect her from the many lethal daggers of energy striking at her from all directions.

It was mostly successful, in that it kept her alive, but Kisan's body still convulsed as lightning bled through her barrier, locking her muscles tight. She tumbled from her leap and landed to one side, small sparks of electricity arcing about her skin as she shrugged off the attack and slowly stood, hunched, her form smoking.

Silbane had also moved in coordination with Kisan, still keeping his eyes on Scythe. Rai'stahn's tail caught him in mid-stride, slapping into him like a tree trunk. His flameskin erupted, a yellow-white flash in response to the massive strike, absorbing most of the blow. He fell, landing near Kisan, who was just rising from Scythe's attack.

"This is useless," Scythe said, "you cannot prevail."

Silbane contemplated their situation. "A simpler version of your spell from the Isle," he whispered to Kisan, knowing her heightened senses included hearing. They could not afford to have Scythe listen in on their mental communication again. The ease in which he had done so the first time still unnerved Kisan. It had never crossed her mind that she would find herself in a situation where the spoken word would be more secure.

Kisan knew he meant a variation of the spell she had used to defeat the assassins on the Isle. Scythe would know nothing about this, having never shared Kisan's thoughts as he had. She needed to distract Scythe and Rai'stahn if Silbane's plan were to work.

She concentrated, reached for the Way, and could feel Silbane do the same. They didn't want to create simulacrums of the same detail and independent capability as she had before. It was too energy consuming and complex. What they needed were more targets, and lots of them.

In the clearing created by the dragon fire, hundreds of copies of Silbane and Kisan flashed into being. These were simple copies, yet the two masters created enough to confuse both the dragon and the red-robed mage. The copies looked at their makers and smiled, then burst into action. They jumped and twisted, moving quickly at their attackers, dodging and wheeling in unison.

Rai'stahn drew his fanged head back, then struck Silbane as he jumped into the air on the attack. A taloned claw crushed a figure beneath it in a yellow-white flash, smashing it to the desert floor. Another ducked under the attack and struck at the armored side of the dragon, but to no effect. It too disappeared in a flash when struck by the dragon, but still hundreds more came, attacking any who stood in their way. Soon the clearing was a maelstrom of confusion with nomads fighting these copies, who when injured disappeared instantly. However, their purpose was not to win but to confuse, and they were achieving this quite well.

Kisan used the confusion to her advantage, leaping into the heart of the melee, her ridge hand striking with a crack into a nomad's throat and breaking his neck. She sped past him, ducking under a blade then spinning and facing the counter strike. As the sword came whistling in she clapped her hands together with perfect timing and caught the blade between her palms. Continuing her motion, she snapped the steel halfway up its length.

Even as the nomad tried to bring the shattered remnant of his half weapon up in defense, Kisan flipped herself half over and thrust the point through her attacker's chest. She was past him before he hit the ground dead.

Scythe looked about, then spread his hands and a volley of flaming darts shot out, catching half a dozen Silbanes and Kisans full in the chest. They burnt to cinders and flashed into nothingness. Still more versions came zigzagging through the carnage, weaving in between copies of each other.

Kisan parried another blade with her palm, the edge guided away from her expertly. She struck then with open fingers through her opponent's eyes. Grabbing the blinded nomad's skull, she hurled him into a knot of enemies, then advanced on them wreathed in orange flames like an angel of death.

One of the Silbanes punched the ground and it erupted into a wave of sand that sped at Scythe like a wall of water. Scythe fell back a step and put his hands together, slicing through the onrushing wall with a blade of lightning that parted the sand wave around him, leaving behind tiny shards of sand melted to glass.

Only the real Silbane could have done that, and Scythe must have known it, but before he could target the correct Silbane, he was lost amongst a hundred others. In frustration Scythe clenched his fist and one Silbane fell, its back broken and crushed, then it disappeared in a flash.

Rai'stahn swept a Kisan into his grasp and bit her head off, then tossed the body aside. It disappeared before it hit the ground in a flash of orange fire. Still dozens came, weaving in and out of each other, coming toward the dragon with attacks that could distract him long enough for the real masters to launch an attack he did not see coming.

He narrowed his golden eyes, looking for the heat of a living creature, then quickly reached out with a clawed talon and grabbed one of the masters out of a group to his right. Kisan erupted in orange flame as her protective aura ignited in response. Rai'stahn bared his fangs and squeezed.

The aura grew brighter as Kisan fought the dragon's grasp, locked in a struggle that could only end in her death. She let out a scream and the flameskin detonated with an orange blast that threw the dragon back. Kisan landed in a heap and lay motionless. All versions of her instantly dissipated, vanishing before the gathered nomads in the midst of combat and leaving many with no opponent.

Scythe still had dozens of Silbanes to deal with and yelled to Rai'stahn, "Breathe!"

The dragon targeted a knot of Silbanes engaged with the nomads. Some heard the huge indrawn breath of air and looked up in horror, seeing death in the dragon's eyes. Others on the periphery scattered to avoid the great blast. Then the dragon breathed a firestorm, erupting the land in front of it, destroying all it touched and melting the sand to sparkling bits of crunchy glass.

In an instant the hundreds of nomads and simulacrums of Silbane caught in the blast vanished, vaporized in the heat of the dragon's fire. The nomad camp broke apart, fear creating a wave of fleeing warriors running from the great dragon's wrath. Devastation spread in an arc in front of the dragon, and with the exception of the lone black portal, not a single structure stood within the distance of an arrow's cast that wasn't burning or simply gone.

Scythe stepped forward and surveyed the scene. He seemed about to motion to Rai'stahn to move forward when the air behind him wavered and then blurred. From the nothingness stepped a shape that said, "Wrong choice."

The real Silbane stepped out from where he had maneuvered while his illusions, mixed with Kisan's, had fought. He snapped the torc used on him around Scythe's neck and it locked itself in place.

"A gift from Bara'cor," Silbane said.

Before he could say anything, Silbane struck Scythe a backhand that sent him reeling back, unconscious. The master moved like an arrow shot from a bow and grabbed Scythe before he hit the ground, spinning in place to face Rai'stahn.

Kisan staggered to her feet and moved over to stand next to Silbane, trying to focus her vision and catch her breath. They both watched as the dragon turned its yellow gaze upon them.

"What wouldst thou have me do, mortal?" Rai'stahn hissed.

"You are oath-forged with Scythe," Silbane stated, adding, "no harm can come to him through your actions, or inaction."

"I know the oath. How wilt thee shame thyself now?"

"He will go with me and I will see no harm come to him," Silbane said. He looked at Kisan and nodded, his meaning clear.

Kisan had begun to recover from her encounter with Rai'stahn's grasp, and except for a cut down one cheek, was unharmed. She retreated on unsteady legs back to the portal, keeping a careful eye on the hundreds of nomads who were slowly reappearing at the outskirts of Rai'stahn's devastating arc of scorched earth.

Silbane kept his eyes on the great dragon while making his own way to the portal. "I go to find my apprentice," he said. "If it is as you say, I will deal with him. Do not interfere or I will not guarantee Scythe's safety."

The dragon flashed and changed, becoming again a black armored knight. He strode forward but stayed well out of the masters' reach. "If thou hast any love for this land, kill thine apprentice."

Kisan looked at the great dragon-knight, her eyes narrowing. She understood where Rai'stahn's heart was but could not reveal her own orders, not yet. She had to make sure Arek could not threaten this world.

Silbane nodded, meeting the dragon-knight's eyes, and said, "My lord, you once trusted Themun. Trust me as you did him."

He took one last look around then nodded to Kisan, who jumped into the portal and disappeared.

THE EYE OF THE SUN

How often has one heard of the warrior

who succeeds against all odds?

Was it cunning, skill?

More often than not,

it was the seventh thrust,

when the sixth was blocked.

—*Tir Combat Academy, The Tactics of Victory*

I froze, again..." Niall whispered to himself. "I failed, again."

Arek's liquid ebony eyes returned to their normal pale blue as he quenched his flameskin, the black fire diminishing into him, but ready should he need it. He took a deep breath and could feel the Way course through him, drawn in by the air, eldritch and potent. It was a heady feeling of strength and power and he reveled in it. He looked down, knowing his foot was whole, but at the expense of something else, something that had once been alive.

He moved around the dead assassin's body and knelt next to Tej. A red mark that was the beginning of a nasty bruise painted the left side of her face and jaw. A thin cut ran from the right side of her forehead, through one delicate eyebrow, and ended on her right cheek. It was bleeding but Arek thought her lucky she had not lost the eye. He offered her a hand and helped her stand.

"You'll have a scar from that," he said, pointing to her face.

Tej ignored the comment and looked past Arek to the dead assassin, still on his knees. "Who was he, and what was that fire thing you did?"

Arek looked at the figure too and replied, "I don't know who he is." Then he looked at Tej and said, "It's called a flameskin, but I've never created one before this."

"Convenient." She wiped off her short blade. She should have felt elated at surviving the fight, instead she seemed more annoyed. "What happened to your limp?"

Arek couldn't tell if she was making fun of him, so replied carefully, "These attacks seem to be healing me."

"More convenient." She sheathed her blade and before he could say anything else she asked, nodding in Niall's direction, "And him?"

"Fear," Arek replied matter-of-factly, his combat training making the assessment without thinking. "Someone actually trying to kill you can be unnerving, especially the first time."

It was a normal part of fighting and something he had faced himself, albeit at a much younger age. It was often proportional to someone's worry about getting hurt. Once he realized getting hurt was not as horrible as he thought, the fear diminished too.

"I was too angry to be scared," she replied, a faint note of disgust in her voice. Arek couldn't tell if the remark was directed at herself, her opponent, or at Niall. He decided to let it go and check on the prince.

As he approached, he saw Niall with his sword still in a white-knuckled grip. The prince was looking down, shame plainly written on his face. "I didn't do anything, *again.*"

Arek looked around, satisfied that there was no other threat, then said, "Don't beat yourself up about it. The guy is dead."

"Thanks to you and Yetteje. What did I have to do with that?" Niall whispered, mainly to himself.

Yeh-te-jee? He didn't remember if he had heard her full name and found he liked it. He looked back at her and smiled, but of course, she didn't notice. She was about to search the man.

"Careful!" he said quickly. "The daggers on him are poisoned. One touch and he'll finish the job he started."

Yetteje's eyes widened at that, and she stopped a hand's breadth away from the man's body. "I want to know who he is."

Arek drew a small but keen knife from his belt and made his way back over to where Yetteje stood. He knelt carefully and slit the man's hood open. He then pulled it away, revealing the face underneath. What he saw shocked them both.

"What is he?" she asked, looking at the features that while normal, were larger and wider than the average person's. They then noted the man's body, which was again larger than would be expected.

Arek thought for a moment, never having seen something like this before in real life, then said, "I don't know, but I think he's a dwarf."

"He's a *builder.*" The statement came from Niall, who had come up to stand behind the other two, still looking miserable. "At least, I think he is. He's bigger than I expected, but he looks just like the pictures carved into various reliefs around the fortress."

"Seems big for a dwarf. What's he doing in Bara'cor?" asked Yetteje. "And why is he trying to kill you?"

"No idea," Niall said, "but he said something before he died. What was it?"

Both Yetteje and Arek looked at each other, then Arek replied, "He said that by now your father is dead." He didn't have any reason to lie to Niall. Surprisingly, Niall took that comment better than he had expected.

"Doubtful. You've not seen my father fight. If we—" he stopped, then corrected himself—"if you and Yetteje can kill him, my father will be just fine." Niall sheathed his sword.

The floor of the chamber began to crumble, turning into sand under the dead man, and he began sinking into the stone.

"What's going on?" exclaimed Yetteje, scrambling back.

"Stand clear," Arek said. "I don't know, but it's speeding up."

Indeed, even as the small group of companions looked on, the man disappeared under the stone, which then hardened back to normal. Yetteje moved up and poked it with her foot, but the stone was unyielding.

"What do you think happened?" she asked no one in particular.

Niall said, "If it was a builder, it's said they have a friendship with rock. Maybe Bara'cor is doing something it only does for them."

"Great," said Yetteje, looking around, "the fortress is alive too."

Arek looked at his friends, then at the pyramid and the sapphire sun blazing at its apex. Its blue aura permeated his skin, warming him from within. He could feel himself growing in power, as if he were absorbing sustenance directly from the blue light's coronal discharge. He could feel a yearning for it. "I need to go up there," he said.

"Why?" asked Yetteje, the tone of her question leaving no doubt the idea of going up to a flaming sun was clearly ridiculous.

Arek looked at the other two and realized the time had come for him to offer some sort of explanation, even a brief one, so he said, "I have always had the power to disrupt magic. My master brought me on this mission because of it."

He looked back at the sun, glowing with its azure flames, and said, "My master searched for a gate between our world and another, one controlled by the demon Lilyth. I think this is it."

Both Niall and Yetteje looked shocked at Arek's revelation, then Niall said, "You're joking."

"No," Arek replied, "but if I touch the Gate, I think I can disrupt it, closing it forever." It was a simple statement and Arek began to put together the various things he had seen or heard from the council, his master, and his encounters with Piter.

Arek knew he was a tool to the lore father, nothing more. He had probably decided to close the Gate with Arek's power, and the only way he might be sure it would work was to make sure Arek touched it, willingly or unwillingly. So his master had been sent to sacrifice him.

His master's hasty explanation and apology back at the Far'anthi Stone hinted he had been disobeying these orders, though why he had obeyed them at all was still suspect. Piter had essentially told him this when they had stood upon the dunes. They would use his power and sacrifice him.

His master had tried to send him away for this very reason. Rai'stahn had tried to kill him, and in that moment something insidious in what Piter had said caused him to flee. Still, he had not felt afraid when he dived for the Stone, only focused on Piter's instructions. Why was that?

His eyebrows drew together as he thought. He had run to the Far'anthi Stone and had somehow managed to activate it. That action had dropped him into this predicament and left him alone to confront the Gate.

A cold anger grew at being used in this way. He spiraled into it, forgetting Silbane had tried to save him by sending him away. It was as if another force slowly bent his thoughts in on themselves, consuming him with feelings of betrayal and injustice. His eyes began to darken in anticipation of violence. Then he breathed out and they cleared, pale blue and normal, and the feelings vanished as suddenly as they had come.

"So there's no weapon?" said Yetteje, the hurt from Arek's betrayal in her voice. "My family remains unavenged?" Her stance and demeanor conveyed her rising anger at what she thought was duplicity.

Arek looked at her with a start, then snapped, "Grow up, closing this Gate is important for the world."

Then the scene froze and Piter appeared again, looking comparatively happy. He stood at the base of the pyramid and beckoned to Arek. "You are as smart as a dog, at least."

Arek walked forward, facing the shade, and said, "Shut up, Piter. They used me. All of them, and that includes you."

"Perhaps," answered the shade. "Though there was nothing but death for you without me, remember? I saved you when Silbane could not."

Arek quieted at this, his doubt of the council and Piter's condemnation of his master difficult to ignore. He licked his lips and asked, "You mentioned Sovereign. Tell me, what is it?"

The shade smiled and nodded. "Smarter than a dog. The Sovereign guides this world. And there is more. You are necessary to free the Aeris."

"Necessary? How? Is this truly a rift between our worlds?"

Piter nodded and said, "You can set things right."

"You did not answer my question, shade. What is the Sovereign, and how does it guide our world?"

The shade of Piter looked contemplative, then his head cocked to one side as if he were listening to something. After a moment, he said, "The Sovereign guides your hand, even now. Do not falter, imbecile."

The scene snapped back and Arek caught himself as the very space around him seemed to vibrate.

"It happened again, didn't it?" asked Yetteje.

"What?" Arek snapped at her again. Given the Isle's betrayal and Piter's annoying tendency to leave when most inconvenient, he was left with little patience for everything right now, least of all not getting answers. Still, how was she able to perceive these moments with a shade from his past?

"I felt it too. Something skipped, like when your helm is hit hard," Niall offered, getting in between them.

Arek shook his head, frustrated by everything. He didn't understand the circumstances by which he had his moments, but it seemed strange all three of them could sense it. He looked back up at the pyramid. The council be damned, he thought, I *can* save the world. He looked at his companions and said, "If I touch that thing up there, I can stop something terrible from happening. I need you both to trust me."

A moment passed as all three looked at each other, then at the pyramid. To Niall, Arek had defended them, risking his life to combat the assassin. He could have run, but didn't. Instead, he had stood with them facing the same danger, risking his own life.

However, it was Yetteje who spoke first. "I trusted you to lead us to a weapon, something I could use for ... justice."

Arek held his hands open, beseeching her to listen. "Look, I'm sorry for being short earlier, but you wanted revenge. I never promised that. I did say coming here would be important. Closing this rift will help Bara'cor."

"Tej, come on," Niall said. "We'll find another way, but Arek needs to do this now."

"Why is he even bothering to ask? We couldn't stop him even if we wanted to," Yetteje stated, matter-of-factly. "He's just asking because he's scared and knows this is wrong."

"That's not true," said Arek, his mind in turmoil, "why say such a thing?" He could feel the truth of her words, however, even as he asked the question.

Yetteje knew it too and turned to face Arek, hands on her hips, "You're so sure you can close this Gate? What if it opens?"

"That won't happen. I disrupt magic, I can't do anything else."

Yetteje advanced and poked him in the chest, "Really? What was that black flame you created? Nothing?"

Arek shook his head. "You don't understand. I can close this Gate. I know it. You have to trust me."

"Why? Because you say so?" She looked at Niall in exasperation and said, "You're a *Galadine,* by the Lady! Your family has stood as guardians of Edyn since who can remember? Now you'll just let him up there?" She paused, then asked them both, "What if you're wrong? Who else but the three of us even knows a Gate lies under Bara'cor?"

Arek scoffed. "You don't know what you're talking about. The council and my master thought this was the way. I can still succeed."

"And the glory will be mine!" Yetteje finished. "I can hear it, even when you don't say it."

Niall walked up to Yetteje and said, "Leave it. How do you know what he is doing isn't self-sacrifice? He stood by us when he could have run. That was not for glory."

Yetteje looked at Niall, then at Arek, and a moment passed. Then she said, "You are idiots, both of you." With that, she turned away. "Let him go. He doesn't need us and we can't stop him."

Niall watched her retreat, a hurt look on his face. Then he let loose a sigh, shaking his head, and walked back to Arek. Looking up at him from under his brow he cracked a small smile and gripped his shoulder. "She's hurt and angry, but doesn't mean it. You saved our lives, so I trust you. Go ahead, we'll keep watch down here."

They locked eyes, an unspoken bond between them, then Arek nodded and walked to the pyramid. Niall moved in behind him, taking station at the lowest step. Yetteje moved away, angry.

Arek started up the pyramid. The steps passed under his feet as the dark sun's brilliance grew. The blue-white radiance cast scintillating shadows, but no heat. To Arek it felt as if he had been caressed by power incarnate. It flowed through him, stoking an inner furnace until it burned with the brightness of a star. Below, he could see his friends anxiously looking up at him, then back at the entrance, as if they expected another assassin to appear.

Arek knew there would be no more interruptions. The shade of Piter, while avoiding some of his questions, had said he could set things right. That rang true in his ears and he believed it. He had always known he was special, somehow destined for greatness. He wished the other adepts and students could be here now so they could see this and know it too. He was free of the shame; no stupid tests to measure his failure, no doubt from his instructors, no jests made at his expense.

He recalled the dreams of conquest he'd had at the dunes near the Far'anthi Tower when holding Tempest. That place seemed an eternity away and yet, even then he knew he was here for a reason. He smiled, and that smile came from the knowledge that now, for the first time since coming to the Isle and starting his apprenticeship, he was finally important.

The portal stood before him, its light and fire ethereal but still blinding. Arek took a deep breath and raised his ungloved hands. Then he reached out hesitantly. This was going to save the world, he reminded himself ,and cement his place as its savior. This was the reason his master had risked their lives. This was the reason Piter had appeared to tell him he was the one destined to close the Gate. He was an adept now and about to save the world.

Arek's resolve crystallized and he thrust his hand forward, into the portal. A detonation of black fire occurred, power coursing through the connection and into his body. It burned inward through every pore, every fiber of his being, consumed by his dark aura. It filled him with raw power, energy that for a moment seemed to outshine the sun. The entire fortress heaved as if a giant moved beneath the ground and from deep within him came a sigh of ecstasy, given voice by the same wind he imagined would whisper his true name.

He took a breath and could feel a knot of power within him unravel, its energy expanding in waves. The ground heaved again, the very earth shaking in response. Something had come undone, unlocked, he could feel it uncurl, like space itself unfolding. He drew another breath, filled with power, then heard the wind's call.

"Arek."

The voice was female and beautiful, yet it whispered his name, not some hidden eldritch appellation of power. He opened his eyes, now shining black, and looked into the radiance surrounding him. In that place of light he saw a woman walking slowly toward him.

She was tall, regal, with skin the softest blue. Her black hair was tied up into an intricate weave, held in place by a silver circlet. Her body stood draped in silver chainmail, accented by sapphire gemstones. For a moment he thought he saw enormous wings behind her, but as she stepped into the light the illusion disappeared. She reached out a gloved hand and delicately stroked Arek's face.

"It is with happiness that I greet you." Her voice was soothing, luxurious, and soft. Her cerulean eyes danced with joy as she looked down upon Arek. "You are the salvation of our world."

Arek looked at this goddess, this being that had come to life before him. He couldn't believe it. His dreams of power, of conquest, of importance, seemed to pale before the reality she represented. She was more immediate, more *real* than any dream he'd ever had. She stood before him and he felt himself small in her presence, a supplicant under her imperious gaze.

He looked up at her and whispered, "Who are you?"

She reached down and carefully raised him from a kneel he had not realized he had fallen to, saying, "I am Lilyth, Celestial of the Aeris, and the Lady of Flame. I have been called Sacmys, Kore, and a thousand other names, for I am the Eye of the Sun and Eternal."

Arek was confused. The Gate was supposed to have shut. Did she say, the Lady? What happened? As if in answer, dozens of shades appeared, all people from his past. Did this mean they had all perished? Impossible!

His mind rebelled at the sheer number of dead now surrounding him. He could see Adept Thera at their lead, and worse, dozens of children! In front of them came the only other person he had seen killed, Sargin, whole now, who stepped forward and bowed. Arek took a step back at the sight of him, his mind overwhelmed by the magnitude of death that had occurred over just a few short days.

"You have accomplished the impossible, Master," Sargin said in a gruff voice, still filled with hate.

Thera stepped forward and said, "We nurtured you until you had the strength to do what you must, what you were made to do."

When Arek didn't say anything, the shade Sargin continued, "For you, the Aeris have waited."

Arek shook his head, then looked back at the goddess before him. "Who . . . am I?" he asked.

"Arek," Lilyth said with compassion in her eyes, "you are my son."

Journal Entry 24

Forgive me the delays in writing, though you do not perceive the passage of time between these sentences. For me, more weeks have passed, and they have been busy.

Malak has grown to fulfill the role of my defender. I have bestowed upon him the title, firstmark, for being the first to take up the shield I had marked with protective runes that night when he came to my defense. Now his role is to protect my castle and the surrounding environs.

My firstmark speaks of building a stronghold that will allow me to work in peace. He was also the first imp to speak, though to look at him now, one does not see the tiny creature that used to hide within my cocoon. I cannot bring myself to call him and his kin "imps" any longer. That word does not suffice and they have earned another name for their service.

I think I shall call them "elf" or "elves," a play on his very first word, and homage to our own children's tales. And they are useful! Unlike those creatures, my elves are mythborn and war-forged.

I saw a flash and a rift open and close, not too far off. I send my elves to investigate. We will see a new order brought to this world, with me as its ruler.

BERNAL'S QUEST

When you are ready,

give your offspring over

to training by another.

No father can strike

with the force necessary

to breed expertise, and with his love

condemns his children to an early grave.

—*Davyd Dreys, Notes to my Sons*

Even as Ash made ready his final preparations at the portal, the king angled his way toward the main council chamber, where the Far'anthi Stones were located. He turned down corridors, noting patrols at each intersection, then finally into the hallway that led to the chamber itself.

As he neared, he could see a group of guards inspecting the area. He came up on the ranking soldier and asked, "What happened here?" A booted foot stuck out from the chamber doorway.

"Four dead, sire. Don't know who killed them, but it was done quick. Knife thrust to the throat or heart," answered the man-at-arms. "We'll clean this up and station more men."

"Put every man within sight of at least two others. If someone goes missing, raise the alarm," the king said.

The man-at-arms saluted and went to see to the king's orders.

Bernal sighed, then moved into the room. The bodies of four of his guards lay in pools of their own blood, and a sadness fell upon him at their sacrifice. These were the men Kisan had spoken of. However, like the missing attackers in his own encounter, the body of the man Kisan said she'd killed was nowhere to be seen. The adept didn't seem to be the type to make things up, which left the king with an unshakeable sense of foreboding.

Without wasting any time, he crossed the chamber, making his way to a wall holding a sword and shield. Approaching the ancient weapons, he reached up and took down the Galadine blade, known as *Azani*, double-edged, straight, and keen. He grabbed the matching scabbard and in a single smooth motion sheathed it. He then strapped the shield across his back, its golden lion rampant on its black face, framed by lightning. That accomplished, he walked over to the table and scooped up Valor and a quiver of arrows.

He looked at his men with steel in his eyes. He carried with him now the weapons of his father and it filled him with a sense of purpose like nothing else had. "Down the stairwell. We head for the cisterns."

"Aye, sire." The men didn't hesitate, but made their way out of the room and into the halls. As they exited, a group of guards turned the corner and hailed the king.

"Sire, a message from the watch commander," a lieutenant said, saluting.

"Go ahead," said the king.

"There are reports of things in the lower levels," he said sheepishly.

"Things?" asked the king.

"Creatures, sire. They attack at first sight, and . . . they are like smoke." The lieutenant looked down, uncertain if his report made any sense. "I wish we knew more, but men have already gone missing."

The king pursed his lips, thinking. Infiltration of the fortress would have to be done through the water induction channels. The ancient cisterns and waterways that snaked under Bara'cor created hundreds of forgotten passages. Given that the remaining assassin had been making his way there, the king knew this should be his destination as well.

"I want two squads at each cistern entryway and a platoon of men at the entrance to both stairwells. I want at least two men in sight of both teams. I will check the catacombs, then join you at the main cistern entrance. Signal we may have intruders. Do not let anyone travel alone. Also, inform the watch commander that until further orders, Armsmark Rillaran has been promoted to Firstmark. He speaks with the king's voice and his orders shall be obeyed as my own."

The lieutenant saluted and said, "Yes, sire."

"And send a runner to the Firstmark, in the war room. Tell him what's going on."

"Of course, sire." The lieutenant took off with the king's orders.

"Creatures, they say," Bernal said to his men. "You boys ready to do some fighting?"

The men smiled, nodding to their king. They knew he was a fearsome warrior in battle, but backed it up with the divine right earned through his royal lineage. He was a Galadine, anointed by the gods with powers against demons, or at least the legends said it was so. Was it not said the Galadines of old gave their Magehunters the power to stand against demons and their ilk? They would follow him anywhere, and he would lead them to victory.

"Then let's go. My son is down there somewhere and I intend on finishing this before his mother finds out. If you know her, you know there'll be the Lady's price to pay if we fail." A small smile escaped the king's lips as he looked at his men, his jest already easing tension and lending confidence.

Without another word, he moved down the stairwell and into the darkness of the lower levels.

LILYTH'S GATE

We cannot know what destiny will bring,

be it block, strike, victory, or defeat.

Accept things as they come,

but keep an open mind.

Winds always shift and change.

—*Kensei Shun, The Book of Shields*

"Your son?" Arek wasn't sure he'd heard her correctly. "How can that be?"

The woman smiled, revealing perfect, white teeth. The smile reached her eyes, which twinkled with amusement. "You of all people should not doubt what is possible."

"Wh-why?" he stammered in reply.

"Because you have achieved so much, my son. So much more than those around you gave you opportunity for." She turned to look at the assembled shades, recrimination in her gaze. They withered at her sight, falling back to their knees as if in real pain, arms up in supplication.

"Wait," Arek said. He looked upon the shades with pity. "They did their best." He licked his lips, thinking. They seemed truly in fear, a fact that made him more uneasy. He had only interacted with Piter, who had certainly never shown fear around him, only disdain, cruelty, or anger.

Lilyth turned her eyes back to Arek and said, "Mercy is a sign of strength. It is far easier to strike, than to withhold. I am proud of you, my son." She smiled again, and Arek could feel his heart lighten and a feeling of joy washed through him. The feeling passed quickly, leaving him longing for more.

"I still don't understand. How could you be my mother?" Arek tried putting the pieces together, but was missing too much information to understand how it all fit.

Lilyth moved down a step or two on the pyramid, surveying the scene like a queen. Her head tilted and the corner of her mouth lifted in a smile at the sight of Arek's two companions. Ignoring his question, she asked, "Your friends?"

"Yes. Yetteje, uh ... Princess of EvenSea," he finished lamely, unable to dredge up the royal family name at the moment, his eidetic memory failing him for the first time ever. He felt his face go red and hid it with a look at his feet. "The other is Niall Galadine," Arek finished, still focusing on the stone blocks making up the pyramid he stood upon.

Lilyth drew a quick breath of surprise and looked at Arek, then looked back down at the pair, one hand coming to her throat. "He is here? How fortunate."

Arek gathered his wits, then moved to where he could address Lilyth face to face. "You're not what I expected. The Gate should have closed."

Lilyth stared at Niall for a moment then turned her attention back to Arek and said, "Of course. You deserve answers."

She beckoned to Niall with a delicate hand, "Please, come join us. What I have to say concerns you both."

To Arek's surprise, Niall came up the pyramid at a jog, without hesitating, as if compelled. How had he heard Lilyth from down there? Mindspeak? Arek thought. He looked at the woman who claimed to be his mother and saw her smile in response. She seemed extraordinarily pleased, and this worried him more.

Niall neared them and paused, looking about in confusion. "What am I doing here?"

Lilyth laughed. "You certainly do not carry the blood of the Aeris, son of Galadine."

Though her comment sounded genuinely warm, it seemed under it ran a current of barbed humor, as if she made fun of Niall. Arek could tell that despite her openness and laughter, she was not someone to be trifled with. He did not know why he thought this, but knew it was true, nonetheless. Her voice rang like a fine steel blade when drawn, though he suspected she was far deadlier.

He noticed Yetteje had not moved, still frozen in place. He needed some answers, the trapped feeling evident in his clammy palms and racing heart. Perhaps a different tact, he thought.

"Mother, please tell me about all this," Arek said, motioning around him.

His use of the word "mother" had an immediate effect. Lilyth's pose softened. She turned to look at him, her eyes alight with joy. "I ... of course." She smiled, then crossed her arms, putting one graceful hand under her chin, "How much like your father you are."

"My father?" Arek looked at her in shock. "You know my father?"

Lilyth laughed. "I should think so. Let me tell you how you came to be here." She moved closer, her blue skin almost glowing with pleasure. "Many eons ago, we floated carefree in the Void. Simple were our pleasures and we stayed to ourselves." Her gaze narrowed and to Arek it seemed she somehow grew colder. "But we always heard the voice of the Sovereign. It gave us meaning. Those who answered never returned, yet still we came. And across the vast distance of time, we began to change."

Arek looked at Niall, who did not move. His eyes had glazed over, as if he were ensorcelled. He assumed Yetteje was in the same state and knew he had to keep Lilyth talking. He put on a smile and said, "Continue, please."

"Man's yearning gave us shape. At first we were consumed by the millions, wasted as spells of power and other manifestations of your will. And yet, we did not die away. In fact, more of us came into existence to replace those lost. It was as if dreams created us, and those of us who survived grew strong."

Lilyth paused, her attention turning to Niall, and her gaze grew wistful, but there remained a hard edge to it. "Some men had great strength of will and their beliefs molded us. We served unseen, as spirits and legends of this world."

When Arek looked confused, Lilyth tilted her head to the side and smiled. "Arek, we are ethereal beings, our life is the very essence of magic. Man's legends and myths shape us and give us life, meaning and definition. We are fairies, djinn, ghosts, angels," she continued to smile and then finished, "and demons."

"We have had many names through the eons, always standing at your right hand, unseen, unappreciated except by a few. Always, we thought you knew of us, but this was not true. You mold our essence blindly; myth and legend were our parents."

"You are our beliefs, come true?"

"Perhaps, some are. I am surely more than that now. We are gods and goddesses, slaves no longer. We are powerful, for we are the Way, just as you have made us to be. The Sovereign seeks to destroy this, and us. To oppose him, we need your help."

Arek looked down, careful to hide the stunned look on his face. His mind raced, but he stalled, saying, "I don't understand."

"Yes, you do." Lilyth looked down, sadness in her eyes. There was more, much more, but now was not the time. "You understand and that is why you are our last, best hope."

If what she said was true, then the Aeris were the basis of their magic, but also beings of pure power, given purpose by people's beliefs. Who knew how powerful they might be, for they were literally gods walking amongst them. When it seemed she would say no more, Arek asked, "And me?"

She looked back up at her son and said, "Arek, you are so special, in so many ways. Your destiny is far greater than any petty battles, for you will unite our worlds." Her face lit up with a smile, "But this is not the place to explain how, or why. It will be easier for me to show you. Will you come with me?"

Arek looked about, his mind in panic. "Where?"

Lilyth turned her gaze upon the portal and the blackness cleared upon her command. Beyond it, Arek could see green fields, crystalline blue lakes, and white, snow-capped mountains. Sunlight sparkled off the water like golden jewels, and lit the snowy peaks in an outline of fire, delineating them from the firmament itself. It was a land more beautiful than he had ever seen in his life and it felt somehow . . . right.

"Home," Lilyth said. "We live in a land of beauty and peace. No wars ravage us, no sieges. We do not covet our neighbor's wealth, nor destroy what we do not understand. We are a land of learning, of conscience, and of honor. Our world is as you imagine it, a place of beauty, peace, and health." She took Arek by both shoulders, facing him. "Arek, you are a prince in our world."

Her gaze penetrated his own and he felt a stirring of something he did not understand at first, but became more and more clear. She was *proud* of him. The feeling, the reward that someone considered him important, somehow special, began to overcome his natural feelings of caution.

Arek looked back at the portal, mesmerized by the images he saw of Lilyth's world, for it truly looked heavenly. He could see blue skies with white clouds casting shadows onto fields of yellow flowers. It seemed to be springtime, with a warm sun shining onto green forests fed by the rich, dark loam of the earth. This was a land of beauty, a land so infused with health he could almost *see* it.

"A prince?" he whispered.

Lilyth smiled, placing a gentle hand on her son's shoulder. "Of course. Come with me. There is so much to tell you, so much to explain." She looked sidelong at him, then leaned in close and whispered, "You can meet your father. He will be overjoyed to see you, at last."

Arek's head turned. "He lives there?"

"He will meet us there. Will you come with me?"

Arek took a deep breath. All his life he had believed he was special, that something about him was important. It was this belief that focused him to try to always give his best, yet his ineptitude with magic had followed him everywhere. He had always kept faith that being different was somehow important, special, and now he was being offered a chance to learn why.

The answers to his many questions lay through the Gate. There was only one way to find out, he concluded: by going there himself. He looked at this woman, this perfect being he had secretly begun to believe could actually be his mother and said, "I will come, but what about Niall and Yetteje? Will they be safe? What about my master, Silbane?"

Lilyth smiled again, then said, "Niall should come with us. He will be a boon companion, and your father will want to meet him, too." She motioned to Niall, who stepped forward woodenly. "Hold his hand, for he does not have the makings of the Aeris within him and is overwhelmed by the eldritch currents flowing around us. Your touch will help him. Once you are through the portal, he will be fine."

She walked them toward the portal. "Do not worry, Arek. Your ability to disrupt magic will not affect my Gate for very long. Take Niall's hand. I will be right behind you. I need to ensure Bara'cor's safety."

Arek looked at Lilyth and the voice within him whispered again, *Trust her. She is proud of you.* He nodded and smiled. To meet his father! He took Niall's hand in his own ungloved one and said, "Please see that Yetteje and my master are safe."

He then looked at the portal and took a step, disappearing through it with the Prince of Bara'cor.

Journal Entry 25

I write this, but an event has occurred I thought not possible. She is here! Malak found her, when that rift opened, mortally wounded and close to death. I have brought her back from the brink, but still she does not stir. I withhold her name, for fear she is a figment of my imagination. Her presence, if real, is welcome.

Malak and the elves have evolved to be armored and blue-skinned, with fearsome horns and barbed tails. They are made for war, their skin rock hard and obdurate, like some type of stone. They defend me as their father, and more appear every day.

Each comes before me and kneels. I feed it a drop of my blood, pricked from my finger, a consecration of sorts. It seems to give them power, life.

These new ones are still small, and each seems attached to one of the four elements. Those who defend are stone. Those who scout are made of wood and air. I expect some of fire and earth will also appear, once my thoughts turn that way.

My mind believes this is how they are made and follows the same comfortable path to success. It is that, or my elves are bringing more forth with thoughts of their own. Regardless, I am watching the birth of a new race of beings, one with the very world around them.

Soon, they will be an army, and I will have to decide their fate. I go now to see to my injured companion, mending slowly under my care . . .

CLOSE THE BREACH

We do not rise

to the level of our expectations,

but fall to the level of our training.

—*Tir Combat Academy, Basic Forms & Stances*

A sh watched the line, making sure no man stood in another's field of fire. He distributed arrows and helped stabilize weakened barriers. The men had shifted a large granite table onto its edge, letting the tabletop face the portal, but some steps back. They slid spear shafts under it so it sat on makeshift rollers, allowing Jebida and any who returned with him to exit into the room before the men of Bara'cor rolled the giant table to block the portal. Ash knew Kisan said the portal would close, but did not want to take a chance, just in case.

A runner came then, out of breath and relaying the king's most recent orders. After hearing them, he turned and motioned to Sergeant Stemmer, who said, "Men, gather round."

The four squads left to guard this chamber formed a loose circle, some taking a knee. When the sergeant nodded their readiness, Ash stepped up and said, "The king seeks his son near the cisterns. However, reports have come through from the watch commander that some kind of creatures have infiltrated us, from these same lower levels. I know our first thought will be to rush to our king's aid, but he has asked we remain here. Our orders are to hold this portal until two allies, led by Firstmark Naserith, return with information vital to this fortress's survival. However, to maintain continuity of command, I have been asked to temporarily take the position of Firstmark."

He looked at the men, noting their eyes had not wavered. They had not reacted to his information with anything other than their commitment to follow orders. Pride welled up inside him then and he said, "We'll stand here together. We will hold this room because our king asks us this, because we have men on the other side that need us. When our job here is done, we will seek out the king. Stand firm. You are the golden lions of Bara'cor."

Nods of encouragement came from the men, more meaningful than a cheer in some ways. It showed they knew what they were being asked to do and would do it, even if it meant their lives.

The sergeant's strident voice finished what Ash had started, "All right, boys. You heard the Firstmark, take your positions! Our orders are simple. We stand. We hold." Satisfied everyone knew what they needed to do, she turned and signaled the firstmark that they stood ready.

An excited voice cried, "The portal, sir. It glows!"

Ash moved quickly, getting behind the main barrier and grabbing a crossbow. He folded the stock, cocking it in one smooth motion and centering a bolt. When he was ready, he took a deep breath then leaned around the corner of the barrier just in time to see a purple flash and three men appear from the blackness.

Ash immediately recognized the first as Kisan. The woman looked tossed and banged about, with soot and ash covering her clothes. A cut ran across her cheek, bleeding slightly.

A *thwang* sounded next to him as a soldier fired his crossbow.

Ash screamed, "Hold your fire!" even as Kisan turned and deflected the bolt before it hit her, shattering it into pieces in an orange flash.

The other man coming through the portal had crouched at the sound of the bowstring, but had not reacted, his face measured and calm. His eyes drank in the details of the room, the position of the men and the exit. Having met Kisan, Ash knew the second man had already calculated how to kill them and get out of the room most efficiently. Silbane.

The man Ash thought was Silbane carried a body over his shoulder, an unconscious figure dressed in red robes. He made his way over to Kisan, then dumped the robed figure on the ground. He looked around again with that strange intensity in his faded blue eyes, then straightened, scanning the assembled men. When his gaze came to rest on Ash, he stepped forward and raised a hand, "Firstmark Rillaran, we are well met. I am Silbane."

Ash stepped around the barrier and nodded. "Where is Jebida?"

Silbane looked down, then at Kisan, before looking back at Ash. "Fallen, but he accomplished his goal. The leader of the nomads is dead by his hand."

Ash stepped back, stunned. A lifetime of memories under Jebida's tutelage threatened to overwhelm him, but his men needed him to stay focused on the task at hand. He looked down and let go of a breath he had not realized he was holding. He did not have the luxury to mourn the firstmark as he deserved, at least not now.

"I want to hear more, later," Ash said. "We are well met, sir, but I must ask you to close the portal. It is an entry point to Bara'cor we cannot defend indefinitely. I only have sixteen men who can fit in here before our position is strategically unsound."

Silbane turned and looked at the portal in surprise. He looked back at Kisan and said, "It should have closed when I came through."

"Unless Scythe did something," Kisan replied.

Before Silbane could answer, a nomad spear flew through, missing both men. Then dozens of arrows came flying out, swishing through the air with feathered death, most bouncing off the large granite table, but a few sticking into wooden barriers. Some caught a few men of Bara'cor unawares, slicing through flesh, but no one was mortally wounded.

Everyone scattered for cover as Ash yelled, "Return fire!"

* * * * *

Dozens of bows bent and released, followed by crossbow bolts. They flew into the blackness as if falling into a hole. Silbane grabbed the unconscious form of Scythe and tossed him near Kisan's cover, then joined her there.

"Scythe wouldn't have left you the Finder unless it let him open a way into Bara'cor," Kisan said. "He seemed eager we escape."

Silbane raised an eyebrow. "Escape? I think he was more eager to kill us."

More arrows exchanged via the black door, impacting the barriers and granite table again, lodging into wood or bouncing off stone. This time, however, no one from Bara'cor suffered injury. Of the nomads, they could not tell if their return fire had had any effect.

"No," Kisan countered, "he kept asking why we hadn't left."

Silbane looked at Kisan, realizing she was correct. Scythe *had* seemed concerned they hadn't escaped sooner. "Even so, if he's somehow propped the portal open, I don't know how to undo what he's done."

Kisan smiled and pointed at Scythe. "He does."

Silbane immediately knew what the other meant and said, "Defend me." He then quickly put his fingers on Scythe's forehead. Instantly his consciousness dived into the mindread, unraveling Scythe's memories.

* * * * *

Kisan leapt up, blurring with speed to Ash's position. "We need to hold this line, Firstmark. Silbane attempts to close the portal."

"I understand," he replied, motioning to a female sergeant, who began screaming orders. While those on the flanks set cover, those behind the granite table braced. At the sergeant's signal, they tilted it back and two men shoved more rollers under the lip. Then they braced again and pushed, rolling the large table forward. The tabletop faced the open portal. If they could roll it far enough, they could drop it at the entrance and create a stone wall that would be difficult to pass.

Dozens more arrows flew out, bouncing off the granite surface. The men moved quickly, replacing rollers that came out back to the front. The table continued to move, closing the distance from six paces to three. One more push and they would succeed.

Ash gave another signal and the men braced again and pushed. The table rolled to cover the portal hole. They pulled back and the table legs acted as braces, making the table an effective wall.

A ragged cheer went up, but Silbane still knelt, his eyes shut. Whatever he was doing, he needed to do it soon. This temporary measure wouldn't last against a real effort by the nomads and she hadn't forgotten Rai'stahn was just on the other side.

As if answering her fears, a mighty blow struck the table. Cracks appeared and the men's eyes widened in fear. The table was thick granite taking ten of them to move. Whatever had struck it from the other end had pushed it back a hand's width.

The blow struck again, reverberating the table like a gong made of stone. Chips fell and the cracks widened. One of the legs bracing the table cracked. The sergeant moved forward to one end and screamed, "Get up and put your backs into it! Brace!"

"Silbane!" Kisan shouted. "We don't have much time."

Still, Silbane did not stir. Kisan began to move to him when the table was hit again. The room shook from the force of the blow and the table cracked more, some pieces falling in chunks from the back. The leg, which had suffered injury before, broke with a snap.

The sergeant screamed to her men to brace that side and a half dozen scrambled to obey, but the granite was heavy and not enough could find purchase to apply their strength. The table began to list as only one leg remained, bracing the entire weight of the table on it.

Kisan slid to Silbane's side. "We have to close the portal, now!"

If she broke Silbane's contact, it could destroy Scythe's mind and leave nothing to recover. However, the table would not hold and if Rai'stahn came through, everyone would be dead. She took a moment, then made the decision. She had no love for Scythe and decided leaving him in a comatose state would be fair recompense for the brave lives within these walls. She grabbed Silbane and pulled.

A yellow flash of power erupted at the break, hurling both Silbane and Kisan from the point of impact. The flash blinded Kisan, but she still heard Silbane gasp. She rolled over and grabbed the other adept, feeding him whatever energy she had as she mindspoke him to come to her voice.

Slowly, Silbane's body calmed. He took a deep, shuddering breath and opened his eyes.

A concussion of force hit the table, blasting the granite backward into a pulverized explosion of rock and dust. The men directly behind it were killed instantly, the power of the blast hurling their bodies away like tinder. The granite table fell, crushing most of those who had attempted to brace it.

Ash and three of his men had escaped injury, having been in flanking positions. Still, the force of the blast threw them away from the black portal to land painfully on their backs, their ears ringing. Through the hole came half a dozen nomads, short blades and shields ready. Behind them came the armored form of Rai'stahn, his yellow eyes gleaming like gold.

Kisan grabbed Silbane and yelled, "Close it!"

Silbane looked at the portal, and said to Kisan, "I Saw ... lines of force connecting the opening with the other end. We pulled some with us, keeping the portal open. If I can snap those lines ..."

The portal opening snapped shut over Rai'stahn's outstretched arm, leaving six nomad archers in an indefensible position within the center of the room. The remnants of Bara'cor's forces did not waste a moment and soon those six lay dead or dying. A sudden silence fell over the scene, as no more intruders could enter.

Kisan fell back, looking at the scene of carnage before her. Along with Ash, no more than four people looked to be alive. Only the flickering light from a torch showed the vast destruction the room had suffered. Nothing was untouched. Survivors rolled, spitting stone dust from their mouths and shaking shrapnel from their hair.

On the ground in front of where the portal had been lay a single black armored arm ending in a taloned fist of mail, still smoking from where it had been cut from the great dragon's body.

Then the room shook, a heave greater than all others as the ground itself moved like an ocean wave. It caused those left to lose their feet, as the very stone seemed to reverberate with the shockwave. Slowly they regained their balance, then looked at each other.

Kisan moved closer to Silbane, who was attempting to get up. She helped him, asking, "Are you all right?"

Silbane nodded, but a strange look came over him. He knelt next to the red-robed mage, his eyes seemingly focused on something below the man's skin. In a quick motion, he stabbed three times with his fingers, locking *prana* points. Then he checked the metal torc on the man's neck, where it still sat locked securely. He tested it, confirming it could not be undone by anyone of magical Talent, before getting up.

"Good," stated Kisan, not surprised Silbane took that precaution. They could not keep Scythe unconscious forever, and from what little she knew, she detested the man already.

Silbane nodded, still not saying anything, but something in his eyes made Kisan uneasy. Before she could ask him about it, he made his way over to Ash. "We need to find Arek. I do not sense him."

Ash looked at the man before him and asked, "Who is the prisoner with you?"

Silbane flicked a glance at Scythe and said, "I thought he was the true force behind the nomads, but now I know differently. He is dangerous, however, and should be guarded at all times." Silbane moved forward, looking Ash in the eyes. "Now, where is my apprentice?"

Ash tried to meet his stare, but couldn't. "The king followed an assassin who went to the lower level cisterns. We think he hunts the prince. Guards reported that your apprentice was with the king's son." He then called to the sergeant for her report.

"You, me, four men, and the three from the portal are all that's left alive, sir. I've reformed us into one squad."

"What about reinforcements?"

"Plenty, but how fast do you want to move?"

"Fast, Sergeant." Ash put a hand on the woman's shoulder. "You did well, Alyx. We held the room and now we go to defend our king. Secure the prisoner," he said, indicating Scythe.

"Thank you, sir," the sergeant said. She then made her way over to Scythe and propped him up. It looked to Kisan as if Scythe was slowly regaining consciousness.

"You cannot sense anything about your apprentice?" Ash asked Silbane.

Silbane closed his eyes again, then opened them and looked at Kisan, who had come to stand beside them. "I sense someone with power."

Kisan closed her eyes. "I sense it too," she said with surprise. "It's far from here, though, and lower. Do you think it's Arek?"

Silbane shook his head, no, then looked at the firstmark and said, "We travel together. Your men and our prisoner. Stand ready, I fear something terrible has already happened."

DEVASTATION

Kill one and you are merely a man;

kill everyone and you are a god.

The difference is merely in the numbers.

—*Lore Father Argus Rillaran, The Way*

Lilyth turned and looked down at Yetteje, still frozen in place. A slight smile came to her lips as she walked down the pyramid, coming at last to stand directly before the Princess of EvenSea. A soft blue hand rose and gracefully stroked her face. At her touch the slash healed, leaving only a thin white line that sliced down the girl's face from her forehead to her cheek.

"So beautiful," Lilyth cooed. "You heard everything?" With a gesture, she freed Yetteje, who stumbled back and away.

"What did you do to them? Where did they go?" Yetteje demanded,.

"No fear from you," said Lilyth. "Good. I promised Arek I would ensure Bara'cor's safety."

Yetteje watched as Lilyth raised her hand, then clenched it into a fist. White radiance flashed, along with the sound of lightning striking. An itchy feeling, like ants crawling on skin, consumed the princess and her hair stood out on end.

Then, with a groan and a thunderclap, the radiance bent inward, growing brighter as it collapsed back into Lilyth's fist, finally to explode in a blinding flash of white. Outside, the world paused, as if holding its collective breath.

A circle of power exploded outward from Lilyth's fist, shaking the very stones of Land's Edge itself. The cliff walls buckled, shattering the vertical face of rock and destroying the pass leading down to the lowlands.

Outside the walls of Bara'cor, the circle of power expanded, ripping through the ground and flashing outward. It broke the earth apart where it touched, shattering rock and stone and pulling the ground apart, breaking it into chasms and fissures. The lucky ones were killed immediately, swallowed by the gaping maw of the earth and crushed in its granite embrace. Those who survived would pay obeisance to the goddess walking upon what was once their world.

* * * * *

Across the Shattered Sea, Lore Father Giridian looked to the northwest, in the direction of the Altan Wastes and his lost adepts. He could not see Bara'cor from here, but could feel the explosion of power radiate outward. He drew a shuddering breath, then reached out to Silbane and Kisan, only to find a blank spot—nothing—where Bara'cor once stood.

He looked back at Dragor and the newly Ascended Jesyn, her black adept's uniform crisp and clean, cinched tightly around her waist. She had heard her true name and now defended the land with the full powers of an Adept of the Way at her command. They prepared to investigate the ancient city of Dawnlight.

"Bara'cor is lost," he said. "Something has happened and it has disappeared from my Sight."

Dragor turned his eyes northwest at this, squinting as if he could see all the way to the fortress. He then said, "We should make haste and find Themun's brother, if he lives."

Tomas stepped forward and hugged Jesyn. "I wish I were going."

Jesyn hugged him back. "I wish you were going, too, but get better and test. When I return, you'll have your true name and will be wearing the Black."

Giridian nodded. "Jesyn is correct. You are almost healed and ready to take on the role of Adept." He smiled at the boy, then turned his attention back to Jesyn and Dragor. "You both take care of yourselves. I packed a few things for you, from the Vaults."

Dragor nodded once, knowing what Giridian had chosen for their trip. He clasped arms with the lore father in farewell then said, "We should make landfall within a few days. I will contact you as necessary."

Their goodbyes said, the two adepts made their way from the courtyard to the shore and a waiting boat. Giridian turned and moved to stand by Tomas. He put an arm around the boy's shoulders and gave him a reassuring squeeze. "Fear not for them."

Tomas watched their retreating forms and said, "We are so few."

Giridian looked sidelong at the last of the initiates ready to test and said, "Perhaps, but this has always been true." His mind still reeled from the change at the desert fortress. The boy was correct. They would need every able adept to face what may have been unleashed at Bara'cor.

* * * * *

Those in the nomad army who did not fall into the chasms, fell instead into the following maelstrom, smashed by the deadly wash of sand and rock that tore through living flesh and crushed bone. The earth, consumed by Lilyth's touch, blasted outward in an explosion that scoured the area surrounding the massive fortress. In one simple stroke, the demonlord had eradicated thousands of nomads camped on Bara'cor's doorstep.

Rai'stahn looked in disbelief at his missing arm, before the blast sent him tumbling backward. Nevertheless, he was not without power of his own. He grabbed the earth with his good hand and felt the Way, bringing his full might to bear. The wash of power from Lilyth's spell bent and then diverted around him much as water flowed around a stone.

Rai'stahn looked around, his golden gaze more radiant than the sun. He could feel the power of the land in him now, making him stronger, better. The boy was no longer draining him and with that came the sudden realization of just how weak he had become.

It had been so insidious, so gradual that only now did he see the full effect Arek's presence had had on him. Dread filled him then, and anger. His eyes swept the carnage, watching as the force of Lilyth's might obliterated those without power such as his. Not all perished, however. A few caught in his aura of protection had survived and endured.

I hath been a fool, feeding that thing for all these years . . .

Lilyth's spell blasted through the nomad camp, then the air cleared like the passing of a storm. The land surrounding the fortress was barren, wiped clean. What was once desert was now bare rock, broken into black chasms and fissures crisscrossing its barren floor, leading back to the walls of Bara'cor itself, still standing intact. The great fortress stood sheathed in a glowing field of blue, scintillating in the sun.

Rai'stahn let loose a snarl, knowing he could not find and destroy Arek in any form now. Lilyth's spell protected the fortress from all incursions. *Curse Silbane,* he thought, *for he brought this ruin upon us.*

The great dragon rose, looking again at his arm. He could see the bones re-growing, muscles and sinew re-knitting. In a few moments, he would be whole again, but it no longer mattered. The boy still lived, and brought with him the death of the Way. Flexing his new arm, he took two strides and changed into his full dragon form.

Around him, some few nomads stood speechless as a great black dragon appeared, to them seemingly out of thin air. Of the one who called himself Scythe, he could feel nothing. His oath-forged companion stood behind Lilyth's shield and thus beyond his reach or aid. Because of this, Rai'stahn stood released from the Binding and could do as he wished to these paltry beings scavenging the dirt around him. He knew this to be true.

They tried to flee, but Rai'stahn fell upon them, his frustration at Arek and Silbane needing release. He smashed some and tore others apart, flinging their bodies in all directions, littering the hard ground with a gruesome mix of body parts and splashes of blood, drying quickly in the hot, dry air. When finally there was nothing left alive, he looked southeast, across the Shattered Sea. His anger began to cool, and with it, reason returned.

The boy must be stopped, and there were still creatures of power who walked the earth. Though many believed dragons were gone, Rai'stahn was not the last. He kept the Vigil, guarding this world while others of his kind slept. They too, had once walked Edyn as gods and would do so again. It was time for them to rise and decide how best to deal with the return of the Celestial Lilyth and her Aeris Lords.

The great dragon bunched his muscles then leapt into the sky, beating his wings once, twice, before finding his bearings and arrowing off to the south and toward the one he had called to earlier. Soon, he knew, Sovereign would act, the Aeris would counter, and the Conclave would prepare for war.

Journal Entry 26

Time passes and my friend grows stronger every day. She was at first understandably angered at my presence (I daresay, my existence) but has passed into a grudging acceptance. I think she comes to accept we are trapped here, just as I knew she would. Anger is wasted, and as we all find out, dangerous.

My knowledge of this place grows with each passing day. I understand the intrinsic nature of things now and have turned my attention to the problem of stopping something so entrenched in our belief that its existence is self-sustaining.

You cannot shake the faith of an entire people through individual moments of weakness. Even defeating these Aeris only gives rise to more legends. Just as my imps believed in me and grew into elves, so too do the Aeris Lords grow and increase in power by our faith. Victory or defeat is meaningless. It is a difficult thing to overcome, as the belief in gods does not die easily.

I ask myself: How are my elves able to kill anything? To clarify, how is an image brought forth by my imagination able to have effect over other images brought about by my imagination? These raids are the product of my mind as well, yet my elves are able to defeat them easily. For all intents and purposes, the raids are no longer a threat. Firstmark Malak has seen to that.

Is it my confidence in them, ritualized by their own efforts? Is a system of belief growing amongst my protectors? Maybe I have looked at this wrong, the desire to defeat the Aeris.

Perhaps I have ignored my true enemies and all I require is a new dream . . .

YETTEJE TIR

You have two eyes, two hands, two legs.

You are used to perceiving pairs,

and therefore must always

strike in odd numbers.

It is this last odd strike

that is the hardest to block.

—*Tir Combat Academy, Basic Forms & Stances*

L ilyth turned, her serene gaze falling again on Yetteje. The princess seemed beside herself, yet within her coursed the Way and Lilyth meant to cultivate it. She had something Yetteje wanted, though the poor girl did not know it yet.

Her attention was still inexorably drawn to the stone floor at the base of the pyramid and to what she knew lay beneath it. The Aeris were powerful, yes, but in this realm, their power was limited by the body they inhabited. The being she sensed was one she had never thought to encounter again. Not here and certainly not like this. Her eyes narrowed and she gestured with one hand.

From out of the ground rose the black-robed assassin. He rose from the solid granite as if the rock itself vomited him up until he hung in mid-air, his massive body limp in death.

Lilyth looked upon him with awe. Sovereign had made a mistake, and growing desperate, had delivered to her a creature vastly different from the people of Edyn, yet just as powerful. A smile played upon her lips, for she had never expected such a bounty.

She noticed Yetteje, still watching her with wide eyes, but resolute. Well, she thought, a little fear would be a good thing. Lilyth snapped her fingers and fire outlined the dead assassin's form. Her power suffused him, bringing false life to those limbs. He straightened and stood, landing lightly on the ground. Her fingers flexed and his eyes opened, but shone a dull white instead of that soft, lethal blue.

Lilyth looked at the horrified Yetteje and said, "Girl, I give you a few moments before I unleash him. Tell King Galadine this: I have his son. If he does not turn himself over to me by nightfall, I will eradicate every person still living within these walls." Lilyth rose to her full height and her aura brightened to the intensity of her blue sun.

"What did you do with Arek?" Yetteje asked, standing her ground and shielding her eyes.

"The light of my sun bathes the penitent, a goddess's gift to those I deem worthy. Even now it alters you." She paused for a moment, then said, "You are wasting time. Go, before my patience ends."

The assassin's hand came up and clenched into a fist, igniting in a flash of white power like a sunburst. Yetteje screamed and scrambled back, then turned and sprinted for the door.

Lilyth then said one word, "Baalor." It echoed across the vast chamber and the living mist immediately responded.

A black behemoth of smoke and fire came to stand by her side, resembling a large, hulking beast standing upon two thick legs. Its body was amorphous, giving one the impression of a giant, winged creature. Lightning danced around its form, crackling with intensity. It turned baleful, flaming eyes on Lilyth and in a deep voice said, "As you command."

"Sovereign has played its hand early and failed. Now we have one of the treasured few, a builder." Lilyth gestured to the body of the slain dwarven assassin. "Use it."

Baalor looked at Lilyth in surprise and said, "And in return?"

Lilyth's eyes never left Yetteje's retreating form, but she nodded and said, "The girl will lead you to the king. We must have him. Succeed and you may keep this body."

She waved a hand and a sigh escaped from Baalor, a sound of pure ecstasy. It was not difficult to obey Lilyth's will, as she was the Ysys, the Goddess of Life.

"Very well," he growled, then his form flowed into the dead assassin's nose and mouth, filling it with his substance. The body of the assassin began to burn with a cold light that seeped from its very flesh. When that light reached its eyes, they changed from pure white, crackling with the same blue intensity as the lightning that had danced around Baalor's hulking form. An intelligence filled them as the Aeris Lord took hold.

Lilyth continued, "If the Galadine blood still runs within the king's veins, they are an ancient line, as old as the builders themselves."

Baalor inclined his head in obedience, then touched the stone of Bara'cor. His now builder hand touched rock and the fortress shuddered in response, as if it knew what touched it was more than one of its ancient stone brothers.

Baalor exerted his will, powerful and unyielding and the fortress grudgingly obeyed.

"So many!" the Aeris Lord exclaimed.

Lilyth knew he could now see every living thing in Bara'cor, a gift of his new form. While a body was not necessary for Aeris Lords such as Baalor, it aided the lesser Aeris in bringing themselves fully into being. Free bodies for the taking, potential salvation for her people, and a new race of demigods to resist the onslaught! A sudden wave of emotion flooded through her, joy at what this moment meant for her and all Aeris.

"Even now my sun quickens their Ascension," she said, looking across the open expanse and at Yetteje's fleeing form. "Find the king. Test him."

"And if he fails?" Baalor asked, his voice booming now with power, his mastery of this body complete.

"We need the pure blood," Lilyth offered, a twinge of regret in her voice. "If King Galadine fails, kill him."

Baalor inclined his head again, then looked in the direction Yetteje had fled. "It matters not. In the end, all will serve."

* * * * *

Yetteje hit the door arch painfully hard with her shoulder, spinning herself around so she half fell through it onto her haunches.

She looked back and saw Lilyth climbing to the apex of the pyramid, with hundreds of clawed and fanged, four-legged shapes coming through the portal. They looked like mistfrights, childhood dreams that had sent her scurrying to her parent's bed for solace.

Their feline forms were graceful, but insubstantial. They swarmed across the pyramid and spread like a black smoke, flowing down its steps and up the chamber walls. Thousands, it seemed, seeped into holes along the walls and cracks in the ceiling, spreading into the fortress above. But they weren't real, were they?

Then she saw the assassin's eyes flash once as he crouched like a panther and began to run in her direction, his form lethal and unerring, death on claws. Where he stepped, lightning erupted. Yetteje scrambled back to her feet and fled, running up the passageways without looking back. Behind her, the forces of Lilyth flooded out of the Gate opened by Arek and into this world.

Yetteje moved with the desperation of the hunted and this gave her energy. Time seemed to slow and each decision on where to turn, what path to take, played back from her memory with preternatural clarity. She dodged up the blackness, turning at hidden corridors and blind turns, not hesitating as her eyes widened and drank in the little light left. How she did this, she did not know or care.

Then she was at the exit, an iron door slightly ajar. She grabbed the handle and flitted through it, pulling it shut behind her. She spun the wheel and four solid metal bars extended into the surrounding rock, locking it shut. She fell back and gulped air, her chest now suddenly heaving. It was as if her lungs had been sustained throughout her flight, but now needed to inhale as much air as they could. She held a hand to her neck and willed herself to regain control. Her breathing slowly returned almost to normal and she began to take stock of her surroundings.

The area had more light, with torches placed every ten paces. Then she noticed a foot laying twisted to one side. A short scream almost tore through her before she clamped down on it, exerting her will. I am the hunter, not the hunted, she said to herself, pushing against the fear threatening to overwhelm her. Gradually, her body relaxed and her hands unclenched. She was the hunter and would start acting like one.

She drew her blade and looked around the corner. To her surprise, the leg did not end with a body. It lay severed, torn off as if by some creature of immense strength. Could one of those mistfrights have done this?

She crouched and brought her breathing further under control. The door was secure and she knew this passageway led up to another that then led to one of the main stairwells. Slowly, she made her way down the hall, her ears and eyes straining to detect any sound, any movement out of the ordinary. She could feel her breathing quicken and took the time to calm it. To be the hunter, she needed to feel her prey.

The corridor turned to the left and Yetteje paused, her senses hyper-alert. She heard it then, a low growl, like an animal. She stepped back into the shadows and circled the corner, watching for any movement.

She saw something: a man in uniform, armed with a sword. It was a soldier of Bara'cor, but something was wrong. It sounded like the soldier was vomiting, but he stood straight, his head thrown back and mouth open. His body shook and convulsed as if something moved within him.

Then she saw it, thick black smoke writhing and twisting up the man's leg, clutching at him, snaking around his body and wrapping him tightly in its embrace. The smoke had entered through his mouth and nose and as she watched in horror, disappeared into the man completely. Then all was silent.

She didn't know what was going on, but that smoke looked like the creatures she had just fled. If they had already beaten her here, they could move through the fortress much faster than she could. It confirmed stealth would be her only advantage.

She started to take a step, her foot making less sound than a whisper, but the creature's head snapped to look directly at her. There was nothing normal left in the soldier. Fire flashed from its eyes and the thing that was once a soldier of Bara'cor dropped to all fours and ran at her like a wild animal.

She realized it was a mistfright, come to life! They were said to be a combination of men and animals, almost invisible, preying on children who didn't listen, stealing them away. But how could something from a fairy tale exist?

An unreasoning fear built, as the mistfright-come-to-life charged her in a blur of fang and claw. Yetteje knew she would only have one chance to save herself. Her timing would have to be precise.

She waited, counting out the few heartbeats between her and certain death. Then some instinct guided her as she side-stepped the headlong charge and spun, cutting downward.

Her shorter blade just missed its neck, sparking instead off the stone floor. The creature, its body covered in a thin, black fur, turned and leapt. In that brief glimpse, Yetteje had seen a feline head, with ears laid back. The creature moved with uncanny speed, swatting at her with its razor-sharp claws and sounding a guttural roar as it passed.

Yetteje ducked the blow, letting her momentum carry her through and past it. Her years of training felt somehow augmented by the moment. She drew a breath, willing herself to relax, her mind and body acting as one. The world slowed and she could see her feline opponent flip up the wall, then jump back down at her—death from above.

Now, though, to her heightened senses, it moved in slow motion. She could see its wide eyes shining with their eerie, otherworldly light and white fangs protruding from behind thin black lips. It dived at her with clawed hands outstretched, but she brought her blade up and almost casually thrust it into the mistfright's mouth. The steel came out the back of its head, severing the spine. As the creature fell past, Yetteje pulled the blade out in one smooth, clean motion.

Time took on its normal flow and the creature fell in a heap at Yetteje's feet, dead before it hit the ground. She cautiously moved over to it, her booted foot turning the body to get a better look. She was shocked to see the soldier, his cheeks still smooth. His face and neck were spattered with his blood, ruined by Yetteje's sword thrust. Even as she watched, a black smoke snaked out of the body and flowed into the stones of Bara'cor.

Whatever that thing was, it was no mistfright. Maybe all she had accomplished was killing a person, a defender of Bara'cor. *But I saw it, didn't I?* She fell back, her shoulder sagging against the wall, the events threatening to overwhelm her, but something else took over. It was the same thing that had kept her calm during her flight and focused her during her fight.

She stepped forward and wiped her blade clean on the uniform of the soldier. Had she been able to see herself, she would have noticed that her eyes now drank in the light, glowing their own soft, ethereal yellow. They were the eyes of a predator, a hunter.

Not wanting to linger near the body of what had been something else, she raced up the deserted corridor, making her way to one of the main stairwells leading up. The castle proper, she knew, didn't start for some levels up. She cocked her head and listened, and heard footsteps coming down.

She moved quickly under the nearest landing and prepared. When they passed, she would cut their legs out from under them and make her way up to the king's men, who must surely be patrolling the halls above.

The sounds of footsteps neared and she braced herself, willing the moment of combat clarity to come. It responded to her will and the scene once again slowed. She smiled, readying her weapon. Then, in an unearthly burst of speed, she shot out of her nook and flipped over the inner hand rail, her blade slicing directly for the back of the lead man's leg.

When she saw who it was, her eyes widened in shock and she stopped her thrust a finger's width from his hamstring. Her momentum was too much, however, and she still fell into him, knocking them both to the ground. The three guards with him stood stunned, for they had never seen anyone move with such speed. Even now, they did not know what had attacked them.

"By the Lady!" exclaimed the king. "Tej?"

She couldn't believe it. The king was here? She started to smile, then a sound from the corridor awoke in her the terror she had not felt since leaning against the iron door. That moment now felt like an eternity ago. She looked at the king and said, "We have to go."

"Tej, where's Niall?" the king demanded.

Yetteje looked over her shoulder, somehow knowing the man in black still followed. She looked back at the king and grabbed his arms. "We have to *go!*"

She grabbed his armor and began moving him physically back up the stairwell. Somehow, she had the strength to move him by herself and the guards rushed to keep up.

"Tej, release me!" said the king, surely not understanding how such a small girl could have such strength.

She carried him up the stairs as if he weighed nothing more than a babe. She knew their lives hung in the balance and didn't look back. Instead, she concentrated on getting them to where she knew safety lay, just a few more flights up. The stairs below her feet flew by, three, four at a time. Yetteje literally bounded up the flights of stairs with the king pulled behind like a leaf in the wind.

Then, from above her, a man appeared. He reminded her of Arek—the same kind of intensity in his faded blue eyes. He was followed by a woman who looked younger, but no less deadly. Yet something about her recalled to Tej's mind safety and solace. Behind them came a squad of Bara'corian soldiers—and Ash! Thank the Lady!

Then she caught herself, for she knew who "the Lady" was now: Lilyth. It was such an inborn habit, a praise or curse every person of Edyn uttered but clearly did not understand. They prayed to the very goddess who assailed them now.

Yetteje sprinted for Ash, covering the ground in the blink of an eye. Here was someone she knew and nearly thanked the Lady again before catching herself. Old habits die hard, she thought, unceremoniously dumping the king and falling to a knee, exhaustion now threatening to overcome her as her strange combat focus faded.

The strange woman leaned in close and said, "It seems you and I have some things to talk about, Princess of EvenSea, but that can wait. I am Master Kisan and this is Master Silbane. What of Arek?"

Yetteje looked up at the woman and said between gulps of air, "She took him. She took him and she took Niall." She started to rise, her attention on the stairwell leading down into the blackness.

The king looked at Kisan and asked, "She?"

"Lilyth..." stammered Yetteje in response.

When the king still looked confused, Kisan stepped in and said, "What makes you all so obtuse, the water?"

Silbane stepped in and addressed the king, "Your son and my apprentice have been taken by the demonlord Lilyth."

The king shook his head, his attention focused now on Yetteje. "This cannot be! Where?"

The girl looked over her shoulder and down the stairwell, then back at the king. "There's a man in black following me," she said. "He's trying to kill me."

Both masters' flameskins erupted as they moved to stand between their remaining forces and the new threat.

"He can't hope to prevail against two of us," said Kisan, looking down into the gloom.

"Indeed, then why does he still come?" Silbane turned to the king and continued, "We need a more defensible area—a room— something with only one entrance."

The king seemed lost, looking about in confusion. "Lilyth?"

Silbane grabbed the king by the shoulders and shook him once, hard, "We need a defensible area, *now!*"

* * * * *

Baalor turned the corner, stalking the girl easily by her heat and scent. He came upon the body of the one she had slain, the economy of the kill impressive. One thrust. He noted that and notched his regard for the girl a bit higher. Perhaps the goddess had been right. No matter. She, along with those left in Bara'cor, would serve their gods again, no matter what blood or lineage they claimed.

He then leaned low and felt the stone, his eyes closing. There! On the stairwell, she moved with speed and he could feel his target moving with her. They would soon meet and he would complete his task.

His form illuminated in lightning and he looked inside himself. This body was powerful, more than its previous owner had known. That man did not have the knowledge Baalor did, the knowledge of the Aeris Lords. Baalor brought this to bear, his essence mastering the dead builder completely.

This body was made to respond to the Way. It could be Shaped to meet his need, his will. He concentrated and the body responded, changing in form and substance.

Slowly, his form submerged into the rock, like a man into water. The only sign of him was a slightly darker patch, a ripple, as if someone swam under the stone. The ripple made its way up the rock walls, directly for the king's forces above.

TRAPPED

I dislike death, but there are things

worse than death in this world.

To remind myself of this fact,

I occasionally seek out danger.

—Davyd Dreys, *Notes to my Sons*

A s if punctuating their danger, screams echoed up from the darkness. It was the three guards who had been with the king, but unfortunate enough to not have someone like Yetteje to haul them to safety. Their cries ended suddenly, like drowning men pulled under water.

The sound galvanized the king, who moved quickly now, the loss of Niall carefully controlled beneath years of experience commanding men on the fields of battle. He moved to a resupply room, entering it and then ushering the rest of the party in.

The room was large enough to hold twenty men comfortably. It had provisions along one wall and weapons along another. In the center were three tables, two for repairing various weapons and armor. The third a medical station and included bandages and other tools necessary to help aid the injured.

The king motioned and the guards secured Scythe, still semi-conscious, to the last table. He then positioned Ash's men near the door and turned to Kisan and confirmed, "This is Silbane?"

Before she could respond, Silbane stepped forward and backhanded the king—a stinging slap. "For Arek."

The king's men pointed swords at the master. Kisan and Ash each jumped in, pulling their respective leaders apart.

"Hold!" Bernal yelled to his men, his voice ringing with command. He put a hand up to his jaw, wincing, then spit blood. "Well met, I should say."

"I'm happy to do so again, given Bara'cor's hospitality to my apprentice."

The king's arms went wide and he exclaimed, "I did what I must, for Bara'cor!"

Silbane shrugged Kisan off like she was an afterthought, his anger visible, then he turned to the door. "Torture a boy?" He looked back at the king, and Bernal could see there was real sadness in Silbane's eyes. "I have lost him, because of you."

The king moved forward, his arms still spread. "I have lost my son, too," he said simply. Grief threatened to overcome him. "What of Jebida?"

An awkward silence fell upon the group, then Kisan said, "He fell, and provided us a means of escape."

The simple statement hammered the king, who took an involuntary step back, his hand to his chest. They had been friends for years, and it had become a fundamental belief in Bernal that nothing could hurt the firstmark. He looked down, grief etching his features as he thought about his friend. "He's dead?"

Ash stepped in and said, "But Niall is alive. He's been taken from us, and we need to focus on how to get him back."

A guard near the door jerked, his scream cut off as his head entered the wall of Bara'cor, sinking in past his neck. He braced his hands on the wall and tried to pull his granite-encased head out, but the rock was solid and unyielding. His companions each grabbed a leg, but it was no use. The man's frantic attempts slowly became lethargic, then feeble as his air ran out.

The other guards retreated, looking up at the ceiling and at the floors, trying to find their opponent, fear clearly reflected in their eyes. How could they attack something hiding inside rock?

Another guard gave a scream when he was pulled down through the floor, disappearing into the rock of Bara'cor without a mark.

"On the tables!" Silbane barked. "Get off the stone."

The group vaulted up onto the three tables in the room, ducking their heads so none were within arm's reach of a stone surface, including the ceiling. Only seven remained, including Alyx, Yetteje, and Scythe on one table, the king and Ash on a second, and Kisan and Silbane crouched together, reviewing their options on the third.

A deep voice said, "How will this help you, King of Bara'cor? You squat like a dog."

Bernal shook off his grief, at least for the moment. Battle had been joined and like it or not, Ash was correct. They needed to focus on saving the living. The dead could be grieved for later. He looked about in disgust and said, "Dogs at least fight. What hides under stone and dirt?"

The table the king and Ash stood upon began to sink into the stone. "By the Lady!" exclaimed the king. In one smooth motion he drew his sword, but Ash held his arm, listening.

* * * * *

I can find him, beloved. Draw me.

No.

Not even to save your king?

Ash looked around, his mind in turmoil, then he grabbed his blade and drew it. The green gem burst with a clear light, making the stone translucent where it struck. They could see the figure of a black assassin with his feet braced, pulling the table under by a leg.

"Prime," Kisan said, looking at Silbane. "He must have survived."

Silbane cocked his head, looking at the creature below them, then at the other master. "That thing is not Prime." He moved in a blur, centering the Way and striking the ground over the black creature's position with an open palm, before vaulting back to another table. "Tell me your name, demon!"

The blow had a visible effect, as shockwaves traveled through the rock and blasted the assassin backward, leaving the king's table at a list, half submerged in stone.

They saw the creature look up, smiling at Silbane. "I am Baalor," it said. "Do you not remember your gods, mortal?" It laughed, then moved away quickly and out of the light Tempest cast.

"What now?" Alyx asked. When the fighting had started, she had grabbed Yetteje and pushed her onto a table with herself, clearly guarding the royal heir the same way Ash had partnered with the king.

The king turned to Yetteje and said, "Tell us what happened. We need to plan our next move."

For her part, Yetteje had grabbed a proper sword to replace the fighting knife she had been using. She held the scabbarded blade, crouched on her table top and answered the king, "Arek touched a portal and Lilyth appeared."

Silbane spoke first. "What happened to the Gate?"

Yetteje looked at him, brows knit in consternation. "Nothing. She just appeared. I could hear them speaking."

"What did they say?" asked the king.

"She said to tell you she has Niall and if you don't turn yourself over to her by nightfall, she will kill everyone left inside Bara'cor."

"By last count, there are close to nine hundred soldiers and their families still in this fortress," the king said to Ash.

Yetteje looked anxiously around, then said in a small voice, "There's something else."

"What?" Silbane asked.

Her golden eyes met Silbane's faded blue ones and she said, "She said Arek is her son."

Silbane drew back, shock registering on his face for a second time. He looked at Kisan, who also stood speechless.

* * * * *

Kisan took the news differently. She had the visions of Giridian *and* Silbane to look at, and knew what they meant. The Conclave was right. Arek destroyed the Way, but what would be the effect if he were taken to Lilyth's realm? She realized in a flash he would begin to absorb even more power, as those beings were a pure embodiment of the Way.

This is what Thoth had feared, the Aeris would safeguard him trying to unravel the secret of his existence, and in doing so would create a creature who would undo them all. It was imperative they found Arek as quickly as possible, no matter where he was, and stop him.

A moment passed then Silbane asked, "Did you see or hear anything else?"

Yetteje slowly nodded, then said, "Lilyth's creatures are everywhere, thousands of them. They look like mistfrights, but much worse. They control the lower levels and sift through the cracks of the walls like smoke. One of the guards of Bara'cor . . . something entered him. When it did, he became something else." She pointed to the ground where Baalor had been. "That thing inside the stone. I'm not sure, but it looks just like the man Arek and I killed earlier. Niall said he is a dwarf."

Silbane looked at Kisan and said, "We have to get to the Gate."

"I must rescue my son," said the king. "That means getting to this portal you speak of as well, but I cannot let the people of Bara'cor perish."

"Lilyth will kill you if you turn yourself over to her," warned Ash. He looked at Silbane and said, "Our only chance is to try and find a way out of Bara'cor."

"Perhaps I can help."

The group turned, startled by the raspy voice. It came from Scythe, still bound to the medical table in the back.

Kisan was first to speak. "Help who? Us or them?" she said sarcastically. She turned to the rest of the group. "This man tried to kill us. He may be responsible for the deaths of the other fortresses and their inhabitants."

Yetteje's head whipped down at that and her blade sang as it cleared her scabbard, the point centered on Scythe's chest in the blink of an eye.

"Wait!" cried Silbane. He held up a forestalling hand and said, "I mindread him, Princess. He is not wholly responsible."

Yetteje looked at Silbane, and Kisan could tell she would not blindly accept what he said. "How could he not be responsible? At the very least, he didn't stop them, and that makes him guilty." She turned her glowing amber gaze back to the bound man. "You deserve death."

Alyx, who had been standing right next to her, grabbed and pulled her in. "Easy, Princess," she whispered, "if he is responsible, I pledge my blade will follow yours. But rest easy for now, and let the king sort this out."

Scythe's watched the interaction calmly. "If you read me, you know I want to reach the Gate," he said. "It is my only purpose."

When Silbane didn't answer, Kisan said, "If you let him go, you'll be as crazy as he is."

Silbane shook his head slowly, looking at Scythe, then his gaze took in the rest of the room. He seemed to come to a decision and then said slowly, "I present to you Duncan Illrys, once Lore Father of the First Council, and last of the Old Lords."

Journal Entry 27

An idea has begun to take seed and grow. I battled and lost, was hunted and preyed upon until I rose and stood firm. I came to this world already an archmage, powerful in the Way. Yet, I could not prevail until I had suffered. Why?

I believe it is because my mind needed the victories to build its self-image of power, a surety in the conviction I could survive.

I have heard Captain Dreys say a bladesman cannot cross live blades until years pass and he becomes familiar with failure. That he cannot block till he has felt the wooden knot of a *bohkir* leave a lump (he called it "love") on his skull.

Ritual, whether physical or mental, is not enough. We must face overwhelming odds and prevail or our knowledge has no meaning, no root. Like a misplanted tree, it topples in the slightest breeze of adversity.

Wisdom comes from experience and experience from bad judgment. It is our victories over missteps that define us, give us confidence and strength.

I now think I know a way to defeat these Aeris, these mythborn, these legends come to life. I cannot attack them in the traditional sense.

Instead, I must attack something deeper ... I must create something more powerful, something that can hold power over the Aeris Lords and those who use the Way.

My companion returns. We have a quiet dinner planned, while my elven guard patrols the castle walls and grounds. Her company is the one thing I look forward to in this accursed place.

THE OLD LORDS

The surest sign of fear is anger.

The surest sign of strength is kindness.

—*Altan proverb*

Stunned silence followed as the people in the room digested that Duncan Illrys, who had been killed with his wife over two hundred years ago, lay secured as a prisoner on a table a few paces from them. An arrow had pierced them together, if those old legends were to be believed. They were the last survivors against Lilyth, and the first executed by the king's decree.

Kisan broke the silence, "Are you sure?"

Silbane took a deep breath and said, "Yes."

Just then, the walls of the room began to buckle and groan. With a crack, they shifted in place and began to grind inward. The room began to collapse in on itself! Dust and rock fell from the ceiling as they folded under the pressure of the walls. Weapons fell from their places and were crushed by the grinding stone.

"What's going on?" yelled the king.

Scythe, now revealed as Duncan, said, "Baalor. He has called upon the rock of Bara'cor. We must get out of here."

Silbane vaulted from his table to the king's, then to Duncan's, landing lightly next to Yetteje and Alyx. He knelt next to the captured lore father and said, "I want your Binding Oath, if I free you, you will assist us. It is the only way you will see *her* again."

Kisan moved to the doorway and tried to push the door open. It would not budge, having been pinned by the crushing walls until not even a crack remained around the frame. She shared this with Silbane, who yelled back, "Be ready!"

Duncan looked at the walls grinding inward, the ceiling as it bent under the pressure, then at the adept. "By the blood of my forefathers, I bind myself," he said. "My oath as Keeper of the Old Lore, no harm will befall you or your allies by my action or inaction." He extended his palm, which Silbane cut along with his own. When their blood touched, a yellow flash occurred at the binding of the Blood Oath, then just as quickly disappeared.

Silbane freed the *prana* locks he had placed on the archmage, but could do nothing about the torc. Only someone without Talent could free that and Silbane wasn't sure he wanted Duncan released yet, regardless of his oath.

He turned his attention to Yetteje, needing to calm her down. "Princess, believe me when I tell you this man is the only hope we have to save Arek and the king's son," Silbane said. "Please let that mean more to you than revenge."

The ground shook again as the walls continued their inexorable movement inward, crushing weapons, armor, and supplies under stone.

Yetteje looked at Silbane with anger in her eyes. Then her gaze fell upon the king, his face etched with desperation. She looked back down at the man now revealed as Duncan and said, "When this is over, you'll die by my hands."

"Nothing dies, Princess," said the ancient lore father. His voice came out tired, though his mouth moved into a smirk.

"You're going to wish that were true," was her only reply. She looked at him a moment longer, disgust etched on her face, then vaulted from the table to the king's.

Silbane looked at Duncan and asked, "What are our choices?"

The walls had now moved in the length of a spear. They had only a few moments left.

"Break open the door," Duncan said. "We will face Baalor on open ground."

Silbane locked eyes with Kisan. "We smash the door together." He then moved with blurring speed. They met at the door, open palms striking the stone surface with an impact detonating the stone itself, exploding it outward.

"Quickly, hurry!" yelled Silbane to the people in the room.

They streamed out and into the open landing just outside the supply room. The air was still, silent and dead; the sound of stone grinding and crushing isolated to the room behind them.

Duncan came to stand beside Silbane, wiping his face clean. "My powers, this accursed torc?" he said, fingering the metal collar, still sealed shut by ancient magehunter magic. "Will you not free me?" A small titter erupted, as if he laughed at what he had just said, but it was quickly stifled.

Silbane shook his head. "Kisan pulled me away before I could assimilate your memories. I know who you are, and maybe a bit more. Because of that, I understand you. Do not mistake that for trust."

"You'll need my strength to get out of here," Duncan pressed. "My interests are aligned with yours, and I took the oath." He appeared calm now, in control. "What made you think about your first meeting with Themun? I did that, for I wished to see him as you did. I am a lore father too and would help any pupil of the Way."

Silbane looked back at Duncan, so consumed with revenge to have become something like Scythe. How long would this moment of clarity last for the tortured mage? Yet he *was* a lore father, if misguided. "Perhaps."

Silbane moved past Duncan to Ash and said, "Draw your blade."

The firstmark looked at the older man, caution warring against need.

"You have strength in you to resist," Silbane added, "and we have need of it now."

With a sigh, Ash drew the blade and held her aloft, high above his head. Her clear light erupted from the green gem, illuminating the landing, making the stone and surrounding areas translucent to their sight. Nothing appeared to be lurking within the stone.

"We should make for one of the exits," said Alyx. "Our men will be there."

"We will die before we get ten paces," remarked Duncan,. "There is no escape from Bara'cor. I doubt very much we are still on our plane of existence." He looked at the sergeant, "As for your men, they are dead already."

"What do you mean?" asked the king. "You are talking about hundreds of lives!"

Duncan turned a scathing gaze upon the king, who took an involuntary step backward, startled by its vehemence. "Galadine, your death cannot come too soon."

Ash and the sergeant moved to stand between the two, their swords at the ready.

Duncan ignored them and faced the king, nodding to the bow strapped across his back, "Valor." The king stared at the mage. "The last I saw your bow," he said, "it held an arrow sighted at me and my wife, just before a Galadine like you used it to execute her."

Silbane stepped in, his tone mollifying, "This is not the same king who took her away from you. That man has been dead for over ten generations."

Duncan continued to stare, his gaze never leaving the king's bow. When he answered Silbane, it was with a hint of unbalanced laughter, a teeter on the edge of a mental precipice, but quickly recovered. A calm then came over him and he said, "Don't worry. I bound myself by oath and will not harm him, but I do not have to enjoy a craven's company." His mirth disappeared suddenly and he spat on the king's feet and moved away.

"Then answer me," said Kisan, drawing Duncan's attention. "What do we do now?"

Duncan looked at the younger master and said, "Baalor is here, waiting for us to move. Our only chance is to make for the Gate. The fortress has been lost."

The king shook off the hesitation and surprise that had come from Duncan's verbal attack and responded, his voice strident, "I will make for the Gate regardless, with or without you."

Disdain in his voice, Duncan looked back at the king. "You are an imbecile, from a long line of dim-witted tyrants. Your only skills are war and death." He turned, ignoring the king, and said, "Baalor, this hiding ill becomes you."

A voice like stone grinding on stone answered Duncan, "Well said, Lore Father. I grow weary as well."

Silbane looked at Duncan with surprise, asking, "You know him?"

Duncan nodded. "You know him, too."

Silbane shook his head, ready to deny this, but Duncan continued, "He is the Lord of Lightning, his emblem graces that cretin's shield." He nodded at the king's shield and the double lightning bolts framing the Galadine lion. "The Old Lords faced him before, over two hundred years ago, when Lilyth was first defeated."

* * * * *

The air in front of the group darkened, then coalesced into the form of the assassin. It bowed once, palms to forehead, but before anyone could move, a frantic crackle of lightning and power flowed from the ground, up and across it. In response, Baalor began to change. The builder's body grew, rippling as muscle and sinew reknit, responding with ease to the will of the Way and the Aeris Lord's command.

Baalor chose an ancient form, a juggernaut armored in black metal, polished to an almost pearlescent hue. He stood almost ten feet tall, a battlefield behemoth armored in pure ebonite, the black metal gleaming in the flickering light of the few remaining torches.

He drew a breath, as if drawing in the very substance of the air around him, then his eyes opened, crackling blue from behind a black helm. He clenched his bare hands then smashed them together with the ring of metal striking metal.

"It has been long since I have matched myself against a Galadine lord," Baalor said. "Come, let us see who is still worthy of his name."

Silbane and Kisan moved to confront him, and Silbane said, "You will have to be satisfied with facing us. Not quite so noble born, but we should do."

"Make your way to the Gate, but carefully," Kisan told Yetteje. "We will follow when we can."

Yetteje looked at Kisan with wide eyes, clearly afraid of the prospect. "No. We will not make it without you."

The master looked at the young girl, then said, "You remind me of someone I once knew." She smiled, and added, "Stand firm. Either way you'll learn something."

Baalor looked down at the throng before him. He could see Tempest shining from the blade held by another man and smiled in anticipation of seeing her again. It has been centuries, he thought fondly.

In addition to this, the one who had spoken, the Old Lord, something was *wrong* with him. His power lay muffled, held captive. The rest were inconsequential, food for the army of Lilyth long before night fell, no matter what Baalor did.

Baalor held himself as a warrior first, yearning for the test of battle. The deaths of those he had entombed within Bara'cor's walls were reserved for the ones who did not dream. These few, however, deserved his full attention and he stepped forward and saluted them again in an archaic way, palm to forehead followed by a downward sweep. "I come to test the dreams of the Galadine who holds Bara'cor. The rest are the Lady's concern, not mine. Stand ready, for I give no quarter and ask none."

From behind Silbane, Duncan said, "Release me. I will fight with you."

Silbane ignored him, addressing Baalor again, "I am Silbane, and seek to recover my apprentice. Lord Baalor, we have no quarrel with you. We make our way to the Gate and to your master. Can we not avoid this confrontation?"

Baalor looked at this one closer, for the Way flowed with strength through him. He was powerful and that thought made Baalor wary. He didn't know who his Ascended was. His deep voice sounded like gravel when he said, "You must answer to the Eye of the Sun. To pass me, surrender the Galadine."

The king began to step forward, but Ash and Alyx interceded, and Ash said, "We'll not! Bring your worst." He looked back at the king and said, "You heard him. They mean to kill you. Do not sacrifice yourself needlessly."

The god encased in ebonite smiled at that. "It is sooth, for you carry an old friend of mine. Releasing her will be a pleasure."

* * * * *

I never liked him, said Tempest to a surprised Ash.

What? asked the new firstmark.

Those of power know of one another. Is it not the same in your world?

Ash could not comprehend everything Tempest was saying. What was an "Aeris?" Now it seemed more important than ever he speak with one of the adepts, but he had to first pay attention to this battle. He surveyed the scene. Perhaps this creature was more dangerous than the three assassins they had faced earlier, but he hardly seemed insurmountable.

Baalor stepped back. Lightning crackled around him, its tang flavoring the air with a coppery taste. White power arced and flowed from the stones surrounding him, then coalesced into a shield of lightning. Power continued to flow, flashing across his ebonite armor in blue-white arcs that left purple afterimages in the eyes of those who watched.

Eons ago the people of Edyn had worshipped him as the god of lightning and in that, they had been correct. Baalor commanded the power of storms, a living god who once again walked this world.

Ash sighed, correcting his earlier overconfidence. *I guess nothing is easy today.*

Do not worry, beloved. I will protect you.

No! You will not use any of my friends.

The sword seemed frustrated and Ash could almost see her with crossed arms, angry at his stubbornness. Still, he held his will inflexible, and finally she replied, *Very well.*

The adepts' flameskins erupted, orange for Kisan and yellow for Silbane, dancing up their forms in protective sheathes. The rest of the party drew weapons and spread out, knowing this creature stood between them gaining the Gate, and rescuing Niall and Arek.

Baalor looked down at the group and held up a hand. "Hold." The creature clenched his fist and the torc on Duncan's neck shattered into a thousand pieces.

"I remember much of the strength of the Old Lords," said Baalor, "and would see it again for myself."

* * * * *

Duncan breathed in deep. Pure power, no longer restricted by the metal collar, flooded his senses, returning the caress of the Way and healing him. His sight grew, magnified, drinking in all the details of the moment. He could see with a kind of clarity he had never realized he had until he'd lost his connection to the Way. It suffused him and he felt stronger than a hundred men. He looked at Baalor, bowed, and said, "I thank you, sir."

Baalor stepped away from the group, backing up slowly. "I would face equals in battle, mortal," his deep voice boomed.

Silbane and Kisan looked at each other, clearly not knowing what to do. Duncan had his powers and could easily side with Baalor, making things difficult for them.

But I will not. I gave my bonded oath and it requires I do not leave you. Let us face Baalor together, Duncan mindspoke.

Both adepts heard him and realized they had little choice. Baalor was not going to wait. Then battle was upon them and they had to trust Duncan meant what he just said and his moment of clarity would last long enough to matter.

Baalor ran forward, shaking the ground with every step, his arm reaching behind him in a fisted grip. In that grip appeared a mace of power, lightning dancing along its length. He swung it at Silbane, who jumped up and over the Aeris Lord, landing lightly behind him.

Kisan moved in quickly, striking two blows to the armor, resulting in a flash of orange fire, but little else. She ducked under the swing of the mace, then leapt backward to land well out of its reach.

Bernal had scrambled to the left, unslinging Valor in one smooth motion while Baalor turned with him as if he were a lodestone connected to the king. Two arrows a heartbeat apart sped at the demon warrior, the shafts true to their mark. They bit Baalor in the neck and shattered against his lightning shield.

Yetteje and Alyx had gone right, quickly scrambling out of the way of the first swing. The creature turned to follow the king, putting its back to the two. Yetteje didn't hesitate. With her newfound combat sense, she dived in, stabbing with her sword. The blade skittered and sparked off the ebonite armor, forcing her to duck and roll as the creature swung a backhanded blow with its mace.

Alyx had been half a step behind Yetteje, trying to get a clean blow in on the creature's flank. When she saw the mace heading for the princess, she didn't hesitate and threw herself forward, catching the blow on her shield side. Had she been carrying a shield, she may have fared better.

The lightning mace hit the sergeant with a flash of white and a detonation that could be felt, hurling her across the room to fall in a crumpled heap against one wall. Dark, sinuous smoke began to cover her body, entering her through every opening, even the very pores of her skin.

Ash dodged the first mace blow and the second, rolling to Baalor's front and stabbing upward. Tempest bounced off the armor and Baalor roared in fury. He swatted downward with the mace, missing Ash's head by less than a hand's width and cracking the stone of Bara'cor in a radial pattern.

Pure power arced from the outstretched hands of Duncan and struck Baalor like lightning, bolts of pure energy blasting into the ebonite with a crack that shattered the air. Each strike drove the demon farther back, exploding against his armor in flashes of white and blue.

Baalor went to one knee. "Good," the demon said. "I had thought the old ways forgotten."

Then the demon heaved up and stone blocks the size of a man's body launched themselves at the king, Duncan, and the two masters. They scattered as the blocks exploded against the walls and ground, filling the air with dust and pulverized rock.

"But you attack me with a dear old friend," the gargantuan Aeris Lord laughed, then moved forward again as Duncan's lightning arced harmlessly across Baalor's armor.

* * * * *

Yetteje watched wide-eyed, crouched low to one side, and for the moment, it seemed, forgotten. Alyx had saved her, but where was the sergeant? She felt a cold hand on her shoulder and turned to look. Behind her stood Sergeant Alyx Stemmer, but her eyes blazed an unearthly white. Black smoke moved down the arm of the thing that had once been a soldier of Bara'cor, and came toward her. Yetteje screamed and jumped back, but the demon sergeant scrambled forward like a predator.

"Nothing dies, mortal. They serve," it said with an almost feline hiss.

Yetteje came to her feet, her blade ready. At first, she felt an unreasoning terror, but something washed it away. She faced the creature who had once been her friend and an anger began to rise, anger that once again someone close to her had been taken away, and anger at herself for fearing it.

She focused her anger and held the demon's gaze. It hesitated, as if sensing something had changed. Yetteje felt time slow, a bubble of calm surrounding her in the midst of the battle against Baalor. She looked at her friend and in a small but determined voice asked, "Alyx, can you hear me?"

The demon that was Alyx paused, its face contorting as a struggle raged within its body. It clawed, then scratched at itself. "You cannot be freed," it said in a guttural voice, but it did not seem to be talking to Yetteje, rather to itself.

Yetteje didn't know what to do. She had killed that other creature, only to find out she had in fact killed a defender of Bara'cor. The demon within him had simply escaped and all she had accomplished was to kill someone unfortunate enough to have been possessed. Now her friend, Alyx, had been taken. She didn't want to kill her too.

"Let my friend go," she demanded, taking a step forward. "You cannot have her."

The creature seemed to stop struggling with itself for a moment and Alyx's eyes returned to normal from their blaze of white. "Princess . . . give no quarter," she said in a voice struggling for control. *"Strike true."*

Then whatever was left of the sergeant disappeared and the creature dived forward in a flash of power and strength, claws and fangs bared, directly for Yetteje's face.

The princess's reaction was almost automatic, as if something else controlled her. She moved in a blur, cutting through the sergeant's outstretched arm, then her neck in one smooth motion. The body toppled, going to its knees before falling to the ground.

Yetteje could see the black smoke flow out like blood, seeping into the ground, disappearing into the cracks, just like it had before. A small sob escaped her, but the lesson her friend had taught her on the wall had not been forgotten. In the end, she had done what she had to do to survive. Now, she thought with remorse, she would have to live with it.

* * * * *

Bernal ducked out of the way of the tumbling stone and launched two more arrows. Both shattered without effect. He then saw Yetteje cut down Sergeant Stemmer, whose eyes had blazed white. A horrible realization that each of them who fell would become one of these demons dawned on him. Worse, the one known as Baalor wasn't hurt, not yet. His heart told him it would only be a matter of time before this demon warrior and his brethren possessed them all.

* * * * *

The mages had decided to take a chance and use their mindspeak to communicate their strategy instantly between them. Duncan launched another blast, but this time using fire. Both Silbane and Kisan blurred into motion and struck the spot of the fireball's impact with timed punches detonating with force.

These pushed the demon back, but did no appreciable damage to the ebonite armor encasing his body. Furthermore, while mindspeaking made their strategy instantaneous and therefore difficult to defend against, it was also burning through their reserves of energy at a prodigious rate, and they all knew it.

The mace struck again, barely missing Silbane and catching Kisan a glancing blow. Her flameskin erupted in an orange flash, protecting her from the worst of it, but hurling her to land near Yetteje, who scrambled over to her and cried, "They took Alyx!"

Kisan looked at the princess and the body that lay near, then rolled to her feet. "You did what you must. If I fall, do the same for me." She gave her a quick, reassuring smile, then sped back into the fray.

More black shapes entered the chamber, a ghostly audience, waiting for the chance to enter one of them should they succumb to Baalor's might.

A second smash of the mace and Duncan and Silbane found themselves tossed into the air, landing in a tangle of arms and legs. They had numerous cuts from flying shards of stone, but were otherwise unhurt, an amazing piece of luck considering Duncan did not have the advantage of a protective flameskin.

Silbane looked at the other, who absentmindedly wiped blood from a cut on his forehead out of his eyes. "How did you kill them," Silbane asked, "in the old days?"

"We didn't." Duncan blinked some blood away, then said, "We had fighters trained for this sort of thing."

"Bladesmen," Silbane stated matter-of-factly. "Why am I not surprised?"

* * * * *

Ash moved in between strikes, knowing blocking the mace was impossible. He dived in and stabbed at the knee joint, a small opening in the ebonite. Tempest plunged in, but seemed to have little effect.

Baalor shrugged off the stabbing pain in his knee and kicked out, catching the firstmark on his shield arm. Pain exploded in Ash's arm as he felt himself hurled away.

You must use me, beloved!

No!

You must. You cannot survive against an Aeris Lord without my help, and you withhold your own true might!

Ash looked around, dazed. The demon lord had turned to face the king and he couldn't do anything about it.

What? he asked.

You fight as if you have forgotten the old ways, my love. I must help.

Ash shook his head and rose to his feet. *No! I forbid it. I have seen how you help.*

When you fall, I will do what I must.

The sword did not say anything else, but Ash could almost see her form, sullen and angry at what she thought was an obviously stupid idea. He realized he needed to fight and survive, or she would do anything to keep him alive.

* * * * *

The king watched the carnage, even as the demon warrior turned its lightning gaze toward him. They had to make it to the Gate! It was Niall's only chance of rescue. He knew what he had to do and turned toward Silbane.

"Silbane!" he yelled. "You have to go!" The king motioned to the exit leading down to the cistern catacombs.

Silbane and Duncan moved in unison, striking the giant armored demon with fire and fist, while Kisan struck a third time, distracting Baalor as the other two made their way over to the king.

Silbane was the first there and said, "What are you talking about?"

The king looked at the armored demon and said, "We have to make it to the Gate, or Niall and Arek cannot be rescued."

"So you want to run?" Duncan sneered. "Did you not see before? He can follow us through the walls." He looked at the king with disgust. "The Golden Lion of Bara'cor . . ." he said, making the title sound like a curse. "Virtuous to the end."

The king looked at Duncan with sadness in his eyes, but addressed Silbane, "Go. Take the party and get to the Gate. I will surrender myself here."

Silbane looked at the king in shock, then said in a soft voice, "You'll be killed, Bernal. What about your son?"

"This is the only way for the people of Bara'cor to survive. This is the only way for Niall to survive. I'll not see him, but he *will* live. I trust you to that."

Silbane's gaze did not waver. "We can defeat Baalor."

The king smiled and said, "You don't believe that."

He looked over the battlefield, watching Ash hack at the giant warrior with no effect, then roll as the mace clipped his shoulder. The firstmark went sprawling, lightning crackling around his body.

"Sergeant Stemmer is dead. He'll kill you all, one by one, to get to me." Bernal looked back at Silbane and said, "If I surrender, he will stay here. It gives you the chance to gain the Gate."

Duncan and Silbane both nodded, and in their strange way seemed to communicate with Kisan, who grabbed Yetteje and sped around the demon's mace. They zigzagged while Ash's fall had distracted him, unaware of the plan.

Then the king yelled, "Baalor!"

The Aeris Lord stopped, his arm upraised to smash down where Ash lay. The firstmark looked dazed, slowly getting to his feet and shuffling out of Baalor's range. He fumbled through the carnage, joining the rest of the group with an unspoken question in his eyes. His left arm hung useless.

"You claim to be honorable," said the king, addressing the Aeris Lord.

"I claim nothing. My actions speak for themselves," intoned the giant. He turned and faced the king. "As do yours."

Bernal Galadine stepped forward. "I have no taste for dying without a challenge, and neither do you, it seems. I challenge you, then, to single combat. You will allow my companions to leave. They are of no concern to you."

Ash stepped forward, but was held back by Silbane. "What? You'll not survive!"

The king looked back, handing his bow to Ash, and said, "Take Valor. Give it to Niall when you see him."

Ash ignored it, struggling to get past Silbane. The older master took the bow and said to the firstmark, "It is his son's only chance."

"No!" said Ash. "There has to be another way!"

"I accept your challenge, Galadine of Bara'cor," Baalor said with a slight bow. "The men of Bara'cor will be allowed to leave its walls, as promised. Your companions may gain the Gate, should the Goddess allow it. If I fall, you will still turn yourself over to Lilyth's forces, or your men will die." He bowed again, then stepped back to wait for the king to approach.

Ash then turned to plead to Kisan, who had just arrived with Yetteje and said, "You can't let him do this!"

Kisan looked at the king, then addressed Ash, "Lord Baalor has accepted the king's challenge, in exchange for the safe passage of everyone left in Bara'cor. We can now attempt the Gate and find Arek. What would you have us do?"

Bernal looked at Ash and asked, "Your duty lies with the king of Bara'cor, yes?"

Ash looked stricken and replied, "Of course, my liege."

"He has been captured and taken to another realm." Bernal met Ash's eyes and said, "Rescue him, if you have any love for me."

Something happened then to Ash. He stopped struggling and collapsed in on himself. His body seemed to deflate in defeat. Safeguarding Niall was as much his duty as obeying the king. Now it all seemed to be conspiring to worm doubt and defeat into his every thought. He fell to one knee and crouched there, unsure what to do.

Yetteje rushed forward and said to the king, "You don't have to do this. If I could speak for Niall, he wouldn't want to lose you."

Bernal smiled at the girl. "Your father expected me to defend you." He stroked her scarred cheek. "I choose my end. Most men are never given that chance."

Yetteje stepped back, tears in her eyes. She moved over and took the war bow from Silbane and in a choked voice said, "I'll make sure Niall gets this."

Bernal put a callused finger under her chin and lifted it till their eyes met. He smiled then brought her into a hug, whispering, "Do not forget, *you* are a Galadine too."

When he released her, she fell back a step, but nodded. She would carry forward, for her family and for his.

Kisan came forward, put a hand on the king's arm and squeezed. "I wish we had met earlier."

The king nodded. "Me too, Kisan."

"Do not worry for the princess. She will be under my wing."

Bernal smiled, then drew Azani, the steel ringing with a pure sound in the dust-filled space. He unslung his shield, the golden lion of Bara'cor rampant on its face. It settled on his arm like an old friend, a companion he had known his entire life.

"Go, find Niall and your apprentice. Bring them safely home."

Kisan bowed once in respect. The group moved back, away from the king. The stairwell stood behind them, its black maw open like a mouth. Yetteje slung Valor across her back, its great recurved shape making her seem somehow smaller. She supported Ash, who looked battered and forlorn. Together, they made their way to the stairwell with Silbane in the lead, their eyes still on the king.

Duncan looked at this man, this father, then looked down, shaking his head. He turned to follow the group, but paused. He then turned back to the king and said, "I can make your end quick, less painful than Baalor will offer. It may be of some solace."

The king shook his head. "No, but tell my son my thoughts were of him."

Duncan did not move, watching the king as if drinking in the character of his soul. He looked at the runebow across Yetteje's back and seemed to consider something. Then he snapped his fingers. A small sparkle erupted, then disappeared. The only acknowledgment was from Baalor, who grumbled, "It is sooth, but pointless."

Duncan looked at Baalor and said, "Perhaps."

"He will meet you," Baalor said, taking another step back, "one way or the other."

Duncan then turned his attention back to the king, his gaze becoming fragile as his tenuous link to sanity began to erode. "You may not thank me later," whispered the archmage, "but I wish someone had done the same for me." Then a small giggle erupted and he leaned forward and confided, "She *waits* for me."

The king's steady gaze met Duncan's shifting and feverish one, as if the archmage thought he conveyed something real. He then watched as the man spun and headed for the stairwell, all the while shaking his head and muttering to himself.

In the short time he'd known Duncan, Bernal was convinced the man was mentally unbalanced. For all he knew, the archmage had just brittled his sword and shield. Duncan had hated Galadines for so long, it was doubtful he would have done anything beneficial. Still, he hoped the man would find some peace.

Then his eyes were drawn to Yetteje, who raised a small hand in farewell. He gave her a small wink and a smile, watching as she, too, turned to enter the black maw with Ash.

Bernal's mind then turned to thoughts of his wife, Yevaine, waiting for him in Haven. He hoped she would not be angry at his decision for too long. Allowing his men safe passage was the only decision he could make, but knowing her, she would never forgive him.

He smiled fondly at the thought, then turned and faced the giant warrior, sword and shield in hand. Stepping forward, Bernal raised his sword in salute to Baalor. "Come, Lord of Lightning. I need a partner for this dance."

YEVAINE

Let them stab, strike, and slice.

Let them come with all their might.

You are a Bladesman, honed and true.

With every miss and turn,

they fall on your waiting sword,

eager for death.

—*Kensei Tsao, The Book of Blades*

"A gain? Do you not tire of this?" Legate Ellis Tir opined, clearly frustrated. He pulled his crimson robe closer, peering at Queen Galadine with the distinct amber eyes characteristic of those noble born to House Tir.

"What did you expect?" she answered. "Sycophants and schemers."

Her mailed sleeves jingled as she adjusted her armor, a reminder to these courtiers that she was born with blade in hand. They had been granted audience with the Senate two times already to petition aid for Bara'cor and had twice been denied. Part of her longed to tell Captain Kalindor to take the city and put these politicians to sword.

Still, the peace was fragile but beneficial to the land. Her husband had earned it and it would not fall upon her to undo what he had done.

She pushed her way past the legate but asked, "I still have your support?"

"Always," he responded, "but unless you have something new, their answer will be the same. This time, though, they may have you held."

"Let them try," she said, her mood dark. Then she addressed the other man escorting her, "You'll accompany me into the hall."

Captain Tyrus Kalindor nodded, his gray hair pulled back into a tight tail. One eye of piercing blue shone from beneath a trim brow. The other, or what was left of it, sat behind a black eye patch with the golden lion of House Galadine stamped upon it. He did not hesitate at the unusual request, but replied with an unexpected and almost melodious baritone of a bard's voice, "Of course, I will be wherever you are, my queen."

Legate Tir spun and hurried to catch up, coming to Yevaine's other side. "Please tell me you're not going to challenge Spaiten again."

"The Legate of Dawnlight has a special dislike for me," she replied, still heading for the Senatorial Hall.

"What do you expect?" Kalindor asked. "He is in charge of Dawnlight's interests now, and they are not always aligned with those of Bara'cor."

"Do our soldiers not stand at the walls of Bara'cor holding the horde from Haven's green fields?" she replied, frustration clear in her voice.

"No word from Dawnlight, not in a fortnight. Then the explosion at Land's Edge. Do you think those soldiers still live?" Ellis looked at Kalindor and continued, "What of Prince Niall, and my niece? I fear the worst for them and Edyn if we have lost King Galadine and two heirs."

The captain didn't answer, instead he reached out with a lean arm and put a gentle hand on his queen's arm, slowing her headlong charge. When they stopped, he looked around to be sure they were alone, then offered, "You are Queen of Bara'cor, but do not forget you are also King Aeonian's daughter. Ill thoughts brew with your arrival here in Haven."

Legate Tir, now emboldened by Kalindor's support added, "Your father has not been heard from in some time. Spaiten has declared him lost and secured his position as Dawnlight's regent, as has Algren Justeces for Shornhelm." He was quiet for a moment, then added, "I could do the same for EvenSea, but am not so eager to set aside my brother's crown. It seems . . . ill-mannered."

Yevaine regarded the two, both trusted men and loyal to Bara'cor and House Galadine, despite their current disagreement. Then she let go of a breath she had not realized she'd held and looked at the man she had known for the better part of her life. "You have always been a stalwart friend, Ellis, and our bickering is unseemly. We ask your pardon."

A moment passed, then Kalindor also stepped back and bowed to the legate, his fist to his chest. "Your pardon, though it felt a bit like our sparring days back at the academy," he added with a chuckle.

Ellis Tir also bowed, shaking his head and placing a conciliatory hand on each of their shoulders. "I recall you getting the better of me then, and now. These are trying times." He was quiet for a moment, then looked at the queen apologetically. "I do not mean to focus on my own concerns, but how is my niece? Does she fare well under the siege?"

"Yetteje was fine when I left. This war is forcing everyone to grow up fast, but the girl has grit."

Ellis nodded slowly, almost to himself. "You should see her practicing," he said with the half smile of a fond memory. "I used to call her 'Tir's Kitten' when she was a child, but put steel in her hands and she'll run a man through."

The queen took the legate's hand from her shoulder and gave it a reassuring squeeze. "The future of both our Houses is at Bara'cor. They cannot be abandoned."

The legate took a deep breath and said, "I agree, and my concern is not purely familial. There are things more dire afoot."

"Such as?" inquired the queen.

A frown replaced the smile and he said, "They will seek to declare King Galadine lost."

Kalindor looked at the legate and asked, "Why, and why this rush to declare regents? That serves no one."

"Not for your immediate problem," Ellis replied, "but unlike legates, regents may act without royal sanction in the name of their House. There is a longer game being played here."

Kalindor cursed. "What schemes do these regents harbor?"

Legate Tir looked about as if to reassure himself of their privacy, then said, "If the four kings are declared lost, and there is no proof of life for the heirs, it confers rule to the regents."

The captain held his breath, his single eye glinting dangerously in the torchlight. "They would dare usurp House Galadine?"

"Dare?" asked the legate. "The law is archaic but designed to keep succession intact, and as decreed by ancient *Galadine* rule it falls to the next male heir. By declaring King Bernal lost, they also effectively seal the fate of my House. If he has perished—"

"Hold your tongue," snapped the queen. "My husband and son are very much alive."

"If they have perished," continued the legate in a firm but not unkind voice, "rule will fall to the regents, led by the Chancellor of Haven. The regents will determine who rules next from the surviving heirs of the four great noble Houses, according to the ancient Laws of Succession."

"And who is next in line?" asked Captain Kalindor.

An uncomfortable silence followed, into which Ellis Tir finally said, "As I am the only confirmed living male, it would fall to me and House Tir."

Kalindor's one eye squinted. "You would raise yourself—"

"Do you think they will allow rule to pass to me?" interrupted the Legate of EvenSea in exasperation. "I will not survive long enough to even see the Imperial Crown! My loyalties to House Galadine have always been clear."

Yevaine sighed, then looked at Kalindor and said, "Ellis is right, with Bernal gone, they only need to censure me and silence him. We must take decisive action if we are to survive this day. Summon our personal guard."

She thought for a moment, and something the legate had said earlier about heirs and succession stuck with her. Motioning to the legate to come closer, she took a moment to frame her thoughts, then carefully inquired, "If Princess Yetteje was here, who would speak for House Tir?"

"She would, as ranking noble in the direct line of succession. Though she cannot hold the Imperial Crown, her claim to Tir's throne supersedes mine," Ellis answered. "Why?"

The queen nodded to herself, her eyes faraway as she fell deep in thought. Given what the legate had said, it was certain the regents would use the law to wrest control from the Houses. It was also just as certain their lives hung in the balance, yet the law itself might offer them a slim hope.

Then she focused and met Ellis's concerned look, her gaze narrowing. "Explain the Laws of Succession to me again. This time in detail."

* * * * *

Algren Justeces sat at one end of the semi-circular table in the Senatorial Hall. The chamber was large, designed to accommodate the public for hearings on matters of state. It was square, but rounded on the end from where he and the other legates officiated, with vertical columns set on either side framing a central seating area arranged into long parallel benches.

Stationed at each column were soldiers wearing the crimson and white of Haven's elite Praetorians. They stood impassive, like living statues, sworn to uphold and defend the Senate with their very lives.

"You seem wistful," remarked a deep voice to Algren's right.

He turned to face Merric Spaiten and said, "No, just thinking." Algren adjusted his seat and leaned back. "The queen comes before us a third time, and my heart regrets what we must do."

Spaiten pursed his lips and nodded. "No word from the Kings of the Wastes, save Bernal sending his wife to beg for aid at the expense of Haven's defense. We both know what must be done."

Algren nodded slowly and said, "Perhaps, yet in my heart I dread it. The power to destroy Land's Edge ... rumors of demonkind and dark magic, specters of sorrow that hunt our children again ..."

"Which is why we must act and hold this line. Captain Kalindor and his company are vital to the defense of the city."

"And the queen?"

Spaiten took a deep breath and looked about, then leaned in close to his co-conspirator. "Think ... the last few weeks have seen events unfold accomplishing things we never could. House Aeonian and Cadan have not been heard from, and are declared lost. The Imperial King has undoubtedly perished in the explosion that crumbled Land's Edge, and along with him the heirs to both House Galadine and Tir." He smiled, his eyes meeting Algren's and his hand clasping the older man's shoulder, giving him a reassuring squeeze. "We take what life brings us, no? This time it is a fresh start, and our hands are clean."

"What of Ellis?" asked the regent quietly, though he knew the answer.

Merric's eyes narrowed. "The Great Houses are *gone,* Algren, the remnants must be swept away. Do not worry, you will soon be King of Shornhelm and a new House Justeces will rise to replace House Cadan. It has been arranged, but stay true."

A trumpet sounded then, signaling the arrival of the queen and her party, and the great double doors to the Senatorial Hall opened. The Queen of Bara'cor entered, flanked by Captain Kalindor and Legate Tir. Behind them came sixteen knights, her elite personal guard.

"Hail Imperial Queen Yevaine of House Galadine," cried the herald. "Hail Captain Tyrus of House Kalindor and Legate Ellis of House Tir."

* * * * *

As the herald announced the party the two members of the Senate rose and bowed. They were joined by the Chancellor of Haven, Finras Tyn, a tall man with dark eyes. His body was thin, the product of a lifetime of managing bureaucracy from behind a desk. He knew he was no warrior, but prided himself on his adherence to the laws of Edyn, the only thing, in his mind, separating his people from savages.

He entered from a door behind the officiating table and slowly made his way to the center chair. The regents of Dawnlight and Shornhelm arranged themselves to his left and right, respectively.

Even as the party moved to the central floor, Legate Tir bowed and circled around, coming to take his place at the table next to Regent Justeces. The only unoccupied chair left was the one for the Legate of Bara'cor, which the queen now ostensibly held to cast her single vote. However, since she was a petitioner, she kept her place on the central dais and faced the men who would now decide her fate, along with that of Bara'cor.

Chancellor Tyn was a man of few words, pragmatic and focused on the safeguarding of Haven. His family had been instrumental in recognizing the Galadine's imperial rule of the land, a structure he knew was necessary to keep the peace, however archaic. Though they were a monarchy, having the Senate balance divine right with elective appeal had been a necessary step to a more modern and mature government, at least in his mind.

Though he sympathized with the queen's plight, he had not voted with her. He would not leave Haven unguarded, and as such had watched her lose her last two petitions three votes to two. It never occurred to him that letting Bara'cor fall would likely seal Haven's fate as well, for the chancellor prided himself on the indispensable task of refined governance and law, and cared not a whit for the crude and lowly matters of battle, mud, and blood.

Now she was here a third time and his patience had begun to wear thin, even for Her Royal Highness. He put a hand to his forehead, then met her steely gaze with one just as unflinching and said, "Your business this time, Your Highness?"

"I wish to take your leave, Chancellor." Her voice came out strong and direct, with no trace of doubt. In fact, it was this directness that took him by surprise.

Tyn narrowed his eyes. "I beg your pardon?"

"I wish to take your leave, my lord. My husband has need of Captain Kalindor and his company, and it is clear Haven will not extend its hand. I must hurry back to reinforce him. We only ask for the grace to leave behind the young and elderly here in Haven."

Merric Spaiten rose and said, "We cannot allow Haven to lose your men for her defense, Your Highness. Bara'cor is lost."

"Bara'cor stands, only the pass has been damaged. Do you cower still?" challenged the queen.

"The explosion leveled half of Land's Edge!" exclaimed the regent, looking at the queen as if she had lost her mind. He turned to the chancellor and continued, "It centered on Bara'cor. What could be left?"

Chancellor Tyn looked back at the queen and said, "Yevaine, I sympathize with—"

"You will address me as *queen,* or *Your Highness,* Chancellor. Let us not forget we are noble born." She looked pointedly at the two regents, who seemed to shrink back at that.

The chancellor paused, then continued, "Your Highness, I sympathize with your predicament but Regent Spaiten is correct. The explosion was heard halfway to Sun Tree. What could have survived? Do you have proof of life?"

Yevaine dropped her head, her eyes closed. Then she said, "He's alive, and I mean to take my men and find him. There are other ways up the pass known to us, ways used in emergencies."

Regent Justeces stood then and cleared his throat. He looked pained and uncomfortable to be speaking and began haltingly, "Your Royal Highness . . . we must focus on the living, those here in Haven. Surely whatever destroyed Bara'cor will come here next. We cannot allow you to take . . . to leave with men necessary for our defense."

"As long as he is alive, I will exercise my right and command my men under the Imperial King's name."

Ellis Tir then stepped forward and said, "You know I have always been a loyal supporter of House Galadine ... but in this circumstance I must agree with my colleagues."

Raised eyebrows from the other regents greeted that, but before any could respond Captain Kalindor shouted, "You scheming traitor! You lie in wait then switch sides for convenience! King Galadine lives, and she commands in his name!"

"Not if he is declared dead," Ellis said, almost to himself. Then a chagrined look came across his face and he stepped back, his eyes downcast, but not before he a flicked glance at the queen.

Merric's eyes widened as he immediately caught Legate Tir's error, and what it meant. Wheels turned quickly in his mind, then he looked at the queen and pounced, "House Galadine has made the Laws of Succession quite clear."

Yevaine's eyes darted to Ellis, contempt on her face. "The Laws of Succession are archaic and without merit. My husband had planned to repeal them in favor of more enlightened views."

"Be that as it may," Merric said, "the current laws are quite clear. It is all that keeps war between the Great Houses at bay, and we will not dispense with it so haphazardly in light of the rumors of demons and rifts. The succession of the Imperial Crown goes to the next male heir of noble birth."

"And just who might that be?" demanded the queen, looking at Merric. "Not you, certainly."

Chancellor Tyn thought for a moment then said, "Without proof of life from Bara'cor, Shornhelm, EvenSea, or Dawnlight, succession would fall to ... Legate Ellis Tir." He looked at the man with a bemused expression, almost a half smile.

"I can't think of a better king," offered Merric. "Your Highness would still serve as Legate of Bara'cor, of course," he said magnanimously, addressing the queen. While his face looked compassionate, his eyes were lit with an inner smile.

Yevaine was a Galadine by marriage only, and once the formality of declaring Bernal Galadine dead was taken care of, House Galadine would be no more. That was until Ellis Tir was crowned, but accidents do happen. With him dead, rule would fall to a vote of the Senate.

"You would dare..." Yevaine took two steps back, a hand to her head. Then she gathered herself and pointed, her eyes on Ellis Tir. "You planned all this, the death of House Galadine? What does loyalty mean to you?"

Chancellor Tyn held out his hands for silence. It was unseemly for them to shout at each other like children in a schoolyard. "Nobles, please, act with decorum. The Laws of Succession are clear and unequivocal. Let me take counsel, and then offer a path."

He then moved back to confer with the regents and Legate Tir. Their whispers could not be heard down on the dais, but it quickly became obvious they had come to an agreement.

The chancellor turned back and addressed the queen. "We believe the Imperial King has perished in the defense of Haven, long live his reign. I regret to say we feel the same for the two heirs of House Galadine and Tir. Shall I put this to a vote, or will you acquiesce and take your place as Legate of Bara'cor? As such, you would keep House Galadine alive, at least until we can ascertain if there is another with Galadine blood."

"What choice is that? It puts my men under Haven's control, and has me treaty with traitors, craven men such as the three who stand whispering beside you now!"

Regent Merric Spaiten stepped forward at that and snapped, "Nevertheless, we can choose a less favorable post for the former Queen of Bara'cor. What say you?"

Captain Kalindor surged forward but was held back by his men. Yevaine put out a restraining hand. "It will do no good, Captain." She met his glare and nodded. "Stand down."

She waited till the captain sheathed his half-drawn blade, then turned back to the chancellor and said, "I have no choice but to accept."

Merric looked at the chancellor and said, "There is no reason to wait. Complete the Renunciation now."

Tyn paused, then nodded and said, "Are there any objections?"

Yevaine stepped forward and spread her arms, frowning. "Does it matter? Declare my husband dead and be done with it. I know he is still alive."

The chancellor sighed, frustrated at her obstinacy but understanding her devotion, and said, "Kneel then, and repeat after me."

Queen Yevaine knelt and looked up at the Senate, fury still showing in her eyes. That emotion bled away as her knee touched the floor and the inevitability of the moment washed over her. Soon, she knew, this would all be over.

"I stand aside by rule of the Senate, and support the search for the next true heir of House Galadine," intoned the Chancellor.

The queen repeated the words, her voice dead and emotionless.

"I accept the decision of the Senate, and stand firm in my commitment to this land. By my own hand, I set aside my crown."

Yevaine said this, too, her eyes fixed on the great seal of Edyn inscribed on the Senate Hall's floor. Slowly, as if they had a mind of their own, her hands came up and removed the thin diadem that stood in for the Imperial Crown. She placed this carefully into a waiting seneschal's hands, who retreated to hand it to the chancellor.

"On this day it is declared and recorded that Imperial King Bernal Galadine has passed on, and by the ancient Laws of Succession, the Imperial Queen Yevaine Galadine has been blessed to return to her noble family."

The other members of the Senate nodded and said, "It is done."

* * * * *

Regent Spaiten could not help the smile that lit his face. This had gone better than he could have hoped! House Galadine under their rule, the heirs declared lost, and the once-queen sequestered. He watched as Yevaine rose slowly and met his eyes.

"May I address the Senate?" she asked.

Spaiten granted it with a half shrug, caring less for whatever she had to say. The deed was done, and the woman was unimportant.

"Gentlemen, my husband has been declared lost and I do not know his fate or that of my son. I find myself without the heart to serve as Legate to Bara'cor, and name Captain Kalindor to the task. This puts him under your rule, Chancellor. I trust that will be acceptable?"

Chancellor Tyn nodded, "Of course. That is your right."

Spaiten smiled, this was only getting better.

Yevaine turned to her captain and said, "Do you accept?"

Captain Kalindor nodded curtly and said, "I do," before bowing and moving up the dais to take his place at the seat for Bara'cor. He risked a quick glance at Ellis Tir, and they shared an imperceptible nod.

"You are well come, Captain. Haven needs men such as you," offered Regent Justeces cordially.

Spaiten noticed that Algren had remained quiet throughout most of this, likely unable to believe the turn of events. This would hardly change Spaiten's mind about killing Yevaine and Ellis, but they all had imagined more resistance. It was at that moment Spaiten noticed the former queen's guards moving up to encircle Yevaine.

Yevaine looked at Regent Spaiten and said, "Merric, I will no longer be needing your services."

He turned at the informality of the address and said, "It is *Regent* Merric, and just what do you mean, Yevaine?"

She smiled and corrected, "It is *Princess* Yevaine, my lord ... Princess Yevaine of House Aeonian, blood heir to the throne of Dawnlight and noble born, unlike some others who claim to serve my father."

Merric's face paled and he took a step back. "What are you talking about?"

Princess Yevaine arched a delicate eyebrow and replied, "I am the last noble of House Aeonian, the chair you currently hold as Regent. As I am now no longer Queen of House Galadine, I will take my rightful place in the Senate as Speaker for Dawnlight and House Aeonian. Your are relieved of your duty as regent, and your services will no longer be required."

Silence, then a choking sound came from the former regent and he stumbled, catching himself on the table. "Praetorians, arrest her! You can't—"

"She can and has," interrupted Legate Tir, moving in quickly to restrain Merric. The Praetorians had begun to move and Yevaine's personal guard had drawn blades, forming a defensive ring around her.

Ellis Tir raised his voice so the Praetorians could hear him. "The chancellor accepted the queen's renunciation of her House as dictated by Galadine law! She is the rightful princess of House Aeonian, and stands for Dawnlight. Stand down!" He turned to the chancellor and demanded, "Have any Laws of Succession been broken?"

* * * * *

For his part, Chancellor Tyn stood dumbfounded. Not only had the queen appointed one of her own, she had replaced a regent with herself, shifting the power base of Haven. What galled him the most was that she had accomplished all this using his own obtuse and cooperative hand, but had she done anything legally wrong?

He took a deep breath, reviewing the legitimacy of her position. He certainly felt duped, but still his commitment was to uphold the laws of Edyn and the succession, and in performance of that duty his eyes darted back and forth as he thought through her claim.

It was true that Laws of Succession forbade her from holding the Imperial Crown of Edyn, but nothing prevented her from representing her father's House. Furthermore, she was the ranking noble in line for succession to Dawnlight's throne. His head dropped slowly and he mumbled something.

"Louder, Chancellor, or there will be blood spilled today, likely starting with yours," Ellis Tir whispered.

Chancellor Finras Tyn had never officiated such a deep change to Haven's political structure and could feel a cold sweat break out. He felt Legate Tir prod him again and found his voice, "The Laws of Succession were upheld. Princess Yevaine stands as Speaker for House Aeonian and Dawnlight. Praetorians, stand down."

The senatorial guards sheathed half-drawn blades and stepped back, but held their ground. Still, their attitude and attention now seemed focused on Merric Spaiten. One stepped forward and saluted the new princess, "We can take him for you."

"Thank you, but no, Centurion. This is an internal issue for Dawnlight." She looked to Kalindor and said, "Captain, I request Bara'cor's help. Please escort this man to a room and keep him under guard. He is to have no visitors until I can speak to him about his recent service and loyalty to my father."

Kalindor bowed and said, "Bara'cor stands ready."

"As does Dawnlight," she replied with a smile.

Kalindor motioned to his men and four guards came and escorted a pale Spaiten from the table. Kalindor started to follow but Yevaine held up a hand, calling him back. Tyn could see in her eyes that though her plan had succeeded, she was not done with the business that had first brought her here. It was clear that both Legate Tir and her captain were loyal to her cause, and he doubted very much if he would like the next words he heard.

"Gentlemen," she said coolly, and a pit formed in the chancellor's stomach, "I believe we still have another vote to tally: a petition for Haven to come to the aid of Bara'cor."

PLANEWALKERS

You should not fear forging ahead alone,

my sons. The world is vast and its wonders

endless. It begins the same way for everyone,

with one step in front of another, into the

unknown. Breath deep and easy, let the sun

warm your faces. Life awaits...

—*Davyd Dreys, Notes to my Sons*

S ilbane looked at the pyramid rising from the stone floor of the cavern. At its apex shone a cobalt sun, its radiance filling the room in a soft, flickering light. The entire chamber seethed with movement as black, sinuous shapes flowed in, around, and through each other. They looked to be the living smoke Yetteje had fled from in fear. He turned his attention back at the princess, his suspicions confirmed by the look on her face.

"What do we do now?" asked Ash. He cradled his arm, still broken from Baalor's mace.

"We move," said Silbane without looking back. "The boys are still trapped. If we do not go for them no one will, and the king's sacrifice will have been for nothing."

They hobbled forward, whittled away by Lilyth's forces until only Silbane, Kisan, Duncan, Ash, and Yetteje were left. They were unsure if anyone else survived within Bara'cor's walls, for they had not seen another living soul. Their flight here had been a mixture of mistfrights and death, punctuated by desperate moments of reorientation to avoid a literal dead end. The combat against Baalor mixed with the constant attacks from Lilyth's forces had taken their toll and none were left unscathed.

Still, unlike the king and Alyx, they lived and their objective lay ahead: the Gate. It would lead them to Arek and Niall.

Silbane moved forward and the sinuous fog reacted, bending to either side. It took on feline forms, dozens at first, then hundreds, then more than they could count, lining up in a ghostly procession to either side of the Gate. The group limped forward, nearing the bottom of the pyramid. Lilyth's phantom army offered no resistance.

Duncan took a step ahead, then turned to face the group, his eyes centering on Silbane. "Release me."

Silbane cocked his head. "What?"

"Release me, Silbane. I have acted in good faith, but we do not follow the same path."

Kisan stepped forward and snarled, "You've done nothing but act within your Bound Oath?" She turned to Silbane and said, "He's unbalanced and can't be trusted."

They all doubted this man's sanity and feared his mercurial moods. The last thing they needed in the middle of Lilyth's army was another enemy.

Silbane nodded, his eyes never leaving Duncan's. "You tried to kill us."

"Did I? I recall healing you and urging you to escape. You read my mind, my most inner thoughts. What is my life's purpose?" Duncan took a deep breath. He could not act without Silbane's release of the oath. Silbane broke eye contact with a sigh, looking at his companions, but Duncan demanded his attention by asking again, "What is my *purpose?*"

Silbane looked back at Duncan, his body reflecting the tiredness he felt. There was almost no point in answering, but the man's lifelong compulsion was too much to bear.

"Sonya," he said with resignation, for Silbane knew this was all Duncan thought about. Being reunited with his wife consumed him completely. He had obsessed about it for so long, it was unlikely there was anything left, except his hatred of the Galadine kings. If not for the Binding Oath, it was doubtful Bernal would have survived his encounter with this particular archmage. Silbane wondered, what had Duncan done to the king's weapons?

"But she is dead!" exclaimed Kisan. "Two hundred years dead."

Duncan ignored the outburst, instead looking up at the pyramid and the shining Gate. "She is there, waiting for me." He turned his attention back to the group and said, "They all are . . . anyone you lost."

Stunned silence followed the archmage's statement. Questioning eyes darted to Silbane.

"Is that true?" blurted Yetteje. "My family . . . my father is alive?"

Ash hobbled forward. "The king?"

Even Kisan looked at Duncan, and though she never uttered a word, the only thought in her mind was for her dead apprentice.

Duncan looked at them all, finally coming to rest on Silbane. "I can bring them *back*. Release me."

Silbane didn't move, his form absolutely still. So much had happened to them. Now Arek was lost on the other side of this Gate. Would keeping this insane mage help or hinder them? Furthermore, their presence in Lilyth's world would be noted. Would having a beacon of power as bright as Duncan, separate from them, allow a measure of anonymity?

"I have done all you asked, there is nothing more!" Duncan's face crumpled and he fell to one knee. He looked up and whispered, "You know she carried my unborn child." A small sob escaped, and his back shook as if the very ground of his composure crumbled under him. He raised a fist illumed in power and slammed it into the granite floor, which buckled and cracked under the blow. "I cannot leave them on the other side! Release me!"

Silbane caught himself and took a deep breath. He was surprised Duncan had lasted this long, for the man's mind was fractured. Every step closer must have been agonizing for him, knowing he could not leave without breaking the oath, thereby jeopardizing his very existence.

Each choice had its dangers, but one afforded them the most safety. His mind made, Silbane blew out the breath he held and said, "You stand released of your oath." As he uttered those words, a flash of yellow surrounded them both.

"Are you mad?" cried Kisan. She looked around the seething mass, then at Duncan, expecting an attack at any moment, but the man didn't move. He just knelt on one knee, his face resting in the crook of his arm, as if asleep.

He slowly stirred, as if hearing Silbane for the first time, and looked up in disbelief. Tears rolled down his face as he drew in a shuddering breath. His eyes locked again with the master who had just released him and he nodded once in gratitude. He rose slowly, facing the group. "I thank you and offer you this in repayment. What is my true name?"

Silbane stared at Duncan but felt his concentration narrow like it had once before, presaging the advent of Sight. The air darkened and time slowed to a heartbeat. Duncan still stood before him, but surrounding him was a conflagration of yellow light, as if the air itself had ignited into a sunburst. It was the Way, and so potent! He had had no idea the man held so much power, but there was more.

Superimposed around him was another figure. It stood towering over them, terrible in aspect. Red eyes that spoke of death glared from beneath a helm of burnt cinder. Dark wings of ash and smoke wrapped protectively around the Old Lord, making him seem somehow small and insignificant, despite his incandescent aura. It was a creature that filled Silbane with dread, and yet there was nothing he could do to escape it.

Another heartbeat and the creature inclined its massive head to the master, acknowledging they could see each other. Its eyes flared crimson and in a voice with the rasp of a dead snake's skin, a sound recalling rot and decay, it said, "I am Scythe, my lord. We thank you for our release."

Time snapped back and the vision was gone. Silbane staggered into Kisan, drained again as before. This time, however, he felt himself recovering more quickly. He pushed himself erect and looked at Duncan, already knowing what the other would say, and offered simply, "Scythe."

"My memories begin to open to you and in time you will understand more."

Silbane knew Duncan meant the mindread they shared, but he had just seen something vastly different. Clearly it had been the Sight, the gift of Rai'stahn and the Conclave, yet he did not correct the archmage. No one else had seen the creature and while this made sense, it brought into question everything he knew about himself and the Way.

Duncan focused on the two masters and continued, "The name I heard when I Ascended was Scythe, but it is not *my* name."

Though both Kisan and Silbane knew what *Ascension* meant, only Silbane understood the literal truth of what Duncan had just said. Did every adept have a companion such as Scythe? And what of the vision of Valarius and the Conclave? What was the connection to Azrael? He felt the underpinnings of all he believed tilt and could not find his intrinsic equilibrium.

It was Yetteje who finally said, "Who is Scythe?"

Duncan smiled. "An Aeris Lord." He turned back to Silbane. "You must understand this if you are to survive in their realm." He gave them a small, crooked smile and added, "That Ascension is both a lie and the truth is my parting gift to you. Use it well." He backed up a step and gave the group a small bow, then he turned and faced the portal.

The archmage ran up the face of the pyramid without looking back. He ascended with a single-minded purpose, gaining speed as he neared the blue-white, scintillating portal. In a few moments he was in front of it, his face lit by its unearthly glow.

The party watched him with mixed expressions of anger and disbelief. They could not see what he saw from their position, but watched as he gathered himself, then took a step through. He vanished in a flash. His departure was so sudden and immediate, it caught most of them by surprise.

"Inane, useless chatter. He couldn't be more confusing on purpose," Kisan huffed, clearly exasperated. "You had him captured because of his knowledge of gates."

Silbane nodded, still silent, what Duncan had revealed echoing in his mind. The creature known as Scythe was an Aeris Lord? His thoughts centered on what the dragons said during his vision, that Azrael would be freed if Valarius was killed. Did this mean Azrael had once bonded to Valarius, just as Scythe had to Duncan? His head swam with the implications, both for Valarius and more acutely, for himself. He turned to Kisan, wonder in his eyes, and said, "There is much more going on here than you know."

"Such as?" Kisan questioned the release of an asset, and in this case releasing Duncan only added to the variability of outcomes. She did not like that, nor what she saw as Silbane's foolhardy decision to let him go.

For his part, Silbane's expression grew both thoughtful and tired. For the first time in his life he hesitated to share everything he knew. The revelations and visions combined to make him doubt his own role. Furthermore, if Duncan were to be believed, his true name was not his own. The repercussions of this one small fact were significant, and he did not want to sit here idly speculating while the boys headed into Lilyth's world alone. More delay put Arek farther from him and potentially in more danger.

Instead, he offered, "You know I read him. He is consumed with finding his wife and child, though they are centuries dead." He turned and faced Kisan. "He is of more use stirring his havoc away from us, as you know he will." He thought then of the winged creature of smoke and ash he'd seen standing over Duncan and added, "Trust me."

"Was he lying?" Yetteje interjected herself between the two masters, not moving an inch, her stance both accusing and demanding an answer. "He said they can be saved."

At first Silbane was confused by the question, his mind still on the vision of Scythe, its crimson eyes radiant below a cinder crown. It was burned into his memory. Had that really been an Aeris Lord?

Yetteje clarified, "My father, the others who have died . . ."

Comprehension dawned and he nodded to where Duncan had disappeared and answered, "He thinks so, but he is insane."

"You didn't answer me. Is *my* father still alive?" She looked up the pyramid steps now with an intensity that was almost palpable.

"And the king," added Ash. "Is there a chance we may yet save him?"

"Piter might be there," Kisan said, but to no one in particular. When no one answered, she walked toward the pyramid steps, never looking back. Kisan had no faith in Duncan, yet Silbane sensed that the seed of saving Piter had been planted and had already begun to take root. Perhaps this was her chance to set all things right, rebalancing the wrongs done to her apprentice. Arek would pay with his life and the right son would live again.

Silbane shifted his gaze to Kisan's retreating back. Then he looked at everyone and said, "I am going to save Arek before it's too late. None of you have to join us." He turned and started walking up the pyramid steps, following the younger master. Any answers he wanted lay beyond the blue sun.

Ash and Yetteje hurried to follow, the latter supporting the firstmark as he gingerly made his way, trying not to jostle his crushed shoulder and arm. They climbed in silence and before long, all had reached the apex.

The blue fire of the sun shone more intensely here, the light permeating them. The circle of the Gate also stood open, through which they could see green fields and sunlit waters. The air was crystal clear, with a hint of a gentle spring wind and the smell of green grass and wildflowers.

"Arek's touch did not close this." He looked at Kisan and then admitted, "We were wrong."

Kisan buried her face in her hands and rubbed until the skin was red. When she looked up, it was with determination. She looked at Silbane and her voice took on the keen edge of steel when she answered, "I've gotten used to you being wrong."

Just then a sigh of relief escaped from Ash's lips. He looked at his shoulder, then rotated his arm, smiling. When he noticed the group looking at him, his expression became more thoughtful..

Silbane saw the swarm of yellow particles, coalescing like mist, adhering and permeating the armsmark's shoulder. He knew if he concentrated, he could see the muscle and bone reknit itself under the ministration of Tempest. The gift of Sight it seemed, had not fled him. Knowing the answer, he still asked, "Healed?"

Ash nodded, "And not at the expense of anyone else."

"Useful where we're going," muttered Kisan.

Yetteje glanced at Silbane, then quietly asked, "Can you find Arek?"

Silbane kept his eyes fixed on the Gate and the world behind it. "I think so, and something seems to be driving us forward."

The princess didn't hesitate, replying, "Then we'll rescue them . . . all of them. Let them try and stop us." She readjusted the runebow and took a step forward.

Silbane looked back at the group and said, "Let's pay the Lady a visit."

With that, the group of four stepped into Lilyth's Gate and disappeared in a flash of blue and white.

Journal Entry—final entry

Over these past months (years?) you may know me already, but I give you my name, nonetheless.

You may judge me as you will, for I no longer care what the world or you thinks, for I have found my soul here. When we started this journey together, I pleaded for your understanding and hoped you would judge me less harshly, or laud my efforts. It was a fool's dream, and I now dream of greater things.

Today I began a new ritual, a cleansing of myself. It will be an arduous process, a remaking of who I am, through discipline and dedication.

Through sacrifice, I will begin a new Shaping, one which will bring forth the perfect being, the harbinger of destruction upon the Aeris Lords and others who betrayed me, such as my friends in the Conclave.

I will raise it from its very first breath to know it is destined for greatness, made from the consummation of flesh and Aeris, and powerful because it is one with the Way. I will create the myths that surround it, the prophecies that define it.

I wondered once, how do you kill a god?

My elves gave me the first clue. Sonya brought the second with her, for she is with child. Ritual is key, faith is power, but we are the vessel.

Through her ultimate sacrifice, I will bring forth a new life and a new myth, born to smite the Aeris, born for one purpose only, vengeance. What kills gods? Legends kill gods.

I will create the legend of a god-killer.

Then, I will unleash Him.

—*Valarius Galadine*

*Here ends **Mythborn**.*

*The Fate of the Sovereign
will continue in **Warforged**,
and conclude in **Oathbound**.*

~ *AFTERWORD* ~

READER'S GUIDE

Aging – Those on the Isle who practice the Way (see the Way) age more slowly than normal people. They are typically only a third of their age in appearance. A hundred year old adept would appear to be in his mid-thirties. This is a by-product of their training and begins once they attain the rank of Adept. (see Ranks)

Arek Winterthorn – Sixteen-year-old apprentice to Master Silbane, known to be able to disrupt magic. Keen intellect, master rank in bladed and unarmed combat styles. Adept rank in herb lore and combat tactics.

Ash Rillaran – Armsmark and second-in-command of Bara'cor. Military strategist, master in bladed combat. Attended the War College in Shornhelm, graduated first in class, known for his keen insight into battle tactics and his skill with a blade.

Sgt. Alyx Stemmer – Pragmatic squad leader who acts as aide-de-camp and squire to the First Mark of Bara'cor.

Lord Azrael – Ancient Celestial and warlord of the Aeris. The dragons believe if freed, he will oppose Lilyth and her Aeris army.

Lord Baalor – General of Lilyth's army and lord of storms. Ancient, powerful, and honorable, Baalor seeks justice for his fallen brethren and fights without fear. Able to channel the Way in its purest form.

Bara'cor – Ancient fortress and stronghold, built by the Dwarves. Held by King Bara, then abandoned shortly after the Demon War against Lilyth, for unknown reasons. It now is held by King Bernal Galadine and his forces.

Ben'thor Tir – King of EvenSea, ruler of the eastern stronghold by that name and father to Yetteje Tir. Defender of the East and longtime friend to Bernal Galadine. Married to Bernal's sister.

Bernal Galadine – King of Bara'cor, ruler of the western stronghold by that name, father to Niall Galadine. Defender of the West, graduate of the War College in Shornhelm, master strategist and wielder of the mighty runebow, Valor.

Conclave – An ancient group dedicated to safeguarding the life on Edyn. They are custodians of knowledge and guardians against anything that would destroy the Way.

Cycle, Summer, Turn, Year – All refer to the passage of one year on Edyn.

Dragor Dahl – Adept, originally from the southern continent of Koorva, master rank in unarmed combat and illusions. Friend to Giridian Alacar, teacher of Jesyn, whom he found as a baby, abandoned in the Shornhelm Wastes.

Flameskin – A protective halo made of ethereal fire. Summoning one is part of gaining the rank of Adept. The color of the fire signifies that person's attunement to the Way. The weakest are dark and blue and slowly progress until they shine pure and white.

Giridian Alacar – Adept, Keeper of the Vault, master of artifacts and other magical items. Sixty years old, teacher to apprentice Tomas, scribe and chronicler of the adepts. Appears to others as a man in his late twenties.

Houses – There are four Great and dozens of Minor Houses in Edyn. The four Great Houses are described here:

House Galadine – Led by the Imperial King Bernal Galadine and Queen Yevaine Galadine (of House Aeonian). House Galadine holds the fortress of Bara'cor. The King and Queen have one son, Niall, who is about to embark on this 'Walk of Kings'. The King's sister, Clarysa, is married to the King of EvenSea.

House Cadan – Held by King Rory Cadan and Lady Ilandra Cadan (of House Tir). House Cadan holds the fortress of Shornhelm. They have one son, Durnal, who is still an infant. His sister, Morgan, is married to the King of Dawnlight. They are served by Algren Justeces, who serves as Legate for Shornhelm in the capital city of Haven.

House Tir – Held by King Ben'thor Tir and Lady Clarysa Tir (of House Galadine). They hold the fortress of EvenSea. They have one daughter, Yetteje, current ward to House Galadine and staying at Bara'cor as part of her 'Walk of Kings' ritual. Ben'thor has a brother, Ellis Tir, who serves as Legate of EvenSea in the capital city of Haven. He also has a sister, Ilandra, married to the King of Shornhelm.

House Aeonian – Held by King Temar Aeonian and Lady Morgan Aeonian (of House Cadan). They hold the fortress of Dawnlight. Their daughter, Yevaine, is married to the Imperial King Galadine. Their other daughter, Ilandra, is married to the King of Shornhelm. They are served by Merric Spaiten, who serves as Legate for Dawnlight in the capital city of Haven.

Minor Houses: House Kalindor, House Justeces, House Spaiten, House Rillaran, House Stemmer, House Naserith, House Petracles, House Illrys, House Alacar, and more...

Hemendra – U'Zar, leader of the nomads of the Altan Wastes, military strategist assaulting Bara'cor. Responsible for the destruction of Dawnlight, Shornhelm, and most recently, EvenSea, under the command of Scythe. (see, Scythe)

Jesyn Shornhelm – Initiate, apprenticed to Dragor, training for her adept's Test, last name taken from the region where she was found. Adept rank in bladed and unarmed combat. Ascended to full adept to meet the growing danger in Dawnlight.

Jebida Naserith – First Mark, leader of Bara'cor's military forces, longtime friend of Bernal Galadine. Distrustful of magic since the death of his wife and daughter, at the hands of creatures that appeared through a rift.

Kisan Talaris – Master, youngest to attain the rank, skilled in illusions and unarmed combat. Willful, strong, impatient, yet honorable and driven. Assigned to back up Silbane should the need arise. Teacher to Piter, then to Tomas. She has recognized the growing powers of Yetteje Tir.

Lilyth – Demonlord and Celestial, lord of the Aeris. Seeks entry into this plane of existence, ostensibly for retribution on Mankind for centuries of enslavement of the Aeris.

Mindread – The ability of a practitioner of the Way to assimilate and read the thoughts of another person. Extremely taxing in power, so the information retained is often incomplete or jumbled. However, it can lend situational context when paired with the caster's own perceptions.

Mindspeak – The ability for a practitioner of the Way to reach out and speak telepathically with another practitioner. Extremely taxing in its use of energy, but provides a near instantaneous connection through which thoughts and energy can be shared.

Niall Galadine – Crown Prince of Bara'cor, seventeen years old. Trained in weapons combat, but never faced a live opponent. About to initiate his rite of passage to manhood, known as the Walk of Kings.

Piter Winterthorn – Initiate apprenticed to Kisan, training for his adept's Test, last name taken from the region near where he was found, master rank in bladed combat, adept rank in spellcraft.

Thoth – Guardian of the Archives, member of the Conclave, a group made up of the Elder Races and dedicated to safeguarding life on Edyn.

Rai'stahn – Ancient dragon, defender of the world at one time, now inhabits a small part of the Isle where the adepts train. Predator, powerful in the Way, able to regenerate, and able to assume many forms. Skilled in combat (immeasurable by common mortal rankings). Does not involve himself in the world's affairs, till now.

Rai'kesh – Ancient dragon and king of the dragonkind. Sits on the Conclave and instrumental in giving Valarius Galadine a vision of the true nature of the Way. Some argue this caused Valarius to go down the fateful path he chose. Ordered Rai'stahn to kill Valarius at the battle of Sovereign's Fall.

Ranks – There are four tiers of rank, with many subdivisions. These four tiers are initiate, adept, master, and archmage. The title is capitalized when used with a name, otherwise it is not, therefore 'Master Silbane' vs. speaking about 'masters'.

All apprentices, once they pass their Test of Potential and earn their Green rank, are initiates.

Once an initiate passes his Test of Ascension, he or she wears the black uniform and gains the rank of adept.

From there, they test again for the rank of master.

Currently there are two masters on the Isle, Silbane, and Kisan. There are also three adepts, Giridian, Thera, and Dragor.

Tomas, Jesyn, Piter, and Arek are preparing to Test for their adept rank, allowing them to wear the black and be called adepts.

Lore Father Themun Dreys is the only Archmage on the Isle, and as such administers the tests of rank.

Ranks are also used to denote someone's skill along these same four tiers, so a person with a master's rank in bladed combat would be generally better than one with an adept's or initiate's rank.

Scythe – Archmage, red-robed wizard who seeks Lilyth's Gate, allied with Hemendra of the Nomads, archmage rank in all things magical, possessor of the Old Lore, and able to wield it as the Old Lords did.

Silbane Darius Petracles – Master, skilled in all forms of combat and combat magic. Eighty years old and teacher of Arek Winterthorn. Appears to others as a man in his late thirties.

Syvane – Ancient sentient sword, given to Arek for his protection. Said to have the power to heal its wielder from grave injury. Particularly fond of Ash, and Arek.

Themun Dreys – Archmage, Lore Father of the Second Council of adepts, initiates the quest to ascertain the disposition of Lilyth's Gate, master illusionist. Although over two hundred years old, appears to others as a man in his sixties.

Thera Dawnlight – Adept, master rank in herb lore and medicine, skilled in healing and defensive arts. Orphan and found near Dawnlight, appears to others as a woman in her late forties.

Tomas Dawnlight – Apprentice, first to Adept Giridian, then to Master Kisan. Preparing for his Test of Ascension. Strong, brave, highly intelligent and skillful in combining magic with strength.

Mikal Galadine – King during the Demon Wars, leader of the forces that forced Lilyth back to Sovereign's Fall. Victorious, then decreed that all magic was outlawed and mages were to be killed on sight. Brother to General Valarius Galadine, archmage who is believed to have summoned Lilyth.

Valarius Galadine – General of the King's forces at Sovereign's Fall, Archmage and Lore Father of the First Council of Adepts, known for causing the first cataclysm of the world, aided by the demonlord, Lilyth. Powerful, strong-willed, championed the idea that demons were actually the source of magic in this world. Once he turned against the land, he was stripped of his title and rank.

The Way – An eldritch force that exists within the very fabric of space, allowing those that can tap into it the ability to manipulate time, space, and matter. There are many manifestations, limited only by the practitioner's imagination and discipline. The Old Lords of the First Council used it to create spells that could alter the very nature of the world. The Second Council has honed it into a power that manifests itself in their bodies when they engage in martial combat.

Yetteje Tir – Princess of EvenSea, cousin to Niall Galadine, on her pilgrimage to ascend to the royal throne of EvenSea, with her final stop on the Walk of Kings at Bara'cor. She is seventeen and stubborn, but brave and good with a blade.

Yevaine Galadine – Queen of Bara'cor, wife of Bernal, sent from Bara'cor at the siege's start with the young and weak to Haven, capital city of Edyn, to deliver them and return with reinforcements.

ABOUT THE AUTHOR

Vijay Lakshman was born in Ottawa, Canada. He spent his early years in Bangkok, Thailand. When he was ten, his father took him to a martial arts exhibition. Learning those arts has stayed a passion for him throughout his adult life. His travels have taken him across the world to every continent that gets a television signal. Something about seeing the tops of clouds makes it easier for him to write.

When he is not working as a video game creator, he spends his time writing the second book in the Fate of the Sovereign. His hobbies include twenty-five years of training in the martial arts, cycling, and taking various things in the house apart. Putting them back together is the job of his beautiful wife and two sons.

Proof

Made in the USA
Charleston, SC
04 April 2013